WILTON TOWN:

THE ANGELS GO MARCHING IN:
Sebastien's Arrival

By Cordelia Malthere

Wilton Town's Spooky Tales

Book Three
Part 2

Published by Malthere Publications Limited

Find out more about the author and her books at
http://www.cordelia-malthere.co.uk

If you want to become a published author visit
http://www.malthere-publications.com

Copyright © 2015 Cordelia Malthere

ISBN:978-1-912143-05-4

Graphics by Cordelia Malthere

Foreword.

Welcome to Wilton Town's Spooky Tales. The readers who have already visited the cemetery of Wilton Town, will know that this instalment is the second story released about that whimsical imaginary town. They will know all about the richest man in town, Abraham Wilton-Cough being shot while protecting his customers in his bank, the very first bank of Wilton Town which he created. They will know about that anti-hero, his great pride for they would have followed him from grave to grave up until his deathbed.

Anti-hero or not, Banker or not, proud or not, Abraham Wilton-Cough is a very much loved character. So much so that he had to have a second writing outing, right from his fans point of view but also from his Author's aims for him. I wept penning A W-C last lines which only implies that his character had grown on me so much. Confession for confession the death of my own father had happened shortly prior to me writing 'Hair Rising, Heir Raising, Erasing,' which speaks about a father dying of an untimely death, leaving three children and a wife, reconsidering his entire actions during his life on his deathbed. If there are many parallels which could be clearly drawn out from my personal story to the one I am writing, I must say that Abraham Wilton-Cough is an entirely different kettle of fish from my father. He was inspired by the Dickensian's Ebenezer Scrooge mainly, with a sprinkle of some traits of my own father here and there.

Here you will find Abraham Wilton-Cough raising once more from the dead as a Ghost setting out on another journey in order to destroy once and for all what is causing his unrest. You will find him using any means to rally the living to his cause. He is a Spirit with an aim and he is not alone...

No, not only does he come well accompanied, you will see him gathering followers. You will recognised most from the first tale about Wilton Town. Some characters, who were just mentioned previously, take centre stage like the good yet curious to a default Doctor Vincent Valdi while others are introduced like the immortal White Witch Whilhelmina.

Teeming with characters from the Past, Present and Future, Wilton Town has many tales in its chest to share. They may lay in a ruined cottage by the edge of the forest or in the cemetery yet for its inhabitants to rest in peace, their stories have to be told.

Spooky: maybe for some, as soon as you speak of Ghosts and Ghouls, some will not read a book terrified by it already. If you don't believe that statement, speak to my mum who will not read any of my books until I create a rosy story of some sort. Then she will read just that one. It would probably go like this: 'Once upon a time Winnie the Pooh shared his honey pot with little red riding hood and they went all Mills and Boon over it. Nine months later the Hundred Acre Wood was full of cute Teddy Bears running everywhere.'

Joking apart, I would rate the level of spookiness in my tales as rather mild. If we had a chilli/chilly chart for scary stories, it would not reach the high end of 'scaryville chill units' of the pure horror type. It would be very mild to medium in some parts, one line or two here and there.

Tragicomedy: definitely. Like the first tale about Wilton-Town this one bestows emotional moments but also lots of humorous scenes throughout. Just like life, tears and laughter are paving the journey into Wilton Town's Tales but sprinkled with just a tad of spookiness.

Enjoy the journey from one's grave to someone else's body...

Spirited away.

Cordelia Halthere

Dedication

To Orlane.

Your hug when I cried at my Dad's funeral meant a great deal of a lot to me. He was your adoptive Grandfather as per say. I remember holding you in my arms soon after your birth, my niece, a beautiful baby which turned to be a beautiful person, a nurse helping others in their times of need. You are not only our Family Angel, you are the one of the many you helped in your profession in this time of pandemic.

Cordelia Malthere

,

an aunt you make very proud.

PREFACE

The Wilton Town Saga continues. The Angels go marching in Wilton Town was written when due to unforeseen circumstances, I partly lost my ability to walk properly. I must confess that I had trouble dealing with my loss of complete mobility then but also now.

'Marching' in the title is almost telling the entire tale of what did happen to my physical life or lets just say giving a clue to the loss of something important to me.

This story took a completely different spin than the one I had in mind and planned due to what happened to me. It is about feelings and physical ones at that, but of course emotional ones as well.

My characters evolve in, sometimes, their own little sphere, space. The Ghost of Abraham is here to provide his help and hard learnt wisdom to anyone who wants it. Doctor Valdi is present of course but also absent... but then present again... His character is a knight in shining armour.

But then his best friend Father Odell, Theo has another time to shine. Theo is weaving his gentle ways throughout the story to bring it to good tidings.

Finally the Angels are marching in therefore Wilton Town will be utterly different for it...

Those new characters, the Angels, are partly based on real humans. I will not start to reveal the guess who. You just have to read it all for yourselves...

This novel is a journey to discover how complicated can be your own patch of the wood. However it is an enjoyment to de-tangle.

Spread your wings...

Cordelia Halthere

To say the least Sebastien and his father were delighted with the outcome and the truce between the white witch of Wilton Town and Doctor Williams over the care of Georgia Marlow. It felt to them like an amiable hand over. During all that time Sebastien bandaged with great care the shoulder of Peter O'Neil, while Father Odell had given a suitable amount of alcohol to the man to make him sleep like a baby despite his injuries. Once Peter dozed off, Sebastien started to look after his most serious wound and repairing it as best as he could. While Doctor Williams assisted him, the angel Mitos appeared within the room. He was welcomed by the Master who briefed him,

-Mitos, I am happy to see you. I have a small case for your expertise. It is purely to be angelic benevolence. The man being looked after by my son was victim of a demonic attack and a collateral damage was his pet rabbit. You know how demons are. They get to someone by who or what they love the most. The demon threw and killed the pet of the man onto the wall before throwing the man in the same manner breaking his shoulder. That man is a pretty lonely one and at this moment in time, well, since a couple of hours ago, all he had in his life to give him a little comfort was his pet. The damage on the animal was extensive but I managed to fix it all. We only need to recall the soul of Clementine, his rabbit.

Mitos transformed himself from his majestic phoenix appearance to a human one. He stated,

-Master, I rarely see you in your human form. I also rarely hear your call about an animal. This is also my second call from you tonight.

The Master picked up Clementine and explained,

-I am needed here. There is some bad activity in that town. It is not only totally demonic. Some humans are preparing to do something atrocious tomorrow night. Let me show you. We have been working almost around the clock to prevent the worst to happen. How did my first call went?

The extremely tall Mitos looked around him and his green eyes met the ones of Sebastien. He bowed to the son of the Master respectfully then told,

-Henry's soul belongs to Sebastien, Master. He chose to regain his memories to be your adopted son in order to stay with Sebastien. Henry's heart is deeply loyal to your son like a guard dog to his master. His deep devotion to Sebastien is quite staggering and dates back to many of his animal lives.

Finishing the last stitches on Peter, Sebastien's head popped up and gave a bright smile to his father. He jubilated,

-It sounds like I just got myself a younger brother. Mitos, I have a question for you, to help me understand my Henry better. During his human life, he always slept in stables, I always thought he was punishing himself for the accidental death of a man he caused. Am I right to think that?

Mitos revealed,

-You are right but it is only part of the answer. The adjustment of his very ancient animal soul to a human body wasn't as smooth as it could have been. You met him when he was a boy of fourteen during his human life. He didn't tell you much about his childhood because it was a very troubled one. His parents were Huguenots. They lost their farm, were persecuted, went to England, couldn't settle there properly, came back to France, try to convert, then went back to England and then back to France again. His animal soul had difficulty grasping the tribulation of being human. He didn't understand either politics or religions. Where he felt the most comfortable was sleeping with the animals and be with animals. Of course Henry was devoid of the knowledge that it was because he was an ancient animal spirit. What didn't help, was that his previous life was the one of a pigeon. Once human, Henry had tremendous difficulty to use his hands. He was clumsy because it didn't come naturally to him. If he had been some type of chimpanzees, a gorilla, an orangutan, then his dexterity would have been there. The clumsiness he suffered from, from the start, made him seek the sanctuary of the stable. In fact, he was hiding himself there, and his shame of being different, more or less with creatures, he did understand and made more sense to him than humans.

Sebastien sighed deeply then demanded,

-Will my Henry cope with his memory back of all his past lives?

Taking the dead Clementine into his arms, inspecting her, Mitos replied,

-Only time will tell. All I can say, Sebastien, is that you

have made a strong angel out of him. I must thank you because it was a pleasure to meet the spirit of an animal reaching your angelic army. What did help is that you met Henry when he was still young in his human life. You were able to educate him on human ways, and the correct ways to do everything more than his parents did, because they were too engrossed in their religious struggle to pay too much attention to their large brood of children. I can reveal to you that your tough hand with Henry was the right helping hand he desperately needed. He has tremendous respect for you from that human life. Now, let me tell you that he reacted really well to having his memories back. It was not an all jumping and dancing moment, far from it, but it was a revelation. For him, it gave him the sense that everything, and I mean everything, was falling into place. Henry had his epiphany tonight. Suddenly all made sense to him. More importantly, he has regained his rightful identity. In my honest opinion, it was the right thing to do. No matter what, The Messenger will remain your angelic messenger and your very gifted fighter, loyal and devoted to you, deep down to his core of his being.

A pleased Sebastien told with respect,

-Thank you Mitos for your help and opinion. They are much appreciated. I am sure you will want to follow the angelic case of our Henry closely. If he is extremely successful, I will want more angels coming originally from animal stock.

The tall angel bowed to him as he answered,

-It will be my pleasure to deliver your order. I will definitely follow Henry's case closely. He is rather exceptional to be honest. But it made me wonder what happened to the seven other lions which protected your dead body in that Roman arena until your father could pick you up. Did their animal spirits tried to follow you as much as the one of Henry did? I will investigate because you may have seven more loyal animal souls in waiting to become human and then angel.

The Master agreed,

-This could be quite interesting to see. I will help you in your quest. Did you find the soul of Clementine and can you recall her back?

Mitos said with a kind smile,

-Her spirit is still here. In fact she is on the lap of her human. She refused to go and rest in peace. I am talking to her right now. She loves that man. She doesn't like him being sad and in pain. She said he cares for her so well. We have a resounding yes from her soul to be back in her body. She wants to stay with him. Well, I can only recall her then.

A great light flashed within the room, and under the hands of Mitos, as a result, the little grey rabbit started moving. He presented,

-Sebastien, you can wake up your human. Here is his pet. The little thing adores him. Put her on his lap, so he will have a pleasant surprise. I will take my leave. Please call me whenever you need me and I will be here.

Sebastien couldn't help smiling when he took Clementine in his arms. He commented,

-That little creature is a small blessing for that man. Mitos, I must thank you for returning his pet to life. I still need you, if you do not mind. First, I have another question for you then I have a task for you to do overnight which is important to my eyes. Mitos, father, let's have a private talk in Peter's courtyard.

Putting the rabbit on the gentle giant's lap, the angel ordered,

-Theo, I am putting you in charge of looking after Peter. I am going to wake him up. Put his shirt back on carefully and make him eat the dinner we brought. Then I want you and Ted to put him in bed. He will be able to lay on his back despite his broken shoulder, I made sure of it. I need you both to stay by him until we close that portal in his house. We may still face demonic activity and attacks here tonight. Theo, I will need you on the ball, ready to exorcise. Miss White, when I am back I want those spells on Theo and Ted done. William give her a hand and reproduce her spell upon her to protect her.

Left with clear instructions, all busied themselves while Sebastien having clapped his hands awoke Peter magically before the angel went outside followed by the Master and Mitos. When Peter O'Neil opened his eyes, the first thing he saw was his pet on his lap, alive and well. With emotion, he stroke Clementine gently, then he looked at Father Odell asking amazed,

-What happened Father?

Theo Odell replied with a reassuring smile,

-Just a little angelic intervention repairing the demonic

destruction. The spirit of Clementine didn't want to leave you. Although dead, her little soul never left you. So the angels were able to mend her body and return her soul into it. Now, as for you, Sebastien looked after your wound on your chest. You have stitches there. So you mustn't do any harsh move. As you know we brought you dinner. Ted kindly warmed it up so I can feed you before we help you to bed. We will stay here until we know you will never be attacked by demons in your home anymore.

The thankful hand of Peter held the one of Odell for an emotional brief moment. Meanwhile in the courtyard of Peter O'Neil, The Master, his son and Mitos were walking together, discussing. Having stopped by the well, and pulling a bucket full of water, Sebastien put his question to Mitos,

-Concerning Henry, Mitos, which animal behaviours can I expect from him?

The Master scolded his son,

-Not again, Sebastien! Henry will not eat mice in front of you nor straw.

With a wicked grin his son corrected,

-I am being serious, here, father, I am asking for a range of skill set that my angel have or will have. But if there are any troubleshooting or flaws as well, I rather know them prior to confronting them. I need to look after him properly, now that he made that big step. My enquiry is simply a duty of care.

A nodding Mitos explained,

-There are some guidelines to Henry, yes. I can reveal to you some skills and downsides that he now bestows. From his very first animal life as a pterodactyl, he will have a predatory behaviour. This will be directed against demons. He will be fearless and fearsome. You can expect him to eviscerate demons like the many birds of prey he has been, eviscerated their own preys. He can see in the dark. He possess the skill of echolocation as well. Like an owl, he can turn his head fully. He mustn't do that in front of humans unless he wants to frighten them.

With a grin Sebastien commented,

-This could be pretty interesting to watch. But apart from being an interesting party trick I doubt that the ability to turn his head in three hundred and sixty degrees could be useful.

His father told sternly,

-You can forget right now to ask Henry to do the head trick for your own amusement. I warn you.

Still smiling wickedly Sebastien defended himself,

-I am just wondering out loud how that ability could be of some help, Dad. It is not my intention to turn Henry into the local freak show. You can rest secure upon it, this will not happen. I am protective of my Henry.

Mitos announced,

-It will be likewise for Henry, Sebastien. He will be protective of you. Let me tell you when that capacity could be useful. Combined with his enhanced sense of hearing, where Henry can perceive the minutest sound such as the movement of a mouse underneath the floorboard of the cellar, rooms away from him, or even a pin dropping in a cottage situated a mile from the presbytery, it can be very helpful. Imagine both of you, side by side, having to face the enemy. He will be able to cover your back. He will know if anyone is trying to creep behind you to plan a surprise attack. He will hear it, and with a quick head spin he can check the danger out without living your side. Adding to that he possess eagle eyes vision and extraordinary sense of smell. Let's just say someone knocks on the door of your house. Henry will be able to tell you if it is a man, a woman, a demon or a possessed human. If he knows the individuals in question, he will tell you before you open the door who to expect, Father Odell, Miss White etc for example. He will recognise their personal scents from afar. If Ivy and Jack get lost in the forest while foraging, he will be able to track them down in no time at all. Your angelic messenger has a natural ability to guide himself anywhere as you know already. As for flying, well he was naturally born to fly. He will always be the most skillful of your angels on that ground in the sky under all weather. He has been flying creatures more than anything else.

The Master confirmed,

-The way Henry flies is faultless. In that regard, I saw him cover great distances, never getting lost in the sky, managing any weather system, this is why we used him as a messenger almost straight away. I can tell you that the penny dropped when he said he must have been a bird in a past life at dinner. It made so much sense I just had to check it out and what I saw blew my mind. We have a very special angel in Henry. His skill set coming from the animal kingdom is impressive.

Agreeing his son enquired further, as they all sat on a small dry stone wall surrounding the courtyard,

-Indeed. I am interested to know if he has abilities from the animals he has been which were not flying and what they were.

Indulging his curiosity the angel of all animals replied,

-Well, Henry was thrice a horse and once your mule. Of that, he has been a very wild stallion, in the steppes of Mongolia. He was leading a large group of wild horses. He was the dominant male, bringing the others to food sources, green pastures, and ensuring the protection of his group. You will find in your angel leading qualities. He can take charge easily of about fifty angels, with your guidance even more, Sebastien. Twice he became a horse belonging to a knight, the same human. Each time he was a battle horse, and was right in the thick of it. He liked that knight a lot. Like many animal spirits, the ones who experienced domestication, Henry has that need, almost an urge to devote himself totally to someone. He did it to that knight. He gave him two of his animal lifetimes. That man is resting in paradise. Sebastien, you will be the recipient of Henry's devotion of all his angelic lives. You will be able to count on Henry to be by you no matter what, through thick and thin.

Sebastien asked with deep interest,

-Does the fact that he has been from the equine family a few times explains the talent Henry has to control and even train horses?

Mitos answered revealing,

-It does explain it, yes, furthermore, Henry has a great affinity with them. A horse will always obey him. Likewise you, Sebastien have that power over horses. Like a fairy godfather I bestowed three spirits of animals at the request of your father to be woven into your soul at the time of your conception, three animals that the Master knew very well. One of them is a stallion.

Grinning sarcastically Sebastien commented,

-Yes, Cadarn, and my father named me after a horse! And my Dad knew Arthus so well that he ended up in the pot and he ate it. But he couldn't have known a sabre toothed cat...

The Master started laughing, he pointed to his son and

stated to Mitos,

-Mitos, this is what you get when you put some human into an angel: an impossible half breed to deal with. He is never content and is always arguing. I wish he kept his fiery temper only to tackle demons. Sebastien, Arthus didn't end up in the pot, he was nicely roasted on the spit over the fire and your mother was basting it with loving care with its own juices regularly.

Sebastien barked in an angry way,

-It makes it all better, does it?

Teasing his son, the Master replied with a wicked smile,

-Oh, yes, it did. Arthus was a delicious cockerel.

Pointing at his father, Sebastien argued, telling Mitos,

-Look at what I have to contend with everyday, Mitos. If I am impossible, so is he! He is an impossible watcher with a cruel streak about him. He ate the bloody animal he wanted me to have the spirit of! It can't get any worse than that!

Mitos started to smile widely. His best friend, the Master, had told him all about the constant bickering he had with his son but also how he enjoyed having them, and was sometimes provoking them and fuelling them in purpose. On his part Mitos, who was a much more peaceful angel, was eager to appease the most important demon killer of the angelic world,

-Yes, it can. Your father could have been a watcher who turned badly and ate humans. Let me tell you a couple of things, Sebastien. First, you are both Punishers. You are correcting angels and you can not escape the fact that both of you have been created with a little dose of cruelty in order to be able to control, curb and deal with cruelty. This is also why you are such an excellent demon killer, Sebastien. Secondly, Arthus's story is more complicated than that. He was an emblem, a mascot to your village and he belonged to your father who never had any intention of eating him. The cockerel was singing at dawn, waking up everyone in the village and they loved him for it. But your mother, a newcomer to the village, didn't know how important the bird was. As a new bride Larra aimed to impress her chieftain of a husband, and she went to cook Arthus. Your father never had the heart to tell her that she did a mistake. But he was sincerely annoyed with the death of Arthus. Hence he demanded me for his spirit to be kept within you as you were to be the chieftain of that village after him. He also asked me to find a cockerel that looked like Arthus overnight and bring it to his village, so no one would know the fate of poor Arthus to protect his wife from facing straight anger from the superstitious villagers who believed that Arthus was bringing them good luck and prosperity. So it was not out of pleasure that he ate that cockerel.

The Master confirmed to his son,

-This is entirely true. The superstition was true as well. I can not dismiss that the curse of the cockerel did happen to that village and to you, my son.

Mitos warned the Master,

-I don't think it is a good idea to tell the Mighty One all about the curse. He is still too young and impetuous. Beside that we tried everything to stop that powerful curse.

An interested Sebastien demanded sternly,

-Who is the Mighty One? What is that curse you two are talking about which affected the village and myself? I need to know.

The Master told to the unresting Sebastien who was turning around in the courtyard,

-Come and seat by me and let me enlightened you a little. You have to know about it at one point let it be tonight so please listen and don't interrupt if you can. I know it will be hard for you to do due to your human blood.

Sebastien sat back by the side of his father and tried to display as much patience as he could. He remained silent ready to listen. The Master started,

-The Mighty One is one of your many names. You are the grand son of the Creator, the One and only. I am one of his sons. The One has three sons and I am the eldest. I am the one who has been creating major angels for my father, hence my full title is the Master of Angels. You are my second son. Your brother, Gael, is resting in paradise, he was a demon killer as well but he didn't make it. He was slaughtered by demons fairly early on. He was also tasked to make angels from human stock but made only two: William and Abigail. After what happened to him, he never wanted to go back on duty. His grand father and I never blamed him but we were left with a huge angelic position to be filled in. I was ordered to create you, Sebastien, and like my first son, you had to be conceived by myself and a human, and you had to become the high angel your brother was supposed to be forever. As I told you, I made a mistake, I didn't check your mother's entire background. She was not fully human, she was part fairy, the daughter of a goddess and a human. This made you far more powerful than you were intended to be.

Appreciating being finally taught who he truly was, Sebastien asked,

--What was I supposed to be?

The Master sighed deeply,

-Just like Gael, only part human and part angel. However, I fell in love with your mother so fast that I married her within a week of her stepping into the village with her father. It was only after conceiving you that I realised that my human wife was not so ordinary. Then the truth came out from her father, that his daughter was part fairy. Further more, Dana the goddess, your grand mother, told me that the inheritance of magical powers skipped one generation in her line usually. So you are the one with powers similar to hers. Beside that not knowing that you had such a grand mother when I created you, I applied to Mitos to impart you the powers of three animal spirits. My reason for that was that I didn't want a repeat of what happened with your brother, I needed you to be stronger. Hence, you, my son, are a rather particularly powerful angel with a combination of powers that set you quite apart from the rest. You are not quite what you meant to be by a long shot. But I dare say that you are a mistake which was most welcomed in the angelic world.

Standing up, Sebastien demanded in an offended manner,

-Am I considered as a mistake?

Nodding his head positively, Mitos revealed,

-You are, but you are also considered a blessing and a miracle. The Master had to ask the permission of his father for you to be when he learnt of your peculiar lineage. Conditions were put upon you becoming an angel by your grand father but he allowed you to be born and to be a human first. The One came to see you thrice during your human life. Thrice, he was greatly impressed by you so much so that at your human death he imparted you to be counted as one of his superior angels. He refers to you often as his mighty miracle.

The Master added,

-How many times did I hear my father say: 'If no one can do it, my Mighty will.' You bestow his highest esteem and the one of all angels. Once you were an incarnated angel, the way you behaved in your many lives brought to you tremendous respect by all and also their constant admiration. If you do not know, but I am sure you must realise it yourself, you are a role model for many angels. Your main angelic name was chosen by my father who I had to confess to that my child about to be born will be much stronger than what we had planned. I told him that the night of your creation you were already kicking and moving inside the belly of my Larra by dawn. You can relate to that because it did happen to you, when you made your little bit pregnant. From the confession of my mistake and the fact that you were going to be much stronger than expected, my father called you the Mighty One and Cadarn became your first human name. He told me in a mighty way what would be your human name by striking my horse dead by lightning and he ordered to Mitos to weave the spirit of that animal into your soul. That Celtic name was also to honour the fact that your grand mother was a Celtic goddess. Your human name changed during your angelic lives to Sebastien which means venerable. It was to reflect how honoured you had become as the grand son of the One.

Sebastien enquired full of curiosity,

-So, I met my grand father without knowing it during my human existence?

His father revealed,

-You did. There are two more instances to add to the three that Mitos mentioned. He was there at your human birth and at your human death. He took the shape of the midwife who delivered you safely into the world. He cut your umbilical cord. He put you into my arms and I knew he was allowing me to keep you despite my mistake. He told me that you'd better be a good one then he pointed outdoors to my stallion who was laying dead on the ground and said that if you didn't pass your grades as an angel during that human life, he wouldn't give you another existence. That human life was your only chance to prove to him that you were a worthy mistake. One major condition that you had upon your head was to be entirely powerless. Before he left he removed your angelic powers. He smiled to you however, and told you in a gentle manner, that he expected great things from you and he needed to be impressed in order for you to become accepted as an angel. He then looked at me and reassured me that you were as handsome as I was, that I was making him proud and that he was sure that you will make me proud. Alone with you Mighty I was trembling with emotion. I was holding you tight into my arms afraid to let go of you. You were a creative mistake which came to pass and had the seal of approval of my father. He didn't come at Gael's birth but he came at yours. Fair to say you intrigued him from the beginning.

Looking intensely at his father, Sebastien asked,

-Did you have to pay for me, your mistake and my mere existence? You always make me pay when I ask you for something. Is it the same with your father?

The Master replied sternly,

-The answer is yes, I did. But do not ask me your worth because for me you are priceless.

Standing up again, Sebastien demanded to know. It was Mitos who confided,

-Your father is totally enslaved to your grand father. His slavery was the price and his loss of free will, however he was allowed to regain free will over time, little by little, by the sum of his actions and yours. He is almost there in that respect. But he will remain a slave for eternity.

Sebastien knelt by his father full of emotion offering,

-Can I be your slave in return, Master?

The Master hugged his son thoroughly giving him his answer,

-No, you can't. I will not allow it and my own father will not either. Just carry on your good work. There is not a day, when I am not proud of you, not one which I can think of, and as a father, this is my joy, my consolation. One of my hardest day was the last of your human life. My father forced me to go with him. We were both side by side in human shape in the crowd watching you being thrown to the lions. He didn't allow me to visit you in jail. He didn't allow me to say something to you. You were human at that time, and all you had to know and remember was that I passed away thirteen years earlier as your incarnated father. So I had to stay put by the One. He never reassured me that you had made it to be an angel. He kept it a secret until your end. When your half brother died I cried heavily. It was a hard blow. But his soul rests in paradise. But for you, there was a risk that my father would dispose of your soul, not let it go anywhere and just destroy it, because you were not meant to be originally. Tears covered my face as I watched you fighting with the lions. You were so brave, so courageous. The Roman threw you in that arena to feed you to the lions and instead you tamed all of the beasts in front of them single handedly. They were impressed. I was. My father gave me the knife which had a spell from your fairy grand mother and ordered me to give it to you. I threw it with all my might in your direction. Then my father told, either you will kill the lions one after the other, become a gladiator, stay a slave all your life and your soul will extinguish itself at your death, either you will do something else with the knife, like kill some Romans and make a useless attempt to free yourself. He said you were capable of doing so and succeed by murdering some innocents in the making. That meant that he would still extinguish your soul at your death and you were simply not meant to be. All the while I kept thinking of the little boy you were, just learning how to walk, and how you would be so pleased to have made it into my arms, and how you would ask to try again and again. The fear of losing you was so strong and then you killed yourself in that arena making your statement to the Romans. You gave me a last look and I knew you recognised me. When you fell on the ground, everyone was in dismay. The lions surrounded you and protected your body. I was a total mess, in complete distress. My father took me then in his arms and told me that you were staying with us; that he will not destroy your soul, that you were to become my angel. He gave me a large sum and demanded that I retrieved your body. No one had been able to approach your corpse because of the lions. But the lions gave me a way and I was able to pick you up. I brought you to my father and he told me to leave you with him. Then you must remember what happened.

Seating back by his father, Sebastien nodded positively, as he recalled,

-I do, like if it was yesterday. I woke up in a pool of light which felt like a cradle of warmth. I saw him, he took me by the hand and gave me a choice to be either a guardian angel or an incarnated one. Whichever way I chose he made it clear that I was to be a demon killer, a Punisher and a maker of human angels. Giving him my choice, kneeling by him, he touched my shoulders and I felt endowed with so much power. Then he told me that I would be pleased to see who would teach me to be a good angel then you came and guided me through my angelic paces. You never told me up until now that the Creator was my grand father. Is there a reason why? When did I meet him thrice in my human life?

Carrying on disclosing important information about him to his son, the Master replied,

-The reason is that the Creator never wanted you to be complacent by claiming you descended from him. However others knew, and this is why you were always met with deep respect. He did the same thing to me. I didn't know he was my father until thousands of years later. Like the One did with you, he observed me, until one day, I was deemed good enough to know the truth about myself. I always noticed that deep reverence were paid to me but I never would have guessed why. In my very first years of conception, I had to be human, just like you. The purpose was that I should never be haughty because I was an angel, the Master of them all and his son. I believed I was an orphan human boy then an orphan entity for so long. An old woman found me as a newborn baby, naked, in a bush on fire. She put out the flames with her hands to save me. As soon as she held me, all the burns that she sustained disappeared and I had no burns whatsoever. Crea was such a kind human. She looked after me until her death when I was seven years old. In those very ancient times, we were living in caves. Without Crea's protection, I had to learn how defend my cave from wild beasts. I was a hunter and a gatherer what Crea taught me to be. One day however I did let my den to be shared by a wounded female smilodon, a sabre tooth cat. Visibly, she bit more than she could chew by attacking a mammoth who pierced her belly with its tusks. She happened to be pregnant. I looked after her last days and helped her to deliver a single cub. One had died inside of her. When she passed away, I raised her cub. I kept him alive and well. I tamed him from the start and we hunted together. My cave was protected, dare I say very well from then on. So to correct your earlier suspicion, yes, I did have a pet sabre tooth cat. The spirit of which is woven to your soul as Mitos can tell you.

Mitos, enjoying being part of the Master's revelations to his son, confirmed,

-Yes indeed, your father did hunt with a large sabre tooth cat which was called Koum-Koum, the life of the mother of which is one of Henry's animal ones. Again this is one explanation why your angel Henry is devoted to you, Sebastien. His ancient animal spirit gave birth to your one. Spiritually you are a family. Your father told me as soon as he discovered it when he put his hands on the shoulders of Henry. He called me out to investigate the matter further. What I found out is that the animal spirit of Henry recognised the one we gave you when he was one of the lions fighting in that Roman arena. It may sound weird but he scented his cub within you. From then on, Henry's animal spirit tried to track you down in all your lives in order to be with you. He succeeded many times to be your pet. Your angelic bond with Henry will always be very strong and protective on both sides.

Sebastien swore in response,

-Good Lord!

Kicking the back of his son's head, the Master scolded,

-Don't swear! Otherwise your grand father will strike you with a thunderbolt.

It send Sebastien giggling widely, yet he demanded,

-So my grand father visited me thrice. Why didn't I recognise him?

It was the time for his father to smile. He stated,

-I never thought you were a little dim witted, Sebastien. Anyhow, the Creator visited you in different shapes in order to test you. First, it was when you were just a little boy. You were enjoying yourself fishing with the other village boys of your age when you saw an old man falling into the lake on the other side. One of your friends said that the man must be drunk, the other that the man must be blind and the last that he must be senile to not see the lake in front of him. You didn't talk, you plunged into the lake, swam as fast as you could to retrieve the old man before he drowned. You managed to save him. You took him to the shore and made sure he was breathing. Then you took him to our home. I knew when I saw the man you were helping that it was the One. You put him by the fire to warm himself up. You told me what happened to him. You went to fetch a cover. You ordered him to give you his clothes so you could dry them for him and you gave him the thick cover to keep him warm. You dealt with his clothes. You asked me if you could give him some cervoise to help warming him up from the inside. I agreed and I saw you bringing the cervoise to my father in such a kind and polite manner, that the Creator gave me a very pleased look. I could tell that you met his approval that day. You enquired about him, genuinely concerned, if he was getting any better, if he was suffering, if he was blind, if he needed help, if he had somewhere to live, if he was lost. The One played the card that he was a traveller who lost his way. When he told you his destination, you warned him that he would not be able to reach it at this time of the day and that crossing the forest at night was dangerous because of the wolves, let alone the boars and you asked my permission for him to stay for the night and that you would show him the way the following day. I agreed and you went running outside saying, that you were quite successful at fishing that afternoon and that you had enough fish for all of us tonight. When you left, my father didn't keep his pretence with me. He told me that he was very impressed by you. He was satisfied that I was bringing you up well. He stated that the mighty mistake I did could turn out to be a blessing. When you came back, you prepared the supper, you gave up your bed for the night for him and slept on the floor. In the morning you showed him the way to the destination he had mentioned and accompanied him all the way. He had ample opportunity to assess you on a one to one basis, asking you lots of simple questions. Do you remember him now my son, the lost traveller that you saved and helped? Well this was the first visit of your grand father when you were about to turn ten years old.

Nodding positively Sebastien recalled,

-I remember him. He did ask me a lot of questions when I guided him through the forest. He gave me his hand to shake when we parted and told me that it had been a very nice pleasure to meet me. I said likewise.

The Master revealed,

-The following day, I was summoned by the Creator. I knew he had assessed you and I was very anxious to know how you did fare in his eyes. First, he asked me why didn't I gave you a surrogate mother. It was a tough question for me. I loved your mother Larra, deeply and intensely, when we lost her it was just you and me against the rest of the world in my mind. I couldn't love anyone else but the son she gave me and to focus on you and to bring you up as best as I could. Then he announced that he was proud to be your grand father so far. He praised the humble way, I brought you up. But mainly he was impressed by your level of care, kindness and mindfulness.

Mitos confided,

-A few superior angels who have the confidence of the Creator like I have, got to hear first hand what he thought of you, Sebastien, at that stage. The Creator had all the confidence that you would be a great angel. One thing that touched him the most, among all the things that touched him and they are plenty like you sleeping on the floor to make sure he had a bed, was the way you refused a coin he was giving to you as a farewell gift for how good you had been to him. You told him to keep the coin for his next meal or to give it to someone that needed a meal. A lot of angels heard about little Mighty said this or little Mighty did that, I can tell you that until your next test came along.

A curious Sebastien asked,

-Did I fare well in my second test?

Replying his father smiled,

-You did. You were twenty then. Do you remember the three milk maids which you protected from being raped? Two of them were apparitions of my father. The third became your first wife. My father knew that she would be victim of a rape during her lifetime. He tried to pervert her fate so she would stay safe. He came forward in the shape of two very attractive girls to be the road companions of your future wife. When the attack happened, the two beauties, he incarnated were bothered first: a simple trick to deflect the attention from the main target, Carantiana. He knew that you were in the wood felling a couple of trees for firewood for the winter. If a terrorised Carantiana lost her voice under attack, he didn't and called for help for her. Sure enough, you came to the rescue carrying your axe. You fought the three men which were attacking the three girls. Not only you managed to beat all of them on your own and made them ran away, my father noticed that as you used your axe, you were careful to not injure anyone with the blade. However the three men were battered enough that they could not go very far. You took the three girls to our village, having given your cape to one to cover her torn dress. You were reassuring them all the way, being protective and ever so attentive to them all. Carantiana who had suffered from a twisted ankle in the attack, you carried in your arms. You left the ladies under my care, having explained to me the situation, then you organised a small group of men and lead them to punish the would be rapists. When you found them, you ruled for them to be flogged on the spot. At the end of their punishments, you warned that if any of them tried to rape a woman ever again, they would be castrated. The shamed faced three never did hurt a lady for their entire lives after that. Now, I knew that one girl was human while I recognised the two others for being apparitions of the One. The following day, sure enough I was summoned to meet the Creator.

Mitos interrupted the Master,

-I was there. I still remember that meeting. The Creator praised the fighting skills of Mighty as much as the way he cared so much for everyone. He said you, Sebastien, could have easily killed the three men because, despite their number, you were the strongest of them all. Similarly, you could have chopped their limbs off during the fight with your axe but instead, you applied enough injuries for them to not go far and recover from them over time and for you to be able to give them a good lesson afterwards. The One concluded that you would make a good Punisher like your father. The fact that you showed pace, strategy, fighting skills, restraint, mercy, and priorities such as looking after the victims before going back to punish the attackers made your grand father praise you endlessly.

Sebastien's father added,

-To be honest with you my son, the result of that test did please me greatly. It was not only because of your success but by the possibility of you becoming a Punisher. It takes a lot of character and at that point I was the only one. It is a rather draining position to bestow so having you my son giving me a hand on that arduous task that still needs to be done, it was happy news to my ears. Also because I became the slave of the Creator, the price for allowing you to be, Sebastien, I am not allowed to have a respite from being a Punisher any longer or any of my other duties.

Grinning Mitos stated to the Master,

-Well, you know what happened when you took a short break of your duties as a Punisher: Some watchers ate humans, literally feasting on all the ones they despised. That was enough for your father to call you back to your duties with immediate effect. To tell you the truth, the Creator needs you all the time on duty call. He realised he couldn't spare you. The Mighty One's birth, being admitted as a mistake by you, gave him the opportunity to unsure that you will always work like a slave by him with no respite to be had. The fact that Sebastien turned out to be a Punisher as well and a very good one at that has been a true blessing for you.

Turning to Sebastien, Mitos revealed,

-Your last test went like the first two with flying colours, Sebastien. I was there with the Creator, witnessing it. It was the last day of your human life. You were upon the chariot leading you to the arena. Your hands were tied in front of you. Your torso was bare to exhibit the severe flogging you received that morning by the centurion standing next to you who was guarding you. You knew you were going to your death but in your mind you welcomed it because for you it meant joining your two little girls and your wife in the after life. Crossing badly the road was a Roman family, a man, his wife, his teenage son and young daughter. The convoy by the side of your chariot had the eight hungry and angry lions in a rather small cage. One lion clawed both shoulders of the driver of the convoy in his rage. The driver in sheer pain dropped the reins. His horses became unruly. The worst was going to happen to that family in front of your chariot and that large cart. You told the centurion that the family was going to die and needed help. You jumped out of the chariot, despite your hands tied together. You rushed to the rescue and pushed them out of the way of the convoy. The centurion followed you to stop the horses of the convoy. You managed to put the father, the wife and the son safely on the road side but the father cried out for his little girl who terrified staid petrified and still in the middle of the road. You ordered him to stay put and safe while you would go and get her. The horses were on their rear legs, upset and would have trample the daughter yet you got her in time and pushed her out of the way bringing her back to his father. You met the grateful eyes of the Roman who asked how could he repay you. You replied by just looking after his own family with love and care because you knew what it was to lose one. You went by the centurion who was guarding you who still had trouble calming down the horses. You helped him out and within minutes you had the two horses being calm. You told him, that the driver of the cart was injured and was bleeding heavily, that he needed help and that you could walk by the horses and lead them and the convoy to the arena. He told you that there was a physician at the arena who would be able to look after the driver and the get go. You did. He watch you leading the cart in dismay and with great sadness. The Roman father went to the centurion and asked, who is that man who saved my family. He replied that you were a Gallic chieftain, that his army killed everyone in your village, that today you were being fed to the lions which you were taking yourself to the arena now. The Roman told that he couldn't understand why such a strong man like you didn't take a bid for freedom, because obviously in the way you came to help you could. The centurion had tears in his eyes when he replied that he knew you wouldn't escape. He confided that his men killed your family in such an horrendous manner, that he felt they were the barbarians and that you were the noble man. He said to the father that you only wanted to be back with your family. The Roman went to the arena that afternoon and wept at your death. Another man who cried thoroughly was the centurion. Unknowingly you taught him to be a better man.

Recalling the event, Sebastien confessed,

-I didn't know it was a test.

His father smiled as he said,

-Of course you wouldn't. It is the all point of them. This one showed that you had a very noble heart. Let me tell you who else shed a tear at your human death: your grand father. Later he gave me the result of your last test to let me in the know because you were already an angel by then. When you were fighting in the arena, you had passed all your tests. You were already an angel for the Creator. He was so proud that you made it.

Smiling blissfully, Mitos confided,

-The One told me, Sebastien, that you simply had to be, for your father, for him, and a great deal of angels and humans. It is getting late. You have a mission for me to do overnight. What is it?

Sebastien shared a vision to the angel of animals by holding his hand then briefed,

-We have a psychopath in town which will be up to no good tomorrow. We protected by spells many places. He likes putting things and animals on fire or hanging them. We do not know what he will be up to once he realise that his plan to burn the tavern will not work out. Will he try to burn the entire town instead? We have no clues. However, we can make the man meet his comeuppance for all the animals he slaughtered in nasty ways in his life. We need to group all their spirits and make them pester the man in a fashion which would slow him down in his actions at the very least or impeach him to do them at the very best. Mitos, I want you to gather their souls and make an army of them overnight. I will flesh them up to be able to bite and claw when the time comes tomorrow night. Find them all, the more numerous, the better. Brief them all. Meet me at the clinic tomorrow morning to report to me how many of those animal spirits you found and got ready to fight.

Mitos bowed to Sebastien saying before disappearing,

-You will have your army of animal spirits, trust me. What Darren Bell did to that poor cat was atrocious. See you tomorrow Mighty One.

#

When Mitos left, the Master praised his son,

-This is an interesting idea to use animal spirits to help out tomorrow. How did you come up with that one? That is what I am intrigued about. However I think it is quite ingenious.

Sebastien gave his father a smile and revealed with some seriousness,

-It was all down to a little rabbit called Clementine. The fact that after suffering a violent death, her spirit couldn't rest because she liked her owner. Now, the cat, which was burnt to death by Darren, was owned by a human who loved him very much and was very upset about his pet's death. I can only guess that the animal loved his owner back and that we will have a spirit which will not be resting. You and I are Punishers, how good will it feel to give that spirit a sense of closure by enabling him to punish the human that did kill him. Imagine Bell trying to light a fire in town, and that cat jumping on his back, clawing him.

Following the thought process of Sebastien, the Master suggested,

-We can go one step further. Fleshing the animals Bell did hurt is an awesome idea. But what if we rendered them invisible or if he can see them one moment and not the next. It will drive Bell crazy to know he is attacked by the very animals he killed but that he can't get to them anymore and they disappear on and off from his sight. They will be able to plague him and attack him all they want. He will be powerless against them just like they were powerless against him during their short lives.

His approving son told,

-This can be done easily. I am sure our good Miss White and myself can work this out together. But I like your idea. That will be a very good punishment for our less than nice man. Now, tell me before we are going back inside what Mitos didn't want you to explain to me about the curse on our Gallic village.

The Master stood up. He had hoped that his son had forgotten about the mention of the curse but clearly it was not the case. It had to be said for his son that he always kept his focus. Instead of shying away, having revealed so much to Sebastien already, the Master announced,

-The curse wasn't only on our village, it affected you as well very badly. What I am going to say will make you emotional. The mistake that your mother Larra done unknowingly by killing and cooking the cockerel of the village was a massive one. You see we had a legend in the village, one which I did not believe but I was keen to maintain and observe anyhow. Let me be give you a bit of background first. When I am fully incarnated, I never have physical human parents conceiving me. Instead I appear as a baby somewhere at the order of the Creator who is choosing the place and the time. This time, he chose that little village of Gaul. The chieftain's wife had just lost her baby in a horrific childbirth. She didn't have any child and she knew she wouldn't have one anymore. The chieftain and her were upset about her inability to conceive any longer. The One aware of their misfortune sent me to them. One morning, three days after their tragedy, whilst hunting the chieftain found me in the woods crying and when he took me in his arms, I smiled. I was adopted into his heart straight away. He brought me to his wife and when she heard that I was a newborn baby abandoned in the forest, she just took me in her tender arms and started to breast feed me. They made enquiries in nearby villages to quest for my possible mum but as I had none, they just kept me and loved me as their own son. Literally I was god sent to that childless couple.

Sebastien giggled, as he commented,

-After a bush on fire, I don't think that a forest full of wolves was safer, grand father knows how to deposit you in the most dangerous places.

His father explained,

-He knows how to appeal to the good heart of a human by putting me in certain situations, that is a fact. When I had to be incarnated to create your brother Gael, I was left on the rocks of a beach and the tide was coming. Same I was a defenceless newborn baby. But I was found just in time by a fisherman. Now in all circumstances of my adoptions by humans, I have always been their grateful good boy. So much so that for the Gallic chieftain, I walked on his footsteps, learnt from him and became one at his death. I was immersed in the Celts's culture. For that particular village, there was a specific legend concerning the chieftain's cockerel.

The Master sighed deeply before he carried on,

-Of course I didn't believe in it but faked all along that I did. Let me tell you how it went. About a thousand years before I arrived, that village suffered a great deal, from bad weather, flood, tribe warfare between villages, poor harvests, hunts which didn't bring any food to anyone. Everyone were so dispirited that they sent their druid on a quest for a solution. He travelled to Britain and came back with an enchanted cockerel, red crested, with bluish black feathers and a emerald green tail. The legend said that the cockerel would belong to the chieftain and change the luck of the village. That if he died, it had to be a natural death and then he will be born again and again and again keeping the good luck on the village. However if the cockerel was killed doom would ensue for the village. Not only that, if the cockerel was eaten the worst fears of the people who ate it would happen. The person who slaughtered the cockerel would die inevitably within a year. Let me tell you my son that everything happened as the legend said. Mitos and I tried to save the day just in case the legend was true by keeping alive the spirit of Arthus the cockerel inside of you. It did not work.

Turning around in the courtyard, the ancient angel told with great sadness,

-Everything came to pass. First, let me tell you that my worst fear is to lose my family, children and the wife I have chosen. When I lost Gael, I was devastated   and the grief staid in my heart. On this occasion, I lost your mother. I could have lost you as well, but because Arthus spirit is within you, it kept you alive and allowed you to come again and again. Larra who killed the chicken passed away within a year of doing so. Her own worst fears passed on to you along with mines. For her, she feared rape since her attack in Brittany, for me, as I said it was losing my family. You lost your wife and daughters and we both know what happened to them. You was conceived on the wrong night. You have been subjected to the heavy hand of the curse during your human life. We also have to acknowledge the fact that the village faced its doom like it was predicted. All the villagers were killed and it was burnt down. The fake enchanted cockerel which Mitos found was just an ordinary one, and yes, the true village cockerel that Larra killed was really enchanted. Your grand mother Dana and the One, put a protection on all your angelic lives to unsure that you do not live through such loss ever again. We were all so pained by the grief you had to go through just by a silly human mistake. I feel responsible as well because, not believing in the curse, I didn't spoke about it to Larra nor warned her. She wasn't aware of it whatsoever. At the time when the deed was done and consumed, I was annoyed but not to the point to even show it to your mother who was so pleased with herself because she had prepared a very nice meal in order to impress me. As I say I also thought it was just a superstition. But as a precaution I invoked Mitos. The decision to keep the spirit of the cockerel within you was taken thinking that this will just do the trick in case there was a curse. The fake cockerel was also to keep the villagers happy so they would not noticed that their enchanted cockerel was no more. At the untimely death of Lara, I had then strong suspicions that we did make your mother and I a terrible mistake. The night we buried Lara in the Forest of Fougères, I told the legend of the enchanted cockerel to Dana. I had to come clean to your grand mother. She invoked my father who came straight away. She made me recount the legend to him and what we did Larra and I. She pointed to the grave of my wife, her daughter, to warn him that a curse was definitely in place. I was scolded right there and then by my father who demanded me if it was the wisest of my moves to keep silent on such a legend then labelled me as a stupid angel. They inspected you as soon as they knew you had the spirit of Arthus within you and sighed with sorrow. The Creator said that at least you would have the stamina to live through all your ordeals. He cradled you in his arms for an instant saying poor, poor little Mighty before ordering me to take you back home. He didn't tell me what would happen. He worked with Dana to alleviate your fate. I was severely punished for my mistake. My father disowned me for years. Not only was I working as his slave, I was now not worth a lot to his eyes. I lost his affection for a while. I was not allowed to speak to him a great deal, I was just allowed to work for him and obey him in every way, shape or form. The loss of his consideration devastated me so much. I passed away soon after you were married. I was working in a field well into a cold night. I kept crying and the tears froze onto my face, then I dropped stone cold dead. My father collected my spirit whilst you found my body. I remember him being harsh for years as he made me witness from above your human life, but also from the ground. He put me inside you when you lost your family and saw the destruction of the entire village. I was mortified at the pain you suffered and at the carnage you had to watch in such a way. I am still trembling about it today. I couldn't talk for days, I couldn't look at anyone especially not into the eyes of my father, I cried blood tears up until your death everyday. When I brought your body to the Creator, he ordered me, to cease crying and to be strong for you because I had a duty of reparation to do to you. He told me that you would be an angel carrying enormous pain in your heart and now that you had made it to be an angel, he didn't want to lose you because of me. So I tried to patch up as best as I could and tried to hide away my emotions.

He stopped and looked at the starry sky before carrying on,

-One night, I crumbled into pieces through the weight of my sorrow. It was about three years ago, you had your accident on the railing. You did spend so many incarnated lives still thinking of your Gallic family. I lay where you did below the stars, I was feeling your pain, and I was about to commit angelic suicide and self combust myself to oblivion. You were being saved at that moment by Doctor Williams and Doctor Fair. My father appeared and ordered me to get up, which I did almost automatically at the sound of his voice. He asked me harshly what I was going to do. Then I dropped to my knees and confessed that I was about to do the worst. He held my chin and demanded if I was sure about it, if I really wanted my son to lose one more member of his family, the only one you knew about now. So I stood up despite being an emotional wreck and I said no, that I will keep on going for you. I felt so shattered at that moment. To my surprise my father gave me a hug, it was the first one since your human death. It was long, it was warm, it was silent and I felt his deep love. Then he told me, that having lost two sons which were now in heaven, he was not prepared to lose his eldest who had been able to work upon earth for so long. He didn't call me slave then, he called me by my real angelic name. It was so long since I heard my name pass his lips. I still felt like I would burn to death in his arms of sheer exhaustion but I hanged on to him for dear life and I begged him to tell me if you didn't lost your incarnated life. He took me to you. We were both human surgeons helping Doctor Williams for the rest of your operation. When you were out of danger, when you were stable, my father, Doctor Williams and I stayed by your bedside. We were fairly surprised to see the human Doctor Fair nursing you throughout the night with us. He kept checking your pulse and your temperature almost every ten minutes. He confided to all of us, that you had to pull through because you meant the world to his daughter. In front of us, he was rehearsing the way he would break the news of your accident to his girl so she could stay strong and not cry. When the Creator and I left your bedside at dawn, satisfied that you would not lose that incarnated life, my father told me in a reassuring manner, that all you needed was love to hang on in there, and that it was just around the corner for you. And well, it was with the young Ivy Fair. You always need to hang on in there to see the happy endings and never quit before you lived fully.

Putting his arm across the shoulders of his father, Sebastien confided,

-I am happy to know that you didn't quit. I never knew how hard it has been for you. How are your relationship with your father now?

The Master replied with a sad smile,

-They are better. The Creator has always been tough but he has always been fair. Somehow, even when he was at his harshest, he has always been there for me and supportive. I am not disowned any longer. One day, I got hurt on duty. I was with Mitos. I was unconscious and he couldn't get a sign of life out of me. He called my father who came immediately. All I know is that I woke up in the arms of the Creator who was crying over me and who was overjoyed when I opened my eyes. He nursed me back to health day in and out like a mother hen. Now, tell me the truth, do you hold any grudges against me for the Cockerel Curse? If you do, I will understand. Then just tell what you want me to do to make it up to you.

Looking at his angelic father, Sebastien replied in all honesty,

-I do not hold any grudges. If it appeases you, I can even say that you bestow my entire forgiveness. Now let's just put the past behind us and work together in the present to build a better future. It is starting here, with this cottage. We need to deactivate that pentagram and portal to hell. We also need to teach Miss White how it is done. Her, Theo are already proving to be excellent assets to my angelic army. Let's not forget that them and Doctor Valdi managed to break a strong curse over Wilton Town. So if you and I have to face curses in the future, we have now the right team in place to deal with them. Moving forward, I will only request one thing of you. You spoke about family and how highly it counted for you. For me, it is likewise. I just want to meet both of my grand fathers, my mother, my grand mother and my half brother wherever they are, paradise or else. Organise that for me. My last request is this one, I would love for your human manifestation to live at my house. As you know, I am restarting a family with my Ivy who is a young orphaned woman with only me in the world. We adopted Jack, a fallen angel in the human body of a eight year old child. My little bit is pregnant with my Theodore who will be a powerful angel like you and I. I will also be given back my two daughters. I want you to be a part of your living family. I want all of my children to know you because I remember how you brought me up and I could have never asked for a better father. I know we enjoy to bicker with each other but the truth of the matter is if you accept to stay under my humble roof, I will not only appreciate it, I will love it because myself, my wife and all my little ones will beneficed from your wisdom and advices. What do you say? Where does your main body live currently?

Slightly emotional, the Master gave his answer,

-I am an owl in a hollow tree in the cemetery of Wilton Town. It has been my main lodgings since you arrived in town.

Sebastien demanded,

-Make your main body this human appearance and live with my family, please. Don't make me beg you, because it will be endless, because I will do so over and over again.

Hugging his son, the father accepted,

-I am here with you, and for you. This is now my main body and I would love to live in your home. Thank you for inviting me in.

A satisfied Sebastien felt that for once his father had properly opened up to him. He was also happy that the Master had accepted his invite to live under his roof. Taking the bucket full of water in one hand, and nestling his free arm within the one of his father, he enjoined whilst teasing,

-Let's go back in. I have the perfect room for you: The

derelict room of Theo. It will be ten times better than a hole in a tree.

The Master shook his head, as he mentioned in desperation,

-I forgot that you are going to be impossible to live with. It is certainly going to be interesting.

Giggling Sebastien replied,

-I am not that bad. I am just kidding you. There are four decent bedrooms on the second floor of the presbytery, you are welcome to any that you like. If it makes it all better, you will still be allowed to give me the slap on the back of my head on occasion to tame my human blood. By the way, what was the name of my human grand father, the blacksmith? Did you like him?

Smiling back to his son, opening the door of the cottage, his father answered,

-His name was Aodhan Gallius and yes, I confess that I did like that human. He was not without flaws but he was a decent man. Most importantly, he had a very good heart. He was skilled, very hardworking, an excellent father to his daughter. I love the way he empowered her to be able to defend herself. Your mother wasn't a shy violet, I can tell you that, she could stand her ground in any fight or any argument. It was all due to him. He was educated. Aodhan had a twin brother called Quentin who was born first. Quentin was supposed to inherit the forge of their father while Aodhan was intended to be a druid. Aodhan was given away aged two. He was taught among numerous things, to read and write, Celt, Germanic, Nordic, Greek and Latin languages, mathematic, the art of making potions, some magic and astronomy by druids. When he was fourteen, his twin passed away of an illness of the lungs. Aodhan's father went to fetch back his remaining son paying an enormous sum to the druids in order to do so. Your grand father was then taught his craft as a blacksmith, all about weaponry and how to fight and use those weapons he forged. I enjoyed many conversations with him. He rests in paradise with Larra. I will present them to you.

When they stepped inside Sebastien gave an appreciative glance to his father, nodding positively. Inside the cottage they found Doctor Williams and Miss White in deep conversation with for main topic the good Georgia Marlow. Williams stood up and bowed at their entrance. He asked,

-Is Mitos gone?

Sebastien putting the bucket of water on the table told,

-We sent him on an overnight mission. He will be back to report upon it in the morning. Did you protect my white witch?

Doctor Williams confirmed,

-I did and she protected me. We did the protective spell as well on Father Odell and Ted. You will find them at their posts by the bedside of Peter O'Neil.

A pleased Sebastien ordered,

-Good. You two follow my father upstairs and wait for me there, I shall not be too long. In the meantime explain to Miss White the process of the proper closure of the hell portal.

Taking the bucket of water with him and a wooden bowl, Sebastien went to the bedroom of Peter. Following the Master and Doctor Williams, Whilhelmina queried,

-Am I his white witch?

Doctor Williams and the Master couldn't help smiling at her question. It was the father of Sebastien who explained as they went up the stairs,

-When you belong to the angelic army of my son, you belong to him. He cares for all his soldiers like a father to his children. He calls every angel and eternal being my this and my that. You will get used to it eventually Miss White. When he does use the possessive article to address you that is when he is prepared to fight to the death to protect you. Whenever he stopped to use 'my' consistently by one's name, this is when it is time to worry as a rule of thumb. It may mean for an angel that he will lose his wings or that the soldier will be demoted, thrown out of his army or maybe ending up becoming a useless soul in paradise.

William added,

-Oh yes, the paradise option, well, never ask that one if you want to keep the respect of Sebastien. He is a grafter. He expects all of his soldiers to be hard working like him and to never ask for a rest. When I requested a holiday in heaven just for a little while after this life, I wasn't his William anymore until the day I told him that I changed my mind about going to paradise to stay on earth working for him. Lord, can he convince any fool that paradise is the option of the lazy good souls who think they have done enough when there is still so much to do down here.

A giggling Master confided,

-I remember the day Sebastien came to tell me about your request. He was truly angry. I tried to explain to him that you did request the same to me many times and that you truly needed a break but it was like talking to a brick wall. His repartee was how selfish can an angel be when he can stay sitting on his arse while he can do so much good instead.

A pouting Doctor Williams stated,

-He is as uncompromising as his grand father.

Interested by the conversation Miss White enquired,

-Who is his grand father?

The Master whispered to her ear that on the paternal side Sebastien's grand father was god himself and that on the maternal side it was a human.

It made Whilhelmina fall backward but the Master and Doctor Williams were quick to grab her wrists to prevent her to fall down the stairs. Bewildered she commented,

-That is why every angel bows to him! I never did, he must think I am rude. Oh, good Lord!

Smiling Williams reassured her,

-Sebastien doesn't know his lineage. Beside that he has been brought up to be humble.

The Master contradicted Doctor Williams,

-I revealed everything to Sebastien tonight. He does know his lineage. But yes, he has been brought up humble and by the way he carried a bucket and went to fetch a bowl to ensure Peter doesn't get thirsty overnight, I can say safely that the revelation will not affect his behaviour in a detrimental way. He will remain as modest as he ever been.

Looking at the amazing eyes of the angel who had put her trembling hand upon his arm to prevent her from falling in the stairs, Whilhelmina queried with anxiety in her voice,

-But that means that you his father is, is, is...

Awe struck she couldn't finish her sentence as the Master showed for a brief instant his full angelic appearance to her. Returning to his human shape, the Master explained,

-Yes, I am the eldest son of the Creator. But if I am the Master of all angels, I am also the slave of my father. Like I brought up Sebastien to be a hard working and humble angel, I had a similar education. Don't you worry Miss White about the way you address my son or me. What is important into our eyes is not the mere formalities but the actions that one's do, like the one you took, of your own accord, to do a protective spell upon Doctor Williams. Your orders were clear and didn't include Williams to be a beneficiary of the spells. First you noticed it. Second you took action to rectify it regardless of your little quibble with him earlier on concerning your Georgia. This shows good character but also you passed with flying colours a little test put in your way by my son. You can go above and beyond of your own accord but also that you care for others. Let me tell you that to look after one another is one of the principles of the angelic army.

Miss White gave a glance at Doctor Williams which she could see him giggling, she demanded to him in a shy way,

-Did you know I was being tested?

The angel nodded positively confessing,

-Of course I knew, I was the main prop to be used in the test. You were under my careful observation all the while but also the one of the Master and his son. I loved the way you said with genuine concern that we'd better protect me as well because you saw the demon that came out of the pentagram first hand that Sebastien and Theo had to fight and it was not a nice beastie. You can expect Sebastien to put a lot of 'my' in front of your surname and title for that for I am the eldest angel being created from a human but also his best friend.

The Master added,

-Let's not forget William that you also have been an angelic mentor to my son for many lives. Now he knows that your creator was his elder brother Gael, he may even start to consider you as family and his orphaned angelic nephew. It will be interesting to watch.

Bewildered, Doctor Williams swore as they reached the corner of the attic where the pentagram was,

-Good Lord! Master you didn't tell Sebastien that! You already know what a mother hen he is with all of his angels. If he starts that with me, he probably is going to force me to live with him and your son has the lifestyle of a monk, a colourful one but still a monk. He made a vow of poverty, I didn't.

Laughing the Master started to remove the planks covering the pentagram, he commented,

-Again, it will be interesting to watch. You have been begging to rest in paradise far too many times for us to ignore it and we know that something is not quite right with you and it has been going on for a while. Sebastien took an informed guess saying that it is the sheer lack of love you experienced throughout your lives. I agree with him. Why do you think, he has been playing the match maker with you? Anyhow, if he ever propose to you to live under his roof, you know that he will never accept a no for an answer. Beside that you will be joining our angelic family home. Let me tell you that I was invited to live at the presbytery myself. I accepted my son's invitation. Hmm, the level of activity of this pentagram is strong. I want both of you to be on your guards. Miss White if a demon comes out, put yourself behind me, I will protect you with all my might. As for you William stay by me and combine your energy with mine. In case of a sudden attack, we will employ the strategy of our good Father Odell, blind the demon momentarily, and call Sebastien to come immediately. I want powerful blinding solar light. Can you do that with me, my William?

The angelic wizard replied positively,

-I can, yes, Master. Definitely, we have some activity, here. Miss White, please, as a precaution, put yourself behind the Master now. Master, I knew you were going to keep a watchful eye on Sebastien and his new family inside his pets.

Correcting him, the Master said with a bright smile,

-No, William, my son wants me in human shape and fully involved within the family he is building up. There is his adopted son Jack which I know he will never give up on to get back as a full angel. Then we have his little bit, Ivy, which is literally an orphan and has only got him in the world. She is also such a young woman that is going to be a mother for the first time this year. And if you want a bit of news, I am adopting the angelic Henry which will become the younger brother of Sebastien and my youngest son. Then we have Ted who has always been an odd ball. Sebastien took him under his wings such a long time ago when Ted was just a little abandoned human boy. In his heart Ted is his adopted son. Since his first human life, this is the first time, I am seeing my boy attempting to have a family again. God knows I want to be part of it and I was only so pleased to be asked to do so. It moved me. Father Odell don't know how much the gift of his home to Sebastien will mean to so many. Miss White, you will need to relate that to him. Theo needs to be aware of this.

Having taken her place behind him, Whilhelmina reassured,

-I will tell my Theo, you can be sure of it. Master, I don't know if it can help but I did develop an emergency spell which involves solar light. You know my daughter was a vampire and if she happened to turn really bad I would have had to kill her demon and mourn her. I didn't know which type of demon she had inside her because she behaved so well most of the time. So the spell is encompassing all demons. If you hold my hand will you be able to see the very spell I am talking about?

The Master turned to the white witch telling her as he held both her hands within his,

-Let me check. This is just what we need! William, grab my hand, I will pass the recipe of the spell to you. Miss White, I am starting to believe my son when he describes you like a walking magical toolbox. He compared you to our angelic wizard, Doctor Williams, which is a very high praise indeed passing his lips. Now let me teach you how we are going to close that portal.

As this took place in the attic, Sebastien was checking that everything was fine in the bedroom. Peter was still awake but being tucked in bed like a child by Father Odell while Ted was tending to the fire in the small fireplace of the room. The giant smiled gratefully to the coming angel. He ventured in a timid way,

-Mr Cotton, I am thankful that you came.

Sebastien, already by the bed, checked the pulse of the human and his temperature. He stated,

-Well, we couldn't let you starve, could we? As you must realise you shoulder will take longer to mend. I will give it three to four weeks. But your broken arm is getting there slowly but surely. Just clasp my hand with your broken arm. Give me the best grip you can do.

Obliging him, Peter asked with anxiety,

-Will Miss White still employ me if I take longer to recover?

The angel nodding positively reassured the man,

-Of course she will. I will ask her to take you on for half a day and half the agreed wages from this Monday. First it will give you a life line. Second, even if you will not be able to help that much, it will allow you to get acquainted with the daily running of the hotel. Let's not forget that it will permit you to befriend all who work there, Miss White, her daughter Mina, Miss Georgia Marlow and Emily. Here, that is a decent grip my man. Don't strain yourself, give it a good couple of weeks but you will be able to use that arm very soon. I hope you enjoyed your dinner tonight. Tomorrow evening I am inviting a few people at the tavern for a meal and I want you to come. Father Odell, Henry and Miss White will be there. I also want you to apologise and make up with Tyrell. It will be a good opportunity for you to do so. Don't forget, you will be surrounded by your true friends and we can support you.

Peter gave a long look at Odell who was telling him silently to say yes. Sighing the giant agreed,

-I will come and I will apologise. You know that I am indebted to you, Mr Cotton. I will do anything you ask me to do. You have all my thanks for Clementine, for looking after my injuries and for the dinner which was very nice. I ate everything because Father Odell said I needed every mouthful to get better.

A satisfied Sebastien told,

-Good, Theo is right. You need to get some strength back. It will come from good nutrition and good rest. I want you to drink a large bowl of water then just to go to sleep. As you know, we will sort out your problem in the attic. Father Odell and my angel Ted will stay by your bedside as we do so, therefore you will be well protected and can sleep in peace.

Then he turned to Odell and ordered,

-My Theo, bless that bucket of water and make it holy. Then, give one bowl of the blessed water to Peter to drink and keep the rest as your ammunition just in case for everyone's protection. Ted, go and get Clementine and put her box under the bed. You have both your orders to stay and protect Peter at all cost. Matthias will be here soon to give you a fighting hand if necessary. When the situation upstairs is over, I will come and fetch you.

When Sebastien left the room, Theo and Ted did as they were told diligently. The three 'M' arrived in the main room of the cottage. Seeing Sebastien the three angels bowed to him before Maximilien briefed him,

-The others are positioned outside as you ordered. The cottage is properly surrounded. I doubt that a demon will be able to leak through that angelic net. The four that were guarding the cottage are here. Dare I say they are upset about what happened in their absences to Peter and are beating themselves up about it. One of them, Lawrence, is so obviously tired that I fear he may become a casualty if the worst happens tonight.

A worried Sebastien demanded,

-What about the other three?

Maximilien answered,

-They all seemed suitably refreshed after the meal they had at the hotel. But Lawrence was dozing throughout the dinner I gave them. He could hardly eat or stay awake which is unusual for him. You know how upbeat he is normally.

This was the last straw for Sebastien as he suspected the demonic possession of one of his angels. He went to fetch Father Odell straight away. He briefed him as they walked together in the main room,

-I want you to come with me, Theo. I fear that one of my angels, who was staying at the cottage all day, has been possessed. He is acting out of character. Maximilien just told me that he is sucked out of his energy. But this is unlike my Lawrence. Please, check him with me. Be ready to perform an exorcism. Lawrence is a rather young angel. It is only his second incarnated life. His first one was cut short when he saved someone, receiving the bullet intended for the human. In his human life he was shot as well during the Cromwell era that affected England. Both times he died aged twenty one. We celebrated his twenty first birthday only a few weeks ago at Doctor Williams's. He is showing unusual signs of tiredness. Even Peter noticed one of my angels yawning very often this afternoon. Before you tell me off, I promise I haven't overworked my angels. This was comparatively an easy and short shift.

The three 'M' giggled at one another and Maximilien commented for the benefice of Theo,

-Yes, we are used to work ten times harder than that, Theo. You will get to adapt to it, eventually.

Odell gave a long look to Sebastien demanding explanations,

-Did you overwork that young angel, Sebastien? You know you can be honest with me. I spent an entire day working in fields with you and you are pretty relentless. The only break we had was when we had finished all the fields. To give you a sense of proportion, you are a strong angel and I am a lanky human, novice at using a sickle. I didn't tell you how many blisters I counted on my fingers, and whenever one did burst, and I did hurt because I was too scared to do so. Is it possible that Lawrence was keen to impress you and didn't warn you that he really needed a little rest?

Put on the spot the superior angel scolded the three 'M',

-Ten times harder, Maximilien, really? Do you want to scare my Theo? No, no it is more or less like twice harder beside that Lawrence is used to pull his weight without complaints and cheerfully. I still think there is something wrong with my British angel and it has nothing to do with me. It has to do with the demonic activity in this cottage. Come with Theo and I, you three. Let's go to Lawrence and find out.

Following Sebastien, Matthias cheekily commented,

-Come Sebastien, we are used to thrice the amount of work at the very least. Admit it and you get yourself a deal. Theo might be very right on the matter. You are saying yourself Lawrence works without complaints, well maybe he doesn't dare to do them. When you think about it, only the angels who have been musketeers with you and knights with you address you almost without fear about anything but the others they are shyer.

A somewhat worried Sebastien, gave a killer glance to his angel as he demanded,

-Thrice! What kind of deal are you talking about? Do you want me to give you another sleepless night on top of the three you had? Because I can, you know? By the way I want you to give protection to Ted, Theo and Peter tonight. I do not think you will have to fight a demon but I can not exclude the possibility. The intense fighting should only happen in the attic while you will stay in Peter's bedroom. Come, I am approachable, you all know that I will be considerate, do you? I want you all to be able to tell me anything. If the trend amongst some is to fear me, I want you three to spread the word and encourage them to talk to me. I am an angel, not a demon, I will not bite the head off any of you if you are a bit tired sometimes.

Curious Theo asked before Sebastien opened the door of the cottage,

-We can resolve the matter easily. Did any of you notice something out of character in Lawrence which is not utter tiredness? It may be slurred speech, being extremely pale, unusual clumsiness, swearing more than normal, showing more temper, or displaying some odd behaviours, total lack of appetite, being unsociable, self harm, the list can be long. In that case it can certainly be a possessed angel and not one overworked by Sebastien. A demon will not care for his host if it is an angel. It will be an inside out job. It could be slow or fast: Slow, if the demon is clever and want to infiltrate your army and spy on you to know your next moves and fast death if he just want a retaliation kill. If Lawrence is still alive by now, I can only guess that you would have a demonic spy inside him. It will be a very conning and dangerous demon. Sebastien you will face in that case another drag to hell scenario. The demon will want to leave with your angel and kill him in hell.

The three 'M' looked at each others worried. Maximilien was the first to speak immensely anxious,

-Sebastien, Lawrence hardly ate but I did feed the lot his favourite dish: sausages, mash and onion gravy.

Matthias added with some emotion,

-I saw him destroying roses in the garden tunnel of Miss White. He said he caught himself on a thorn but there were probably twenty white roses littered on the ground by his feet. I put his bout of anger down to his tiredness. I didn't think more about it.

Then Maurice shared,

-Sebastien, when my brothers were preparing the meal, a waiting Lawrence played with a knife over his spread hand on the table in the dinning room. I had to remove the knife from him when he stabbed his hand with it. He didn't want me to look after his hand saying that it was a mere nothing.

With a heavy heart, Sebastien ordered the three 'M' and Theo,

-Let's be clever about it. We do not want the demon to

run away with Lawrence's soul and body. So the plan is to pretend that we are having a spot check review of the army. As we will check everyone it will not arouse suspicion to a demon keen to learn about us. Theo, your part is to be the novice who is learning how to be an angelic soldier, hence that is why we are showing you how to present yourself as an angel. We have to check the other three that stayed in the cottage by precaution. But if we exorcise one in front of the others we will have trouble if we have more than one demon out there in our army. We need to devise a fast way to separate them from the others, let alone recognise them fast enough.

A brainstorming Matthias proposed,

-We can always question them separately.

But Sebastien objected,

-We haven't got all night. We still have to close the portal upstairs. We need a fast system of recognition.

Maurice expressed himself,

-That is going to be tricky.

In desperation Sebastien barked,

-Thank you for your participation which is hardly helpful, Maurice. We need ideas here and not stating the obvious.

Thinking out loud Theo Odell advanced,

-There is a possible quick way. When we touch a possessed person's skin with holy water, the area affected emit some smoke. If you wash your hands with holy water then shake the hands of your angels, you will then know who is possessed and who isn't.

Sebastien argued,

-Not a bad contribution Theo but not an adequate one because shaking hands make them see what we are doing and we certainly don't want that. We want to assess them without them realising we are doing so. Secondly in the angelic etiquette we bow to one another. We only shake hands to humans.

Having an epiphany Maximilien told with some excitement,

-I know how we can pull it off! Playing on the army

review, and on the idea of Odell, we can, with our hands washed in holy water, adjust the collar of our four, back and front. We can just touch a little of their skin at the back of their necks and see what will happen without them knowing we are assessing them.

Pleased Sebastien patted the back of his angel and messed up the hair of Theo. He ordered,

-This is what we will do then. Well done you two. Theo, did you had time to bless the bucket of water I gave you?

Theo nodded positively. Then Sebastien enjoined,

-Gentlemen, let's wash our hands and proceed with our plan.

Once all of them stepped outside, Sebastien could only notice that Lawrence was further away in the yard than his other angels, leaning against an oak tree, but that he also was partially asleep. This shouldn't happen to one of his angels on duty. Sebastien ordered for all to make a line in order to review them. Everyone rushed to the command while Lawrence took his time and was the last of the line. With the three 'M' helping Sebastien, he soon arrived at the inspection of Lawrence. Sebastien was satisfied that the other angels that spent the day in the cottage were not possessed. However it was not the case for Lawrence who failed the test. When he did the collar of his angel and saw the smoke coming from the skin of his neck, he sighed deeply with great sadness. He ordered sternly as he quickly thrust Lawrence onto the ground,

-Theo, you know what to do. Maurice, Maximilien help me to hold Lawrence still. Matthias stay by Theo and protect him. For the others I want three quarter of you my angels to focus on the cottage and the rest to help us.

Father Odell proceeded with the exorcism immediately. Soon a demonic guttural laugh came out of Lawrence who swore, tried to stand up, pushing and kicking. Sebastien worried for his young angel wanted the demon out as soon as possible from his incarnated body. He provoked the demon with all might in a vociferous way. Eventually with the help of the exorcism taking place, the provocations of Sebastien worked, a colossal demon appeared behind Theo Odell and Matthias. Sebastien warned them immediately,

-Behind you, Theo watch out, he is here!

In a fast move before the demon could grab hold of him,

Theo took two pointed crosses from his jacket and planted them into the legs of the giant demonic entity who screamed in pain and threatened to kill the nasty vicar. Matthias reacted quickly, he pushed Theo out of the way, yet he found himself in front of the demon doing so, he ordered in a desperate tone,

-Theo, carry on with the exorcism. Send this one back to hell.

Odell shouted,

-Matt, duck!

Father Odell through the content of one of his holy water bottle on the large sexual organ of the demon before throwing the content of another one straight into the eyes of the demon. The loud growl of the giant sounded like thunder. Theo grabbed Matthias and dragged him away from the hurt demon. Sebastien couldn't help giggling at the resourcefulness of the vicar as he went to attack the demon with all his might. Maurice upset to see Lawrence almost lifeless went to support Sebastien in his fight. While Maximilien stayed by the young angel monitoring him, Theo carried on his exorcism which was diminishing the strength of the enormous demon. An angry Sebastien and an equally angry Maurice didn't let the demon to gain any advantage. Soon Sebastien delivered the killer blow breaking the neck of the horrible giant which fell to the ground and turned to dust. Maurice having held strongly the hands of the demonic beast in order for Sebastien to finish the fight fast with a straight kill was satisfied to see the dusty pile at his feet. However he warned Sebastien with sadness,

-It doesn't look too good for Lawrence.

Going straight to his young angel despite bleeding from his flank fairly badly, Sebastien knelt by him and asked Maximilien,

-How is he doing?

His upset angel answered with tears in his eyes,

-Not good at all. I have a very low pulse that is weakening by the second. I think we are losing him again. But his soul is still there. You managed to get that demon out of him with Theo. At the worst he can get another incarnated angelic life.

Sighing deeply, Sebastien started to rescue the young angel, inspecting him all the while. He found deep slashes on

Lawrence's arms and ankles. Sebastien announced,

-Lawrence has been bled most certainly by that demon on top of the pentagram. I want all of your angelic energies powering my healing one, we may be able to save him.

Maximilien put his hand on the shoulder of Sebastien who had his upon the heart of Lawrence. All his angels formed a chain, hand in hand where the last hand was given to Maximilien. A flow of energy went through that angelic chain of hands. The result was a powerfully glowing Sebastien as he healed his young angel. Soon the pulse of Lawrence improved, then his cuts all across his limbs sealed themselves into healed scars. When the youngster regained consciousness, he asked feebly,

-What happened?

Sebastien replied while stroking the dark blond hair of his angel,

-You suffered from a demonic attack. You have been possessed and bled. Do you recall anything that happened to you this afternoon after I left?

Struggling to remember anything Lawrence however told,

-I was ordered to put the planks back on top of the pentagram to keep it close. Then I did it but that's it. It is a total blank.

Taking the young angel into his arms carrying him, Sebastien ordered,

-Maximilien, I leave Lawrence into your charge. Take him to the hotel, feed him, put him to bed and stay by his bedside. He is still suffering from a severe blood loss. He has to rest for a good couple of days, make sure he does and make sure he eats. If he deteriorates, call me as soon as. But we managed to stabilise him all of us so there is good hope.

Maximilien took his angelic shape, opened his arms and received Lawrence within them. He answered,

-I will look after him like if he was my own son, Sebastien, you can be sure of that. I will keep you inform on how he is doing.

Flying away with his charge in the night sky, Maximilien

gave Lawrence a kind smile as he revealed to him,

-Sebastien, my brother Maurice and Theo killed the demon that possessed you. We will make sure that you recover from your ordeal.

Lawrence put his head against the chest of Maximilien seeking to be comforted and confided,

-I feel so drained, Max, so drained. My hand is in pain. I can't move one of my fingers. The other hand hurts as well.

Maximilien explained,

-Once in the hotel I will have a good look at your hands. I know that you stabbed one of your hands with a knife. You lost a fairly dangerous amount of blood, this is why you feel so drained. We will have to keep an eye on you. You will be under my care for a good couple of days so I will have to request from you your total obedience during that time.

Lawrence nodded positively with hope in his heart.

In the cottage's courtyard Sebastien ordered a few of his angels to follow him into the house, warning them that this was the second large demon he had to deal with coming from the hell portal in the attic therefore that they should not expect the demons to be of a manageable size. Hence they would need to attack one demon in pair and not alone to try to prevent angelic casualties. As they stepped into the cottage, turning to Theo and Matthias, Sebastien smiled while he stated,

-My Theo, I definitely like your fighting moves. Personally, I would not attack the genitals of a big angry demon but I can only admit that your trick managed to get Matthias out of the way to safety. It was brilliant. Where did you get all those little pointed crosses by the way?

Father Odell explained,

-I used to be attacked by thieves on the streets back in the days. Doctor Valdi taught me some defencive moves and Peter O'Neil made me those. Each time he came to help me prepare my church for the Sunday service, he brought me a cross. He told me that if I poke those into a leg or a thigh from an attacker, I will be able to run away faster than they could pursue me.

Giggling Sebastien commented,

-Crafty. Go back to Peter's bedroom with Matthias and look after him for me. You shouldn't be under attack but it is better to take precautions to be safe than being sorry. So I want you all to stay on your guards at all time.

#

When Sebastien and his angels arrived in the attic, he saw his father, Doctor Williams and Miss White fighting demons. The Master turned to him, flustered and demanding,

-What took you so long?

His son just pointed at his injury before he replied,

-A little big demon situation down there. It is sorted but we nearly lost an angel. I will explain it all to you later.

He rushed to attack the demons coming out of the pentagram, ordering,

-Forward Soldiers! Dad, close that entrance as fast as you can. I would call the Creator if I was you. It is necessary, trust me.

The Master seeing his son bleeding badly dragging a demon and killing him neatly did as he was advised. Ready for another kill, Sebastien ordered,

-Send me another one, Soldiers. As soon as you are injured and bleeding I want you off that pentagram. Do you understand me?

Understanding the situation and watching Sebastien slaughtering demons away from the pentagram, the white witch did a quick spell to prevent blood from dripping inside the pentagram. Drops of blood and pools of it were sent levitating in the room to the amazement of some angels. She sent a telepathic message to Sebastien,

-No blood will go inside the pentagram. I made sure of it but that spell only last twenty minutes.

A pleased Sebastien was then able to kill the demons as soon as they came out. While the Master and Doctor Williams put all their energies into closing the pentagram, a great light appeared in the attic. Then an entity with the appearance of a very tall and strongly built man who looked like the Master came to them commenting,

-It looks like hell broke loose.

The Master relieved to see his father, bowed his head to him before saying,

- Don't tell me about it. Doctor Williams, Miss White and I have been killing a good dozen of demons in the past half hour. We are desperately trying to close that hell portal that is leaking a hemorrhage of demons. We have been so busy defending ourselves that we have been unable to do the spell to erase that pentagram.

Pointing his finger towards the pentagram, the Creator threw a thunderbolt at it which closed the portal instantly. Then he ordered,

-Come with me, with your two, my son.

But the Master declined with a plea,

-Please save my two, they are not fighting angels. They are part of the healing team of Sebastien and we will need them because my son is injured and we have another angelic casualty. I am staying here to help killing the half a dozen demons that are left in this attic.

The Creator nodded his consent and glanced at his grandson who was tackling two demons at once. He stated,

-The way your son fight, I would not have guessed if I was an angel that he was wounded. Come to me with him when the skirmish is over.

Bowing the Master replied,

-He lives up to the name you gave him. Miss White, Doctor Williams follow my father and stay safe by him.

The two did as they were told. Whilhelmina was in awe of the Creator, especially since she witnessed his thunderbolt coming out of his finger while Doctor Williams remained silent knowing that any conversation with the Supreme Being had to be started by him. When they arrived in the main room of the small cottage, the Creator sat at the head of the table, smiled amiably and invited,

-Please, be seated. Miss White, you are proving to be a nice new addition to my grandson's angelic army. How do you feel to not be an angel but still be part of it?

Looking at her hands instead of the intense gaze of the

Creator upon her in a shy way, she answered,

-I feel very honoured. Sebastien repaired me as a woman and my future husband and I intend to devote ourselves to his army.

The Creator smiled kindly commenting with a blissful air upon his face,

-I am glad to hear it although I know it already. My intentions are to come to your wedding which will be performed by my son. You see, Whilhelmina, the Master rarely do unions, however he had been watching Theo Odell for a very long time. Therefore for a very long time, I was told that Theo will be an angel. We also knew he would cross your path one day and would win your sore heart, bringing love and faith back to you. My son reported to me how my grandson rated you. He said you had flaws but you also had mainly right intentions and that your actions were speaking for themselves. Let me tell you, if you are in any doubt, that the Mighty One rates you greatly. Ultimately he wants to make an incarnated angel out of you. This way all your lives will match your husband's incarnated ones. You will forever be together. Your souls will be completely united, angelic life after angelic life.

Her eyes full of hope lifted to the Supreme Being as she asked,

-Who is the Mighty One?

With a signal of the head from the Creator, Doctor Williams replied,

-This is the angelic name of Sebastien, given to him by the Creator. It is his original one and true name. Like the Creator, he has many names. He is also known as the Venerable One amongst angels. As Sebastien means venerable, it is a human way to address him. If you ever make it to his confidence, you may call him Mighty, like his father and I do. His little bit is allowed to do so as well but she thinks it is just a nickname for him. Now, the Mighty One knew he was a very important angel, superior to many, but he never knew to which extent up until today. All other angels had the knowledge of his noble origins but were sworn to secrecy. Only the Creator and his father were allowed to tell him who he truly was one day. The Master of all angels decided to reveal it all tonight to my great surprise.

The Supreme Being vented,

-It was overdue. My son could have told his origins to the Mighty One two angelic lifetimes ago. But he had that undue fear that Mighty would become brash and proud. Miss White do not mind us talking thus, you are part of the angelic clan of my son and grandson. William as the best friend and mentor of my grandson has been monitoring him for me for a very long time and we enjoy having regular conversations about Mighty.

A few angels came into the room from the attic. If two carried one badly injured, the five others did sustain wounds. Doctor Williams took charge of the situation straight away, standing up, he ordered,

-Lay him on the table. The rest of you seat down and wait your turn. Miss White, I need some sanitised bandages, plenty of hot water and for you to prepare plenty of potions that numb the pain.

While Miss White got up from her chair, Williams clapped his hands together many times. Multiple things appeared as he did so: a couple of buckets full of water by the stove, a cauldron in the fire place, a fire underneath it, a little table full of the ingredients needed for the potions and its recipe, bandages, strong alcohol, and two medical bags, his one and the one of Miss White. The white witch of Wilton Town busied herself straight away with her given orders. Doctor Williams was already breaking the leg of the trousers of the angel on the table carefully revealing the entirety of his thigh injury. He sighed deeply as he assessed the extent of the damage. The femur of the angel was visible within his torn apart muscles. He garroted the top of the leg to stop the hemorrhage and announced the bad news sternly,

-I will do my best but the honest truth is that if that wound, after what I will do, is not sealed and healed in three to four weeks, you may have to face an amputation.

The pale angel complained,

-I will then become useless. I dedicated my life to the army of Sebastien.

As Williams went to pour some hot water in a bowl then washed his hands, he tried to comfort in a scolding tone,

-Fighting is not the only way to help Sebastien. If you ever lose your leg, you will have to use your hands and your brain. You will have the choice between becoming a healer for the army or be part of the logistic team. Losing a limb is not the end of it all, it may be a new chapter in your life. Beside that in your next life you will be whole again. However you will have a scar on that leg. But there is nothing like a good battle scar to impress others.

Not entirely convinced the angel pouted before asking,

-Let's just say if all goes well, will I be able to walk again.

Preparing his surgical instrument Doctor Williams replied before starting to divert the mind of his patient from what he was about to do to him,

-Prop yourself up a little for me. Miss White, would you be so kind to bring the bottle of alcohol to Daniel. Now Daniel, you suffered extensive damage. Although you haven't got a broken femur, it will take you three to six months before you will be able to walk again. You will not be able to run anymore and you will have to use the support of a walking stick until the rest of this life. You will limp. Here, now, drink. Thank you, Miss White. Tell me, how is the situation upstairs?

Daniel starting drinking, mulled over the informations he had been given before he answered,

-It was fierce but when we were ordered to go down and be seen to, there were only two demons left being tackled by Sebastien, the Master and Maurice. One of the surviving demons is the one that was starting riping me apart. I was saved by Sebastien, just in time, I would say. I made a massive error of looking at the eyes of my opponent. He is one of those demons which paralyses with their stares. I was literally pined down and immobilised by him. He started destroying my leg with one clawed hand and with the other one he was about to rip my heart off my chest. I was petrified, terrified and I saw all my lives passing before my eyes. But then Sebastien charged the demon, pushed him against the wall with such brute force, and kept him there under the ceaseless attack of his fists. He ordered to all the injured angels to get out of the attic. It was all of us apart from the Master who was still safe and well, but Maurice disobeyed the order and protected our retreat and then went back to keep protecting the Master. The last glimpse of the fight between my demon and Sebastien was that the Mighty One was blinding the demon with his fingers pushed in the demonic eyes while the claws of the demon were desperately trying to dig in to the back of Sebastien. I am shaking just thinking of it.

Doctor Williams ordered,

-Then take another large sip of whiskey. The Mighty One is a well seasoned demon killer. When he will come downstairs I am pretty sure, he will stand tall despite his injuries and try to pretend that he is alright at the end of the day.

Smiling the Creator stated,

-You are so right William. You've got to know my grandson by heart. Here he comes, walking tall and helping his injured angel down the stairs.

The Great Being stood up and went to welcome them, addressing himself to his son first,

-Raguel, is the situation sorted?

The Master replied with a sigh,

-In that cottage, yes it is. In this town, it isn't. I will have to give you a full brief up about it all.

Turning to the angel that Sebastien was helping, the Creator told,

-You would be Maurice, one of the three 'M', my grandson is so proud of his angelic fighting triplets. Come and let me guide you to my chair. Thank you for protecting my son and grandson the way you did. It is called dedication and it will not be forgotten.

He took charge of helping Maurice to the chair as he ordered,

-Master, Mighty go and wait for me in the courtyard.

His son and grandson obeyed. The Creator then said to Doctor Williams,

-Feeling all of their injuries, after Daniel, you must tend to Maurice. He has three broken ribs, two on the right side and one on the left side. Then you have Fabrice with a dislocated shoulder. For the rest it is bruises and very nasty demonic scratches, Illiad has the most of them and a ruptured artery which need to be seen to.

The Great Being left the cottage. Doctor Williams felt overwhelmed and ordered as he was cleaning Daniel's wound with great care,

-Miss White, please, could you tend to Illiad immediately

so he doesn't bleed to death on the floor then give the potion to all of them as soon as, because I will be a while with Daniel. It will soothe their pains as they wait to be mended.

Whilhelmina diligently did as she was told then went to help at the operating table by Doctor Williams. They cooperated their efforts and by dawn they had sorted out all the injured angels. When Williams flew back to Boston, it was with Daniel in his arms whom he had decided to look after from now on.

In the meantime, when Sebastien arrived in the courtyard with his father, he dismissed most of his angels ordering them to get a rest before the following night which would request them in town. He kept two of his angels behind to look after Peter overnight and for the day to come. Once his couple of angels went in the cottage, the Master went straight to the well and brought a bucket of water by his son. He ordered,

-Let's have a good look at you. Let me help you to remove that shirt.

As the father removed carefully the lacerated shirt of his son, the Creator stepped into the yard demanding,

-How is Mighty doing?

The Master replied with a deep sigh,

-Still standing, but he has been bleeding profusely since a while. He has multiple wounds to be seen to. His shirt was white this morning and is almost totally red this evening from his own blood and the one of demons.

Seeing his grandfather, Sebastien bowed profoundly to him, in the knowledge that if he had been allowed to exist it was because of him. The presence of the Creator made him humble. It didn't help that his torso was now naked and all his bleeding wounds were visible. Taking the damaged shirt from the hands of the Master, the Great Being inspected it and teased,

-It is a shame that it was your last good shirt since your other one was sneezed upon by your little bit.

This made Sebastien smile despite his pains. He recollected the moment it had happened in the coach on its way to Wilton Town. It made him think of Ivy with great tenderness and in his mind all the visions of the demons he had just fought with just washed away. He confided,

-It reminds me that I need to wash my shirt when I am

back home to get it ready for my day at the clinic in a few hours.

Turning around his grandson, looking at him from head to toe with eagle eyes, the Creator could see in him the same nine year old boy Sebastien was as a human, the one which was hardworking and didn't mind chores. He suggested,

-You should wake up Jack. Grab some sleep yourself. I can feel your exhaustion. You need to be ready for tomorrow night and you have a few wounded angels in there being looked after by Doctor Williams and Miss White. You have a diminished army. The rest of your soldiers will need you tomorrow on good form. Master, start to heal your son.

Sebastien replied,

-I will be there tomorrow night for the fight regardless. I do not want to wake up my Jack. I will cope, I always do. As for my army, the best were in the courtyard to provide a strong backup in case the demons made it out of the cottage. They are now resting for tomorrow. To be honest, I expected the task to close the portal to be a much easier one. But the pentagram was opened further because one demon came out of it this afternoon and bled one of my young angels, Lawrence, upon it. This changed the level of the portal we were facing compared to what it was that I saw that afternoon. Not only that, the demon possessed the angel he bled in order to know the next moves of my army, to spy within him. Hence the demons came out 'en force' in order to prevent the closure of the pentagram but also to come out whilst they could. On this occasion my Lawrence and my Daniel were the biggest casualties. The demon I killed which possessed Lawrence is the same type which damaged Daniel badly. They are strong and powerful because they can paralyse their prey. I do not know how many of those are in Wilton Town since the creation of the portal we had to deal with.

His father was cleaning Sebastien's torso using water with great care, assessing the seriousness of all his wounds. He commented,

-That would explain the bad situation we had up there. Listen, Mighty, you had a rough time almost the entire day. Call it a night and rest. My father is right. You need to wake Jack up and grab a little rest while you can. From seeing your wounds, I would ground you myself for an entire day at least like you have done for Henry to give him time to recover. Are you that proud that you can't accept a little help? Stay still, your back is very damaged. I was so scared for you with that last demon. But you managed it so well.

Sebastien confessed with some emotion,

-Father, I was scared for you all the way through. As soon as I tasked Maurice to your protection when we entered the attic, I saw him almost becoming your angelic guard dog, fiercely protecting you with all his might. Even injured, he was not prepared to leave the attic without you. He impressed me by his sheer courage because like me you were under ceaseless attacks. However you dusted demons with that bright solar light coming out of you. How do you that? Father, I am not proud and I can accept help. You've got me wrong for refusing to wake up my Jack. The thing is, the thing is, I learnt recently that he will pass away aged sixteen trying to protect and save my wife. Both are not making it. I know that fallen angel Jack never experienced to be cherished in a loving family. I adopted him because I want to give him that, because I am convince that it will raise that angel from the ground and bring him wings again. But I have only eight years to do so. I want him to feel like my beloved son, not like a servant and not like a slave. He is still a frail boy beating himself up from his past mistakes. I need to help him to correct his mistakes he did as an angel, and to regain his wings, but I certainly will not wake him up in the middle of the night to wash my shirt. Jack is ever so helpful that if I ask him he will do so. But as his adoptive father, I want him to have a good night sleep and I know that tomorrow my rested little boy will propose his help to me willingly without even being asked for it. When his little hardworking self sets about to do a task of his own free will I know that his soul is mending itself. My Jack needs love not orders. When his time comes I will have an angel back by my side.

While the Creator was listening attentively to the conversation, the Master proposed to his son as he started healing him thoroughly,

-Then let me clean your shirt for you because as your father I want you to have a good sleep so you can be in fighting form tomorrow night. More, you can let Ivy run the clinic in the morning with Jack and I only for you to come at midday fully rested. As I am only applying your own principles of love and care, you can only accept my son. Now let me tell you something you must know. It is important and you must spread that tactic to your entire army. However I do not believe that all will succeed to reproduce that spell. Miss White developed a spell to kill demons with solar light. It is intricate but it works on many demons. She shared it to me and Williams and this is why we were able to stay alive and to not be harmed until your arrival in the attic. We dusted a dozen demons together that way. Basically, Miss White created that strong spell to deal with Mina if she did turn badly out of control. Having tested her magic spell

I can tell you that it kills demons that can possess someone. For you, it will be child play to use that clever spell. I must praise Miss White to you for multiple reasons, but also tell you that I think she is an excellent new recruit to your army. First when Doctor Williams and I explained to her the process to close a pentagram, she was a very attentive listener, she didn't interrupt, and asked questions at the end. Secondly, she thinks fast upon her feet, she is resourceful and is keen to help which all are qualities that her future husband possess as well in abundance. Thirdly, when we had to tackle the demons coming out fast and in numbers from the portal, she held her nerves and stood strong with us. When Williams was going to be attacked by two demons at once, she shouted to him to kill the one on his left while she will kill the one on the right. Her focus and courage under pressure is commendable. Mighty, I sealed your back and treated you, but I am afraid to say that you will still be in pain for a good couple of days. It will be pain potion time for you at least for the rest of the night and this morning. Now let's deal with that flank and that shoulder.

Sebastien turned around and smile to his father with tenderness and gratefulness, showing him his badly wounded flank. He told the Master,

-You know Dad, if I haven't told you already, I appreciate you so much. Always, I may end up getting slaughtered but I want you to know that I love you and respect you enormously. I know we always bicker and that I have a tendency to argue a lot but there is not one day when I am not blessing having you as my father. For you to accept living with my new family made my day, today. It was the highlight of my day in fact. Another thing which gives me joy and hope is the fact that you are adopting Henry and will make us come as brother and be our incarnated human father in our lives to come. I have the fondest memory of being raised up by you and I am looking forward to have that feeling again.

Looking at his son with intensity the moved Master asked him,

-So you thought you had a close call today?

Nodding positively Sebastien admitted,

-Yes, father, twice. I had a couple of close calls. This is why I don't want to leave things unsaid and want you to know that I love you so much, that my admiration for you runs very deep. I need to beg of you and plea to you, that if the worst ever happens to me, please would you look after my new family, my little bit, my Jack and my future son Theodore. Because you are such a good father, I know they will be loved, cared for and protected.

The Master saw by the blood tears of his son, how emotional he was, therefore he reassured,

-Sebastien, I vow to you that I will look after them. Let us dry your tears now. You are still with us and you are still standing. Do you want to speak about your close calls with me or is it to early for you to share them?

As he saw the father dry the tears of his son with his thumbs, the Creator could see the powerful bond between the two of them. He wished he had that strong bond with his eldest son but after treating him like a slave for so many years, the Master was withdrawn with him and hardly shared the intensity of his feelings at any one time. He recalled the night Raguel was ready to commit angelic suicide, when he had to stop him in extremis. He had deep regrets to have witnessed the state of his son and the way he wanted to end his life without telling him or even sharing any of his emotions with him prior to the event. The Great Being honestly thought watching the Master's interactions with the Mighty One that his son was a better father than himself. He listened as Sebastien willingly confided to his powerful father,

-Master, I was saved, rescued for the first time. I made the same mistake that Daniel did for a split second with my demon that had attacked Peter O'Neil and killed his pet rabbit. I gazed at his eyes and became paralysed. It was such an atrocious feeling: a sheer sense of helplessness and that my death will be inevitable. But I had Theo Odell, my god send good Theo, who intervened and blinded the demon momentarily. It was enough for me to regain control of the situation along with my mobility. Theo saved me today. Then a similar demon that was ready to kill Daniel, presented another tough challenge. I had a short window to blind him and kill him, but as I did, he went for my back and was starting to rip it apart with his claws. I saw my past lives before my eyes, I had thousands of thoughts rushing in my mind, one of them being that I didn't want to die because of you and my family, that I had to fight and fight harder and harder to stay with all of my loved ones. Now, the demon within Lawrence was of the same type, a terrifying giant with the capacity to paralyse if you meet their gaze. This is the demon that got his nasty claws into my flank. He appeared behind my Theo and my Matthias during the exorcism we did on Lawrence. Oh, father, you should have seen how Theo reacted to my warning! Hold my hand, I've got to share it with you. I had to stay serious because it was my time to fight but the manner both of them got themselves out of the way of the beastie was quite something to witness. I must confess when I was fighting my last demon who tried to rip my back, I used the genital kick to make him drop his grip and it worked a treat.

When his father got the vision shared by his son, he smiled, commenting,

-I like quick thinking Father Odell. He possess such a good soul. The way he helped Matthias makes me want to swear but I can't with your grandfather by us.

The Master, still giggling, gave a side glance to the Creator who however demanded,

-Come, give me your best one, Raguel.

The son of the Great Being tried to bargain,

-Only if you promise me to not get me thunderstruck.

His father gave him an enigmatic smile while he stated,

-You do know that I cannot promise you that. However I made you a demand.

Sighing the Master responded, as he was healing the flank of his son,

-One can only have hope, heart and faith. I also do believe in miracles. My favourite swearword is God almighty and I also emit a good Lord once in a while.

Rather pleased with the answer, the Creator stated, while he came closer to inspect the healing which had been done on the back of Sebastien,

-As I consider both as compliments rather than anything else, feel free to carry on swearing that way. Now, Mighty, your father told you about your true identity. How do you feel about it all?

Sebastien replied in a humble way,

-To be honest, I didn't have time to process it all yet. I need to get my head around it. Because of the enormous respect I was always shown and given in my angelic lives, I guessed I was different but I didn't know to what extent. To say the least I am very appreciative to have been allowed to know my true identity. It makes me feel humble and has given me a will to rise to any expectation which has been placed upon my head. I am only slightly confused if I should change my address to you or not.

Putting his hand on the damaged shoulder of his grandson, healing it completely, the Creator enjoined,

-Between you and I, you can call me whatever you prefer: Grandfather, Grandpa or Grand Dad. I do acknowledge that I can appear or sound a little daunting. However I want you to feel free to come to me or call me whenever you need me. You can confide in me exactly like you do with your father. Let me tell you a few things that you should know. First you are not only the pride, joy and solace of the Master, you are mines just as well. Watching you from your human birth up until now has been a real pleasure. When I held you for the first time I recognised my beloved son, your father in you. After that I would not let any one else but me and my son to help at your angelic births. Without knowing it, you have been our treasure and every first breath you took at each new life, we were looking down blissfully at you in my arms. Like I helped delivering you in all your lives, I demand to be the first to hold my great grand son Theodore. I was there at your wedding to Ivy Fair among the angels. This is why the doors of the church flung opened before us. Your father was there as well but he was so emotional that we couldn't go at your wedding reception. I had to take him away with me so he didn't ruin your big day by his endless tears. You see we waited for so long for you to allow yourself to love again and build a new family. I knew it would happen but your father had to see it to believe it.

Sebastien looking at his father with tenderness commented,

-And because I didn't see you at my wedding, father, I thought all along that you disapproved of my wife or of the way I married disregarding the human convention about grieving for an entire year.

The Master shook is head negatively then revealed,

-I disapproved of nothing at all. I didn't take my usual human shape so you wouldn't recognise me as your embarrassing very emotional dad. I adore your little bit. She is fragile and strong all at once. She is courageous and hard working. She is so bright yet never shows off. Ivy had the best education one could wish for and has been given a good childhood by her late dotting father Doctor Fair. However when she became destitute overnight at the death of her dad, her true colours shown through, she was brave, and full of fortitude. Being rich is not a goal for her whatsoever but being a good

Doctor is. Last but not least Ivy is a very sweet and decent human being. Because she was a young adult orphan with only you and Doctor Williams as friends, I was elated when you took the decision to marry her to look after her. You did the right thing to a lovely individual. Mighty, your marriage have my entire blessing all the way. Like my father, I can not wait to hold little Theodore, my grandson.

Miss White came running outside towards them. She bowed before them and gave a large bowl of potion to Sebastien then she announced,

-The operating table is ready for your son, Master. Sebastien, you must drink the potion, it will knock you down enough for all of us to proceed with the operation on your flank.

Sebastien asked his father,

-Is my wound that bad?

Nodding positively, the Master demanded,

-Yes, can't you feel it? I just repaired your veins and arteries there.

His son replied,

-Isn't it just a big scratch, like normal? I don't really feel it.

The white witch looking at his torso answered,

-It is a gaping wound, Sebastien, that needs to be looked after and closed. Master, his insensitivity is abnormal. Daniel showed such stamina on the operating table as well despite not being knocked down completely. Kick your son on the flank for me. Sebastien, wait before drinking the potion.

Sebastien gave a killer look to Miss White as he vented,

-When I started to like you, my white witch, you demand from my own father to hit me!

Whilhelmina explained herself with some anxiety,

-Your numbness before even drinking the potion is worrying, Sebastien. You tackled the same demon as Daniel and he showed extraordinary courage on the table, not a scream of pain. Doctor Williams praised him saying that he never saw that in his entire career. We need to assess you as soon as possible. You may have been rendered insensitive by the very claws of the demon, which means that when they damage you the demons can carry on before you can realise it or react. In the animal world, certain predators possess the ability to numb the area they attack on their prey. It can be by some sort of venom or poison or else. You and Daniel had massive injuries yet both are not feeling the entire pain of them. It rings alarm bells to me. You may need to be treated for more than just your wounds. There is a possibility that Doctor Williams and I will have to find an anti poison. The sooner we know, the better.

It was a plea which was convincing enough for the Master which gave a hard slap right on the wound of his son before Sebastien could object to anything. His son didn't feel any pain nor batted his eyelids. The father repeated the gesture with a harder kick. His son didn't screamed in pain and didn't react. The Master was about to give yet another kick, but his fist was held in mid air by Sebastien who told sternly,

-You proved her point, Dad. Let's not play kick my son all night because at the end of the day, when my sensitivity will be returned, I am the one that is going to suffer. Miss White, how can you see if I have been poisoned?

The Witch approached him and inspected his wound. She replied after a little while,

-It is a very clean wound. Your veins are fine. On Daniel, the blood was almost black. We took a sample to analyse. You may be fine if it didn't touched your bloodstream.

His anxious father announced,

-I cleaned his wound thoroughly and repaired all his veins. He may still have been infected. He has lost a lot of blood. His shirt is covered in it.

An eager Whilhelmina demanded,

-May I see his shirt, please?

The Great Being gave it to her with an appreciative smile. Miss White took the shirt and inspected it closely sharing out loud all the informations she could gather from it,

-There is a lot of different blood on that shirt. I can feel different demonic blood. Here is Sebastien's one, and there and there. That black stain that's his, that's recent. It's black. It turned black just like for Daniel! Oh, Sebastien, you have been affected. Something is up like Doctor Williams and I suspected. I will try something to know more but I may faint, just pour water over me if I collapse, please.

Making the shirt levitate in front of her, she touched the shirt again but this time her hands, glowing, were going through the fabric assessing every bit of it. She carried on with a voice which was more ethereal than her normal one,

-Your blood is poisoned, Sebastien. You have been poisoned thrice during the night by the same type of demons. It's the type you warned Theo and I from when we were in the courtyard kissing. They do bestow poisonous claws. I can feel it in your last stains of blood, I can feel it in the lacerations on your shirt. Their claws will always aim to dig in their victims to infect them.

The witch collapsed on the ground, pale and weak. The shirt of Sebastien fell by her. Tears appeared in her eyes. Sebastien ran to her help and ordered,

-Pa, fetch some water. Whilhelmina, stay with us. I can slap you a little to make sure of it if you want? I would get my own back then.

This made the white witch smile despite herself as Sebastien lifted her up and guided her to the dry stone wall and told her to take a seat by him. When the Master presented her with a bucket of water, she washed her face and drank a little with her hands. Then she asked wildly,

-How many of your angels have met the demons, of the type I am talking about, and have been injured by them?

Sebastien replied with a sad sigh,

-As far as I know only two, Daniel and Lawrence.

Miss White demanded firmly,

-You need to send a telepathic message to all the rest to ask them if they have been clawed by those specific demons and then to report to you immediately if so. I need to work on a counter poison for all of you affected but also to protect you all from them in the future. I have been impeached to see the result of the poisoning, Sebastien, it usually means the worst and we need to react fast. It can imply death, it can imply something else nefarious. I wish I could have seen what it does but I was spiritually knocked out for a split second. This is when it is dangerous to continue.

A comprehending Sebastien told,

-I know what you are talking about. I just called my Ted. With both of your powers combined, you may be able to see the effect of that poison. The big question is how would you be able to work out the counter poison, Whilhelmina?

While she was thinking as hard as she could, Theo and Ted came to the courtyard. Both bowed to Sebastien respectfully. Ted reported,

-All of the angels injured are now sorted and asked for your permission to leave and rest for the remainder of the night. Theo suggested that they all stay at the hotel, because Miss White who is a nurse and him will be able to care for them and their recovery. However Doctor Williams had requested to be in charge of Daniel. Williams has to speak to you fully about Daniel's case who will not be able to walk for months. You requested me, Sebastien?

Nodding positively, the angel replied,

-Yes, I did. To cut the matter short, Daniel, Lawrence and myself have been poisoned by a particular type of demons. Hold my hand and see for yourself the three demons I am talking about. We need to find out what will that poison do to us. We already established that it numbs us from pain which makes us slow to respond to a physical attack by the demon in question and that it turns our blood black. Our Miss White tried to see what the poisoned will do but she has been spiritually impeached to do so and she collapsed. You know more than any angel about those spiritual attacks since you had them very often my Ted. I want you to join forces with our witch in order to find out as much as you can.

Once Ted released his hand, having seen the three demons concerned, he went to Whilhelmina, picked up the shirt and demanded,

-Hold the other sleeve of that shirt with your left hand, Miss White and hold my free hand with your right one. Now we will see what we can achieve together.

While they started their process, Sebastien turned to the Master and then to Theo, ordering,

-Father, please, can you hold their shoulders, give them your energy and protect them both against attacks. Theo, come with me, I want you to do as you said and take my injured angels to Miss White's hotel. They must all walk with you and not fly. Flying takes more energy than walking and they need their energy in order to recover fast. Show them to their rooms and make them feel at home.

Addressing the Great Being, his grandson asked,

-Do you want to follow me grandfather? I need to check and enquire about my Daniel. I am deeply concerned about him.

The Creator smiled to Sebastien. He made a black and burgundy cape appear out of nowhere and fastened it on Sebastien's shoulders as he replied,

-I will follow you. Here, put this on you, Mighty. This cape given to you by Father Odell will protect you from scaring all your angels left in this cottage because of the sight of your wounds.

Odell looking at the gaping wound on Sebastien's flank became pale and wondered,

-How can you stand Sebastien? Doctor Williams said he needed to operate on you urgently. Now I know why. This was done by Lawrence's demon, wasn't it? You can't go back to the presbytery in that state. If you meet someone on the way what will they think? I have a shorter distance to my new home than the one you have to yours. You have to cover that torso after your operation. Please, have my shirt. I am tall enough for it to fit you. My jacket can close up but your cape can not. I must insist for you to accept if for just one reason, gossips are spreading fast in Wilton Town. It is enough for one to see you badly wounded to tell about it all. If the news reaches the members of the gang, they will surely strike tomorrow assuming that you are at your weakest. We must take all precautions. Like your angels can't fly because it uses too much energy, you will not be able to after the surgery. You will have to walk. No, actually I can fetch you in my phaeton with my old Rosalie and drive you home.

Sebastien messing up affectionately the strawberry blond hair of Odell proposed,

-Grandfather am I allowed to introduce you formally to my newest angel? He saved me tonight. He carries a bag of caring thoughtfulness attached to his heart. If I am naming my son Theodore, it is in his honour. I hold him in high esteem.

While Father Odell couldn't help blushing under the praises but also the gaze of the grandfather of Sebastien, the

Great Being announced,

-You may tell him who I am. But I know who Father Theo Odell is by heart. Before you met Theo, your father was already very fond of that human now angel. He is a precocious one to earn his wings during his human life just like his best friend Doctor Valdi. Theo Odell talks to me everyday since he was three years old. I greatly enjoys all of his prayers. I am sure that I will enjoy his conversations as well because I am planning to visit him often.

As they stepped into the cottage, Sebastien revealed the identity of his grandfather to Theo's ear who swore in great awe out loud,

-Oh, Good Lord!

Sebastien giggled as he commented,

-Yes, that would be him. Now, I have to accept the gift of your shirt because your reasons for it were so valid. If I can't return it to you for some demons fight of mine, I will get you another one at the first opportunity. But don't come back to fetch me with your phaeton. I need you to rest. The truth of the matter is I do not how long I will be after the operation. Two of my angels and myself have been poisoned by demons. Miss White and Doctor Williams will try to work on a counter poison. Once this poison problem is sorted, I will bring Miss White back to you at the hotel. You have Lawrence there who will need his dose of antidote.

A baffled Theo enquired, while he took off his jacket to give his shirt to the angel,

-You do not seem to panic at the fact that you have been poisoned, Sebastien? If I were you I would be frantic.

Holding the jacket of Father Odell and his dog's collar, Sebastien replied,

-Panic is a waste of anyone's time which at the worse can add more damage. To stay cool, calm and collected is the best option, to think clearly of solutions to a dilemma. I am more worried for my two angels than for myself. I mustn't panic in order to resolve the situation in an efficient way for all of us. Beside that Ted showed me a vision this week of the future where I am still standing tall surrounded by my wife, my two sons and one of my daughters planting cherry trees all around the cemetery of Wilton Town. It is in eight years time. So I have faith in Doctor Williams and Miss White to come up with an antidote.

While Odell took his shirt off, a more pessimistic Williams, bowing to the Creator and his grandson, announced,

-Sebastien, I have difficulties separating the poison from the blood. If I can not do it then we can't find a counter poison. Not only that the blood seems to transform itself into demonic blood slowly but surely. I am worried that our unconscious Daniel is becoming possessed as we speak. He is in a near coma at the moment which shouldn't have happened.

Giving his shirt to Sebastien, grabbing his own jacket back and going to the angel laying on a blanket on the floor, Father Odell did the quick check on the wrist of Daniel with holy water and confirmed as he saw smoke coming from it,

-He is possessed. Sebastien, it has to be your turn. Show me your wrist.

Obliging him, Sebastien however refuted,

-But I feel fine.

Odell told him firmly,

-Well, let's confirm that you really are fine.

Doing the small test on Sebastien's wrist, it came clear to the satisfaction of Father Odell and Doctor Williams. Theo stated,

-This may mean that the black blood has nothing to do with being possessed. Without stating the obvious, it may means that Sebastien having less human in him than the other angels is having a different reaction. To assess what we are facing you need to take a sample of blood from Sebastien and one from Lawrence, Doctor Williams, to do a compared analysis.

Sebastien contested,

-Your future wife wanted me slapped and kicked which my father enjoyed doing and now, you, my friend who knows how much blood I lost today, want me to lose some more! I protest.

His grandfather crossed his arms upon his chest in a disproving fashion. The Master who had arrived into the room followed by Miss White and Ted, seeing the dark air upon his father demanded,

-Father, is something wrong?

The Great Being pointing with his chin towards Sebastien confirmed sarcastically,

-Yes, your son. Our great demon killer is being finicky about having his blood taken as a sample so we can find an antidote for him. He is showing signs of noncooperation.

This displeased the Master straight away who scolded his son,

-If you do not let Doctor Williams take a little of your blood now, I will have no problem to rip the repairs I did on your veins. Go and take a seat by him. If I hear one complaint, just one from you, Cadarn, I will punish you in front of everyone. You will also not like having black wings for a very long while. Know that Lawrence has only up until dusk to live and that Daniel will be dead by midnight tomorrow. There is a time for everything and this is not the one to play the uncooperative brat upon us.

Doing as he was told, Sebastien was going to argue that he was not a brat but seeing the harsh stare upon him by his father and grandfather, he abstained and retained his silence. He gave his arm to Doctor Williams who had already prepared a syringe. As his blood was taken, Sebastien confided to his best friend,

-William, I don't feel quite like myself. Something is happening within me.

Then he shouted,

-Father! Help me! Theo, do an exorcism right now upon me!

Pulling the needle out of Sebastien's arm which was full of black blood, Doctor Williams cried out,

-He is possessed! Mighty has no pupils.

The Creator and the Master rushed by Sebastien and held him as he was convulsing. While the Great Being poured out intense energy into his grandson ordering the demon to come out. The Master ordered,

-All injured angels go in the courtyard now, out of the way. Odell, in the corner of the room and start the exorcism.

Prepare yourself to be attacked. We will face two demons, the one within Daniel and the much stronger one within my son. William, join forces with Miss White and get my smilodon and Arthus out of my son, they will protect him and us. Ted, stay by me, do what you do best, predict the demons next fighting moves and give us all the information via telepathy.

Everyone took their orders and positions. Doctor Williams demanded via telepathy to all,

-Let's kill the demon within Sebastien and paralyse the one within Daniel. With a live dissection upon him, Miss White and I can locate the glands which secrete their poison. It will allow us to work upon an antidote for it.

The Master agreed with the request before giving a warning to all in the room which he send to their minds,

-We will keep one alive and paralysed for you William to work upon. Remember all of you that looking at them in the eyes will paralyse you, avoid it at all cost.

While Father Odell started his exorcism, the white witch made her magic wand appear within her hand, with a fast spinning motion of her wrist she almost sang a spell,

-Eu-Mo-Va-Te, Te-Va-Mo-Eu, Mo-Te-Va, Reflectus!

All in the room found themselves kitted with a large rectangular shield which outward surface was made of mirror. Miss White explained quickly,

-The mirror shields are indestructible. They will reflect their own gaze to the demons and maybe immobilise them for split seconds.

Ted considering the solid Roman shape of his shield felt somewhat more protected especially since the Great Being had succeeded in ousting the demon possessing his grandson from his body. The colossal demon stood in the middle of the room took a chair and threw it towards the exorcising Odell with great violence. Whilhelmina reacted ever so fast to protect her Theo, with a move of her magic wand, she stopped the chair in mid air, and ordered,

-Return to the Nefarius!

With great speed the chair went back to break itself on the angry demon, who then turned himself around to face the witch. Doctor Williams instinctively put Miss White behind him and his shield. He shouted an incantation as fast as he could as he saw the demon coming towards them. The result of which was that the spirit of the sabre-tooth cat and the one of Arthus the cockerel appeared into the room. While this feat was done, the Great Being carried an unconscious Sebastien and disappeared with him from the cottage.

#

Taking his grandson far away and into safety, the Creator reappeared with his precious load into the cabin of Doctor Valdi on the ship of Captain Hansen. Amelia Valdi was alone, working on the diary of the corsair when she saw the great light and as she adjusted her glasses, she witnessed for a split second the true form of the Creator carrying what looked like a lifeless angel. She stood up from her chair straight away, she showed the double bed in the corner of the cabin with a gesture of the hand, and pulled the cover. She enjoined with an anxious voice,

-Please, lay him here. I will fetch my husband immediately. It is Sebastien, isn't it?

The Great Being nodded positively yet remained silent. Amelia nodded likewise, put her shawl upon herself and rushed away from the cabin in quest of her husband. She found Vincent within minutes who was teaching the rise and fall of the Roman Empire to Zachary Wilton-Cough and his brother Josiah in the Captain's cabin. She failed to speak for an instant but rallied herself up,

-Vincent, you are needed immediately. Someone is wounded.

Valdi stood up and told the boys,

-We will pick up the lesson where we left it at Julius Caesar tomorrow.

Zachary enquired with his desire to help,

-May I come and be useful?

But Amelia desperately intervened,

-No you may not, it is, it is rather unsightly.

Sensing that something serious was up, Doctor Valdi ordered to the youngsters,

-Captain Hansen wanted to teach you both how to use a

compass, now is the time, run to him.

While the boys tidied their notes and books, Vincent followed his wife to their cabin. Amelia confided to him in a secretive manner,

-We have a badly wounded Sebastien on our bed. He is an angel like our Abigail. A very glowing angel without wings or a kind of supernatural being brought him to us. Sebastien is unconscious and his flank has a wound which is very serious.

Hurrying and intrigued Doctor Valdi arrived in his cabin with his wife who locked the door behind them. Vincent asked the Great Being, while going straight to the injured Sebastien,

-What happened to him?

As Valdi checked the pulse and temperature of his angelic patient then the wound on hid flank, the Creator replied,

-Sebastien fought with Nefarius demons. They are pretty violent. They rip with their claws which are poisoned. He has been possessed by one for a couple of minutes but if I took the demon out of his body, my grandson is now in a coma.

Doctor Valdi went to fetch his medical bag then washed his hands quickly yet thoroughly while he told,

-I am going to seal his wound first while he is out of it. He has a steady pulse but not as strong as what it's used to be. Tell me about the poison. How does it affect someone, well an angel in that case? Is there an antidote for it? Amelia wash your hands, I am going to need you as my nurse.

While the Great Being watched the Doctor's wife diligently doing as she was told, he replied,

-There is no known counter poison for it. Doctor Williams and Miss White will work towards finding one as soon as they stopped being embattled with demons. The poison numbs straight away the area of the body being attacked by the demon which makes the victim slow to protect themselves. The poison turns the blood black. Two angels of my grandson's angelic army have been affected by it. Both suffered being possessed, both acted out of character just like the Mighty One. Both are going to die tomorrow if we don't find the antidote in time.

Cleaning the wound Vincent demanded,

-Pray, who is the Mighty One? Sebastien's injury is pretty clean but there are several signs of inflammation. There are all coming and spreading from his liver. Something is up with this vital organ. I need to investigate and most probably operate if we don't want to lose him. Amelia, did you sterilise my surgical instruments?

His wife brought to him his medical tools on a tray when the Creator answered,

-The angelic name of Sebastien is the Mighty One. Like a few superior angels, he has multiple names. The Venerable Mighty One is his full name. Cadarn and Sebastien are his human names.

Doctor Valdi started to cut the skin of the torso to check the liver while he commented with a smirk on his face,

-That is a mighty mouthful of a name if I may say.

Readjusting her glasses, Amelia commented,

His human names are almost translations of his angelic ones, Vincent. Cadarn is the Celt for mighty and the first name Sebastien has a strong association for being venerable. So I understand that poor badly injured Sebastien is an important angel then?

The Great Being smiled to Amelia Valdi and replied,

-He is very important. He is the only demon killer left in the angelic world. His eldest half brother who was one as well, was slaughtered by demons a very long time ago. Sebastien was training a young angel, who is called Henry, to be one but Henry has been wounded in an attack last night, well two nights ago. The Mighty One makes angels from good humans which then become either guardian angels, either soldiers in his angelic army. He educates and trains the human angels. He is also a Punisher like is father the Master who is the Angel of Justice and a Watcher.

Vincent Valdi stated sternly,

-Demons certainly did have a good go at killing one of your major angels. I can tell you there was a plan behind it all. They removed the strong sidekick Henry, or disabled him for a while, in order to have a crack at your grandson to get rid of him. Here, look at that demonic claw embedded in his liver. That gaping wound was just a mere distraction. I can put my hand in the fire and swear that the other two angels who are going to die tomorrow have a similar claw in their livers. You will need to get them operated as soon as. Were they important as well?

As Doctor Valdi removed carefully the claw from Sebastien's organ, the Creator answered,

-Not really. Young Lawrence is not and has never been a mature angel. All of his lives even his human one did stop at twenty one. As we speak, he did turn twenty one only a few weeks ago. Theo Odell suggested that his possession was to allow a demon in him to spy on the angelic army and to know all our next moves. While for Daniel, he was a strong and bold fighter, a fearless one which is rare to find. It feels like losing a knight on a chess board. If we manage to save him, he will not be able to walk properly anymore so fighting will be out of question for him.

Putting the demonic claw in a dish presented by his wife, Vincent ordered,

-Amelia, don't touch this, please. Put it in that drawer we will study it later. Please bring me a bowl.

As his wife did so, Doctor Valdi turned to the Great Being giving him his fair comment,

-Pawns or knights, all pieces on a chessboard matter. At the end of the day, the queen is here on my bed, wounded. Lawrence may have been a pawn but he was in a very strategic place at the right time for the demons. They saw it and you lot didn't. They removed two knights and a pawn to get to the queen. This was a fast and possibly lethal move to sustain on our side of the board. Amelia hold the bowl for me, what I will do may make you feel sick, so please look away. I have to drain his liver.

Taking the bowl from Amelia, the Creator ordered,

-Please go and fetch hot water, Mrs Valdi, we will need it. I will hold the bowl for your husband.

With the nodding consent of her husband who demanded a bucket full of it, Amelia ran out of the cabin to go to the ship's kitchen. Once alone with the Great Being, Vincent did the gruesome task of emptying the liver of Sebastien, mouthful by mouthful, like if he was treating him for a venomous snake bite. It took time. He was getting pale yet he stated,

-We will save him. He is strong. We will have to do the other two angels.

When it was over, Doctor Valdi mended the liver and the gaping wound. With the finishing stitch he looked at the Great Being and recommended,

-Let's leave Sebastien here to rest in my cabin. His pulse is already getting stronger while his temperature from high is getting back to normal.

A satisfied Creator asked, when he transformed Sebastien back to his human shape,

-You do not mind losing your bed, Doctor Valdi?

Preparing a bandage, Vincent replied,

-Of course I do not mind for who needs that bed the most at this moment in time? It is most certainly your grandson. May I enquire about one thing which puzzles me?

-You may.

-Why did you only transform him into a human now?

The Great Being explained,

-If the Mighty One is strong as a human, he is even stronger as an angel. With what happened to him and the operation he had to undertake, his survival chances were increased in his angelic shape. Not only that Vincent, it is good practice for you to work on healing an angel. You did brilliantly.

Doctor Valdi smiled sadly as he said, whilst bandaging Sebastien,

-When I will see Sebastien being conscious, up on his feet and talking, this is when I will be satisfied with my work. Until then may I offer you all my help for the situation you are facing? It doesn't seat well with me that Whilhelmina and Doctor Williams are facing demons of the kind that Sebastien fought with. I can operate on Sebastien's wounded angelic soldiers, then I can help William to find an antidote for the demonic poison. The more hands on board, the better we have a chance to find a counter poison fast enough.

Touching the shoulder of Valdi, the Creator made his wings appear on the back of Doctor Valdi and replied,

-Your help is more than welcomed, Vincent, it is appreciated. Here are your wings. When we are out there just fly by me and mimic whatever I do. Our first port of call will be at the hotel of Miss White to operate on Lawrence. He was the first angel to be possessed by a Nefarius today and he isn't doing too well I am afraid. Sebastien managed to kill the three Nefarius demons he had to face today but one must only admit that the three demons left three badly injured angels behind, one of which who is the main fighter and leader of the angelic army.

The hand of Sebastien moved slightly on the bed. His unusual two different coloured eyes flicked opened, and he started talking in an anxious way with great difficulty,

-I must go back to work. I must. I mustn't lose any of my angels. Where am I? What happened? Where's my Dad? Is he alright? How's Daniel? I must get up. I must check on them.

Coming to his grandson, the Great Being holding his hand firmly, ordered,

-Mighty, what you must do is rest.

An unusual knock on the door disrupted them. Doctor Valdi reassured as he went to open the door,

-Don't worry, it's my Amelia with the sterilised water. We use Morse code between us on occasion.

Sebastien, looking at the Doctor and his wife and the diligent way he took the bucket out of the hands of Amelia in order to carry it for her, while she locked the door behind herself, realised where he was. His grandfather had his hand firmly upon his, while his other hand was stroking his forehead with concern. Sebastien felt unsettled yet reassured in the same time by the presence of the Great Being by his bedside. His fingers pressed the one of his grandfather with affection and gratefulness but also to indicate that he pulling through while he asked, his voice still weak,

-You saved me, did you, grandpa?

Nodding positively, the Great Being smiling to him with tenderness, explained,

-I did. I can not let you to be taken by demons. You are the 'Raison d'être' of my son. If we lose you, the Master will be so inconsolable that I will lose him. Without you two, I would be left without my heart and soul. Doctor Valdi helped tremendously to save you. How are you feeling? What do you remember?

Still struggling to speak Sebastien answered,

-It feels like I am coming back to the surface after drowning. I remember calling my father for help and our Theo to do an exorcism on me. I remember that something was coming over me fast and strong, almost like a gut feeling that a demon was inside me coming out from within me to take over my entire body. Then I don't remember anything at all after that.

He stopped, coughing a great deal. Doctor Valdi came to him, giving him a cup of water with an order,

-Here, here, drink slowly. Breathe and pace yourself. You mustn't exert yourself too much, Sebastien. You just woke up from an intense operation which just happened literally five minutes ago. Like your grandfather ordered, you must rest. Amelia, please fetch me the pine forest honey pot and a spoon.

Looking at his grandfather, after having drank a fair amount of water Sebastien demanded,

-Why Doctor Williams didn't look after me? Why didn't he do my operation? He is, he is my best friend.

The Great Being scolded Sebastien, tapping his hand,

-And he is still your best friend. It is all due to the circumstances when we had all to rally together to protect you. Your father, him, Ted, Miss White and Father Odell had to tackle two demons, the one within you and the one within Daniel. Once your demon was out, it was essential to remove you from the room, you were unconscious, you had collapsed, you needed immediate care and you would have been the best and easiest target for a couple of demons to finish you off. Doctor Williams, Miss White and Theo Odell provided the best distraction they could under the telepathic instructions of your father and the helping ones of your Ted. So I took you far away from your demon to get efficient emergency care but also to protect your full recovery. The demons will never find you on this ship on the ocean. You are safe here. You need to focus on your recovery. It is an imperative. Your father stepped in charge of your army up until you can fight strong again. Doctor Williams has teamed up with Miss White to employ magical warfare on the demons. They are fighters in their own right but not as you know it. As for you, if you really want to get involved in the fight in Wilton Town tomorrow night, I suggest you to not you use fist fighting this time but the full scope of your magical powers. Your fairy grandmother Dana will come to visit you. She was really worried about you. Take the opportunity of her visit to learn from her what you can do with your strong magical powers. But also, just get to know Dana. She took a strong interest in you since your birth. Your father and I visited her many times, sometimes together, sometimes apart. You are her only grandson and you have a special place in her heart.

A very concerned Sebastien demanded,

-Have you got any news from the cottage, Grandfather? How are they all doing? They are not really physical fighters.

While Doctor Valdi spoon fed some honey to the convalescent angel, Sebastien's grandfather replied,

-There are many ways to help and fight, Mighty. As I said your father coordinated everything as soon as you asked for his help. He kept me updated. The demon inside you first went for Father Odell who was doing an exorcism with extreme gusto. I can reveal to you that Theo is a powerful priest who can tame demons and send them back to hell. By far he will never be the weakest in your angelic army. His astuteness makes him a real asset. So my power felt his own power when we got rid of the demon inside of you and made him face us. Of course with a choice between me and Theo, the demon went to attack the weakest one, the one who meant a trip for hell to him. He threw a chair at Odell in order to bring him down in the aim of attacking him full on. However Miss White intervened with her magic wand and protected Theo. She stopped the chair in mid air and sent it back to the demon with the same strength and velocity. The chair hit and broke itself upon the demon who now had his attention on the witch. That diversion allowed Doctor Williams to release two spirits from you, the smilodon of your father and Arthus the cockerel but also for me to save you and bring you here.

Puzzled Sebastien asked,

-Why releasing my animal spirits from me? Why only two and not the third one?

Pulling the bed cover up on his grandson with care, the Great Being explained,

-Cadarn had to stay within you because he is a stallion that survived all the battles he went through and we needed you to survive this one. Animal spirits protect you and all you care about. With the wizardry of Doctor Williams, he made the two other spirits corporeal. The sabre tooth cat was reunited with the Master which he takes orders from and therefore became a lethal weapon within his hands against demons. While Arthus and his claws had the task to blind those dangerous demons.

Now, let me tell you the result: both demons were killed and dusted. However a gruesome undertaking was done on them. Both lost their clawed hands before becoming a pile of dust. This was done in order for Doctor Williams and Miss White to work on a counter poison which they are busy right now as we speak to try to find. Your father told me that none have been hurt during the fight that they are all without a scratch. He says it is due to the fact that all had each others backs at all time. They outwitted the demons. When one of the demons, yours, went to attack Miss White, Williams shielded her. Now the white witch had provided everyone but herself with an indestructible mirror shield. Our clever Miss White wanted to try if their own gaze could paralyse the demons. Her speculation worked beautifully and was tried and tested by a brave Doctor Williams. The reflection of his stare immobilise the demon. Your father threw Arthus at his head who took no time at all to blind the demon in a very gruesome way using claws and beak. When the bird was done, of course, the demon wasn't paralysed any longer but the sabre tooth cat pinned him on the ground in such an efficient manner, on his back, with his teeth sank into the demon's neck ready to tear it apart at the order of the Master, his claws digging into the shoulders of the demon, that your father only had to take his angelic sword to finish off the Nefarius. He cut both arms of the demon off. At the click of his fingers, his smilodon riped the throat of your demon turning it into a pile of dust. By that time, your brave Theo had successfully exorcised the demon from Daniel and initially tackled him on his own so the demon would not join forces with the other one. He first blinded him with holy water, Ted came to help him bringing the cockerel which he threw on the head of the demon. Arthus did his work and while he was doing it, a courageous Ted and Theo joined forces to floor the demon. Your fast thinking Odell used his trick again harming Daniel's demon by throwing blessed water on his genitals. In pain, being blinded, the colossal demon fell on the ground unable to fight his opponents. Theo threw a pointed cross to Ted, and took another one in his hand and both pinned the arms of the demon on the ground with them in a coordinated forceful move. When your father turned around having finished off your demon, he found that Daniel's demon was well under control and properly blinded. The Master removed the arms of the demon before letting his sabre tooth cat killing the Nefarius. Theo and Ted stood up, both, without any harms done to them. Those two angels have done you proud, Mighty. They work well as a team.

This made Sebastien smile with relief and happiness. He confided,

-I would have been so distraught if any harm had happened to any of them. I would have beaten myself up for it.

My Theo keeps amazing me. Who would have thought that Ted would start fighting one day?

His grandfather stated,

-Miracles do happen. Ted was distressed when he saw you on the ground almost lifeless. You mean so much to him. You are undeniably his second father. However I felt his strong will to honour you by making sure the logistic team you have been building would work together in an efficient manner. Seeing Theo in action, empowered our Ted. He wanted to be by his side and provide all his help to him. Ted took ownership of the logistic team tonight. From an angel who always had to be looked after, he finally took a forefront fighting position to look after a new angel.

Satisfied Sebastien told,

-I followed the advice of my father about Ted and he was right all along. He told me to stop smothering Ted like if he was still the abandoned human child he was. He ordered me to give some tough responsibility to my angel, to make him step up to the plate and watch him grow from then on. It works.

Standing up the Great Being confirmed,

-Yes, it always works. You and your father are living proofs of the method. I never spoilt your father and he never spoilt you. Your senses of responsibilities were anchored down on you from a very young age. Right, now, Mighty, you must rest. You can not fly or transport yourself somewhere until either your father or me give you the all clear. I made sure of it: those powers are deactivated in you. Get strong for tomorrow that's the aim of the game.

He then turned to Doctor Valdi after bowing to his grandson, enjoining,

-Vincent, let's sort out Lawrence and Daniel. Are you ready?

Doctor Valdi replied,

-Almost. Amelia, come and take a seat by Sebastien. Monitor him for us. It's only water and honey for him at the moment. In six hours, then he can start eating properly. Give him a porridge laced with honey, a large glass of milk and the apple compote of that Canadian cook. Then three hours later ask the Chef to prepare some scrambled eggs with smoked salmon and chives. Say it is for you, pretend it is a craving of yours because you are pregnant and then feed it to Sebastien back in the cabin. He must stay in bed for as long as possible. His liver was perforated and he has suture points upon it, let alone the large new scars on his flank. My Darling, I need to operate on two angels and help out in Wilton Town for a little while. I do not know when I will be back but I will do my best to be by your side within forty eight to seventy two hours. Now you must promise me two things: First to look after yourself, remember you have been sick twice today, take it easy, no promenade on the deck without me to look after you, beside that Captain Hansen forcasted two days of rough sea, so stay in the cabin apart to fetch meals. Second, look after Sebastien and keep his presence a secret and him locked in here. The only one, you can tell the secret to, is our Zachary Wilton-Cough. He will know how to keep it, like he never told to anyone that Mina was a vampire. He will also be ever so willing to help you both which can be very handy. Last but not least, give me a big hug. I won't be long, I promise.

Amelia nestled in her husband's arms, impressed by his wings, she caressed them gently. Then she ordered,

-And make sure you come back to me without a ruffled feather. I will check them, you know my Vince, one by one. The penalty will be very harsh, you will be grounded by my side, at least for an entire day, and you will have to pay for each damaged feather by a kiss. Now go and try to stay safe.

They kissed each other. Their hands pressed one another with tenderness before Doctor Valdi went to the Great Being who took him away, disappearing from the cabin. Left alone, Sebastien smirked to Amelia while he commented,

-Mrs Valdi, punishment by kisses, really? That angel will certainly come back to you with plenty of ruffled feathers!

Amelia sat by the bed while she replied,

-The point is, Mr Cotton, my husband will come back. He has something to look forward to. Your voice is still a little rough. Here, have a little water.

Sebastien obliged her, drank and told,

-Thank you. Looks like we are stuck together for a little bit. My grandfather went on a live today, fight tomorrow scheme upon me. Let's chat, I am far from being tired. I am far from being able to sleep. I am far too worried about my angels at this moment in time. How do you feel about your husband being part of my angelic army, and being my angel?

Amelia Valdi answered with her deep honesty,

-Like you are worried about your angels, I am worried about my angelic husband especially since seeing you so hurt. However, my first husband was a soldier and I do understand what duty is. He died on the battlefield a hero. I am so proud of him. As for my Vince, I know he has already the will and want to serve your army well. We had the heads up from Father Odell's letter that Vincent had no choice but to become an angel. The news were not unwelcome by my husband, although we discussed them all night when we received them. Vincent was mainly worried about me, you see, if I would cope during his absences. Of course I reassured him and I said I would.

Giving her back the empty glass of water, which Amelia filled up again, Sebastien engaged the conversation further,

-As you know, your husband is one of my newest angelic recruits with Father Odell. As his General, I am keen to know more about Vincent Valdi. Would you be able to enlighten me about him?

The chatterbox that Amelia was, had just been given a subject of conversation that she was most passionate about. She started with eagerness and a rosy blush on her cheeks, giving the tell tale signs to Sebastien of how much in love she was with her husband,

-What can I say? Where do I start? Vincent was born in Sicily during the Napoleonic wars. When he was a toddler, his parents sought to leave the Italian peninsula but their carriage was stopped crossing the alps. The French Napoleonic army murdered the couple in front of their only child. A distraught Vincent was going to get stabbed by a bayonet and disposed off but a soldier of an elevated rank took pity of the toddler. He took Vincent to the nearest orphanage. The maternal aunt of Vincent, who was the school teacher of a village in Sicily, at the news of the death of her sister, walked the entire length of Italy to retrieve her nephew. Something also happened to the aunt on the way back, robbed and raped, she did hid Vincent in the bushes in order to protect him. She was left for dead on the road bleeding heavily. Vincent went to fetch help in a nearby almost derelict farm. Luck was that it was the one of a medicine woman or a white witch of the like of of our Miss White of Wilton Town. She took care of the aunt and her nephew for a while. From the traumatic events, he had seen, Vincent had ceased to talk altogether. From the orphanage his aunt had tried to make him talk to no avail. But the old woman of that farm managed little by little to make Vincent speak again. The way she saved the life of his aunt inspired him to become a Doctor.

Sebastien commented pensively,

-I was told by Doctor Williams that Doctor Valdi had a tragic start in life but never in such great details. I only knew he had been an orphan for an extremely young age. But my father warned me that Vincent had no faith because his parents were killed before him.

A nodding Amelia added,

-You see, Mr Cotton, the only faith my Vincent have, is medicine and sometimes the good will and acts of people. That old lady who helped his aunt to recover and looked after him for example showed him that not everyone was bad. The same goes for that French officer who prevented him to be killed and took him by the hand to an orphanage instead. Then there is his maternal aunt, who despite being poor, went on that relentless quest to find him and take him back to Sicily, brought him up and gave him a solid education. For my Vince, there is no god, only good hearts out there once in a while.

The angel couldn't help giggling. Then he started to laugh, yet it did hurt so much that he soon stop and confided instead to Amelia,

-Mrs Valdi, your husband is flying back to Wilton Town with the Creator himself, my grandfather.

She swore,

-Oh! Good Lord! My husband is an atheist or was or is still a bit! I wish I was a bird mite on his wings to know what will happen.

Sebastien laughed irresistibly, however he tried to comfort,

-Amelia, your husband is already so valued by all high beings that I would not worry for him. After all the Creator brought me to him to be saved. As I am talking to you, Doctor Valdi did a pretty good work on me. Waking up five minutes after an operation is good going. I am wondering what he did?

Mrs Valdi explained willingly,

-Well, I can tell you. I was there for part of it. Your grandfather gave Vincent the heads up about what happened to you. My husband examined your flank wound. He saw signs of inflammation radiating from your liver. He opened you up to investigate it further and he found a poisoned demon claw perforating your liver embedded within it. You can see it, but you and I mustn't touch it. Then Vincent asked me to put it away in the drawer and to bring him a bowl which is now on that console over here with lots of smelly goo within it. I was about to stay and be the nurse of Vincent but your grandfather hearing that I may be sick and had to turn my head to not see the rest of the operation sent me away to fetch hot sterilised water. When I came back, you were awake, barely, but awake.

The angel ordered with a warning,

-Bring those to me but be careful to not have contact with the demonic items, Mrs Valdi.

Amelia obeyed, taking first the plate containing the claw of the Nefarius demon to him, saying,

-Here. This is the claw found in your liver. Vincent thinks that your two other angels that are on their way to die who met a Nefarius demon have both one of those in their bodies. He is going to operate on them and try to save them both. He said that your wound distracted from your main injury which was to your poisoned liver.

His hand trembling above the claw, Sebastien confided,

-I can feel its power yet when it was within me I couldn't feel that it was there. My very father cleaned my wound but if he repaired my veins, he didn't spot the claw.

Showing her perspicacity without knowing it to the angel, Amelia commented,

-From what your grandfather said the claws were numbing the area of the body they damaged which made one slow to react to the attack because they simply couldn't feel what was done to them. When you think about it, Mr Cotton, if you do not know that you have a poisonous claw in you, it could kill you more effectively by letting the poison do its work. Those Nefarious demons worked out a clever way to kill, with the victims unaware of the full damaging scale of their encounter with them. Look, you see that flabby thing at the base of the claw. Vincent looked at it closely when the claw was still within you. He gave a long stare to your grandfather. I think he found the pocket which was containing the poison which was then dripped into your liver via the claw. As for your father, he couldn't have seen the claw for it was further up. Vincent had to open you up to find it. But by repairing your veins, your father reestablished your normal circulation of blood which could have meant two things: first that the poison went faster within you leading to your sudden collapse soon afterwards. Second, it allowed signs of inflammations to be visible from your wound later on. I doubt anything could have been spotted when your father looked after you.

Sebastien taking a closer look at the base of the claw demanded,

-Mrs Valdi, please bring me a knife, a spoon and a little container of some sort. You seem to know a little bit about medicine?

Amelia opened the medical old leather bag of her husband and took out everything requested, saying,

-I just pay attention and I listen. My husband has been my friend for years before I married him. Every morning, he brought me the newspaper and we chatted about everything. Him being a Doctor, medical subjects were often discussed. Now, that we are together, I told him of my wish to be able to help him at the clinic when he needed me there. So he has started teaching me everyday about medicine and medical treatments for different ailments.

Dissecting the demon's claw with great care, the angel gave an approving sign of his head as he commented,

-I can see you being more than a nurse, Amelia. Like my wife, you could become a Doctor in your own right. We have still got some poison in that gland. Hold the container for me, I am going to pour it in there. So tell me, you had a long courtship from Doctor Valdi?

Doing as she was told, seeing the black viscous liquid coming out of the dissected gland, Amelia recounted,

-It was not a courtship. It was a deep friendship. Vincent has always been very proper with me since the first day I met him. I never knew he was in love with me until the day he asked me to marry him. At that time, I had lost my Harry and was pregnant with my Abigail. I thought Vincent just wanted to look after me from the goodness of his heart but I soon realised he had secretly loved me all the time but ever so silently, with so much care and so politely. Let me confide to you that his hand is the one I trust the most, his arms are the most comforting ones, his shoulder is the most supportive one, his smile brightens my day, his wit makes me smile endlessly, and the level of his care is such that many times I thought to kneel by him to rest my head on his lap, just being grateful. I value all the moments we had together simply chatting at my doorstep every morning. Sometimes, I asked myself, there must have been a clue that he was in love with me that I failed to spot. I always thought of his morning calls as just a simple check that I was alright. But for both of us, we enjoyed so much our morning conversations, that it left us with a bright smile all day. I considered him like my best friend and confident. I never thought once that I could be his love interest. However I was the only woman that he paid a visit daily. Yet all was very proper and polite, in view of all, on my doorstep.

Sebastien smiled to her and shared,

-For my Ivy and I, our love developed from a strong friendship as well. I must say that I knew I was in love from the minute I saw Ivy and I knew it was very deep from how protective I felt about her. When I saw you and Doctor Valdi in Boston for the first time, not only could I feel the deep connection you had for one another, but I could clearly see, how protective of you your husband was. Now, confide, can you remember the first time you met Doctor Valdi?

A thoroughly blushing Amelia confessed,

-I do. I must admit that I do. My friend Angela Wilton-Cough gave a tea party to welcome the first Doctor of Wilton Town at that time. Dare I say, that I found him a very dashing young man, not only that, he was witty with a great sense of repartee. I must say that when he arrived in town, he excited all curiosity. We never hoped to have a Doctor in Wilton Town. Abraham Wilton-Cough was the first to welcome Vincent with open arms, so, of course, his wife had to throw a little party to introduce the newcomer to the gentle folk of the town. Well the young ladies almost threw themselves shamelessly at his feet during that party so much so that sick of it, Vincent took his seat by the stern Abraham, the welcoming Angela and myself at our table. Abraham asked him if he was a heartthrob. Vincent was almost offended by the question. He replied that if he had been a little religious which he was not as an atheist, he would have been a monk to escape the vicissitude of life. By the mournful way he said it, I was struck by what it seemed to me such negativity for such a young man with his life in front of him. Angela scolded him saying that he didn't realise how handsome he was and to expect to be chased by young ladies. Vincent replied that if they were only concerned by beauty, as beauty was ephemeral, he would ignore them all. Which he did, like the man of his words he is. Angela truly thought that Vincent was queer while Abraham was worried to lose the Doctor if he didn't settle with a wife at some point because Wilton Town would not be attractive enough. However, Vincent reassured him saying that he didn't need to marry to stay in Wilton Town that it was enough for him to know that there was no Doctor there to stay here for a very long time to help the people. He added that if he ever found the right companion, a soul mate, a partner which had character, intelligence and was not shallow and materialistic then and only then he would consider marriage. I must confess that I did find him deeply interesting then. But as a married young lady at that time I never entertained loving thoughts about him, none whatsoever.

The angel gave the little glass flask to Amelia asking,

-Would you be able to label this for me, Mrs Valdi, as Nefarious demon poison, found in Sebastien? Then if you bring me a handkerchief, I would be very much obliged to you. You see, I found the canal within the claw where the poison pass to the body of its victim. Look, here it is.

A curious Amelia took a glance before doing what she was asked for with diligence. Sebastien told her,

-Mrs Valdi, I have heard about you for a very long while. You see, Doctor Valdi wrote to Doctor Williams weekly. William, being my best friend, used to read his letters to me by the fireplace. Let me tell you that Vincent never failed to mention you in all of his letters with such affection. One day, a long time ago, he confided that the only woman he wanted to marry and spend the rest of his days with was you, but as you were already taken he was resigned for a life of celibacy. He told us when your father passed away, when your brothers and sisters went back to Ireland or went elsewhere, when you were increasingly lonely but always did put a brave face on, when he asked Father Odell to take you as his chief organiser of his charity events, when you suspected that something was wrong in some families of Wilton Town and that you were rarely wrong in any of your worries about someone. About the way you smiled and laughed, the way you put your glasses back upon your nose, the way you constantly fiddled with your bonnet, the way your apron was patched up, so much so that it was a mismatch of patches and colours, Doctor Williams and I had all the details.

As she handed to Sebastien the little flask of poison which she had labelled, Amelia confided thoroughly blushing,

-I did notice a few times the particularly kind attention Vincent was paying to me. But as he was teasing and mocking me in the same manner as he did with his best friend Father Odell, I never thought it was love. Only that I was his second best friend.

The angel put the wrapped dissected claw and the glass flask on a shelve which was used as a night table by the bed. He revealed,

-Let me tell you something Amelia, in which Doctor Williams and I had been involved and investigated for Doctor Valdi and bring me that bowl of goo please. One letter of Valdi told us how he found you in tears walking back from the bigger neighbouring town. It happened about four years ago. You were expecting Harry Bates back that day, like the many soldiers which had been discharged but instead one of his lieutenants gave you a letter from your former husband. Disappointed from broken expectations, you went back to Wilton Town reading the letter on the way which put you in tatters. Harry wrote to you that he had been promoted and that he will stay posted and will not come back for a few years. Meeting a concerned Doctor Valdi, you showed him the letter of Harry, and he tried to make you see the positive side of the letter in which your husband had been promoted hence he did have higher degrees of responsibilities which didn't permit him to take a short leave to see you. However he told us of the matter, and that Harry's letter clearly mentioned years in being unable to see you which was irregular because any soldier is entitled to short breaks to see their family. Valdi even spoke of the matter with Abraham Wilton-Cough who thought that this was highly unusual of his best friend Harry. So a few went to investigate what was truly going on and we know why Harry didn't come back to you for altogether five years. The truth maybe unpleasant because we all know how highly you regard the late Harry Bates.

Giving him the bowl Amelia demanded,

-Unsavoury or not, I rather know the truth. This bowl contains what was found in your liver.

Sebastien, his hand hovering above the bowl magically analysed its contents while he told,

-We found out that your former husband had been victim of trickery during his last years. He was Captain of a small mission which took from the enemy a very important bridge. Not only was he successful, there were no casualties in his ranks. It only confirmed his status of hero. Harry was awarded a very princely sum. Of course that type of money attracted scoundrels of all sorts. In the very ranks of his battalion was a soldier named Francis Hay who was such a scoundrel but also a pimp. He plotted against Bates to get his money. On a celebratory evening of another victory of Harry, he spiked his drink. Bates fell unconscious. Hay carried him into a bedroom of the Auberge they were celebrating. Hay ordered one of his favourite and most cunning prostitutes to carry out his plan for a thirty per cent share of Bates' newly found good fortune. So Harry woke up the following morning in the arms of the naked Sandra who pretended that they had made love all night and that he had promised her almost the moon, and that he had also given to her his wedding ring as token of his affection. None of this was true of course but the drugged Harry couldn't remember anything. Hay made sure that Sandra would fall pregnant, from himself, to ensure that his prostitute could use her situation to get the most out of Harry Bates. Their ploy worked on Harry who felt ever so guilty. A baby was born, ten months later, a month too late to really be the daughter of Harry Bates but they managed to make Harry believe that it was his baby girl: Sandra called her Harriette Rose. Now, your husband was ashamed to meet you ever again despite loving you dearly from that day on. He never came back to Wilton Town. Hay and Sandra broke up your first marriage literally by their greed. Not only Harry recognised Harriette Rose as his daughter legally, he provided for her and her mother Sandra who demanded his entire fortune or almost. Almost, because Harry made sure that you kept receiving his soldier's allowance. He kept writing to you, he kept loving you but his heart was heavy with guilt and shame because he knew that you wanted a child and a family so much and he thought he had one with a prostitute. It distressed him greatly.

He paused seeing a lot of emotions passing on the face of Amelia. She wiped her tearful eyes but asked,

-What happened next?

The angel revealed,

-Well, not very long afterwards Harry Bates died on the battlefield. Hay died by his side as well. The soldier was protecting your husband like if he was his asset and livelihood. Let's just say with just greed on his mind. By that time, Hay and Sandra had used up all the fortune of Bates. Hay wanted Bates to bring another glowing victory under his belt and another princely reward but if they won the battle, they were not alive to reap the rewards which went to the entire battalion of Harry Bates that time around. Sandra who loved her Francis Hay and knew that she couldn't apply her wit to get money from your dead husband hanged herself. Abraham Wilton-Cough which had been left in charge to deal with the affairs of Harry Bates, his best friend, learnt at his death of the existence of Harriette Rose which he kept from you. A week after the funeral, he went on a business trip to New York where he found out about the death of Sandra. He took Harriette Rose from the brothel she was going to grow up in to an orphanage-boarding school. He paid her fees personally for up until she would be sixteen years old for her to be educated, all in advance. He added a close, that if she was adopted the fond should remain for her education wherever she would go. Spiritually, Sandra who had her first symptoms of syphilis by the time of her death and Francis Hay who was such a dissolute and fairly bad character are serving time in hell. Harry Bates became a ghost at first because he thought he was guilty, so he refused to go to heaven. He used the body of his friend Abraham Wilton-Cough at his own funeral, in order to give you the child you always wanted to have. Abigail was his parting gift to you. It was granted by high above and we gave you an angel. Harry, now rests in peace in heaven but he occasionally wants to help out as a spirit down here upon earth. He is also fully aware now that Harriette Rose is not at all his daughter. First she doesn't look like him whatsoever. She has flowing black curls, olive green eyes and a naturally tanned skin. Doctor Williams who couldn't and has never been able to curb his curiosity went to give a medical inspection to all the children of that orphanage just in order to see that specific little girl. He confirmed that she was solely Francis Hay's and Sandra's daughter, that Harriette had syphilis and that she looked like a gypsy. He doubted very much that she would ever be adopted. However he suggested that after her education, depending on Harriette showing a good character and morality, he may give her some employment of some sort to help her with the illness which will plague her life.

Taking a seat silently, feeling somewhat nauseous, Amelia pondered on all of what had been said. Sebastien ordered,

-You must drink some water Mrs Valdi, you are looking very pale. Being with child on a rolling ocean is difficult enough, so I hope I didn't made it worst by delivering all that information at your doorsteps.

Amelia drank an entire cup of water before she replied firmly,

-No, don't feel uneasy, I ought to know what happened exactly. Of course, I am deeply annoyed by the entire matter but it makes me understand, comprehend why Harry was so aloof the last years of his life. I must confide that I thought it was my fault that as a woman I was lacking in graces the older I got, that I was not attractive enough any longer but also that I consistently failed to give him a child. If he would have confided to me the matter, I would have forgiven him readily but I would also have taken my own life in a manner which would have looked like an accident so it would preserve him from guilt. Me, knowing now is best because I can deal with it all. I also feel so sorry for that orphaned little girl which was only conceived not out of love but just out of greed. The fact that she inherited that terrible illness from her mother as well is so disheartening. I need to speak to my Vince but on my side I would be willing to adopt her because for me a child is always innocent from the faults of his or her parents.

Looking at Mrs Valdi with his amazing gaze, Sebastien told with gravity,

-Amelia, I am glad no one did tell you earlier. Your loss would have been a great one for humanity. I am sure that if you appeal to the good heart of Doctor Valdi, you will both become the adoptive parents of that little orphan girl. I never considered you as a human that could have entertained suicidal thoughts? You always seems ever so jovial with a constant bright smile on your face.

Amelia giving him a sad negative nod answered,

-In the past five years, I did become depressed and yes, I did try to end my days. But with Vincent visiting me every morning, he spotted easily that something was up and wrong. I did stop eating one day, I had no will to live any longer and as I was living on my own, I thought it would go unnoticed. A few days later I collapsed but unfortunately or rather fortunately, it was a Sunday morning. Of course I failed to go to church. Father Odell went to report the fact straight after his mass to Vincent. Both went to call on me, immediately and as I wasn't answering the door, they broke their way in. They found me unconscious on the floor. Vincent took me to his clinic and both men nursed me back to health. After that episode, I was hardly left alone. Both organised for me to be watched almost constantly. I had friends and neighbours visiting me. Father Odell kept me busy helping in all sorts of events he was organising for the parish. I hardly ate on my own after that, it was invitation for dinner after invitation for dinner which I was not allowed to refuse by many in town. All was because Vincent and Theo realised that I tried to let myself fade away. I must say that their methods worked on me and that they did snap me off my bad under the weather moment. You see, Mr Cotton, I am a usually very happy being but I am not the most confident woman in the world and I couldn't help feeling rejected and neglected by my Harry so I couldn't see the point in carrying on without him. When I shared that to Father Odell, he gave me a right scolding and when he told Vincent I had another telling off, a proper one. But he told me that I and my conversation were brightening his days, that my friendship was the warm rays of sunshine in his life. What he said to me did touch my heart that day so much that any thoughts of ending my days disappeared altogether.

The angel ordered holding his hand out to Mrs Valdi,

-Give me your hand, Amelia.

While she done so, he held her hand tight, and glowed before he said with some sadness,

-Oh, Amelia, Amelia, I can feel your great lack of confidence. I can realise that the long absences of Harry contributed to increase it. But let me tell you from an angel to a lovely human soul the truth. First you possess a very decent and good soul. I can't tell you enough how rare it is. Part of my work consists of making angels out of humans, and if you fulfil your destiny, I can reveal to you that your soul is made of the right material to be one. Now, Vincent has done enough and is already my angel. For you, you must run your path as a human, succeed in what has been mapped out for you, which is going to fully use your good soul and heart. Let me tell you that you did a prayer one day, a big wish you repeatedly done over and over again afterwards, it has been granted and is coming in your future. Can you guess what it is?

Mrs Valdi stroke tenderly and instinctively her pregnant belly, replied, her eyes glistening,

-I always wanted a large family because I had so much love to give.

Sebastien smiled to her while he confirmed,

-That is right, and you proved it again because despite it all, your good heart accepted orphaned Harriette Rose within it as soon as you heard of her story. You will become a mother to many. Some are your biological children, but you will provide a home and lots of love to many abandoned and orphaned children. You have a mission in your human life. The success of it will mean that you will become an angel in your own right and therefore be granted to be incarnated again and again by your husband Vincent. Now, let me tell you this Amelia to boost up your confidence: if two excellent men chose to marry you it is not surprising. The first, Harry, was adamant that only you could be his wife, despite a difference of status. He opposed himself to the disapproval of his wealthy family to stand by you and give you his hand anyway. It made him become a soldier of fortune. While the second, Vincent loved you silently so much that he was determined to never marry unless it was with you and he waited patiently, politely, settling on being your protective friend. You have qualities in abundance, from your kindness, your good temperament, your intelligence, your humour, your humbleness, from the way you are selfless, helpful and caring. I could mention more but I will stop here, scold you and tell you that you have all the rights to be confident. Now, I need you to fetch Zachary Wilton-Cough for us and bring him to the cabin so I can brief him into our confidence.

Giving the angel a grateful smile and a small courtesy, Mrs Valdi left the cabin to obey her order. Left alone Sebastien closed his eyes thankful that he had been saved in extremis and was only hoping that Valdi would be able to do the same to his other two angels. Death by a demon meant the total loss of an angel and vice versa, so it was crucial that Doctor Valdi arrived on time in Wilton Town.

#

Having a crash course about flying delivered by the Creator himself, Vincent Valdi had still no idea who he was addressing himself to. For him it was just the grandfather of Sebastien, hence a being of some sort or another. Therefore he was behaving in the most natural way possible, which pleased and amused the Great Being, who wasn't eager to reveal his true identity. This way he had time to observe the only atheist angel in his grandson's army. Once they both appeared in the thundery sky above the Atlantic ocean about a mile away from Captain Hansen's ship, he stated,

-You have a nice stormy weather system to contend with for your first flight, how do you feel about it Doctor Valdi? Deploy your wings now and stay by me. Mimic as I do.

With his hand released Valdi could only feel the strength of the wind pushing him away from the Being yet he was quick to watch and learn and made his way back with a struggle to the side of what he thought was possibly an angel. He replied sternly,

-Well, I will have to deal with it. Life is full of ups and downs and has never been fully rosy. Stormy or not, we have to get to Sebastien's angelic soldiers as soon as possible to help them. I hope to prove myself to be a fast learner on this occasion, I need to be one for the others.

Appraising that Valdi showed no fear, the Great Being ordered,

-Follow me. Get a feel for the air currents and use them to the best of your abilities. I like your attitude. Your praises reached my ears from many, Doctor Williams, my son Raguel and my grandson among them. Your fortitude is greatly admired.

You never had a very easy life, I must admit.

Vincent, getting a good feel of his wings copied the expert moves of the Great Being despite the challenging winds, commented,

-If I do know Doctor Williams very well, I am afraid to say that it is not the same for your son and grandson, the later which I first met a few days ago for the first time in Boston. However I heard of Sebastien via Williams very often. Surely your son and grandson can't both sing my praises knowing me not at all for one and the other so little. At the moment I am wondering what do you know about my life, because I don't open up about it very often. I rather have no one but my very close ones to know just a little about it. I abhor pity especially if it is shown towards me.

The Creator gave an amazing glowing glance at the new angel who was now flying by him rather well as he revealed,

-I know everything about you, Vincent, everything. If you want proof let me give them to you or just one which could be sufficient. As a little boy you used to pick up all the snails from the road and put them back on the surrounding stone wall of the small school and cottage of your aunt, saving them from being crushed by carriages wheels after rain showers. You did it to keep them alive until any hard day your aunt and you may face which meant that they would become a last resort pauper's meal.

A gob smashed Valdi almost lost his pace, but regained it fast enough, demanding,

-Who are you? Whenever I did that, I always made sure the road was clear to protect the pride of my aunt, so no one knew we had to resort to do that in the village.

Smiling enigmatically the Great Being questioned,

-Do you rate pride more than pity, Vincent? I could do the apology of pity over the one of pride with you if you want me to. Let's just say that pity brings the consideration of one another. It may be welcomed or not welcomed but it usually says from one soul to another: I feel for you, I know you are in trouble, let me commiserate with you or even try to help you. Pity should not be put in the same bag as false pity. Well checked, pity is a decent sentiment which only shows an active good heart in someone. I would be most worried by a lack of pity or its disappearance in the world. However, I would not miss seeing humans with too much pride being stripped of it, the same goes for all my created angels. Despite being atheist Doctor Valdi, I suppose you do know the story of fallen angel Lucifer? Or do you want us to discuss the point between pity versus pride further?

His head shaking in disbelief Vincent replied with his natural honesty,

-No there is no need to argue the point further. Deep down I am convince you are right and that any of my attempts to prove you wrong would be fruitless. However I do enjoy a good debate once in a while. But what is unsettling me greatly is that you know all about me without me knowing anything about you. By the example in my childhood you recounted, I believe you do and I find that a little unnerving. If you have the knowledge of me being an atheist and all of my past, all I gathered about you is the assumption that making angels must be a family trait. As for the story of fallen angel Lucifer, your supposition is correct, I am acquainted with it. Would you be surprised if I told you that I read and studied different religious texts but I doubt you would because you know me from Adam and Eve it seems? How does your son know me? Is it in details like you?

The Creator laughed before he revealed,

-For my son Raguel, the father of Sebastien and the Master of all angels, he is a Watcher. He can see everything and be everywhere at anytime, like me. Ahead of us, five kilometres away, from the eyes of a seagull, I can see a clear corridor between the two weather depressions. Stick to me like glue, it will be a tough ride until we reach it. As for the power to create and make angels which I possess, it only goes to the line of my eldest son Raguel. My other two do not have that power. I bestow three sons and a very extensive descending family. You will become yourself a father soon, of your first child, Scott, but also of a large adopted brood. You and my grandson will get on very well together when you return to work to Wilton Town. He will become the father of his first son only a mere four months before you. Sebastien has a heart of gold, throughout his incarnated lives, he tends to adopt souls to look after them. His latest adoption was the one of a fallen angel currently named Jack Malt which you have heard of via the letters of Father Odell. Jack is a little human boy of eight at this moment in time. So both of you, will have a lot in common bringing up your children in the same time, both sharing a similar sense of humour and also working to save people. Do you want to know what my grandson said of you?

Despite being intrigued, Vincent doing his up most to

keep up despite flying against the wind gave his answer,

-It will not be necessary. He will tell me of his own accord if he feels the need to do so. No, what I am most eager to know is how can I help him to the best of my abilities in his army? What will be his expectations? What would be my duties? Is there a pecking order in his army and a hierarchy amongst angels which I need to be aware of to not alienate anyone unknowingly or are all angels equals? I am so sorry to ask so many questions. I guess I require to be educated in angelic matters. A few months ago I didn't believe in lots of things until I saw the ghost of Abraham Wilton-Cough and the angel Abigail. Dare I admit that it worked like revelations in my eyes. Recently learning that I earned my wings and was already an angel surprised me beyond belief. I am still trying to make sense of it all. But seeing my wings and using them today makes the fact that I am now an angel sinking in.

Pleased with the attitude of the new angel of Sebastien, the Great Being explained,

-Let me enlighten you then. Do not be sorry for showing your desire to be educated. It is welcomed. I can give you some answers for the time being but know that your full angelic education will be given to you by the Mighty One and the Master. Sebastien has already a plan and a specific role for you in his army. Your numerous qualities will make you a versatile angelic soldier. The angelic army of Sebastien consists of angels which are made from humans. The Mighty One has been especially created to have human blood within him for him to understand from the get go the human plight. His first life was fully a human experience where he had no angelic powers at all. The angels he makes are given two choices: either to become guardian angels, either to become Sebastien's soldiers as incarnated angels. There is a third option that one human angel can opt for at anytime which is going to paradise. But for Mighty, he considers that option as a resignation where a soul rests on its laurels instead of being useful and helpful towards their human brothers and sisters. The aim of Sebastien's human angels army is specific. It is to provide help, support and protection to men, women and children. It also deals with demons that are incarnated and walk upon earth along with the ones possessing humans. The advantage of an angelic soldier made from a human is that he or she will retain freewill and has the ability to intervene and interact directly to any human affairs and problems.

He paused considering the storm building up then ordered,

-Doctor Valdi, I need you to be as fast as you can following me. We have to ascend right above the thunderstorm. I don't want you to get you close and personal with the lightnings which are about to surround us. Remember the words of your dear Amelia, she wants you to come back to her without a ruffled feather. Stay right by me because I will have to shield you. Do not reciprocate, first because you will die on the spot, second because it is unnecessary to protect me as I am the Eternal One. It's a vertical ascent, move your wings like I do.

Vincent didn't have time to reflect on what was said, as the Great Being started ascending, and as Valdi heard the low, long growl of thunder around them, he followed suit with no further a do. Within seconds a lightning seemed to tear the dark grey cloud they were flying through. Aware of the rise of electricity, with great anxiety in his guts Doctor Valdi did as he had been ordered to do as a matter of survival instinct. He learnt to ascend vertically very fast. The storm was no longer brewing, it was upon them, strong, powerful, frightening. The thunders became louder and louder. The bolts extremely close, so close that Valdi could feel his hair rising across his entire body. Then one lightening came fast, blinding, straight toward him. He retained his breath, fear in his belly, despite how fast he was flying, Valdi was too slow for that bolt. But, the Great Being intervened. Vincent witnessed him catching and gathering the lightning bolt within his powerful hands before throwing it below them. Valdi gasped when the Creator turned to him with tremendously glowing eyes scolded him,

-If you don't want to burn a feather, you need to put more velocity into those wings, angel, you just had a close call. Stay by me, I will be your shield.

As they ascended, Doctor Valdi had two more close calls which were each time deflected by the Great Being. When they finally rose far above the storm, his heart was still pounding in his chest in a very painful way. He was pale and felt drained. He didn't realise that his protector was flying still waiting for him to catch up. Vincent's vision was impaired by the frequent lightnings he had been confronted with from so close. One moment he could see and a second later, he couldn't. It was the same for his hearing. Therefore he collided into the Great Being, almost like a blind and deaf man could have done. The Creator receiving him in his arms without being cross stated with some amusement,

-Looks like you had a bumpy first flight, my angel. Let me check you out.

Vincent obliged him willingly,

-I can't see that well, neither can I hear properly. I am so sorry, I must be such a disappointment. Will I still be able to help your grandson? I bumped into you, I was blind for a good five minutes, now I can see a little and it is very blurry. I've got to do those operations, I need to see what I am doing. I need to make those angels feel better not worse. I must thank you with all my heart for saving me thrice. It will allow me to see or rather feel my Amelia and to tell her all about being within a thunderstorm. I saw my entire life passing before my eyes at one moment. I thought this was it. But I could still see myself teaching to read and write to my Abigail and my Scott and to walk them to school. I had another little boy, of a similar age of Scott, give or take, I was carrying him on my back. I had a strong feeling that the boy couldn't walk. I, I am confused. Too much electricity maybe...

The Great Being smiled as he scolded,

-Vincent, you talk too much. Take a little silent break and just breathe. The worst is over, well we are above it. Just recuperate a little while I inspect you.

He proceeded to turn around the new angel who flew as still as he could. The Creator checked the wings of Valdi, putting out a burning tip with his own hands, then lifting the chin of the Doctor, he looked deep into his eyes. He was about to give his reassuring result to Valdi when he saw the diligent Henry the Messenger coming towards them. When Henry was by them, the Messenger knelt profoundly to him in the sky as only he could do with his flying expertise. Seeing the signature respectful acknowledgement of his presence by the young angel, the Eternal One greeted,

-Henry, my Messenger, I have never been so pleased to see you. How are you doing since the attack? You were supposed to stay in bed up until noon today, recuperating. What made you disobey the Mighty One? Give me your best excuse and a hug because my son is adopting you which makes you my third grandson on the angelic side.

Grateful for this warm greeting, Henry went to the opened arms of the Great Being replied,

-Lord, thank you for accepting me into your family. It is such an immense honour. You know I couldn't stay in bed when I heard what happened to Sebastien. Restless, as I was feeling better, I begged the Master to let me help. When he received a telepathic message of his son who was making sure to reassure him and to give him the particular of the operation, the Master asked me to go to Sebastien. An inquisitive Mighty has dissected the claw which was found in his liver and managed to obtain from it a pure sample of poison. My mission is to collect those items in order to bring them as soon as possible to Doctor Williams and Miss White so they can work on the antidote. Doctor Williams even suggested to try to find a protective vaccine against the Nefarius demons' poison to protect all angels in the future. So it isn't disobedience, it is a mission given by the Master.

Pleased the Great Being commented,

-Raguel couldn't have chosen a better angel for the mission. Over the Atlantic we have a perfect storm today. Only consummate flying angels like you could do the task properly, with speed and without getting hurt. Most of the others would have attempted to go through the storm rather than making their way high up and above all clouds where it is safer. You have already met our Doctor Valdi, Henry. He is doing his baptism of the air with me. This is his first flight.

Henry giggled as he stated,

-This is the worst weather for a first flight but one may argue that being thrown in the deep end tends to work. Sebastien was a believer of that method though at the last resort, but it didn't work for our Ted to his dismay and sorrow. May I enquire how is it going with Doctor Valdi? Was it a last resort for him? The Master, Sebastien and I were looking very much forward to teach Valdi how to fly for the first time. I hope they will not be too disappointed that you had the honour of being his first teacher. I expect seeing silent sighs from them though.

The Creator, deeply amused, told with a half smile,

-Well my son and grandson can sigh all they want. I know they take great pleasure being at the first flight of any angel but I had to do it this time around by necessity. It is not the last resort for Doctor Valdi to be thrown into the deep end because of an impediment wing wise. No, he has done beautifully well through a very tough ride as a novice. The truth of the matter is we need him to save Daniel and Lawrence, the same way he did save the Mighty one. We haven't got the luxury of waiting for beautiful weather for his first flight. What about you Henry, have you got a pinch of disappointment of having missed Doctor Valdi's first flight?

Shaking his head negatively the Messenger replied with his genuine honesty,

-Of course not, beside that, I am here, seeing him doing rather well the standstill position during his first flight. How was his ascent to high above the clouds? Did you had to hold his hand for it is a difficult technique to learn without training? Mine, today, was hazardous, I am not as fast as normal due to my convalescence but I managed through it all. The thought of seeing Sebastien drove me to take immense care and also the importance of the mission. Somehow, something strange happened, I saw a lime butterfly caught in the storm ascending like I did ahead of me. I told him to land on my shoulder, that I would get him out of our dangerous position. He did accept my invite. Then it felt like no thunderbolts could touch me. Their paths were diverted. The butterfly is still on my satchel and hasn't left me since the ascent.

Giving a quick glance at the butterfly, the Great Being revealed,

-Henry, you are transporting the great Celtic Goddess Dana. She is the grandmother of Sebastien on his mother's side. I warned her about what happened to him and she wants to help to look after her grandson as he recover. Obviously she protected you with her magical powers as you are giving her the ride to him. She knows you are considered to be the adopted brother of Sebastien now. You will make her full acquaintance soon enough. As for Vincent Valdi, he is a very fast learner, I show him and he replicates the gestures like a perfect mirror. I never had to hold his hand once during the flight and he can hold his nerves very well in bad circumstances. I had to deflect lightnings from him, but if another would have lost his resolve and fall into the vortex of the storm, he stayed by me. He just suffered a few hiccup on the way up here but nothing major, sight and hearing troubles which will adjust itself within minutes and the tips of the wings did feel the heat a little. Here, take this burnt feather to Mrs Valdi and reassure her that her husband made it through the storms above the Atlantic Ocean. We will expect you to be back in Wilton Town as soon as you can, Henry, with the goods to deal with. Now, go!

The Messenger bowed profoundly to the Creator, gave a smile and a salute to Valdi, before flying away at great speed. Turning to the Doctor, the Great Being enquired,

-How are you feeling, Vincent? Are you suitably rested?

Valdi responded by a positive nod yet he remained overwhelmingly silent. It finally had dawned upon him that the superior Being maybe God. While he was watching intently the interaction between Henry and the Being, Vincent assembled all his clues he had heard or seen, like when the Being told him he couldn't die because he was the Eternal One, the way Henry knelt in his presence and the way he called him Lord, his ability to handle lightning combined with the fact that he seemed to be all knowing, and his capacity to be in multiple places at the same time, last but not least if his eldest son Raguel was the Master of all angels then surely who else could be more superior than that apart from God himself. The conclusion of Doctor Valdi's silent reflections unsettled him greatly. He didn't know how to address the Being before him, let alone that, he was curbing an internal urge to demand confirmation of his conclusion.

Knowing the Doctor's silent realisation and struggle with it, the Creator smiled to him enigmatically while he demanded,

-What if I am really by you at this instant, Vincent, will your atheist self cease to talk to me?

Struck by a certain fear Valdi stammered,

-Oh no, no, no, I will certainly talk, I, I am just, just confounded, so confused I am shivering. But, but you said 'if'?

Seeing the new angel trembling before him, the Great Being took a reassuring and Cartesian rationalistic tone, one which Valdi used a lot himself, to say sternly,

-Yes, I said 'If'. Your shivering is due to the high altitude. Here lets cover you up a little more. You were so eager to help that you forgot your coat in the cabin, then we have to keep you moving. It will warm you right back up since we have to carry on with our fast pace.

With a wicked smile, he made an ancient coat appear upon the back of Valdi, then talking to himself out loud, he commented, teasing the non-believer,

-No, the multicoloured cloak of Joseph doesn't suit you. It is a little too garish for someone like you who is used to wear mainly black and brown over impeccable white shirts. Let's change that.

Doctor Valdi who had taken a good look at the antique garment with amazement saw it disappear to be replaced by a brown leather hunting coat. It came with matching leather gloves, all doubled up by insulating sheep wool. The Great Being wrapped a white scarf with care in a Byron's fashion around the neck of the Doctor as he stated with a pleased smirk on his lips,

-Here, Vincent, you are more suitably attired for those great heights. Now, let's keep you warm by moving. This time you can fly by my side and we can have a conversation, you and I. As you enjoy a good debate once in a while, here is the perfect opportunity to assert for yourself whatever you want. If you did retrieve your art of argumentation and your sarcastic tongue, pray do start. Come!

Leading the way the Creator waited patiently for an answer to his invite. Doctor Valdi, covered up, felt like a child by his father and could not shake away that impression. However he defended himself, in a tone which he wanted to be firmer but which was a little shaky,

-I, I, I haven't got a sarcastic tongue!

Giving him a long amused glance, the Great Being stated,

-Vincent, did I made such a deep impression upon you for you to still stammer? Pull yourself together. Argue with me like you debate with that poor Father Odell, it is an order. One day you made him doubt so badly that he went to bed in taters. He didn't pray that night. The following morning, he announced to you his intentions of not doing the Sunday mass, quitting the order and leaving town altogether to quest for himself. You didn't feel like the winner of the debate that day. You didn't know what to say to your friend either. That afternoon under the pretext of repaying part of your loan, you went to see Abraham Wilton-Cough and confessed to him the entire matter and how important it was for Father Odell to stay in town and a vicar. You received a right scolding by Abraham along with a back of the head slap but he told you that he would give you one chance and one chance only to make things right. He devised that you should convince Theo to stay the vicar of Wilton Town that very evening at his dinner table where the both of you would be invited. You ate humble pie that night, and made the apology that religions had some advantages in appeasing people and giving them hope, while eating chicken and leek pie which Abraham had ordered to his cook with irony on his part. The dinner finished with an apple pie as well. Wilton-Cough presided to that new debate, and helped you out whenever you struggled to convinced Theo to stay. Do you remember his argument?

Valdi recalled that episode very well, amazed that the Great Being knew about it all,

-I do. At the end of my apology about religions being somewhat beneficial and of the necessity of having a vicar in town, Theo just told that he will make sure that he will find a good replacement to his post for Wilton Town before he went. After the forty five minutes that I exerted myself to somehow preach to Theo, his answer left me speechless, dejected and truly about to cry. I would have kicked myself if I wasn't at the dinner table of Abraham surrounded by his family. I was about to lose my best friend. Abraham realised that I was feeling too emotional to carry on talking for a while so he took the charge. He wasn't going to let Theo Odell go. First he ridiculed the idea of soul searching when the soul was within one's body, to try to look for oneself anywhere else was sheer stupidity for him. To be honest, the way he said this, made me dry up my coming tears and I couldn't help smiling at his argument. Then he spoke about the decent house Theo was living in as a priest, the very house of the founder of Wilton Town, Abraham's ancestor Noah Wilton, and that he would have trouble to find somewhere to live of that quality especially if Theo ceased to be a vicar. Abraham then demanded to know what Odell wanted to do to prevent him to become a pauper overnight. What was his skills apart from reading the bible, knowing Latin, preaching, and performing the rites? So Abraham gave Theo the concrete idea of results from a possible brash decision without having done proper plans beforehand. Then if I dare say, he went for the kill. He told Theo that he had saved a large amount to build a meeting hall on a field he possessed right at the end of the cemetery. He intended that building to serve as a Sunday school but also to be used for the charity events Father Odell was doing monthly. But he said firmly that without Theo, the project will not take place because he needed someone he could trust to run that meeting hall and that Father Odell was the only one he had faith on to do so. His arguments rendered Father Odell indecisive, but eager to stay. Abraham finished by bringing to Theo a little notebook that we had fastened together and made that afternoon. I had one half in my clinic while Abraham had the other one in his bank. We asked anyone coming there to write a farewell to Theo. The result showed how much the people of Wilton Town loved Father Odell. Seeing that Theo decided to stay and remained the vicar of Wilton Town. To be honest Abraham saved the day that night. As for I, I experienced the possible bitterness of winning a debate.

The Creator told sternly,

-The lesson you had, wasn't learnt however, because you kept teasing Theo.

Smiling Vincent commented,

-Perhaps but I did tone it down a fair bit.

At the scolding glance of the Great Being, he admitted,

-Maybe I didn't tone it down enough.

-Sebastien described Theo as your martyr to the Master, a willing martyr maybe,
but a martyr nonetheless. As Raguel is the angel of Justice, as him and his son are Punishers, I would be a little worried if I were you. They monitor angels closely, if they think you are far too demeaning to Theo, like a bullying elder brother, you may face the risk of being separated from him for decades if not an entire lifetime.

Seeing the worried look of Doctor Valdi, the Great Being carried on,

-I am just giving you the heads up. Let me tell you the formal plan so far that the Mighty One has for you and Theo. Sebastien is building up a unit within his army dedicated to logistics. The leader of the unit is an angel called Ted who has a gift of visions, which means that he can predict enemies' moves and works out ways to prevent them. Ted who was a monk in his human life is not a fighting angel. Theo who is pacific but can fight cleverly if he has to, joined that unit. The White Witch of Wilton Town is part of it as well. Whilhelmina has already done some excellent work for the Mighty One in that team. Although she is not an angel, but an eternal being, she has become part of the angelic army. Sebastien wants you to join that special unit in his army for multiple reasons.

Doctor Valdi told eagerly,

-I would love to. May I know his reasons?

-You may. First, you will be assigned to the protection of that unit, its bodyguard. Ted, Theo and Miss White are not fighters as per say, but they are essential to prevent, plan and find solutions. You, on the other hand, are an excellent fighter. Second, you are not only a physical asset as an angelic soldier. Your intellect and your power of deduction can contribute greatly to the logistic unit. Third and to continue in the line of multitasking, you and Miss White will be the first aiders in your team. You two can be deployed to the healing unit of the angelic army if or when necessary. The healing unit is lead by Doctor Williams. Sebastien and the Master are also part of it. That is all. That unit has been targeted and decimated by demons. They didn't get Williams yet but he is a walking and flying target for them because he is our most eminent physician in the angelic army. In terms of chess, Doctor Williams would be a Rook, Sebastien the Queen and his father the King. That would be the current state on the board of the healing unit.

Vincent dared to ask,

-I would have assumed you would have been the King. Which chess piece are you then?

The Creator replied rather sternly,

-I am not on the board. Above it, I play with my King, Queen and pawns.

Intrigued Doctor Valdi enquired,

-Pray what would be Theo, Miss White and myself's roles on the boards? For if I understood correctly there are multiple boards for the different units of the angelic army.

The Great Being confirmed,

-Yes, there are. On the healing board, Miss White would be a bishop, while you would be a knight. While on the logistic board, if it becomes a nice combination, Ted will be the King, you will be the Queen, and Theo and Miss White will be the Rooks. There's potential for Mrs Valdi and Jack Malt to come on board as bishops. Last but not least, another reason is that Sebastien tends to keep individuals with friendship or affinity to one another together in the same team. From experience he knows that those units work better with soldiers who bestow solid bonds. For the logistic team, you and Theo are best friends. You and Miss White have excellent working relationship as Doctor and nurse. Theo and Whilhelmina will be very shortly husband and wife. Ted and Miss White can both predict the future. Ted and Theo both are or have been priests. Now you have no obvious connection to Ted and this is worrying the Mighty One.

Acknowledging what had been told, Vincent queried,

-Why would Sebastien be worried? I can build bridges and connect with Ted over time.

The reply which came forward warned him,

-The reason of his concern is that you are a strong individual with an indomitable character. The way you behave with Theo Odell can be praised but also criticised. Sebastien who spent time with Theo and befriended him since he arrived in Wilton Town will speak to you about it all. I can warn you that it will be a dressing down. There is a fine line between teasing and demeaning someone constantly. Theo may seem to take it with good grace and just accept it as his common currency, because for him you are is only true friend and confident, but, and this is a very big but: Do you know that Theo during all those years, harbouring a crushed and bruised ego, with no sense of his own self worth, contemplated to hang himself all along? The plan was there in his mind, with the perfect tree in his cemetery which had a nicely inviting protruding branch.

The revelation shocked Vincent so much, that he became pale and stopped flying. Free falling, grief in his heart, Vincent repeated wildly,

-Theo, my Theo, not my Theo!

The Great Being came to his rescue before he could fall back within the storm. Leading him by the hand he scolded Valdi,

-Get a grip on yourself, angel! The Mighty One spotted that suicidal lingering thought in Theo. He has started dealing with it to nip it off him. Unfortunately, it was found not in a budding stage but at a rather mature stage. Theo who is such an excellent soul, a charitable, kind and generous one, a cleverly resourceful one may disappear in front of all at anytime. However Theo received a saving grace, he loves and he is being loved back by Miss White. Their marriage has the power to heal the self deprecation of Theo over time. But his wound runs deep, it started since he was an infant. He didn't make a single step up until he was three. He didn't utter a single word up until he was five. His parents, especially his mother, were the first to demean him in front of everyone. One would lament loudly what would the boy would or even could become with great despair, the other described her son as a simple minded clumsy donkey. The parents came to the conclusion that someone would have to possess the patience of a saint to deal with Theo. He was about seven when he was given as a servant to a vicar that battered him. When that vicar passed away of a heart attack, Theo was passed on to the new vicar like a piece of furniture coming with the presbytery. He was fourteen, extremely shy, forlorn, only talking and praying to me. His prayers have never been about him since the day he could pray. He wanted nothing for himself and expected nothing for himself. The new vicar took him under his wing, for yes, he was an incarnated angel and he taught to Theo his vocation. As all parishes were claimed after he was ordained in his country, his only option was to accept the remote post of becoming the vicar of Wilton Town in the new world that no preachers really wanted. The point here is that Odell has a sensitive soul and that words can inflict to him great damage. They can push him over the edge. They can be the kick which removes the stool from under his feet to make him hang faster. In consequence you, my dear Valdi, must watch your tongue when you are with your friend. Sebastien will make sure of it. If you don't, if you carry on teasing and demeaning Odell, prepare yourself to face severe consequences.

Still pale, his lips trembling, Vincent promised,

-I will not tease Theo anymore. I didn't know. I thought it was harmless. He never told me... He never told me about his past fully. He never told me when I did upset him. He never told me he had, he was thinking of suicide. I would never have guessed.

Releasing the hand of Doctor Valdi, The Creator told sternly,

-The signs were in front of you all the time. The fact that he wasn't eating properly. You thought it was because he didn't know how to cook. It was more due to a lack of appetite for life itself. As for confiding about his past, of course he would keep away from you details which you could have used for your sheer amusement from his mother calling him a donkey to the fact that he was slow to develop as a child which made him so vulnerable to his parents and others. Lastly, let me ask you, how do you think Theo felt when he learnt that you did a bet that he would never marry because he was such an impossible case? Wasn't it such a harsh comment and belief coming from his best friend supposedly? Wasn't it a little cruel? Wasn't it putting Theo as the butt of all your jokes? Did you show him a little consideration then when you did that, 'harmless bet'? Let me tell you how it went. He smiled and put on the face that he was used to your antics. But his heart sank a little bit more. Thankfully, when he learnt about the bet, his marriage proposal to Miss White was accepted. If it had not been the case, Theo would not be alive today.

He paused, giving a glance to Doctor Valdi who was sighing deeply, sadly with remorse in his heart. He then resumed,

-Vincent, the imperative for you is to tame your cavalier attitude towards anyone. You can stay witty but always make sure you remain kind at all time. To be considerate, you must watch your tongue. If you fail to do so, Sebastien will take you into his angelic boot camp up until he sees you fit to leave it. Because he is not only worried about Theo Odell. He is concerned about how you will behave with his angel Ted. Here is the corridor between the two perturbations. Let's go down there. Follow me.

Doing as he was told, Vincent asked in a subdued way,

-Please, tell me how should I behave with Ted? I have no cues of angelic etiquette.

The Great Being explained,

-It has nothing to do with angelic etiquette. All which is required consist of a combination of respect, kindness and comprehension from you towards Ted. Let me brief you about him. Ted is not the strongest angel about by far. He is actually the weakest. Ted possess a gift of vision so powerful that it affects him physically, but also mentally. Ted is prone to depression, solitude, incontrollable frights and nightmares. After some visions, he can collapse, faint, be unconscious, worse enter into a coma or suffer from epileptic convulsions. His lightest symptoms are severe headaches and temporary blindness. Ted has a hard time coping with his gift. He resorted to chain smoking and drinking heavily which is damaging his incarnated human body. Lately, the Master gave him a new lease of life by healing him. While the Mighty One has decided to home Ted in order to monitor him closely to not let him fall back into his harming ways. So Ted needs support and the last thing Sebastien wants Ted to face is someone with a demeaning attitude towards his angel. This is a concern to him because he considers Ted almost like an adopted son. He is extremely protective of him.

An intrigued Vincent was eager to know more while he was amazed by that corridor almost without winds compressed between the two storms. He could see numerous sea birds flying within it and far away the outline of a distant land. He asked,

-Pray, may I enquire how protective are we talking about in terms of gestures? As Ted will be the leader of the unit I will work for, would you be able to tell me more about him? I can already assure you that I will be on my best behaviour. From what you told me about Theo, I am deeply saddened and ready to make amend to him. As for Ted, I want to start on the best footing possible. My dearest wish is to help and to not hinder by a stinking attitude. I will be on top of that, regulating myself by limiting my impulses but also by thinking twice or thrice whatever I want to say. Am I right in saying that I can see a coastline in the horizon or is my eyesight still playing up?

-We are half way through. This is the coast of Greenland. Your senses did adjust themselves. You will be able to operate on the two angels of the Mighty One with no physical difficulties. Let me tell you more about Sebastien and Ted then. It was during the end of the dark ages and the beginning of the middle ages that Ted met Sebastien who was a monk in a monastery in charge of educating youngsters to read, write, pray, learn Latin and sing. Those children were intended to become either monks or priests. Often they were abandoned there by their parents. On that account Theo has a similar start in life with the one of Ted. This is giving us one more reason to believe that they will get on well together. Ted was a seven year old child with a heavy stammer, shy beyond belief, with a clumsiness depriving him of confidence. He had lost his human father and his mother was eager to get rid of him in order to remarry. The unwanted Ted found a surrogate father in Sebastien who was moved by the awkward little boy who seemed to be scared of his own shadow. Since the day Ted did put his little hand within the one of Sebastien, the teaching monk, a strong bound developed between them. On the part of Sebastien, it is ever so strongly protective. On the part of Ted, Sebastien is his only family in his heart. He has no one else and that for centuries. Sebastien represents all at once his mother hen when he is recovering from his damaging visions, it will be Sebastien that will nurture him back to health, be by his bedside, pulling his cover upon his cold chest, reignite the fire, aerate the room, spoon-feed him, I pass all the tender care my grandson provides to that angel which he adopted in his heart to go to the fact that Sebastien also represents a strong father figure for Ted, one who encourages, guides, scolds when needed, but one which is always there when he is in trouble to pick him up in his strong arms and take him to safety. From that you should pick up that it is certainly not advisable to tease Ted at any point in time for Sebastien will be at your doorsteps and will certainly show you the rough end of the stick.

Doctor Valdi told with certainty and a smile,

-I will be good, I promise. Something is intriguing me. Does angelic gifts hurt their hosts as a common currency for having them? In a sense do you have to pay for what you get? It doesn't make sense to me that Ted's gift should hurt him so much.

The Great Being revealed,

-Vincent, a gift is a gift, you do not pay for them. However, of your own free will, you can give a gift in turn to the person that bestowed you one either in kind or in actions. The case of Ted is highly peculiar. He is the son of an incubus demon and a woman. He is a cambion. Ted could see the future and have visions from the start, from his birth, before becoming an angel. His power is demonic in origin. When he was part human, his visions would not hurt him. His only problems then was nightmares and sickness when what he saw was highly distressing. But when he became an angel, his gift of vision increased tenfold, it is then that he started to suffer tremendously and physically. The fact is cambions are created by demons to help and serve them. They are extremely useful. However my grandson meeting that one wasn't going to let him work for demons. He managed to make him worked for angels however Ted is paying the hefty price for his choice to be loyal to the Mighty One, the Master and myself. Not only that, Ted doesn't know how to fight nor fly. He is a vulnerable angel to say the least. To make matters worst, demons did put a price on his head. If he is ever captured, he will be dismembered and eviscerated with his severed head displayed in hell. Ted has been a demonic target for centuries because demons do not forgive him to work for angels. If he is ever taken, he will suffer the most horrendous death. Sebastien has been able to protect Ted during all his missions. He has trained a strong angel, Rob, to serve as a bodyguard to Ted during any fight. Expect Rob to train you in turn to secure the protection of Ted's unit. Robert used to be a musketeer in his human life. This was when he met and fought alongside Sebastien.

Curious, Vincent queried,

-Even with demonic blood someone can become an angel?

Giggling the Creator replied,

-Yes, and even when someone is a determined atheist, he can still become an angel.

Doctor Valdi looked at him and smiled, taking the hint. He admitted,

-What can I say apart that seeing is believing for me.

The Great Being argued with an impassible air,

-You and I both know that it is not always true in your case. Sometimes you believe in something giving it the benefice of the doubt like for the germ theory of disease. You believed in germs before Doctor Williams showed them to you in his laboratory.

Vincent defended,

-This is different, I am a Doctor. Beside with observations of the physical type of the symptoms of the patients, one can deduct the presence of germs which later experiments can prove using microscopes and other methods. We can hardly put the concept of god through any tests and experiments. The benefit of the doubt here, for me, didn't apply. If tests of the existence of god could be done via answered prayers, apparitions when he is called or miracles on occasions then I would have been bitterly disappointed.

From his angelic shape, the Creator took his true appearance for a blinding second to the great awe of Doctor Valdi who withheld his breath for as long as it lasted. A surreal voice coming out of the great ball of light proposed,

-Let us argue your points Vincent.

Taking back his angelic shape, the Creator continued,

-If seeing is believing, now do you believe? Close that mouth Doctor Valdi, you look like that basking shark swimming below us. Based on your principle, basing belief and faith on sight only is very restricted and a little short-sighted, don't you think? Especially when many senses were created. You did hear me a few times, and I was labelled as the inner voice of your mind by you. Can you remember those particular times?

Valdi apologised, stammering once more,

-My mind, my mind just went blank. I am so, so sorry. I usually have an excellent memory.

-Let me refresh it then. You were only too little, hiding in the bushes like your aunt told you to for your protection. You witnessed the horrendous rape which she was submitted to and when the men were out of sight, you bravely went to check upon her. Your distraught soul kept asking yourself how you could help her because she was in such a bad state. I told you then to go and get an adult to look after your auntie, to run to the first house or farm you saw and to lead the adult by the hand to her. You obeyed to my suggestion. The Master, my son helped you just as well, he was the large hare that crossed your path in front of you. Your surprised eyes followed where he went. He crossed a field of wild flowers, a vegetable garden and then you saw a derelict little farm where he stopped by the opened door and a dim light glowing from the window. You ran across the field and garden and fetched the only adult there: the old medicine woman, white witch of the village. When she saw the state of your aunt after following you, she just knew what to do. Some of my interventions are by mere suggestions to one's soul when they face a dilemma.

Finding the courage to demand answers from the Creator, Doctor Valdi asked in a bitter tone,

-What about all those unanswered prayers?

The Great Being replied sternly,

-I am the Creator, not Santa Claus. You did only one prayer with your aunt, one which was dealt with but not according to your insane expectations. I concede that you were only seven years old but asking for no rain whatsoever for months because the thatch roof of your aunt was leaking badly, the consequences of that prayer would have been devastatingly deadly. No rain would have meant failing crops for all in your village, famine, thirsty animals and cattle that would have starved to death. The adequate solution wasn't no more rain, it was the reparation of that roof. The night of your prayer, I answered it by sending a heavy hailstorm. The rainfall that night was the equivalent of the amount of rain which fell in an entire month where you were living. It made the roof fall therefore there were no longer any options but to repair it. Your proud and poor aunt at the misadventure still wasn't going to ask for help. I made her have a little congestion, nothing too serious but serious enough to pass it on to a couple of pupils which were the very children of the thatcher of the village. I knew your aunt though unwell would still deliver her tuitions to the village children. She would not have been able to pass her ailment to anyone else due to a little trick of mine. Seeing his children both coughing and sneezing, learning that the school mistress was unwell and probably should have dismissed the class until she was recovered, the thatcher was ready to give his piece of mind to your aunt. However when he saw her visibly ill correcting a pile of homework and you forking and trying to dry the hay of the collapsed roof by the fire place, his former intention of scolding the teacher of the village vanished to be replaced by pity. What happened afterwards you know and remember with gratefulness. Your prayer was answered in my mysterious ways. You must admit that the heavy rain bestowed upon your village was a blessing in disguise at the end of the day for your little household. Of course, you never prayed afterwards because you asked for no rain and I gave you plenty of it instead. Funny enough this little event, and I am enjoying the irony here, confirmed to you in your belief that god didn't exist. You also used that example in your many debates about religion with Father Odell speaking with great gusto about the inefficiency of prayers.

A bewildered Vincent reminisced out loud with some emotion,

-I remember Luigi Carnolli with great affection till this day. He came to the cottage of my aunt, saw the state of our collapsed roof and demanded from my aunt when did she plan to tell him that he had his work cut out to repair her roof, mentioning that the storm happened four days prior to his visit. He asked her with grave seriousness, if she waited for all the children of the village to be ill and to not be able to go to school. He spoke about his little Ludovico and Olivia being sick and for my aunt to not expect them to attend school until they got better. He didn't hide the fact that my aunt should do the same. In her defence, my aunt, who was fairly diminished, coughed that she wasn't planning to ask for his help because she couldn't pay for a new roof nor could she afford to miss school for a day. Carnolli stood firm as he demanded, pointing at me to my aunt: 'So you are determined to let that little charge of yours, that little fellow, your nephew to sleep under the stars in that pigsty. Shall I demand a couple of coffins to be prepared in advance to the undertaker for you two not making it during winter without a roof above your heads?.' My aunt tried to reply to him but just ended up coughing. I brought hot water to her and the thatcher took a lemon from his pocket, cut it in half and squeezed the juice inside the hot water, he asked if we had either honey or sugar. We kept bees so we had honey. He put a couple of spoons in the glass and handed the concoction to my aunt. He reasoned with my aunt for a good half hour where he explained that she owed him my help because Ludovico being unwell would not be able to help him for a while, like he always did after school. He settled with her that my wages would pay for the roof's repairs. With that agreement in place I went to work with him after school in the quality of his apprentice. He kept me on even when his son worked back with him and after I paid for the roof telling me that my wages would improve the situation of my aunt and I. He was such a decent man. I must concede that you brought the right person in that moment in time to my aunt and I.

From then on Doctor Valdi went from admissions to concessions passing by confessions in his enlightening discussion with the Creator. When both landed side by side in the courtyard of the Crying White Doe Hotel, the Great Being smiled with the satisfaction of having converted the only atheist angel.

#

While the Great Being considered the stately hotel, Doctor Valdi was up the entrance stairs ringing the bell in his usual forceful manner when he was signalling to Miss White an emergency. In her kitchen with Doctor Williams and Father Odell preparing some potions, the white witch lifted her head, surprised, announcing,

-It can't be possible! We have Doctor Valdi at the door.

Theo stopped stirring the potion he was doing and lifting his wooden spoon up in the air, he confirmed,

-It's definitely Vincent. It was firm, sharp and loud like when he wants us right here right now.

Both gave their spoons to Williams and ran to open the front door of the hotel. The race in the corridor was won by Miss White but as she unlocked the door, Theo rushed outside and threw himself at the neck of Vincent Valdi, exclaiming with sheer joy,

-Vince! What's bring you here? I thought you were already on the other side of the Atlantic, near the Portuguese coast. Look at you! You are all angelic. What happened to your wings?

Under the flow of questions Doctor Valdi tapped Theo's shoulders in a friendly manner yet replied firmly,

-I will tell you all later. Please show me the bedroom of Lawrence. How is he doing? By the way, Miss White and you have my congratulations. I will not miss your wedding for the world. I am so happy for you two.

The couple blushed under his stare, and Vincent smirked teasing,

-You will have to tell me later about all the kisses you shared before wedlock and I will make you recite a paternoster for each one of them before god. Did you meet him already or shall I do the presentation?

Miss White and Theo held their hands to give each others support and bowed to the Great Being who was standing behind Vincent. He looked at the couple with benevolence stating,

-We met earlier on. There is no need for formal presentation. They both belong to the angelic army of my grandson, like you.

Doctor Williams who had ran in the hallway, not far behind the couple asked with some anxiety,

-How is Sebastien doing?

It was the Creator who replied,

-Valdi saved the Mighty One. We left him to rest. He was conscious within minutes after the operation. He will pull through. Where is my son?

Doctor Williams, giving a deep bow, briefed,

-Raguel is in the garden my Lord. He is busy preparing the operations for tomorrow night. I must warn you that he is extremely tense. I think that when he will be reunited with his son and see him alive and well, will be the only moment when he will feel reassured. Our worry is that our two angels under this roof are deteriorating under our eyes. Lawrence is on death's door. He is in and out of consciousness, but he hasn't opened his eyes for the past hour. Maximilien is by his bedside, monitoring him and trying to apply some minor relief that we can come up with. As for Daniel, he is starting to take the same path as Lawrence. He has moments of absences, but they are short and he screams in pain waking up from them. I think he will lose his damaged leg. We made all efforts to try to ease him but to no avail. His restlessness woke up the only customer of the hotel, a Mrs Toad, a kind human, who decided to give us a hand. She is looking after him. She doesn't know we are angels whatsoever.

The Great Being ordered,

-Williams, Miss White show the room of Lawrence to Doctor Valdi and follow his orders. He will start operating on him immediately. Father Odell fetch Mrs Toad from Daniel's bedroom, get her to help you monitor and stir the potions you all have been busy doing. Then prepare some strong coffee for Vincent, he will need more than one cup for what he is about to do after flying the entire Atlantic ocean in record breaking time especially since we faced storms.

While all obeyed immediately, the Creator went to his son Raguel who was doing the hundred paces in the pretty garden of the white witch of Wilton Town. When he saw his father, the Master knelt to him, begging,

-Please tell me, will Mighty make it?

Making his son stand up, giving him a strong hand, the Great Being reassured,

-He will. Keep my hand in yours to see how his surgical operation went. Remember that Sebastien is strong and heals fast. When we left his side, Mighty was fully conscious. I had to make sure he was going to stay put and safe until we can give him the all clear: no wings and no transport here and there with angelic will power for him for the time being.

The Master commented,

-Sebastien will not like being grounded but he is already using his standstill time in an efficient way. He dissected the demonic claw which was embedded within him and managed to retrieve poison from it, he told me via telepathy. I hope this will help Doctor Williams and Miss White to find an antidote. I kick myself for not seeing that claw when I started healing my son.

Putting his arm around Raguel's shoulders in a comforting manner, the Great Being explained,

-It wasn't visible. Don't be harsh upon yourself. What you did was reestablishing the proper blood circulation of Mighty. It helped us. If you didn't have repaired Sebastien's veins and arteries, Doctor Valdi wouldn't have been able to find where the true damage was. Demons are cunning, their large wounds inflicted to their victims distracted from the point where their attacks were the most lethal. Valdi had to open up further Mighty in order to find his true ailment. As you can see he put himself in danger to save Sebastien, but his drastic method worked. Standing by Doctor Valdi, I was amazed by his sheer tenacity as he spat mouthfuls of poison onto the bowl I held. Pale, about to be sick, Vincent carried on despite me enjoining him to take a little break. He replied that the poison was too potent for him to stop, he needed to remove all the poison he could from that liver as soon as possible without failure. His determination impressed me.

Walking towards the hotel by the side of his father, Raguel enquired,

-It sounds like the only atheist angel did meet your approval? I know that Doctor Williams swore by Vincent Valdi when he was his medical student. Myself when William warned me that Valdi will earn his wings during his lifetime yet being an unbeliever, I was highly dubious. However we all saw it happened. William was jubilating with a 'I told you so'. I was simply wondering how a Valdi would integrate in the angelic army of my son. While Sebastien was all smiles and didn't have that concern. He told me that all Valdi needed were a sound heart and an excellent soul to fit in. Sebastien added that by judging the letters of Doctor Valdi sent to Doctor Williams over the years which he knew the contents of, he was confident that Vincent possessed both. I would be interested to know your first opinion about Vincent Valdi now that you have met him, Father.

At the top of the terrace balcony, the Great Being smiled with kindness as he demanded,

-My Raguel are we having a conversation finally? Do you want me to talk to you more than just giving you orders? Will you care about my opinions? I remember a day not so long ago when communication ceased, when you didn't care if your death would break my heart or not. Tonight wasn't it my grandson who knowing how dangerous the situation was prompted you to call me? Do you know that you can talk to me, confide in me and that I will always be there for you?

Looking at his Father with great emotion, Raguel replied in a defencive tone,

-Father, please it was about a decade ago.

The Creator commented sternly,

-Pray what is a decade for the Eternal One? A drop in the ocean, a grain of sand in an hourglass. Tell me what it would be compared to the loss of a most beloved son for the rest of eternity? Beside it was three years ago not even a decade. When I saw our Sebastien falling unconscious within my arms as I ousted the demon from his body, my fears then were that if he ever died, you would follow suit because you can not envisage your eternal life without Mighty anymore, as much as I can not envisage mine without you and him.

His son went to nestle silently into his arms, so he carried on, stroking gently the long grey blond straight hair of the Master,

-Our Sebastien is not only safe and recovering for at his bedside will be his grandmother the Celtic goddess Dana. She will be able to provide to him her magical protection while he is not by our sides. She hiked herself a ride on the Messenger's satchel as a lime green butterfly.

Raguel breaking the embrace with a soothed smile on his face asked eagerly,

-So you met Henry on the way? I was worried about him. He is recovering well and fast but when he heard about what happened to Sebastien there was no way of keeping him still because he wanted to help so much. So I reluctantly sent him on a mission to fulfil the last orders of Sebastien regarding the collection of the poison sample to bring to Doctor Williams. Dana should have come from the East of the Atlantic not the West. Did she relocate to the New World?

Admiring the garden of Miss White from her terrace, the Great Being informed his son,

-We met your Henry half way through the ocean. He was fine, efficient as always, flying like an albatross. Safe, high above the storms, Henry was only too eager to see for himself Mighty so worried he was about him. The loyalty he has for Sebastien life after life does him credit. Such devotion is rare and to be praised. As for Dana, she still lives in Old Europe in a forest in Brittany. I had to send to her a telepathic message about what happened to her only grandson and descendant while I was carrying Sebastien to his remote safety on board of Captain Hansen's ship. She decided to come to help looking after him but before she transported herself to Greenland to see the important wizard Filemonsen who possessed an artifact which could protect and promote the recovery of the Mighty One. Hence this is why we met her coming from the West rather than the East on my return to Wilton Town. The garden of this hotel is truly enchanting. The shame is that the ruins of that cottage over there, which Miss White tried to make a folly of in her garden, are still haunted. The body of a very small girl is buried there. Her remains need to be given a proper burial on consecrated ground with a ceremony to allow her soul to finally rest in peace. Her anger and unrest has been given energy and fuel by demons to the point that she has become a damaging spirit. Upset and cross, she hates seeing happiness and is set to destroy it when she can. She makes wishes to demons who obey her nasty whims and wants. When someone witnesses her ghost, it is usually a bad omen for them. She is responsible for the would have been fatal illness of Miss Georgia Marlow. She wanted her dead because she was jealous of the tender affection the old maid surrounds the young Mina White. Because she was wronged during her life, she turned into a nasty entity. She will plagued this hotel in a manner or another.

The Master briefed his father,

-The re-burial is on the map, we know it has to be done but we haven't established a date for it as we speak. Since he stepped foot in town, Sebastien has been extremely busy. The demonic activity in Wilton Town is rife. You've seen for yourself what we had to deal with tonight. The Mighty One has been killing demons almost everyday here. When it is not demons, there are troublesome humans to contend with, who in a gang think that they can rule the town since Doctor Valdi is away on honeymoon. Tomorrow we are expecting the worst from them, a retaliation for a lesson Sebastien inflicted to them a few days ago. The vision Ted gave us as a warning was dramatic with the loss of two incarnated angels, two strong fighters, Rob and

Callum. We prepared some protection spells in many places in town, however will it be enough? We don't know. The gang leader is an erratic pyromaniac and a psychopath. The angelic army counted on Sebastien to lead them tomorrow. With what happened tonight, I am taking charge of the Mighty One's army and the operations of tomorrow night up until he is well enough to take the helm again. When I will be fully acquainted with the consequences of the fight due tomorrow, then I will fix a day for the burial of the little girl but also of the ceremony to appease her soul. May I asked why did you bring Sebastien to Doctor Valdi and not to Archangel Raphael?

Sternly the Great Being told,

-Raguel, do not delay the re-burial too long. The girl has a hatred of Father Odell since he has done the exorcism on the ruined cottage. He got rid of many of her pet demons in one go sending them back to hell. She ordered her favourite and strongest demon to drag Theo with him to hell. It failed because Sebastien intervened, killed the demon and saved Odell. Father Odell who is marrying Miss White very soon and has already taken his lodgings in the hotel of Miss White will be in great danger here up until the skeleton of that little girl is placed in the cemetery of the town and that her soul has been dealt with to be able to rest in peace. Theo brought happiness to this hotel since he has been stepping within it frequently of late courting Miss White. The entity of the girl will aim to annihilate Father Odell and to render his life in this house a nightmare. Make sure the re-burial is done before the wedding of Miss White to Father Odell. Is it understood? Because if you don't you will endanger the life of that excellent new angel Theo Odell.

Pausing he saw his son nodding positively only to confirm,

-I will do it, Father. I promise you. Also Sebastien would be very grieved with me if I don't do it. He is absolutely fond of Theo. I must confess as the Master of all angels, that the newly recruited Theo did put more than once a blissful smile upon my lips, an amused one just as well but more than that like the Mighty One, I can already witness what an asset Theo is for the angelic army. I would be ever so sorry to lose him especially since he has such a beautiful soul as if he was born to help with all his heart, selflessly.

Satisfied the Creator announced,

-Then you, Mighty and I share the same opinion about Theo Odell. Concerning Doctor Valdi, my opinion of him is thus: Having observed him during his life, he already had my consideration. Having met him many times, without him knowing, my consideration deepened over time. Tonight's meeting started with Valdi not knowing who I was exactly to have him then realise everything little by little during the journey to Wilton Town. Do not be surprised if I reveal to you that he is a superior angel in the making. Having been left to his own device, a free spirit 'par excellence', I am satisfied with the progress Vincent has made so far...

Interrupting his Father, the Master enquired intrigued,

-It sounds like you do know something that I do not?

The fast response came accompanied by an ironical smirk,

-Raguel, how long do you have to live to realise that it will always be the case? Does one of my qualifications of being the All Knowing ring a bell to you?

Shaking his head in false shame and amusement, Raguel persisted in order to have an answer to his curiosity,

-I surrender to you, I concede that I should have formulated my query differently. My question then is, if I am the Master of all angels, let me correct this slightly, of all your angels, then surely you should share with me the information about any new superior angel so I can do my work and duties according to your plans but also to what you have in mind? Here I will not play the card that I am your loyal son to obtain your consideration although I could. Instead I will say that I am your devoted slave, you order and I obey. Also I will add a small confession you should know about: being at your service keeps me going as much as my Mighty does. It gives me the hope that all my exertions and my good work, one day, will grant me your forgiveness for that shameful and sad day when I was about to commit angelic suicide unable to see a point to anything in my grief.

The Great Being turned around his son, observing him with a gaze as sharp as surgical instruments doing a detailed autopsy of the mind. He then stopped in front of Raguel, put his hands on his shoulders in a determined manner to make sure his son would look at him in the eyes and listen to him attentively, but also a tender one, as he started removing specks of dust of his son's cape and readjusting his shirt's scarf in a Byronesque fashion. He started in his stern voice,

-If you harbour the thought that the making of another superior angel is to replace you because of your past suicidal mishap and your obvious depression, you are highly mistaken. If I may remind you for a fact that things do not turn out very well when you are not here: Do you remember how the watchers behaved when you took your short break, your holiday of your angelic lifetime? The main cause of your enslavement, my child, is that I can't spare you for one moment. I need you at the helm of my angels. You have my divine justice and powers to control those strong entities for that reason. So you are far from being replaced.

Taking a pause, the Creator pointed towards the ruined cottage in the garden then he continued,

-You see, my son, unfortunately, sins do exist and one of them is jealousy combined with envy. That little girl's soul, the one buried in those ruins, is almost entirely rotten by it. She compared her life to the one of her neighbour, the young Mina White. When one was spoilt with love and affection, the other one starved from it. That haunted spirit is willing to hurt the entire White soon to be Odell family to afflict serious pain to Mina. Who would have thought that a child of that age could be thus consumed by such jealousy and hatred? Well, I spotted with great sadness in one of my best angels the rise of jealousy coupled with envy.

The Master turned pale while he exclaimed,

-No, it can't be possible, can it? I would know about it! Our angels are above those sentiments, I am sure... It can't be serious amongst angels. Who would be jealous of who?

The Great Being took the hand of his son within his and tapped it gently as he corrected,

-It is possible Raguel and it is happening. I disbelieved it at first as well, dismissing the idea to the back of my mind until, of course, paying more attention to the individual in question, more evidences came to light. Trust me when I say our angels are not above anything. In two examples, which I will not go into details about because you know them as much as I do, I can prove my point: First, the way the watchers reacted at your short absence; second, the case of our fallen Lucifer. As for the seriousness of the matter under my scrutiny, well the archangel in question, although doing so in a very covert manner, sabotaged and keep trying to sabotage my plans. The object of his jealousy is you, my son, and it has and had repercussion to your children.

Trembling of rage Raguel demanded,

-Mighty!? His state, we nearly lost him tonight. Is it due to... I can't express it. Surely it was a normal working day for a demon killer... If an angel wants the skin of my Mighty, he will face severe repercussions. I will not let it pass.

-Me neither. But if we act as if something is up now, we will miss the opportunity to find out who are all of his accomplices. Now, calm yourself down and listen to me attentively.

Surrounded by intense light the Father and the son disappeared from the terrace becoming invisible to all. The bubble of light transported them not only out of sight but also out of ear range, up above in the sky, at such an altitude that the earth's curve could be seen and appreciated with great awe, where the firmament with all its stars was shinning above brightly. The Creator didn't wait any further to announce,

-You are victim of a plot Raguel. By targeting you, those angels are also defying my authority and my entire creative work, which they think they are the best part of. Let me tell you, first that I carried out my investigation over a long period. So let me establish the history of the matter. You were not the first angel, I did create. The first ones were made from fire but you my son was from my flesh, blood and fire. You were made their Master. You bestow my justice within your hands forever. Your conception bothered some angels for a couple of reasons: you came later and yet you were to have the ascendance upon them all. No one came to speak about their unease overtly apart from Lucifer who always wore his soul and heart on his sleeve at that time. However he let you be, but he warned me one day. He reported to me the success of a battle, where you were overwhelmingly victorious but got wounded protecting Archangel Raphael. Lucifer spoke almost cryptic words for a few seconds before telling me: 'Your son is not perfect. He lacks flaws. An archangel who thinks that he is perfection incarnated hates your son with a passion. That angel thinks that he is the perfect one and not your son, but to his frustration Raguel is the better angel of the two. Beware, the life of your son is in danger.' When I probed him of who he was talking about, he just replied to prepare myself to be surprised. Do you remember that battle, my son, the one that prompted Lucifer to warn me? He saw in our ranks your personal enemy.

The Master shook his head in negation before replying,

-I couldn't fault anyone that day. I wouldn't know. Even Lucifer fought by my side brilliantly. It is a shame that he became such a loose cannon which had to be thrown to hell.

Sighing deeply, the Great Being corrected,

-Lucifer is far from being a loose cannon. Do not underestimate anyone, my son, may it be foe or friend. Now, let me tell you, did it not astonish you that the consummate warrior Raphael came into such trouble that you lent him a hand exposing your flank to the enemy? Who was the only wounded on the angelic side? Who was victoriously wounded? Being the healing archangel, Raphael looked after you with all the affability one could give in the aftermath of the battle. Let me tell you that you were not getting any better under his hands, on the contrary, he reported infection, and that if you were made of pure fire you would have a better chance of survival. If I did spot the covert criticism, I didn't pay attention further to it. I was just worried about you. When you asked me for your break, still struggling with your battle wound, I gave it to you. You went far away from anyone even myself and only I knew where you were licking your wounds. Strangely enough, without potions, magical or not, you looked after yourself and made a full recovery faster than the weeks of angelic care you had received. When I fetched you back to return to your duty, I was astonished to see you well and full of health while you explained to me that you only used honey and resorted to sew your own skin like human did. Now, I know you have great respect and reverence to archangel Raphael, but he is the one who wants you harm. He has been relentlessly scheming. I am the first to confess, that even I, didn't notice until very late what was going on. But once you piece everything together the complete picture is staggering and sickening. Like I, you remember the death of Gael, your eldest son. Think of the inefficiency of Raphael when you brought Gael to him to be saved. Like when it was you, the best healer of all angels couldn't do any good and may have done some worse because he had our blinded trust. Gael died in agony. I had to retrieve his soul in hell because the demons claimed him.

The Creator paused, observing the affected traits of his son before he pursued,

-Lucifer on a throne was waiting for me. Demons attacked me from everywhere, but he clapped his hands, made them cease and shouted: 'Bow maggots to your Creator, for you owe him your very existence.' They all did so and Lucifer came to me, knelt by me, looked at me straight into my eyes and begged that I had to forgive them because most had forgotten who they were and that the same applied to him. He asked me to follow him to his infernal suite. He kept looking at me with some joy and some deep sadness. He confided that he always harboured the hope that I would step in hell to pay him a visit in honour of the old days when he was good or just to check upon him, if he was doing fine. He was saddened that my visit was only due to my half breed of a grandson being dead. His ambivalent self once more gave me warnings, advices and coded messages. In essence, my plan to create angels from humans and have an army of them walking the earth looking after humans and helping them had caused an up row in the angelic world and Gael who was the first angel in charge of that mission and able to bestow wings to humans became the first casualty. You were next. The counsel I was given to preserve you, I followed and it worked.

An unsettled Raguel demanded,

-Do you follow the advice of a Lucifer?!

-A fallen Lucifer is still my creature. He has a peculiar devotion to me and a high respect. Anyhow, the matter at hand was that the angels were highly vexed about the idea of an army of angels made from originally humans. Their pride was bruised, none more than the one of archangel Raphael. His criticism of that plan rallied other old angels made of pure fire in a scheme to prove me that angels made from humans are worthless. They didn't leave time to Gael to perform his duties for very long. The only legacy he left us are the two angels he made from human stock: Doctor Williams and Abigail, both who passed the test of time successfully to the disarray of archangel Raphael. William, especially, an eminent physician in his own right in his human lifetime, descendant of a goddess which made him a powerful wizard became the much needed healing angel for my human angels. William is a prime target for Raphael. Do you remember his accident in Boston when Sebastien had to save him? I will not go to the details but something fishy was on. To go back to our Gael's death by demons and me questing for his soul in hell, I learnt there that a pact was passed between Raphael and Lucifer which resulted in the murder of Gael.

Pale, the Master of angels trembled as he demanded,

-Tell me about it all, Father. Do not spare me. I want to know, I ought to know what really happened to my son.

The Creator revealed,

-Archangel Raphael sought Lucifer and demanded the death of Gael to him. Lucifer refused unless Raphael would pay him in a manner that pleased him. Trying to not even bargain, the haughty Raphael advanced that it was in Lucifer's best interest to get rid of Gael because the later was born to be a demon killer. Unphased, Lucifer replied that he still needed a price for Gael's head pointing that first of all, Gael was not his problem, demon killer or not, that demons were vermin multiple enough to always crowd hell and that if a few were missing, it would provide a few breathing spaces to enjoy the odour of sulphur better. Secondly as the half breed was still the grandson of god, the price should be very high: The loss of an angel for the loss of another angel. Because Raphael made the plea for the kill, only his soul should pay the price by being sold to Lucifer. Archangel Raphael refused the price, went, pondered for six months, then at the creation of William as the first human angel made by Gael, he went back to Lucifer in order to accept his terms. I was shown the signed contract stamped with the seal of archangel Raphael. He sold his soul to Lucifer who will take it at Raphael's death.

-Raphael signed a pact with the devil! I feel so betrayed, you must as well?

Nodding positively the Great Being agreed,

-Of course I am. To make things worst, Raphael arranged the 'guet-apens' to set up Gael to face a full blown demonic attack on his own. Your eldest son was literally sent to his death. Lucifer confided to me that my grandson fought bravely until he couldn't lift any part of his body. He presented me with Gael's soul and told me, that he didn't find in himself the will or want to either pervert Gael's soul or to exterminate it totally. Lucifer gave Gael's soul to me with a sad smile and his recommendation to not let him reincarnate because he would be obliged to kill him again and again in the most horrendous manner but that I could rest assure that he would always preserve the soul of Gael intact. Anyway, what happened to your eldest marked him so much that Gael had no desire to join the battle once more. For him it was over. He just sought peace and solitude in heaven. When I asked Lucifer if I had to pay for the retrieval of Gael's soul, he replied with tears in his eyes that Gael belonged to me and that he only returned my belonging. He also assured me that as his part of the pact had been fulfilled, he will gain an archangelic soul, the one of Raphael, which would do less harm in hell than upon Earth. He didn't know when but he was looking forward to it for my peace of mind and to make Raphael pay the full price of his evilness.

Raguel commented thoughtfully,

-This is why you took my Mighty to Doctor Valdi and not to Archangel Raphael because you knew Raphael was a traitor. I am deeply unsettled about it all but also by the ambivalence of Lucifer. Can I trust him?

The firm reply came immediately,

-You? No. I can only advise you to approach him with great caution if you ever has to do so. However, his advice to me to treat you as a slave for a while since the birth of the Mighty One worked as a treat to preserve and protect you. Let me explain. I never wanted to give up my plan to have angels made from humans despite what happened to Gael, we needed to rise up and fight on. I asked you to conceive once more a maker of human angels and demon killer. Despite frowning a fair bit, you agreed, for centuries had passed and the bereaved father that you were had so much love to give to another little one. Sebastien came to this world. I faked being crossed for the spurious reason that you didn't check the human mother's ancestry properly and took the opportunity to punish you for it by enslaving you. Let me tell you that demeaning you deflected the attention of the pure angels from you straight away, they concentrated their attentions to your new offspring. You are at the end of the day the one who can make those powerful demon killers and maker of angels, so will your descendants. The jealousy of Raphael towards you diminished because of my sometimes harsh treatments of you. The malignity of Lucifer worked to protect your life for thousands of years. However, the attention turned to Sebastien...

Sighing deeply, Raguel asked,

-So for tonight?

-Well, no, since he arrived in Wilton Town, Sebastien faced many demons, many. My suspicion is that this is not very catholic and that something is up. I will pop in hell later to interrogate Lucifer about it. You see Raphael has already sold his soul for the death of Gael. I wonder who has sold his soul for the death of Sebastien. My suspicion is on archangel Michael. I saw him having a long discussion with Raphael one day and when I came to them, they stopped talking immediately with both showing some embarrassment.

Almost begging the Master demanded,

-Let me go with you in hell. Please!

The Creator looking at his son in a severe manner conceded,

-You can come but you must be on your best behaviour and let me do the talking. Remember, Lucifer tolerates you but hardly much more than that. If an angel would sell his soul to him for your death, he would have no problem to accomplish his part of the bargain only to spare your soul because you are my son. If you throw all your grievances at his door, he will not help you further than he already have. Beside any erratic behaviour of yours down there and I will warp you out of hell with immediate effect to protect you from getting slaughtered. Now, let us check on how Doctor Valdi is performing.

As they descended back to the hotel of Miss White, Raguel asked,

-So Valdi is to become a superior angel. Will you be so kind to tell me more about him?

The Great Being replied with a winning smile,

-Vincent Valdi is one of my projects. I destined him from his mother's womb to become the first of the human angels to be an archangel. The beauty of him is that he is purely human from the start. If he ever fulfil his destiny, what a blow would he be to the vanity of all the angels of old made of fire who caused us so much grief. His avant will teach many a lesson rightfully. Free willed and spirited, he has so far accomplished so much like becoming an angel during his lifetime. The little guidance Vincent had without him knowing came from Doctor Williams, our William who lead him and promoted his medical skills to become an excellent Doctor. The true punishment of Raphael will come when he will see his place taken as the leading healing archangel by human born Valdi. I will avenge the death of Gael and all the culprits despising angels made from humans will be very sorry for their pride for I will replace them one by one. As for you my son, you are welcome to help me in my scheme. Your first task will be to train that rough diamond of a Valdi as an archangel. He has big shoes to fill but I am convinced he is capable of doing so. Here, no more words, we are arrived.

#

Both appeared within the ballroom of the hotel. Raguel showed the way to Lawrence's bedroom to his father. The conversation he had with him, not only enlightened him thoroughly but gave him a perspective to look forward to. The Master felt mixed emotions of anger and joy at a possible revenge. His father was giving him vindication and his own back. Raguel opened the door of the bedroom and invited the Great Being in.

The sight before them with an unconscious, livid Lawrence on the bed looked bleak. Like if he read their thoughts, Doctor Williams announced,

-The fight for his life is not over. We still have a small chance to save Lawrence. We are trying, we are trying...

As the voice of William fell into a sob, Miss White explained as she was performing a massage cardiac on Lawrence,

-We are trying a desperate measure. We have retrieved his pulse since a couple of minutes. It is weak but it is there.

While he went by his bed side and stroke worryingly the pale forehead of Lawrence, the Master, concerned for his angel, enquired

-Pray, tell me what are you attempting to do right now?

It was Doctor Valdi who replied with a deep air of concentration as he injected blood within the veins of his angelic patient,

-We are doing a blood transfusion.

Spotting a couple of buckets full of stinking black liquid, the senior angel demanded,

-What is that? The rotting odour coming from that is vile! I never heard of blood transfusion. What is it?

Doctor Williams explained with some anxiety as if he waited for either condemnation or approval,

-In the buckets is the poisoned blood. Doctor Valdi managed to drain almost the entirety of it from Lawrence. We had to keep just a little of his blood inside his body to keep him alive. We are replacing the contaminated blood with my blood and the one of Maximilien inside Lawrence's body. Blood transfusion is not a widely known practice, Master. But I dare say it has passed its experimental stages with Doctor Blundell from London. He saved someone suffering from haemophilia by it not so long ago. Doctor Valdi and I have been in touch with that British pioneer obstetrician since the publications of his results of his earlier transfusions during the past two decades. I myself acquired numerous instruments for blood transfusion created by Blundell which we are using now. Here, our aim is to give time to Lawrence. If you see by the buckets full of poisonous blood, he literally had none in front of him.

Bending over the buckets and about to put his hand in one, a worried Raguel stated sternly with consternation,

-So you are not saving Lawrence right now, just buying him time.

Doctor Valdi grabbed the hand of the angel before it could touch the black blood and holding it firmly in his grasp retorted firmly,

-Keep your angelic paws away from the poison unless you have a death wish! I do not perform instant miracles but we are doing our best to save your angel. Upon thorough assessment the strategy we took to save Lawrence is to first stabilise him. By draining him we removed most of what was killing him but we are resetting the countdown for him. Time is not a negligible factor here. Every second counts. Henry will come back with the pure sample of poison and Doctor Williams will be able to work out an antidote which we will inject to Lawrence. It is a step by step rescue operation. Step one was the assessment of the patient resulting in step two which we are currently performing.

The Great Being came to his son and Vincent. Smiling and shaking his head irresistibly he scolded,

-Raguel, meet your new angel. Thank him to have prevented you to put your hand in that poison, you, stupid boy! I can think of a back of a head slap which would not go amiss from my part. Come, shake his hand. Do not expect to babysit him for it will be the reverse before you know it. Train him fully, like you did with Sebastien. Do not spare him, he will be able to take anything on board.

Repositioning the hands of the two protagonists into a handshake, the Creator continued,

-Doctor Valdi, meet my eldest son, Raguel, also known as the Master, Master of all angels, angel of Justice, Punisher and father of the Mighty One, aka Sebastien. Beside that he is a Watcher. Raguel will teach you thoroughly all there is to know about being an angel. Follow his league and the leadership of his son.

Doctor Valdi considered the tall angel with some scrutiny as he held Raguel's hand this time in a welcoming manner. He recognised the features of Sebastien in the handsome Raguel. However the air of joyous impertinence that the Mighty One possessed at times was totally absent from the traits of his rather stern father. Vincent, although not a psychologist, could feel a great sadness emanating from the gaze and posture of the angel. It was as if an immense burden was upon Raguel's strong shoulders, an unbearable weight which he eventually had learnt to cope with, and to carry without a word. He reminded Doctor Valdi of the mythical giant Atlas condemned to carry the celestial heavens. In front of the deeply silent angel, Vincent felt obliged to break the ice between them, shaking his hand with some warm vigour,

-Doctor Vincent Valdi, at your service it seems... Angel Raguel. You will have to forgive me about formalities, like your father has to, I am afraid to say, I come as I go without knowing how to address anyone adequately.

With a wink and an amused smirk Valdi added to get the angel to react,

-To be honest, one can only feel rather shy to address any member of your family from the Mighty One passing by the One and Only to you, the Master. Do I have to call you Master like Doctor Williams did?

This time, the ice broke as Raguel warmed to his new angel who had managed to put the speck of a smile to his lips. He acknowledged,

-Well, you haven't got to deal with Tom, Dick and Harry in all honesty but I concede that our names can be a bit of a mouthful to digest to any Tom, Dick and Harry, especially if one possess the pride of a former atheist. But let me tell you, my dear Doctor Valdi, I will let you call me all the names you want to under the sun until you feel up and comfortable to call me by my proper appellation just because of the help you gave to my son tonight. I promise you I shall not be offended nor take umbrage for I owe you more than you can think of.

Vincent felt the strong amicable pressure upon his fingers. A glance at the eyes of the angel did let him know that he bestowed heartfelt appreciation. Valdi smiling humbly replied firmly,

-You do not owe me anything. I did my duty as a Doctor. Beside that I happen to be acquainted with your son. The adagio the friend of a friend is my friend goes as a rule into my eyes especially when it concerns a friend of Doctor Williams. I was sorry to see Sebastien in such a state but he is of a robust constitution therefore it is my belief that tomorrow to everyone's surprise, he will have done a complete recovery and be able to fight for another day.

Withdrawing his hand, sighing deeply the angel questioned with great sorrow,

-Only a belief? I lost a son before, almost as robust as this one. Physical strength doesn't constitute the assurance policy that my Sebastien will survive.

Doctor Valdi returning to his patient, monitoring the flow of blood going into his veins, argued in his polite yet firm manner,

-Maybe but his strength can still be a contributing factor to his survival which is not negligible. In terms of assurances, I wish I was able to give you your son in full health right here, right now, but let me give you the realistic facts instead. Comparatively speaking, although your son was poisoned, his state was not so advanced as the one of the young Lawrence laying before us. When one needed almost total drainage of his blood from his body, the other was at such an early stage that the poisonous material only needed to be removed from his body. In terms of survival probability, this young angel is still not out of the wood. He is in the thick of it while your son's state is right by the edge and about to come out of the wood. All we need for Sebastien is the antidote and he will be out of the blue, standing tall once more. Another harsh fact is that drained of his poison, your son pulled through to regain consciousness, however as you can witness, it is not the case for Lawrence. This angel has been plagued by demonic poison far longer in terms of hours, which means his entire system was contaminated. I can tell you that Sebastien's system is in a far better condition and if it has still any poison within it, it will only be traces of it, I made sure of it. Now I need to make sure this youngster of an angel doesn't join your eldest son in heaven. We need to give him more blood. Maximilien are you ready?

The angel Maximilien, anxious and tired, came to Vincent Valdi like a lamb ready to be slaughtered. He asked in his soft voice,

-Will Lawrence live, Doctor?

Making him sit on a chair by the bed, Vincent gave him a half confident smile and positive nod of the head with his answer,

-We are working upon it you and I. Put your sleeve up. Did you drink all the potions as asked?

-I did Doctor Valdi, all of them, even the bitter one.

The angel presented his arm while the Doctor checked his pocket watch for a second then announced,

-Cross fingers and toes, our Lawrence will receive not only your blood to keep him alive but also the medicine his body needs right now. Let's proceed.

While Vincent worked on the feat, he demanded,

-Whil', pulse?

Miss White smiled giving her answer,

-Weak but steady.

Valdi ordered,

-Write it down along with all the potions given, then if you could prepare the heartiest oxtail soup for those recovering angels and the ones giving their blood away, you will bestow the gratitude of all.

The white witch obeyed and left the room with a short courtesy. The Great Being went to inspect the notes which she left behind on the chest of drawers. Reading, he asked,

-So Lawrence had a demon's claw as well within his body?

Doctor Valdi confirmed,

-Yes, he had. The entrance point and wound was upon his back right shoulder. The claw was found in his right lung which it had punctured twice. Doctor Williams, please, would you show our surgical finds. We repaired the lung. But if Lawrence recovers, it will take him a good six months to a year to be fully fit to fight again. He will suffer from shortness of breath from now on.

Bringing the claw on a dish for the Creator to have a close look upon, Doctor Williams added,

-If the boy is making it, I think he should stay under the tutelage of Sebastien and Doctor Valdi. He could work as a receptionist at the clinic or develop as a nurse. I doubt he could be a Doctor but I could be wrong, if he is given the right monitoring. But his days as a fighting angel are truly over. He would be a weakest link which we couldn't afford in any fights. It would be better to reassign him as soon as he is awake. If he awakes that is. At this moment in time blood transfusions' success rates are about fifty fifty. But under our circumstances, it is our only and last option for Lawrence.

Raguel going to his father to inspect the content of the dish enquired with some anxiety,

-Fifty fifty! With that poor boy being born outside of luck... Why such low success rates?

Doctor Williams scolded with his reply,

-Master, please, it is not the right time to remind us of the would be curse of Lawrence. We are trying to keep our hopes up here. But for blood transfusions, one main problem resides in the compatibility of the blood used to replace the old one. In previous trials animal's blood were used on humans with very mixed results and a high death rate. Here, it is angelic blood to replace angelic blood so our expectations of success are much higher.

Monitoring the transfusion, Doctor Valdi corrected,

-Not that higher, no. The ratio will probably be similar to the one from human to human. Not forgetting, in our case Lawrence has been bled substantially during the day in a ritualistic fashion henceforth we have an extremely weak individual to save on our hands.

The Master demanded,

-How did you gather that information Valdi?

Lifting one hand of Lawrence to exhibit the young angel's healed but slashed wrist, Vincent replied,

-By examining him. From the bump behind his head, I can tell that Lawrence was attacked by surprise and that he probably didn't realise it until it was too late. I would not be astonished if he suffered partial memory loss. What is sure is that he didn't struggle when he was bled. The cuts on his wrists and ankles are precise. Lawrence was either unconscious or unable to defend himself. He suffered a puncture in his heart. This was repaired twice during the day. The first repair was a rough cauterisation, the second, I can not define but it soothed the wound greatly and fixed it properly. On his abdomen there is the outline of a sigil. He is the claimed victim of a magical ritual. From the spread of his cuts, I can tell he was bled above a pentagram. Both his hands show some damages which look self inflicted and came after him being bled. One hand was full of embedded thorns, rose bush thorns, the other was stabbed through rather neatly but by a blunt knife with a round tip blade, a dinner table knife. He tried to eat but his poisoned self couldn't digest and had difficulties to swallow food. He threw up at some point this evening a meal which consisted of onions and sausages...

A pale Maximilien interrupted him,

-Doctor Valdi is right, Master, for the kitchen knife, the rose bush, the dinner, my brothers and I witnessed Lawrence being erratic, certainly not being his usual self, stabbing his own hand waiting for the dinner which was of sausages and onion gravy. Sebastien healed Lawrence as much as he could after he was exorcised before he handed the boy to me to look after. Lawrence told us he didn't remember anything after his order to cover the pentagram in Peter O'Neil's cottage with planks.

Suitably impressed Raguel was about to touch a red stone within the presented dish but, again, Vincent Valdi went to hold his hand in mid air to stop him doing so. The senior angel giving a deep look at the Doctor asked with a marked impatience,

-What now, Doctor Valdi, a precious gem, surely, can not be poisoned?

Handing Raguel a pair of tweezers, Doctor Williams replied for Vincent who went back to his patient,

-Considering the state of Lawrence, Master, we can not be too careful. Please use this instrument to avoid the contact of any items in this dish with your skin. You would be surprised by the amount of cases of death caused by the lightest contact with a poisoned object. Having lost my first human life to poison I made it a point to learn everything about that toxic subject. Not only that I can tell you that gem stones can carry very potent spells. We need to investigate this one, this garnet, to understand why we found it in our young angel.

The Great Being ordered in a commanding tone,

-Pray, Doctor Williams start your investigation on that garnet now, in this room. Let us know as soon as you find anything. Raguel, stay by my side, stay safe and do not touch a thing: you are worst than a five year old sometimes. I am truly reconsidering taking you on my trip to hell. You are going to be a nightmare to look after there. I will not have the good Doctor Valdi to babysit you either.

Doctor Williams who made appear magically upon the chest of drawers all he needed to study the precious stone and the demonic claw, rose his head intrigued at the mention of hell, to enquire,

-A journey to hell undertaken with the Master of all

angels, my Lord, this is unprecedented and unexpected. May I ask if what happened to the Mighty One is the reason for that dangerous trip?

Taking a good glance at the industrious and inquisitive Doctor Williams, the Creator revealed feeling deep sympathy for him,

-William, the Mighty One is one of the reasons but you are another one. Do you remember who made you an angel?

Nodding with sorrow, Doctor Williams placed the garnet on his microscope and sighed,

-Only too well, sadly. I miss Gael. He was so, so unassuming, kind and reserved. I go and see him in heaven regularly but he is an angel of a few words only, without any interest to engage with what is happening in the universe. Strangely enough we always end up chatting about botany and entomology. Last time I went to see him, he was writing a study about ants which was quite fascinating. Please tell me how can I be a reason for you two to go to hell because this is the last place I want you to step in?

The Great Being sat on a brown leather armchair by the bed. As he stroke the cedar wood of the arms of the chair admiring silently its quality, he commented,

-Your concern does you credit. I will be fine.

William gave a quick glance to the Master who stood by the armchair of his father silently before he insisted,

-My concern is only natural. What about Raguel? Will he be fine as well?

Taking a good look at his son, the Creator gave an enigmatic smile with his answer,

-Only if he behaves which can be problematic for him. I guess this is what you get creating a son by mixing fire and the original blood: an angelic bundle of impetuosity to tame and harness constantly. Anyhow he wants to come therefore he gave me his word that he shall do as I say or else I will send him away immediately back to safety.

Doctor Williams felt a little reassured. He probed further as he drew the stone he was observing under a microscope,

-What is the motive of the expedition to hell? Again if I

am one of them, it makes me feel unease and extremely worried. Am I even allowed to ask? The demonic sigil clawed on the abdomen of Lawrence is carved on that garnet. This is definitely a stone with a purpose and a spell.

Suddenly getting up, the Great Being removed carefully the bed sheets covering Lawrence unravelling the marks on his body. He inspected the sigil with great care while he replied,

-Doctor Williams, know that you are allowed to ask. That you, Maximilien will be allowed to give the information to your two brothers but will have to be sworn for the three of you to keep the secret, and that you, Doctor Valdi, will be aware of the secret and can only share it to Father Odell and Miss White. What I will reveal will eventually spread but let it be in a controlled manner in order to retain or gain the upper hand. My human angels, let's consider yourselves at war. The enemies we are facing are traitorous. They are the pure angels made of fire who wants the annihilation of any human angel. The creation of human angels did upset them so much that one archangel, my best one, sold his soul to Lucifer for the death of the angel charged of making them, Gael.

At the announcement Doctor Williams dropped his pencil, stunned. He uttered almost silently at the tip of his lips with fear,

-Raphael!

-The very one. Bring your drawing of the sigil to me, Doctor Williams. I know the two of you do not always see eye to eye. When I thought it was only pure rivalry between you on the medical front, I was far from envisaging the pure hatred of Raphael towards you. Esteem yourself lucky that he does not have another soul to sell for your annihilation as an angel. I saw the very contract with his archangelic seal and blood signature in hell. Now let me tell you of an appallingly sad fact, which you have to know about, and which demonstrate of a most intense jealousy and hate, it was your creation as a healing angel by Gael which prompted Raphael to sign the contract which killed ultimately my angelic grandson. By the death of Gael, he thought it would stop the creation of more angels from human origins.

Trembling, Williams handed over his drawing to the Creator. The old angel was saddened about the revelation. He commented with a deep sigh,

-Here, my Lord, the demon's sigil. I will never esteem myself lucky, my Lord, just upset that the hate of an archangel of me being, caused the murder of your eldest grandson. Archangel Raphael always had a specific way of showing me his dislike when he was not showing me his contempt or ignoring me, it went as far as drawing his sword to make the promise that it will hack me off into a thousand little pieces one day, so basically there were physical and verbal threats. I knew Raphael hated me all along since his nickname for me was 'Maggot'. His demeaning behaviour had its effects upon me, your son can confirm that I asked many times, even begged Master to send me to heaven for a break. But Raguel always kept me to do my duties, dissuading me in one way or another. So here I am, the devoted servant to you both. Let me tell you about what you asked me about the garnet. Its carved sigil indicates that we have to deal with a demon which has the capacity to come back to life by his invocation or the simple mention of his name. His sigil is his portal. By marking the body of Lawrence, like he did, he aimed to appropriate his physical appearance for his next come back. The use of garnet stone in the case of our boy is multiple. By hovering my hand above the stone I could feel its aim. First it is to inflict a deeper and deadly blow to its victim. Second it regulates the blood circulation to create a slower death in order for the demon to use the body of his host for longer.

Maximilien who despite his drowsiness was paying attention to the important conversation interrupted,

-The demon used Lawrence to spy on our army, Sebastien said. He possessed him and tried to get informations by observing us from within. Demons knew what we were doing at the cottage of O'Neil, the closure of their hell portal but they wanted to have an idea of what our next move would be. Sebastien and Father Odell did a thorough check on the angelic army's soldiers but only Lawrence showed himself to be the possessed spy amongst us. Keeping that young soldier weak but alive as long as he was discovered was probably the plan of the demon, yet he had no problem to start killing his host from the inside as soon as the plot was up and discovered. I dare say Lawrence has been a walking time bomb since he was bled above that pentagram. Master, when Sebastien killed the demon which was inside of Lawrence, we all thought the boy would make it. But dare I say, having seen the demon with my own eyes, he was such a beast! It took the help of Father Odell, Matthias and Maurice given to Sebastien to get rid of him. Then also after the fight, the Mighty One came to me who had the order to look after the exorcised Lawrence. Sebastien had sustained a wound on his flank which was gaping, but he remained brave as always, he ignored the fact that he was badly injured to care for his soldiers and give our next orders. Mine was to take care of Lawrence and to bring him at Miss White's hotel. However I can say that if the boy had regained his own self, I could only observe his decline by the hour helplessly.

Deeply interested Doctor Valdi stated in an encouraging fashion,

-Maximilien, observe now Lawrence picking back up some colour by the minute. Look at his cheeks. It is all down to you and your strong blood helping him through. The blood transfusion has positive effects so far.

Taking the pulse of his patient and noting it down Valdi continued,

-Lawrence is responding well. For one thing his pulse is stronger. Now, let's check yours, Max, so we can call it a day when it goes down but is still within safe level. Remember to drink plenty of fluids after the transfusion, but not alcohol and take a good rest for at least a day.

Turning to the Master, Doctor Valdi demanded,

-I know there is another fight tomorrow evening, Angel Raguel, and that the angelic army of Sebastien has suffered a few casualties including himself but I must request that this angelic soldier, Maximilien, stays out of it. It is preferable to let Max rest and look after the recovery of Lawrence. If you are short in the number of soldiers for the fight, take me instead.

The Master noticed that Valdi truly struggled on how to address him which meant that the new angelic Doctor had therefore decided to settle on calling him Angel Raguel. If anything this made him smile internally. Raguel was still pondering if it was to be due to some pride of some sort on the part of Valdi or the shock of the new order of things surrounding all of a sudden the head strong atheist, empirical and rather Cartesian Doctor. After all Doctor Valdi's well ordered world which was based on science, mathematic, proofs by experiments and so on, had turned on its head the day he encountered the ghost of Abraham Wilton-Cough not so long ago, when he was forced to accept the metaphysical along with the paranormal. Basically for the Master, he faced a new angel which had to adjust fast to his novel reality but he also guessed that Valdi would be a very solid character by his side ready to support him and help. Raguel replied to the demand firmly after a long minute of silence,

-Doctor Valdi, I agree with you: Maximilien depleted of part of his blood should stay here to look after our Lawrence and stay out of any fight tomorrow. He will be far more useful here at the bedside of the youngster.

He then turned to Maximilien to carry on,

-Beside that, Max, you know we did put a magical protection on this hotel and outbuildings against any fire. If the fire we expect in town tomorrow reaches uncontrollable proportion, the hotel will be the post of rescue for the town's inhabitants. I want you to be in charge of this outpost. Prepare it to receive casualties and homeless humans. Get your brother Maurice involved in the defence of this outpost. It will keep him out of straight fight bearing in mind how injured he is, but I know how much he will want to get stuck in what we are doing to help this town in a manner or another, no matter how poorly he is physically. As for your brother Matthias, he will be on the fighting front with me but deployed to lead the humans who could be affected by tomorrow's conflict to safety, hence he will bring them through the forest up to the hotel. Depending on how bad things are, he will have to do many journeys. These are your orders. Deploy them to your brothers. How is Maurice?

The angelic soldier replied affirmatively,

-I will do so, Master. Maurice is sleeping soundly but he had to be drunk to do so under Doctor Williams's supervision. My brother can not lay on his back. He is downstairs in the pretty drawing room of Miss White tucked in one of her armchairs as comfortably as we could make him be. He will patch up fast, he always does.

Doctor Williams confirmed,

-Maurice will be back to his full strength, Master, in a matter of hours not days. I went a little magically heavy on him to repair his ribs. As we speak the fractures he sustained are healing themselves.

The Master only nodded to Williams his appreciation before he returned his entire attention to Doctor Valdi as he welcomed,

-I can not hide from you, Doctor Valdi, that a fair few valuable soldiers of my son's angelic army are a bit down and under at the moment, wounded. Therefore, it would be with thankfulness that I would accept your help for the coming troubles in Wilton Town. Beside that we couldn't help to notice that your reputation in town is that you are the one who imposed a respected justice. You are the policeman of the gentle folk of the town. They are all looking up to you. Your absence, however short it may be for your honeymoon, created such a vacuum that all the rogues, thieves and up to no good, felt that they were finally free to do as they wanted. Without you in Wilton Town, all hell broke loose. I am afraid but also pleased to say that you are the guardian of the peace in this little town whether you want it or not. You are their hero, their knight in shinning armour. If you appear tomorrow, in the middle of the expected troubles, you will be seen as the bucket of water to put down the flames. Your presence will be the cold shower that all who are relishing your absence to do the worst they can do deserve. To be honest, I will be internally rejoicing to have you by my side to punish those scoundrels. If your living legend is true, you fight very well.

Washing his hands, Doctor Valdi replied with some embarrassment at the praises laid at his doors,

-Let's just say that I know how to use my fists when I need to. May I ask a few questions since I am stepping into a scene? First, about my young patient, Lawrence, I gathered that there could be a curse upon him: what is it about? Secondly, many of you mentioned a potential fire to have to deal with tomorrow, can you tell me what we are talking about precisely? Thirdly, last but not least, I seek more explanations about the 'consider yourselves at war, human angels', being a new angel, it is kind of a big deal which I need to grasp fully.

Doctor Williams with diligence, bowed to the Master to propose,

-May I enlighten Doctor Valdi upon the first point, Master, as I fear I may be responsible for his query?

Raguel accepted with a solemn nod of his head therefore the old friend of Valdi started his explanations,

-Vincent, as it stands we do not know if Lawrence is suffering from a curse, however the idea, the thought of it crossed our minds many times. We dismissed it however, brushed it under the carpet without any investigation on our angelic parts. We labelled as pure coincidence or bad luck that Lawrence died at twenty one during his human life and then again during his first reincarnated angelic life. This is only his second angelic reincarnated life, right now and Lawrence's twenty first birthday was celebrated at mine only a few weeks ago. You can easily understand our concern that we never saw the boy grow any further to full adulthood. Him, laying here, in that fateful age, seemingly struck down, reignited our questions and suspicions about a possible curse upon him, that is all. Another thing that we noticed, well, couldn't help to notice is how unlucky Lawrence is. It became quite a talking point in Sebastien's army of angels, a notorious one for the wrong reasons, the soldiers are betting on the bad fate of Lawrence and usually win. I can give you some examples, for there are many to chose from but the latest one was a prank we did for his birthday. Purposefully we did cut his cake short of one slice compared to all the guests around the table. We drew straws to decide who would be without a slice of his birthday cake and surely enough, Lawrence picked the shortest straw without knowing it. When the Master says that Lawrence was born outside of luck, we all deep down believe it somehow.

Maximilien added with a sad sigh and a giggle,

-I remember when we had to storm that tavern's cellar one day, we all descended the old staircase to the basement without problems but Lawrence broke his ankle on the only step which gave way under his weight. He was the lightest of us all! What about the time we were hiding in the bushes spying on the Duchess when her Beauceron guard dog decided to relieve itself by the bush where our boy was. He took the shower of pee in deep silence to not blow our cover yet we all laughed internally but his poor forbearing self didn't. Decidedly the lad has never been very lucky. However my brothers and I can't think that it is due to some curse because who would curse Lawrence? He is such a decent and kind individual.

This statement made Doctor Valdi shake his head negatively in disbelief to correct sternly,

-My good angel, don't be so naive. Of two things, a curse or the group or person doing it will disregard their victims. It doesn't matter to them how good or bad is the target of their curse. I will just take an example, the curse which condemned the children of Wilton Town born during a full moon to become ghouls at their deaths. The curse lasted for centuries, affecting many blindly, regardless of anything. Secondly, let me ask you, how many coincidences of bad luck events could constitute as evidence that something definitely wrong is affecting Lawrence which need to be taken seriously and investigated do you need?

Vincent Valdi paused to address again his last question to all present with a dark look which was screaming silently to them: 'Come on!'. All of a sudden, the ghost of Abraham Wilton-Cough appeared by Doctor Valdi. His lanky almost skeletal self presented himself, his tall hat held in his pale hands before him respectfully, however his eyes displayed a tamed anger towards all the angels present. Doctor Valdi presented the ghost to everyone in the room with some deference,

-Please, meet Abraham Wilton-Cough, the descendant of Noah Wilton, the founding father of Wilton Town. Us speaking of a possible curse is upsetting him since his eldest son was affected by one. He wants to offer his help.

Shivering despite himself, the surprised angelic soldier Maximilien commented demanding an explanation,

-Doctor Valdi, this ghost came from you!? I saw him. He was inside you, I swear he was!

Vincent Valdi couldn't help his ironic giggle as he confirmed to the worried soldier while he made a connivance sign of the hand to the almost transparent Wilton-Cough to let him deal with the query,

-Max, there is no need to be afraid. Abraham is my resident ghost. His spirit stays with me.

Bewildered Maximilien asked,

-Possessed! You are possessed, Doctor Valdi!? Are you? Look how fierce your ghost looks!

Shaking his head hopelessly, Valdi laughed out,

-No, I am not possessed... Abraham's soul is just hiking a way through my body to look after his loved ones. We are friends. We understand each other. It is just a pure symbiosis between ourselves.

Maximilien, dumbfounded to say the least, gave querying looks to the Master, the Creator and Doctor Williams. He repeated at a loss,

-Sym-bo-bio-sis, what does that mean? Doctor Valdi, I am an angelic soldier, a former musketeer of the time of Louis the thirteenth, I am not Galileo Galilei.

Doctor Williams intervened with his explanation to the help of both, his friend Vincent Valdi and the soldier to the benefit of his comprehension,

-Max, Doctor Valdi is not possessed, I can assure you of that firmly for when he visited me in Boston lately with his wife and the son of Wilton-Cough, the Mighty One assessed Vincent without him knowing. No, what you have before your eyes is a true partnership of souls. Both respect, look after and protect one another. Symbiosis is just a scientific term when we can observe in nature a beneficial partnership of some sort between animals or organisms. For example, from my time living in Egypt, I witnessed crocodiles from the Nile opening their jaws to plover birds, not to eat them, but to let them remove leeches off their gums. The birds were having a free meal while the reptilian predator was getting the riddance of his nagging blood sucking troubles in his jaws. There, we are witnessing on a higher level a symbiosis of two spirits who mutually work for one another's best interests. It is no possession, it is a positive collaboration.

Giving a second long and worried glance to the ghost not far from him, a circumspect Maximilien commented,

-I would be worried to collaborate with a spirit which looks like the Cardinal Richelieu... Why does your ghost look so cross Doctor Valdi? Can he harm like in the example of the crocodile given by Doctor Williams?

Valdi took the hand of Wilton-Cough within his to reply,

-Maximilien, please feel free to address any of your questions to Abraham himself. What I can tell you is that yes, he has the capacities to hurt emotionally and physically anyone. But it is not in his best interest to do so nor his intentions. Forgive him to be a little upset. It is only due to his concern that the possible curse on Lawrence hasn't yet been investigated.

The Great Being, coming to the ghost, took Wilton-Cough's tall hat, shook invisible dust from it then from Abraham's shoulders, each time making the ghost more visible and corporeal, saying as a matter of fact,

-Maximilien, know that our Abraham Wilton-Cough is not only tolerated but appreciated. Just consider him as a soldier within an angelic soldier like the Mighty One does.

Giving back his top hat to Abraham with a warm smile, he asked,

-My dear Wilton-Cough, still fighting with the living, when will you call it a day? What stirred your old guts this time around?

The ghost, pointing with his hat at Lawrence laying on his bed while following the Creator who was going back to his chair, replied with great energy,

-On this occasion, I would say still fighting with the dying! What stirred me is the sight of that angel. When I complain to have been shot dead too early, and I look to that lad who never makes it past twenty one, well, I am honestly gutted.

Taking a seat with some majesty, the Great Being

haughtily demanded,

-And what would your torn guts suggest, Abraham, apart from sincere commiseration for Lawrence?

Still waving his hat towards the unconscious angel, Wilton-Cough fiercely replied in an argumentative manner,

-Well, well, well, for a start, it is not good for that angel of yours to be all drawn upon like that by demons! I would remove that gibberish scribble from around his belly button.

The Master interjected,

-Easy to be said, but to be done is another matter. There are powerful demonic magic in those symbols.

Abraham grew angry,

-Are you saying that you can't help him because a big dead demon put a claim on your angel? The demon is dead until someone say his name right. The sigil is used as a portal by that demon and you want to keep the boy alive with that threat upon him if he ever survive? Whatever demonic seal or stamp it is on Lawrence's belly, it has to go. You must work it out for his sake!

-How?

The Master exclaimed incensed as he went to consider the marked sigil on his angel. Wilton-Cough pointed to Doctor Williams with his hat as he answered,

-You have an excellent wizard and a witch in your crew to work it out. Miss White does wonders. She is unassuming about her craft but show her the sigil and watch what she tells you about it. She knows always far more than she let assume. You have a bible of witchcraft in your hands with her.

Williams coming forward told,

-Master, I know of a ceremony to remove any sigil embedded within the skin, but whoever performs it dies in the end.

The dark look of Raguel was covered with sadness as he announced,

-I don't want to lose anyone anymore.

Putting his top hat in front of his waistcoat, turning it in his hands, Wilton-Cough proposed,

-Would it work if someone already dead could perform the task? Because I am here, I can be physical enough, I could do it.

Doctor Valdi interjected,

-No! Ab! You could lose your soul, you don't know...

But Abraham turned to Vincent in a resolute manner to say,

-I know that I have you to look after my children. I know that you will be a better father than I was. I can do this with peace in my heart because of you. If I don't lose my soul, I will return by your side and follow you like a shadow, trust me, I will. You are devoting yourself to my children, I am devoting myself to you.

Valdi gave a manly hugged to the ghost feeling deep emotions before asking to Doctor Williams,

-Is what suggested Abraham possible? Could he lose his soul?

Walking about the room in deep thoughts, Doctor Williams made two attempts to answer, but then each time stopped short to do so, only his pointed finger waved in the air for a few seconds before he carried on walking from wall to wall. Then Williams with a grave air went to Abraham Wilton-Cough demanding,

-Please Sir, would you mind me assessing you as a ghost? It will not take long but it may be a little inconvenient and embarrassing. However it may help me to answer adequately to your proposal and Doctor Valdi's question.

The old banker put his hat back on top of his head consented,

-If it has to be done, so be it. I will be your patient patient. God only knows I wasn't like that during my lifetime.

As the ghost surrendered himself to the investigation willingly, the Great Being chuckled with a condescending smile,

-I am not the only one to know upon that subject. Doctor Valdi, I am sure can tell many stories of your infamous impatience...

Surely enough, Valdi couldn't help smiling as he replied,

-Oh dear Lord, I can!

His joyous eyes met the ones of the Creator for a split second and suddenly he blushed at the realisation that he gave the proper title to the entity before him almost naturally. Raguel by his father commented not missing anything of the interactions within the room,

-At least Doctor Valdi can swear by your name without an inkling of a problem, Father. It is something, I guess.

The Great Being only gave his son his traditional enigmatic smile before he announced,

-It is definitely something to behold. I believe your new angel might learn to swear by your name as well rather sooner than later. My divine inclination is to take Doctor Valdi with us to hell as for him seeing is believing, the trip can only prove to be educational.

The reaction of the Master was to give a wild glance to Valdi then back to his father with his interjection,

-It will be throwing that angel straight into the deep end. It is far too dangerous. If we lose him there, Sebastien will be months before addressing a word to me, as for Williams it will take years.

But his father replied sternly,

-Therefore you will have to make sure you look after Doctor Valdi very well during our journey to hell back and forth. Train him like you did with the Mighty One. Train him like if he was a Punisher, like your son. Vincent will be up to it, I am sure of it. I rough trained him to fly above the Atlantic and he managed it almost perfectly well. He is an angel that can take a lot in his stride from the start, isn't it Doctor Valdi?

A reflective Vincent Valdi smirked as he argued,

-I do not know about that. My Lord, after all, we are talking about a trip to hell. Saying that I can take it all might be flattering my wings with more feathers than they bestow. Without you, a thunderbolt would have rendered me just a pile of ashes on the surface of the ocean. May I decline the offer of a trip to hell on the ground that I do not need to see it to believe in it now?

The Great Being laughed. Raguel stated firmly,

-You can not decline an order from high above my angel. The question was can you take that trip in your stride? If not, I will have to make you do so and make you cope with it all.

Doctor Williams looked with sorrow to the ceiling before he told,

-An order is an order, Vincent.

Defending himself Valdi argued,

-William, I heard correctly, it was a divine inclination to take me to hell not an order. Despite it being expressed with the assumption that I will accept the proposal without thinking, I still possess my free will and my common sense. We are speaking about hell, William, it sounds far less appealing than having a glimpse of paradise, now does it? Or do you want me to swear like hell about it all?

Doctor Williams answered in a pondered manner,

-There is no need to swear. All angels are going through training whether they want it or not. Training takes all shapes and forms which I can not describe as a walk in the park. A trip to paradise will prepare you to be utterly useless. You might as well train yourself in that case to pick up daisies and watch butterflies... A trip to hell on the other hand is a crash course in survival which is not given to all, because they will not survive it. But considering the two mentors proposing you the lesson, if I was in your wings, I would think twice before declining the offer.

Under Williams's inspection, Wilton-Cough commented,

-Vince, I will come with you. If it may help, if I may help you in anyway, you know I will.

A dubious Doctor Williams wondered out loud,

-I do not want to sound negative Mr Wilton-Cough, but as my hand can go through you fairly easily, I do not think you could be of much help to Doctor Valdi.

As soon as he said that the old Doctor found himself levitating from the ground, thrown upon a wall and pinned to it by extreme force. Abraham holding him a few metres up in the air demanded,

-And your point is, Doctor Williams? I am fairly transparent, I can be totally invisible but I am still here and stronger than when I was alive. I can tell you that. I consider Vincent like a son and if someone dares to touch him, he will have to face me. If he goes to hell for training, I will go too to make sure he survives.

An impressed Doctor Williams feeling the strength of the ghost gasped,

-I understand. Please, let me down. I didn't mean to offend you.

His plea was joined by the one of Valdi,

-Abraham, you made your point known, please don't fiddle with his internal organs to make it go deeper. William is a dear friend of mine who means well.

The ghost dropped the old Doctor who fell to the ground. Wilton-Cough then presented his hand to help Doctor Williams up with his apologies,

-I am sorry, I forget myself sometimes. Being invisible most of the time and all, it is easily done, I guess, although I am not a psychologist.

Taking the offered hand, Doctor Williams felt the power of it as it pulled him up back on his feet. He knew then that the ghost of Abraham Wilton-Cough had enough power to be very potent therefore he announced,

-Mr Wilton-Cough can help us to remove the sigil from Lawrence. I believe he can help to protect Doctor Valdi as well. He has enough physical strength, I can tell you that. What I can't answer for is for the loss of his soul in the process either in hell or during my magical counter spell.

The Master having witnessed the scene with some worry gave his opinion,

-Wilton-Cough is a far too wayward soul to be a reliable soldier. If it was up to me I would discard his help altogether. He is all impulses.

While all eyes turned to the ghost, the Great Being came to his defence,

-I would call his impulses, all of them, the pulses of his heart. He acts upon love. He reacts. He protects. He puts himself forward to take the bullet for others. This is how he lost his life. I would never discard the help of Abraham Wilton-Cough. He saved the day of many at the cost of his own days. His soul is not wayward. He thinks forward with his sacrificing heart.

Not really satisfied, especially since having seen one of his elder angels ghost-handled, Raguel walked to Doctor Williams with concern. After ensuring William was alright, readjusting his angel's jacket a little and his neck scarf, the Master gave a dark look at Wilton-Cough but addressed his father,

-Under which jurisdiction that spirit that needs a leash goes under, pray? I hope it is not mine, for it is clear as water to assess that he is no angel. To consider him as part of my son's army, as a soldier, is just about reaching the extremities of my toleration, but more importantly it is filling me with worries. If Valdi is an asset to the army, the ghost that comes with him is a dangerous liability.

Under the stare of the major angel near him, Abraham Wilton-Cough didn't buckle, he stood tall despite being far less proud than during his life and defended,

-All I can do is offering my help. Inconsequential or great, I don't know yet what it will be. It all depends on what I am facing with by my friend Doctor Valdi. All I can say is that I want him alive at all cost for him to stay the guardian of my children. And, and I rather enjoy his friendship, I can't put it into words. Wherever he goes, I will go. If it is hell, I will go there too, if it is to mix with haughty angels and rough angelic soldiers...

Raguel lifted his hand in an authoritative manner which stopped the ghost of the former banker to finish his sentence. With a piercing glance which made Abraham shiver to his bones, he told coldly,

-Do you know what a Punisher is, Wilton-Cough? You have one in front of you. I can tell you right now that you do not belong to heaven. I can tell you that if you step out of line in my son's army, I will drag you to hell. You can not flap your wingless way in his army like a flea trapped into the feathers of one of his angels unnoticed. You are granted toleration by the Most Gracious One and by my son, but fall short of their estimations and I will fall upon you like a ton of feathers. Is that understood?

Abraham felt a knot forming in his translucent throat, yet he replied with a makeshift confidence which had more to do with bravado rather than anything else,

-I do understand. You can hit me with your feathers all you want if I fail to help properly, which is not my honest intention. Feathers sound somewhat better than bricks.

Doctor Valdi came by the ghost and putting his hand on his shoulder corrected,

-A ton is a ton, Ab. It weighs the same either in bricks or feathers.

Then he addressed himself to the Master,

-I vouch for Abraham Wilton-Cough. I will keep him in check if needs be but I doubt it will ever be the case. I trust him with my life like he trusted me with his although I couldn't save him from a certain death.

Faced with the new angel and his ghost, a conflicted Raguel repeated as a surprised demand,

-You vouch for him!?

An adamant Vincent replied with a certain fire in his voice,

-Oh yes, I will. Abraham is the father I never had. Again, I trust him.

Wilton-Cough gave a paternal smile to Valdi and explained to the angel,

-You must understand, Master, that Vincent was only a toddler when he lost his father. He very vaguely remembers his real father. I took his place in his heart somehow. I won't defect Vincent, ever. I am proud of him. If he had been my real son, I would have been over the moon with pride. You must know as a father how it feels especially with your boy Sebastien. I met your Sebastien in Boston, he asked me to move on but I told him I couldn't. I couldn't possibly. It is like my heart is sown on to the ones of the living, my wife, my sons, my daughter, my aunt and my Vincent. I can not cease to care for them all. I simply can not rest. I need to love them from beyond, help them from beyond...

His voice failed him. With his rising emotions, his appearance flickered between a ghost full of flesh and a skeletal cadaver. Abraham repeated, tears burning within his eyes sockets,

-You know as a father what loss is. I don't want to lose

any of mines. I want to stay and protect them with all my might, even if it is not much, even if it is not enough, even if it may be too late.

The sight of the spectral Abraham filled Raguel with compassion. More than anyone he understood the meaning of loss and the dread its perspective could cause. He sighed deeply before offering his hand to shake with slight reluctance to the ghost with his order,

-Do not disappoint me nor mines. Know that I accept you with a very limited tolerance that is all. The less I hear of you, the less I see you the better I will feel. For me you will always be a lose canon until you prove yourself to be something else. For me you will only be tolerated until you repay as a soul, and you have much to repay, so much so that I don't think you can ever achieve to get your redemption. If you ever lose my consideration, know that you will become dust under my feet. Am I clear?

The ghostly banker, with great sorrow in his heart, reached for the hand of the commanding angel, trembling, yet he replied giving a somewhat firm handshake,

-Angel Raguel, you are very clear. I wish you had more faith in me but I don't blame you to have none as I can only offer you my good intentions at this moment in time. If you have an angel of redemption, please tell him to be on my case. I will be ever so obedient and do whatever he says to get better for the sake of my Angela and my children.

The Creator couldn't help giggling at the situation. He coughed bringing the attention to him before announcing,

-My son Raguel is the angel in charge of redemptions.

Devastation appeared upon the face of Abraham at the statement. He looked upon the implacable Raguel and his heart sank. His head bowed so low that his hat fell on the floor. He picked it up slowly, hiding his disheartened tears to all. He dusted his black velvet top hat as he stood back up ever so silently. His mind tormented him with thoughts that he would never be given a chance to redeem himself with the Master. When his eyes met the one of the angel again he pleaded in a desperate fashion,

-I will do whatever you say to save my soul. I will make myself small, and scarce if it is what you want. I will not talk in your presence if it offends you. I can stay invisible by my Valdi. I can work as his shadow helper. You won't hear me, you will not see me until you ever find in your heart the ability to give me just the speck of a chance to redeem myself to your eyes.

Taking the hat of the ghost before placing it firmly back on his head Raguel told sternly,

-Abraham, I am taking your soul under my jurisdiction and my wings. We will work on your redemption together. Do not disappoint me. Obey. Scarce is good but I prefer you to be present to take orders and please no aggression towards my angels in the future. Just be on your best behaviour.

For a few seconds only, Abraham Wilton-Cough felt his physical heart beating in his chest. His surprise at the fact made his wild look encountered the glowing eyes of the Master. Although regaining his human heart did hurt, that minute of intense feeling brought pouring thanks at his lips and tears at his eyes,

-Thank you Master. Hand on heart I promise you to be on my best behaviour.

Abraham made the vow with a hand on his chest, as much to prove how sincere he was at that moment as to catch the already extinguishing heartbeats. Still in owe of the powerful angel, he corrected the position of his hat before he was hit by a sudden idea which he proposed in a hurry,

-Lord, your son did revive me for a split second, I swear! I felt it fully. If he can do that again, I could be fully used to do the removal of the sigil on that young angel of yours!

While the observant Raguel saw the repositioning of Wilton-Cough's hat as a marked sign of a truly independent spirit, while his eminent father considered the ghost with interest, while Valdi was pondering on what happened between the ghost and the dominant angel, Doctor Williams reacted to the proposal thoughtfully,

-You could Mr Wilton-Cough, you could, you definitely could but your soul, your soul can be lost in the entire affair. You are already stuck in between worlds. For the help you would give to angels, you will be fair game to demons, they can drag you to hell for their loss. The risks are great. I can not answer for your soul.

Faced with such warnings, Abraham bowed his head thinking out loud mumbling,

-I am willing to try. Look at him, Lawrence, young at the

prime of... He is an angel, I am not. His soul already made his proofs, mine hasn't. He is only a boy for crying sake out loud. I did my time, I did. It was cut short, yes, but not as short as him. I am willing to risk my soul for his.

The Great Being's eyes shone watching Wilton-Cough with deep intensity before he proposed,

-The solution is simple. Your soul needs to be claimed by a higher being. Their seal would protect your soul, Abraham, but you would become their eternal servant. It is better than your lost soul having a permanent dwelling in hell.

His son interjected straight away with pessimism,

-The question is who would want to claim such a soul, even as an eternal servant? No angel in his right mind would want to inflict upon himself the eternal ordeal of Abraham Wilton-Cough's company. I certainly wouldn't. You certainly couldn't.

Correcting his son, the Creator replied,

-I could but I will not do so, not because his soul is too lowly spiritually to carry my seal. If Abraham Wilton-Cough choose to become the eternal servant of an angel to keep his soul, my dear Raguel, you will have to find his soul a master. You will have to ask around the angelic community and if you fail to find him an eternal master, I will have to force you to accept him for Lawrence's sake.

Raguel looked at the ceiling in sheer desperation as his father asked the humbled ghost in the room who had tears in his eyes,

-Abraham Wilton-Cough, what is the choice for your own soul? Do you want to take the risk of losing it to demons or do you rather take the humiliating path of becoming an eternal servant?

The old banker wiped his tears with his hand which felt so physical. Downtrodden, feeling deeply unwanted, it took only a look to the pale unconscious Lawrence for him to reply,

-I will take either for the angelic boy. If he was my son, I know I couldn't leave him like that. If my soul is such an inconvenience to all, I am ready to lose it. I'd rather not, but I am ready.

The Master with a deep sigh turned to Doctor Williams

and asked,

-As the most senior entity in this room after my father and I, William, would you consider that soul as a possible eternal servant to yourself?

The old Doctor fiddled with his medical instruments, gave a furtive look at the ghost who had handled him rather roughly earlier and shook his head negatively. However he apologised,

-I am sorry Wilton-Cough, I could not deal with you eternally.

Raguel put the question without further a do to Maximilien who was prompt to reply with his natural gusto,

-Oh no, no, no! Don't even ask my brothers you will have the same answer. Give us a Planchet or a Mousqueton anytime as servant but, him, not him. He looks like the ghost of Richelieu so much that we would have sleepless nights.

An upset Doctor Valdi intervened, conscious of the distress the entire bidding conversation had on his old ghostly friend,

-I claim him! I want to claim him! Can I claim him? He is my friend. He was my mentor. I will treat him with respect forever as an equal and not as a servant.

Smiling the Great Being stood up before his son could say a word, lifting his hand with majesty only to rule,

-Granted. Abraham Wilton-Cough, do you consent for your soul to belong, be protected and serve the angel Vincent Valdi?

The ghost turned to Valdi full of emotion and couldn't refuse, truly grateful for his friend's intervention,

-Oh yes, I do consent to it.

Raguel tried to object,

-My Lord, we didn't ask senior angels who have a priority upon the matter.

Giving him a stern look, the Creator stated,

-I am only saving you the time to go through the list of

all the angels in order of ranks which would have anyhow decline the honour of possessing such a sacrificing servant. Our discerning Doctor Valdi would have been the only one to preserve that soul anyway. He still has a living heart. Vincent, Abraham, come to me. Let me seal the deal between your souls.

If the Master sighed deeply, he saw the proud new angel and the ghost go to his father who performed the biding rite. When it was over, the ghost of Abraham had embedded on both his palms the angelic seal of Vincent Valdi. By curiosity, Raguel went to inspect the hands of Wilton-Cough. There he saw a fighting rooster with a fighting bee protecting the cockerel carved within the ghostly flesh. He nodded positively understanding the meaning of both symbols, yet he asked his father,

-This is the seal of my new angel Valdi, a cockerel and a bee?

When the Creator nodded positively, Doctor Valdi inspected the seal assigned to him silently, while Doctor Williams went by him to satisfy his own curiosity and interpreted for his sake,

-Vincent, the cockerel was assigned to Sebastien as well, the grandson of the Lord and to two of his three sons. It means so much, you can not start to understand, you will bestow the power to bring light after the darkness and the bee, the bee...

Doctor Williams smiled to the ghost of Abraham before he revealed,

-This is your bee, Vincent, Abraham is your bee attached to you forever. The symbol of the bee means that when there is a will, there is a way. The bee is a strong protector to have, they defend fiercely whom they love. It means so much more too, so much more.

Wilton-Cough looked intrigued at his own hands, he repeated with disbelief,

-So I am represented in my angelic master's seal... the bee is me?

Closing the ghost's palms firmly, Raguel replied only to order,

-Yes. It means that you are the industrious one. You

were during your life, and you started your afterlife in the same fashion. Now, let's put you at work with no further a do. We have that young angel of mine to deal with. I am going to give you back your beating heart for much longer than before so that Doctor Williams can proceed with his removal spell. Follow his orders to the letter and do not argue. I am afraid feeling your heart again will hurt you. Can you deal with that for as long as the sigil takes to be removed?

Abraham nodded positively as he confirmed,

-I can. From experience I dealt with a painfully slow agony. Valdi can tell you all about it because he witnessed it.

Doctor Valdi gave the Master a very sad glance to agree with Wilton-Cough's advances before he added,

-Abraham is much, much tougher than he looks. He has resilience for a hundred men put together.

With that further confirmation, the Master rubbed his hands together with satisfaction to enjoin,

-Let us proceed.

Doctor Williams prepared everything for his spell with the help of Miss White which he went to fetch. Straight away, Whilhelmina gave him access to all he needed from her herbal garden to her pantry. Soon enough all surrounded the bed of Lawrence. A grave Doctor Williams proceeded giving his precise instructions to a willing Wilton-Cough. Abraham couldn't help looking back to Doctor Valdi to gather more confidence. Vincent reassured him,

-I have your back, Ab. Your soul is mine, remember, you can't be claimed but by me. I will fight for you.

The hands of the Creator and the Master tapped the shoulders of Doctor Valdi. Raguel confided to his ear,

-We will show you how. Trust, follow, obey to my orders and act as quickly as you can at all time. Stay sharp.

Doctor Valdi sighed knowing by intuition and by the warning that a steep learning curve for him and his ghost was about to happen. He watched with great attention all the moves that Abraham performed under the strict instructions of the wizard Williams. He could see the trembling hands of Wilton-Cough as the old banker braved all his fears. When the last performing act was done, all the candle lights in the room extinguished themselves.

In the deep darkness, Maximilien shouted,

-What is happening?

Doctor Williams had only to clap his hands to restore the light in the bedroom as he answered,

-A miracle, we are reclaiming an angel from a demon.

The soldier looked at Lawrence. The young angel showed signs of life, moving his fingers ever so slightly and his eyelids. Yet he turned to Williams to demand with some distress,

-Where are our Lord, the Master, Doctor Valdi and the ghost? They are no longer in the room.

Facing the anxious look of Whilhelmina White as well, Doctor Williams replied,

-All on a trip to hell to make sure Wilton-Cough doesn't pay the price of saving an angelic soul.

#

If Wilton-Cough felt like falling helplessly in a maelstrom made of wind and fire, if his entire body was dragged by demons downward, the Great Being, the Master and Valdi were in his hot pursuit not far away. Raguel was the first to reach the poor banker. With great strength he took one of the harassing demons off him. The battle that ensued was fierce but short. The punishing angel disposed of the demon like if he was a rag doll before he went to attack another demon dragging Abraham.

By that time Valdi arrived to attack the last demon who was taking away the soul of Wilton-Cough. Abraham kept falling down to the great worry of Vincent which was recalled by telepathy by the Master,

-Concentrate on your demon, Valdi! He is a scorpion demon so watch his tail. My father will look after the soul of your servant. Fight like you have not another day to live, fight.

Doctor Valdi thus told was obliged to focus on his demon within his hands. He realised fast enough that he needed all his attention. The stinging, swirling tail of the demon was giving him the valse of his lifetime to avoid it. Even the lovely valse he had at his wedding couldn't compare in intensity with the one he was having right now. But with his thinking cap on, Valdi was quick to grab the tormenting tail with both hands.

Maintaining his demon that way he swirled it around him with great force to get the scorpion demon so dizzy that when he pushed the tail into the demon's entrails it was almost child's play. The demon succumbed to the move instantly.

When Valdi turned around, he saw a pleased Master of all angels watching him with a satisfied smile who told,

-You are a natural born fighter. Like my father said, you can save and kill with the tip of your fingers. After all your own father was a soldier. Come, it is time to claim your servant. Shoulder to shoulder, I will have your back down there if we need to be forceful to reclaim our Abraham.

Flying by the majestic Raguel, Vincent questioned him,

-Our Abraham? Our? I thought you couldn't care less for him.

The Master corrected,

-What made you think that? I never expressed such an opinion of Wilton-Cough. If you'd listened carefully you would have realised that the soul of Abraham has been given a chance to get his redemption. As the latter is one of my many duties, I will be on his back like a rash for him to get it. As I shall not be lenient with Abraham nor with any soul, you can call what I give as angelic tough love. Did you miss the part when I clearly stated that I was taking his soul under my wings? Hence I haven't given up on him as of yet. I do not kill demons for my pleasure yet two were dusted by my hands for the sake of Abraham. Realise Vincent that his soul has devoted itself to your service, that you are an angel in the army of my son, not only that as an angel, like all angels, you belong now to that peculiar extended feathery family that we are and of which I am the head of, hence my angelic name as the Master. Trust me when I say that I will protect your servant like I will for you and that is with my own life.

In owe Vincent Valdi admitted out loud,

-I have much to learn, haven't I?

Agreeing Raguel pointed far ahead of them, to reassure Valdi, to the ghostly soul of Abraham, which was by now guided and protected by the Great Being,

-Yes, you have but you have an eternity to do so apart if your life is taken by a demon. Please be as careful as I will down there. My father has secured your servant. Let's join them to be their bodyguards. My Father is pretty immune in hell like everywhere, but we never know. Something dark is brewing up hence you had to save my son and you've seen the state of one of many angels which has been wounded in the past few days. It all happened in Wilton Town where a portal to hell was opened. There is a definite sustained daily attack on the angelic army. The angelic casualties have reached a number which we can't ignore. If my father is getting involved and wants to interrogate Lucifer skillfully, I can only warn you that we have an ample problem on our hands on earth and maybe everywhere. We already know that one pure original archangel is a traitor and sold his soul to Lucifer to claim the life of my eldest son. My Gael is dwelling in heaven since a while now, but as you witnessed the state of my last and youngest son you can only guess that the treason runs deeper. My father and I will not get any sleep until we will find out what we need to in order to stop this decimation of angels. As much as you can, just let the Great Being lead the conversation, the covert interrogation, like me, although, I swear, I would love to hit the ground and eviscerate the fallen angel who rules hell, the one who made sure that my eldest was dwelling in heaven. I am sure he knows very well what happened to my youngest son and that his dirty hands engineered it all upon the wish of another traitor.

Vincent Valdi saw the fire within the eyes of the major angel. He realised that this visit to hell was something extremely personal to Raguel. He recalled the Great Being's worries about taking his son to hell with him. He remembered how he employed the word to babysit his son. So it dawned on Valdi all of a sudden that he had a duty to look after Raguel to prevent him to be rash and irrational, to protect him, to halt him to make excess mess which would injure any chance to get crucial information in the enemy's nest. Vincent understood why he was requested to accompany them to hell: as much as the Creator trusted him to save his grandson, as much as he brought Sebastien to him, as much he needed him, the humble Doctor Valdi, to keep a close eye on his son, Raguel. With that realisation in mind, Vincent advised,

-Do you play chess, Master? Do you know how to lay low, lose face by losing a pawn in order to save your queen later? We have a chance to save your entire angelic army by not acting without measures right now. We have to keep this mission as a recognition one at all cost. Remember this quote from Sun Tzu: 'If you know the enemy and know yourself, you need not fear the result of a hundred battles. If you know yourself but not the enemy, for every victory gained you will also suffer a defeat. If you know neither the enemy nor yourself, you will succumb in every battle.' Your father is giving you a chance to know your enemy better. He is putting a sword in your hands for you to be able to strike later with greater might. Do not lose this given opportunity.

Raguel gave an overall look at the new angel at his side and just knew his father had placed a very important spirit in his angelic ranks. He replied,

-We will not. Together as one.

He presented his fist to Valdi who replicated the gesture and touched the angelic fist with his own. When they reached the Great Being and Abraham Wilton-Cough, they were in the midst of hell. The ghost was holding the hand of the Creator, all his bones trembling, he repeated wildly as he took in the sight of hell,

-I am not daunted, I am certainly not daunted, I am far from daunted. Oh good Lord, what is that demon doing to that soul? Oh my, oh my, oh my!

Giggling the Master answered with some sarcasm,

-Do you really want to know Wilton-Cough?

The Great Being intervened straight away with a dark glance to his son,

-We have more pressing matters at hand than tormenting poor dear Abraham's soul, Raguel. Follow me. Remember, let me do the talking. I want all of you to respond as less as possible to any taunt.

Keeping firmly the hand of Wilton-Cough as if he was a child within his strong hand he moved forward and showed the way to everyone leading them to a throne room with bleeding walls. Vincent Valdi looked in owe and disgust at the entire vaulted ceiling made of human bones in a Gothic cathedral's style while Raguel's glance was searching for Lucifer who wasn't on his impressive throne also entirely made of bones. He soon noticed him. The awfully handsome fallen angel was kneeling to his father at the base of his own throne. Lucifer welcomed the visitors,

-My Lord, I wasn't expecting your visit so soon. You are not coming alone?

The Great Being looking around haughtily replied,

-You should run away from me Lucifer, not bow. If you can not accept the basics, you should leave your post.

Standing up, the defiant fallen angel argued,

-Where would I go? Have I not fallen low enough for you?

Without touching Lucifer, the fallen angel was thrown and pinned to the vaulted ceiling by the Creator with great might who replied,

-My dear locust, there is one thing I am good at, I am so gifted, that I can turn water into wine, wine into blood and angels of fire into piles of ashes. The least of your concern is where you will go for you will not exist any longer. I am ready to show you how low you can fall further.

His divine power holding Lucifer on the ceiling released the angel to let him fall on the ground. Sustaining the heavy fall, Lucifer re-assumed a kneeling position by the Great Being told with emotion,

-I will not run away. I admit it, I did it. I submit.

Seeing the blood tears appearing in the eyes of his fallen angel, the Creator demanded lifting in an authoritative manner the chin of Lucifer,

-Let's dust you then. I grant you a little privacy to save your pride from all your demons. You will creep out of life with your great infamous pride intact. Show me where you want to end. My suite will be your only witnesses to your death.

Facing his fate, Lucifer rose and showed the way to his private room inviting,

-Please, follow me, my Lord.

Crying almost silently all the way the fallen angel stated,

-I am so sorry to have upset you. I do not deserve any forgiveness but just know that I am sorry to the Master and to yourself.

An incensed Raguel seized Lucifer and pinning him to the wall of the tortuously long corridor barked,

-We don't need your fake crocodile tears along with your fake sorrow. You are such a despicable filthy disgrace on the face of the earth that I will rejoice over your ashes! Who do you think you are? Act truthfully or I obliterate you right here with great pleasure.

With no fear within his eyes Lucifer retorted,

-I need you to understand Master that I will not beg you to spare me, you are holding a broken angel within your hands, my life is as much yours as your father's. Kill me now, and you will take away all my guilt with a pure erasure. By pleasing yourself, you will please me just as well. I am feeling so unbearably low with an intolerable burden of sins on my shoulders. If I have one prayer to be granted it is for my blood to soil your hands to repay for the life of your son. If I have one plea Raguel is for you to take away my shame and misery weighing down on my soul. Your pleasure will be all mine.

Standing tall, fierce, the son of the Great Being, his hands on the throat of the fallen angel, pressed to choke him to just an inch of his life before he released his grip and threw Lucifer away from him disgusted. Raguel during all that long moment could only acknowledge the true will to die of the fallen angel who didn't lift a hand or a finger to protect himself from the sustain assault. The thought of giving an easy way out to Lucifer only had stopped the Master of all angels to take revenge in that manner. However Raguel did let his frustration of not finishing off Lucifer by kicking the fleshy wall which was looking like the inside of an artery. His fist pierced it easily. From the hole a cascade of maggots poured down. He stepped aside in sheer disgust to ask out loud,

-What is that?

Standing up from his fall, rubbing his extremely bruised throat, trying to catch back his voice and breath, Lucifer answered,

-Everyone needs an army. They trickle down like honey cleaning the place of rotten flesh and organic matter. They are soldiers which know to discern between the garbage and the garden, what to destroy and what to keep. Let's make a move, if you are safe, Master, I am not. You must have pierced the guttering in your bout of understandable anger. That human dead soul with you lot is not safe either. I refused his entry to hell not so long ago.

Taking his advice, the group followed the fallen angel with no further a do. Valdi, full of his natural curiosity, dared to ask,

-Well controlled maggots are safe. They can clean a festering wound properly. Surely they cannot attack a fallen angel nor an immaterial ghost?

This question brought the attention of Lucifer upon Vincent. He gave him a long glance from head to toe before he commented,

-We have a newcomer in our midst, shinning like a brand new coin, glistening feathers, a staggering aura, a knowledge of medicine and demon blood already on his hands. By the way, whoever you are, you need to wash that with holly water as soon as you can for a scorpion demon's blood eats the skin away slowly but surely. Now, this new angel will annoy a good couple of archangels. May I know his name, my Lord? I must say he is a very dashing creation which will bring to him many envious, lots of jealousy and enemies in his trail, just like your Raguel.

An offended Master commented with gusto,

-I haven't got a lot of enemies in my trail!

Lucifer snapped at him,

-Deny it all you want! Be proudly blind and believe that you are loved by all! How do you explain one son in heaven and one that was about to join him but for that new angel's intervention? Down here in my gutter, I see more than you think I do and I know much more. Your lineage has been attacked. No enemies, I have been an instrument of your enemies! I have two archangels that sold their souls to me. Your father possess seven. I dread to see the next one that will come to ask for you. Just to let you know the truth and be truthful as you required, we are not on sweet terms together. I will never be good enough for you, and you will never be good enough for me. Look at what you didn't take from me, my life, yet I am a plague that will plague yours because I would have loved to be a son of your father. I believe I would have done a better job. Why do you think you are tasked to do angelic humans? Why are you not tasked to do good traditional angel made from pure fire?

Raguel was about to strangle again the fallen angel walking by him but Vincent intervened, holding the Master's hands up in the air before they reach their target. Valdi only gave a reminder with his prompt gesture,

-Taunts!

Regaining his countenance immediately, Raguel gave a dark glance to Lucifer with a warning,

-Trust me when I say that I will plague you as much as you plague me.

The fallen angel grinned as he stated,

-Reciprocal hatred, welcome to hell and my universe.

Lucifer opened the door to a room which looked like a prison cell and invited the group in with a theatrical gesture. The Great Being entered with Wilton-Cough which he was still holding the hand to. Valdi followed suit while Raguel held the door to invite his enemy in, not trusting him for one second,

-After you, Lucifer.

Once the fallen angel was within the room, the Master destroyed the wooden door into little pieces. Lucifer commented with a smirk,

-As if I needed more combustible elements to sustain the fire in hell! When you have finished to make firewood you can come and join the talks with the devil, Raguel.

If the Master gave a dark look to Lucifer, however he came into the suspicious room, small, almost bare, so humid that green moss was growing on the stone walls enclosing it. The single bed consisted of planks, with the luxury of fresh hay as a mattress and an almost torn to pieces red blanket. At the bottom of the bed, a nicely carved chest made of the darkest wood was the only piece of furniture which didn't scream poverty to the visitors. Lucifer got busy presenting wooden chairs and stools to his guests in an affable manner before picking up the shards of wood from the broken door and lighting a fire with it in the sturdy fireplace made of unpolished black granite. The Great Being seeing his unease commenced the talks,

-Our new angel is called Vincent Valdi. He is solely of human stock.

Lucifer stood up, smiled with generosity to Vincent, welcoming the fact that he was allowed to know his name. He gave a thankful look to the Creator as he announced,

-Solely, he smells slightly divine to me. He will create a stir, I can tell you that, my Lord, already. I can also tell you that you lost Michael's soul over the Mighty One. I cannot fathom yet what the consequences of Sebastien staying alive will be but him living may prevent another deal done attacking directly Raguel. No archangels dared to attack you so closely my Lord. But I am afraid all the time that it can happen. But their course of action are and will be lowly therefore through me.

Going to his chest, making a magical key appear within his hands, Lucifer opened it before he took a parchment from it and brought it to the Great Being. Kneeling by the Creator, the fallen angel presented the document,

-Here, my Lord. You can check for yourself. All I can add is that there was no way of stopping Michael.

The Great Being opened the scroll in an affected manner stating sternly,

-My belief is that you didn't try hard enough. Why do you think you dwell in this cell in hell? Why are you not tasked to make angels? Isn't it because you are only good to rip their wings and make them fall in your trail? How can I be more blunt? What can you create apart from chaos? Can you impress me by clearing up your trail and repair it, even if it is little by little, step by step? How dare you boasting to my son that you would have done a better job than him when you obviously can't do yours and is handing me, yet again, the soul resignation of another archangel. You can only dream to create angels therefore destroying any you see is your only course of action. But even if you were the only one left, I would destroy the living day out of you for all the loss you made me suffer.

Standing up from the wooden armchair, the Creator turned about the room, handed the rolled parchment back to Lucifer demanding with a cool yet mounting anger,

-Is your gift of persuasion lost in your own pockets, Lucifer? Have you completely lost the sense of yourself? Because I can tell you that my patience is lost. My last grandson!!! What were you reasonably thinking? That I would let it pass? Respond, you, Locust!

As much as the ground started to shake under the divine wrath, the fallen angel began to tremble. He went to hide his fear by placing back the precious scroll in his wooden chest and tried to gather himself up to give a reply,

-My Lord, as I said earlier, I was expecting you to come because I knew you would not let it pass. Believe it or not I was being your Locust, your maggot, your soldier when I performed what I did. You have another angelic rebellion brewing all around you this time more nefarious than the first for they are attacking your descendants. I have to play a serious and credible double game in order to inform you. And, yes, yes, you are right, if I can not make angels at least I can warn you of all the traitorous garbage of archangels you have in your garden. How is the Mighty One doing?

Lucifer casually went to a small book shelve full of manuscripts, hoping that his plea would have calmed the grief of the Great Being. But it didn't calmed down Raguel who barked at him but was held back by his father,

-How do you care? How dare you asking about my son?

Taking an ancient leather bounded black book, Lucifer gave his acerbic answer along with an incandescent look to the Master,

-Because I do care about him. Unlike you and your eldest, this son of yours doesn't take a break. He doesn't go to his father to beg for holidays complaining how hard his work is, leaving the place to become totally chaotic. Even pinned on a pillory, he always find the strength to carry on. Therefore I care to repeat: How is the Mighty One doing?

Hit by the home truth blow Raguel became pale and silent. However his father never losing his north, south, east or west responded by another question,

-What do you expect, my Locust?

Lucifer gave a grin with his educated reply, his eyes desperately searching the ones of the divine entity in front of him for confirmation,

-My Lord, I expect the Mighty One to survive anything thrown at him. I didn't gave him my best shot, by a long shot. No, the best shot would have been myself but, well, I would be ever so reluctant to do it. Like your other Punisher, Mighty is capable to erase me without any due respect. At least, your gracious self had a care for my pride by asking me where I wanted to die and telling me that you would do so in the privacy of your small entourage. But I am digressing. I expect Mighty to survive the blow is my answer, and I, nasty locust that I am, threw at him one strong enough to keep him aware and on his feet in the future. He must never let his guard down. As I smell his blood coming from you three, apart from your ghost, I can only guess that this valuable lesson will be taken in a serious manner.

His answer fuelled the anger of Raguel who was ready to assault the fallen angel again but Vincent put himself in front of him to prevent any rash action, however Valdi took it upon himself to argue with Lucifer,

-You are a liar! You intended to kill Sebastien. You said Mighty was about to join his brother in heaven if it was not for me!

A deeply interested Abraham Wilton-Cough went by the side of Vincent Valdi forming a wall with him to keep the son of the Creator away from any harm or a fight. He put in his own strongly opinionated word,

-Of course he is a liar! Devil, D-E-V-I-L, what can you expect from him?

Lucifer confused the both of them by opening the book within his hands in a self secured manner before replying with great calm,

-Angel Valdi, I clearly said 'about' but also 'heaven'. Of course I knew the risk, I caused it. But I also believe in my Lord. He and you saved the night and the Mighty One. Sebastien was strong enough to be saved which I expected. But in the worst case, my intention would have been to give his soul back to his grandfather for him to take him to heaven. Because the Mighty One deserves heaven not hell. Like you, ghost, you saved many souls therefore I rejected your entrance to my realm. But you are not good enough to go to heaven yet. Like me you are a grey area, neither entirely black, neither white, just a servant that will do time to hope to reach the unattainable.

Slightly baffled Wilton-Cough questioned in an argumentative tone,

-You do not know me! I would remember you if you rejected my soul from here. But I do not recall your face. You are lying again. You don't even know my name. You just said your ghost this and your ghost that! I am no servant! You do not know me! You do not know Valdi! You had to ask for his name. So stop pretending, be truthful like the Master ordered. Lies and pretence will get you nowhere.

This intervention made Lucifer grin with some hilarity before he corrected the ghost in earnest,

-It lead me at the helm of hell along with my great pride. Abraham Wilton-Cough, son of Terah, proud descendant of Noah Wilton, your mother dwells in my realm. Know, my dear soul, that I am a shape shifter and assume many forms. You may recognise me as the gatekeeper of hell.

For a split second Lucifer assumed that shape,

becoming a colossal multi headed demon with limbs the size of Doric columns. This startled Abraham who stepped backwards almost into the arms of the strong Raguel who put his hand on the ghost's shoulder to reassure him. Abraham admitted in a trembling voice,

-I do recognise you!

An amused Lucifer turned back into his very handsome angelic form stating,

-Here we are, now you remember me. I will not start shape shifting into a snake to give you the apple of knowledge but nonetheless to joggle your memory further, my ghost, I will only mention that I handed you to the gracious angel Abigail.

An already pale Wilton-Cough turned to Valdi and Raguel to confirm with a vehement positive nod of his head,

-He did. He gave me to Abigail who took me to lay in my grave.

Approaching slowly but surely, Lucifer carried on,

-So you can not pretend any longer that I don't know you, Abraham Wilton-Cough. As I said I know much more than I usually let appear to do so: Your long agony, your feverish nightmare that made you change your dreadful first will, your eldest son whose cursed soul you saved. Shall I carry on or shall I stop here? Are you convinced enough of my truthfulness, your former atheist angelic master and you?

Before any of them could answer, the fallen angel exhibited the palms of Wilton-Cough in a firm manner demanding,

-How dare you calling me a liar when you lie yourself, Abraham? How do you explain those, servant? Is your memory that challenged that you can't remember belonging to an angel?

Reclaiming his hands from the cold grasp of Lucifer, and rubbing them together with some anxiety, Abraham replied,

-It's a technicality. Angel Valdi will never treat me as a servant.

His begging eyes met the ones of Vincent who confirmed immediately,

-Yes, it is a formality. I respect him too much to treat

Abraham as a servant.

Lucifer commented with an evil grin,

-So his soul is not yours if your seal is just to make one believe it is the case.

Valdi corrected putting Abraham protectively behind him swiftly,

-Oh, I can assure you he is mine. He is family. Do not lay your evil paws on him anymore, for you will pay and you will pay dearly!

Raguel stepped forward, protecting further with his angelic body Wilton-Cough with an order,

-Vade Retro Satana!

It threw Lucifer against the wall of the cell violently. When he was back upon his feet, the fallen angel looked in sheer pain at the Great Being to demand an explanation,

-You held the hands of Abraham. Why?

His answer came as a riddle,

-A damn will never stop the water flowing if I wish to.

Lucifer shook his head in desperation yet smiled giving his assurance,

-Your wishes are my orders. I will stay away from this servant of yours.

Without realising his hands were bleeding, Lucifer wiped his forehead before he added,

-I know he helped to destroy an important demon, but I relinquish my fair claim on Abraham's soul. Taking Raguel in hell was enough of an incentive to make sure I let Wilton-Cough go back with you. Although Abraham has an interesting personality which would have mildly amused me for a while, I will be happy to see him leave hell.

Raguel asserting his ascendance over Lucifer went to him to check both his bleeding hands asking with some annoyance,

-Now, why are you bleeding so much when I barely

touched you so far? Give me your hands.

The fallen angel obeyed without questions silently avoiding the harsh stare of the Master. What the Master saw surprised him, and he dragged Lucifer to the Great Being to exhibit his palms to him and his discovery. Lucifer fell on his knees without a word but full of shame.

The Creator only commented without showing any emotion,

-Those must hurt.

Lucifer agreed silently with a positive nod.

Then the Creator taking a good look around the almost monastic cell proposed coldly,

-Do you want me to remove your deed?

Standing back up, almost trembling from an indescribable passion, Lucifer replied hurriedly in a begging voice,

-No, please no! It will hurt me more than having them. I'd rather suffer a thousand deaths.

If Raguel found the answer suspiciously brave, his father who seemed totally detached from the situation however told,

-Lucifer, you are treading a very thin and narrow line. Let me resume, you are helping my enemies very well, so well that they come back to you for more. What do I get in the entire affair is just a who did it and was a villain in hiding all along, but also warnings and casualties. If you can only put yourself in my shoes for an instant, imagine my wrath, I would still follow the first advice I gave you when I saw you, if I were you, which is to run away from me, very, very far away as fast as you can. I think it is grand time for me to have a toast, a toast on the ashes of all the creations I did of pure fire which for some reason or another find themselves much more superior to my other creations and want to jeopardise my rather beautiful world.

Silence fell on the entire cell. All eyes were on Lucifer. Either from good acting or truthfully, the fallen angel went to the Creator knelt and bowed his head saying in almost a whisper,

-I am yours to be disposed off.

Raguel was uneasy about it and made it known by punching the fallen angel with great strength in the face shouting,

-What do you have to say for yourself? What? Don't even dream of an easy send off! A thousand deaths is what you'd rather suffer you said, I will give you a taste of it. What do you have to say, scumbag?

Faced with rage and anger, Lucifer fought back crying loudly,

-I have nothing to say for myself, nothing! Sorry is the only word you will get from me. Sorry, that's it! I am his creature, let me die a thousand deaths under his hands.

Both angels were fighting on the ground with a palpable and physical hatred so fierce that blood soon poured on both sides. Valdi helped the Great Being to separate the two protagonists. It took a good minute for both angels to calm down after being split up. While Valdi maintained Raguel and was already assessing him physically for any wounds, a very damaged Lucifer was under the hands of his Creator. Loosing consciousness the fallen angel met the eyes of the Great Being thinking with honesty that his last moment had come, knowing that he had sustained a wound too close to his heart to probably be fatal, he told without strength,

-Sorry.

As Lucifer closed his eyes, Raguel shouted to his father,

-He is faking it! Smack him!

Giving his son a disapproving yet worried look The Great Being ruled,

-Raguel, you know what I told you. Valdi take my son to Williams and provide him first aid care. Do not worry about leaving Wilton-Cough behind, I will bring him back to you once I have finished with Lucifer.

He made a vortex spiralling upwards appear on the ceiling of the cell. Valdi bowed respectfully to him before taking away Raguel who was leaning heavily upon him. Abraham saw the two angels leave via the vortex with some concern but he went by the Great Being rallying himself together with his soldiering on spirit to ask,

-How may I help you, my Lord?

-Bring me a glass of water and that white cloth.

The Creator smiled kindly as he watched the ghost obeying with diligence before returning his attention back to Lucifer whom he slapped back to consciousness.

#

Appearing straight into the bedroom of Lawrence the two angels made quite an impression. Miss White was utterly worried by the amount of blood which covered both of them while Doctor Williams went straight to them querying,

-Where is the Great Being? What happened?

Helping Raguel into an armchair Doctor Valdi informed,

-The Lord is still down there, in hell. He is with Wilton-Cough. The Master and Lucifer did fight and when we left Lucifer was properly out of it.

Still feeling some rage, Raguel corrected,

-Knowing Lucifer, he can fake it! He can play dead for all I know and my father is still with him.

Valdi taking the shirt off the angel, who had resumed his human appearance, scolded,

-We would still be down there by your father if you haven't played rough and tumble with the devil. We would have provided him back up if needed and carried on helping him to gather information. Now let's mend you. It looks worst than it is. But your shoulder is definitely dislocated.

Turning to Williams, Doctor Valdi ordered,

-We need to do a garrot to stop the bleeding on his left arm. Then we have to put his shoulder back into position. With a few suture points here and there, he will be almost as good as brand new. However I suspect he has a fractured rib.

Doctor Williams, getting all that was required, demanded,

-And you, Vincent, are you alright?

His request was joined by an anxious Whilhelmina who commented,

-Vincent, are you hurt? Do you realise that you are covered in blood as well?

Doctor Valdi replied with certainty,

-I am fine. Do not worry about me. It is mainly the Master's blood as I helped him out of hell.

But the Master contradicted his angel straight away,

-William, Valdi is not fine. Some of the blood on him is of a scorpion demon he killed and highly venomous. We all need to wash ourselves in holy water. He also helped to separate the fight between Lucifer and I. He received a share of scratches and bruises to be looked at. If you take the shirt off our proud Italian angel you will find that his blood was shed as well.

Reacting immediately Doctor Williams demanded the shirt of Valdi who reluctantly gave it displaying his muscular torso with its fighting credential. It pleased the Master who boasted,

-Wasn't I ever so right? Here, here, look at that wound, William, that needs stitches and that bruise, massive, I knew I missed Lucifer at one moment but did hit someone. I knew it wasn't my father for, well, he would have let me know in a very harsh way. That will require some ice. Lord! Does his torso remind me of the one of my son?! Those scars, Valdi, you have a map of them just like my Sebastien! What have you been up to?

Miss White replied for Doctor Valdi taking the shirts of both angels with care,

-He embodies the law and order in Wilton-Town. Sometimes he gets hurt doing so. This nasty scar above his heart, which missed it by less than an inch he received it protecting a young lady from being raped by the gang of Wilton-Town led by Darren. The girl was saved. The members of the gang had a serious beating including Darren but Valdi suffered a severe stab wound in his chest. He only collapsed at my doorsteps after ringing the bell of my hotel. I was able to tend to his wound. Doctor Valdi is made of resilience and courage.

Raguel nodded his agreement as he ordered,

-I have no doubt that it is the case my dear Miss White. You should have seen that brand new angel killing that scorpion demon. He used wit, 'savoir-faire' as well as strength. Burn those shirts for us please and may I ask you to demand to the good Theo to sort us out with a lot of holy water?

With diligence Whilhelmina left the room after a courteous bow and her positive answer,

-I will see to it.

While Doctor Williams applied a garrot to the arm of the Master, Valdi asked him,

-How is Lawrence doing since we left?

Giving a glance to the bed, William told,

-Much improved. We have signs of movements but he is still not conscious. I was waiting for your advice to stop the transfusion. All I can say to you is that what we did to remove the sigil under the advice and with the help of Wilton-Cough had its impact on the boy, a positive one, as he became more responsive. It is all written in the notebook.

As Doctor Valdi going through the notes smiled with satisfaction at the improvements witnessed during his absence, Maximilien added whilst yawning,

-Lawrence muttered my name, Doctor Valdi, he even pressed my hand.

Putting the notebook down back upon the chest of drawers Vincent gave his verdict,

-Then Max, it is grand time for you to go to bed and have a rest. Beforehand I want you to grab a large bowl of soup in the kitchen and drink plenty of water.

The angelic soldier stood up as soon as his arm was freed. He gave a look to the Master in a silent need for confirmation, which came promptly forward,

-Do as he said, Max, you have before you a future archangel and Punisher.

Maximilien bowed with profound respect to Valdi then the Master before giving a firm and warm handshake to Doctor Williams before he left the room. An impressed Williams asked the Master once the door was closed,

-Is that true?

Submitting himself to the medical care of Doctor Valdi, Raguel confirmed,

-Yes. Archangel Raphael sold his soul for the death of my eldest son Gael. Lucifer fulfilled his part of the deal. Raphael is lost. My father has enough of the pretentious angels made of pure fire who believe they are superior. From what he said down in hell I can tell you that he has a harsh punishment in store for them. It will not go pass him if he replaces the entire lot. We learnt from Lucifer that archangel Michael sold his soul for the death of my youngest son. We know that the deal nearly came to fruition.

Giving a helping hand to Valdi who was doing suture points on the Master's arm repairing a gaping wound, Doctor Williams amazed enquired,

-Michael, a traitor? I find it hard to believe.

Raguel replied with great sadness in his eyes,

-However it is true and verified. His seal is on a pact with the devil.

Williams shaking his head in disbelief with tears in his eyes of incomprehension cried out loud,

-But why? Why?

The Master explained with great calm,

-I will tell you why. You have sentiments called jealousy, envy and pride out and about everywhere. Mix the three together in someone and you obtain a lethal cocktail. Look, Raphael lost his soul because he was jealous of you and your very existence hurts his pride. Your medical expertise is equal to his if not superior in many aspect and respect because you are out there in the field constantly practising while he is sitting pretty in the thought that he has done enough for eternity. He ordered the killing of who made you an angel to prevent any more angel like you to come into existence. You put in jeopardy all his pretences. This is the fact of the matter and you will have to promise me to be careful because I believe Raphael having lost his soul, has not a lot more important to lose, therefore he potentially can put you under his sword like he said he would. He has always been an angel of his words.

Looking at the neat stitching on his arm Raguel paused before he continued his explanation,

-As for Michael, I am afraid to say that the same lethal cocktail must have come into play. My Mighty has been such a successful fighter, killed so many demons that I am afraid to say he has become more glorious than Michael who, again, has sat upon his laurels for a long time. However if my father gave me the cues and clues to understand their traitorous behaviours, he also hinted that our Doctor Valdi was meant. He was meant to be and by him. You can guess what this means William. At the death of Gael, my father gathered what was going on with the original angels and as much as they were plotting the undermining of his creations, he created ways to foil them hence standing here we have one of his first new knight on the chess board. Valdi is probably the first of the new set of archangels which will replace all of the old ones who defect. Hence my father brought my son to be saved by him. Hence Valdi was my bodyguard in hell. Hence he took care of teaching this angel how to fly himself. How often does my father take charge of the tuition of an angel since I exist?

Doctor Williams gave a good glance at Doctor Valdi who was busy dealing with the next wound of Raguel seemingly ignoring the conversation, then commented,

-Master, you are in charge of the tuition along with Sebastien of all angels since a very very long time. Your father usually never take part in the schooling of an angel. So Vincent is meant?

The Master confirmed with a firm positive nod of his head, but Vincent Valdi dismissed,

-Come on you two, I just happen to be, that is all. As for your father, his flying tuition was just a crash course because I had no option but to come and help with the situation you are dealing with in Wilton Town with your angels being attacked left, right and centre.

Cocking his eyebrows, Raguel smirked as he stated,

-You can be in denial all you want, my angel, for as long as you want but I am telling you: if my father said you were meant, he means it because he had a hand in your creation. Beside that let me remind you the words of Lucifer concerning you: he clearly said that you did smell slightly divine. He was not speaking of perfume let me assure you, not after your long flight across the ocean. No, that fallen angel has a canny capacity to know everything about one in a matter of minutes if not seconds. I can tell that he was interested by you.

Again Vincent Valdi replied by a dismissal,

-Don't be ridiculous! Lucifer paid more attention to Wilton-Cough than me.

The Master who strongly withstood any stitches done to him corrected,

-Isn't it you who said we were down there to learn about the enemy? Well, let me tell you what I learnt and what I know from knowing that fallen angel way before the day you were born. Lucifer paid so much attention to Abraham first as a test put at your own doors but mainly to check which type of new angel you were. He realised, in that gruesome corridor of his, by the way my father was keeping the hand of Abraham in his own hand that something important was there. Even when I tried to take his attention away from it all, to keep his sens of deduction at bay by pinning him on the wall, he knew that something of significance was on the palms of Abraham.

The curiosity of Valdi was at his pick as he asked,

-Surely, your move in the corridor was just made of pure impulse? You just wanted to finish Lucifer off.

The Master smirked with his reply,

-If I managed to fool you as well, my dear Vincent, I was pretty convincing then. Well, I had no problem to play the part of a father seeking revenge for his sons because ultimately I truly am one. But even so, given my physical state which tell another story, I do have self control.

Vincent couldn't help laughing irresistibly begging,

-Come, you had no self control down there! You are kidding me? Have you seen the bruise you inflected to me? That was a true punch. That was not fake!

It was the turn of Raguel to laugh while he said in earnest,

-The last fight was part punishment, part diversion, Vincent. I had to take you back above as much as you did have to take me back above. I created the situation.

Valdi regaining his countenance demanded,

-So tell me what truly happened down there?

In a very serious tone the Master replied,

-When Lucifer checked the hands of Abraham, he discovered your seal within them. It is an extremely important one. You can not start to realise how significant your seal is. The rooster means that you comes from the Lord. It is a symbol shared by my two brothers and I, and my two sons. It isn't given to anyone, trust me. Williams will teach you all the significance of it. But my angel, you did a big mistake, you answered that Abraham was family to Lucifer. Treat the one you love the most in a condescending manner in front of an enemy. Lucifer knew from that moment that if he attacked Wilton-Cough it would have stirred you enough to fight with him and then you would have both become fair game for him. This is why I stepped in to protect you both from his possible intention.

Understanding, Valdi commented,

-That was the Vade Retro Satana that sent Lucifer flying across the room, wasn't it?

When his last stitch was done, the angelic Master stood up from the armchair confirming,

-Yes, it was. Clever you, I would pat your head but unfortunately my shoulder needs to be seen to. I am glad you kept the worst to the last. Now, I discovered something very important, something that my father did hint me about previously, that it was the case about Lucifer.

As Doctor Valdi was preparing to relocate the shoulder of the tall angel, he gave the signal to Doctor Williams to distract the mind of Raguel from the procedure which William did with diligence but also true curiosity,

-What did you learn about Lucifer that we don't already know?

When Valdi performed the brutal putting back into place of his shoulder, the Master replied,

-My William, as bad as he is, Lucifer is a true servant of my father. Do you remember that the Creator removed his marks from his palms? No, you can't, it was before you. Lucifer, remembering the seal of the Great Being, carved it on the flesh of his own palms back. His wounds are not sealed so he keeps digging at them but they are old, very old, we are talking more than thousands of years. He has deep respect for my Father. His sore heart and soul are still belonging to him deep down. He is such a conflicted angel, with double standards, double rules and I can tell you that he is so worn out that he seeks his death but at the hands of my father. He knows he can never be a son to the Creator, not even an adopted one, that even as a servant he was rejected. He has no wish to live any further because my father is his only hope. He justifies, somehow, all his actions by him. He isn't even asking or begging for forgiveness. I saw true sadness in his eyes and whenever he said sorry, it was not faked but truly meant. Now, I know what the seal of god does, because I have it being his slave and servant as well as being his son.

He showed his marks within his palms to Williams and Valdi before he continued moving his shoulder,

-That feels much better! Valdi, you are a true angel. Now let me tell you that each time you step out of the Creator's desire, the seal will bleed and that the pain will be excruciating. Lucifer's makeshift seal bled profusely because his intentions were sincerely to hurt you, Vincent, by attacking Wilton-Cough, then you. This is why I dragged Lucifer to my father for him to acknowledge the fact. But also to let him know that I was going to do something drastic and fake a situation to take the danger away from you, Valdi.

A stunned Vincent Valdi watched the senior angel already punching the air with expert boxing moves. Full of questions, he asked,

-Surely, you are not the servant of your father, his slave? In all honesty, you fooled me beautifully down there.

The Master explained,

-Sometimes you have to do whatever is necessary to protect someone. You claimed Abraham Wilton-Cough to protect him and his soul. Well, the same happened to me a very long time ago. My father felt it necessary to give me this extra protection. I do serve him most loyally. In my heart I am his true slave because I will do anything for him. I am his servant and I have no shame to admit it because my soul belongs to him. In regards to you, my angel, you need to learn how to use your poker face when you are in front of the enemy. You, who seems to be a keen chess player, must know that your opponent will strategically remove the best pieces surrounding your King and Queen before going for them. Learn from the old angel that I am whose first son has been removed from the game and the second one nearly followed suit. It was a very good attempt as well. They removed some very decent soldiers of Sebastien by wounding them before going for him. Why do you think my father got involved to save the situation? The next major piece on his board is myself. Lucifer stated clearly that no one came for me yet. The yet gives it away. He expects it. If he gets to do a deal to bring my end, he will help with pleasure whoever wants me out.

Sighing deeply Raguel added,

-If I am out of the picture nothing will stop any primordial entities to go for my father. Lucifer made it clear that he was facing another angelic rebellion more serious than the first one. The first happened when I took a leave after being wounded in battle. But, what I want to say to you, Vincent, my message is that Abraham is the first soul you are taking under your wings as an angel and if you show like you did down there how much you care for him, your opponents are going to try to destroy his spirit in order to get to you. So just be a clever player. Lucifer knows that Wilton-Cough is your Achilles heel now. He knows Abraham is stuck as a spirit because decently enough he refused him at the gates of hell. He can send legions of entities to harass Abraham. It is within his power. You must know how intransigent Wilton-Cough was within his lifetime about the repayments of his loans. It caused more than a couple of suicides. One father of a large family died of exhaustion in his field, dropping dead like a fly from a cardiac arrest, causing a dozen orphans, just because he tried to meet his repayment. But the widower just couldn't do so even with all the strength his limbs could give him. Like Lucifer said Abraham Wilton-Cough is a grey area. He is not the worst soul by all means but he has a lot of amends to do. Trust me when I say that your servant will be visited by the ghosts of his past. You and I will have to make sure that Wilton-Cough keeps it together despite the torments he will face. A way to do that is to task your servant, not to keep him focused and busy, although this can work, but to allow him to redeem himself faster. If I still stand by what I said that Wilton-Cough is a liability, I also agree with my father to recognise that he is indeed a soldier within a soldier. Abraham's will to help is truly present therefore we must let him do so, under supervision, as much as we can. I know you are rather new to all this, but as I trickle down orders for the angelic army, you will pass down his orders to Abraham. I do not care if you treat him as an equal or family in my army or if you show him respect. In the army of my son, it is the musketeers way of one for all and all for one. We stand for one another and by each other. Just remember to treat him condescendingly in front of an enemy who could think that his soul means a lot to you. By doing so you may hurt Abraham's pride a little, but as it will protect his soul much better from any harm or attack, you can only recognise and admit that his pride is a small price to pay for his safeguard.

Taking the talk with a very serious demeanour Valdi

answered,

-I promise I will be more careful in the future.

At the last word of his promise, Father Odell arrived with a large bucket of water and a worried look on his face. Putting the bucket down, he was about to give a manly hug to his friend, at the sight of him, asking with anxiety,

-Vince, how was hell?

The Master interposed himself to prevent the embrace to happen,

-Not now Odell! You can do all the welcoming embrace you want after your friend is clean from any venomous demonic blood. Otherwise you will have to prepare another bucket for yourself.

Father Odell took the cue while the senior angel presented the bucket to Valdi to wash himself. Vincent started with his hands before thoroughly cleaning his torso while he replied to his friend to relieve him from his unease,

-It's alright my Theo. The Master is only too right to be cautious. As for hell I found it frighteningly interesting in my honest opinion. As for Lucifer, his guts make me cringe.

Showing his great surprise, Father Odell screamed with curiosity despite himself,

-You saw Lucifer!?

Within the bed in the room, a great stir happened, Lawrence responded to the scream by his own,

-I am free!

All heads turned to the young angel and Doctor Williams stated the obvious, going to the bed immediately,

-He is finally awake! Lawrence, my boy, Lawrence, how do you feel?

If Lawrence smiled to the old Doctor, it was not him that answered to his question, it was the Great Being who appeared in the room majestically, along with the humble ghost of Wilton-Cough at that instant,

-He will feel much better, my William, his soul which was

held in hostage in hell has been released. His body which has been saved by Doctor Valdi and yourself will recover much faster and with the pugnacity of Abraham the curse on the boy angel has been lifted.

The Master had a much relieved smile on his face at the sight of his father, standing tall within the room, safe and well. Valdi expressed his own relief along with his curiosity,

-How did it go since our departure?

With great excitement, Abraham Wilton-Cough recounted,

-It was the Lord's justice through and through. It started with slaps and Lucifer's feet were put on fire and...

However he couldn't finish the tale as the Great Being ordered with authority,

-Quiet, Abraham! Raguel, how are you doing?

The son smiled to his father giving his answer,

-I am surviving for another day. To be honest there is no need to worry. First because I have seen much worst. Second, because of the expertise of Doctor Valdi and Williams, I will be able to fight tomorrow.

The Creator turned to Valdi, appreciating him from a head to toe glance before he stated,

-Then it is your turn to be looked after Vincent. For your first trip to hell ending up with just a few scratches is not a bad outing. You did pretty well. You stood your ground and were not afraid to get involved when needed. You will make a good Punisher like the Mighty One and the Master. Follow their tuition to the letter. Doctor Williams, please tend to him. Abraham, go to your angelic master and help Williams to look after him. Vincent still has to take a good look at our angel Daniel as soon as he can. Raguel, Father Odell follow me.

#

Following the Creator to the garden of the 'Crying White Doe' hotel, Raguel asked his father for confirmation,

-So Valdi is definitely to become a Punishing Angel?

The Great Being nodding affirmatively ruled,

-Yes, he is. You witnessed as well as I did that he showed no fear in front of anything or anyone in hell. Not only that, he is a born protector.

Joining the conversation as best as he could about his best friend, Father Odell told,

-Vince is fearless. But he is not all fists and fights, he is fair with it all. He delivers when needed, only when needed.

Raguel gave a condescending smile to Theo with his agreement,

-We know that, Theo. Us, taking him to hell was a test and he passed his test with flying colours. I will let you in a little secret of ours, your friend will become an archangel.

While the Great Being opened the back door leading to the garden, he made an inviting gesture to let his followers enter first. Father Odell turned to the Master with great surprise to question,

-Vincent, an archangel? But, but a few days, hours ago he was an atheist!?

Raguel replied to him as they followed the Great Being to the well,

-It doesn't matter. All that matter are his heart and soul. He wears his heart on his sleeve. Like my father said, Valdi is a born protector. Down in hell, he protected the soul of Abraham Wilton-Cough from Lucifer with a fierce warning to him. He pushed Abraham behind himself and was ready to fight for his soul with the ruler of hell himself.

A pale yet curious Theo asked,

-What happened then?

While the Creator got a bucket of water from the well, his son answered,

-I intervened. But I am pretty sure if it did come to it, a fight between Lucifer and Valdi could have turned to the advantage of your best friend. When Vincent separated me from my own fight with Lucifer, he was fearless enough to put himself in between and I saw him protecting me from more blows, acting as a shield. His hand stopped the fist of Lucifer at one moment, he grasped it in the air and I could swear he twisted it and I heard it crack.

His father putting a bucket before him confirmed,

-You did hear it as I did. Vincent broke the right wrist of Lucifer. It will take the fallen angel a good six months for his wrist to heal. This fracture as well as your last couple of blows were enough to make Lucifer feel faint, truly in pain, but also to call a time out. He wasn't able to fight any longer.

Raguel gave a winning smile with his conclusion,

-So he faked death, the scoundrel. I told you he was! How cowardly can you get?

The Great Being replied sternly,

-If everyone is treating you like a bug to squash, you can get a survival instinct very fast. Is it being a coward or being intelligent under the circumstances? My son, Lucifer has learnt the lesson to live to fight for another day a very long time ago.

Turning to Theo Odell, he ordered,

-Theo, hold both of my hands, I will impart you with this angelic gift: Whenever you will touch water, it will turn holy from now on.

Father Odell did as he was told. Blue bolts of electricity passed from the hands of the Creator to the ones of the vicar of Wilton Town who was all at once in awe and overwhelmed to the point of tears. But once the deed was done, the Great Being smiled to him with such kindness that Theo looked at his own glowing hands with amazement yet confidence. He asked,

-Are my hands holy?

The Creator took Theo by the hand and lead him by wilted flowers, demanding,

-Touch those daisies, Theo and see for yourself how holy are your hands.

Obeying Odell went wild with happiness when he saw the flowers reviving under his touch. He revived all of the flowers in the border before returning by the Great Being like a child to his father, beaming with pride to ask with great interest,

-What can I do with those?

The Great Being smiled to him warmly as he answered,

-A fair few things. At the touch of your fingers you will be able to revive vegetation from a tree to a fern passing by an entire field. If you take a small animal within your hands, let's just say a little dead field mouse, or a sparrow who did hit a window during a storm, you will give them a new lease of life. For larger animals, you can help but you will have to add prayers and get my agreement or not upon their lives. As for humans, their hearts will have more chance to restart under the pressure of your hands, although it will not be a given, and you will have to pray me as well.

Taking a large dead white moth from the gravel on the path within his hands with utter care, Father Odell looked at the lifeless insect with sadness stating,

-I guess it doesn't work with insects.

But the Great Being corrected him,

-No, it does. You have to wish its life to be restored to me. You can do it, just do a silent prayer from your heart and soul. Then you will see it happen.

Enclosing gently the night moth in his hands, Theo made the wish. As soon as he did so, he could feel the gentle flickering of the wings of the moth brushing against the skin of his fingers. With trepidation, he opened his palms to see the creature alive within them. He gave a joyful look to the Creator as his gratefulness poured out,

-Thank you, thank you so much, thank you so so much.

His happiness pleased the Master who told,

-We thought it would be the perfect angelic gift for you. I've seen you caring for birds and other animals big and small. You love and respect my father's creatures. Now, my Theo, I will develop your hands into healing hands. Like Doctor Williams and Vincent, you will be able to do wonders on humans and angels. With your future wife Whilhelmina, you will become a nurse of the angelic army of my son. That role will not cancel the one you both have in the logistic team that Sebastien is forming.

Agreeing Father Odell confirmed,

-I understand, Master. You know, I don't look like much, but I am hardworking and I intend to help you and Sebastien. You can count on me.

Raguel smiled kindly giving only a knowing 'I told you so' look to his father who stated,

-We already know we can count on you, Theo. You proved yourself to us. You bravely helped Sebastien with your clever use of holy water on demons yesterday so much so that he came up with an idea well actually a fair few ideas. Now, put your hands in that water, make it holy for my son to have a good clean from all that demonic blood he and Valdi faced then take a turn with me in the garden and I will tell you all about the ideas of my grandson.

Theo Odell obeyed. Not only did he marvelled at the water within the bucket bubbling at the contact of his fingers, he could see light coming from the tip of his fingers. Father Odell then followed the Great Being when his deed was done to leave the Master of all angels wash himself with some privacy. Theo was still full of wonder about his gift but was ever so pleased and peaceful to possess it. He noticed that the large white moth had landed on his shoulder and settled there quite happily despite him walking fast enough to catch the pace of the Creator.

After a few paces, the Great Being turned to his smiling companion to comment,

-Your suicidal thoughts are truly gone, Theo.

It took Theo by surprise, so much so that he stopped walking for an instant, but for instant only because he knew who was addressing him, so he started walking again to confess,

-Yes, they are. Your grandson helped. He helped me greatly to gather confidence, some confidence. I am still not totally confident, you see, but, but, I can be loved, I learnt that I can be loved and I am loved by none than my Whilhelmina. I will not go and ruining it all now, I will keep strong, I promise I will keep strong and not falter. It is not only me anymore.

The Great Being scolded him,

-It has never been only you. You had to see beyond your limitations and how you fitted perfectly well in the entire jigsaw. How your piece with all its particularities completes the entire picture in a sense. Let me tell you that my grandson in and out of consciousness when I took him across the Atlantic Ocean spoke about you.

A curious Father Odell enquired,

-Did he?

-He did. He mentioned your help, how brave you were and that he could not have survived without your intervention.

This straight answer made Theo blush thoroughly as he diminished himself,

-I am sure he could have, he is strong. He is called the Mighty One after all.

Stopping, the Creator put himself in front of Odell to repeat firmly,

-He could not have survived without your help. Mighty maybe strong but when he was in difficulties you were there with your quick thinking solutions. Not only you bestow his esteem, he wants you to train his army to think outside of the box like you do. He was impressed with your jacket full of little bottles of holy water. He thinks this can help with the situation in Wilton Town because he does not know how many humans have been possessed since the opening of that hell portal at Peter O'Neil's cottage. The Mighty One, the Master and I are putting you in charge of creating this type of ammunition for his angels and to teach them how to use it. Your gift gives you the capacity to do your mission at the tip of your fingers.

He then carried on walking and talking in the direction of smoke which could be seen coming from the ruins of the Oggins' cottage in the vast garden of the hotel,

-Come with me. As you know something bad will happen tonight in Wilton Town. As much as the Master and Mighty were reluctant initially to get you involved in the event they are fearing, it has been decided, due to your resourcefulness that not only you will be able to cope but also to prove yourself to be helpful. Raguel, who took over the logistic of tonight's operation until Mighty is well enough to come back to the fore, wants you to participate in three ways this evening. The first part of your own mission is to determine from the remainder of the gang who is possessed and who isn't. You will be flanked by two angels in order to do so: your friend Valdi, who killed his first demon a few hours ago and had kept that gang in check for all the years he has been in Wilton Town, and the angel nicknamed the Messenger.

Father Odell acknowledged with a deep positive nod,

-That would be Henry, the angel with golden eyes who,

with Sebastien, helped killing the demons dragging me to hell after an exorcism not so long ago, the one I did in the ruins of that cottage.

The Great Being confirmed,

-Exactly. Henry is an excellent angel as well as being a good soldier. Mighty taught him how to fight. Along with Valdi, he will unsure that you stay safe during your mission tonight. He is an ancient animal spirit who made it as a human then as an angel. He has a deep loyalty to my grandson which has been going on for a very long time. If he is considered by Sebastien as one of his best friends, my Raguel has developed a paternal affection for Henry so much so that when Henry reincarnates he will be the son of Raguel along with Sebastien. This is a very high endorsement which means that in his next life, I will call Henry, my grandson. I can only recommend you to befriend Henry. As a new angel, within the army of Mighty, you will need to find your way around and grounding as soon as you can. Henry is an angel who despite being peculiar, is not haughty whatsoever. You can ask him anything regarding the angelic army during your flying sessions he has proposed to give you.

Taking the advice, Theo asked with some curiosity,

-I will. May I ask how peculiar he is? Do I have to address him in a certain fashion?

Smiling kindly, the Creator answered,

-You don't have to address him in any fashion at all, you can whistle to him and he will come to you, you can make a coming gesture of your fingers and Henry will be by you in seconds. He still possess his animal instincts. Beside being truly kind, truly loyal and truly protective, Henry has gifts from the animal kingdom in abundance. Tonight, trust his instincts, if he can hear something that you can't, if he can see someone in the dark that you can't, if he can smell danger like a barrel full of powder, just trust him and follow him to safety. If Valdi takes another direction or directive, take my cue: follow Henry. Vincent can be mobilised to fight and receive a call for fight, but we need you to stay on the logistic side at all time to defeat the enemy.

The worried face of Odell frowned as he enquired,

-Will Vincent be alright?

To which the Great Being replied,

-If you are doing as you are told, yes. If you are putting

yourself in danger when he needs to focus on his own mission, you will jeopardise yourself and him. If you want to help Vincent, you will have to follow Henry. You can then prepare with all the other angels the counter attack 'en masse' to reinforce what Vincent and Mighty will be doing with the Master.

Full of hope, Theo asked with eyes filling with tears,

-So Mighty will be here? Sebastien will come? He is alright!?

Entering the ruins where the White Witch was burning the shirts of Raguel and Vincent, the Creator replied,

-I know my grandson will be here even if it means he can die. He is not alright, not yet, but near enough. Your friend did wonders.

Odell wiped his tears with the back of his hand and was ready to listen to more orders, but another tear pearled at his eyes and rolled upon his cheek. Whilhelmina seeing him crying came to him and held his hand asking gently,

-What's up Theo?

Odell with a deep sigh informed her,

-Sebastien will come to fight tonight despite it all. We need to help him with all our mights. You know we are his logistic team. He isn't fully recovered yet but he will be here to save Wilton Town.

The White Witch looked at the Great Being for confirmation ever so silently, which he was more than willing to give her,

-My grandson will be here, tonight. He never misses a fight, even covered with wounds. I have a little something for you Whilhelmina to help the Mighty One. Your future husband is going to prepare all day ammunitions of holy water for the angelic army ready to be used for tonight. But I have a very special task for you. Here, you must copy this as fast as you can and as accurately as you are able to. As soon as it is done, burn the original in the very chimney, you've burnt the shirts in. Keep the copy, but hide it and hide it well. A spell may be in order to do so.

He gave her a heavy manuscript which she inspected with great care and curiosity. Shivering, s
he stroke the black leather of the cover and realising

slowly what it was, tears came to her eyes. She muttered,

-It is made of human skin. What is it?

The Great Being confirmed,

-It is indeed a manuscript made entirely of human skin, from the cover to every single page of it entirely written by Lucifer. It is a nomenclature of all his demons, their specific assets, their weaknesses and how to dispose of them. A ruler of hell needs to know his demonic crew and how to control them. He wrote over a very long period this little handbook for himself. Abraham Wilton-Cough stole the book when we did our little hell trip. He handed it to me while we were returning with a sorry I couldn't help being bad down there.

This made Whilhelmina and Theo retrieve their smiles as both uttered together,

-Oh, good old Abraham!

With a grin the Creator agreed, before informing,

-Yes, we all need an Abraham Wilton-Cough. He had noticed in the chamber of Lucifer, how the fallen angel knowing he was about to die reached for that book almost as if it was a bible and concentrated on it while talking to us, looking, searching within its pages. When the book fell on the ground from Lucifer's hands, it was opened on the page on how to kill an angel made of human blood. It happened when my son stepped in to protect Valdi, Vincent who is an angel of human blood. You both know what this means. Whilhelmina, this manuscript will be sought by Lucifer himself so you must dispose of it, discard it as fast as you can after having made its copy. As for the pages about killing angels, transcribe them differently in your copy but do a proper transcription for the Master and the Mighty One. Under no circumstances you must retain that book any longer than three days, three hours and three minutes. This is when the discovery of it being missing will occur. If Lucifer mustn't retrieve his manual expertly created from his centuries of experience, we must unsure that a copy stays with us for the use of the angelic army.

While Whilhelmina gave her agreement to perform the difficult task, Theo Odell took his turn to examine the manuscript at the light of the fire provided by the burning shirts. As he turned the pages slowly of the volume, he shared out loud his thoughts about it and concerns,

-I must say for Abraham Wilton-Cough that even when

he was alive not only was he an excellent judge of character, able to know what a person was mainly about, but he also spotted the valuable objects in their surroundings. If Vince always found those qualities remarkable, because Abraham was usually dead right and accurate, I always thought that Abraham had just turned completely into a cynical banker with the complete skills set that comes with it. But this, this book is definitely a devil's bible. It is so detailed, so precise, so intricate. It is partly written in latinised tongue, proper Latin, Greek, Coptic and even hieroglyphs. I wonder why Lucifer didn't simply wrote it all in demonic tongue? Most is written in blood...

Raguel who was standing at the entrance of the ruins, his naked torso still glistening of droplets of water in the morning light, had listened enough of the on going conversation to have gathered what it was all about. He joined in with his speculation while his father made a linen towel appear out of nowhere for him and gave it to his angelic son to dry himself off,

-Lucifer could only have used different languages to make his book more complicated to read.

Father Odell, turning more energetically the pages, and looking at the book from different angles expressed his slight annoyance,

-Yes, but, yes, but why is avoidance of the demonic tongue altogether? When you expect evil to speak evil, it is bewildering! It like a French speaking a crooked English when he can do so well in his native language which is beautiful by the way. Which blood is it written with? Look, look, it is written the upside down way as well but with invisible ink. If you give that book to Vincent he will have so much fun decrypting it! Or even his wife Amelia, who is very clever indeed and as curious as her husband about almost everything.

Drying himself, the Master of all angels approaching the priest to inspect the manuscript as well, suggested,

-If the time limit for transcribing the book is so short, the help of Valdi and his intelligent little wife could be a good idea. We need to get the most informations from it while we can. For the blood ink, I can tell by the acrid smell of it that it is the one of Lucifer himself. I clean away some of it from my skin just now. His blood is as bitter as his owner's spirit. There is one way to find out for sure. Give this book to me.

Handed the manuscript, Raguel put his finger on an heavily drawn capital letter in one page, he followed the curve of the large c with the tip of his finger before he announced,

-It is definitely his blood, father, it gives me the unmistakable strong stinging and burning sensation. My pure guess is that he used his palms, he carved with your seal, as an inkwell. This is why his hands never healed.

Stating the obvious, Theo commented,

-This must have hurt a great deal. This manuscript was truly a painstaking creation of Lucifer. Can I touch the letter too?

Raguel closed the book at once and scolded,

-Don't be a curious child, my angel. The very handling of this book for too long is dangerous. It is the property of the devil, remember. Beside, Lucifer will hunt for it, and when he will, you will not want to have a speck of smell of his blood upon you, trust me. You will not want him to skin you alive for him to create his new book to replace his stolen one as punishment for handling stolen goods, will you?

Becoming very pale, Odell shook his head negatively while trembling all other, querying,

-He can't do that surely?

The Master replied only too sternly,

-For his painstakingly handmade bible, the price will be the life of the beholder. Trust me, when I say he can. He has no regards for human angels. He has no regards for my youngest son, if he is paid to kill him, he will try by all means possible. He had no regards for my eldest one, which he managed to kill and he has certainly no regards for me. We can engaged to the death at any point in time. For you my Theo, he will have even less regards not because you wear the dog collar, but because you have been efficient at sending his demons back to hell. Do you think, he will not have noticed by now the demons sent back to the sender with a thank you very much but not wanted? Lucifer is not stupid and if he put his hands on you, it will be very painful and slow because your dear friend Valdi managed to wreck one of his wrist. So it will be a skinning session with one hand only.

-Raguel! Stop scaring your new angel like that!

The intervention of his father nonetheless didn't discouraged the Master who retorted,

-I prefer an angel aware and warned of the dangers,

than ignorant of them, tortured, and facing a slow death. Look, tell me if Lucifer will not be overly joyful if he catches one of my incarnated human angels and skins him to replace his old manuscript? For him it will be upgrading his game from humans to angels. Do not forget that he has already one soul of an archangel fully paid for and another one in the balance. Theo and even Vincent are baby angels to my eyes who needs to grow up fast with the reality of the danger they are and will be facing. I will not let anyone molly cuddle them like we did with Lawrence. Because let's be honest, we always felt sorry for the boy. It was such a touch and go to save Lawrence this time for him to not be completely lost.

The Great Being agreed adding,

-You will have to thank Abraham Wilton-Cough for the full retrieval of Lawrence. He didn't have to do it. He knew the risks to his own soul however he took them. It was the pure kindness from one stranger to another for he didn't know Lawrence whatsoever. I will also tell you, that Abraham behaved as my servant when you left with Valdi, on his own accord. He could have been a coward and nestle in a little corner but he didn't. He stepped forward to the plate and performed whatever I asked him to do. I found him useful and helpful. If he ever ask to help you, do not refuse, you will not be deceived. He may do a little bit more than the ordinary like stealing Lucifer's bible but he will come clean with it and tell you and give away the good to your responsibility.

Lifting his eyes to the sky in slight exasperation, Raguel couldn't help to mention,

-Yes, yes, but what responsibility it is! I am scared for the lives of everyone that will handle the book. Truly, I wish it burnt right here right now.

Grinning the Creator scolded his son,

-That would be dismissing what a precious mine of informations has befallen onto your hands. You have within them the complete handbook on how to kill every type of demons hell bestows. You couldn't wish for a better treasure to preserve all of your angels. The manuscript is a grey area, a liability, just like Abraham is but it has its uses which you mustn't neglect. You must take full advantage of it. Beside that let me tell you something, Lucifer was created an angel, not a demon. He never trusted demons this is why his precious book is not in an understandable tongue for demons. He always feared rebellions under his volatile hellish roof. You have in your hand the manual for his own self preservation down there. It was conceived for no one else but him. In fact what you possess in this book is the Achilles heel of Lucifer where he has patiently wrote how to kill his legions of demons but also his ways to kill your angels.

The Master still grumbled despite admitting the points made by his father,

-Yes, yes, but still the danger associated by possessing such a book is such that I would strangle Wilton-Cough if he was not already dead. What was he thinking? Certainly not the rage and rampage Lucifer will do when he realise his precious book is missing.

With his fists upon his hips the Great Being disapproved,

-Surely you don't mean that! Abraham was only thinking of helping us.

Sitting on the ruined stone wall and almost sulking in front of his father, Raguel put the book down by his sides to finish to dry himself and argued,

-By stealing! And what happened to the 'you shall not steal'?

Still taking the defence of Wilton-Cough, the Creator explained with the shadow of a smile appearing on his lips,

-Under the circumstances, I see it like intercepting an enemy's missive from reaching its destination, a missive which contains all the enemy's next moves for about everything. It was opened at the page of how to kill an angel of human blood when Wilton-Cough picked up the book from the floor, the very page Lucifer looked when he addressed Abraham with the intention to attack Valdi in fact.

This made Raguel smile with irony as he commented,

-A missive from Lucifer to Lucifer!

This time the Great Being took the book back and placed it opened on the lap of his son to the said page with some impatience demanding,

-Here! Do I have to spoon-feed you a little bit of intelligence or do you want to show your stupidity to Lucifer by handing his manual of how to destroy everything back to him with apologies from Wilton-Cough saying that he took that book by mistake? Read, Raguel, read!

The Master started to read, and after a few lines, he stood up and turned around his father with a worried face, as he continued reading with deep interest. He stopped to ask bewildered,

-How did Abraham figure out this information was important to us? This page is so crypted. How could he have made sense of that hieroglyph and that one?

The eternal being that was Whilhelmina answered him,

-I have lived in Wilton-Town from its beginning, I can tell you that I saw Abraham grow up. He was very disliked by his mother and then his father. The only love he received was from his aunt Josephine Cough who took him on holidays with her everywhere. He visited Egypt with her. Abraham is far from stupid, if he knows mathematics to the tips of his fingers, it was also the case for Latin. As he went to Greece with his aunt, I am sure he picked up a few words there too. Abraham realised full well the importance of what he saw on that page.

Father Odell added in the defence of Wilton-Cough with emotion,

-Master, don't forget that Abraham Wilton-Cough was killed by a thief. He received his mortal blow by one. He led a life where he was so up-strong on values such as hardworking, and earning all your pennies and your worth. Stealing is not in his morality whatsoever. If he took that book from hell, the only reason is what he saw had to be known by you from high above. He handed it over to your father with his apologies, there is no better proof than that for his honesty.

Softened up on the case of Abraham Wilton-Cough, the Master of all angels turned the pages of the manuscript and directed them to the light of the sun. He put the book upside down and swore,

-Lucifer could not have been more stupid! The way to murder my every single angel is here. I found the page for Lawrence. He knew our boy was plagued by a curse.

Satisfied to see his son realising the importance of what he had within his hands, the Great Being took the book from him and placed it in the hands of the White Witch with his orders,

-Look after it for me, Miss White, write fast and well. We want just a copy not a translation. This book has to remain crypted. Do you understand? You have your orders, see to them. Remember, you have three days and a few minutes. We will try to get you some help for that important task.

Miss White bowed to him with respect and ran with the manuscript back to her hotel. The Creator turned to his son, threw his towel to the fire commenting,

-You took your time to see some reason upon the matter at hand. You haven't seen the pages regarding the archangels, nor the one concerning you, I have. This is why this is intercepted war communication and not theft. It is fair game. But yes, it also means that anyone who handles that book will be in great danger of reprisals from Lucifer and your task will be to unsure their protections. Let me warn you, don't be harsh about it with Abraham. He took the manuscript, he will be in more trouble than anyone else. Don't let my ghost fall into the hands of Lucifer. Come, Father Odell, please do follow us, I have still to brief you on your other two missions for tonight.

Theo looked at the burning flames in the old fire place with concern but he didn't need to worry for when the Great Being flicked his fingers, it ran heavily extinguishing the fire. He followed the Master and his father without a word, obedience in his heart. Raguel killed the silence with his question,

- 'My' ghost, father, are you sure?

The sharp reply came fast like a snap of a whip,

-Wilton-Cough belongs to Valdi therefore he belongs to me. You granted to take Abraham's soul under your wings to be redeemed then do so and put a shirt on.

The Great Being made a white cotton shirt appear within his fingers which he handed to the Master before he turned to Father Odell, re-engaging the conversation with him,

-So we are clear on the ammunition making of holy water which has to be done for this evening, Theo? It will rain all day so the well of Miss White will replenish itself as fast as you will have to take a bucket full of water from it to do your task.

Odell catching the fast pace of the beings before him answered,

-Yes, this is fully understood. I will do so but what about the containers? We need quantities of small bottles and what about the jacket for your angels to carry them? How many angels are going to need those specific jackets for tonight?

Putting his new shirt on, Raguel turned to Father Odell to reply in a hurried fashion,

-When the Messenger is back, I will send him to you. He will get everything you will need. I have seventy six angels due to arrive in Wilton Town tonight, that is without counting the dozen already here, my son, Valdi, you and I. Oh! And Doctor Williams, do not forget Doctor Williams! If you are not sure of anything ask Henry, if Henry is away then come and fetch me. Even if it is something randomly stupid that you can solve by yourself, don't be afraid to ask and bother me with it. Also do not worry about jacket measurements to fit each of my soldiers, we can resolve the discrepancies for each of them by a little angelic magic. I want you to concentrate on the creation of the ammunitions. Do you understand?

An anxious Theo nodded positively with his answer,

-I do, I do.

The Master continued,

-So my father filled you in with your first mission for tonight, correct?

Odell replied as firmly as he could,

-Correct. I have to determine of all the members of the gang who are possessed by demons.

Arriving by the well and closing his shirt Raguel stated,

-Good, I like angels who pay great attention to their orders. Now, listen to me, the reason I want you involved tonight is because you are the shepherd of your parishioners. If fire is in town, and spread throughout the town, I want you to lead them to safety, to reassure them as much as you can, to tell them that what is destroyed can be rebuilt but that life once lost is lost. I am counting on you to manage your flock with a firm hand that save them from danger. You will be flanked and helped by the Messenger and the angel Matthias in that second mission. Once you rounded up all the town folks in danger, then your third mission will start. You will have to take them here, to this hotel who has been protected against fire. Consider this house as a Noah's ark, lead everyone in danger here with the help of Henry and Matthias through the forest. You may need to go back in town to fetch the missing and the unaccounted for. There are always some, some who will hide in fear, some who will go back to save a pet, some who will go back to protect some family treasure or heirloom, some who will want to take the opportunity to loot the abandoned houses... I trust your knowledge of your parishioners to make sure that at the end of the night when all is over, we can established who was saved from the casualties and the dead. Can you do that?

A trembling Father Odell nodded his ascent, fearing for all in Wilton Town, then rallying himself up answered,

-I can and I will. You can count on me, Master, I will not let my people down.

Satisfied Raguel ordered,

-I am sure you will not, my angel, I don't expect any less from you. See to your ammunition task. I will check on you later. Don't forget, if you have any queries, do not be afraid to come and ask me.

Handing a bucket full of water to the vicar of Wilton Town, the Creator smiled to him with great kindness adding,

-Rise above and beyond, you are my angelic Theo, I expect wonders from you.

Father Odell saw the two beings leaving him by the well to go back to the hotel in their fast paces. He closed his hands into fists and talked to himself in a low voice,

-Well, let's get on with it then, Theo. For all the good people of Wilton Town, let's do it.

He then plunged his hands in the cold water and saw the magic happened, the bubbles and the blue light coming from his fingers turning it to holy water.

#

When the Great Being and the Master entered the bedroom of Daniel, they found him surrounded by Doctor Williams and Doctor Valdi who were performing an amputation on his leg. The brave angel was bitting the leather scabbard of his dagger to prevent himself from shouting. Raguel asked immediately with great sadness,

-His leg can't be saved?

Valdi replied sternly,

-It will be the death of him.

Williams added,

-Its flesh already turned black in areas. It's fully poisoned, Master.

While his son closed his eyes of sorrow, the Great Being went to hold the hand of Daniel and stroke his forehead with gentleness reassuring him,

-Trust me, sleep my angel, sleep and be brave for me when you wake up. You will be alright, you will make it.

He removed the scabbard from Daniel's mouth who managed to smile to him before falling into a deep sleep. Behind the Great Being a little woman with an apron covered with blood marvelled,

-How did you do that? I tried vainly to knock him out with strong alcohol for ages!

The Creator turned around to appraise the woman talking to him. She was wearing a night gown and dress. Her plaited hair revealed that she had a dishevelling night at the hotel. Despite it all she seemed in good spirit so much so that despite his unwillingness to acknowledge the human, the Great Being faced her small hand presented to him in a jovial manner with her invite to get acquainted,

-My name is Mrs Toad. I am a guest here, a customer. I couldn't sleep. The poor man was screaming so much, you see. So I came to see what was wrong and staid by his bedside to look after him.

Apart from Valdi who got on with the preparation of removing the leg of the sleeping angel, the others in the room were interested to see how the Creator would react to the friendly human before him. When he offered his hand back to shake the one of Mrs Toad in her similar amicable way, they felt some relief. The Great Being presented himself,

-My dear Pamela, this is a very eventful time you have here in Wilton Town but I hope it will not prevent you to come back here. I must thank you to have looked after Daniel tonight. He is one of my valued soldiers. I am the grandfather of Sebastien whom you have made the acquaintance of.

A delighted Pamela Toad after the warm handshake confided,

-You must forgive the state of my apron, Mr Cotton the

elder, I am helping those two gentlemen, the Doctor Williams and the Doctor Valdi. Your grandson is the most gallant, charming and amiable man, I ever saw in my entire life. He is ever so polite and ever so helpful and his young wife Ivy is such a gentle soul. She is a sweet dear little thing but she is a Doctor in her own right as well. May I say that I do not spot your French accent if it is not being too curious?

The Great Being who didn't mind for one bit the triviality of the conversation despite the gruesome operation taking place behind him answered

-Ah! Madame Toad, this is because I am very well travelled. I am pleased that my grandson and his wife made such a good impression on you. Did you meet my son, Raguel? He is my eldest and the father of Sebastien.

Making a sign for his son to approach, the makeshift 'Cotton the elder' played his role in front of the human with some amusement as Mrs Toad replied,

-I didn't have the pleasure to meet him yet. Although I saw him doing the hundred paces in the garden of the hotel for a very long time tonight. For a moment I thought he was talking to himself. Raguel is a very interesting name. How did you call your other children, I wonder?

The Master getting close to his father could see the enjoyment on his face to be talking to the jovial Pamela Toad. His father answered with an amused smile,

-I adopted my second son called Adam, my youngest is named Joshua. Raguel is the name of the archangel of justice, no less and no more, who is all about fairness, vengeance and redemption. But it pales in comparison with your own first name, Pamela, which means 'all sweetness'.

Mrs Toad smiled widely, proud to know the meaning of her name. She presented her hand willingly to Raguel to shake while she said,

-No daughters, Mr Cotton the elder? Nice to meet you Raguel, I am sorry I wasn't presented to you earlier.

As the Master kissed her hand instead of shaking it, his father told,

-I am not ruling out a daughter yet, Mrs Toad. Everyone needs a little bit of fresh air in a room. Please do not be sorry to not have been acquainted with my Raguel yet. He is a very taciturn one who talks to souls, spirits and ghosts, so you may very well have seen him talking on his own. He has lost two wives and his eldest son. So that doesn't help him between you and me.

Offended, and shaking his head in disapproval, Raguel defended,

-I am not taciturn!

Protectively Pamela touched his arm in a maternal manner and reassured,

-It is alright to be so under your circumstances. You know I do talk to my dead husband sometimes. It is partly missing him and wishing him to still be there, but one has got to move one eventually. You resemble so much to Sebastien. Your youngest son is your very portrait almost line for line. You must be so proud of him. I have a son, you know, and he looks so much like his father and I think that there is still a bit of Mr Toad living through him. Life continues and goes on.

As Raguel sigh deeply unable to put any more complaint forward in front of the little widow full of fortitude, his father took him out of his misery by enjoining,

-Mrs Toad, we must thank you for all the help you provided to Daniel overnight but it will be unfair to prevent you any longer from resting and finally gathering some sleep. We will take over to assist the operation he has to undertake. Unfortunately the gruesomeness of it all may not be for all eyes.

The tired Pamela insisted despite herself, full of kindness,

-You are talking to a fisherman's widow Mr Cotton the elder, I never shied away from gutting fish, I shall not pass out at the sight of blood. I can help.

Smiling to the human with sympathy, the Great Being replied,

-Then you may help us later once you are fully rested. Because we will need helpful hands and hearts like yours tonight. You see, we are mercenaries hired by the town to get rid of a gang who is causing problems. We discovered that the gang is planning to cause havoc in Wilton Town tonight. We will send any of the wounded town's folk here to the good nurse that is Miss White. If you care to help her, it will be most appreciated, but as it will be a long night, you must rest now, to be a soldiering nurse with her all night.

With that incentive in mind, Pamela Toad bowed to all and retired from the room saying,

-You can count on my help tonight, Gentlemen.

When Raguel closed the door carefully behind her, he questioned his father,

-Mercenaries? Really?

But the Great Being was already by the bed helping with the amputation when he cared to reply,

-Could you think of something better? Stop arguing and give us a hand to save your angel.

Worried the Master came near his father demanding,

-Is it that bad? Are we losing him?

Valdi replied with severity,

-No, but he is losing his leg. I am about to severe the bone. Hold his leg for us, please Master.

Williams added, pointing to a demonic claw embedded within the top of the thigh to the genitals of Daniel,

-We have to castrate him as well. It is as bad as it can get for Daniel. Your father wasn't making chit chat with the nice lady for the fun of it, I asked him via telepathy to keep her away from what was happening here. We didn't want her human self to see that large demon's claw we've found, did we?

Still vindictive, the Master held the leg of his angel firmly commenting,

-It would have been nice for one of you three to have informed me of what was going on.

With a sheepish look Doctor Williams explained,

-I was busy inspecting the damages done by the claw, Master.

Doctor Valdi gave his no non sense excuse,

-I could hardly tell out loud that we had found a large

demonic claw embedded in the patient's testicles, in front of that lovely lady, now couldn't I?

Raguel giving him a severe look retorted,

-No, you couldn't but you could have used telepathy.

Holding his saw in place, below the garrot on the leg, Valdi, undisturbed replied,

-What part of new angel do you not understand, angel Raguel? The technicality of angelic telepathy I have still to learn. I am afraid all my tools are still mainly human, my brain, my muscles and my hands. Now, are we all ready because I am going in at the count of three with a very human tool.

The Great Being holding strongly the shoulders of Daniel told,

-Ready. I will keep him asleep all the way through.

With the positive nods of Williams and Raguel, Doctor Valdi started in earnest the amputation. To alleviate the seriousness of it all, Doctor Williams, who was so used to surgery, engaged in small talk like he used to do during operations in his Boston hospital with his then surgeon Sebastien,

-Mrs Toad is a very helpful soul, if ever so chatty. Sebastien spotted the loneliness of the widow and has been playing his matchmaking game again with her.

The Master commented straight away,

-I told my son to stop playing the love angel with humans. He is so stubbornly French, just like his mother. What has he been up to with Mrs Toad?

A smiling Williams revealed,

-Well, he found that for such a lovely lady, she had a very unfortunate surname so he did set to change it to the one of Berry. Sebastien is matchmaking her to a dairy farmer of Wilton Town, a widower, who is an excellent fellow apparently. According to your son the match is made in heaven and the attraction being mutual between the two gentle souls, he expects wedding bells in town soon enough.

Doctor Valdi, sawing the bone neatly, enjoined,

-Mr Berry is a very good man. I can vouch for him. That little widow Toad from Boston if she loves him really will be treated like a queen by him, with tender, love and care for the rest of her days. There is nothing wrong with uniting two lonely and lovely souls together in my view.

The Great Being stated his opinion firmly on the matter with his agreement,

-Nor in mine. I rather find this matchmaking hobby of Mighty sweet, charming and amusing. This is far better than the passion of his brother Gael for ants and their observation. At the very least some interesting results come out of Sebastien's endeavours.

Raguel, maintaining the leg of Daniel and about to see it completely detached from the body of his angel, told gloomily,

-Yes, perhaps, but Mighty isn't always successful with his matchmaking skill. I have seen some broken hearts as a result so I wish he would leave this hobby alone. At least Gael playing with his ants didn't affect the humans in this world.

Gazing at his son, the Creator retorted with a smile,

-Practice makes perfect. I have been recording the successes of my Mighty against his failures on that front and I am happy to report that he gets it very right far more often than he gets it wrong. There are a lot of happy little children running upon this earth of which parents, grand parents or great grand parents have been matched by Mighty. Playing with hearts shows a welcoming humanity in an angel. Playing with insects shows a disconnection with humanity which is a bit alarming, in heaven or not. I wonder if the telling off of one hobby over the other one is utterly misguided in this case.

The pacifier that was Doctor Williams announced bluntly to the father and the son to divert the attention from their obvious tension on the subject of Gael,

-Mighty decided to play with my own heart and I am falling head over heels for it. I dare say I feel love, real love, like if I was alive for the first time. He matched me with a lady that makes my very ancient heart sing with love and trust. Trust, a feeling which I could not give to any women till this day, not after what happened during my human life, is running through my veins again. I did contact with a living heart, an eternal one. I held her hand with trust and we will see where love is carrying us.

A very surprised Valdi, putting his saw down in a dish on the bed table to attend straight away to what was left of the thigh of Daniel, exclaimed,

-You, old boy you, William, in love!? This is a miracle by all means! Who is the lady in question, dare I ask?

Raguel's attention was also caught by the surprising news. The dawn of a smile played on the Master's lips and tears pearled at the corner of his eyes as he demanded,

-Come, my William, you have to tell us. Valdi, Valdi, you can't even start to understand what miracle this is! Dear William was poisoned by his wife in his human life, way, way back in ancient Egypt and ever since, ever since...

The voice of the Master failed him overtaken by emotion. Doctor William helping Vincent with the intensive care for what was left of the leg of Daniel answered willingly to the demand,

-The Mighty One matched me with the good and so straightforwardly honest Georgia Marlow. We made her an eternal being recently to save her from her ultimately lethal illness. I am having breakfast right now with her and the two little girls Mina and Emily in my breakfast room. Some strands of her hair are escaping from her bonnet in pretty curls. She took some care to present herself this morning. This comes after the talk we had yesterday night about seeing how we will get on loving wise. She keeps looking at me, and dare I say that she is smiling and blushing.

A confused Vincent demanded,

-What are you talking about William? You are here with us.

With a soothing voice, the Great Being explained,

-William is a special angel. Like me and Raguel, he can be everywhere at the same time. Our presence is complete wherever we are. Although he helped all night long in Wilton Town, William was also still at his home in Boston. He is here and there presently. This is an angelic gift which I scarcely give away. But you will bestow it, Vincent. Raguel and William will teach you all about it in time. But what my son will show you first is how to use telepathy for you do possess the gift already but you do not know how to employ it at will yet. However I want you to master the use of telepathy before tonight. It is important for your own safety and everyone's else's. So how are we doing with Daniel, Doctor Valdi?

Vincent, looking at the severed leg, responded straight away,

-It went rather well, the amputation I mean. It will be a clean, seal and wrap from now on. Williams and I are used to them. However I want to clean the scar tissues with holy water. If it works against the venom of scorpion demons, it may help against the poison of Nefarius demons. We will never know until it is tried and tested and we have the occasion, here and now. Then we have to perform the castration and wait until Daniel wakes up to his new diminished self and deal with his anguish about it all. For his severed leg, I will autopsy it to know how the poison spread.

A couple of hours later, a yawning Vincent washed his hands by Doctor Williams who had kept smiling throughout the surgical operations. He mentioned,

-You are definitely falling in love, William, to keep smiling after what we did to that poor angel.

As Doctor Williams answered, some motion came from the bed where Daniel was waking up,

-I am, but in Boston, I have just checked the eyes of Emily. She will not be blind as I first feared. My expert optician confirmed it as well. We are going to get her a good pair of glasses. Her problem is solved and it makes me happy to see the shy smile of gratefulness on her little face.

Both Doctors returned to the bed. Raguel standing by Daniel was holding his hand firmly while his father was on a chair by him. Daniel's first words were for the Master,

-I am so sorry, Master. I got caught out. It was a schoolboy error. It was. I gazed into that demon's eyes. He was able to paralyse me just like that. Just like that, I couldn't move. If it was not for Sebastien, I would not live to tell the tale. If it was not for your son, I wouldn't be here at all.

With an emotional knot in his throat, Raguel gave a comprehensive smile to his angel as he demanded kindly,

-I know Daniel, I know what happened. I was there. We were so worried about you, Mighty and I. Mighty was the closest to you and reacted as fast as he could. That demon you tackled nearly killed Mighty. He put poisonous claws in the body of its victims. You had one lodged in your body so did Mighty. Now tell me how do you feel right now? You had a major operation...

Daniel sighed as he spelt out with some dread,

-The amputation. I still feel my leg.

But when he looked below the cover, the angel stated sadly,

-Nope, it is definitely gone. And, oh good Lord! No!

Doctor Williams with his satirical affability common to him confirmed,

-Yes, it had to be done Daniel or it was you gone for good. I can show you the black and blue poisoned flesh of it all which was ready to contaminate the rest of your body.

Daniel shook his head negatively stating,

-You've been thorough. I believe you. I don't need to see anything of me black and blue. I was in agony and now I am in pain but it is bearable. Where is the sweet old lady that held my hand when I couldn't bear anything anymore?

The Master answered,

-Mrs Toad is in her bedroom getting a rest. We had to send the little widow away because Doctor Williams and Doctor Valdi found a demon claw embedded in your body, in, well, a part that is now missing.

The amputated angel sighed deeply and expressed his sorrow,

-Well, that is it for me then. I will have no little wife. I will not know the joy of fatherhood in this lifetime. I might as well become a monk!

Intervening the Great Being smiled,

-Come, come, Daniel, you have never been an angelic monk. You know it. But what you don't know is that you are already a father.

Daniel looked at the Creator with tears in his eyes and demanded,

-How? I have been careful apart with the woman I intended to marry, but when I came back to propose to her she was in a grave, dead and buried.

The Great Being stood up and went to hold the hand of the grieving angel revealing,

-What you don't know is that Sarah Kay died in childbirth. Her parents ashamed that she wasn't married gave the child to an orphanage, your child, your daughter. She is only three years old and her name is the one of her mother, Sarah Kay. You will find her in an orphanage in Boston. She has your green eyes but she bestows the frizzy red hair of her mother. She hasn't been adopted yet, not because she is naughty, for she is clever, one must admit, but because everyone considers her as a freckled little 'thing'. I suggest you to take residence at Doctor Williams's in Boston and to adopt your little girl as soon as possible. You and him can see to her education.

The announcement made Daniel cry,

-Sarah gave me a little girl, a little bit of herself.

Returning to his chair, the Creator confirmed,

-Yes, she did. But to correct you, Sarah gave her entire self to you, not just a little bit, and at the end of it all she died. Her parents are very cross with you and your offspring because for them you took their daughter away from them so they took yours away from you in return. The grandfather of your girl has been visiting the little girl in the orphanage regularly as an anonymous benefactor. He made sure she was properly clothed and nourished. He is a vindictive man but he is not a bad man. He grieves in the worst way possible his only child, his daughter. As an angel, your duty is to unsure that love is law. You must repair that distressed human family. Take your child under your wings, make her be the joy of her grandparents.

Daniel nodded positively, taking the demand as an order he replied,

-I will.

Turning his head to Doctor Williams, drying his tears, Daniel asked in a most humble way,

-William, will you look after me, my recovery and my child?

Plumping the pillow of Daniel to make him more comfortable, the ancient angel reassured,

-Of course I will. I told you so already that I will take you with me. We will go and get your daughter together. As soon as I saw your wound, I knew that leg wasn't going to stay. I will make sure you have a wooden leg perfect for you which will allow you to walk. I will reeducate you as for your walking but also to redeploy you in the army of Sebastien. There is a new logistic team being created and my own healing team can do with some help and more hands. The choice will be up to you, but you can be part of the two teams like the skillful Miss White or like Doctor Valdi, presently here.

The hazy eyes of the weak angel looked in the room and met the ones of the tall Vincent. He appraised him, from his torso full of healed and fresh scars to his leather apron stained with blood. Daniel enquired,

-Are you Doctor Valdi? We meet at last. I heard about you a great deal. The people in this town sing your praises. Williams did forecast that you will be an angel in your human lifetime as soon as he met you ages ago. He was right. The feat has been talked about greatly in the angelic world and everyone is dying to meet you. Your name has reached almost mythical proportion among us. It didn't help that the Mighty One meeting you in Boston was very impressed by you, so much so that you had his immediate approval. He said you had all the attribute of a great angel. Come and shake my hand, in my normal state I would have done you that honour immediately. It is always nice to meet a new brother in arms.

Presenting his cleaned hand to the angel, Valdi commented with an apologetic smile,

-Please just call me Vincent since I pulled your leg. But please don't treat me like a mythical creature. I am just me, Vincent Valdi, just humble me.

While they shook hands, Raguel came by the bed and refastened the cover over his angel like a father. He told in a manner that didn't allow any questions,

-Daniel, humble Valdi is an archangel and a Punisher in training. You know what that means. As for the mythical creature that he is, hear this: his first angelic flight was across the Atlantic Ocean during a storm with my father. Not only that he saved the Mighty One, then helped saving you and the young Lawrence. He slaughtered a scorpion demon with his bare hands and without help on his first trip to hell. Last but not least he broke Lucifer's wrist with just one hand to protect me when I sustained a dislocated shoulder. He then repaired my shoulder and my wounds before he did let himself to be looked at for his own battle scars. Like my son, I can tell you, Vincent is a major angel. Now, you will have the pleasure to work with him in either team you chose to be with. I also have a particular task for you, Daniel, a very important one. It is actually a crucial one.

The Master took a deep breath as he posed checking that Daniel had his full attention. The green eyes of his angel were fixed upon him and he could read within them the hope he expected from him, the hope that despite his severe injury he was not useless. Raguel delivered his order with his natural authority,

-Daniel, you have been a corsair countless time, captain, sailor, fisherman, well, you travelled the world far and wide. Your knowledge of different languages is right up there. Doctor Williams can get you acquainted with, teach you much older languages. The reason for this is that we have in our possession a manuscript written by Lucifer on how to kill his demons and all angels. It is in multiple languages. It must stay as crypted as it is but I want you to learn the book by heart from start to finish, be the living translator of it. My angels will come to you to learn how to kill a particular demon or how to protect a particular angel. You will become the living beholder of an extremely big secret. The book itself comes from hell and will be destroyed as soon as a copy is done. In three days time, it will be only ashes. Miss White is in charge of the copy. You will be in charge of being the living copy of the book and then to pass on that knowledge from generation to generation to only one specific angel, precisely, to the letter with no mistake. It is a big ask because if enemies manage to know that you behold such a secret you will become a target for them. At the moment, you are counted as one angel down. They will disregard you as just an invalid. This is an opportunity for us, angels. When we fall, we can rise again. You, Daniel, can help us fight, by being the living copy of that book, you can save many, many brothers in arms doing so. What do you say, my angel?

Daniel propped himself up on his elbows for a few seconds as he delivered his answer with all the strength remaining in his body,

-I say that I am your angel, Master, I will always be yours and the Mighty One's. I will help. Despite the danger, I will be your living book.

Satisfied Raguel tapping the shoulder of his angel with appreciation welcomed,

-Good! I didn't expect any less of you than to rise to the challenge. My father will brief you fully upon your mission.

The Great Being, bringing his chair closer to the bed, added,

-It is also grand time, you and I, Daniel, have an in depth conversation. It has been a while since your last misgivings and a lot of water flowed under the bridge since then. A thorough catching up is in order, don't you think?

Daunted the angel looked at the enigmatic eyes of the Creator, but nodded positively and silently. At this gesture, the Master ordered,

-Right, father, make sure my angel is able to rest and recover from what he went through at some point. Williams, Valdi follow me.

The two Doctors obeyed without a word when the senior angel opened the door to them and led them away from the bedroom. Once in the corridor, once the door was closed, Vincent asked with curiosity,

-What is this all about? Daniel had fear in his eyes at the prospect of a conversation with your father. What will happen?

With a snapping noise of his tongue, Raguel sharply replied,

-To answer your first question, this is none of your business and to reply to your second I will say this, only god knows. Where is your servant?

A disappointed Valdi answered,

-I don't believe that, you must know something. You mean Abraham. Please, call him Abraham when you are with me, you know he isn't a servant in my eyes. Abraham is with Lawrence. He is looking after his sleep. If the boy shows deteriorating signs all of a sudden, he will come and fetch me.

The Master gave a warning glance to Valdi as he told,

-I am training you to protect your Abraham. If you get into the mode, the pretence of treating him like a servant he might escape from being severely hurt. If you couldn't save his body, you might be able to save the last thing he has: his spirit. Your ghost stole a very important manuscript from hell belonging to Lucifer and written by him. The reprisal Abraham will face may range from losing his soul to eternal torment passing by countless other horrible things that Lucifer indulges in. So the time to be finicky with the word servant is gone. The word slave might even save him better than servant with the deed he has done. So you tasked Abraham like I asked you to?

Taking the severity of the matter in his stride, Vincent, removing his dirty leather apron, gave his reply,

-Yes, that I did.

Doctor Williams, joining in, stated,

-Master, you must bare in mind that Vincent is a very recent angel who has got much to learn. It will help him to understand everything if you don't hide from him anything he should know. If he is to be an archangel and a Punisher then teach him to be one by sharing all he should know about us and our past. He will pick up where we are at very fast then. Start by answering his genuine question about Daniel. It shows a care to understand what is happening under his nose which mustn't be sniffed at.

Raguel, walking down the stately stairs of the hotel, gave a sigh and a look at Williams but consented,

-Alright, my wise William, you win the call. Valdi, I do know partly what will be going on in the room between my father and Daniel.

Vincent smiled asking for a confirmation,

-You do?

Turning to him while leading everyone outside to the large terrace by the ballroom, the Master nodded positively,

-Oh yes, I do. Come.

Once outside, Raguel looked at the grey sky for a long minute with intent, but seeing nothing, he enjoined his companions to take a seat on the marble bench while he was himself doing the hundred paces back and forth along the beautiful alabaster balustrade,

-Please, please, take a seat and have a slight rest, you two. Let's cover you up with a shirt, Valdi. Williams, you should have attended to that.

Flicking his fingers a white shirt appeared within the Master's fingers which he gave to Doctor Valdi. As Vincent put the shirt on he commented,

-This is a nice little trick, can I do that?

The Master replied, returning to the edge of the balustrade checking the horizon,

-You will be able to. You can already but it will take some training. First, you can only give to someone else but you can not provide to your own self. This is the basic rule. It means that angels have to look after each other. Secondly, there is a vow of poverty amongst angels. We are all living modest lives but this doesn't apply to Williams who didn't take the vow and his a provider for the entire army of my son. William, why was my angel not properly attired?

Without losing his nerves, despite the reproaching tone, Doctor Williams gave his answer bluntly,

-Vincent was for what he had to perform. Giving him a shirt before the amputation would have been a waste of a perfectly good garment, which would have ended up covered in blood and in need of being changed again, but also a waste of my magical powers. I can only point out that I didn't have any rest or hardly any for the past week like many angels of Mighty. I can not afford to be without powers when you need them the most tonight. We already have weakened soldiers left, right and centre. I had to be economical, I am afraid, not because I was mean and wanted to but because I had to.

Valdi with his shirt on, which he was already rolling the sleeves of, added,

-William said he would fetch me a shirt after the amputation, I told him to not bother because I was going to borrow one from Theo.

Looking at the two angels on the bench and acknowledging their friendship Raguel ruled,

-I let it pass because I can not fault you my William and I need all your magical powers right now to work on that counter poison for us. Henry should arrive soon. He sent me a message via telepathy. He has the pure poison of a nefarious demon with him that my son managed to get from the claw embedded in him. As soon as you work it out, I want you to give the potion to Daniel, Lawrence and my father and Valdi will bring the rest to my son. Make as much of that counter poison as you can for any other casualties we may sustain tonight. As for you my Vincent, I really want you to rest as much as you can before you are being called to fly across the Atlantic Ocean once more. But prior to that you shall have a breakfast of oxtail soup with Henry and I when I will both brief you with your mission for the day and tonight.

Vincent asked,

-What about William having breakfast?

Doctor Williams replied with a kind smile,

-I had it in Boston, with Georgia and the two little girls, remember? Come, Raguel, you have to educate Valdi. He will pick up everything very fast if you do so. Start by the story of Daniel while we are waiting for the arrival of Henry.

Consenting with good grace, the Master of all angels started whilst keeping watching the sky,

-Vincent, Daniel is a very ancient angel. You can not guess it because he hides that fact very well to all the new recruited angels since thousands of years. He was one of the original watchers, like I. We watched over earth. I watched over the angels as well but after a battle I was wounded. The main healing angel at the time was Raphael, whom you know sold his soul for the death of my eldest son. As you can guess, I wasn't getting any better under his hands. My wounds were festering. I demanded from my father then a time off my duties. I isolated myself and mended myself back slowly to health. When I came back to my duties, the watchers were so unruly, earth was in chaos. I brought back order. Lucifer became a fallen angel and many others lost their wings. Daniel was one of them. However his punishment, like the one of others were not to dwell in hell but to simply become human. Daniel after his human lifetime gained back his wings, but my father transmuted that to just another human life, so Daniel reincarnated again and again and again because after each of his human lives, he earned back his wings. When the Mighty One came into being, Daniel joined his army. He has been a very devoted soldier. He doesn't spare himself. No one can fault his courage nor his sense of duty. More than that he carried himself honourably and humbly for so long that forgiveness is in order. That is without mentioning his constant loyalty despite his   punishment and having to gain just another human life all over again when in fact he had earned wings. I put a plea to my father to reconsider his case. This is what he is doing now with Daniel. But also he is giving him the full brief of the mission Daniel accepted to undertake. It will not be an easy task by all means. It will put his life in constant danger but we believe that he has the maturity and the right devotion to carry it through. We will rely on you Valdi to protect him as you will be working in similar teams.

Valdi agreed before Raguel continued,

-Good, I know I can trust you. Let me tell you a bit of the character of Daniel. He used to be a very friendly and joyous being who enjoyed life to the full prior to his punishment. But he is now tamed miles down, miles down, frighteningly so. Daniel who could teach all about the sun, the constellations, the stars, the planets and the moon, who could make anyone dream about his astronomical knowledge, is the shadow of himself. His character is still excellent, he can be there by you fighting without you noticing he is protecting your back like a lion, well could. His physical fighting days are over.

Standing up from the bench, Doctor Williams swore,

-Lord! This rain is constant! I am getting soaked through. Why don't we wait for Henry indoors? As for Daniel, Master, you would make a mistake to think that his fighting days are totally over. When I was giving him first aid at Peter O'Neil's cottage, I told Daniel that he would have to use his brain and hands more. Well by hands, I meant that Daniel is an excellent shot. He is a sharp shooter: give him a musket, a pistol, a bow, a crossbow. He rarely misses his target. Strategically placed, this soldiering angel can still do some damage.

The Master, eyes upon the horizon, smiled,

-My William, Mighty and I will consider this utilisation of Daniel. However my concern is that once spotted, Daniel will become himself an easy target which can't run away very well any longer. Now, don't let me catch you swearing by the Lord again, nor let my father hear you. You have a special grant with me but do not push it. Beside, the rain is good. We need the rain especially today in Wilton Town. This is a gift from my father. First, it will provide all the wells of the town, the supply of water needed to tackle any fire we face tonight. Second a damp ground or roof take longer to be set aflame. Thirdly, it will help Father Odell to provide our angels with his ammunitions of holy water. Here, I think I spotted Henry but he is flying much higher than normal. The weather is not that bad.

Williams came by him, as well as Valdi, to tell,

-The rain is very good indeed then. I like the thoughtfulness behind it. Speaking of which, I thought long and hard about the dilemma of the locomotion of Daniel and I think I have the solution. What if he could be here and there at the same time like us. So you could have multiple sharp shooters

Daniels placed skillfully. And what if, I devise a spell to allow him to be invisible at will for his own protection. Therefore he will not have to ran away from danger but just to put himself in a safer position. This spot in the sky looks like an eagle, if you don't mind me saying, Master.

Full of suspicion, Valdi commented,

-That would be a very large eagle flying very awkwardly, then William, come put your glasses on. I think it's our angel alright, and I saw him flying better than that above a storm. I believe he is in trouble. Look at that leap he just done sideways, something is up.

It was enough for the Master to become fully winged and to order,

-Valdi, come with me. William go indoors and stay there. Keep Theo inside until I give the all clear. No trips to the well until I say so.

While the old angel did as he was told with a sense of urgency, Vincent's wings appeared. He followed the Master into the sky, flying as fast as he could to keep up with him.

#

Soon the Master and Valdi reached the Messenger who was indeed in a spot of trouble. Henry felt relief at the sight of Raguel, yet he warned,

-We mustn't stay here. Someone shot me in the left wing.

Feeling upset for his angel coming to some harm, the Master demanded,

-Where did come the shot?

As Henry replied, Valdi inspected his left wing as fast as he could, supporting the angel all the while with his own strength,

-The bullets came from that grove on that hill just outside the boundaries of Wilton Town. I managed to escape three shots but not the fourth.

Dislodging the bullet from the wing with his bare fingers, Vincent informed,

-I know the culprit by his bullet, I saw many like this one

before. He is a hunter and a farmer who lives outside of Wilton Town and outside of the next town who believes he owns everything in between. Amos kills eagles, owls and nails them to his farm and barns as trophies. He also shot children who he said were poaching on his lands. I operated on two young boys and it didn't go well with me when one passed away in my arms. Amos is a troublemaker which I had to throw out of Miss White's hotel many times. Barred from it, he killed one of the white deer of the garden of Whilhelmina in retaliation with the false excuse that it had strayed into his territory. He is one nasty fellow. The question is did he believe Henry was an eagle or else, or he saw what he saw an angel and decided to shoot nonetheless?

Raguel looking at the grove, fields and farm in the distance told sternly,

-Whatever the answer to your question is, Vincent, it sounds to me like another possessed farmer. I am going to check him out. Take Henry to be looked after by Williams and come back to me with Theo and a little supply of his holy water.

Valdi securing Henry firmly, expressed his concern,

-Master, don't go alone!

But the reply he got was as fast as Raguel flying away to investigate the area where the danger came from,

-Then be prompt in accomplishing your order.

Vincent sighed deeply worried but executed what was demanded of him swearing,

-Bloody hell! If something happens to him, tonight we will be without the strong angels.

Henry smiling at his helper reassured,

-No, we won't. Since you looked after him, Sebastien is doing very well. He is rearing to go into battle and just wait for his all clear, authorisation from his grandfather. Then the Master knows how to look after himself. Then a lot of us are going to be deployed tonight, and you must remember that there is strength in numbers. Then, you are here with us.

Shaking his head in disbelief Valdi replied,

-I am happy to hear that Sebastien is feeling ready to fight again tonight but I still wish his father would have waited to be surrounded by other angels before going to confront Amos.

He is and has the master plan for tonight. As for me fighting with all of you tonight, I am still just a new angel.

When they landed on the terrace, when Vincent made sure Henry was safe on the ground, the Messenger told,

-You maybe a new angel, but you have already earned your angelic name which is no mean feat.

Intrigued Valdi asked as he helped the angel with his damaged wing going inside the hotel,

-I am not aware about that. My name is Vincent Valdi, that is all. What is an angelic name?

Henry smiled kindly to him,

-An angelic name is given to an angel by the Creator or the Master. It usually reflects the line of duty of the angel in question, like I am called the Messenger. When your angelic name is given to you, you also receive your angelic seal. It is an important step in the angelic community, a little like a baptism, or a rite of passage is in the human world. It is a step up. Take it from me, an angelic name and seal give you instant respect and recognition among angels. I will take an example for demons, it is their sigil, a demon without one is considered a minor one or just slightly above a malevolent entity. It is a little bit of the same in the angelic world. You can also think of it that way: You have just been knighted by the Creator himself. If it is performed by the Master, it is a great honour already, but done by his father, it is significant. It is the difference which can equates to being made a Captain by Raguel or a Colonel by the Great Being. This, my angelic friend happened to you today. I received the telepathic order from the Master to give the news to all angels which I duly did.

As they entered the ballroom of the hotel by the double doors windows, Vincent enquired further, grateful for the informations given generously to him,

-Pray, what is my angelic name, Henry?

It was Doctor Williams who had been waiting for them impatiently in the ballroom who replied,

-Vincent, you have been dubbed the Protector. It means a great deal, it not only reflects how you lived your human life so far but how you started your angelic one as well. Up until now I can tell you that you live up to your angelic name. Now, I received some orders from the Master. You must go back to him immediately. I told Father Odell to wait for you by the well and to be ready to go with you. He has the ammunitions requested by the Master. Promise me to be careful and to look after your friend Odell. He is not as good as you flying wise. To give you the heads up, Raguel has been shot at but escaped all the bullets since his last telepathic call. I took the liberty to call reinforcement but they will arrive a quarter of an hour after you and Odell at the farm of Amos. Go now, I will look after Henry. One more thing, keep me informed, via telepathy, think of my human name Williams thrice to establish communication or of my angelic one once, the Wizard, then follow through with what you need or want to tell me. You don't have to spell anything out loud, think your words and they will reach me. Go, and bring everyone back safe and well. Live to your angelic name.

Giving a short and firm positive nod of his head to Williams, Valdi left the ballroom. He found Odell, wings on, waiting for him by the well anxiously. Both departed with no further a do. But at the clumsy taking off from Theo, Vincent knew he had to keep a good eye upon him straight away. His lips curled in an irresistible smirk as he stated,

-My Theo, we are both angels now, but as I arrived in Wilton Town before you, and helped you settling there, as I earned my wings before yours, I still consider myself like your elder brother. Follow me and do as I do and you will be alright. I will protect you. The wind comes from the west. Position your wings as I do and you will not struggle. I will go at speed because Raguel can be in danger, so I expect you to keep up. Flap right and flap fast.

Theo, happy to fly with his old friend for the first time agreed and did his best to keep up the pace.

Meanwhile Henry was guided from the ballroom to the kitchen of the hotel by a cautious Doctor Williams who probed,

-Does it hurt? Where is your wound? The Master told me you received a bullet in your wing. Which one?

A smiling Henry replied to all the questions,

-It does hurt a bit but the Protector removed the bullet from my left wing. I have seen far worst as a bird and recovered. In your expert hands, Williams, I know it will not be the end of my flying days. It is nice to see again the lovely hotel of Miss White after all the weather fronts of the Atlantic Ocean. It is warm and cosy here. I think this is a very decent new home for the humble Theo, don't you think so?

The old angel who couldn't resist a good chit chat especially with the Messenger who carried all sort of informations, gossips and rumours agreed,

-I think so as well. But what a gesture of generosity from Father Odell to give his presbytery to our Sebastien and his forming family, a family which you are now part of. Come, how does it feel to have the Master adopting you as a son?

The golden eyes of the Messenger lit up at the question when he stepped into the large and well furnished kitchen. He stood by the hot stove, putting his cold hands above it to warm them up then replied,

-I feel accepted. I am no longer a beast or an animal. I am family, a brother, a son and a grandson. You know I always felt awkward. But the Master figured out why and sorted it out in the most unexpected way. It has been mind blowing. He made me retrieve my entire memory as an animal spirit and he adopted me. When I was shot, soon after I saw the Master and Valdi. I can only confess that I knew I would be alright in their arms. I saw in Raguel's eyes how angry he was that I got hurt. I saw the Punisher in his gaze. He went straight to give a piece of his mind to a so called Amos which Valdi described as a nasty fellow.

Doctor Williams went to look at the damaged wing of the Messenger as he commented,

-You have been accepted well beforehand. I can tell you that, being a friend in the confidence of the Mighty One, he spoke highly of you even during your first human life. He said from very early on 'My' Henry. Well let me tell you something, confidence for confidence, the family, grandfather, father and son, have been calling our two new angels, 'My' very often. It has been my 'Theo' or 'My' angel and the same goes for Valdi. Your wound needs good cleaning then I will repair it but it is not as bad as I imagined. You will not be able to fly tonight but in a day or two, you will be as good as new.

Turning to face the old angel, pouting Henry confided,

-But I wanted to help tonight...

Williams presented him a chair by the kitchen table and invited Henry to take a seat before he reassured in his affable manner,

-There are many ways to help. Only, you mustn't use your wings tonight. At least you have your two legs and can run as fast you can unlike our poor Daniel.

This took Henry out of his self pity immediately as he enquired sadness in his voice,

-I heard by Sebastien who saved Daniel, that if he had not intervened Daniel would be dead, that his injuries were very bad.

Making his Doctor's leather bag appear upon the table and already taking from it what he needed to mend the wing, Doctor Williams informed,

-Bad doesn't qualify what I saw. His leg injury was horrific. When he was brought to me his thigh was opened by a gaping wound. The flesh surrounding it was lacerated to shreds. You could see his femur, Henry, his thigh leg bone! I struggled to close and mend that wound, but for all I was doing I had the gut instinct that it was only temporary, that his leg would eventually have to go. That was before the discovery that Nefarius demons were poisoning their victims by leaving a claw inside them. When Valdi arrived, who made that discovery by operating on the Mighty One, he quickly set himself to save Lawrence who had been infected by the poison the longest. He found a claw piercing the lung of the boy. It was an uphill struggle which involved a great deal like removing almost all the blood of Lawrence and replacing it but the boy is pulling through now and he has a fair chance to make it. As for Daniel, he had to have his leg amputated and as the claw was embedded in his manhood, he was castrated as well. From the time I looked after his wound to the time Doctor Valdi came, Daniel's entire leg was almost black and blue, eaten away from the inside by the poison, which would have spread to the entire body. So unfortunately the leg of Daniel had to go and Valdi performed the amputation with my help, assisted by the Master and the Great Being.

Henry sighed deeply as he commented,

-Poor Daniel, he was already not one of the happiest angel. I never seen him smile very often, especially since the little red head laundry girl he wanted to marry passed away three years ago. He doesn't speak a lot but with me, he shared a few things here and there on occasion. You know when I was sleeping in the straw in Sebastien's stable, in my first human life, he came on occasion to check on me. He brought me a cover and showed me how to make a bed with the straw which resembled human beds. He even has a nickname for me: Odd, because I partially grew up in England in that life. What a tragedy it must be for Daniel! I must go and see him. What will he do from now on? In which bedroom is he resting?

Because Henry was about to proceed in his quest for the room of Daniel and stood up, Doctor Williams stopped him, pressed his hands on the shoulders of the Messenger and made him sit back on the chair, querying in a commanding voice,

-Where do you think you are going my young angel? You will stay right here with me and get mended. You don't want an infected wing that need to be chopped off, do you? What would a messenger be without his wings? S-L-O-W, slow. Beside that the Creator is talking to Daniel, therefore you must consider that bedroom as having a do no disturb sign on its door.

Doing as he was told, Henry asked with anxiety,

-Will I lose my wing? It is very serious for Daniel for the Great Being to spend time with him?

Doctor Williams reassured as he started cleaning around the wound,

-The answer is no, you will not, I will see to it. I have to use a little magic to help the bone regrow where it has been damaged however. As you always respond well to treatment and mend fast, I expect you to fly again in forty eight hours. I can also see your flesh restoring itself. Have you been in contact with a higher Being recently?

Breathing with more ease, Henry answered,

-Well, yes, I met the Great Being on my way to Sebastien. He hugged me saying to consider him as my grandfather from now on. Then, I transported the goddess Dana to see her grandson. She gave me protection against lightnings whilst she was with me.

Stroking the damaged wing gently, Williams assessed it again before he declared,

-You pleased a Celtic Goddess, it seems, I can feel it. She was so worried about her grandson that she got into trouble in a storm vortex on her way to see him, but you saved her, you happened to be there at the right time, you took care of her, you gave her a ride. She put a protection on your wings. It is a strong spell. I can feel it.

-What does this mean?

Doctor Williams couldn't help smiling apposing his own healing hands to the dented part of the wing bone, replied,

-It means that you will be able to fly much sooner than expected. Your wings have the ability to self repair. With my magic added to hers, it will be a matter of minutes. It is a lifetime protective spell that Dana put on your wings. She rewarded your kindness to animals big and small, because when you met her she was simply in the shape of a humble butterfly, am I not right?

A pleased Henry confirmed,

-You are right. Dana was a little lime butterfly when I met her. I had no clue who she was until I met the Great Being over the ocean who told me then. I was properly acquainted to her when she took her usual physical shape in the cabin where Sebastien is recovering. She was ever so kind and courteous to me all the while I stayed there which was not too long.

The old angel could only comment,

-My dear Henry, you are being adopted by the Master, you will see many being very courteous to you in the future. You've just entered the most royal family of them all. Almost everyone will pay you the greatest respect from now on. Now tell me, how is your brother? How is Mighty?

As he could feel his wing getting better, Henry confided,

-Sebastien was smiling when I arrived. He was in the company of Mrs Amelia Valdi and Zachary Wilton-Cough. Both were looking after him and he seemed to enjoy it. The human wife of the Protector was showing him an ancient book of some importance about a secret island. The eldest son of Wilton-Cough was behaving like a servant, fetching this and that almost without a word. He has been told that Sebastien was an angel and you could tell by his entire demeanour that he was very impressed by it. He was literally subdued by the Mighty One.

This made the old Doctor give his opinion,

-I met Zachary Wilton-Cough in Boston, and I must confess that I like this lad very much. There is something about him, an honesty that is pleasing to see but not only that, I could feel that he had a good heart. What did you think about him? Here, I am going to apply an unguent on your wing and we are done.

A satisfied Henry told willingly while his wound was soothed by the application of the unguent,

-Zachary has certainly honesty in abundance, I agree. He has a humble demeanour about him. He is also generous with his time and care. He missed his own meal in order to provide one for Mighty. He gave his own one to him. As I was about to depart, I saw Zachary munching on a sailor's biscuit on the deck. He was obviously starving but he didn't let me know, apart that I could feel his entire young body being depleted of energy, me being an angel. He gave me the rest of his biscuit before I flew away on my long journey. He discussed with me a little, not much for he is shy. He asked me random questions about how long would it take me to travel back to Wilton Town and so on. I must admit that I like that boy on first impressions. May I advance that I can see a potential angel in him? But you know better than I because you are an angel spotter. Anyhow I have a couple of letters from the boy for you, a rock with some lichen and a sea shell from Iceland. He asked me to tell you to forgive the simplicity of his style and any possible mistake in his letters.

The Messenger found the items in question in his satchel then handed them to Doctor Williams who smiled kindly. The old angel confided,

-Mighty gave me the permission to participate in educating Zachary, to become his pen pal as well as one of his mentors. And yes, we do see something in that boy, something good. We felt like we met an awkward but deeply interesting caterpillar when we saw Zachary for the first time. We will help him develop into a beautiful butterfly, soul, angel. Now, Henry you are sorted, let the magic and medicine work for a few minutes. Take a well deserved rest meanwhile.

Henry stretched his wings before folding them neatly on his back. Then as he watched the old angel put his letters and presents from Zachary into his medical bag, he told,

-Well, now, for the most important, I have the flask of neat poison from the Nefarius demon that infected the Mighty One. This comes from the claw which was embedded in him. We have lots of hope resting on you, Doctor Williams on that one. I have a few recommendations, well, I will say orders, from Sebastien to you. He wants you to analyse any claw found in any of his angels in the future. The aim of the game is to analyse if it is the same poison used. The claws numb the area they are lodged in. The angel will not feel, he or she has been infected. Mighty wants you to change that. Even if his angels feel pain when attacked and infected, he prefers them to have the ability to raise the alarm about what happen to them. Here I have the claw he dissected and his notes, his observations about it.

The Messenger presented the flask, the claw and the notes on the kitchen table before Doctor Williams who inspected everything one by one carefully. William making his laboratory equipments appear in a corner of the kitchen enjoined,

-You must be exhausted, Henry, why don't you rest for a while as I deal with this?

The yawning golden eyes angel replied with a smile,

-I have to stay awake if just to reassure the Master about his son.

Interested as ever, Williams queried as he started studying the notes of Sebastien,

-So there is reassurance in the air. Last time I saw Mighty, I feared for his life. He was totally unconscious, transported out of harms way by his grand father.

Henry pouring himself a glass of water told with a smile,

-I can confirm to you that Mighty is pulling through. Whatever Doctor Valdi did to save him worked. Sebastien is in good spirits if just pinning to go back to the fore front and fight again. Beside that I found him being well looked after by Mrs Amelia Valdi and Zachary. Do not forget, I also brought the goddess Dana, his grandmother to his bedside who soon tended to him like if he was her own baby. I heard that you and Miss White fought extremely well together against the demons coming out of Mighty and Daniel...

Blushing the old angel confessed while he started working on a counter poison,

-Well, let's just say that when one has to defend himself, he'd better do it. Miss White and I have magical powers almost complementary of each others. We were protecting each other as well as the others. I can tell you that she was very fast to protect Father Odell, her Theo, from any harms. He was doing the exorcism, you see, and the demon attacked him with a chair. The flying chair went straight back to its sender at the move of her wand.

With a giggle Henry commented,

-That would cross an angry demon alright...

Williams doing different tests on the poison agreed with a tell tale look upon his face,

-It did. I feared for the woman's life so much, I put her behind me while the demon came to destroy her. But we managed alright. We kept our nerves. We used mirror shields to paralyse the demons momentarily. At the order of the Master, I removed the animal spirits protecting Mighty out of him. They had to do their task: protect Sebastien at all cost. This time, it was to facilitate the fast removal of Mighty from the scene to prevent him to become a sure casualty. They provided the right diversion. The Smilodon spirit went to save the white witch and I from the attacking demon, assaulting him from behind while the cockerel went to blind the other demon that was going to kill Father Odell. And Theo, Theo! Oh Theo! He helped the Master killing the demon.

Full of curiosity, Henry demanded,

-He did? How? I heard he had lots of tricks under his sleeves and that he was quick thinking. Mighty rates him very highly. Theo Odell is right up there in his estimation. I helped Mighty to save Theo on his descent to hell, and I could see his determination not to lose him to demons.

Doctor Williams grinding part of the demonic claw with a pestle and mortar gave his answer with a knowing smile,

-I will tell you one of my little secret guesses. Theo Odell is like his friend Vincent Valdi, an angel born to protect, but I suspect their higher aim is to protect the angelic bloodline of the Creator, the one which is in great danger right now. They don't know it, but I am sure they have been conceived for that purpose.

-What if they have?

The solemn voice of the Great Being entering the kitchen startled a little Williams who only answered with assurance,

-I am all for it because we need them, right here, right now at this moment in time.

Sitting by Henry, the Creator asked,

-What is your own opinion, my Messenger? I heard you've been shot in the wing. My Raguel was so upset about it that he asked me to check on your welfare.

When the Messenger was ready to stand up and bow, the Great Being stopped him with the order to be at rest and just to reply to him. Henry obliged him with his great humility,

-I agree with Williams, my Lord. But have they been conceived by you?

With his enigmatic smile on his lips, the Creator replied,

-Everything has been conceived by me, even free will which can be a little problematic at time, I must confess. Even you, my Henry, I conceived you. Now tell me, how do you feel and what shall I tell my son who is worried about you?

Full of straight honesty, Henry replied, his golden eyes shinning with a glow of devotion,

-My Lord, reassure him. Tell him that I am sorted. Tell him that I want to help him tonight and that I can. Doctor Williams did wonders, so did the Goddess Dana it seems, not forgetting Valdi who removed that dreaded bullet from my wing. I will fly again my Lord, soon, very soon.

Tapping the hand of the young angel with approval on the table, the Great Being told,

-Consider it done, my Henry. So to satisfy the curiosity of both of you who are considered as family by my eldest son, let me reveal that, yes, Valdi and Odell are the first two of a dozen of newly created angels called the protectors. They have been conceived to protect my creations.

Doctor Williams offering a beautiful smile to the Creator commented while holding a large syringe in one hand and the flask of poison in the other,

-I knew it! The gut feelings I had when I saw Vincent Valdi for the first time couldn't be dismissed. I knew, he was one of us and more. I just had the belly butterflies, my Lord, but stronger than ever, similar to the ones when the Master presented me his youngest son, the Mighty One, back in the days to ask me to stay on Earth if only for his little one and to carry on serving. Sebastien was just such a clever toddler. The Master put his young angel in my arms, both giggled, and I was won over to stay forever at their service. For Valdi when he came to me in my hospital, he had that irrepressible same giggle. He said he came to ask me for work, and when he saw me busy operating and understaffed, he helped straight away.

He even ordered me to tell him, teach him what to do. But his efficiency was clear to see from the get go. During that operation, he impressed me with his skills, great attention, care and cleanliness. He was young, yes, but clearly he was something else. He was certainly not the son of the worst butcher of Boston. I always thought he was god sent. I needed so much help in that hospital at that time...

Coming to Williams, the Great Being told,

-I know you did. This is why I sent you Sebastien when Valdi had to leave for Wilton Town. Now, that Mighty is settling here as well, I am giving you, my dear angel spotter, another angel. Teach him as well as you did with Vincent. This one needs to be taught almost everything from scratch but you will find his willingness not wanting. You know who I am talking about do you, my William? Make an angel out of that boy. His wish of an hospital for Wilton Town has been granted. You are one of the many angelic cogwheels that will help him make it happen. Vincent is another.

Doctor Williams, putting carefully some demonic poison in the syringe, replied with certainty,

-I do know, my Lord. I will make an angel out of Zachary Wilton-Cough. You can count on me for that. That boy has such a decent heart that it will be a crying shame to overlook him. I did manage to get his friendship. Although he is shy, I received two letters from him and a couple of gifts. So he is opening up to me. I will mentor him, I already made that decision. My Lord, may I be so bold to ask you a few questions?

With his unfathomable look the Creator agreed,

-Fire away my William, I know those questions are burning your tongue. But do not let my answers make you lose your concentration on the creation of the antidote.

The old angel smiled with eagerness to please as he started to ask, whilst keeping working on the counter poison,

-About Vincent, the Protector, will he be at the head of those new angels?

Going by the window of the kitchen and opening it, the Great Being replied,

-Yes, he will, but he is Vincent. He will treat them all as equals. You have seen the respect he shows to Abraham, his servant ghost. Don't expect that archangel to lord it around like a Raphael. Vincent can be a little brash at time but that is nothing in comparison to a Michael. Also I lectured him upon the way he talked to certain people. The lecture went straight to his heart. We will have to accept a certain cockiness from that angel. He will also be more self secure, more daring than others and take charge of situations in the blink of an eye, naturally. I made him that way.

Doctor Williams doing different trials and noting the results conscientiously questioned,

-Will the Master accept such an imposing archangel in his stride?

Turning to face the Doctor a giggling Creator revealed,

-He has no choice but to do so. Virtually, Vincent is his half brother. You looked after the second part of the education of Vincent. The Master and his son will look after the third part. The fourth part will be done by myself.

Full of questions, fiddling with his instruments, a curious Williams asked further,

-Vincent is the half brother of the Master, this can't be true, surely? Is he to be considered on the same footing as the Master? Is he above the Mighty One? Who looked after the first part of his education?

Going back to his seat by Henry, the Great Being confessed,

-Vincent Valdi is my son. I loved his mother so much that I took the body of a human to be with her for a while and to conceive him in a human manner.

Doctor Williams dropped his pencil at the announcement. His pale lips moved but pronounced nothing for a few seconds while Henry, slapping the table with his hand swore,

-I'll be damned!

With his enigmatic smile, the Creator corrected,

-Of course you will not my Henry, you are part of my confession circle. You should have seen the mother of Vincent, bright, witty, beautiful, and she was kindness personified. She resides in heaven where I visit her very often. Must love be forbidden to God? Anyhow I am planning her reincarnation to have a daughter with her.

Finally Williams came up with some words, still baffled by the entire confession,

-But Valdi, Vincent, he saw his parents being shot in the carriage crossing the Alps. He never believed in God because of it! That event made him who he is.

The Great Being admitted,

-This is the irony. Having a son that don't believe in you but he is good enough to be forgiven in my books. As much as I enjoyed conceiving him, I enjoyed watching him from above growing up. And to answer your questions, his first education was given by his aunt who is a lesser angel, but an angel nonetheless. He also met Abigail on his way back to Sicily with his aunt. She is the one who inspired him to become a Doctor and to help people. Now, both of you mustn't reveal to Vincent who he really is, nor to the Master. All revelations have to be done in the right time. I will deal with that. So, how are we doing with the antidote?

Giving a shy smile, Williams answered,

-I think that we are getting somewhere. I just need a few more minutes but I am pretty sure I have the solution. I did wonder if Abigail was involved because, Vincent told me why he became a Doctor and he described how a woman saved the life of his aunt that was left for dead on the road. The techniques she used were the ones of healing angel Abigail. I also know that the last incarnated life of Abigail was in Tuscany, so it does fit. And now, well, now, her new life is to be the adopted daughter of Vincent.

Fingers tapping on the table, his eyes set on the tall wooden clock in the kitchen, the Creator asked with concern,

-Remind me William, how long did my Raguel leave?

Doctor Williams turning to check the time replied reassuringly,

-About forty five minutes my Lord, this means that the Master will now be with Vincent and Father Odell. I made the telepathic call for other angels to go and help them out. They should arrive in that farm within minutes now. May I ask if the other angelic protectors will be your children? Is Theo your son?

Smiling the Great Being told,

-No, the other protectors are just my angelic creations made out of humans. It works with the same principle as Gael made you. You are not from the bloodline as per say, but you are still considered as family. If my Raguel ever considers the adoption of any of the protectors, then I will consider them as family as well. So to answer your question, Theo Odell is not my son but I do like that angelic human dearly. If the Master happens to be fond of him like he is of you, I will have no problems to consider him as my son as well. To begin with, my grandson, the Mighty One, absolutely likes Theo. This is not forgetting that my youngest son Vincent befriended Theo to the point that they feel like being brothers...

He was interrupted by a jubilant William who claimed,

-I have it! My Lord, I have it! The counter poison for Mighty! Now, I need to work out if this will work for the other angels. I need to analyse the claws found in Lawrence and Daniel.

Putting a precious liquid, the antidote, in a silver flask Doctor Williams was beaming as much as the Messenger and the Creator.

#

Meanwhile, Vincent Valdi had landed in the ploughed field of the farmer Amos followed by his friend Theo who touched the ground less gracefully and kissed the mud. Valdi couldn't help giggling as he reminded,

-Theo, you mustn't forget to use your legs when you land. Deploy them before you, it will prevent you from kissing the ground.

Father Odell stood up, brushed himself off the mud and told a tall tale,

-I just wanted to feel like being ordained again. All over again, to feel the humbleness of it all.

Vincent came to him, started to help brushing Theo's back off the mud asking yet smiling,

-I hope you didn't hurt yourself doing so? Move all your limbs for me. Why have you got a large white moth on your head? I saw it flying by you the entire way.

With an apologetic grin, Theo Odell did as he was told and replied,

-Everything is in working order. I will probably have a couple of bruises but nothing to worry about. For the night butterfly, it follows me since I gave it back its life. I found it dead in the garden of Whilhelmina.

An intrigued Vincent observed the moth attentively, stating,

-This is a Thysania agrippina, a White witch moth. You shouldn't have found it in her garden because it is situated too far in the North for that species. How did you manage to bring it back to life? Let's make our way to the farm and stay on your guard.

Following Valdi who was now scouring with a vigilant look the boundaries of the field, Odell explained,

-I just held the moth in my palms and wished it was alive. It is the Creator, you see, he gifted my hands. They can bring back to life small creatures. They will be able to heal but the Master, Sebastien and Doctor Williams will teach me how to use them properly. Finally if I plunge my hands in water, it makes it holy straight away.

Turning to him Vincent commented while pointing at marks in the mud,

-That's what I call handy. I can tell you that us knowing that lot, our lives are going to be totally different. I think our daily normality went out of the window as soon as we met Sebastien, the Mighty One, grandson of god. The good thing my Theo is that we are in it together, you and I. Therefore we will both learn to be good angels at the same time. Look, do you see those prints on the ground? A fight took place here.

Theo looked around with great care along with Valdi and interpreted out loud as he picked up a feather from the field,

-The Master had a fight here, most certainly. By the look of things, he lost only one feather on the battlefield and I can't see any blood, but this rain is so persistent that it could easily have washed anything away. For Amos to fight with an angel something is wrong with him. Raguel obviously had wings when he landed. So when Amos shot at the Messenger, he must have known he was shooting an angel too...

Valdi took some ammunitions from the ground then went to fetch a long pistol which was a few steps away and stated,

-Amos was clearly disarmed by Raguel. Here, Theo, take the gun, let me show you how to use it quickly. When we go at the farm, stand back, protect yourself and us with the pistol. You don't have to kill, aim for the legs. An enemy that cannot run is always a good idea if we need to escape from the situation.

Returning to his friend Valdi showed him how to shoot and to reload warning him,

-And for Christ's sake do not kill the eldest son of God otherwise we will be in deep trouble. As I say aim low at the legs of the enemy. Think of it that way as well, the lower you go, the enemy can still talk to us and give us the information we need. If Amos shot the Messenger knowing he was an angel, and maybe knowing he was carrying something essential for the recovery of the Mighty One, we have big trouble on our hands in that farm.

After a couple of trials which missed the target of a tree by a fair few centimetres, Vincent proposed with a giggle,

-Theo, maybe if you aim for the heart, you may hit the legs.

Odell, reloading the pistol ready to be use, and putting it safely away in his belt, scolded,

-Right, I take your point. You will have to give me lessons that last more than five minutes in the future so we can cover each others back properly.

Tapping the shoulders of Theo in a friendly way, Vincent reassured,

-Trust me I will. Come. Stay behind me and safe. Remember, you are our back up if I need to remove Raguel from danger.

A worried Theo followed and became increasingly tense as they walked in the farm yard. A large dead eagle was pinned on the side of the barn of Amos. The hens running about were famished and almost featherless. A large rottweiler with flanks full of fresh and old scars came to inspect the newcomers. Valdi warned,

-That's Amos dog, Satan. Amos won many dog fights in the neighbouring towns with him. Just don't show to this dog that you are scared and your calves may escape some bite marks.

An unnerved Theo commented,

-Great! What a lovely name that dog has and you want me to stay in the yard with him?

Turning to his friend, Vincent told firmly,

-I can hear fighting going on. I've got to go in. Get rid of your wings like me, you don't want them injured if we need to escape fast. Make them appear only when needed. For the dog, as I say, don't show your fear. If you must, feed him with one of those barely alive chicken. It will give you some practice at shooting accurately. It will keep the dog busy with bones. Stay back and stay safe.

Father Odell saw Valdi entering the farm, flinging the door open doing so. Inside Theo could assess that a dozen demons were attacking the Master who was putting a mighty fight. Theo cried out,

-Oh damn, oh damn, oh damn!

Trembling Odell did shot a chicken, went to throw its carcass in the barn and locked the hungry rottweiler within it. He reloaded his pistol and took position by the window of the main room of the farm. From that point he could assess the situation properly. The intervention of Vincent had been quite effective. Valdi was by Raguel, defending him with all his strength. Theo witnessed the two angels fighting together, like if they had known each other for a very long time, and were aware of their next moves. Therefore they could compound their individual strength to better efficiency. Breaking a panel of the window with his elbow, Odell joined the fight by shooting at some attacking demons.

By Raguel, Valdi asked,

-That's not just Amos we have to deal with?

Pointing briefly to a body in the corner of the room, before punching another demon, the Master replied,

-Amos is dead. I got rid of him. He created a demonic nest here. We are dealing with his brood. Amos was no human. He was a demon through and through.

Valdi answered to that by strangling the demon he was tackling,

-Well, he was a bad kettle of fish. That is all I can say. Apart from that, he will not be missed in the neighbourhood. Is it me or something smell in here?

Finally terracing a large demon that had been bothering him for while and breaking both of the demon's arms with a gruesome bones cracking noise Raguel replied,

-Trust me, you don't want to know what is that stench.

He took a large axe which was exhibited on the wall like a prized possession and threw it to Valdi with his order,

-Use that! You don't want to be too close and personal with those demons.

Grabbing the axe in flight, Vincent retorted,

-You've to tell me more than that. If I am to be in the thick of it with you and your son along with my Theo, I've got to know. Your father gives me the harsh truth of things, I expect it from you as well.

As Valdi started using his axe with efficiency against the next demon attacking him, he saw three demons going outdoors. Punching a demon far away from him and throwing him inside the fireplace, Raguel shouted,

-You, stupid angel! Now, they know Theo's here with you. They are going to get him!

Swinging his axe right in the face of his assailant, partly splitting it, Valdi then rushed to the window and opened it. He dragged Theo inside and ordered him,

-Close the window and the door! Quick! That's three less demons to deal with for the time being. Then behind me, Theo, behind me! Stay there.

He protected his friend with his axe as he obeyed his order. The diligent Odell putting a large wooden bar across the door announced,

-I killed two inside and one going for me just now. Let me kill the other two outside, I have still some ammunitions, I can do it from the window.

Raguel placing himself by Valdi to protect Theo ordered,

-Do it Odell! I trust you! Those bastards are banging on the doors. Fast, my angel, faster!

Father Odell reloaded his pistol with great efficiency before going to the window, aimed and fired. He cried out,

-I've got one! It's a belly wound. He is crawling on the ground.

Valdi shouted at him, while axing demons away from Odell,

-A wound is good enough, Theo. Just reload as fast as you can.

Father Odell did as he was told, but the last demon outside showed his face by the broken window pane. Holding his nerves, the vicar kicked his head with the pistol with great strength. As the demon retreated from a couple of steps, Odell threw a bottle of holy water at his face blinding him. It gave him the time to aim and shoot again without missing. He jubilated,

-I got him, Vincent, I got the last one outside. He is dead, a bullet between his eyes.

But Valdi couldn't answer as he was being tackled by two demons at once who were ready to slaughter him with his axe. Odell reacted as fast as he could, threw holy water into the eyes of the demons, grabbed the axe back and gave it to Valdi asking wildly,

-Are you hurt, my Vince?

Raguel culled the two blinded demons in no time at all and repeated the same question to Vincent,

-Are you hurt, my Angel? We got them all.

Standing up but dropping the axe, Valdi replied,

-I think I have a dent on my shoulder, that is all. I saw my entire life before my eyes, I swear.

The concerned Master came to him, opened the damaged shirt of Valdi and looked at his wound, demanding,

-Did you look at the demons' eyes, Valdi?

Vincent grumbled trying to hide that he was in pain,

-I did.

Putting his healing hand on the bleeding shoulder,

Raguel told,

-That's your mistake but we always learn by our mistakes. Some demons paralyses with their stares. Eye contact with demons as a general rule is best to be avoided. The good news is the axe didn't reach your bones but you are going to need stitches for that one. I will help you to fly back to Doctor Williams. You did really well, both of you. We got them all in the end. There were two dozen of them in here at one point.

Looking around him, Father Odell tried to count the dead and wounded demons but couldn't, he asked,

-Do demons smell like that? The stench in this house is unbearable.

Raguel making a makeshift bandage with the sleeve of his own shirt for the shoulder of Valdi replied sternly with a deep sigh,

-No, the stench is from humans.

Vincent demanded,

-Humans don't smell like that!? Do they?

The Master fastening the bandage tightly answered,

-They do when not kept well. Humans are here. I can smell them. Those demons we killed eat humans. They dismember them and feast on them. We have to search that farm. There's a larder somewhere full of butchered but kept alive humans. Do not even look at what is inside that casserole on the stove.

Father Odell disobeyed and went straight to lift the lid of the casserole, closed it again and felt utterly sick. A worried Vincent asked,

-What's in there Theo?

Crying, Odell replied,

-A dead baby, Vince, stewed to death!

While he was shaking his head in despair, Valdi saw the Master letting in the farm main building a handful of angels. Raguel told them,

-We have humans in distress here, find them. Follow

the flies. Check all the barns. Two of you come with me. I want three of you to sort out those demons from the dead to the wounded and be careful.

He went back to Valdi conceding,

-You are right my angel, both of you are in the deep end with me and my son now. Both of you need to to know the harsh truth of things. Come with me, let's find those humans in need. Theo, put your hand on the bandaged shoulder of Vincent, you will do wonders as we go along.

Doing as he was told, Odell enquired,

-Will I?

Raguel leading them to the back of the house and down a dark stair case replied,

-You will. You have been touched by my father this morning. You are full of his healing power right now.

A wondering Vincent asked,

-If your father can heal why didn't he cure Sebastien?

Upset the Master turned to Valdi, tears appearing in his eyes,

-We are givers, we can not help ourselves, or only to a certain extent our loved ones. Mighty is his bloodline. We have to rely on someone's good graces for any given help. My father can't save his bloodline directly when they have been hit. But he can indirectly. He created and keeps creating healing angels. Theo just turned into one this morning. Vincent, the rules are complicated and I will teach them to both of you in time. Trust me when I say living to those rules hurts me deeply.

The more they descended the darker it became. Father Odell touching the walls commented,

-Something are on those walls.

Making a torch appear and giving it to Odell, Raguel ordered,

-Don't touch the walls. Hold the shoulder of your friend and the torch only. The walls are full of dead animals in different state of decomposition.

Thrusting the torch in the hand of Valdi, Theo told wildly,

-But I am full of him, I can make them live again. Master help me! Take them off the wall, we will free them back into the forest where they belong!

The Master smiled at Odell's enthusiasm and helped taking all the carcasses down. Valdi, holding the torch, could only see the magic happen as his friend was touching all the dead animals, they were brought back to life. A couple of angels coming down gave a hand leading the animals out of the farm. When all the creatures were resuscitated Theo gave a satisfied grin to Raguel who taped his shoulder and stated,

-You just did your function fully, angel Theo: looking after my father's creatures. He gave you a lot of power within your hands. He trust you and your judgement.

Vincent enquired,

-Does he trust me? I can't bring anything back to life like Theo just did.

Raguel reassured taking the torch and leading the way down the stairs,

-He brought my son to you. You don't need anymore sign of trust from him. He also took the pleasure out of Sebastien and I to teach you how to fly. We were looking forward to that moment, but he did it himself. It only happened to Joshua and I, his sons. He never gets involved to teach an angel the basics. I do. Anyhow your line of work is utterly different from the one of Theo. I am the Archangel of Justice and you will be by me delivering it. I have to train you as a Punisher. You can forget, like I do, resuscitating hares and rabbits to focus on killing demons.

Still feeling sheer pain in his shoulder, Vincent stated cockily,

-I do like the line of work of Theo better. I would not get dismembered with it. Can we swap?

His offended friend shouted,

-No way! You fight better than I do!

The Master turned to them with a disapproving look to tell them off,

-Shush you two! Theo, you killed five demons by yourself today, from the dozen we were dealing with it is a fair share. Vince, you are stuck with it like I am, and like my son is. You are an angel of Justice and that is all there is to it. Deal with it as best as you can.

Entering a large cave, Raguel went to lit every corner of it. As the light came into the room, the horror of it appeared in full sight. On all the walls, humans were either chained or pinned by large nails. Some had lost their limbs and were barely alive with their stomps eaten away by maggots. Some women in chains were in various stages of pregnancy. All the humans were naked and in appalling conditions. Raguel sighed and told,

-I could smell them from their flesh to the feeling of their pains. Let's free them. We have to turn the hotel of Miss White into a hospital for their recoveries.

A tearful Odell who was already helping to free everyone commented,

-My Whil' will look after all of them. I know she will. I will do so too.

The Master ordered as he made a pile of linen covers appear on a torturing table in the middle of the room,

-Let's start now. Valdi, I want the name and a full check up of all the victims, bring them to the table one by one. Theo with me, we are going to apply basic healing care. I will show you how to do so. We want to get those victims on the move as soon as possible. Stanley, arrange a couple of carts for all of them. In their state very few will be able to walk and follow us to the hotel. Roger help Valdi taking the victims off the walls. He damaged his shoulder badly demon fighting with me.

This started a military operation in the cave where all the victims, were counted, assessed, seen to and then their nudity covered before being transported in the outside world. For some their trust was so inexistent that they would shout and scream all the way through the process. While others were mute and docile like little lambs. A little boy missing half a leg and half an arm, born in the farm, of about five years old, had no name whatsoever. When Roger carried the child out of the farm to the cart, he couldn't retain his tears. He handed the boy to Stanley who put him in the cart with a warning,

-The boy is a cambion. He has no name. If he don't answer to you, it's because he has no tongue. They ate it, like they did with his missing limbs.

Stanley shook his head in desperation as he commented,

-Cambion's tongue is a delicacy for demons. They pay a lot for it. We had one wounded demon and we made him talk. He had received a bullet in his belly out in the yard. Amos was their butcher providing them human meat. Interestingly, because of Valdi, Amos didn't prey on the inhabitants of Wilton Town, he had to go further afield in the neighbouring towns for his victims. We found his shop entrance in one of the barn, a pretty large one. How are we doing down there? I am ready to go as soon as. I have Williams who duplicated himself again for the operation, well triplicated because he is also in Boston. He is manning the other carriage.

Roger, seeing the older angel making cushions and mattresses appear in his cart, gave him a profound bow while wiping his own tears away. Roger confided,

-Those victims need him. I am glad he came forward. We will be a little while down there. The Master is taking care of the humans, cleaning their wounds with Odell.

Stanley smiling sadly replied,

-Williams is a most devoted servant, he will never miss an important call from the Master. But we also have the Lord here. He came to close the shop down, well, the entrance of it, the one which has been found in the barn. That portal has been anointed by babies' blood, many, we are talking about hundreds.

A good hour later, Raguel carrying a little girl in his arms, followed by Valdi and Odell, who were helping a heavily pregnant teenager walk, came to the farmyard. There he found his father waiting by Doctor Williams who was busying himself making the victims in his cart comfortable. The Master went to him straight away with an apology,

-I am so sorry, Father, I didn't expect my farm trip to take that long neither to find so many human victims.

The Great Being took the little girl from the arms of his son into his whilst he replied,

-Well, with demons, it can not be helped to have to expect the unexpected. They had established a very large human butchery here. No wonder Amos was shooting anyone crossing his land. We have another nice little cambion here. What is her name?

Raguel tossing the black curls of the girl answered,

-That's another one with no name. We might as well call the first one Meat and that one Lucky because she was lucky to be found before she was mature enough to be eaten and become one of their demonic delicacy. She is about three. Her human mother has been confirmed dead by the others, bit by bit, eaten away. We have other cambions on the way. Six women have been impregnated by demons, well when I say women, some are just young girls, the one looked after by Theo and Vincent is only thirteen and about to give birth in a day or two.

Looking at the child in his arms, the Great Being stated,

-This one is Lucky Esmeralda for her eyes look like emeralds, but we can not call the boy Meat. Your angels will have to look after those cambions. Those children can't be fully looked after by human parents.

An interested Father Odell who had listened to the conversation with an equally curious Vincent whilst putting the last teenage victim in the carriage asked,

-Why can't they be looked after by human parents? I can easily find adoptive parents for the boy and the girl.

It was the Master who replied to his query,

-Cambions are part human and part demon. They are special children in per say, they do have some powers. Have you ever heard of Merlin? He is a powerful cambion.

Theo interjected, his eyes wide opened,

-Merlin, Merlin the wizard, but that is a fairy tale, surely?

This made Doctor Williams laughed as he put Lucky Esmeralda in his cart,

-Father Odell, haven't you seen enough angels and demons to not believe in cambions and wizards? You are soon to marry a witch and I am a wizard. I can also tell you that if Merlin would have heard you doubting his existence, he would have been mischievous enough to transform you into a toad on the spot with for only counter spell the kiss of Miss White to return you back into human shape.

A blushing Theo commented,

-I would not mind too much the last part.

Putting his hand out to Father Odell, the old Williams enjoined,

-Come and take a seat by me and let's take our wounded to our good nurse. We did let her know of their numbers and she is preparing her hotel to receive them all. Let's give her a hand, shall we. Depending on how diligent you are, it may grant you a kiss from her.

Odell climbed in the carriage by his side with no further a do but turned to Vincent asking,

-Are you coming Vince?

The wounded Valdi gave a look to the Master and the Great Being before replying,

-I may still be needed here. Go and look after all of them. And please name that little cambion of a boy with something better than Meat before I come back. I am sure Whil' will think of something.

Raguel gave the order for the two carts to leave the farm yard. Full of the victims, some silent, some crying, the carriages headed for the hotel of Miss White. Once they were out of view, the Great Being told Valdi,

-You are coming with me, Vincent. I have the counter poison for Mighty. We will bring Sebastien back to Wilton Town for tonight.

Putting his arm across the wounded shoulder of Valdi gently the Master opposed his father,

-Take me with you. Let Vincent rest. He is wounded. He needs stitches. He hasn't slept nor eaten for hours. Or delay the departure with him until I can look after him properly. Mighty is doing a good recovery according to Henry. A few minutes of delay will not hurt him.

The Great Being was rather pleased to see that paternal intervention of his eldest son for his unbeknown younger brother. He conceded,

-I accord you a few minutes to look after your angel, an hour and a half, two maximum. But you, Raguel have to stay here to monitor the preparations for tonight. I will take Vince with me and bring you your son back for tonight and Vincent if he doesn't collapse of exhaustion along the way.

Pushing Valdi closer to him in a caring way, Raguel asked him,

-My angel, Vince, listen to me now, can you push yourself to that extent or shall I beg for you to stay by my side?

Vincent felt the strong care of the Master. He looked at his honest kind eyes before he replied,

-I want to bring your son back to you. I really do. I want you to hold him, just like you are doing with me now. I never had the chance to know my father, I never knew what paternal love was, but I kind of felt it with Abraham Wilton-Cough and I kind of feel it with you right now. I want you to have your only son left back by your side. I will get him for you, I will.

Raguel messed with the hair of Valdi in a sign of affection and demanded,

-Father, fly with him to the hotel, I will catch you up on the way. He is damaged as you know but his wings are not. He was clever enough to advise Theo to retract his own wings too to prevent them from damages. Look after him for me while I make sure that this farm is a close and clean site.

While the Master turned around and fired orders by the dozen, Valdi a little bereft looked at the Great Being making his wings appear asking,

-That means we have to be off?

Smiling kindly to him, the Creator told firmly,

-Yes, we haven't much time before us. Come. If you are struggling up in the air, don't be brave, don't be shy, just tell me.

Both flew away from the farm yard together. Valdi although in pain was not struggling and kept up with the Creator who engaged the conversation with him,

-This was a bit of a situation in Amos's farm, wasn't it?

-It was but Raguel kept it under control. There was a dozen dead demons when I stepped in and a dozen left.

Smiling with some pride the Great Being told,

-I must say my son is a very good demon killer. Mighty is like him in many ways. While you haven't done too bad yourself on your first outing as an angel. How do you feel about the entire experience and working under Raguel?

It took no time at all for Valdi to reply,

-The entire experience is a little overwhelming, I must confess, but I will adjust to it fast. Somehow what I need to do comes to me almost naturally and when it doesn't Raguel is there to pick me up upon it. I feel safe by him. He has watchful eyes. When I make a mistake, he lets me know. If I may say I am learning under his wings. I hope I will learn fast enough to please him.

Turning to Vincent in mid flight and not seeing him struggling, the Great Being gave him one of his bright grin as he queried further,

-So you want to please the Master of all angels? Interesting, I thought you found him haughty. Have you still got difficulties on how to address him?

A giggling Valdi answered,

-I will probably always have difficulties to address any of you lot with your mighty titles, but with no disrespect intended. As for Raguel, I do not find him haughty, not at all. I just saw him cleaning wounds and limbs of humans from maggots with the care a mother would have for her children. The thing is your son is caring, and he is caring intensely so. Sometimes I may think he is acting brashly or with a hot head but that would be me being wrong because he is a multi levelled thinker and he is just playing a game and the best poker face in front of demons. From knowing him, for such a short while, I learnt a lot from him. He put his life on the line in the flick of an eyelid to protect. I admire that and respect your son greatly.

The Creator demanded,

-So you have no problems or arguments to work under him and to protect him then?

Valdi, seeing the hotel of Miss White in the horizon, replied with certainty,

-Of course I haven't. I would lay my life for him like he does for me.

What Vincent failed to notice was a red winged

blackbird flying by their sides all the way since the farmyard. He had no ideas that it was the Master who could be omnipresent like his father in different shape or form that was with them. To the reply of Valdi, the Great Being announced bluntly,

-Good. I am pleased to hear that because Raguel is your older brother.

A baffled Vincent interjected,

-It's impossible. I was the first and last child of my parents.

The blackbird transformed itself into a fully angelic Raguel who was quick to say,

-That is entirely possible knowing my father.

Valdi surprised to see the Master uttered,

-You are here!

Raguel explained, stabilising Vincent who was losing concentration on his flying,

-I have always been by your side since you left the farm in case you would need my help. Remember I can be present everywhere at the same times like Williams. I am also a shape shifter. I can take any animal shapes. Now watch those wings movement. You don't want to fall into the canopy of trees, do you?

The recalled Valdi looking into the confident and reassuring eyes of Raguel regained his composure while he demanded,

-Are you really my brother?

It was the Great Being who replied,

-Yes, he is. All of my children have been created differently. Raguel is your older brother. He was conceived from my blood and fire whilst you have been created from my blood and a human mother and in a very human way. You may remember me into that physical form.

Briefly he took the shape of the human father of Valdi before regaining his angelic shape but it was enough for Vincent to have tears appearing at the corner of his eyes. The Great Being continued,

-You were early for everything as a baby Vincent, from your first tooth to your first steps. It amazed your mother who didn't know who I really was then and subsequently who you really were. You were such a good little boy from the get go but you shared a similarity with my Raguel, you were brash at moments and I had to look carefully at your every footstep. I had to grab you out of the pond of your maternal great grandfather one day. You took a dip trying to grab a carp. You loved nothing more than being on my horse 'Il Tuono' with me and riding in the countryside or on the beach. If I launched Tuono into the waves, you kept laughing. Do you remember? You were ever so young when we were snatched away from you. Your Ma is in heaven. She is still my beloved human wife. I can make you visit her when you are ready.

An emotional Valdi replied,

-I would love to see her. I have vague memories of everything. I remember 'Il Tuono', how black he was with his white marking like a thunderbolt on his head. I can recall being pulled out of a pond, I do. I was just a toddler. And everything after your deaths I do remember more vividly. But only you didn't die.

The Creator corrected,

-My human body did so did your mother's.

Retaining his tears Vincent did let the information sink in before he said with a spike of disbelief in his voice,

-So I am not an orphan...

Raguel taking the hand of Vincent and understanding his emotions, gave it a firm nudge of compassion as he explained,

-You have been a human orphan, yes but you belong to the original family, if I quote your words, you belong to us lot with mighty titles. Let's say you have a special family. We all have been brought up in different ways but they are usually not easy ways. My youngest son only knows from yesterday night who is grandfather is. He spent many incarnated lives not knowing his true and full identity. We did that because we wanted the Mighty One to remain humble. Others knew of his noble origins but were sworn to remain silent about them. You will find that Sebastien, your nephew, and I are not pretentious whatsoever. We are down to earth. I was made to be closer to humans and to know their plights deep down. Our upbringings can be pretty lonely but eventually we meet Him. So, all you must take and think is that you are part of us but also that I am extremely happy to learn that you are my younger brother.

When all of them landed by the Crying White Doe Hotel, Valdi hugged Raguel silently then his father. The Great Being couldn't help smiling as he told,

-You knowing your true identity, Vincent, is my belated gift to you, first for marrying your true love then because you are going to be a father yourself therefore making me once more a happy grandfather.

#

If in the Crying White Doe Hotel the sudden burst of activities seemed suddenly chaotic at the arrival of so many victims to look after, in its kitchen the peace reigned. There Vincent Valdi had taken a seat at the order of the Master of all angels. Fairly subdued, still digesting the news that he was a member of the Great Being's family, Valdi was unusually silent for once in his life. Standing still upon his chair, he did let Doctor Williams take the bandage off his shoulder to look at his wound. The old angel assessed the damages with a sigh as he stated,

-That is going to be an eternal scar, I am afraid to say. But it could have been much worst. A couple of millimetres deeper and your bones would have been damaged, Vincent. I can feel your physical pain. Let's give you some alcohol before I stitch that wound.

An adamant Valdi refused point blank,

-No, I will cope. William, go ahead with whatever you have to do. I need to stay sober to assess Sebastien later.

Looking at his younger brother with pride and approval, Raguel ordered,

-Do as he says, my William. My brother is brave enough to sustain the inconvenience.

Doctor Williams smiled as he started to clean the wound of Valdi with great care. He gave a knowing wink to Henry who had brought to him some hot water. It was the Messenger who acknowledged out loud with a question,

-So you both know you are related?

The Master went to the stove to check the food which

was simmering gently, and replied,

       -Yes we do. But let's keep it within the family. Your vows of secrecy are still maintained. This oxtail soup smells delicious. Henry, fetch our bowls so I can serve it to everyone of this family present in this room, that includes you and William.

       While the diligent Henry obeyed, Valdi enquired rather shyly,

       -Are William and Henry my family too?

       Raguel smiling to him whilst stirring the soup explained,

       -Both are not blood related to you like I am, but you can consider them as family. William, although not the son of my eldest son, has been created by Gael. Since Gael's death, I consider myself as his next of kin, his relative, his grandfather if I may say. William has always been close to my son and I. He is family. As for Henry, he is a very ancient animal spirit turned angel and I am adopting him. So you can consider him as your nephew, like my Mighty is your nephew.

       Nodding positively Vincent took the information in,

       -I see. Is there anything else I should know about my new family?

       The Great Being taking a seat opposite him told,

       -Yes, there is. I adopted my human creation Adam who is now long dead and in heaven. But the ruler of heaven, Joshua is my other very famous son. So both are your brothers as well as Raguel who is my eldest.

       As Doctor Williams started to stitch his shoulder, Valdi commented,

       -So this is a fairly large family...

       Raguel giggled while pouring ladles of soup into bowls when he confirmed,

       -Yes, especially if you count humanity within the line of Adam. As for Joshua, he did roam upon earth long enough to have descendants. But we kept all of them secrets for none to be crucified.

       Bringing a bowl of soup to his father, Raguel continued in order to take the mind of Vincent away from his pain,

-So my dear brother, now that you know a little more of the 'lot with mighty titles' which you are part of tell me a little bit more about yourself.

Vincent pulling a face told,

-In retrospect I should not have said that, should I? It would have probably been better if I did bite my tongue at that moment. There is not much to say about me really. I just am what I am.

The Great Being smiled irresistibly as he thanked his eldest son before commenting,

-Biting your tongue is not preferable to honesty especially when Raguel wants to feed you so you are adequately fuelled up for a journey back and forth across the Atlantic. Come, now, my son, there is a lot to say about you. You can start by telling us how you are enjoying your honeymoon trip so far.

Raguel took on the opportunity to add upon his father to encourage Valdi, who was clearly suffering, to talk,

-Yes, you recently married, Vincent, you can speak to us about your wife, Amelia, if I am correct. I heard that she was clever.

This was enough probing for Valdi to talk passionately, his cheeks blushing as he did so,

-Amelia, oh Amelia, she is my everything, my light in a dark room, my sun when the sky is grey, my shining moon in a starless night...

A satisfied Raguel returning to the stove to serve Henry and the others commented,

-You clearly love her. I heard that you waited for her until her hand was available, patiently, for years. Don't look at my William like that, of course he is telling me everything he knows, especially since you were going to be one of my angels. Now, that I know you are my brother, there are even more reasons for you to be entirely honest with me. I can take all the good, the bad and the ugly. Look, Henry killed a man by mistake and clumsiness but I am still adopting him.

Looking across the table to a red face Henry full of shame, who dropped his spoon in his bowl of soup, Vincent knew it was a fact and the truth. The Messenger explained to the querying glance of Valdi,

-It was a long time ago, in my first human life. I've never been a human before only animals, mainly birds. Therefore I wasn't proficient with my hands for a long time. Being on a battlefield, very young, with a pistol I didn't know how to use was a very bad combination.

Putting a bowl of soup in front of Vincent, the Master revealed,

-To cut a list of excuses short, the Messenger shot dead one of the best Musketeers of my Sebastien. Mighty was mightily incensed as you can imagine. But nonetheless, he educated the clumsy and guilty lad and took him under his wings. Now, tell me more about Amelia, especially the fact that she is intelligent because I may have an urgent mission for her. How is the stitching going on, William? I need Vince to have his soup whilst it is nice and hot.

Doctor Williams replied straight away without losing his concentration,

-I am getting there, Master, a few stitches left. You can get some bread for his soup in the meantime. I used my magical thread. His wound will not reopen during his long journey, I can reassure you on that.

Valdi couldn't help commenting,

-I am very happy to hear that. Having the bloody wound reopening in mid air, in mid trip, is something I could do without. Thank you, Raguel, for the soup.

Making a basket full of warm little bread rolls appear on the table the Master replied,

-It was your order for my recovering angels, it is only fit that you should have some as you are my recovering angel about to go on a long journey. We haven't got much time, tell me more about Amelia, because I need to make a decision on getting her involved or not with something of great importance. We were talking about how clever she was...

Thus urged Vincent told with concern,

-Indeed my Amelia is very intelligent. The fact is she keeps reading, almost everything, from the newspapers to novels passing by treaties of laws and sciences. Most of what she knows is self taught because she left school at a young age. Her mother passed away giving birth to her last child who didn't make it either. So the Elroy family was strong of eleven children with no mother. Three of the little girls of that Elroy brood dropped out of school to look after their siblings and Amelia was one of them. What is the something of great importance, pray? I hope it doesn't involve any demon to come close to her because she is with child.

Raguel putting a couple of bread rolls by the bowl of soup of his brother didn't reassure him at all,

-It potentially could put her in great danger. The reason is that she would then bestow forbidden knowledge. Is she proficient in different languages?

A worried Valdi demanded,

-She knows Spanish, Irish, German and Latin. Amelia can also guess many words of other languages. She works their meaning out. She got a knack for it. You didn't answer me. We are talking about my Amelia. What have you got in mind? What do you want her to do?

Doctor Williams with the will to defuse the situation announced,

-We are all done here! Give or take three weeks and this shoulder should be as good as new. Vincent, you will keep feeling the pain but your wound will seal itself slowly but surely. It will leave a scar but when you have the scar your shoulder will not hurt anymore. If I remember right your Amelia read the Illiad and the Odysseus of Homer in ancient Greek? Please tuck in to your soup. You need to go soon.

A starving Vincent obeyed after replying,

-Williams, once more I owe you. Thank you. And yes, my Amelia did read Homer but what has it got to do with what the Master has in mind?

Serving a bowl of soup to Doctor Williams, Raguel answered,

-A lot. We have a book to translate and copy that your servant Wilton-Cough stole from hell. We have only three days to do it. Miss White has been hard at work with it, but with the numbers of victims we brought to her hotel, she returned to her primordial role of nurse for the time being. Lucifer will notice his manuscript missing in three days time and will definitely quest for it. So there is enormous danger in beholding the book and handling it. However it is important to have a copy of it before we destroy the original. It has to be a very conscientious copy, faithful to the original because the manuscript is literally a guide on how to kill every kind of demons but also Lucifer's techniques on how to kill angels. So we do not want that bible of a book back into his hands however we need to keep the informations from it.

Valdi breaking his bread roll reflected for a minute before he posited,

-We will have to ask her but her decision will have to be respected. If she says no, it means no. However knowing my Amelia, I can fairly say that she is a bit of a dare devil, so she may say yes. I have also no doubt at all that she has the skills required to perform that task. But if she ever accept I want to be at her side at all time to protect her. I can also help her performing it because two minds are always better than one.

Finally taking a seat by his father at the table with his own bowl of soup, the Master told,

-Miss White was the one mentioning Amelia to help her with the task. When our White Witch has a spare time from nursing and hosting, she will be by your wife. Whilhelmina seems to admire Amelia a little.

Speak of the devil and he does appear. Miss White stepped into her kitchen along with Father Odell. Having heard the last of the conversation, she corrected,

-In fact I admire her a lot. Which woman wouldn't for her marrying the best man in town?

A lot of eyebrows raised around the table while Raguel checked the effect of that honest outpour on the face of Theo. He saw Theo's smile vanish for a few seconds but only to return as soon as Whilhelmina turned to Theo realising her blunder. She kissed his freckled nose and tried to get away with it all by saying,

-Vincent will be our best man at our wedding, will he?

Watching the confusion of Odell, the Master intervened to help his angel to sort out his emotion,

-My son wanted to be the best man at Theo's wedding. Can we have two best men or more, Miss White?

With a heavy heart, knowing that what she did say may have saddened her future husband whom she sincerely loved dearly, Whilhelmina replied almost with a sob in her voice,

-We can. Can't we Theo? There are a lot of best men in the world, isn't it?

Pulling through out of his mixed emotions, Odell reassured with his usual kind smile,

-Of course, there are lots of best men in this world. We mustn't overlook anyone. We can have two best men at our wedding, even three or four or more.

Vincent noticed the apparent sadness in the tone of his friend and was lost for words. The Master, again, stood up to diffuse the situation, went to the stove and stated,

-Our Vincent will not mind not being the only best man since he wasn't my only best angel this morning. Our Theo, if he hasn't told you yet, Miss White, killed five demons and helped to rescue Valdi who managed to find himself in a spot of trouble. Come, you two must sit with us and eat. We do not know when we will be able to grab our next meal for tonight will be full on.

The Great Being standing up presented a chair at the head of the table and called Whilhelmina White to take it while Theo Odell sat by his friend who had pulled a chair next to his for him. Soon Raguel served them bowls of soup before getting back to his own seat by his father and ordered,

-Please, eat whilst it is hot.

Whilhelmina puzzled asked,

-I only had a table of four in the kitchen. What happened to it?

The Master, the Messenger and Doctor Williams all giggled at her question. William answered with a beautiful smile,

-I upgraded it to a table of twelve. Think of it as one of my early wedding presents, Miss White. You are soon going to cater for a family, Father Odell, little Emily, Mina, the giant Peter O'Neil, and well any little children coming out of your union with Theo since the Mighty One restored you.

Turning her spoon in her soup, Miss White corrected him,

-You are forgetting my Georgia.

Doctor Williams took a serious air to reveal,

-I am not. I am courting Georgia with the intention of marrying her. If she accepts me, she will become my wife and not be your servant any longer. But she takes you more like a mother, let me correct that, hold you in her heart like a mother, and I will never destroy that bond between you and her. Whether she decides to live with me or stay with you out of sheer loyalty, I am an angel that can duplicate myself and be where I want at the same time. So I can easily be in Wilton Town and in Boston, like I am doing now.

With tears appearing at the corner of her eyes, Whilhelmina asked,

-Is my Georgia responding to your advances? If so, will you be good to her, deep down I know you will but your word in front of the Creator and the Master will mean a lot to me?

Nodding positively William reassured with certainty,

-You have my word that I will look after your Georgia and make her mine. She makes my old angelic heart sing with her sheer honesty. We made her an eternal being. We can't let her be without love for eternity. I, I know how hard it is and you know just as well. I am willing to be her companion and embrace her into her journey as an eternal Being. So far, she is responsive to my courtship. Since I said I have a loving interest towards her, she does her hair in a pretty fashion. You and I know that it says it all.

Miss White could only agree, wiping her tears,

-Oh yes, I know, I do know. She never cared a fiddlestick about the way she looks. Doctor Valdi could tell you that she is considered as a fierce woman in Wilton Town, not just because she broke the arm of a man during an arm wrestling contest. If you manage to bestow her heart then you can be sure to have my blessing, Doctor Williams. If she ever consent to marry, I will give her a way because she has no father to do so.

The Master interrupted giving some bread rolls to Whilhelmina,

-No, I will give a way to your servant if she marries my William. By the way, who will give you a way at your own wedding? If you have no one, I will stand by you. Eternal Beings falls under my jurisdiction, I treat them like my angels in a paternal manner. Now tell me how are you coping with all the humans we brought to you?

The White Witch took the bread and answered, admiring the thoughtfulness of Raguel deep down,

-I would be very honoured if you give me a way for I have no one, for I, I have been the head of my family for so long.

Reassuring her, The Master commented,

-Then you have me. Likewise, it will be a honour to give you a way to the altar, as well as performing your wedding to one of my best new angels I have seen since a very long time. Right, what about my wounded humans? Brief me.

Whilhelmina replied full of subdued awe,

-They have all been made comfortable here. Some have to share rooms and some have mattresses on the floor and covers... The healthier ones. They are in a state of shock, most of them. Abraham is talking and reassuring everyone of them one by one. He is doing wonders. He asked us to fetch some food for them all. This is why Theo and I came to the kitchen. I have to prepare something to eat for those poor things. I don't know what yet but Theo said if we go to fetch the eggs of the hens of Doctor Valdi we could feed half of them. Market day is a week away from now...

Raguel putting his spoon down ordered,

-My Wizard, please, replenish this delicious soup for all those humans to be fed. Ensure that the pantry of Miss White has enough for the next few days to deal with the demand put upon her. Miss White, if you need anything for those humans ask Doctor Williams, he will furnish you with everything, everything to look after them properly.

Doctor Williams with a wand appearing in his hand made a spell toward the stove. Immediately three more large casseroles were simmering away filling the kitchen with the delicious smell of oxtail soup. A satisfied Master continued,

-Miss White, this soup is delicious by the way. You are doing really well without your maid.

Whilhelmina blushing slightly under the compliment confessed,

-My Georgia taught me how to rustle up this hearty soup. This is one of the favourite in winter in this house and of Doctor Valdi. But you would be wrong to classify Georgia as my maid, she is family to Mina and I. There are no tasks that she does in my hotel, that my daughter and I do just as well.

Doctor Williams commented,

-With a large hotel like you have however having the help of someone comes handy. The little Emily and the Giant Peter will provide you with the help you will need to replace the one of Georgia and then you also have Theo. What is the favourite dish of Father Odell by the way?

Put on the spot with red cheeks, Miss White who didn't know looked desperately at Theo who was waiting for her answer with some eagerness, suddenly she received a telepathic message from the Master who told her,

-According to Vincent, his favourite dish is simply sausages on a bed of mash potatoes with thick onion gravy.

With that angelic lifeline given by Raguel, hoping to save her potential future marriage, Whilhelmina finally replied, gathering up courage by knowing she had strong allies at the table,

-My Theo's favourite dish is sausages and mash with an onion gravy, a nice thick one.

This pleased Theo, who smiled but yet remained shyly silent and carried on eating his soup without even looking at her. Seeing that, the Master sent another telepathic message to Miss White,

-Theo's silence says miles. He is still hurting deep down. If you really love him you will have to work on that one. Theo has never had a huge ego and you almost destroyed it with one sentence. My son destroyed the tree branch your future husband wanted to kill himself by hanging. Make sure my angel doesn't find another perfect tree to end his days.

A silent tear rolled upon the cheek of the White Witch unchecked. Doctor Williams, on her left gave her his handkerchief before carrying on the conversation,

-My intentions were for Georgia to not lift a finger at my home but I realised that she needs to help to feel wanted.

Her tears keeping on rolling despite her drying them as they appeared Whilhelmina commented,

-Then you realised a lot about my Georgia. It is intrinsic with her, she helps. She based her own worth, her own value upon her help. But she enjoys cooking most of all. There's nothing that she loves more than pleasing people with her delicious dishes.

Williams then demanded,

-Which is your favourite dish that you will miss the most Miss White? Maybe Father Odell knows it and will prepare it for you?

Lifting his eyes from his soup, Odell almost caught unaware replied, still lost in his sad thoughts,

-I do not know Miss White.

When all faces turned to him, he corrected,

-I do not know Miss White's favourite dish.

This sent Whilhelmina crying even more. She didn't hear her first name, or Whil' or my Whil' in the mouth of Theo. Shivering and despaired, she covered her face to hide her flowing tears. It was too much for the good Theo who went to her and asked in his calm but cold voice at that moment in time,

-What is up Whilhelmina?

Miss White tried to dry her tears as fast as she could but they kept coming and found the strength to lie to explain her behaviour,

-I must have something in my eyes.

Theo stated with a kind smile,

-We can't let you in pain, show me, my Whil'. I might be able to take it out although I am not a Doctor or Doctor Valdi.

Standing up, coming closer to Odell, seeing him so forlorn, Whilhelmina just pushed herself against him and just let herself sob thoroughly. Her despair was such, that after a few seconds of standing still and silent, Theo finally enclosed her into her arms and told sternly,

-Come with me in the garden Whil', we need to talk or at

least dry your tears.

He turned briefly to everyone at the table who were watching them to say,

-If you will excuse us. Please carry on eating.

Father Odell and Miss White left by the French window doors, Theo holding Whilhelmina close to his chest, his hand tapping her back gently. When they were gone, the Great Being asked,

-Vincent, how does this make you feel?

Valdi mopping the rest of his soup with his bread replied,

-Uneasy, uncomfortable and very worried for my two friends.

Raguel commented strongly giving his opinion,

-Well, I would not be as worried as you, my brother. Now, that the blister is pierced, they will feel better with one another. We all know he loves her and despite her obvious blunder we also know she loves him sincerely. The poor thing was in such a state when I told her that Theo had suicidal tendencies.

Joining in, Doctor Williams told,

-I know, next to her, I could feel her pain. She was so sorry for what she said and beating herself up internally for it. I can tell you that she is clearly scared to lose Theo over it and is inconsolable. But he, he was visibly mulling over it all, wasn't he?

Henry agreed,

-He was. I think that small blunder may have cost her greatly. He was avoiding eyes contact with her at the table. He seemed to be in his own little world and he took his time to call her back by her first name. The 'I do not know Miss White' was clearly a blow from a hurting Odell. My bet would be a cancellation of marriage between the two.

Raguel firmly disagreed,

-My bet would be for the opposite and I can all tell you what is happening because I am a wet little bird outside watching them.

A surprised Vincent demanded,

-You are not watching them?

His older brother confirmed,

-Oh, yes I am, like a good Watcher of my eternal beings and angels. Miss White just dropped upon her knees in front of Theo. Tears are still running on her face. She doesn't care for her dress to be muddy. Her sorrow is so palpable and she tries to explain to Theo who is turning around her, not standing still, his emotions all torn apart. But he doesn't help her up, he doesn't give up an inch to her. The rain is strong and getting stronger but they are staying underneath it lost in their mixed emotions. Here, Theo take his jacket off and is putting it across the shoulders of Whilhelmina. He makes her stand up and is taking her under the tunnel of roses which is not the prettiest site since the rampage of Lawrence yesterday. There are a lot of damaged flowers. It must hurt the poor Miss White to see all her carefully tended roses broken like that. She kneels back upon the white rose petals as he argues with her. He is upset and he is letting her know. She is sinking further down, she is covering her face with her hands. She remains silent, all in her emotional pain and Theo walks away from her. He stops for a few seconds, look back but walks away again. Whilhelmina runs after him, she falls. Theo comes to her side straight away, he helps her up but he is still cross about something. He is about to walk away again but she holds his hand, she drops on her knees and good Lord!

Valdi hanging onto every word of his brother asked,

-Good Lord what? Tell us.

The Master smiled, very pleased, and revealed,

-Whilhelmina is proposing to Theo. She had two wedding rings made for them. She is showing him the box. He is opening it. He remains silent and is giving the rings back to her. He is walking away. She is prostrated on the ground. She is a pure picture of sorrow.

Vincent stood up demanding,

-We've got to intervene.

Putting his hand up, the Great Being ordered,

-Sit down my son. We have to let it run its course. Carry on, Raguel.

While Valdi took back his seat. The Master told,

-Theo has stopped again. He is in tears. He is looking back. He sees her and he comes back to her. She didn't notice that he turned around. She is crying so much the poor thing. He is stroking her back gently. He is kneeling by her. He lift her face up. He is kissing her tears, her lips and that is it my children, nothing more for you to know, eat your soups before they step back into the room. Of course keep the secret: we know nothing about what went on outside. Eat up, eat up. Vincent, I want you to have another bowl of soup. We need to fuel you up for the road, my angel.

Raguel put another bowl of soup in front of his brother before going back to his seat with a smile as he said,

-Here, Vince, eat and do not worry about what happened here. The fact of the matter is that yes, Miss White did love you silently and respectfully for years and she never ever told you she did, nor anyone until now. Firstly because she knew you loved Amelia. Secondly, she never wanted it to be a hindrance to you to not affect your work as Doctor with her as a nurse. Thirdly, because she didn't know what were exactly her feelings for you, it was new to her. She regained trust in men by working with you. When you married and when Theo did dare to manifest his sentiments for her, she did let herself fall in love with Theo. And gosh, I can tell you she loves him now, very, very deeply. I will not repeat her proposal to him, but when she thought all was lost, she even begged him to let her be his silent shadow, so she could stay by his side forever. She made a full confession to Theo, and he was deeply upset about it at first but his love for her prevailed as I knew it would. Henry, you lost your bet and I win my one.

The Messenger finishing his soup queried,

-What do I owe you Master?

The senior angel giggling replied,

-Well, you just have to work for Theo Odell the entire afternoon. He is going to prepare holy water ammunitions for tonight's probable fight. We need specific jackets like his and a large supply of small bottles for our angelic soldiers. You are in charge of providing him with everything that needs to be ready to be used to, at the latest, nine o'clock. Also when you deliver to every angel their special jacket, tell them to use the water to blind any demons they could face.

Pushing his empty bowl away from him, Henry assured,

-I know where to get everything quickly. I just need Theo's jacket and I will be back very fast with everything for him and you, Master.

As he finished his sentence, Odell and Miss White stepped back into the room soaking wet with sheepish smiles upon their faces. Raguel came to them, he removed the jacket of Theo covering the White Witch's shoulders and gave it to Henry who stood up. He ordered as he made a warm woollen white cape appear from thin air and covered Whilhelmina with it,

-Miss White, take your seat and warm yourself up. You need it. Eat your soup, it will help you. We have a big day of work in front of us. Henry, off you go and promise me you will be alright?

Henry came to Raguel and gave him a warm hug, silently, and nodded his head positively before leaving by the garden doors and deploying his wings. Once the Messenger was off carrying the jacket of Father Odell in his hands, once he closed the door windows, Raguel turned to Theo and demanded,

-Did you find out what was Miss White's favourite dish? For she will miss her Georgia dearly and to know the comfort food of someone goes a long way.

Odell understood all the double meanings straight away so he replied in a similar way,

-Her favourite dish is humble pie, the humble apple pie I mean.

Turning to him, a tear in her beautiful eyes, Whilhelmina agreed,

-Yes, it is with a dash of cinnamon in it to sweeten and spice things up a little.

Theo smiled to her and went to kiss her forehead firmly as he said,

-Eat, eat my Whil', warm yourself up. I promise you that I will learn to do apple pies for you to feed our family. Our Mina will teach me how to make them.

When he stood back up, Theo saw Raguel holding a new jacket and shirt in his hand who told him,

-You look like a wet dog, my angel, here, put that on and we will let that shirt of yours dry by the fireplace. Then you need to eat up because you have heaps to do ammunition wise today for my army. The little delay at Amos's farm didn't help us in regards to timing for the preparation of tonight.

While Odell obeyed, and the Master took back his seat by his father, Doctor Williams enquired to start back the conversation at the table in a casual way,

-Did you find a name for that little cambion without a tongue, an arm and a leg?

Miss White answered straight away with some emotion,

-That poor little boy! Yes, we did. We are calling him Mitchell. To be honest, it was Abraham Wilton-Cough who found that name when he and I heard the story of the little cambion.

Going back to his place at the table, with his new clothes on, Odell explained further with a deep sorrowful sigh,

-We couldn't escape thinking of him being called Meat to be truly honest. Although we knew it wasn't appropriate. But Abraham who is helping us looking after everyone upstairs came up with Mitchell. As we couldn't find anything better, we agreed to call that little boy like that. The short of his name will be Mitt, of course, which sounds like Meat.

With a despairing smile, the Master vented,

-Dear old Abraham! He had to get involved. Well you mustn't tell that child about the meat part. But Mitchell is an acceptable name especially to the eyes of my father as it means the gift of god. But isn't Wilton-Cough making it worst for the victims with his ghostly appearance tending to them?

The White Witch confessed,

-No, he isn't scaring them. As he was helping looking after Lawrence, Abraham asked me how he could become more physical to give water to your young angel when he needed some. So I worked out a fast spell to render him fully physical when he wants to for the next twenty four hours. So far he has been fully physical and helping out.

Father Odell added with emotion in his voice,

-Abraham reaches out to the victims. To all the ones that can talk, he made them share their stories. Believe it or not he provides them with moral comfort. The man with one arm left, the one which was screaming all the way to the hotel, is now deeply asleep, pacified. Abraham held his hand until the man was sleeping. He told him and the two others in the room a fairy tale, like if they were children, but they are grown men who happened to have horrendous things done to them. But it worked, it just worked like magic. His voice, his presence soothed them all.

Giving a warm bread roll to Theo next to him, Vincent told,

-If he proves helpful here with Amos's victims, I want Abraham to stay in the hotel rather than coming with me over the Atlantic especially if I am too weak to make it back.

The Master ruled with some severity,

-My dear brother, you told me that you will come back with my son, so you will. If you rest yourself back on your honeymoon I will be highly displeased.

It was the Great Being that spoke for Vincent,

-Your brother doesn't mean that at all, Raguel. No need to go on your high horses here. What he meant is that he is scared not to accomplish the return back, to fall from exhaustion from the sky into the deep ocean. This is why he wants to protect Abraham from plunging with him and witnessing his death. Do not forget his torn shoulder muscle.

Raguel looked at Vincent with deep sorrow and told,

-If anything untoward happens, I will look after your family, your Abraham and keep an eye on his sons and little widow.

Theo added,

-And I will keep looking after your hens.

Valdi smiled and tapped the hand of his friend on the table in a grateful manner. The Master expressed out loud his trail of thought,

-Well, I hoped you and Sebastien would have been able to bring your intelligent Amelia for her to help us out but it would be too dangerous to even attempt that mission in your state and his.

Dropping his spoon inside his soup, Theo bursting with joy claimed,

-I have the solution! I have it! I have it! It can work, it can!

Raguel looked at his happy outburst with suspicion and demanded,

-My dear Theo, explained yourself, for right now, I believe you stayed too long under the rain and therefore are a little feverish.

Theo shook his head negatively defending himself,

-I am not! I am not! I can assure you, I am not but I have worked out the solution to our dilemma. Listen, your son, one day made my old Rosalie fly along with my phaeton. He did put his angelic wings on my mare and off we were flying above the forest. My Rosalie is far too old to make the crossing above the Atlantic, but Fair Wilton, the Appaloosa of Sebastien, that is a stallion that can. It is a horse that made the trip from Boston to Wilton Town without any problems. It is a fine stallion and you must know that your son has a keen eye for his horses. As his stallion, Fair Wilton is also used to have wings on. Now, if the shoulder of Vincent is damaged, his wings are not! We tidied them up before entering into any fight to his advice. That is when his advice is paying off! He can use his wings on Fair Wilton. The beautiful flanks of the animal will do all the work and not Vincent's back and shoulders. So those could rest. If taking my phaeton, then Amelia could be brought to Wilton Town safely. If Sebastien join his wings on his stallion, giving it four wings, there is enough room for three in the phaeton so for his recovering self not to strain himself either. A four winged Fair Wilton will also cope with the weight of everyone on his way back across the Atlantic. What do you all think about that suggestion?

While the Master was nodding positively pondering silently, an interested Vincent asked,

-But how do I put my angelic wings on a horse?

Theo retrieving his spoon from inside his soup admitted,

-When there is a will, there is a way. I am too new as an angel to know exactly how it works but I have seen it and experienced it. Sebastien did it, he knows.

Doctor Williams proposed,

-Let's contact Mighty via telepathy. I am sure he will see the necessity of you using his horse to get to him and talk you through it all, Vincent.

Raguel ordered,

-My William, contact him and explain the situation to him. He will understand and help his uncle. Vincent, when Mighty makes contact with you follow his voice and guidance. I know everything is a steep learning curve for you two, my new angels, but you are doing fine. Vincent, this exercise will also teach you to learn how to use telepathy effectively while on the way to my son. My Theo, well done. When the Mighty One said you were a logistic angel through and through, he was right. You have proved yourself to his eyes and mines to be the most resourceful angel we ever encountered beside our William. Now, where is the stallion of my son?

Blushing under the praise, Odell replied in a shy manner,

-I believe he is in the stables at the presbytery. My phaeton is in the stables of the hotel.

The Great Being stood up and corrected him,

-Not any longer, they are both right outside waiting for us. Vincent are you ready? It is grand time for us to depart. Theo, if you keep on the good work, you will be an archangel in no time at all. Raguel, Williams, Mrs Odell, we will see you all on our safe return thanks to the ingenuity of Father Odell.

Vincent hugged Theo before he followed his father. Passing by Raguel, his older brother stopped him in his track, embracing him warmly, he told,

-Come back to me in one piece with my son. I will keep a close and kind eye to your Abraham while you are away.

This made Valdi smile and say with some cockiness,

-Well, if you are kind to my Abraham, you can be sure that I will bring your son back with all my might.

He left closing the garden doors behind him. Raguel looked at Vincent's bowl and stated,

-At least my angel has eaten if he haven't slept. What do you think my William? Is Vincent going to be alright?

Doctor Williams starting clearing all the empty bowls from the table answered,

-He will especially with his friend's idea, that is a game changing move. Beside that he is with your father. It is going to be alright, Master. Mighty has been quick to respond too. He has already given instruction for his stallion to be docile under the lead of Vincent which is something. He has spoken to his animal.

A smiling Raguel commented while helping to clear the table,

-I wish Mighty chose his horses a little bit more manageable but he loves powerful beasts, he always have.

Father Odell enquired with deep shyness, feeling he was intruding into a conversation he wasn't allowed to join,

-I believe Vince to be more than capable to deal with Sebastien's stallion. He is a veterinarian as well as a Doctor. But I must ask you a couple of things. Did your father meant it that I could become an archangel?

The Master stopping what he was doing, considered the timid Theo from head to toe before he replied,

-Of course he did. You would do a very fine one as well, let me tell you that. Now fire away your next question because we have a lot of work to do.

A fidgeting Theo enquired,

-Is Vincent related to... to... I couldn't help noticing, listening...

Raguel putting bowls in a deep sink answered with ease,

-It happens that Vincent is my brother, my blood brother on my father's side, well my only side for me. He is much, much younger than I am of course, because he has been created only a few decades ago from a human mother and is on his first life. But it is a brilliant life so far, I must confess, for he is also like you already on the path to become an archangel. We learnt that we were related only this morning. Our father broke the news to us both.

A giggling Doctor Williams queried,

-How did Valdi took the news, I wonder?

The Master starting to clean the dishes alongside Williams revealed,

-Well, I wish I could say like an atheist learning that his father was god, but he took it all pretty well in his stride. Now this has to stay between us that Vincent is the son of my father. I am only telling you because Vincent considers you, Theo as a younger brother and you, Whilhelmina as an older sister. Therefore you are considered as family and allowed to know. But I expect from you two silence about it. The blood line of my father is in great danger right now and if the news falls onto bad ears the life of Vincent would be jeopardised. So it has to stay a family secret.

He stopped for a few seconds before saying, giving a full brief to Odell and Miss White,

-Right, let me say this, the secrecy is between the family members and we do adopt people in our hearts, so they are included. So far, I know, you two know, Williams and Henry know about it. It will be extended to the Valdi family, the Wilton-Cough one and my son's family. William is allowed to include whomever he wants to the secrecy, because he is my safe servant. Now, my Theo, it is time for you to get back to work. That well outside must be full of water to be transformed to holy water. Mrs Odell, get plenty of bowls and spoons, you are coming with me to feed all our human victims.

Both obeyed straight away. Father Odell went outside and Whilhelmina followed Raguel who was carrying a large casserole of hot soup upstairs. The Master turned to her asking quietly mid stairs,

-How are you doing, Whilhelmina, after that trying time outside in the garden?

His question made her cry. Reaching the landing Raguel, put his casserole down and took all the bowls of Miss White to put them on the ground then he offered the space of his arms to her, demanding,

-How do you feel, my Being? Tell me, I am here for you.

Miss White cried within his arms confiding between her

sobs,

-I am not rejected. I am still his. I am still my Theo's. I was so scared. I thought I lost him for good.

Tapping her back, the Master reassured,

-I know you did, I know, but Theo can see through everything and he truly, deeply loves you. As I told you this angel of mine has no confidence at all. You will have to bare that in mind when you talk to him. Look, it was just a blunder on your part, but it is a good blunder because it got you talking to him in all honesty. What did you get from that conversation?

Whilhelmina replied as she dried her tears,

-That I love him so much it hurts. I didn't know what to do to retain him and what I said seemed wrong and to angry him further. And the further he went from me I felt at utter loss. He has become in the space of a few days my anchor. If I ever lose him, I think I will be lost at sea.

Raguel proposed,

-Come and sit by me on the stairs for a minute, talk to me. First, I want you to know one thing, you can always confide to me and my servant Doctor Williams but also my son Sebastien. Whatever happens, you will never be left alone, you have us to rely on, we will be there for you.

Taking a deep breath, the White Witch accepted the invite and sat willingly by the Master of all angels. She felt that she needed that moment of pause deep down. Once she was settled, Raguel revealed,

-Before you say anything, know that I am a Watcher and I do know exactly what happened between you and Theo in the garden. I can be anywhere at the same time. I know for example that Peter that will work soon for you is up and about. He is in pain but he is feeding his little rabbit right now. While Mina, Emily and Georgia are by the sea side collecting shells on the beach. All have a smile on their faces, enjoying the day out despite the wind. You can confide in me, my Being, whether you are wrong or right. I have seen and heard almost anything so if there is an angel you can talk to, it is me.

Her tears coming back, Whilhelmina just started by her first confession,

-I find it hard to deal with emotions. I tried to retain

them. I tried to retain them for so long.

The Master gave her a kind smile and wiped her eyes while he commented,

-I can understand that, because I know where you come from and the start of your life hasn't been plain sailing. So you didn't retain your emotions for Theo. When he said he didn't want to marry you any longer, you run after him, fell, and you actually proposed to him. A beautiful proposal, I must confess, and coming from you, most rare and unusual.

Whilhelmina looking at her shivering hands confided,

-I would do anything for Theo. He has such, such a beautiful soul. As an eternal being I saw a lot of humans, a lot. But Theo, oh, Theo, I feel soothed by him, I want to devote myself to him completely, entirely and yes, if he don't like me anymore be his serving shadow. I am hopelessly in love with him. He means so much to me, so much. He gave me back hope. You know I have been guarded against men because of what happened to me.

Taking her hand within his, Raguel told,

-I know, Noah Wilton was the first to inspire you to be the nurse for the town he was creating. He restored a little bit of faith of humanity to you. Then it took my brother...

Miss White trembled as she confessed,

-I did fall in love with Vincent, but I stayed silent about it, to him and to everyone, and I know how to behave, I do, I've never done anything with him, never. We just worked together and he is more than a good man but I knew he wasn't mine so I've been good. I have, I am also scared of love. He married the love of his life and Theo soon after started to pay me some attention. I was worried of Theo before because he is a priest and I am a witch. So I never really met him, I never gave him a chance to get acquainted with me by fear for my daughter and I. But Theo is not like that and he made his way right to my heart and yes, I could kneel by him because my heart belongs to him and no one else. When I never had hope, I just look at his eyes, and I have some again.

Helping her up, Raguel commented,

-I will tell you what, my Being, your wedding is still on and yes, you may have hurt Theo's feelings, but they will heal over time. If you want to be cheeky you may ask him if he didn't love a little girl called Clara when he was a schoolboy and she didn't looked at him at all because he was lanky and a 'freckled thing'. He loved too but nothing happened there as well. There's a thing that is called life. You happen to love his freckled nose and are willing to kiss it, and more than that to devote your entire self to Theo. Odell will never receive a declaration of love like you did to him today, never. If he had ignored your heart put on a plate in front of him, I would have branded him a fool. But thank God, he has a heart that loves you, very deeply just like yours, this is why your blunder did hurt him so much. But I am very confidant that you will both work it out and be happy together.

Whilhelmina sighed before she asked,

-You know I am losing my Georgia who will probably live with Doctor Williams. So I am losing my confident and closest friend. Would you mind becoming my confidant?

The Master giggled at the timidity of her demand while he took the large casserole back into his arms, and answered,

-You have me, my William and my son as confidants, Whilhelmina, don't forget that. You are not alone. You have become a part of our angelic family. Now, why don't you grab a nice little rest, especially after all those emotions? You have been working tirelessly so hard. Sleep because we are going to have a long night tonight and I will need you to stay in your hotel to look after all the rescued I will send here. Grab five to six hours of sleep now, change your dress, feel fresh and come back to me for your orders. I am staying here to keep an eye on your hotel and all those poor humans. I will be there when you get up. Go sleep now. And, remember before you close your eyes, your Theo will marry you, he will. I know he will because my father called you Mrs Odell before he left us, this was not a mistake on his part, this was a clue of what was in store for your future. So you can dry your tears, my dear.

The White Witch bowed to him respectfully but also gratefully. She took the bowls back from the floor, and told,

-Thank you, thank you for everything. Who will help you? Let me take that to the corridor upstairs, there is a little console there.

Welcoming her care, Raguel replied with a wry smile as he carried his casserole of soup up the stairs,

-Don't worry about me, Whilhelmina, I will have plenty of help. First, the one of the ghost you decided to render more physical for twenty four hours. I would say god help me there but my father is away to finish the rescue of my son, so I will have to cope with an Abraham. Then there will be the one of that good human, the kind Mrs Toad, which my son likes a lot, that he is trying to wed to a dairy farmer called Berry so her surname isn't Toad anymore. But I also have my William, and my angels will come to the call for tonight one by one. So I am good. Put all the bowls on the console and grab a rest while you can, Mrs Odell, this is all I can say.

She did, looked at Raguel and confided, before going to her bedroom,

-I would have loved to have a father like you. Thank you again.

When her door closed, left alone in the corridor Raguel talked to himself,

-Funny that they are all saying that.

Appearing, passing through a door, a ghostly Abraham Wilton-Cough demanded,

-What are they all saying?

The Master sighed deeply at the sight of the apparition before asking sternly,

-I thought you had been rendered more physical, Wilton-Cough?

The old Abraham made himself more physical at once, took his top hat off to bow to the senior angel then replied,

-Yes, yes, I have been made more physical but think of it like a full bank account, you need to use the money sparingly so it last longer. I appear fully when I need strength to do something.

Raguel couldn't help smiling at his answer and ordered,

-Well, grab those bowls and follow me, we are going to feed all those human victims. Your master is away to fetch my son with my father and you have been left in my care in case he doesn't come back.

About to drop all the bowls but managing to secure them, Abraham demanded wildly,

-But he will come back, will he? My Vincent will never leave me stranded like that unless it is something very serious.

The Master reassured,

-I have all faith that he will come back safely. He wanted you to stay here because there was a risk to his life and we needed help here. I promised Vincent that I will look after you if anything happens to him.

The ghost with a sad grin confessed,

-You know, I am going to be extremely worried for Vincent until I see him back. What is my brave boy doing now?

At this confession Raguel realised that Abraham truly loved his younger brother like a son, so he replied,

-As you know we had to fight demons to save those humans you have been helping. Vincent sustained an injury. It is not life threatening in itself and we looked after it but he hasn't got his full strength. He is crossing the Atlantic back and forth again to fetch my son to face the problem we will have in Wilton Town tonight. Although I fed him and I fed him well, exhaustion is a danger and above an ocean, it is a real one for an angel. He could take a diving dip to his death. But we think we worked out a solution, a trick my son uses. He puts his wings on a horse on occasion, you see. With this method of transport, the horse is doing all the physical work and this should spare Vincent. So there is plenty of room for hope. Now, brief me about our victims. Which should we attend and feed first?

Abraham told while showing the way,

-The two children, Mitchell and Lucky Esmeralda, then the pregnant girls, then the rest. What happened at that farm is appalling. I went to my bank and looked at papers I had regarding it. Please have a look at them when you have time. The rolls are there, in the pocket of my tail coat. So the land Amos had was all mine but on a lease dating from the time of my father Terah. The entire lot now belongs back to my family, in fact to my eldest son, Zachary. I know he has his heart set on creating a hospital for Wilton Town. This is the perfect place for it. There is the scope to build a large one with gardens even, some for the recovering to wander about and some to sustain the kitchen and the land is large enough to add an orphanage for the town. The orphanage could become a pet project for my widow and Amelia Valdi. Both love children and have mother's hearts.

Entering the bedroom where the two children were, the Master of all angels smiled at Abraham Wilton-Cough confided,

-My dear Abraham, I must admit that I like your way of thinking. Feed that little girl while I give his soup to Mitchell.

The ghost obeyed yet he warned the angel,

-Don't let me hear you calling him Meat because I will haunt you forever.

Raguel gave a glance and a giggle at the old ghost and didn't argue. From that point that spirit was truly accepted by him as family.

#

Since having left the yard of the hotel in the phaeton pulled by Fair Wilton, flying above fields, forests and villages, the Great Being and his youngest son had been chatting. Vincent was getting the grip of making the appaloosa of Sebastien fly. Not willing to talk about what he had witnessed with his brother at the farm which saddened him greatly, he engaged a conversation about the stallion,

-For sure this is a fine animal. Sebastien arriving with that horse in Wilton Town must have made quite an impression.

The Great Being corrected,

-He was actually in the carriage with the ladies, so he didn't swan about with his beautiful stallion.

Vincent enquired with a giggle,

-I wonder why?

His father scolded,

-Vincent, you are so encourageable and incorrigible. Well, if you must know, the little Miss Fair had a cold and as she is his wife now, it goes beyond explanation. Sebastien was just caring for his future wife, even offering her his sleeve for her to sneeze upon because they didn't have any handkerchief. The rock bottom fact is that your nephew wasn't doing the 'Beau' to the ladies. To be truly honest with you, it is beyond him but, like you, he is extremely handsome and can not help the attention of women. May I remind you, what happened in Miss White's kitchen this morning. Do you want to discuss it with me?

A blushing Vincent replied,

-I'd rather not but I will. I was surprised. I would never have guessed, with all those years working with her that Whilhelmina had sentiments for me. It came out of the blue and it was rather a shock. Not only that, I felt so bad for poor Theo who really loves her. I didn't know what to say so afraid I was to make the situation worse. But I was sorry for them both all along.

Surprised that his younger son chose to confide, the Great Being knew that the entire matter had been affecting Vincent more than he expected. He told,

-Your restrained attitude was the best to have to be honest with you and it did sort itself out in the end. My Raguel had a talk with Whilhelmina afterwards to make sure she was alright. She was still emotional but she is okay. As for Odell, Raguel, Henry who will work with Theo all afternoon and Doctor Williams will keep their eyes on him. We certainly don't want him to do something stupid over the entire matter. So you can rest assured that he will be watched closely. The three will also probe Theo to see if he is ready to confide his feelings.

Valdi told with a deep sigh,

-This is the problem with Theo, he bottles things up until it is too late. He is shy and never wants to be a bother, never. I remember once, he organised a tea party for old ladies for one of his charities, the one for homeless people. It was to encourage the ladies to knit large woollen covers for the people of Wilton Town without a roof before the winter. During his trips back and forth to organise everything, he tripped, damaged his ankle badly, and said nothing to no one. They were even missing a chair for the meeting so good old Theo stayed standing without a word about being in such pain. When I visited him that evening, he had been standing against the wall of the corridor of his presbytery unable to walk since those dear ladies left. It was three hours later, three. His ankle was literally black.

His father reassured,

-Well, this time it is not a physical pain, it is of the emotional kind which could be worst for someone like Theo who has suicidal tendencies. However, according to Raguel, he did express himself fully to Whilhelmina when they were in the garden. He didn't bottle things up then. She did a full confession to him that she had harboured sentiments for you for a long time but as she knew that your heart was already taken and engaged, she always behaved appropriately and professionally.

Pulling the reins Vincent confirmed,

-I can testify to that. She did behave correctly. I would never have guessed she loved me all along. She never battered her eyelids to me or played flattery games upon me. Look, our line of work is not always rosy, sometimes we cross muddy fields to help a mother to deliver her child when it is not to help a cow to deliver her calf. I would describe it as mud, blood and sweat. We always had a good understanding that's for sure and she taught me a lot about medicinal herbs of which I am grateful because it is ever so useful. I consider her as my nurse but also as a friend. Like with Theo, I witnessed life and death with her. One thing I am scared of...

He stopped talking, drying a tear with his hand. The Great Being took the reins from his son and encouraged him to share his sentiments further,

-Come, tell me, Vincent, you are not one who is scared easily, what are you scared of?

Valdi confessed sobbing,

-Losing their friendships. Both matter to me greatly. I have a wife which I love passionately. So if my best friend Theo sees me working with his wife or talking to her, will he now consider me as a threat? Of which I am absolutely not for I love my Amelia.

Wings appeared on his father who reassured,

-Theo is intelligent, Vincent. Yes, his ego is a little bit bruised by that discovery that his future wife had feelings for you but he will get over it. Theo has known you for more than a decade, and he knows how much you love your Amelia. You will not lose his friendship over the matter. Now, I think it is grand time for you to take a nap. I will be in charge of that phaeton. Lay your head on my shoulder, sleep and have faith that everything will turn out alright in the end. Just think of this, you will be the best man at Theo's wedding this Sunday while your wife will be the maid of honour along with Georgia Marlow, Mina White and Emily.

The strong left wing of the Great Being protectively covered the shoulders of Vincent and pushed him against his own shoulder. Vincent didn't struggle. He closed his eyes and was soon fast asleep, his head resting on his father's shoulder.

A few hours later the phaeton stopped in a grass field in

the middle of a large cumulus cloud. Gently waking up his youngest son with his wing the Great Being told,

-Vincent, we are here, wake up my dear child.

Opening his eyes, Valdi was amazed to find himself in green pastures within a cloud in the sky. He looked at his father with wonder but didn't ask any question. He retrieved his wings from Fair Wilton and freed the animal from the phaeton. The stallion took no time at all to rest and graze on the lush green grass, while Valdi followed his father and went to 'the Neptune'. The ship, full sails on, benefited from a fair wind. Soon father and son caught up with it and went to the cabin where Sebastien was, without being noticed.

The knock on the door was responded by Zachary Wilton-Cough who hugged Vincent as soon as he saw him. He then turned to Amelia to announce with joy in his voice,

-Doctor Valdi is back!

While Amelia rushed into the arms of her husband, Zachary presented his hand to the tall angel behind Vincent with his welcome,

-Please, come inside. I will make sure that the coast stays clear. If you need my help tap thrice at the door.

Not leaving the hand within his, the Great Being appraised the son of Abraham Wilton-Cough on the spot. He smiled to him as he asked what he knew already,

-And your name is, young man?

Intimidated, Zachary stuttered,

-I am Zach. Zachary Wilton-Cough, at your service.

The Great Being smiled further and replied,

-This is very good to know. I am very much obliged. I know your father.

Zachary corrected without thinking,

-Knew, my Pa passed away a little while ago.

Messing the hair of the young man who was holding the door of the cabin open, the Creator stated,

-No, know. Your father is a helpful spirit attached to one of my angels, Doctor Valdi.

Zachary nodded with respect, guessing he had an important angelic entity before him. He told Amelia Valdi quickly before he left the cabin,

-Mrs Valdi, knock for me if you need anything. I will go and fetch.

Amelia went to the boy, held his hand with gratefulness before she closed the door as she said,

-Thank you so much Zachary, we will. You are our guardian angel. Make sure no one enters but you.

She then turned to the Great Being whom she recognised and courtesied to him, still struck by his awesome presence. Vincent made the presentation,

-Amelia, this is my father. Dad, this is my wife.

Extending her hand to the Great Being, a baffled Amelia enquired,

-But I thought you were an orphan, my Vincent?

This made Valdi say seriously,

-My father will have no problem at all to explain the situation to you for he can answer for all things.

Vincent then went straight to Sebastien whom he found well and up, while the dumbstruck Amelia had her hand held by the Great Being who told her,

-I heard a lot about you.

Adjusting her glasses upon her freckled nose, Amelia apologised,

-I am so sorry I never heard about you apart for seeing you last time briefly.

A giggling Sebastien reassured,

-Mrs Valdi, I know he is my grandfather since yesterday only.

Pleased to see his grandson back upon his feet, the

Great Being went to hug him and demanded,

-How are you doing Mighty?

Sebastien replied as he was released from the embrace,

-Much better. But I can still feel something wrong with me. But I am myself. However I have moments...

Amelia came to explain with eagerness,

-He has dizzy spells, not very often to cause alarm but they do last for a good quarter of an hour. Vince, I wrote it all down for you. What he had to drink, what he had to eat, the hours he slept and the time he was out of it.

Valdi went to fetch her notes and going through it with care, he ordered,

-Let's give him the antidote without delay.

The Great Being handed to Vincent the potion and told,

-Mighty, Doctor Williams worked hard for that one.

Sebastien checking the antidote in the hands of Valdi commented,

-I am sure he did. He is such a loyal servant of my father.

While Doctor Valdi put some of the glistening liquid into a syringe, he announced,

-You will then be happy to know that your love match you did with him and Georgia Marlow is working.

Smiling endlessly, and punching the air with joy, Sebastien jubilated,

-I knew it would! I just knew! She is ever so honest and he needs honesty most of all. I knew it would work.

The Great Being laughed at the happiness of his grandson before ordering,

-Mighty, take a seat and give your arm to Vincent. Your father is still disapproving of your matchmaking hobby although I am not. I did find your will to transform the name of Mrs Toad to

Mrs Berry quite amusing. There again it is working. I must admit Pamela Toad is a darling of a human being and when she couldn't sleep because your angel Daniel was screaming in sheer pain in the hotel of Miss White, she just went to look after him out of her good heart.

Giving his arm and seeing it garroted tightly, Sebastien answered,

-She is a good woman. She was a lonely heart who needed a good man, which Mr Berry is. Pa is from the old school of angels who did let everything happen by themselves but I think there is nothing wrong to make one meet another person you know they are going to either like or love. It is just a little push in the right direction that is all. Anyhow, most importantly, how are my Daniel and my Lawrence? So Daniel was screaming. His wound was really bad when I got the demon off him.

Valdi replied as he injected the anti poison in the arm of Sebastien,

-Daniel lost his leg. I had to amputate him. His leg was black when I arrived at his bedside. There was no recovery possible for it, I am afraid. For Lawrence, it was in extremis, but we saved him by doing an almost complete blood transfusion. Both of your angels are alive and recovering. Doctor Williams said that he will employ Daniel who can't be a fighting angel any longer in your army. One of the lungs of Lawrence is in a poor state, and it will be better to keep Lawrence away from fighting in the future. Williams suggested to recycle that young angel as a nurse in our clinic.

Sebastien demanded a little astonished,

-Our clinic?

So Valdi confirmed to him,

-Yes, as I know now, that you are my nephew, as you are already doing me the great favour of looking after my clinic while I am away, as I also know that you will stay a while in Wilton Town in order to protect your little wife, I thought it fair to give you a wedding present showing you my appreciation. Instead of working for my clinic, would Ivy and yourself become partners of it? It will be our clinic from now on. This will give you an instant status and respect in town. It will not give you wealth, I can tell you that, but it will give respect to your name all across Wilton Town. What do you say?

While Vincent put a small bandage across his arm his nephew gave his answer,

-I can only say that it is most appreciated and accepted. My Ivy will be pleased as well. How is she? She must be so worried.

The Great Being announced,

-No one told what happened to you to Ivy by order of your father. Jack is in the confidence though. He is keeping an eye on her and both opened the clinic for business as usual this morning. But I can tell you that with every minute that passed without seeing you, your Ivy has been increasingly worried. She is very busy but she keeps looking at the clock.

Standing up from the chair he was being treated, Sebastien told,

-I must go back to her. This was a bad decision from my father. I want my Ivy in the know at all time. She will be biting her nails right now but if she knew she would man up and be strong, be strong for me. My Ivy may be a frail woman but she has bags of character and she can take a bad news hitting her doorstep.

Valdi ordered,

-Sit back, I haven't finished with you yet. We want Ivy to see you fine, now do we? She has done enough worrying, so let me finish up fixing you. You can be as brash as your father when you love. I can tell you that the apple on this occasion hasn't fallen very far from the tree. I can see Raguel in you. In the defence of your father, he was also very worried about you.

Sebastien sat back on the chair willingly but with a pout, arguing,

-I can see my father in you just as well. You are a commender in chief type, aren't you?

While Vincent prepared a glass full of potion, the Great Being announced,

-Mighty, you are not wrong. Valdi's archangelic name is the Protector, he will lead a group of angels that will protect your angels and your father. Your dad and him gave a good beating to Lucifer because of what happened to you.

The Mighty One's smile returned as he told,

-I wish I had seen that. What was the score?

Casually looking at notes by a manuscript and reading them, the Great Being replied,

-Your father gave Lucifer a right rough and tumble. He had the upper hand up until he dislocated his own shoulder. But we intervened to break the fight and Vincent broke the wrist of Lucifer single handedly. He took your father away and looked after him. Raguel is fine before you ask. You know he is made of tough skin and blood like you.

But Sebastien still demanded reassurance,

-So Pa is alright?

Valdi giving him a glass of potion to drink reassured,

-Raguel is strong and still standing. He is alright. I fixed his shoulder. He killed many demons afterwards, more than a dozen. But in the heat of the moment I failed to keep the count. Here drink that, this will clean your liver of any remaining poison. Then take your shirt off and let me examine you. My stitches are not the magical ones of Doctor Williams. I must assess if you are fit to fight tonight. But I can tell you one thing if you are fighting or not, your father wants to see you. Your absence hurts him. He just wants to see you alive.

Sebastien did as he was told while a beautiful goddess stepped into the room from the opened next door cabin, a child in her arms. She addressed Vincent straight away,

-You haven't got magical stitches but they were perfect and I made them to be magical. My grandson will be able to fight tonight despite his injuries. But it will be better if he doesn't get too physical. I taught him a few magical tricks which could help him greatly. But if you could remind him to use them instead of his physical strength, it will be most appreciated, Doctor Valdi.

The Great Being presented,

-Vincent, this is Dana, Celtic Goddess and grand mother of the Mighty One. Dana, this is my youngest son, the Protector.

Dana, giving a head to toe glance to Vincent, told,

-I heard and hoped for his coming. He is most certainly

needed. He is also absolutely dashing.

Valdi couldn't resist not to the beautiful goddess but to his adopted baby which he took in his own arms with delight welcoming,

-Come to papa, my little Abbi, come to papa! Did you miss me? For daddy missed you a great deal of a lot. How is your little tooth, did it come through? Oh yes, it did! It did! Who is papa's big little girl? It's Abbi! It's Abbi, all the way to the moon and the stars and back.

His wife went to him and related, stroking the fair curls of the child with tenderness,

-We had to look after her in the other room because she was crying so much, poor thing, and we needed Sebastien to rest. Dana put a balm on her sore gum and it helped.

Vincent turned to the goddess smiling gratefully to say,

-I thank you for your help, Dana. I am most indebted. And I do want the recipe for your balm because my little princess has more teeth to come through.

Before the goddess could reply, the Great Being put the little Abigail back into her arms with a look of emergency as he told with great certainty,

-Of course Dana will give you that recipe out of her good heart, she will also look after your child while we are 'all' away, for you must ask Amelia to join us.

While Dana nodded her consent to the Creator, Vincent turned to his wife. He explained to her the situation as briefly as he could and the result was Amelia putting her bonnet on, along with her cape and then she told,

-I am ready when you are, gentlemen. Let us save the day, the night, Wilton Town and anyone we can!

Sebastien smiling to her reaction stated,

-This is what I call a trooper.

The Great Being informed Dana,

-We need Amelia Valdi for three days. The couple will return in four days. Dana look after their little angel with your life. They were only two angels created by Gael. She is one of them, and you know how much it means to Raguel. At her tender reincarnating age, Abigail is at risk. But I trust you completely with her.

Dana held the hand of the Great Being with respect and told,

-I have two fairy knights on their way to the Neptune. Tell Raguel that Abigail will be fine, properly guarded and looked after.

Amelia eagerly added,

-Do not forget, Dana, you have our Zach. He will fetch anything you need and want.

With a smile the goddess conceded,

-I know, I have. He is such a sweet boy, endearing, really. Now do not worry for Abbi and me, we will be fine and wait for you here safely. But time is the essence and you must all make your way back to Wilton Town as soon as possible.

Amelia kissed Dana on her cheek in her amicable way and thanked her again before she was led outside by her husband and the Great Being. A fully winged Sebastien embraced his grandmother before he departed from the cabin that had hidden his recovery. While his grandfather and his uncle were already flying away holding Amelia, he went to find Zachary on the deck to give him a clear set of instructions before giving a thankful manly hug and farewell. Soon Sebastien was flying by his grandfather, catching his fast pace up, and he confided to him,

-I must thank you. Taking me to the 'Neptune' saved my life.

The Great Being replied, pleased to see his grandson flying again,

-You are welcomed but it was more a case of taking you to the individual the most capable of saving your life who happens to be your uncle.

Sebastien confided a little disgruntled,

-I wish my own father would have thought of saving me.

His grandfather corrected,

-Raguel did the fighting lion share of it all. He provided the diversion for me to take you away to safety, putting his own life in danger for yours. You mustn't blame your father for not carrying you in his own arms for he used them to protect you with all his might. I can tell you that he was really upset with what happened to you. He was scared to lose you just like he lost Gael to demons. Sebastien, your father loves you. He may not be demonstrative but he loves you more than you can imagine.

Getting involved in the conversation as they arrived to the fields in the clouds Vincent told,

-Your father taught me a lesson, my very first angelic lesson, it is that the more you love or care for someone, the less you show it, especially in front of your enemies because they will attack the people you love the most. If Raguel is not demonstrative, it is because he loves you most of all and is protecting you. I have seen how your father gave a correction to Lucifer because of you. At the end of it, Lucifer felt he would pass away.

Sebastien landed first then opened his arms in order to receive Amelia to protect her from a brutal landing. Still unsatisfied he retorted,

-But my father didn't come to visit me once at my bedside. Pass me Mrs Valdi so she doesn't hurt herself.

While Amelia was being given a smooth reception in the arm of the strong angel, the Great Being scolded,

-Mighty, if your father had come to see you, it would have been a direct giveaway of where we were hiding you to give you time to recover. It would have been leading our enemies straight to your bedside to finish you off. Beside that Raguel wanted to come, but I ordered him not to do so. But by all mean if you want to carry on your ungrateful child stance, you are free to do so. But I can tell you straight now, that if you want an arm and a leg from your father, your prayers will not be answered.

Putting Mrs Valdi on the ground safely, Sebastien replied with a pout,

-I am not an ungrateful child!

Amelia ran to her husband as soon as he landed gracefully, checking his wings with great care but also curiosity while the grandfather told sternly to his grandson,

-Then prove it to me because for the last ten minutes you didn't. When your father endangered his own life for your sake in the past twenty four hours, you dismissed it as nothing just because of your desire to be fussed over. Well, let's just say that Raguel fussed over you in a meaningful way with his own life. Does it please you better?

Sebastien admitted walking by his grandfather towards the phaeton,

-It does but it also makes me feel bad about what I said.

With a smirk the Great Being told,

-It was intended, go and get your horse. Fair Wilton did have a small rest in those pastures. I will keep that field in the sky to allow us to bring back Mrs Valdi to carry on her honeymoon with her husband after her mission.

Whistling, Sebastien brought his stallion to him. The appaloosa recognising his master ran to him. Once by his side, Fair Wilton nudged the Mighty One with his head in a display of affection. A pleased Sebastien stroked the stallion telling him,

-It looks like you missed me my Fair Wilton. Come, let's go home together.

As he attached his horse to the phaeton with efficient care, the Mighty One commented,

-This is Theo's phaeton. How he is doing?

Watching the tenderness of Vincent helping Amelia to climb in the phaeton, the Great Being informed his grandson,

-He is still alive and hasn't been killed by any demons, instead he killed five under the protection of Valdi who did got hurt doing so. Theo is physically fine but he is a little down hearted at the moment. Let me show you what happened this morning around the table so you can understand better, hold my hand.

Getting the full vision from the hand of his grandfather, Sebastien commented,

-My low confidence Theo certainly didn't need that. When I am back, I will have a good talk to him. He listens to me.

The Great Being welcomed with a positive nod adding

in confidence,

-Good. He has archangelic potential, losing him for that matter would be dreadful. Your father is already watching Theo carefully. Miss White made full amends to her future husband and their wedding is still on the map. I can tell you also that nothing at all irregular happened between Miss White and your uncle. She kept her heart's feelings for herself knowing that Vincent's heart deeply loves Amelia. I must also tell you that your uncle was rattled by the morning scene and fears to lose both of his best friends.

The Mighty One reassured,

-I will make sure that those friends stay friends.

A happy grandfather then ordered,

-Perfect. Climb in the phaeton. Let's get a double pairs of wings on Fair Wilton and let's depart.

Sebastien did as he was told and asked,

-Are you not joining us?

The Great Being taking off replied,

-I will fly by you all.

Soon the phaeton was off and within it between her husband and Sebastien, Amelia was amazed as she gasped,

-We are so high up in the sky!

The brash Mighty, keen to impress made the phaeton fly even higher and faster for the rest of the way. While Sebastien was informed of most of the things that happened in his absence during the journey, courtesy of his grandfather and uncle, in Wilton Town a worried Raguel kept regular checks on Theo Odell.

In one of those checks, the Master of all angels, found the vicar silently still, crying and contemplating the deep water of the well of the hotel. Coming by him, almost without a noise, he startled Theo who had been lost in his thoughts,

-I bet that well is deep enough and has enough water today to drown any man without any will to live, any will to love, any will to help his fellow human beings and any will to make his life count for something. My father did his job well to fill up all the wells in this town so we can save as many inhabitants as we can tonight, don't you think?

Thus taken off his suicidal haze, Theo turned to the senior angel. Tears were still running upon his face but he tried to gather himself up as he replied with a stutter,

-Oh, oh, yes, yes, he did, he did. If we have that amount of water everywhere in the town's wells, we can hope to tackle any, any fire.

Raguel dropped a bucket in the well, filled it and hoister it back up while he asked,

-Why are you crying my angel, before seeing any casualties before you?

Theo answered as he tried to dry his tears up as fast as he could,

-I am not crying. It is the constant rain.

Giving a stern look to Odell, the Master replied as he pulled the bucket full of water up,

-One thing you have to learn Theo is that you are talking to me, the angel of Justice and a Punisher. A lie, sweet or not will get you nowhere with me. Hit me with the hard truth, forget the pretence, and just talk to me. Why are you in tears? It is no longer a question, it is a demand. Come with me. How much preparation have you done for tonight? Show me your work.

Raguel took the full bucket and led the way back to the hotel. Because Theo Odell was slow to follow him and remained silent, Raguel told with impatience,

-I am waiting.

His imperative tone made Odell move faster to keep the pace of the senior angel and also say,

-It is nothing.

Stopping and turning abruptly to confront Theo, Raguel stated,

-Look if it makes you cry, it is not nothing. If I have to stop my work to cut your suicidal thoughts over a well, it is not nothing. Again, I am the Master of angels, you can turn to me and confide. Look this morning you had a most beautiful eternal

Being, down on her knees, in front of you, in the mud, under the rain, begging for your consideration, begging to be with you for eternity.

With trembling lips Theo demanded,

-You do know about it?

Putting on of his arm around the shoulders of his newest angel reassuringly, Raguel answered in a softer tone of voice,

-Yes, I do. I happen to be a Watcher. You see that bird on that rose bush by the well, that is me, who has been keeping an eye on you. There is a lizard on the stone walls of that ruined Ogin cottage, that is me as well keeping an eye on the spirit of a little girl who doesn't like you very much at all. Now, did you hear a voice nagging you inside your head? Tell me what did she say to you?

Theo looked around him baffled but then his eyes met the ones of the Master again and he felt safe and secure. He stuttered,

-She, she said it would be fast if I jumped in the water. She said the pain would be over soon and that everyone would forget about me the following day. She, she said I wasn't truly loved, that nobody loved me and would ever love me.

Raguel ordered in a serious tone,

-Come with me. Let's go inside. You are victim of a spiritual attack. I will explain it all to you and deal with it. You will feel much better afterwards.

Odell followed the strong angel to the kitchen of the hotel. As soon as they stepped in, he saw Doctor Williams close the door behind them then throw salt at the threshold who told,

-That will keep that little pest away, Master.

Closing the other entrance door to the kitchen Raguel demanded,

-William, do the window then this door too so we can keep Theo fully protected.

While William acted swiftly, the Master presented a chair to Odell,

-Sit down Theo, we need to have a good talk you and me. My William, when you have finished, this angel of mine needs one of your nice lemon and ginger teas with a good dollop of honey for he is soaking wet then come and join us at the table.

Theo sat silently without discussion feeling worried and safe at the same time. Raguel took a seat opposite him and didn't lose any time to brief him,

-My Theo, this property, the hotel and the ruin in the garden in particular has a ghost. A little girl couldn't rest in peace, like Abraham Wilton-Cough couldn't. If the ghost of Abraham decided to deal with angels, her ghost decided to deal with demons. I can explain that to you in a factual way, both died very badly but one, Abraham, had love in his heart for his family while that little girl didn't. She didn't love her family for what they did to her. She has been buried, in a rough way, in the ruined cottage in the garden. She have hate and jealousy in her spirit and heart.

A puzzled Odell enquired,

-Did I know the girl? Was I aware of her plight? Why is she asking me to kill myself?

Kicking the table with his fist, the Master replied with gusto,

-I knew she did! William, we have an evil spirit in the making in this property. I will need you to protect it with all your might until we are making her rest in peace. Theo, you didn't know that little girl when she was alive. She was born centuries before you. But she knew Mina White and her mother. The poor girl was jealous of Mina because of the love she received from Whilhelmina, because she wasn't receiving any from her own mother let alone from her father who was beating his entire family. She doesn't want to see Mina happy, she doesn't want her to have a complete family nor a happy one. She will be a destructive spirit around here and you have to be aware of that my angel. That little girl doesn't like you at all, first because you managed to exorcised the demon plaguing the ruins she inhabits which was her friend. This is when you nearly lost your life if it was not for my son and Henry. Second, you are the piece of the jigsaw which will make this mother, Miss White and her daughter very happy, and a complete family. As I said, she doesn't want happiness in this household and you killing yourself will give her great satisfaction.

Doctor Williams who started preparing on the stove

added,

-With what happened this morning between Miss White and yourself, that spirit must have thought you would be prime to be her prey, Theo. Now, tell me did you hurt yourself, cut yourself or have a rash upon you that is bleeding?

Father Odell intrigued replied with his own question,

-Yes, I have. Why do you ask me?

William came straight to Theo demanding,

-Because I am a Doctor and a Wizard. Show me where you are bleeding. Did it happen whilst you were working in the garden or whilst you were fighting at Amos's farm?

Raguel told firmly,

-He didn't get hurt at the farm, William. Vincent was protecting Theo like a lion. He could have lost his life doing so as well. He didn't want one speck of hair of Theo being touched by a demon that's for sure. He was tackling three demons at once, one moment, then two after he killed one, then he lost his axe and that's when my little brother got his deep wound on the shoulder.

Theo confirmed when he showed his left hand to Doctor Williams,

-Yes, it wasn't at the farm. It was in the garden. I have just got a small rash.

Williams observed the grazed hand carefully and demanded,

-It is slightly more than that I can tell. What did happen to you out there? From the three pieces of gravel embedded in your skin, I can guess that you fell at some point. I have to tend to your hand before it gets infected.

It was Raguel who replied for his angel,

-I can tell you what happened, William. Theo was mulling over again on his own his relationship with Miss White, making himself cry doing so. Meanwhile the ghost of the little girl appeared to play in the garden in a somewhat destructive way...

Cleaning the hand of Father Odell with care and removing the gravel from it Williams enquired,

-Destructive? Destructive, how, in a poltergeist way?

The Master went to look after the infusing tea as he answered,

-Yes, exactly, in a poltergeist way. When Theo was busy pulling the bucket up from the well, she threw the rake that was against the wall across the gravel path. A crying Theo didn't notice anything, blinded by his tears, he didn't see the rake and he fell over it. Not only that, with the weight of the bucket, he fell partly in the nettles bed. Why would you grow nettle, of all things?

Doctor Williams concluded,

-That would explain his rash. Nettle is good nutrition wise. You must not forget that Mina White was a vampire. Her mother gave her nettle soup to overcome her anaemia. In this garden, nettles are not weeds, they were staple food for this family.

Feeling guilty Odell confessed,

-And I squashed a lot of them! Oh, will Miss White forgive me?

Raguel and William gave each other a knowing look. Serving the infusion, the Master of all angels told,

-You can call Miss White Whilhelmina with us, or even, my Whil' like you used to. Drink that, it will warm you up, Theo.

Presented with the porcelain cup, Father Odell took it with his spare hand trembling as he said,

-She is not my Whil'. She will never be my Whil' apart for her name. She will become Mrs Odell but her heart belongs to another. The other happens to be the son of god, how can I compete with that? I am just the lanky freckled thing, I have always been the lanky freckled thing...

Taking a napkin and wiping the teary eyes of Theo, Raguel corrected,

-I know for a fact that Whilhelmina never called you a lanky freckled thing and I also know that she doesn't think of you that way. Her entire heart belongs to you and to no one else. Clara, the little girl of your childhood you liked and loved secretly, silently may have called you that way but not

Whilhelmina. If you want to hear the truth, as a Watcher, and you being my angel, I can reveal it to you.

Still a little shaky, Theo looked into the deep eyes of the Master and the reassurance they spelt without a word being said. He nodded positively, begging,

-Please, please do tell me...

Raguel going to tend to the fire told sternly,

-Whilhelmina never, and I repeat never, knelt to anyone, to any men, but you, let alone in the mud and under the rain. You mean to her more than you can imagine. She is not the little Clara of your childhood, Whilhelmina is far, far beyond and better than that. By the way, Clara, the pretty little Clara you fancied, married a butcher who killed three of their born babies to have less mouths to feed. Clara knows. She did let it all happen under her eyes, her pretty eyes. Well, less said about that is better for as the angel Justice I will give her her due and the one to her husband. Let us talk about an eternal being who really loves you and considers you more than a lanky freckled thing.

The Master went to sit back opposite Odell before he continued,

-My dear Theo, as you were in love with Clara in your childhood but you are well past it now, that you did nothing about it, you will understand that it is the same with Whilhelmina and my brother. She is well past my brother. She always knew his heart belonged to another woman and she always respected that. You, as the best friend of Vincent knows who he talked to you about the most. Who was she, if she was not for dear Amelia? Nothing happened between Whilhelmina and Vincent. Miss White may have harboured feelings about him but that was it, just like you with Clara. How can you say, that Whilhelmina is not yours after her honest confession to you? Did you tell Whilhelmina you liked someone else previously and happen to like her now? I am asking you this, who loves better: the person that throws his or her dignity away to be totally true to another or the one that put back the wedding rings into her hands and took minutes to go back to her...? Whilhelmina is an old being. She has been upon earth a while. She has never given her heart up like that. She didn't do it to my brother. Theo, she loves you, she truly loves you. And you must stop comparing yourself to my brother because you have been amazing this morning. You must be yourself. Whatever that spirit said to you, I can deny it. You are loved and you will always be loved. Now there is your Whil' in her bedroom and she was shaken with the events of this morning. When I talked to her she was still trembling with the fear of losing you for she loves you, truly, deeply, madly. If I was you I would go to her, lay by her side, get warm and reassure her about my love. That is if you only have a little consideration for her.

Drinking his infusion in one go, Theo stood up and told,

-I will go to my Whil', right away.

#

It was dusk when the phaeton landed back in front of the hotel. Raguel, who had been patiently waiting for its arrival welcomed first his father who had been flying alongside it. The Great Being embraced his eldest son warmly giving him a reassurance,

-Mighty is sorted. He will make it. But be warned that he is still recovering. He may tell you that he is fine but I can tell you that he is suffering still from some symptoms, one of them being the loss of consciousness for a few seconds if not minutes on occasions. However brave he is, do not let him work on his own tonight. Stay with him.

Raguel nodded his ascent and comprehension before he went to the phaeton. He greeted as he helped Amelia Valdi down,

-Mrs Valdi, it is with great pleasure that I make your acquaintance. I am Raguel, Angel of justice, Master of all angels, your brother in law. I am delighted to see that you decided to come to help us.

A little intimidated by the tall and handsome angel, whom she recognised the traits to be very similar to the ones of Sebastien but older, Amelia nonetheless presented her hand to him and courtesied,

-Nice to meet you. Please, call me Amelia, since we are brother and sister. I honestly couldn't refuse you my help under such circumstances.

Stepping down, and standing by his wife Doctor Valdi told putting an arm around her waist,

-I told you my Amelia would be up for the mission.

Raguel smiled widely, revealing,

-Amelia, I heard a lot about you, a lot. According to the

rumour you are a very clever woman and my son could do with the like of you in his army, did he tell you that?

A blushing Amelia replied,

-He did. I am engaged to be a member of his logistic team, the same team as Father Odell, my husband and Miss White.

The Master told leading Mrs Valdi inside the hotel,

-Good. It is a new team but it is a good team, the leader of which is an excellent angel called Ted. He is a rather gentle character and will not be bossy with you all whatsoever. He suffers from forecasting visions which are very helpful when logistic is concerned. You will meet him in due time. For now I want you to have a nice cup of tea and get warm inside before you start your mission. Vincent, see that Amelia is comfortable. You will find Miss White, Theo, William and Henry in the kitchen.

When Vincent took his wife into the hotel, Raguel walked back to the phaeton who was tended by his son. Raguel opened his arms to Sebastien who silently nestled himself within them. Tapping gently the shoulders of his son, the Master asked,

-How do you feel my boy? And remember to not hide anything from me because you know it will not work.

Sebastien replied while leaving the embrace,

-I am better Father, much better. I can fight tonight. But I must confess that I will be given the all clear by Valdi in twelve to twenty four hours from now. I suffers from episodes...

His father demanded, as he started to free Fair Wilton from the phaeton with his son,

-What sort of episodes?

Stroking his stallion, Sebastien revealed,

-I suffer from blackouts. They are much less frequents now that I had the counter poison. Vincent and even Amelia kept a good eye upon me. Vincent wants me to have another dose of the antidote for me to be on the safe side.

His grandfather told sternly,

-And your uncle who is an excellent Doctor is right, you

must admit, especially since you nearly sent him and his little wife swimming in the middle of a cold ocean.

Raguel folding his arms upon his chest demanded,

-Mighty, did you put the life of my brother and Amelia in danger?

Put upon the spot in that way, Sebastien led his stallion in the barn and explained against his own will,

-The truth of it is, yes I did. I was leading the phaeton most of the way because I wanted to protect the shoulder of Vincent which, as you know, has been injured this morning. So I was holding the reins. Beside that my stallion is quite a beast to manage. Unfortunately at one moment, I did suffer from a blackout...

His grandfather continued for him,

-When the phaeton was going down fast, Amelia realised that Sebastien's chin was on his chest and that he was clearly out of it, she reacted quickly and took care of the reins while warning her sleeping husband of the matter at hand. At her alarm I realised what was happening and I intervened to stop the plunge of all in the ocean, grabbing the neck of Fair Wilton to lead him upwards. Vincent woke up fast enough and took over the entire situation into his hands. He had some practice with me on how to make the phaeton and horse fly beforehand when we went to get Mighty and he did pick it up in his stride well. While he took control, his little wife took care of Sebastien to make sure he would not fall from the phaeton. She put him in the middle of the seat, between her and Vincent. She was so brave doing so. I can tell you that her husband was watching the entire operation with fear in his belly. Then she tried to recall Mighty from his blackout with her scented salts bottle but it didn't work until Vincent demanded for her to slap him strongly. This did work.

Sebastien giggled as he commented,

-Yes, I can tell you that it did work. Amelia may be small but she is mighty. I still feel my cheek if you know what I mean, Father. In my entire eternal life, I never been slapped by a woman like that.

His father couldn't help laughing as he enquired,

-Is she angelic material?

As they arrived inside the barn, Sebastien looked after his stallion and replied with certainty,

-I dare say she is. Having been looked after by her for almost twenty four hours, I can tell you that this woman has a huge heart. She is not only clever. Her intelligence is impressive, but she thinks quickly just like my Theo. I have no wonder why Valdi likes them both. Both have good natures, both have excellent souls, both have wonderful hearts. Now, let's talk about my Theo. Did you have a good conversation with him about Miss White?

Raguel answered bringing hay to the horse,

-I did. I actually talked to both of them. The situation is resolved properly. However we need to get that spirit in the ruined cottage to lay to rest properly. She is becoming evil. I do not know how long she has been talking with her demonic friend you got rid off, the one Theo exorcised but I reckon it has been at least for a few hundred of years. She is set on killing Theo and if I didn't intervened, I think we would have found him in the bottom of the well. She works by giving nasty suggestive thoughts. For Theo she played on his suicidal tendencies. She wants Theo dead and with him living in the territory she haunts, you can imagine the danger that will be constantly above his head.

While he was cleaning his stallion vigorously, the Mighty One commented,

-I can't have that level of threat on that new angel of mines. We have to deal with this situation tonight. We have to go to town anyway tonight. I want that girl's body buried properly in the Wilton Town cemetery right now.

A noise came from the corner of the barn, Sebastien came to investigate it, speaking out loud,

-That's Mr Berry's carriage. What is it doing here?

His father giggled as he answered,

-That would be because Mrs Toad is here, and both have been helping us today. Vincent must have informed you of the amount of human victims we have found in Amos's farm. Their willingness to give a hand with the situation was most welcomed. Mr Berry, there is no need to hide, it is only my son and my grandfather. Did you manage to fix your wheel?

Appearing from under the straw, Mr Berry replied with

red cheeks,

-I, I, I did. The carriage is ready for tonight. I guess, I guess I heard things which I shouldn't have.

Coming to him the Master of all angels helped the man up only to reassure,

-Do not worry too much, my human, you and the future Mrs Berry are considered as safe humans. My son would not have chosen you as his best man otherwise. You can know a little angelic secrets here and there. We have a small situation with the spirit of a little girl. She died many, many years ago in a bad way, and she is haunting this hotel.

Mr Berry finished up,

-And she wants to kill our Father Odell. She needs to be stopped. Father Odell, well, Father Odell is such, such a nice man. I remember once, I am talking about it because, since the death of my wife, I wasn't going to church often, but when I saw what he did, I made a point to attend to his sermons. I remember once, an old drunkard, he fell in the mud, late at night, and people teased him and some threw stones at him, telling him to go home and that he was a disgrace. Father Odell made the stoning stop. He made the crowd vanish around the man by quoting to them Matthew 7:5 from the bible. He told them to go home, that they were disgraceful themselves. He helped old Tom up. He made sure the old man went home and put him to bed. I was there because I proposed my help to Father Odell. In the garden of Tom, when we left, we found a very fresh grave, with a written cross upon it. Tom had lost his companion of fifteen years that day, his most faithful shepherd dog. Father Odell told me then that there was an explanation for everything and only comfort and help to be given as much as we could.

Raguel enjoined the man,

-Then you will not mind helping us to protect Father Odell and to make his new home less haunted?

Taking his old hat off, the dairy farmer agreed willingly,

-Of course I will help but, but does this mean that Abraham Wilton-Cough will have to go to? I have seen his ghost in this house. He saluted me politely in the corridor, he even shook my hand, I could have fainted. He was helping Doctor Williams and Mrs Toad with all those poor, those poor...

Finishing his sentence up the angel of Justice told,

-With all those poor humans. I know. Let me tell you that there are good ghosts and there are bad ones. Wilton-Cough is a good one who is working for an angel. We will not be dealing with him on this occasion. We will only be dealing with the evil spirit of the little girl who wants to kill Father Odell.

Delighted to be within the confidence of the angels Mr Berry commented,

-It surprises me because Mr Wilton-Cough was dreaded and feared during his living. When I saw him I was spooked beyond belief but he reassured me, hat in one hand, and offering me his other one. He even asked me how I was doing with my farm. Back in the days, he helped me to keep the farm and my living. I lost my dear wife, you see, and was so bereft and devastated that I didn't want to get up. He came one day, not to ask for his money but with Doctor Valdi and Father Odell and he told them, that I was a mess of a man and that they needed to sort me out. Then they both did as they were told and here I am ready to help you, years later.

Having listened carefully, Raguel stated,

-My dear Mr Berry, the difference between a good ghost and a bad one is just this: One cares for the living, while the other wants to send them to their graves. Abraham Wilton-Cough, to give him justice, cares, and he cares a hell of a lot. The way he died speaks volume about his soul. He gave his life to save others. Yes, he may have been tough and wanting everyone to account for everything and quite a scary figure in Wilton Town but at the end of the day, he had a heart, although he had difficulties to show it, because he was such an unloved child. But he did care and he still cares beyond his grave. Let me reveal to you that he is the servant ghost of Doctor Valdi, who is an angel. So Wilton-Cough is not to be feared. He is a good ghost.

Mr Berry putting back his hat told positively,

-I am happy to hear that. It is true that the day Wilton-Cough passed away was a very sad instance for Wilton Town. He died a hero although no one ever knew in this town that Abraham would have the guts to be so brave to protect others. He suffered a terrible agony, you know, a terrible one, Doctor Valdi, Father Odell and his dear sweet little wife were there to tell you all about it. By respect for the man, a lot of people turned up to his funeral, more than I would ever imagine for that man, like I said because he was feared, but no, no, there were not enough benches in the church to sit down, even I was there standing up by a pillar. If he became a servant to Doctor Valdi, it is not surprising you know.

The Master knowing the particulars of the entire affair of Wilton-Cough becoming a servant giggled but was interested nonetheless to hear of the dairy farmer's assumptions so he prompted,

-Why isn't it surprising?

Mr Berry explained in a gossipping way,

-Well, you see, when the young Doctor Valdi came in to town years ago, Abraham Wilton-Cough helped him with all the financial advices he could to make sure the clinic of Valdi stayed in business. He said, and that I got it from Valdi, himself who delighted us with the details, one night at the tavern with Father Odell, so Wilton-Cough apparently said over dinner one night to Doctor Valdi, who was his guest at his family table, that Wilton Town needed a Doctor badly, that fit people worked better and if they did so, they could repay what they owed to him faster. Wilton-Cough was a banker through and through, you know. So he knew the small town might not have been appealing to the young Doctor Valdi and he was scared to see the Doctor we needed all depart one day. So he made sure that Valdi's clinic was financially viable but also that Doctor Valdi would be welcomed, accepted, by all kind of circles in town. Not only that, Wilton-Cough always liked hard working people and, well, Doctor Valdi is one of them. Somehow he heard that the young man Valdi had been an orphan from the Napoleonic wars, and from that moment he kind of behaved like a father to Valdi. Doctor Valdi was invited frequently to have dinner at the family home of Wilton-Cough, weekly or if not twice weekly, if the banker was worried that the young Doctor didn't have enough to eat that week. The little widow, Mrs Thicket, who loves a good gossip, told me one day a conversation she had over the counter in the bank of Wilton-Cough with him, personally. Now, you must know that Abraham Wilton-Cough was not sharing a lot about how he felt but Mrs Thicket is a hardworking little lady who was a good customer of his and she did have his appreciation. So he told her in all confidence, that if Vincent Valdi would have been his eldest son on top of his other two sons, he would have been an extremely proud father. He also said that he would have loved to have given to his wife Angela a little girl for her not feel lonely in an all boys and men household.

Raguel who didn't lost his smile despite the length of the gossip, put his arm across the shoulders of the man in an amicable way and tasked him,

-Right, Mr Berry, I am glad to know that we can count on your help for tonight. Can we ask you to bring the remains of that little girl to town for her to be given a proper burial?

Daunted the farmer asked with a shiver,

-Will her spirit try to kill me, like she wanted to do with Father Odell?

The Great Being replied with certainty,

-I will make sure she will not, because I will come with you, along with Doctor Valdi and Wilton-Cough.

Feeling reassured Mr Berry told to the Master,

-I will do it. I will prepare my carriage. You will find it in the front of the hotel within fifteen minutes.

Raguel tapped the man's shoulders with appreciation as he welcomed,

-We will thank you for that Mr Berry, we will. Father, Mighty, let's get the remains of that girl.

As the three impressive beings left the barn, the farmer started to attached his own horse onto his carriage while talking to himself,

-Oh good Lord, what did I fell into, angels, ghosts and demons roaming about in Wilton Town...

But outside the Great Being, his son and grandson went straight to the garden of the hotel chatting together casually. It was the grandfather who enquired the first,

-Raguel, you made quite an eloquent speech to convince the human that Wilton-Cough was a good ghost. I know that you didn't have that opinion of Abraham before. What did change until I last saw you?

Raguel gave a deep sigh as he replied,

-Well, you know I promised my brother that I will look after his servant ghost if something happened to him. And of course, I had to warn Wilton-Cough about the risk of Vincent not coming back and my promise to him. I made Abraham work alongside me most of the day. What I saw, father, was that not only he was helping me thoroughly, he had also begging eyes when he came to me to ask for his next task because he had accomplished his last one. If as a human he did like hardworking as a value he cherished, as a spirit, it is still so. Not only that, I witnessed how he behaved with all our human victims as he looked after them. He reached out to them, like a good father would do, he cared for them all like a mother hen. He came to warn me when one was not doing too well and that Doctor Williams would be required. He was on the ball all the time with all those poor humans. Father, Abraham Wilton-Cough was kind and humble. I did actually regret to have turned him down as a soul servant when the opportunity was there, because he has a spirit that truly wants to be redeemed. He will do anything for redemption. Having spent time with Abraham, I am convinced of his good heart.

Leading the way towards the ruins of the Ogin cottage, Sebastien turned to his father enquiring,

-On my way here, Vincent told me what happened and how he decided to claim the soul of Abraham Wilton-Cough as his servant in order to protect it. I must confess I was surprised by the harshness of everyone but Valdi when it came to take on board his spirit. I felt sorry for the banker who had to face so many refusals, even the good Williams, your own servant, father, refused to take on his soul.

The Master gave his explanations firmly,

-In the defence of William, he was ghost handled quite harshly by Wilton-Cough. The problem with Abraham is that he reacts very fast on impulse. He can become a liability quickly. Now, if I refused first of all his spirit as my servant, I didn't refuse to take him under my wings to redeem his soul.

The Great Being making three shovels appear out of thin air distributed them to his son and grandson, told,

-Mighty, Abraham Wilton-Cough's soul needed that little dressing down from your father, my angel of justice. With the knowledge that Vincent will intervene in the favour of Abraham, I refused him as well.

Sebastien started to dig in a muddy spot and couldn't help to express himself,

-But what a downcast blow for that banker's soul who gave his life for so many.

His grandfather who started digging by his side explained,

-But I needed Abraham to be attached to my youngest son for Vincent's protection, well, for the protection of both really.

Raguel smiled putting his fists on his own hips as he stated,

-I knew you had something on your mind all along! You kept delivering subtle cues for me to be kinder to Abraham. The biggest one of all was how you looked after his soul when we were in hell. The way you kept him by your side, even holding his hand which had been noticed by Lucifer.

Giving him a long knowing look, his father commented,

-I am glad you were intelligent enough to notice the cues. Like you have William as a devoted servant, like Joshua had his own, Vincent had to have one. Like the other two servants, I selected Abraham Wilton-Cough very carefully. Yes, he is far from perfect but he is a spirit that cares so much. If we compare him to your Doctor Williams who never left the materialistic side of life and always lived in a lavish way, Abraham has not the same ego, although he has some pride. He has agreed to tag along with Vincent whom he knew lives a very simple hardworking life.

Putting his shovel in the mud deeply, Raguel replied sternly,

-That's because Abraham loves his children and he wants to keep an eye on them beyond the grave via Vincent.

His father confirmed,

-Exactly. Abraham Wilton-Cough is motivated by love and love only and this is why he does not rest. This is why he is still with us in spirit. As you realised yourself, spending time with him, he is a soul who cares, and cares so deeply that he will not care of how he is treated himself. He will even accept servitude under your tough rules as long as he can help. This is why I held his hand and protected his spirit in hell. His soul is blessed by me, my son. If you hold my hand, you will hear all of his prayers during his life to me, and you will know a good heart when you meet one.

Doing as his father demanded the Master of all angels, held the hand of the Great Being for a few minutes. When he released the hand, Raguel had tears in his eyes. He wiped them off quickly while he stated,

-So Abraham's last living prayer to you was coming from his heart: 'Dear Lord, let those good humble people live, take my life instead.'

The Great Being nodded positively whilst he carried on digging. He confirmed,

-That is right. No one else, in his bank, in their time of struggle thought of anyone else but Abraham did. He thought of them all and of ways to protect them. That day, he was the most courageous of them all, the most selfless. He had the heart and guts to protect them. But I will tell you one thing, my son, no one, no one would have dared to protect him the way he saved them all. With free will ruling, no one could have stopped the robber if they didn't want to. Abraham did, and I also answered his prayer. Now go and get him, tell him that we need a large blanket for the remains of that little girl.

Raguel went with a heavy heart to fetch Abraham Wilton-Cough. He found the ghost of the old banker by his angel Daniel who welcomed him with a query,

-Master, Abraham just told me that the hotel was turned into a hospital for the time being?

The Master replied,

-This is partially true. There is still one guest, however.

Daniel answered with a giggle,

-Who has been a very kind nurse to myself and others, I understand, the good widow Mrs Toad who will probably soon be Mrs Berry.

Smirking, Raguel told sternly,

-Most probably yes, due to the matchmaking skills of my son. Now, I need to borrow Wilton-Cough for a little emergency situation, if you will excuse him to not entertain you any longer with any gossip.

With the sheer strength of his arms, Daniel sat by the side of his bed, pain showing upon his face, but with determination, he answered back,

-Abraham wasn't gossipping. He informed me of what happened at Amos's farm and why the hotel was turned into a hospital. Please let me help you Master, I am dying of restlessness here in my bed. Let me be useful so I can bare my pain better.

Raguel looked at his barely recovering angel with sadness, but he proposed,

-Mrs Amelia Valdi is here to make sense of the book from hell you need to learn by heart, the one Abraham stole from Lucifer. We are burning that book in three days time, if you want to help her right now despite your state, let me and Abraham, take you to her.

With thankful eyes, Daniel demanded,

-Please Master, do so!

The Master ordered Abraham Wilton-Cough who was ready by his side to do anything he wanted,

-Abraham, go on the other side of my angel, and help me carry him with all your strength downstairs.

As Wilton-Cough obeyed, Raguel asked him,

-We are going to need a large cover afterwards, will you fetch it for me as fast as you can?

The ghost of the banker helping the amputated angel down the stairs reassured, but enquired as well with emotion,

-Of course I will. You, you mentioned Amelia but not, not my Doctor Valdi. Is he alright? Is he alive?

The Master of all angels probed the ghost mercilessly,

-What if he wasn't?

Abraham missed a step at that moment. His eyes filled up with tears. He held onto the wall and onto the angel he was helping. He looked desperately at Raguel and demanded,

-Tell me my Vincent is still alive? Tell me he is... He is the anchor of my heart, he is the anchor to my love ones. He is a son to me. Oh my Vincent!

Before the physical ghost collapsed in distress, Raguel told him, reaching and tapping his hand maintaining Daniel,

-Vincent is alive. He is downstairs with his wife. He made it. There was trouble along the way though. My son is still recovering but also suffering from blackouts, and Vincent is still recovering from his own wound he sustained this morning at Amos's farm. Both are here and still standing but both need help, although they will never ask for it. You will need to keep an eye on Vincent for me while I will need to keep an eye on my son. Do you understand me? If anything happens to Vincent tonight, you must come and get me as fast as you can. We are going to be separated and in teams. But Vincent may be called out of his team, being the strongest, to provide for the retreat of the others. If this happens you must stay with him. Be my eyes and look after him.

Wilton-Cough agreed straight away,

-You can count on me! I will be his shadow. I will be his dog following him faithfully. I will look after him with all my might. If my might is not enough, I will run to you, well, I will glide to you to tell you, because I glide faster than I run nowadays.

The Master couldn't help but smiling at the willingness of the ghost while Daniel told with a smirk on his lips,

-Be glad to be able to glide, Abraham, I wish I could at this moment in time.

Looking at the amputated angel, the old banker reassured,

-Daniel, you must be patient. Doctor Williams told you that he will look at ways to make you mobile and independent again. You must stay strong for us all for we need you. Look in your next incarnated life, you will be walking on two legs while I will still be gliding. My physical appearance has only been strengthen by a spell which will stop in a few hours, while you, you have been saved. You are still alive and you will get to meet your little daughter, you will be able to hold her in your arms and kiss her cheek. I, I can't do that with my own little girl, I can only watch her be.

Raguel feeling the emotion in the voice of Abraham enquired,

-How do you feel being physical again for a little while, Wilton-Cough?

The ghost replied with a sad smile,

-Good, I feel good but it would have been miles better if it had been done by my wife and children so I could hold and hug them all one last time. But I guess one can't wish for everything to be perfect. But I can still be invisible and gain minutes for the spell to last longer. However I failed to render myself invisible in front of Mr Berry. He came so fast up the stairs that he saw me. He is sweet on Mrs Toad, if you haven't noticed, he rushed to see her. He knows I am dead, he was there at my funeral and I fear I may have spooked him a fair deal. I tried as much as I could to calm him down. I like Mr Berry, you see, he is a very decent man, always amiable, kind and helpful.

A reassuring Raguel told,

-You did scare a little Mr Berry. But he is a sensible man. Beside that like Mrs Toad, I made them to be in the confidence of the angels. Now, both of them knows about the existence of angels, demons, spirits and ghosts. So you mustn't worry too much when you meet Mr Berry next and you will, because Valdi and you along with my father are going to take charge of transporting the remains of that despicable little girl, which tried to kill Odell, in his carriage. We will bury her properly in Wilton Town cemetery tonight.

As they approached the kitchen, Abraham asked,

-What is the name of that little ghost?

The Master replied with some annoyance,

-I don't know and I don't even want to know. All I know is that she tried to kill Georgia Marlow because she was bringing love to this household and that she is doing the same to Father Odell for the same reasons. All I can tell you is that she is an evil spirit. She has befriended demons for centuries.

Then the old Wilton-Cough told firmly,

-If angels did give her a chance and learnt her first name may be they would not be dealing with an evil spirit. You always need to know who you have to deal with. As a banker, I always made sure I knew my customers, the one who could pay back a loan, the ones who couldn't, and the ones who were worth a gamble. Of course, there is always a risk to get too involved but sometimes it pays off in the end. Sometimes it doesn't, this is why I am a ghost. But what I am saying is if you are dealing in human's souls, as an angel, it might be worth your while to know where they came from a little more, what were their background, what were their plights as humans to understand their paths as ghosts or spirits.

Raguel gave a long dark angry look to Abraham before

he conceded,

-Maybe just maybe, you are a little bit right. Then, let me give you another task: learn all you can about that ghost, because where she will rest is literally the backyard of my son. I do not want her to pester my son like she pestered Father Odell. Then report to me, because I will live with my son, so I can deal with her in the future if necessary.

Abraham who was about to open the kitchen door enquired,

-How is your son? I like him very much. He has a no non-sense attitude like you. I was sorry to see him so hurt on the ship. But Valdi, well, Valdi did wonders. You can count on me for that new task. I will do it and I will do it thoroughly for you and for Sebastien.

The Master of all angels looked at the ghost with a kind smile and welcomed,

-Thank you, thank you very much. You met my son but I haven't personally met your children yet, the reason why you are still with us. Tell me about them.

Wilton-Cough corrected keenly,

-Let's not forget my wife Angela, she is another reason. She is so frail, I constantly turn in my grave about her welfare. My eldest son is called Zachary. Doctor Williams and your son met him in Boston. He is not the cleverest, I must admit, but he is a bit like me. He did hide his shyness and clumsiness like I did with proud manners and a haughty air but we managed Valdi and I to get rid of that false pretence and brashness in him. Now what is left is just a good willing boy with a good heart. Then there is my younger boy, Josiah. Unlike his brother, he is clever. He knows what to say to everyone and dare I say, that he is a natural crowd pleaser. Both of my boys are fairly handsome, but one of them is clumsy and the other isn't. Josiah is very talented. He plays the piano like no other in Wilton Town. Unfortunately, I didn't connect with my Jo' as much as with my Zach' during my lifetime. I wish I did. Because I love my little Josiah as much as I love my Zachary but I never had a proper chance or time to tell him. Instead, I took him away from his Ma and put him in boarding school for her not to pet him like a circus act every Sunday for her tea parties. I regret all that very deeply. Angela was displaying little Jo' like the next Mozart. Then there is my little mistake, that came after I was dead, Abigail. You know I always secretly wanted a cheerful little girl which looked like my Angela. But at the birth of Josiah, it was clear that my Angela couldn't have anymore children so I was careful because I didn't want to lose her. I really, really, didn't make love to any over women from then on. But it just happened that my best friend died, his widow cried on my shoulder and I comforted her a little too much. And then, then the little Abigail came. I was so riddled with remorse when I realised that Amelia Bates was pregnant. I was thinking of my Angela, I was thinking of Amelia having to explain everything, I was so distressed at my death. But, but there was Father Odell and Doctor Valdi and they took care of everything and everyone I left behind...

A compassionate Raguel told firmly,

-Abraham, Abigail is an important angel that reincarnates over and over again. She was created by my eldest son Gael. She was due back on earth and she chose to fulfil the dying wish of Harry Bates who knew that Amelia was desperate to have a family and a child. He didn't want his widow to be all alone. He possessed you the evening of your mistake and Abigail did the rest so she could come back forward within the loving arms of the good Amelia. You were an instrument in their hands so do not blame yourself for it. I can tell you a little more about it but we are rushed for time. You have your orders for tonight?

Opening the door of the kitchen the ghost confirmed a little unsettled but like a perfect soldier,

-Yes, I have. I need to get the cover for the remains of that little girl first. Then I must get acquainted with her spirit and tell you all about it, when I can. Thirdly, I must be the protective shadow of my Vincent and rush to you if anything happens to him.

The Master of all angels smiled as he thought he had a ghost he could truly count on. He confided, tapping the shoulder of Wilton-Cough,

-We got on the wrong foot together, Abraham, partly because you went rough on my most beloved angelic servant Doctor Williams. But although I am the angel of justice and you have to fear me, I want you to know that if one day, and I don't wish it to happen, but if one day, you have to become my ghostly servant, I will welcome your soul with open arms. You have a protector in me Abraham Wilton-Cough.

Abraham had a humble smile and a tear rolled upon his cheek as he entered the kitchen. They were welcomed by Doctor Williams, who rushed to them, asking and helping to carry Daniel to the nearest chair,

-Master, how is Mighty?

Raguel making his angel as comfortable as he could be upon the kitchen chair replied with a distinct sadness in his voice,

-Better but not perfect. He suffers from blackouts. I will have to keep a good eye on him all night. As you know a loss of consciousness at the wrong time can be costly.

Bitting his lips the old William asked,

-Is it why Wilton-Cough is crying? I heard that they nearly fell into the ocean on the way back because of a blackout of Sebastien.

The Master gave a look at Abraham, took a handkerchief from his waistcoat pocket and dried the tears of the ghost with care as he replied,

-No, Abraham feels emotional because I basically told him that he was part of my angelic family and that he was welcomed within it. Where are the others, Valdi and his wife?

Doctor Williams rejoiced as he went to shake the hand of Wilton-Cough in a friendly manner,

-Don't cry Wilton-Cough, the Master is tough but fair. I have been under his protective wings for a very long time now and I am ever so happy to serve his family. You will not get a lot of rest with them but as you are out and about not resting in your grave, you might as well join our grand angelic family.

Raguel recalled,

-William, less said the better, we are pushed for time. Where can I find Amelia Valdi? Daniel will help her with the book from hell. Abraham, fetch that cover and bring it to the garden, you will find my father and my son there waiting for you.

While the ghost obeyed without questions and left the room. William answered,

-You will find Vincent and Amelia in a little hidden office of Miss White. The White Witch is with them, she has been woken up by Theo at their arrival. Whilhelmina is briefing Amelia of all the work she has done so far on the manuscript. Although I found Mrs Valdi a little cold, suffering from hypothermia, from her trip over the Atlantic, she is from a hardy constitution. You can't beat the blood of the Irish, I guess. I gave her tea, some bread, butter and jam and she was ready in no time at all to do her task. But good Lord, she is the most talkative women I ever met! I couldn't stop giggling when she told me about the episode of Sebastien losing consciousness and how she dealt with it. I started preparing a potion for mighty because of it. I think it could be the right solution for him for tonight at the very least. But there is a downside to it, he will not sleep for forty eight hours. But it will get rid of his blackouts.

A satisfied Raguel went to help Daniel back up and enquired,

-Good work, William, as always. We will be leaving in no time at all. Where is Theo and how did he get on with his mission?

The angelic Wizard was prompt to answer,

-Theo with the help of Henry got everything done, in good time. The army of Mighty's human angels is all kitted for tonight, down to the last. You will find Theo and Henry sleeping in armchairs in the drawing room of Miss White. They had no rest for a while so I sent them to have a restorative sleep to be ready for tonight. It is a little brief yet powerful spell of mine. I can wake them up whenever you want me to. May I ask something, Master?

-Of course you can.

-About Abraham Wilton-Cough, is he really considered as family?

With a deep sigh Raguel replied,

-Yes, he is. Just like for yourself, I will fight to the death for his soul. He is far from perfect but he has a heart and a good one at that. He would love to hold his children and wife for a last time, if you can find a spell to make it possible, my William, I will appreciate it greatly.

Giving a profound bow to the Master of all angels, Doctor Williams told,

-Consider it done! I saw the way Abraham looked after those humans upstairs. I do not know if it is out of his good heart or because he truly wants to be redeemed but it moved me.

Raguel stated,

-It is out of his good heart. Abraham, a little because of me, unfortunately, does not believe that he can be redeemed. But he never gave up helping us for one moment. However I found him wipping for Vincent at the bottom of the stairs this afternoon. He was crouched upon himself and his soul felt ever so lost. At that moment I captured the essence of his true heart as I helped him up and he has an excellent one. Of course, I told him off, to get on with it and to not cry until he knew something had happened to Vincent for sure. He did and carried on. He is a deeply caring spirit, this is what I can say for him so far. We will look after his soul.

Daniel added,

-If I may share my opinion, Master, I had Wilton-Cough tending to me. He didn't only help me physically, he helped me morally as well. His words made me want to get up and go, just like your own words.

The senior angel accepted his opinion with a positive nod as he took Daniel with the help of his servant to the little office of Miss White.

#

Arriving in the little office unannounced the three angels found Amelia Valdi already hard at work on Lucifer's manuscript, monitored and guided by Miss White and Doctor Valdi. She wanted to courtesy at the entrance of the Master of all angels but he prevented her to do so by a simple but effective gesture. Raguel told in his naturally commanding tone,

-My dear sister, there is no need for you to bow to me each time you see me, especially in your condition. Please take a seat. Unfortunately, I have to take your husband away for the night and we do not know when we will be back or if we will be back. But I can reassure you that my father, my son and I will protect your husband to unsure that he will come back by your side.

With a pounding heart, Amelia went to hug her husband immediately and warned him,

-Honey Bear, be careful out there, please, be careful. You know your shoulder is pretty bad right now so don't go all fighting mad because you can't, you just can't. Don't be head strong, listen to the angels who will look after you. Promise me at once once otherwise I tie you upon the chair so you can stay with me forever!

Understanding her strong display of affection and

knowing that Amelia had already lost a husband, Vincent embraced his wife to give her a most passionate kiss. Then he reassured her in an affectionate way touching her pregnant belly,

-I will be careful, my Love, for all of us, for our growing family, I will and I promise.

While Amelia released a big sigh trying to retain her coming tears as best as she could, her angelic brother in law made a beautiful purple pashmina cashmere shawl appear out of thin air. Raguel covered her shoulders with it from behind and told in a comforting way,

-Amelia, I saw your husband killing demons. He will be careful and he will be fine. I will make sure he is. He has his mission and you have yours. Accept this little token from me to keep you warm meanwhile, a belated wedding present. I understand you were a little chilly when you arrived from your journey to help us. How are you getting on so far?

Thus recalled Mrs Valdi, like a true soldier, manned up. She answered in the strongest voice she could manage at that moment in time,

-Thank you, yes, I was a little cold. It was fairly breezy over the ocean. But Doctor Williams sorted me out on arrival. However that beautiful shawl is most welcomed. I thank you, my, my dear brother...

Looking for an instant at the quality of the silk upon her shoulders with awe, Amelia then continued,

-I think I am getting on fine. Whilhelmina briefed me and I know how far she managed to go through the manuscript. I will carry on from there. I already started. But if I may say or advise. There are two books in one there. Maybe it could benefit to split the both apart in their copies. You see, Lucifer made the guide to kill demons visible, with proper ink but for the way to kill angels, it is created with invisible ink. One can suggest, it is because he doesn't want that part to fall into the wrong hands, like a form of protection to his former kind. But it could also be a way to disguise a proper plot against angels. I need to go through it all to tell you more about it, but I found a paragraph saying that anyone reading the angelic part of the manuscript risked death at the hands of Lucifer, and if they killed any angels following his instructions even more so.

A deeply interested Raguel ordered,

-Show me that passage, Amelia. You must bear in mind that Lucifer is a fallen angel. He is ambivalent. I do not trust him myself, having lost my eldest son to his dealings but my father has not lost faith completely in him. To Lucifer's credit, he does keep hell in good order, and it is a tough job. However as we have seen in Wilton Town or nearby at Amos's farm, he doesn't mind, letting some demons lose to prey on humans. He never liked the human kind. For him to murder my Gael because he was part human was not a problem whatsoever. But back in the days, we fought alongside each over and he was one angel I would have trusted with my life, but that is the past. Come, show me what he wrote.

Putting her glasses upon her freckled nose, adjusting her new shawl, Amelia obeyed and replied,

-Here, have a look.

As she presented the manuscript at the right page, she added with eagerness,

-I think he has a classification system going on as well. You see, he is using Roman numbers for all the pages, but he is also using them by the names of demons and angels. My belief is how he sees everyone in some sort of ranking order of importance. Now, I have been told by my husband that he accepted to do pacts with the souls of Archangel Raphael and Michael. In here, there is a symbol at the bottom of their pages a serpent looking like a S, when there is a straight line going through it I believe it means when Lucifer accomplished his part of the deal, because it is present for Raphael but not for Michael. With our current situation, it explains it all. But then I found a S with double bars underneath the name of an angel, here, here, that one. Do you know what it could mean?

An impressed Raguel examining the book told,

-If we follow your theory, Amelia, the S with a double bars means a soul taken. Because that angel became a fallen angel back in the days not long after Lucifer. He died and his soul dwells in hell, a slave to Lucifer. You must carry on the good work for me, Mrs Valdi, I count on you. To help you with the task, I brought to you my excellent angel, Daniel. He is a very ancient one and he can identify all of the angels mentioned in this manuscript, let alone all the demons. Not only that, he knows different languages like no other. But as you can see, he has been badly wounded yesterday and had to suffer the amputation of his leg, so I will beg of you to tend to him like a nurse tonight.

The good natured Amelia presented an armchair by the large rococo writing desk, put a cushion on it only to invite,

-Please, make him sit down. Daniel, it is nice to meet you. I am Mrs Amelia Valdi, the wife of Doctor Valdi, but as we are going to work together, please just call me Amelia.

She presented her hand for the angel to hold with a simplicity that pleased him straight away. Daniel smirked as he vented, holding the presented hand with respect,

-If you could find me a little wife like your Mrs Valdi, Vincent, I will be happy for you to cut my other leg.

This sent Amelia blushing, while Raguel gave her the manuscript back with an explanation,

-I forgot to mention Daniel has been a sailor for most of his incarnated lives, he can swear like one, and behave like one but you must forgive his manners for he is a good angel, Amelia.

Helping Daniel to sit on the armchair, Doctor Williams added,

-He is also a grieving angel. The woman, he loved passed away giving him a little daughter, Sarah Kay who is three and waiting for him in Boston.

The Master of all angels recalled his servant,

-William, we haven't got all night, although I know you like gossipping, you must go and wake up Theo and Henry now for we are living in a few minute. Mrs Valdi, Daniel, I will check on the progress of your task when I can. Let's say first thing tomorrow morning.

He then turned to Miss White and told,

-I would have loved to have you in town tonight Miss White for your magical powers, but you must stay here and protect this house with all your might. Your hotel is going to be a refuge and a hospital. You are a dedicated nurse so I do not have to beg you to look after all those victims we have upstairs. They are all stable at the moment. I am afraid that we may have more wounded to send to you tonight. I trust you to care for them. You are the leader in chief of the medical operations tonight. I am leaving you a couple of angels for the protection of the hotel but they will also give you a hand to look after everyone. Order them and they will obey. I am afraid to tell you, however, that I am taking Theo with me for he is the right individual to shepherd the inhabitants of Wilton Town and to lead them where they can be protected. If you want to say goodbye to him, now is the moment because we are leaving soon.

The White Witch bowed to the Master before running out of the room after Doctor Williams as she said,

-You can count on me, send all those poor people to me, I will look after them.

When she disappeared, Raguel genuinely smiled and stated turning to his brother,

-This is definitely a woman in love. Vince, Whilhelmina truly loves Theo. I felt her heart earlier after the little episode this morning by touching her hand. I can tell you that she was so distressed by the possible perspective of losing his love. She did hurt, hurt very badly because she loves him completely. If she didn't have a daughter, that pain was close to push her over the edge, and by that I mean kill herself. I also had a good talk to Theo. Let me tell you all about it, Honey Bear, as I walk with you to your next task. Amelia, I promise that I will do my up most to bring him back to you. Come on, Honey Bear, come with me.

Vincent kissed his wife one last time before following his older brother. In the hallway, after closing the door behind him, Vincent gave a dark look to his brother as he argued,

-I am called Vincent, not Honey Bear.

Raguel gave him a teasing smile with his reply,

-My dear brother, as long as you can't call me by my angelic title or anyone else by their titles or adapt that you are an angel, I will carry on calling you Honey Bear.

Valdi catching up with the fast pace of the Master retorted,

-Hold on, you gave me a leeway about calling you because I looked after the recovery of Sebastien!

Raguel turned and replied strongly with a serious air,

-My dear Honey Bear, my son is back but not fully recovered. He suffers from blackouts and as a Doctor you can figure out how dangerous that is, in a night like tonight when we face full front danger. Not only that he is a major angel which I can not deploy on his own. I will have to stay by him to supervise Mighty to ensure we do not lose him for he his a prime target for Lucifer to finish off. This means that I will have to deploy you instead but you need supervision too as a new angel and one with a wounded shoulder. How are you doing? Tell me now. How do you feel?

Walking by his brother finally, Vincent confided,

-I am feeling better. I would lie to you if I said I wasn't in pain but I can cope with it. I am ambidextrous and can punch with my left as well as with my right. But father, can I call him, father now?

Giving a kind look to his brother, the Master told,

-Of course, you can and if it is easier for you, you can call me brother. Carry on, what do you want to say to me?

This encouraged Valdi to reveal,

-On the way to the Neptune, father did let me rest on his shoulder. I slept thoroughly and peacefully for a few hours. He ordered me to do so because of your concern about me. So I can tell you that I am fully rested and quite ready for tonight. But I had a strange dream.

A curious Raguel enquired as they reached the kitchen,

-Do you want to share your dream with me, now, little Brother? I remember a time when you were not thinking much of me.

Almost blushing under the intense stare of the Master, Vincent confessed,

-Well, I had to prevent you twice to do something stupid. But since we fought by each other sides and you save my life at Amos's farm. I will never forget that I owe you. But beside that your will to look after mines if something happens to me touched my heart. Also I am learning so much by your side. I have confidence in my abilities, yes, but I am not a proud man, well, let me correct that to angel. To come back to the dream, it was all about the creation of angels and I got to shake their hands, to all of them. It felt like I knew them all by heart by the touch of the hand.

Opening the kitchen door Raguel asked further,

-Did you happen to meet any archangel in your dream?

Valdi nodded negatively with his reply,

-I would not recognise one but Henry, Daniel, the young Lawrence, Doctor Williams, a grown up Abigail and lots more were there.

The Master then explained as they entered the kitchen,

-That would be our father introducing you to the entire angelic army of the Mighty One, my Sebastien. Consider your dream as part of your angelic education. A few angels can give very meaningful dreams to people usually the ones that are destined to be angels, it usually happens by a simple contact, like the brief touch of fingers, holding a hand or, in your case sleeping on dad's shoulder. By the way, you do not owe me anything. In hell, I did get carried away and with you breaking the wrist of Lucifer, you saved the day. With my dislocated shoulder, I was seriously diminished. It was me owing you, Honey Bear, big time at Amos's farm. Beside that, I must congratulate you on your choice of wife. Amelia is so likable.

Standing by the stove, holding a cover close to his chest, Abraham Wilton-Cough commented,

-That is the problem. She has that twinkle in her eyes. She has simple manners but is so bright, that her intelligence can in a few words outshine any other women in a room. Her laugh is also infectious but I never saw her laugh very much. She has been a pretty lonely thing, although married, until Valdi took her as his bride.

Slightly startled by seeing the ghost of the banker, Raguel scolded straight away,

-Wilton-Cough! That cover is needed right now in the garden! What are you doing standing still?

Abraham looked at the Master of all angels bitting his own lips with guilt and explained,

-I was caught by the scent of those stews. They smell delicious. I guess I missed being physical too much, I am so sorry. I wanted to taste, just a small spoonful to know if I could remember what it was like to be fully alive...

A tear ran upon his cheek unchecked and Raguel came to the ghost straight away to hug him tight. He comforted,

-Abraham, know that my servant will be working to find a solution to make you stay physical much longer than just a day. I want you to hold your children and your Angela once more. Your wish is in my heart, it will stay there until it happens. We are working upon it. My William knows the spell of Miss White, he just needs to work out a way to extend it. Trust me, he will. Now, you've got to stay strong for all of us. I would let you taste that soup, but it was made for all the human victims who need it a lot. Also, if you have a little of that soup now, it will make you crave to have your life back more strongly than ever. If you take my advice, I will say, stay strong, wait until we sort you out, and come with us. We have a big night in front of us to deal with.

Putting on a brave face, Abraham replied as he wiped his tear,

-Please forgive me. I will wait. I will stay strong for you all. I just had a moment. It will not happen again. I will keep going. Let's sort out Wilton Town and the spirit of little girl.

Raguel already opening the French window garden doors called,

-Then let's go you two. We have work to do. Abraham, you've been briefed. Go ahead. I still need to give his orders to your angelic master.

The ghost left with no further a do. When he was out of sight, Raguel turned to his younger brother and said,

-Your servant is very devoted to you, Vincent. I must tell you that he cried of worry for you when you were away. I had to pick his spirit up, like I just did now. He really considers you as one of his sons. His heart has adopted you fully since a very long time. From what I felt, it was about twenty years ago. There are two instances, when his heart was moved by you. Do you remember the time, the first time, you were paid with a chicken for your medical services in this town? You told him that at the very least it will give you some eggs to eat, and that it was an asset to keep you going. He liked you from that point on. But then he saw you working in the field of a farmer with a broken leg. You helped that man until he could deal with his farm once more. From then on his heart had fully adopted you as a son, a son he wished to count amongst his ones. It really made me understand what a strong bond you have to one another. So tonight, you and Wilton-Cough are going to be paired again which is how it is going to be from now on. You will protect each other. Do you remember what I told you about acting in front of your enemies?

Valdi recalled,

-I certainly do. You chastised me verbally for it.

The Master told sternly,

-Good, I am glad you do remember it. The more you show affection to someone in front of your enemies, the more they will attack that person. Remember also one thing, our Abraham Wilton-Cough is known by Lucifer and he stole his manuscript. Consider him as a most wanted soul by hell demons from now on. Protect him by not demonstrating too much care for him in front of others you don't trust. I had that conversation with Abraham today and he understood me perfectly when I explained what happened to my eldest son but also when I took my own case as an example. Our father treats me rather roughly in front of others, like a slave, but it is for my protection. He may have ignored you for part of your existence but this is why we are still alive. Outside of those doors, our father will not treat you like a son, I will not treat you like a brother but like a normal angel like all others and you will treat Abraham like a servant because this is a way we can carry on loving each others and be with each others.

Vincent replied slightly moved,

-Trust me I know, brother, I had to remind the same lesson to your son. He was slightly upset to not see you at his bedside when he was recovering. But our father and I reminded him why. When all this is over, you will need to find some time to spend with Sebastien.

Raguel embraced Vincent,

-Thank you for telling me. I know my boy will not have shared anything about it to me, due to the way I brought him up. I will see to it. To my great pleasure, not long ago, he invited me to live with the new family he was building. God knows it took him a while to create another family. He has been mourning for centuries, his former wife and two daughters. They were raped and killed in front of him by the Roman army whilst he was nailed to a pillar. The fact that he couldn't help them has been haunting him throughout all his lives. If your friend Theo is suicidal, my youngest son had moments when he truly considered death as a better option to living. Sadly, he has a tendency to brood and he made an attempt on his life only a few years ago, in this very incarnated life. However the plight of the young Ivy Fair, who suddenly had no one in the world, became destitute and was in danger if she stayed in Boston was a strong enough incentive for him to look after her. My boy loves her to bits, hence I have been called to Wilton Town to live in his forming household because he dreads for Ivy to suffer like his first wife did in Roman time. He also took on a little boy called Jack who is in fact a fallen angel made human. He loves that boy and treats him as a son. So as I will live in Wilton Town for a while, I will find time to talk to my boy. Now, my dear Honey Bear of a brother, you are acquainted with some facts about my family.

Whilst he opened the door to the garden, the Master added,

-Now, our first mission is to deal with the remains of that little girl and to bury them properly for her spirit to rest. My father, Mr Berry, Wilton-Cough and you are in charge of transporting them to the cemetery of Wilton-Town. We will meet there for I will fly to town with Theo, Sebastien and Henry. We will all meet afterwards Williams and the other angelic soldiers at a pretend dinner at the tavern of Tyron Tyrell where we will wait for the reprisal of that gang Sebastien dealt with last time. For sure, you will give the gang a big surprise when they thought you were far away to bring justice back to town. Now, I will allow you to show yourself as an angel to them, a little flash of the wings will suffice, but withdraw them almost as soon as to keep them undamaged in any fight. They are your get away plan to get you to safety if needed. A word of caution, my son and I encountered many possessed humans in this town for there were an entrance to hell but also a demonic butchery nearby which we got rid of this morning, so one human may hide a demon inside him, be warned. Those discoveries, in my honest opinion, are only the tip of the iceberg. Are you ready for the night?

Valdi nodded positively when he replied,

-I am, a little fear in the belly but nothing comparable to confronting Lucifer.

Raguel smiled as he enjoined,

-You gave him a beautiful broken wrist, I must say. What a way to make him take his hands off me! Come, let's go, my brother, and sort this town out. One last word of advice, don't show your fear to the enemy. Just do like I do pretend that you are rough, fearless and ready for the kill if necessary. From experience, I can tell you that destabilises even your toughest opponents.

Vincent followed his eldest brother to the ruined cottage ready to face a night of upheaval, happier to have had that little chat with him. On the face of everything, he found Raguel someone to look up to. He understood his abruptness but also the loving care he had for his angels and humans deep down. Arriving at the make shift burial, they found that all the remains of the little girl were dug out and they were being placed carefully upon the cover by the Great Being himself.

Sebastien briefed his father,

-We are nearly ready to go, dad. All her little bones are here and accounted for. All we need to do know is bringing them to the cemetery.

The Master's answer came fast and forward,

-That duty belongs to your grandfather, Valdi and Wilton-Cough for you are coming with me. We will be flying into town with Williams, Henry and Theo supervising their operation from the air. If anything happens to the carriage of Mr Berry on the way, we will be able to intervene fast enough. Also do not forget, Theo is still a novice angel flying wise, we must keep him in the sky away from that spirit who tried to kill him. You and Henry will be his bodyguards for that flight, while Williams and I will intervene on the ground if necessary.

A dubious Sebastien questioned,

-Shouldn't you go with one of my angelic soldier? Williams isn't a fighting angel, father.

But this was dismissed at once by Raguel firmly,

-My William can teach you that there are multiple ways of fighting, my son. He has magical ones up in his sleeves, the ones that allowed him and Miss White to create a diversion serious enough for the Lord to take you into safety to get mended.

Sebastien putting his shovel down went to his father and held one of his hand strongly, before hugging him with some emotion, telling,

-That's when, I heard, you fought like a lion to allow me to be taken away to save me, risking your own life, which you risked once more confronting Lucifer...

Raguel almost tearful tapped gently the shoulders of his son before pulling away from the hug,

-Yes, enough about that my boy, enough about that, it hurts me to think of you in the state you were in. Let's move on, we've got to move on. Come with me to fetch Henry and Theo.

Father, I will meet you at the front of the hotel. We will depart at the same time.

His father made a military sign of agreement before folding carefully the remains of the little girl in the blanket and giving them for Abraham to hold and to carry to the carriage of Mr Berry.

When the Master and Sebastien went to the drawing room, they found Doctor Williams and Henry standing and discussing by its close door. Raguel demanded,

-Where is Odell?

Henry replied with a giggle,

-Still inside the drawing room, saying goodbye to his future wife, properly.

A blushing Williams confessed,

-You know when I told you, Master, that I gave Theo and Henry a power boost nap well... Theo is making love to Miss White right now as his farewell.

A swearing Raguel banged his head on the door,

-Good Lord! What I am going to do with all of you children if you do not know to behave!? We have work to do!

His son smiled as he answered,

-Well, swearing will amount to nothing. If we have to go, we have to go. Beside I have been willing to see some action for the past few hours when I was stuck in bed.

He put his hand on the clutch of the handle. Raguel warned,

-Don't you dare disturbing them!

Sebastien gave him a wink, and retorted,

-I will because caught into the act, they will have to marry and marry fast, solving the little issue between them.

Without waiting for an answer Sebastien stepped in without caring to knock on the door. His father had his eyes raising to the sky in desperation. Henry was smiling from one ear to the other while a sheepish Williams tried to say,

-Mighty does love matchmaking, Master. He can't help it. You must remember that his mother was French.

An annoyed Raguel answered back,

-Gallic, she was from Gaul. What can I say apart that Sebastien is impossible like his mother used to be, bless her soul.

Meanwhile, stepping into the cosy drawing room, Sebastien found the pair in a loving embrace. He coughed out loud before saying in a stern tone of voice yet with a smile,

-Father Odell, you must marry this woman at the first opportunity. I will see to it.

His intervention sent the couple blushing thoroughly. While Theo tried to hide his manhood as fast as he could, Whilhelmina was putting all her petticoats and her dress to a correct order. Both sighed at the same time and Miss White said first,

-We will marry!

And she gave a desperate look at her future husband who confirmed,

-She is my wife in my heart already. She carries my child. Of course I will marry her. I want to spend an eternity with her, hold her tight, make her feel safe and simply love her by caring for her everyday of her eternal life. Mina is already my daughter too, in here, deep inside here.

Theo tapped his heart as he said so and an emotional Whilhelmina hugged him for one last time before he went to follow the Mighty One dutifully.

#

As soon as the carriage of Mr Berry was loaded with his very specific load to take to Wilton Town and passengers, it went away from the front court yard of the Crying White Doe hotel. Soon afterwards it was followed by a few angels flying over it, keeping a good eye upon it from above. Sitting in a lotus position at the back of the carriage, the Great Being was watching over the covered remains of the little girl. By him, a crouched Abraham asked in a soft voice minding to not wake up the dead,

-Is the spirit of the child attached to her skeleton, my

Lord?

The Great Being replied looking at the good old banker with compassion,

-Not exactly, but she never strayed far from where her body was. She doesn't know any better unlike you. She is with us already, rather lost, angry and wondering what we are doing. Her intentions are to push Mr Berry who is driving the carriage under its wheels but she hasn't got the strength to do so after having used most of her energy this morning with her evil plan to end the life of Father Odell.

Abraham unable to see the spirit yet, however told her off,

-You mustn't push, Mr Berry. This is not nice and good little girl don't behave like that! Show yourself. What is your name little Miss?

Wilton-Cough knew that if she did as she was ordered to do, her ghost would lose the rest of her energy in order to sustain her apparition. To his surprise, the little Ogin girl appeared before him. She was poorly dressed, not cleaned just like the day she passed away. Her pale blue eyes were seriously angry while her closed fists by her side displayed a defiant attitude. She shouted,

-I don't know you!

Unshaken but pleased to see her ghost, Abraham pursued in a very certain and demanding tone of voice,

-Let's address that then young Lady. My name is Abraham Wilton-Cough and my credentials are that I used to be the banker of this town. Now what is your name and what are your credentials apart from the ones to talk to demons, and wanting to harm and kill people?

Shamed, red faced, the ghost of the girl, tried to tidy her poor little dress while she explained with a palpable sadness,

-I don't know my name, Sir. I don't remember it. My father used to call me the thing. He said often take the thing out of my way to my mum and she pushed me. I try not to remember much.

Wilton-Cough invited showing the little corner in the carriage by him,

-Come and sit by me. You know, you are not the only who had an appalling childhood. Like you, I wasn't loved as a child. My parents sent me far away from them. But I don't roam the earth with the intention to attack people, I just got over it. Tell me what is that kind of solution, if I wasn't love so I will kill? It doesn't make sense. It is mathematically and morally wrong. First, it doesn't solve the fact that you were not love. Second, you will not be loved any better afterwards. You will only get hate from it. Now, we can't have you being called a thing. Let's find a name for you. Come and sit down. I will not bite you. You are a ghost just like me.

Thus encouraged and somehow trusting Abraham, the ghostly girl went to sit by the old ghost. As she did so, she asked shyly,

-Are you going to find me a name? It won't be thing anymore?

Nodding positively Wilton-Cough confirmed with a benevolent smile,

-Yes, I will find you a name before we reach town. And, you, little Miss, will help me too, you will chose the name you prefer. Now, all the important ladies in my life have a first name starting by a A, but one, my aunt, by a J. So what do you think about Amy, or Anna? And with J in mind, Jenny or Joanna?

By the old banker the little ghost was pondering about her name, with all of her anger vanished into thin air. The satisfied Great Being sent a telepathic message to his angelic eldest son who was flying above them,

-The situation is under control in the carriage. Abraham Wilton-Cough has her little spirit tamed in the nicest way possible. She doesn't pose a threat to Mr Berry any longer. He forced her to appear. She is losing all her energy doing so. Abraham pacified our evil spirit. By talking properly to her, he is getting to the bottom of her soul. He is finding a name for her at the moment.

Raguel turned to Theo who was flying by him trying to keep up with the Master of all angels but with great effort. He asked Odell,

-Will you do the christening of the ghost that tried to kill you? It will help to make her rest in peace. Wilton-Cough is finding a name for her right now.

Without hesitation Odell replied,

-Of course, I will. I definitely want her to rest in peace.

Raguel giggled at his answer and gave a good look below inside the carriage where he could see Abraham holding the hand of the little girl in a paternal fashion. He remembered seeing the good old ghost doing the same with the human victims of Amos's farm and he thought to himself that Abraham Wilton-Cough was an asset rather than a liability.

The little ghost thought long and hard before confiding to Abraham with a slight pout,

-I like Amy but I like Joanna as well. I do not know which one to pick.

A conciliatory Wilton-Cough proposed,

-Why don't you have both Amy as a first name and Joanna as a middle name?

Smiling the child enquired with some joy,

-Can I?

It was the Great Being who confirmed in order to validate whatever Abraham said,

-Yes, you can. Actually Amy Joanna Ogin sounds pretty.

The little ghost frowned as she retorted,

-But I don't like the Ogin part of it. I hate it. My father never wanted a girl. My brothers bullied me and my mother let all of them kill me. When my father decided to stop feeding me, to only feed the boys, she agreed silently with it. I resent being called Ogin.

Tugging her small hand Abraham told in a soothing voice,

-Well, my parents didn't love me, as I said. My mum ended up in hell. But I still carried their family name: Wilton and Cough. I didn't cause a big fuss about it. Do you want to know why?

With enquiring eyes, the child demanded,

-Yes, why? Was your mummy that bad?

Wilton-Cough replied,

-I don't want to talk about my mummy, because the past is the past and we have to move on to make the future better for one another. By the way, your own mummy did repent and has been trying to repair her mistakes ever since. We have been helping her doing so. Now, for my surname, if my mummy and my daddy were far from perfect, they are people from my family carrying my surname or part of it which were or are very good people. My aunt Josephine Cough for example, the sister of my mother, was a second mother to me when I was alive. Then I have a few ancestors named Wilton who are quite honourable, notably Noah Wilton who founded this town. So you, Amy Joanna must have some ancestors named Ogin who were very nice and decent individuals. You may not have known them because you died far too early, a little like me because I was killed too, but unlike you I was a grown man when I was murdered.

The ghost did thrust herself against the arm of Abraham asking,

-Who would have wanted to kill you? You are so nice! I wish you would have been my father.

The old banker told sternly,

-That is the thing my child, sometimes people put their own agenda before any one else's and they are prepared to kill randomly people. They do not care if they are nice or not, that is not in their selfish interest. Did you care that Theo Odell is a very decent man when you tried to kill him? No, you didn't care. You were just jealous that Mina White was going to get a decent father whilst yours has been an appalling one. You don't want that little girl happy because you were not happy and you are prepared to destroy anyone around her. Let me ask you something straight: what will you get from destroying the life or happiness of others? What will be your reward apart from hell? If you think you are going to rejoice, I can correct you immediately that you will not. I have been to hell and came back, and it is not a happy place for a little girl like you to be. Beside that you may meet your own father there that will give you a hard time like he did during your lifetime. That's a sweet perspective in front of you but I guess demons would never have warned you about it. You can miss your pet demons badly but trust me when I tell you they are not to be trusted for their advices. It's the same thing they have their own selfish agenda and they will not care a speck to what will happen to your soul. When you will be down there, in hell, they will leave you there to be hurt forever.

Silently the little girl cried, yet she kept leaning upon Wilton-Cough who put his arm around her shoulders and cradled her. He gave a begging and desperate look to the Great Being who said,

-Her father is in hell. She will definitely meet him back down there. Her spirit, I am afraid is condemned to hell for all the mischief she has done for centuries. Last but not least was her attempt to kill Father Odell, prior to that was the illness she caused to the Georgia Marlow. Not only that she always tried to create chaos in the hotel by pushing drinks and creating brawls which ended up with wounded men.

The child hanging onto Abraham turned to the Great Being to tell him strongly,

-You are so mean!

To which he retorted firmly,

-The same could be said about you. But I am not mean, like Abraham Wilton-Cough, I am just being frank and honest with you. With centuries of demonic lies feeding your soul, you may not be used to it, that is all. Look, you haven't chosen to be a good spirit from the get go and there are consequences about it. That is all there is to it.

Amy bit her lips and sighed sadly before nestling herself within the arms of Abraham as she vented with tears in her eyes,

-I wish I had a nice daddy, so I would have been a good girl and a good ghost.

Then she thoroughly sobbed. Wilton-Cough took the opportunity to ask while he hugged the desperate little ghost,

-You can't blame on someone else the fact that your are bad. I know many victims who stayed good despite their ordeals. Now, given the chance, could you only be a good ghost? That means no talking to demons and not trying to hurt anyone.

Shivering at the perspective of encountering her father again, Amy confided,

-Oh yes, I could. I would be a very, very good ghost given the chance. I really don't want to meet my father in hell.

Abraham probed further in an encouraging way,

-Tell me about your Pa. My one was not that bad but he loved hunting with a passion. He liked killing animals even taking their hearts out when they were barely dead. I wasn't that sort of boy. I didn't enjoy killing anything and I always missed my targets on purpose to let the animals live. So I was a bitter disappointment to my father so he just sent me away. I was just his son in name but in his heart, there was no love there for me to be found. But he didn't hit me, he just ignored me, my mum ignored me as much as she could and battered me once when I was in the same room she was with her lover. I happened to be there by mistake but he was enough to unleash her fury against me. So tell me about you, now that you know a little about my childhood. How was it for you?

Settling on the lap of Wilton-Cough, the little ghost told,

-My Pa was a force to reckon with at home. He battered all of us. He said he never wanted a little girl, that two boys were enough. Apparently he did something to my mum so she couldn't give birth again after me. I don't know what it is but it involved a knife. As I said he never recognised me as he child because he refused to have a girl. I was a useless mouth to feed in his eyes and the usage is to provide a dowry for the girl. My father wasn't ready to do any of it. We had a big famine and he decided to feed his boys but to let me starve therefore I died slowly under their eyes. I simply wasn't wanted. But all of them did eat my flesh at my very end. Because I was never taken into town no one ever knew that I existed there. So when they got rid of me, it was easy. But I played with Mina White a couple of times at dusk. She was hanging bed sheets in her garden. She knew I was living but she didn't notice when I was gone.

The Great Being commented with severity,

-This is why you held a grudge against her, not knowing that that little girl had terrible predicaments of her own to deal with. Your death wasn't caused by her but by others yet you took it upon her. You will pay for the misery you created in the White household.

The sighing Amy did burst to tears before hiding her face within the arms of Abraham who tried to comfort her a little by tapping her back gently. Then the old banker asked for her, giving a knowing wink to the Great Being,

-Is there any way she could redeem her soul and escape going to hell and meet an atrocious eternity at the hands of her father, my Lord?

Reading the mind of Wilton-Cough, the Great Being smiled with benevolence, and winked back to him as the little ghost was still nestled, distraught, into the arms of Abraham missing any signs of connivance between the two. The Creator replied in an imposing manner,

-Where there's a will there's a way. But the will has to come first and forward.

This had an immediate effect on the child. She rose up to face the Great Being and half choking on her sobs she enquired with disbelief,

-There's a way I can escape hell?

Wilton-Cough making her sit by him and wiping her tears with his old handkerchief told firmly,

-The correct question is, my child, what do you have to achieve in order to do so. Your mother is still trying very hard to undo her wrong doings but she is getting there. Another question is what can you do to help others? The last but most important question of all is have you even got the will to redeem yourself?

Amy, full of sudden hope, tears in her eyes, answered quickly,

-Yes, yes, yes, I have the will, I have. Tell me what to do. I don't know what to do, but please tell me what to do and I will do it.

Putting the little ghost between himself and the Great Being, Abraham ordered,

-All you have to do is to listen to him, and to listen to him very carefully. If you obey his orders, you will be redeemed Amy.

A subdued Amy spent the rest of the way listening to the Great Being. She was attentive and kept holding the hand of Wilton-Cough whom by his mere presence gave her some courage. When they arrived at the large iron gates of the church's courtyard and cemetery, the Great Being jumped off the carriage and helped Amy down while he ordered,

-Vincent, Mr Berry, please, go to the tavern and wait for us there. Vincent, I am borrowing your servant but I will return him to you, just like I brought him back from hell. Abraham, you stay with me, you are in charge of Amy for the time being. Last word of advice, my son, if I want you to order dinner for

everyone, I also want you to be on your guard. Don't let it down.
Don't let me down.

Vincent Valdi nodded positively and firmly to his father.
He shook the hand of Wilton-Cough briefly saying,

-Abraham, you are at my father's orders until I meet you
again. I trust you to not displease him.

He winked at the old ghost who smiled back. Wilton-
Cough jumped down. Amy rushed to hold Abraham's hand who
accepted her little hand with some tenderness, as he reassured
her,

-It is going to be alright, Amy. Just like me, you just have
to be a ghost on its best behaviour. If I can do it, you can just as
well.

The trusting Amy nudged her head against him while
the Great Being took charge of her remains with a care that
touched her deeply. The carriage departed and she waved
goodbye to its driver and Valdi. As they entered the church yard
they saw four angels landing before them: the Master, his son,
the Messenger and Theo who as usual didn't use his legs and
landed flat on the cobbles. If Raguel and Sebastien giggled
together, Henry was prompt to pick up Odell and to tell him,

-Practice makes perfect, my friend. I will see that you
have some. Obviously your landing is an issue to look into, but
your flying is not that bad. You kept our pace throughout which
was not a given so well done to you.

Theo Odell stood up, brushed himself of any dirt, his
pride a little shaken but still slightly alive by the encouragements
of Henry. But what he saw moved him almost to tears, and took
his mind off his faulty landing. Almost as soon as Sebastien
landed, his wife and Jack appeared on the threshold of the
presbytery. Jack ran to Sebastien and held him tight in his little
arms, crying. Sebastien could only smile kindly and mess with
the hair of the boy as he said,

-You didn't think I will be gone forever, did you? It takes
more than one demon to bring me down. I am back my Jack.
How is Mummy? Did you keep a good eye upon her for me?

Whilst Sebastien picked up the boy in his arms, Jack
replied, drying his tears,

-I confessed I was ever so worried for you, I was. They
told me what happened but I wasn't allowed to tell Mum. Ivy

worked at her best at the clinic but she kept looking at the clock and I saw her cry. I held her hand and I reassured her that you will come back each time she did so. It was ever so hard.

Kissing the forehead of the boy, Sebastien put him down to run to Ivy who met him half way. They embraced each other silently for few seconds before Sebastien confessed,

-I heard they didn't tell you what happened to me. My little Bit, I was wounded and poisoned. Doctor Valdi saved me. I have more to tell you, much more but it will be for later. Something bad will happen in town tonight and I have to help as much as I can. I want you to stay indoors because the presbytery is protected, and keep Jack safe. We will send victims to Miss White's hotel but our house is a port of call too and the ones that are too wounded to make the trip to the hotel will be sent here. Prepare yourself, my Love. You know what I mean?

His little wife sighed deeply in his arms, but with her chin up she replied,

-I guessed that marrying an angel would never be plain sailing. I could see at Jack's worry that something was utterly wrong. And, yes, you will have to tell me what went on, because, because, I swear I was worried sick and not just because of your baby in my belly! But I will do what you just ordered, I will prepare for tonight. I have my Pa's medical satchel. We will boil some water. We will prepare some bandages. We will prepare some beds. I will keep Jack safe with me. He is such a brave little boy. He is ever so helpful you know. Before you go back into the night fighting demons can you just tell me how you are?

Sebastien holding her tight answered,

-Little Bit, I must admit that it was a close call. I have a faster healing process than humans but I am still not fully recovered. I will be careful tonight, I promise you. Beside I am not alone, my father is here to look after me and my grandfather. Come and meet my grand dad, Ivy. Jack, come with us and be on your best behaviour.

The three went toward the tall Great Being. If Ivy courtesied by him politely, she was surprised to see Jack kneeling to him and staying down with tears in his eyes. Sebastien told in a most casual manner doing the presentation,

-Grandfather, please meet my wife, Ivy and my adopted son Jack.

Giving the blanket containing the remains of Amy to Theo Odell to hold, the Great Being went first to hold the hand of the wife of his grandson. He greeted,

-Mrs Cotton, I am delighted to meet you at last. Dare I say, I know everything there is to know about you but do not be alarmed or worried about it for you have my complete approval. The day you accepted my grandson truly made my day, a better day. But it was also the same for the spirit of your father who rests in peace. He was overjoyed by the news and confided to me that you could not have found a better man. He also said that he could see wedding bells between you two a very long time ago. Was he right?

A blushing Ivy replied,

-I did admire Sebastien since I arrived back in Boston. I loved him silently, Sir, in my heart while becoming his friend.

Releasing her hand from his warm one, the Great Being comforted,

-Although we have to steal again your husband from you, as duty calls, we will make sure he comes back to you in one piece. I would not wish for my great grand children to grow up without their father. I heard you were expecting and I am truly overjoyed.

Then turning to the little Jack who was still on his knees, he added,

-Well, we meet again. You have a new name, a new body, let's hope that you do not mess up this time around. You seem to have encountered the pity of my grandson. Disappoint him and my wrath shall fall upon you. Stand up and take care of the mother that has adopted you. She mustn't leave this house tonight. If any errands are to be done, you must do them, to look after the wounded.

A trembling Jack stood up as he replied humbly,

-I will my Lord, I will. I am still a servant, in here.

The boy tapped his heart with his hand. Softening up a little, the Great Being ordered as he dried the tears of Jack with his thumb,

-You must understand that it is hard for me to see one of my fallen angel reduced to be an orphan human boy. You must also understand that you have been given a chance to work your way back up the angelic ladder. Follow the guidance of my grandson and serve him well. If you are under his protection by charity, you are still not under mine. You will have to work very hard to get my appreciation back.

Jack tried to stop crying as most as he could but with his human child constitution, he could not. However he felt the strength to look at the Great Being as he made the promise,

-Dear Lord, I will work very hard, I can promise you that. I don't deserve your appreciation, I know, but I will just work very hard for you and your grandson because I am still yours deep down.

Turning around the fallen angel turned human, the Lord answered,

-Do you know that even Lucifer still makes those kind of pledges, yet when one archangel decides to sell his soul to him for the death of my grandson, he has a good go at it.

Falling back on his knees Jack cried thoroughly out loud,

-This is what happened to Sebastien, then. No, no, how terrible. No, no, oh, no.

Sebastien picked up the boy and carried him into his strong arms to only reassure,

-Jack, I am still here. The plot didn't work.

Putting his arms with true affection around the neck of Sebastien, Jack cried upon his shoulder. Sebastien told firmly,

-We are agreeing on this point, Grandfather, Jack has another chance. Leave it to me. He is human and he is a child now. He may still have his angelic memory but I can tell you how lost he was when he appeared. If I have a plea for him to make it is to give him time. I will look after him. I can promise you that he will get his wings back.

The Great Being conceded,

-I am not going to argue the matter. I will agree with time in good faith. Now, Jack, pick yourself up, take your adoptive Mum indoors and come back to us for I have a task for you. We will be in the church.

Once back on the ground, Jack bowed profoundly, still

tearful, before taking the hand of Ivy and leading her back to the presbytery. Once inside, in the hallway, Ivy demanded,

-Why are you so upset, Jack? What did just happen out there?

Jack revealed with eyes still glistening with tears,

-Ma, you just met God. He is the grandfather of Sebastien. Sebastien is really called the Mighty One amongst angels. I am a fallen angel, but fallen so low that I lost my wings and I am now only human. I must go back to them. If the Lord is giving me a task, I have a real chance to regain my wings one day. I mustn't disappoint him this time, I mustn't. I thought he would ignore me altogether but he didn't. Ma, for any angel, the Lord talking to you is a privilege. He usually doesn't take his human appearance very often.

Wiping the tears of the little boy with kindness, Ivy probed further,

-This is why you knelt to him, isn't it? Sebastien never told me about being the grandson of...

Pale, she couldn't finish her sentence, with the realisation of it all dawning upon her. Jack told enjoining her,

-He didn't know. All other angels did all along. It was the wish of the Master of all angels, his father, that Sebastien should be brought up in a very humble way, and a very human one. That made the Mighty One such a good angel. Obviously, he knows now who his grandfather is, but I can tell you, he had the revelation not so long ago, probably just hours. He will not be more proud as a result. His heart is so set in goodness and benevolence. We must work for him together. For tonight, it means that we will have to be prepared to receive some injured humans. I will be back by your side as soon as I have finished my task.

Ivy kissed the boy's forehead before he left, saying softly,

-My son, know that you have my love with you. Make them proud for me, make them proud of you.

Jack went away with a smile on his face and was no longer tearful.

#

When Jack came into the church, a baptism ceremony

was in full swing, and the Great Being made a gesture with his hand for him to go by his side. The boy obeyed straight away in a most willing fashion, his little cap in his hands. In no time he was by the Great Being and asked him in the most subdued fashion,

-Did I miss something my Lord?

The Great Being looking down at the most willing little boy replied to him in a whispering fashion,

-Not really. We are just performing the christening of a Spirit, well, Father Odell is. Follow me so I can task you in private with Sebastien.

The three left the church together, Jack holding the hand of his adoptive father all the while. Once in the little stone garden by the presbytery, the Great Being invited,

-Pray, sit on the bench by your father, Jack and don't be uneasy, I do not have a tendency to bite the head off little human boys.

If Jack did as he was told, he kept his hand locked within the one of Sebastien who could feel him trembling. His adoptive father reassured,

-It's okay, Jack, stop shivering like a leaf. You are with me and belonging to my household. You are facing the Lord, not my father, the angel of Justice, he is the one that you should fear now. Be a brave little boy for me.

Jack tried his up most to straighten his back and to calm his nerves down while he said,

-I will. I will do anything for you.

The Great Being couldn't fault the willingness of Jack and his desire to please his grandson. But he could also feel a true and deep affection between the two so he started,

-Jack, I am glad to hear it. Because we have an issue, which with your past as a guardian angel, you may be able to help us with. You dealt with Mina White when she was a vampire, you kept her soul and managed to prevent her to do much damage. This is to your credit. No one asked you to look after her soul but you did, from the kindness of your own heart for centuries. I want you to look after another soul.

The boy with tears of joy asked with eagerness,

-Am I to be your angel again, my Lord? Am I to be a guardian angel once more? Will I be accepted?

Turning in the little garden, considering everything, the Great Being told firmly,

-Don't get ahead of yourself too fast. First, you are already accepted back in the angelic community because you are under the wings of the Mighty One. He wants you to get your wings back and I am pretty sure if you follow what he says you will get them back. The task I am giving you can only help you achieve that a little faster. Now, all will depend upon your delivery of that delicate mission.

Jack was all ears at that stage as he begged,

-Please, task me, my Lord.

The Great Being could see in him a truly repentant fallen angel with a good heart, so he continued,

-Jack, your mission will not be easy. We have a very young ghost on our hands. You must have encountered her for she did plague the White's household being jealous of Mina White.

Jack nodded positively as he answered,

-Yes, I did. She was eaten by her family during the famine. They starved her to death. She became a very angry spirit.

Satisfied by the reply the Great Being pursued,

-That is right. She also befriended demons during her centuries as a ghost. One can only guess what type of advices they delivered to her spirit. This morning she tried to encourage Father Odell to commit suicide. This was adverted by my son. Now, her terrible past is not negligible and we are working to put her soul at peace. First, we are doing what her parents didn't do, we are giving her a name. She is being christened right now in the church as Amy Joanna Ogin. Abraham Wilton-Cough, another ghost, is her appointed Godfather. As you must know the spirit of that little girl is pretty evil and needs to settle down. If we send her now, on her way to the other side, she will go straight to hell. However we want to give her a chance purely because of what happened during her life. I don't know any guardian angel who would look kindly to that little girl who had demons for best friends and tried to kill people but I know, you,

Jack, are capable of consideration having dealt with a young vampire for a very long time. So I want you to look after that ghost, to turn her spirit around, so much so that when we can lay her to rest she will go to paradise and not in hell. Are you up for the task?

Jack accepted straight away, rising up from his place on the bench,

-Yes, my Lord, I am up for the task. I must confess to be well experienced with children's souls, especially the difficult ones, with my last undertaking being to preserve the soul of Mina White. I have enough compassion in my heart to help them out and give them a much needed hand. Being a human child now myself, I will be able to relate to her better. If I can allow myself to do an assumption, it is that if Amy made demonic friends, it is probably because she didn't have the choice of any other friends. Demons are also notoriously famous for preying on stray souls and spirits. With her age at time of death being so young, from a toddler just about to become a child, her level of understanding being not mature at all, she was a prime prey for demons, an easy one. Of course now with centuries as a ghost under her belt, she will have acquired some knowledge under demonic hands but the wrong type of knowledge making her an evil spirit. But at the end of the day she is still a child that has been given an horrendous life, an horrendous death and a miserable after life. I can certainly help her spirit out. For one thing I know about her to some extent and know what she is capable of.

Smiling the Great Being demanded,

-Will you be able to work with human limitations? You are not an angel any longer.

But a determined Jack replied,

-I know. It comes with limitations but not without compassion and understanding which is what that ghost needs. I will painstakingly undo the bad undermining the demons did to that spirit.

The Great Being went to tap the shoulder of the boy with kindness as he revealed,

-This task alone, Jack, will make you earn back your wings. I have faith in you. Take back your seat, I need to give you more information on your mission.

The boy obeyed, full of hope in his heart, and put his

young hand back inside the one of Sebastien who held it in comforting way. The Lord continued,

-Amy responded really well to Abraham Wilton-Cough. He was bluntly honest with her, yet he showed her what you promoted as your skills, compassion and understanding. He is no longer a human, he is a ghost and he used his talking power to soothe to some extent the spirit of Amy. I saw him building bridges to her soul just with his voice alone. I believe you can do so as well and with your expertise as a guardian angel, you will achieve wonder. Now, Amy has been warned that she will end up in hell and meet her father there. She fears the idea and became extremely subdued ever since. She has been listening to us willingly and attentively. Now, if she responds positively to attention and conversation, she still had years of brainwashing by demons. Therefore I had to limit where her spirit will be allowed to roam. Her ghost is literally within the prison of this cemetery, her bed will be her coffin. She will not be allowed in the house of my grandson. However she will be allowed to go inside the church accompanied by either you, the Master or the Mighty One. Abraham Wilton-Cough has a positive influence on her, and you can allow him to spend time with Amy, ghost to ghost. She is a poltergeist ghost. She is able to move things and also appear but when she appears her energy is depleted therefore she will not be able to hurt anyone. I want you to educate her properly but most importantly she needs to learn to care and to see further than her own belly button. You need to dissipate the hate in her heart to allow that soul to go to paradise. The Mighty One will be the supervisor of your progress on that task.

Rising to the challenge, Jack enquired,

-So her spirit will be a prisoner of this cemetery? She will not be allowed inside apart from the church, am I right?

The Great Being replied firmly,

-You are right. These are the rules.

Jack contested,

-That child needs to know what love is. Spending her after life amongst graves, I don't think she will get any sense of the meaning of the very word. So we will have a little ghost roaming outdoors in all weather...

Sebastien intervened,

-I agree with Jack, this is a very harsh sentence for that

soul.

But the Great Being faced both of them to retort,

-This is that or hell for her. Shall I remind you both that she tried to kill a man this morning? Her bed will be her grave until I meet her again and she meets my requirements. Then I will reconsider her case. As for you, Jack, if her plight moves you that much, you'd better get her settle in her new environment soon enough so she doesn't plague it. Teach her to be useful: Tending to the graves for example, keeping them flowered. And don't let her befriend any demons ever again. As for you, Mighty, don't let that girl into your household by charity until I say so, until Jack has done his work with her. At the moment she is tolerated. She has been given a chance but she is not to be trusted. She will harm any happy households she witness because she didn't have one. She can attack your pregnant Ivy without any remorse. I know your father has decided to accept your offer to live in your home. He will keep a very good eye on the situation as well as an eternal Watcher. This is why we are letting little Amy in your backyard. By all means, you can both befriend her, but just be reminded that she has been talking to demons for centuries. Wilton-Cough had a tough but right approach with her. I want you both to do the same. Let's go back to the church. Her baptism is over. Jack, I want you to take over from Abraham the care of her spirit.

Sebastien took the hand of Jack in his as he enjoined,

-Come my Jack, you had your instructions and I had mines.

As the boy followed his adoptive father, the Great Being added,

-Trust me when I say that she will be much happier here than in hell meeting the father that decided to let her die of starvation to feed her to his sons. She is exhausted because of her exertions of today. She has used up all her energy to appear by the clever demand of Wilton-Cough who knew as a ghost what it took to do so. All we have to do know is to put her to rest in her new bed and get on with our demanding night. Jack, you will have to help your adoptive human mother to look after any seriously wounded tonight whilst the Mighty One will be on the front line with his father to resolve the situation in town.

Jack nodded positively agreeing,

-Yes, my Lord, you can count on me.

Turning to the fallen angel turned human boy, the Creator stated,

-You never truly left my service, did you?

Jack admitted with tears in his eyes,

-Never, but sometimes I wasn't good enough. I made bad mistakes. Because I lost my wings I did find it hard to carry on and I did try to end my life that was when little Mina was unguarded for a few hours and that was when she created two vampires out of the Ogin boys. I beat myself for it, my Lord. My heart is very heavy with remorse. I should be brave all the time and carry on but I have moments when, when, I think I am not good enough, would never be good enough or just be good enough for a hole in the ground to hide my shame of being a fallen angel. But the Mighty One is giving me back my strength, my hope and my will. I will continue to continue not for me but for him. He has, he has...

The Great Being demanded taking the other hand of the child encouragingly,

-He has what? You must know something, Jack, you are not lost any longer. You are not alone. You can talk to us freely because you are part of our family now. Wings or no wings, you must grow higher than your inner shame. When you feel low, confide, we are here for you. You know, you can always pray to me and I will listen.

Thus encouraged Jack confessed,

-The Mighty One has my entire devotion. I want to serve him for my entire human life.

Sebastien messed the hair of his boy with tenderness while the Great Being welcomed,

-I am glad to hear it. Now, be strong for him. Accomplish your given mission. Earn back your wings and then you can dedicate more than one lifetime to him but many as one of his incarnated human angels, be part of his army. Now, let me present you formally to your mission. A last word of warning, she may be small but do not underestimate her.

The boy took a deep breath at the church doors giving his reply,

-Yes, my Lord. I will not forget it. I will be vigilant. I must confess one more thing to you... It has... It has been an honour, a privilege to talk to you again let alone to be tasked by you because, because, I didn't think I deserved anything not even yourself addressing me, nor even noticing me.

Before Sebastien opened the church doors, the Lord put both of his hands on the shoulders of the boy making him face him and locked his eyes with the child's ones, before he told firmly with his enigmatic smile,

-Jack, you will not be surprised if I tell you that I have more faith than you. I never lose hope on any of my angels, even the ones lost or fallen. You can't go more fallen as an angel than Lucifer in hell but you may be astonished that I have still conversations with him. I will always give a hand and opportunities to my old angels to get back their former status. Now, it is up to them if they grab their given chances or not. Now, mistakes on tasks do happen, but I will not beat around the bush with you, and recite you two old adagios: first, that we learn by our mistakes, second that practice makes perfect. Come, have a little faith in you and have a little faith in me. Let's step in together. Give me your hand.

Jack gave his hand willingly and entered with the Great Being. They were closely followed by Sebastien. The scene they all witnessed was the ghost of Amy by the side of Wilton-Cough apologising to Father Odell. Abraham bowed to the Lord as he explained,

-Amy is fully baptised now. She also said sorry to Father Odell.

The Great Being demanded,

-Was it from the goodness of her heart or was Amy enjoined to apologise?

His son responded before anyone else,

-Amy Joanna was asked to do so by Abraham. I would say she was willing to comply to his request. It was half hearted apologies: The ones that you are feeling obliged to do but don't really mean.

The little girl gave Raguel a dark glance. Seeing that the Great Being told her sternly,

-Amy, this is the angel of justice and a Punisher. I would play nice in front of him if I was you, unless you want to see your dad in hell of course, faster than you can imagine. So you said sorry, that is a first step and I will accept that, half hearted or not. But I want you to do more than that. Every Sunday morning, Father Odell is doing a mass. I want you to help him preparing his church for it from now on. What do you say?

Sighing deeply Amy looked at Theo and at the goodness of his benevolent eyes before she answered,

-I say that I will do anything that keeps me away from my father. But you know I did mean to be good, just now. Father Odell christened me despite what I did to him this morning and it means to me. It really did mean something. I can't describe it.

Abraham Wilton-Cough put the words to the feelings of the young ghost,

-Well, Amy, Father Odell just showed you his forgiving heart. Forgiveness is one thing you need to learn badly. By helping him, you can only learn how to do that.

Amy tugged his hand in agreement before facing back the Great Being with a knot in her throat, truly intimidated. But she saw a glow in his eyes which was sympathetic rather than damning. He invited her to hold his hand which she did willingly yet reluctantly leaving the hand of Wilton-Cough. When her little hand reached his and was nestled within his, the Lord presented,

-Amy, I want you to meet Jack. He is going to be your guardian here. If you follow his instructions to the letter, you will not go to hell. Jack, this is the spirit in your charge. She became malevolent because of what happened to her.

Faced with such an introduction, Amy's eyes started to well up as she retorted,

-I am not malevolent!

Raguel corrected her sternly,

-You are. If you were not given a chance to behave better, I would take you straight to hell. Because you were killed, you tried to kill others. Pray, tell me how good does that sound to you? Very benevolent? Try again to do it just once and you will meet your father in hell my little Darling. You have one chance in my books, just one, take it or leave it. But you will face very harsh consequences if you are leaving it. I will show you no pity nor mercy.

This made Amy sob heavily. Jack naturally came to her and hugged her. He soothed,

-Amy, you will be fine. We will show everyone that you can escape a hell sentence, and you will be good, so good that you will earn a place in paradise instead.

Her eyes met his then she rested her head on his shoulder with the confidence that she found a friend. A happy Great Being enjoined,

-It is getting late and it is time for Amy Joanna to have some rest. Come my child, let me show you your new resting place. Your little bones are not hidden under a muddy floor this time around ignored by everybody, no you have your proper resting place.

Amy took the presented hand again, totally subdued, whilst her other hand was held by Jack. She followed them to her grave. Doctor Williams and Henry made it whilst she was baptised. They stood by it with a solemn air. Raguel demanded as he saw them,

-Is everything ready?

Williams, his servant, responded straight away,

-Yes, Master. We have a nice oak coffin with white velvet lining ready for Amy. I can change the colour to her own liking. We also marked her grave by an engraved stone with her name upon it, her date of birth and the day she died.

While the Master gave a nod of approval, Amy looked with tears in her eyes to her proper grave. It was no longer a hole in the mud. Her remains had been placed carefully within the coffin. She was deeply touched. She asked bewildered,

-Whom I am to thank for this?

Raguel replied in his commending way,

-That would be the Lord who is giving you a chance to redeem yourself.

Amy went to hug the Great Being silently crying then she promised him in a whisper,

-I will be good from now on. I promise I will be a good spirit. I will follow the footsteps of Abraham to be a good ghost and then maybe I can go to heaven one day.

Picking her up, the Great Being put her in her coffin.

The child put no resistance at all. When she was there, Father Odell performed the rites and she laid quietly all along. When all was done Raguel told Amy,

-You now live in the restricted area of this cemetery. You will only be allowed to go to the church accompanied to perform your duties. Just know that you have two punishing angels living in this property. Me, being one of them, I will only accept your best behaviour. Constantly, I will be watching you. Stray from being good and I will have no remorse to send you to hell.

Somehow, appeased by her burial ceremony, a subdued Amy answered,

-I can only say to you that I promise to be good.

Only responding with a positive nod to the girl Raguel ordered,

-Let's not waste more time on that spirit tonight, we have work to do. Jack, stay with Amy until she is asleep then help your mother.

Everyone followed the Master leading the way out of the cemetery but Jack did as he was told and remained by the little girl. He asked her with compassion,

-How do you feel Amy?

She looked at him from the depth of her coffin before she answered with honesty,

-Grateful but so terribly fearful at the same time. Who is that very severe angel? Is he really living here?

Jack sitting by the open coffin in the grave replied,

-He is living here from now on. He is not only the angel of justice and a punisher. He is the Master of all angels. He kills demons like if it is a pass time. We call him Master in the angelic world.

Amy enquired shyly,

-Do you think if I call him Master, he will be less harsh on me?

Shaking his head negatively, Jack told,

-This is not how it works with him at all. You can flatter

him with his titles all you like, it will get you nowhere. No, with him, it is all about your actions and your deeds, nothing else. With him only your best behaviour will do. But you are in his very bad books at the moments for trying to kill Father Odell, something which he had to stop from happening today.

The little girl sighed deeply as she confessed,

-I am not feeling proud about that. Abraham told me off about it. What he said was true. I was so jealous of Mina that I didn't want her to have the perfect father adopting her. But, but, when I faced Father Odell again, he was all forgiving, he baptised me, he gave me a proper burial as well. It moved me a fair bit. I don't see kindness very often. I feel bad about what I did to Father Odell because he is such a good man.

Jack corrected her,

-He was such a good man that he is now an angel during his own lifetime. It does happen, but not very often. You can count those instances with your two hands only.

Amy enquired with some curiosity,

-You seem to know a lot about angels?

Putting a large and thick white woollen cover over Amy as if he was tucking her in bed in her casket, Jack answered,

-I do. I work for them. Now, you look very tired. Do you want me to tell you a bedtime story?

The little girl clapped her hands with sheer joy while she exulted,

-Oh yes please! Miss White always tells some to Mina, and I am often in a little corner, in the shadow listening to them when she does it. My Ma never told me any bedtime story.

Jack smiled as he prompted,

-You must have heard many tales then since Miss White and her daughter are eternal beings?

Amy argued,

-Maybe but it mustn't stop you telling me one! Even if I heard it before. I like stories especially fairy tales.

So Jack settled himself back in a lotus position then

started,

-This is a story that will be new to you. Close your eyes and imagine everything. Once upon a time many angels were watching upon the earth, walking among humans...

Amy did as she was told. It didn't took very long for her to be deeply asleep and to gradually fade in her coffin. She had lost all energy and all physicality. Jack closed the lid when he knew her spirit was at rest. He put large slate slabs to cover the grave then walked to the presbytery thinking that the little spirit he had the guard of was not the most evil one and that he could definitely revert her to be a good spirit. She had the willingness for sure and with Raguel making such a strong impression on her, he was certain she would stay in the right path.

He stepped in the presbytery to find Ivy hard at work to prepare herself to receive casualties. The living room table had already been dressed as a make shift operating table. Ivy welcomed him immediately,

-Jack, how did it go? Tell me everything. I prepared us some tea and we will have a small supper. Come.

The boy followed her willingly as he confided,

-I have been given a task, Ma, which may give me back my wings. It is not an easy one by all means but I think I can do it.

When they arrived in the kitchen, Ivy enjoined,

-Please, sit down Jack. You have been working all day like I did and it sounds like we will be working all night. You and I need a little something to keep going. I can tell you straight it will not be as good as Pa's food but it will have to do for us for the time being.

Jack smiled as he put plates and cutlery upon the table. He commented with an irresistible giggle,

-Ma, Pa has been born in France over and over again. He knows his food from A to Z. I would not even venture to compare myself to him culinary wise. Beside that he is an angel approximately 2000 years old, give or take a couple of centuries, which means he has lots of experience under his belt.

Frying some bacon and eggs on the stove, Ivy confided with a shy smile to the child,

-When I fell in love with Sebastien, I had absolutely no idea whatsoever how important he was. For the young girl I was then, I found him as dashing as a Prince Charming, but also honourable, brave, hardworking and his sense of repartee won me over. But he always looked after me as if I was his young sister, with care, tenderness and sometimes a fair deal of teasing on my inexperience in the general things of life. But I will try to not let cooking be one of his opportunities to tease me endlessly. He knows so much and comparatively I know so little.

Jack told trying to help,

-You know enough, Ma, trust me. You are clever but you are not pretentious about it. In the angelic world, we never thought the Mighty One would set eyes on a woman after the loss of his first wife and his two daughters. He grieved for centuries. He lived almost like a monk as well for centuries until you. I can help you for the cooking you know. When I was within Mina, I learnt a fair few things because she enjoys cooking especially baking. Georgia Marlow who is a fabulous cook taught her great deal. I must confess I encouraged Mina in that pursuit which would make her love proper food instead of craving human blood. Also the servant of the Master, Doctor Williams possess a very comprehensive library. He has cookery books in there dating from Roman time, one from Apicius, up until books from the present. He is a wizard, you know, and legend has it that he also possess books from the future. He did home you for a while when you lost your father and your house, when you became destitute. Just ask him, he is one of the most erudite angels around. He knows you well and he will help you.

Ivy enjoined him,

-Slice some bread for us, Jack, everything is almost ready. We have some butter, if you can fetch it on that shelf. It was from the lovely lady who couldn't pay with money this morning at the clinic. I didn't know Doctor Williams was a wizard. But it is a good idea, I will ask him if I can borrow some of his cookery books. You see, Jack, I would have never guessed Doctor Williams was a servant either. He lives in a very lavish way and has lots of servants himself.

The boy felt obliged to explain as he did get the bread and the butter to fulfil his orders,

-This is because Doctor Williams has been chosen by the Master of all angels to be his servant. That makes him in angelic terms, the top of the class in per say. Angels are a usually a very obedient kind and we do attach ourselves to an other more senior angel if we can or if we are accepted by that more eminent angel. Henry, the Messenger, is a servant of your husband and Ted has recently become one. This is why they are now living here. The servants you saw at Doctor Williams's house are younger angels in different stages of reincarnation that have devoted themselves to him who his an older entity. If I earn my wings again and I am determined to do so, I want to serve Sebastien. When we serve one another it is usually for eternity.

Serving their dinner, Ivy commented,

-The Master of all Angels, this is the father of my husband and his own father is God himself, this is what I understood so far. Jack, you will have to brief me about all I need to know as the wife of Sebastien. What is surprising me, is although, he has an awesome presence which could be slightly daunting, the Master has a humbleness about him and dare I say, there's extreme sadness in his eyes.

Jack slicing the bread then buttering it revealed,

-The Master's angelic name is Raguel. He is an Archangel. He is also the angel of Justice and Punisher. That is why there is something always somewhat daunting about his presence. Last but not least, he is a watcher who can be in multiple places at the same time in different shape, animal, human or else. Ma, for his humbleness, you spotted that well. He is the servant of his father. Raguel could wear rags that it will not bother him at all. However he does have pride but one that comes from his actions and achievements alone. He taught that his son. Both are not materialistic for one bit, both deal with souls, angels and humans. They are helpers. The Master didn't impose poverty on his servant, Doctor Williams. He has been very generous and indulgent to Williams for as as I know. First, it is because Williams has the capacity to heal his angels, the human ones and the other ones created with fire. Second, it is because Doctor Williams has a very profound knowledge and is also being used to educate angels. If you do not know, Williams has been the personal tutor of Sebastien for many, many lives. Thirdly, Williams is totally devoted to the Master and his son. I would say myself you could not wish for a better servant. He has been stretched beyond and above. Williams is renown for his capacity to work tirelessly and going without sleep for days. So yes, Raguel is giving him some slack by letting him live the plush lifestyle Doctor Williams always loves. As for the Master's sadness, he had two human wives, you know. He truly loved them. The first one was the mother of his eldest son Gael. Years later it was the Celtic Gallic mother of Sebastien. I would say he was passionately in love with the last one but she died not long after Sebastien was born, I think it was three or six months later.

So he raised his baby boy on his own instead of having the happy family he wanted for his youngest son. Not only that, having lost his eldest son to demons, he was forced to watch the end of the first human life of his youngest one, unable to intervene. However Sebastien's soul did pass the grade to become a reincarnated angel at that stage. But, yes, the Master of all angel carries a lot of sadness in his heart. How do you feel about him living with us, Ma?

Taking a seat, Ivy replied with confidence,

-I think it was very nice of Sebastien to invite his father to live with us. Having learnt what you told me, I am very happy he did so. It sounds like this old Archangel could do with a bit of nice family time. Now, I do not know how good I am with being a mother of a family, because I was brought up without a mother for she died at my birth, but I will give it my all and my best. Sit, my Jack and help yourself to dinner. I promise you we will have something better on the table once we will get properly established in this town. But I do understand Doctor Valdi accepting whatever the people can give to him as thanks for their care.

The boy answered back, smiling,

-And I do understand why the Mighty One chose you as his wife. You mustn't put yourself down for not having been brought up by a mother, because it is the same for him. He only had a father figure just like you.

Ivy still grieving her own father changed the conversation while serving tea,

-So, tell me, what is the task that was given to you which may get you back your wings?

Enjoying very much the company of Ivy whom he trusted completely, Jack confided,

-Well, it is a complicated mission but as I used to be a guardian angel, I have the skills to do it. We have a spirit of a little girl to lay to rest but if we do it now, she will go straight to hell. I have been tasked to turn her spirit around from evil to good.

A surprised Ivy enquired,

-A little girl spirit can't be evil, surely?

Putting his cup of tea down after a sip, Jack replied with

sadness,

      -Ma, you would be surprised of the amount of evil spirits on this earth. Evil disregard gender or age. It accepts every soul it can pervert in its stride. In this case, the one of Amy Joanna Ogin, she was about three to four years old when she died centuries ago. It was during the foundation of Wilton Town. There was a famine at that time which lasted a long time. Her father who didn't want a girl and who had two boys to feed decided to let her die to feed his family. He starved her to death and they all ate her body afterwards.

      This made Ivy drop her fork as she expressed her sentiments,

      -This is horrible! Poor thing!

      Jack agreed carrying on eating,

      -Yes, it is. Her horrendous death is the cause of her spirit not resting in peace.

      He took another piece of bacon to put on his plate with his fork before he added,

      -A bad death is the main cause for ghosts. Abraham Wilton-Cough for example is a ghost. He was shot in his guts by a robber and died after a long agony that lasted hours. He created the bank in this little town, who by the way had been created by his ancestor.

      Ivy recalled,

      -I have heard of him, many times since I arrived here. Didn't he die a hero?

      Jack answered straight away,

      -Yes, he did. He protected the customers of his bank from being killed. From what I know he can be considered as a good ghost. But our little Amy since her death as been befriended by demons for centuries. It doesn't take a wit to figure out what kind of damage this does to a soul. She tried to persuade Father Odell to kill himself today. She would have been successful if Raguel didn't intervene.

      A baffled Ivy demanded,

      -Why would she do that? Father Odell is such a nice person. I mean we live in his presbytery because of his generous heart.

After finishing his egg, the boy replied,

-She is jealous and envious. She didn't have a nice childhood as you now know. Her little neighbour was Mina White who is much loved by her mother and others like Georgia Marlow so Amy, jealous of Mina, tried her hardest with the help of demons to ruin any chance of happiness in the White household. The deadly illness of Georgia was caused by her evil doings and as for Father Odell, he is about to become the adoptive father of Mina because he is about to marry his mother so Amy wanted him dead.

Ivy nodded her comprehension of the entire matter before she asked,

-What could you do to change her and what can I do to help you, Jack?

The fallen angel smiled at his human adoptive mum. He liked her so much. However he told her firmly,

-Don't help me, not for the moment. Ivy, mark my word, Amy will hurt you. Let me deal with her first. I will tell you when she will be safe for you to approach her. But I have a little plan already in my head to make that spirit enter paradise instead of hell. If you really want to help me, could you create a rag doll, a special rag doll for her. It will be filled full of demon repellent which I can get from Doctor Williams. She never had a toy and she will cherish it. She is resting in a casket in the cemetery at the moment, totally exhausted. Before she was resting in the mud where her remains were. So a velvet lined coffin feels like luxury to her. I covered her and I told her a bed time story. This made her spirit peaceful and she slept. Amy needs to have her childhood. It will be an after life childhood but it will soothe her. I can give that to her and I am sure her spirit will go to paradise in fifteen years from now.

Admiring his determination, Ivy enjoined,

-Have one more cup of tea before we have to prepare all the bedrooms. I certainly can create a rag doll. I know how to stitch bodies fairly well. So Amy is in the cemetery?

The boy chuckled on his cup of tea,

-I know you can stitch. That arm, this morning, of the lumberjack, you did an excellent job. Poor man, I was hurting for him to just see his wound but he was so brave because you were so brave too. You reassured him very well. For Amy, yes, the cemetery is now her new home. It was too dangerous to let her stay by the White household due to her jealousy to little Mina. Now, she is being given a chance here. We must be careful because that spirit may have died aged three-four but she is a ghost old of a few centuries, who indulged talking to demons during all that time. The cemetery is in effect the prison of her spirit. She will not be able to cross the boundaries of it, the Great Being made sure of it. She will not be able to enter the Presbytery but she will be allowed to enter the church accompanied by either the Master, the Mighty One or me.

Finishing up her plate, Ivy confided,

-I don't know about you but I am still starving. It must be the little one inside me. Who is the Great Being?

Jack sliced another piece of bread and buttered it for Ivy before he replied,

-Here, Ma, have another piece of bread. Put some jam on it, let me fetch the pot for you. Do want the plum jam or the bramble berry one? The Great Being is God. In the angelic circle, we always refer to him as the Great Being or the Creator and when we address him, we call him my Lord.

The young woman touching her belly with tenderness confessed,

-I hope I didn't make a fool of myself out there in front of him. I will have the plum jam, Jack. Do I have to call Sebastien the Mighty One? Will our baby have a title? Do you have an angelic title?

Jack bringing back the pot of jam to Ivy smiled to all her questions full of curiosity. He reassured,

-No, you didn't make a fool of yourself. For what I witnessed, I can tell you straight away that you made a good impression on him and that he likes you. The fact that he told you, he spoke to your father, maybe because he did show your wedding to Doctor Fair from the above, from heaven. You don't have to call Sebastien the Mighty One. You can call him like you always used to. Beside Sebastien doesn't care too much for titles. But I will tell you a secret, all his first names, his first Gallic one and Sebastien mean mighty. Also his father calls him affectionately Mighty, just Mighty. He is so used to that you may call him that way if you want to. For the little baby in your belly, for sure, he will have a title for he is the great grand son of the Lord. As for me, I used to have one. I was a good guardian angel before, well, let's not talk about it.

Ivy insisted slicing another piece of bread for the boy, and preparing it for him before handing it to him,

-Jack, you know you can always talk to me. We are family now, you, Pa and me. Oh, we mustn't forget Raguel, my father in law. I don't want to hear your story if it makes you uncomfortable, just the title you had that is all.

Reluctantly, with tears appearing in his eyes green eyes, Jack confided,

-I was called the Heart's Guardian back in the days. I earned that title because of my good heart and protecting the ones of others. But, but I made a few mistakes, it broke my own heart and I lost my way for a bit which made me lose my wings. But I tried to correct my mistakes on my own. It was hard, but if I patched some, some have long lasting consequences. I have a very heart about it.

His adoptive mother came to him straight away and hugged him. She comforted,

-I can't start to tell you how much Sebastien was so happy and touched to have discovered you were not lost but that you protected the little Mina's soul all along. So chin up, finish your bread while I clear up, and let's get back to work. Do you want to know what I think? I think that the angelic community missed you a great deal of a lot. I can see it in the eyes of my Sebastien and how he speaks volumes about you but also, none that Doctor Williams appeared to me to tell me all about you.

Jack finished his piece of bread in an instant before he demanded with curiosity,

-What did Doctor Williams say? What did the Mighty One say?

Ivy clearing up the kitchen table actively, revealed,

-Well, first both were happy to find you. I think they thought you were totally lost. Doctor Williams confessed that he cried for a while after the whole event, after you appeared back as a very badly burnt child. What I gathered is that angels did quest for you for years without success. What Sebastien said was that all angels wanted you back as one of them. He told me that he didn't only took you under his wings, he made a plea for you which was also done by all angels in his army and two very major angels.

Sighing deeply but smiling shyly Jack told,

-Those two major angels would be Doctor Williams and the Master. This is probably why I was tasked and given a new opportunity to get my wings back. Let me clean the dishes for you, Ma. There is a strict order for you to stay inside tonight because this house is protected. Mayhem will hit town. What you said will explain why I started to receive telepathic messages back from the Master of all angels and his servant. They both truly want me back.

His human mother confirmed,

-Doctor Williams said something along those lines although he also told that this time around you will have the choice of who you want to serve and which angelic career path you want to do. Now, you asked me how did I feel having the father of my husband living with us, let me return the question to you?

The boy bit his lips before he provided an answer,

-He is the angel of justice, Ma. I am daunted. But all the same, I like Raguel, I like him a lot. You may not understand me because what I am going to say is pretty much an angelic feeling. But angels do have loyalties, strong ones, well, some of us do, and although I did make mistakes, my one is still there. I would give my life to him or his son in a heartbeat, for you and your future baby as well because you belong to the Mighty One.

Ivy hugged her adopted son with tenderness whispering to his ear,

-You will get your wings back, I am sure of it.

#

In the tavern of Tyrell, it was busier than usual. Tyron still recovering from his injuries welcomed everyone in his premises with a friendly smile. But when he saw Sebastien and Doctor Valdi, his joy was visible on his face. He demanded straight away,

-Mr Cotton, I heard you were out of town. One rumour said that you were back in the hospital in Boston but not as a surgeon as a patient... I was worried for you, very worried. Your little wife and your boy were working alone at the clinic for the past day. A lot of people went there with little nothings today to know what happened to you apart from John our lumberjack who was really seriously wounded. I went there myself but Mrs Cotton changing my bandages didn't enlighten me about your whereabout or your welfare. What happened?

The cocky and brash Sebastien gave a bright smile to Tyron as he replied lifting his own shirt exhibiting the latest large fresh scar on his flank,

-This one happened. I added one scar to my collection. So the lumberjack was seriously wounded you said, what happened to him? Come and sit with us. I brought a large party here.

Tyron looking at the amount of people in his tavern asked,

-So all those are your friends? I don't recognise a lot of them being from Wilton Town.

Sebastien winked at the tavern owner in a jovial manner as he gave his answer,

-That would be because they come from all over the place, and by that I mean the world.

Valdi couldn't help smiling by the side of Sebastien, while Raguel just listened with a stern air about him. However the Great Being behind them enjoined,

-I can see that Ted did reserve a large table for us.

Tyron replied showing them to the table,

-Yes, yes, he did. This is my largest table. If you need more chairs or stools, I will bring them for you all.

Pleased with the obliging human, the Great Being told,

-Mr Tyrell, you must let the friends of Sebastien do that task. You are injured and you must not exert yourself too much. Please take a seat by my side.

As he sat by Ted, who was full of confusion and awe to see the Lord in human shape, Tyron Tyrell took his seat by him willingly. The owner of the tavern confessed as he did so,

-I feel bad sitting down because I should really be hosting.

Raguel taking a seat by Tyron told in a firm manner,

-No, you should really be resting. My son, Sebastien told you to do so.

Tyrell at the tone of his voice understood he was amongst angels. He presented his hand to Raguel to shake,

-I presume you are an angel like your son. Nice to meet you. My name is Tyron Tyrell, the owner of this tavern. I must say something about Sebastien, you must be so proud of him. He helped me so much the past few days. I was so worried to not see him in town, worried for his welfare.

The Master of all angels shook the presented hand firmly, knowing that his son wanted to make an angel of that man. From the simple contact, he knew he had an excellent human before him and most certainly that he had angelic potential. He introduced himself,

-Nice to meet you, Tyron. My son spoke very highly of you. I am Raguel, the angel of justice. On your left is my father.

The polite man turning to the Great Being presented his hand warmly while he asked,

-How do you do? Tyron Tyrell at your service this evening. I will unsure that you all eat very well at my tavern.

The Great Being considered the hardworking injured man with some benevolence before accepting to shake his hand. His handshake was mild and caring, enclosing with his two hands the hand of Tyron. He could feel that the human was and had been in pain each time he had given his handshake for the past few days yet that he had remained sociable nonetheless despite him suffering. The Lord answered with a kind smile,

-We should really ask this question to you, Mr Tyrell, how do you do? For us, we are doing as well as one can do under the circumstances that my grandson considers you as possible angelic material, you, an Atheist and a Publican.

Tyron's gaze went to search for Sebastien, who was still just by the entrance of the tavern, welcomed by all of his angels who were relieved to see him alive and standing tall once more. Slightly moved, Tyron told,

-I didn't know that your grandson appreciated me that much. I am touched but nobody's perfect, and I know I am not. I would not know how I would stack up as an angel with my atheist credential on my shoulders. I would say I gave you, angels, enough trouble as it is, for you to be good enough to sort the problem in my tavern. I will remain a Publican who will serve people and try to make them having an enjoyable time in my premises.

Giving a long look at his son, the Great Being sent Raguel a telepathic message,

-I can only agree with you and Mighty. This man is absolutely decent. If you two really want him as an angel at some point in the future, you have my seal of approval. There are no bad bones in his body apart for his fractured shoulder and broken ribs. He will make a good angel. His soul perspires sadness and lonelitude along with his goodness. That human could do with being introduced to the great family of incarnated angels that is the army of your son during his lifetime. Tyrell's tavern is not a problem, it could be used as a canteen for the angelic army and a meeting point like tonight.

With this agreement, the Master said to the man,

-Tyron, you do not mind me calling you Tyron, do you? If my father may be able to claim to be perfect, us, angels, we can only strive to do so. Look, my Sebastien is not perfect exhibiting his battle's scars at every opportunity, like he is doing right now, again. If you join his army during your lifetime, atheist or not, we can provide you with the angelic training. If it doesn't work out, it doesn't work out, but if it does you will become a reincarnated human angel in my son's army in your next life and the next and the next. Ted, sitting at the table, comes from very long time ago, before the middle ages. He was abandoned by his mother to a monastery where my son was a monk and a teacher. Ted is not perfect, far from it, but he is still a most cherished and valuable angel. What motivates all of us is helping humans and humanity. Ted with all his imperfections did that in the bucketful. You said you do not know how you would stack up as an angel. I would say the most important thing is to give it a good go and a good try.

Doctor Valdi arrived at the table and took his seat opposite Raguel. Vincent was all smiles as he reported,

-Lord Almighty! Gosh, is there a celebratory welcome to the walking wounded out there! I hope I am not interrupting anything?

Raguel gave him a slightly amused smile when he answered his younger brother sternly,

-You are just interrupting a conversation with a potential new angel, and swearing in front of your father, that is all.

Not really apologising, Vincent swore again before asking,

-Damn it! Sorry! Who is to be a new angel?

While the Master shook his head in a desperate way, the Great Being told,

-Your friend Tyrell.

He then addressed himself at the owner of the tavern,

-You see, Tyron, my youngest son, Vincent is far from perfect as well and was an atheist for many years. But he eventually still made it as an angel during his human lifetime. Like my eldest son said the most important is to give the angelic incentive a try and earn your wings.

A confused Tyrell looked at Doctor Valdi in dismay and enquired half hazardly,

-I thought you were human Vincent. I thought you were an orphan. I thought you were on honeymoon with Amelia. I had so much trouble here without you but, but Sebastien and his angels came to the rescue. So did you tell me lies all the time when I thought we were good friends?

Seeing the emotions passing on the face of his younger brother, Raguel took it upon himself to reply for him,

-Tyron, there is no need to get upset. First, Vincent only learnt he was an angel extremely recently. In this human life which is his first, he has been technically an orphan who was brought up by his aunt. He wasn't aware at all of his angelic family until virtually just hours. He was on his honeymoon but when my son and a few angels were injured, the Doctor that he is helped us. Literally he saved my Sebastien. He is here tonight to give us a hand because we know we are going to have trouble in town again with that gang. I am pretty sure he would rather be on the ship off the coast of Spain with Amelia enjoying the scenery rather than being here preparing himself mentally to protect people, by intervening, fighting most probably, and that is without mentioning the aftermath we will have to deal with therefore looking after the wounded. No, my brother never lied to you Tyron. I sincerely hope on that basis that you will both remain friends.

Tyrell replied straight away,

-Most certainly, we will. Please, Vincent accept my sincere apologies. Let me make it up to you.

He called a young waiter who was behind the bar who came running to him with great eagerness. He told the red head boy to take the orders from everyone, food and drink, to be liberal for everything was upon the house that night. The waiter bowed, smiled to him and went about the room to announce the good news to every single guest and taking their orders.

Raguel demanded,

-Haven't you got a business to run, Tyrell? This will cost you a great deal of a lot. Your offence to my brother was small. Can you afford a night on the house?

Tyron almost blushed under the stern angelic gaze but replied in an adamant way,

-You brought an angelic army to protect this town, this is my thanks to you all as a resident of Wilton Town. I may feel the pinch later, but it will be a much smaller than the one I could feel if all inhabitants leave town because of that gang. The good old Abraham Wilton-Cough would have replied to you that we have to put things into perspective all the time.

A smirking Master commented,

-But Wilton-Cough died applying this concept to the letter.

Undeterred, Tyrell retorted,

-But he died a hero. Look, you can not question generosity especially when it is not blind. I know the cost but I am fully prepared to pay them.

Raguel turned to his brother with a smile and told,

-I approve of your choice of friends so far, my dear Vincent. Your vicar is an angel now and your Publican has all the qualities of an angel. He just has got to decide to become one.

Taking the slight hint, Valdi decided to encourage his friend,

-Tyron, first I must tell you that I am sad to see you in that state. I didn't know that my absence would have such an effect in town. When I saw Sebastien and how wounded he was, I was chocked. I just knew I had to come back. The good thing about being an angel is that you have wings and can travel fast. Despite the Atlantic being fairly stormy, I am here, ready to help. Look, this is the main aim: Being an angel is all about helping others. I know you always help people. You care for them. Tell me about your red head little waiter. He is new. I never saw him in town. By the way he responds to you I can guess that you did something good to him. Am I not right?

Tyron opened up willingly, glancing at his waiter who was very busy taking orders,

-Vince, the boy is called Rick, short for Richard. He came to Wilton Town about ten days ago. First he asked for work to our black smith then to all the farmers without success. I saw him sleeping under a bridge two nights in a row. He pretended that he was just sheltering from the rain whenever I asked what he was doing there. Then on the third day, he sat on the church steps begging any church goers. I did what Abraham Wilton-Cough would have done, offering a meal to the lad in exchange for work. I made him swept my entire tavern and gave him a good meal for it. I sat with him and, when he was willing to open up a little, I learnt his story.

A very interested Vincent demanded whilst Sebastien, Father Odell and Henry took their seats at the table, along with Mr Berry,

-Tell me, what is his story? What is his surname?

Tyrell sighed deeply as he revealed,

-I still don't know his surname but it is early days. I know he is scared of something. From what I gathered, his father and elder brother were black smiths in Boston. His father was a gambler and went into bad debts to a gang there. He couldn't pay and got killed. The same happened to the eldest son. Now, the gang has their black smith business and this young lad, his youngest son, my waiter has been on the run to save his neck and he ended up here in Wilton Town. For the mum, she was killed as well as a warning to the father if he didn't pay his debts. You can only imagine what this young lad went through. He is rather tall and well built but he is only fourteen and no one to answer for him any longer. So I took him in and because he is a lad that doesn't accept charity, I gave him work for his full boarding and his wages. At least I know he doesn't sleep under a bridge any longer and he is not starving. He has a very good and very willing temperament. Everything I taught him, he took on board.

Vincent looking at the new waiter who was giving drinks to everyone diligently commented,

-Well, we will have to look after little Rick to make sure he stays safe here.

Sebastien picking up on the conversation proposed,

-His story is similar to what my Ivy faced in Boston. If he is shy about his surname, he has a death sentence above his head by that gang. He is young enough to be adopted but who would do so in Wilton Town? He needs to change his surname to be fully safe.

Tyron replied straight away,

-I am willing to give him my surname and adopt him. He is a very nice hard working lad. I want him safe, here, under my roof.

Vincent approved,

-That is the case of Rick sorted. Will you send him to school?

Looking at Rick who was busy serving behind the bar with the angel Callum, Tyrell answered,

-If the boy wants to go there, yes, I will. He is bright enough, a little shy, but he knows how to write and checking on his notes when he takes his orders, I can tell you that he has a decent and clear writing hand, not only that you can't find any spelling mistake whatsoever in them. For his mathematical skills, let's say between you and I that the old banker Abraham Wilton-Cough would have been proud of that boy's skills with his numbers. I gave him some complicated additions, substractions, multiplications, divisions and even fractions to work out, all in the line of my business of course and for my account books. So I was able to verify the ability of Rick on the subject and work out that he has been educated when he was in Boston. When I give him a little break, he likes nothing more than sitting by the chimney fire on that little stool and reading books, the ones I have one the shelves for the customers. At the moment, I know he is half way through the Frankenstein of Mary Shelley. It is not the easiest book to read for a fourteen years old.

Raguel paying great attention to the conversation

demanded,

-You said Richard was shy and scared of something. Can you elaborate on that for me, Tyron? There is a situation with gangs in Boston, a nasty one and we will resolve it, I can assure you of that. We lost the excellent Doctor Fair to it and my good friend, Doctor Williams, who lives in Boston did receive death threats and not just the one.

The tavern owner complied willingly to the request,

-Well, for a start, he doesn't let people know his full name. If you ever call him Richard, he will look at you with frightened eyes. I did that once, when he was in the basement, dealing with the bottles of wine. I asked him to tidy them a bit. He was very methodical about it, dusting and accomplishing everything with great precision. I have an alphabetical order now in that basement for my wines. Anyhow, it took him some times so I went to check on him and at his full name Richard being called out, he was so scared, he went to hide behind a huge casket and crouched as if the worst would happen to him. It took me a good five minutes to reassure the boy that it was only me checking up on him and to coax Rick out of his little corner. Also, he mentioned that his real nickname was Dick but that he didn't like that one any longer. One can ask the question, why? Finally I took him once to the market with me to carry my baskets, and I can tell that he was afraid. He was looking behind him constantly and I could feel his hand holding the lapel of my jacket to not lose me in the crowd. He was ever so anxious on that outing.

Raguel stated at the end,

-Something definitely happened to that boy. For a start, from Boston to here, it is quite a way to do on foot for a young lad. We will get to the bottom of this together. At least he found a good Samaritan in you, Tyron. Keep an eye on that boy and if you ever learn anything new, come and tell me, I will reside at the presbytery. If you don't find me there, you can talk to Henry who is the angelic Messenger, or Jack, the little boy with striking emerald eyes which has been adopted by my son. Both will deliver your informations to me. As for you, my dear Tyron, I will give you time to think about becoming an angel. Whenever you make your mind up, just tell me straight, if it is a yes or a no. If it is a yes, you will become part of the army of my son, and his angels will train you. You can still stay a Publican by all means. Look my son is a surgeon, my younger brother is a Doctor, Henry is a post man. What I am trying to say, is that we have human vocations, still, despite being angels. First it allows us to blend in, second it allows us to help humans. I will accept a no from you with some understanding and no hard feelings because you are such a good man. You will not lose my appreciation.

Tyron told him frankly, immediately,

-I will do as you said before, I will give it a good go and a good try. I want to try to be an angel and if I can't, I will settle for helping you all with the best of my abilities.

While Sebastien and Valdi went to hug the man, Raguel gave a winning smile to his father with his telepathic message,

-We will make a good angel out of that human. He has such potential already. His generous and caring heart speaks for itself. I like him. I had reports from Rob and Callum who have worked with him for the past few days. He passed everything with flying colours. I know my Mighty will be ever so pleased to count him in his army.

Rick came to the table with paper and a charcoal pen to take the order. He watched the effusion given to Tyrell with some timidity and waited politely and ever so silently. Raguel who noticed the presence of the boy addressed him first,

-Rick, we are ready to order. For our table, it will be four racks of roasted pork ribs, the 'Gratin Dauphinois' that Callum swears about that it is delicious, about two of them, make it three. Then we will finish the dinner with the baked apples. My table will get more heads during the night so just keep the count and add more of everything as you see fit. With all that you can start with bringing us jugs of the best cider in the house. I heard that you came from Boston what brought you here? Fleeing? I am a soldier, like Callum and Rob and we will protect you. You can confide to any of us or Tyron who is considering adopting you to protect you fully. Come and sit by me for a little bit. I can see what I told you upset you a great deal.

The red head boy did as he was told and burst into tears. Raguel comforted the young lad, putting his arms across his shoulders,

-Rick, you are here, amongst friends. We will have your back and watch it, so you don't have to turn around every five minutes when you are in the great outdoors. You do not have anyone any longer. Mr Tyrell wants to adopt you, give you his surname so you can feel safe here in Wilton Town. You are not the first person coming from Boston, having lost everything and everyone. My son married Ivy Fair, to change her name to protect her. She is destitute and had to run away from Boston too. You can confide to us. Trust me we will understand even if gambling was involved. For you see my daughter in law's father was maybe a gambler but still an excellent man, a Doctor who saved many lives yet he died because of his gambling debts. His daughter, Ivy who is now a Doctor in this town, cannot live in Boston any longer for fear of her life. Like we are protecting her, we can protect you so you can open up to us.

Taking the encouragement the youngster confided,

-It was all about gambling debts. My Pa refused to pay his debts because he said his loss was fool play. It was supposed to be settled by a duel which my father won by injuring his opponent. But the following day, they kidnapped my mother, tortured her, raped her, killed her. We received a letter. They told us what they did to her. Inside it were all of her fingers cut with missing finger nails, one with her wedding ring so we would know it was her for sure. I thought it was the worst day of my life. My father tried to report the case to the authority of the town. But that was the last time we saw him. They arrested him for injuring a man, the murder of his wife and debts. They hanged him. My brother tried vainly to protect the forge but it was taken away and he was beaten up to death in the street. He told me to run away, to save myself. I did and I was followed. I went into an alleyway but there was no way out apart from getting inside the sewers which I did. They teased me out loud calling me a rat and if they ever caught me they would do exactly what they did to my mother and gut me alive. Two of them went into the sewers in my pursuit. I only escaped them by holding my breath and laying flat under the filthy water of the sewers. After they passed, I backtracked to the nearest ladder to come out of the sewers. I then left Boston as fast as I could.

Satisfied that Rick opened up, the Master tapped his shoulder gently and told him,

-The important thing is that you were intelligent enough to follow the order of your brother. You made it, you are here with us and we will protect you. Are you happy to stay under the guardianship of Mr Tyrell?

The boy nodded positively as he answered,

-Yes, Sir, Mr Tyrell is an excellent man. He took me off the street.

Raguel pursued,

-I know that giving up your family name maybe a hardship, but for your protection I will advise you to do so. If you are scared to tell your real name, you have already figured out that it poses a danger to your life. Tyron is offering you his own name and adoption. Tyron, do you want to add anything about that?

Tyrell agreed before he told,

-Yes, I do. Rick, I will treat you as a son. I am a Publican as you know and your home will be here with me. I am not the richest man in town but I am not the poorest either. You will have a roof above your head and food everyday. I haven't got any children because the woman I loved died not so long ago. Trust me when I tell you that you will be a son to me. Under my roof you will receive tender love and care. I will not impose my views upon you. I want you to tell me what you want to do and become when you grow up, and I will help you to achieve that. I have the means to send you to school and university. You will be well looked after here and respected. I just want you to know that. When the threat over your head is gone, you can take your family name back again. I will help you do it.

Acting as a middle man, the Master demanded,

-Rick, what is your answer? Are you up to be adopted by Mr Tyrell?

With tears in his eyes the teenager replied as he went to kneel by Tyron and took his hand within his,

-Thank you, Mr Tyrell, thank you so much. I will never forget your kindness. Yes, I do want to be adopted by you. It will be an honour. I will not disappoint you, you know, I am a hardworking boy. I used to go to school, work at the forge, do my chores and do my homeworks.

Tyrell ruffled the red hair of the boy with affection when he told him,

-Call me Ty, from now on. Forget the Mister, we are now family, you and me. You will be safe here. Now, run along and tell the cook the order for this table.

Rick obeyed with a smile and diligence. Once he left the table, Raguel stated,

-Tyron, your boy is definitely not naturally shy, he is just reserved because of fear. But he will open up more and more to you. Most importantly, in just a few days, you did manage to get his trust. By touching his shoulder I have seen his past and what he went through: horrific. I am glad that young lad found you in his path. I can reveal to you that he genuinely likes and respects you a lot. I also believe that you will get on very well because your character and his are not that dissimilar.

He turned to Henry and ordered,

-My Henry, tomorrow, I want you to fetch the adoption paperwork and to bring them to Tyron. The sooner it is done, the better for that kid.

Tyrell agreed with him silently but ask with curiosity to the angel,

-So when you touch my hand, you gathered who I was deep down. Your son bestows a similar trick. May I asked what you gathered for Rick and I?

Raguel, far from offended by the question replied,

-A few angels possess that gift, by a simple contact we know what a person is made of, their character, and we can even see their past. Yes, my son possess that gift. For Rick and you, you are both honest, courageous and hard working individuals. For you, you are naturally generous, with your time, your help, your service. You are extremely lonely and that boy will change that. For him, his heart is grieving bitterly. He is cross with himself to not have fought by his brother but to have listened to him instead and run for his life. He is not proud of that. But you must teach him the concept of fighting for another day, Tyron, this way, Rick will cope better. He has a very lonely, struggling soul at the moment however your help did touch his heart and made him hang on in there. As for intelligence, he is clever, way beyond his age. He doesn't really need to go to school any longer. Just get him books. My servant can provide you with those, he can also provide tutorials if the boy wishes to have them. It will be wrong to think of him as just an intellectual. He is very much hands on as well. He knows how to craft weapons better than any other and his late father who taught him the art. Fencing has no mystery for him, you can consider him an expert. His father was a former soldier. Horse riding and the care of horses are other skills of his. The boy knows how to repair his own clothes, and he learnt to cook with his mother. He can make excellent breads, especially a sourdough one. He dreamt of being a baker but everything has been put on hold in his mind since the tragedy that happened to his entire family. He just needs to get his footing back and you, Tyron can provide that for him.

Impressed Tyrell remained silent. Sebastien took his opportunity to express himself,

-We need to tackle those gangs in Boston. If my Ivy's story was bad enough, Rick's story's is far worst.

The Master told firmly,

-Leave it to me. I will deal with it all. I gathered most of the names of the culprits I needed from the boy's memory.

Extending his hand across the table, Sebastien demanded,

-Show it to me.

His father refused to hold his hand and share the informations he had just gathered. Instead he ordered,

-You, my dear Mighty, will stay here and look after the problems in this town. They are bad enough to keep you occupied. I will deal with the problems in Boston myself.

Sebastien tried to argue,

-But my Ivy comes from Boston, I owe it to Doctor Fair to avenge them.

Raguel's fist slammed the table, while he corrected,

-You are out of your depth, Son. What you owe to Doctor Fair is to look after his pregnant daughter and making sure she stays safe in this town. What you owe to him is making the town you will bring up his grand child and mine an haven of peace. Boston will be my responsibility and I want you to look after yours. Right here, from right now. Since your face is so recognisable in Boston, I suggest you do as I say and stay away from the place. You have target written all over you there. For your wife, for Doctor Fair, for Jack, for me, you are staying here in Wilton Town. Beside that, for nearly getting killed you are grounded.

A pouting Sebastien retorted,

-But I made it. Look, Pa, here, at the table, good old me. You can't stop me from helping you to crush those Boston gangs.

His father argued, making a pinching in the air gesture with his fingers,

-You narrowly made it, like that narrow. If you can't

survive in Wilton Town what are your chances in Boston? You stay put, it is an order and try to do a better work here at staying alive. The Lord is my witness.

A shame faced Sebastien stated almost surrendering,

-Of course you had to bring grand dad into the conversation. Needless to say, I lost the argument as soon as you did that. But what you can take from me is half of my army to help you in Boston. At least, don't go alone, just for my peace of mind.

Raguel accepted,

-I know there is going to be violence in Boston. I am willing to take your offer. I will bring with me half of your angelic army. Are you satisfied? Will you stay put and look after this town with all of what you've got because it will need it?

Sebastien nodded positively as he replied,

-I will do as you tell me to do.

While Callum came to the table carrying a tray with jugs of cider and glasses, Father Odell advanced rather shyly,

-Since what happened to Doctor Fair in Boston, I made enquiries to my fellow priests and vicars there by letters. I must say, I have been inundated by their replies. Not only do I have the names of their parishioners being gang members, I have the ones of some of their victims and the ones of their intended victims. One vicar told me that a few senior members of the town were corrupted. That could explain the senseless hanging and conviction of Rick's father. He mentioned three but had suspicions on a fourth one. I can give you all the letters.

The Master of all angels told him,

-As you read them, I will read them, just give me your hand, Theo.

Odell obliged him straight away. After a few minutes Raguel imposed,

-I will have to take your priest to Boston with me, Mighty, I am afraid. He not only detains valuable information, he also has valuable connections.

Pouring himself a pint of cider, Sebastien contested,

-No, you can't take my Theo. He stays here with me, in Wilton Town.

Doctor Williams who had arrived at the table and sat by the Master commented with eyes to the sky,

-Good Lord! Did I arrive just in time to witness another father and son bickering?

The Master and the Mighty One gave him dark looks whilst the Great Being smiling at his comment responded,

-My dear Williams, you only just missed the first argument which was settled amicably between the two. The second one only just started.

Raguel fired away,

-We are not bickering nor arguing we are discussing matters.

Putting his pint of cider down after a good sip, giggling, Valdi stated,

-William, lets just say they are discussing matters in a very bickering way. To give you a short brief this one is about Theo going to Boston helping Raguel with the problems there.

Whilst the Master held the hand of his servant to pass him the entire account of the situation, he persisted,

-Vincent, I can assure you this is just a discussion.

Doctor Williams chuckled, having caught up with everything. He explained,

-Vincent, this is what happens when you create an angel from a feisty French woman. You end up with a Sebastien with a spirited temperament.

Williams served the Master cider who giggled despite himself. Raguel addressed his son again, sternly asking,

-Pray, Mighty, what are your reasons to keep Theo by your sides when his skills and the work he has already done will help greatly with the Boston situation?

Father Odell was curious to see how the situation would turn out. He didn't particularly want to go to Boston, but he felt compelled to help as much as he could to resolve the problems there. Sebastien posited,

-He is getting married to Miss White. It will be unfair to take him away from her.

Raguel gave a disappointed look at his son,

-What kind of argument is that? Mighty, this one is solved already. I am marrying that couple in the next forty eight hours. You don't want them to spend their honeymoon in Wilton Town, do you? Going to Boston and see the Ocean could do a world of good to Miss White who spent centuries in Wilton Town. They can reside at Doctor Williams's during their stay. It will also reassure Miss White about the house where her Georgia Marlow will live in the near future. Because your match making game you played on my servant and hers worked. Have you got another reason which is reasonable to throw at me, Mighty?

A pouting Sebastien gave an outcry,

-So you are claiming my witch as well! You already have a wizard! That's being greedy now!

While Williams started to laugh, Raguel smirked as he retorted,

-I have witnesses around the table who could quote you, my Mighty, saying that it will be unfair to take Theo away from Miss White, therefore, I will not separate them, and take them both. Beside that, technically speaking, as she is an eternal Being and not a human angel, she is free to chose any jurisdictions, yours or mine, she wants to work for at any time. So this was another lame argument from you. There is also a little magical word called training. Your grandmother Dana showed you a few magical tricks that you can perform when she spent time at your bedside. I would assume that you didn't waste the time and energy of a goddess by not wanting to practice your own magical powers. As for the 'my witch', let me tell you straight that she is not a pawn on a chess board, she is a Being with a heart that belongs to Theo Odell. If you haven't got any valid reason to throw at me, I am taking them both.

Mulling over his answer, Sebastien gave a long look at Theo before he pleaded,

-Father, my Theo is my newest angel, my newest recruit. He hasn't been fully trained yet. I would hate it if something happens to him.

The Master of all angels replied sternly,

-And what do you plan to train that angel by molly cuddling him: Near death experience? It will be an educational field trip for him. I saw him killing five demons and I can tell you that Theo knows how to look after himself. He thinks on his feet. He will be fine and I will make sure, he and his wife will come back to Wilton Town in one piece. I will be their personal bodyguard, I can give you my word on it. Theo has crucial informations which can resolve the problems in Boston, I need him for a few days. I will bring him back to you with his Whilhelmina, both, safe and well.

Sebastien sighed deeply before he demanded again for confirmation,

-I don't want to see any of their fingers in an envelope is that understood.

His father answered strongly, in a scolding way,

-Mighty! Is my word not enough for you? Without my careful watch, and my intervention, Theo would not be sitting here with us. He would have fallen victim of a spiritual attack and killed himself. I promise I will bring them back with all their limbs still attached and intact, two arms, two legs, all their fingers and their toes. Does that suit you? Can I borrow them for a few days?

Reassured and now teasing his father in an unashamed way, Sebastien demanded,

-Their eyes, their eyes are most important and their tongues too, I want your word on those as well.

Raguel gave him a dark look yet started giggling, only too happy that he had his son back in front of him and was able to joust again with him. He scolded,

-Mighty! Don't push it!

Valdi, fully amused by the conversation, joined in,

-I agree with Sebastien those body parts are most important and deserve your words. If my best friends are going to dangerous Boston...

Giving his younger brother an annoyed look, the Master commented sternly, his smile growing,

-Vincent, don't you start! Mighty is incorrigible and encourageable enough on his own. I give my word and my pledges for all those parts too. Are you both satisfied?

With a very serious air, Sebastien replied straight away, point blank,

-No.

His father and even Vincent blinked at him with disbelief. Sebastien explained,

-My new angel is still human, fully human, therefore he has free will and it will be his decision if he wants to go to dangerous Boston or stay safe by me here in Wilton Town.

The Great Being stated,

-Your boy has a point, Raguel. There is free will. Theo Odell has the ultimate decision of what he wants to do.

Sighing deeply Raguel told with exasperation,

-Father, I wish you didn't have to throw your weight on the table sometimes, especially if it is to side with Mighty.

An amused Great Being retorted,

-But it happened that Mighty was right this time around.

He then addressed Theo to ask him,

-So my dear Father Odell, the question is down to you. What do you want to do: Staying in Wilton Town or going to Boston for a few days?

All eyes turned to Odell who blushed with shyness. But he rallied himself up soon enough, turning his pint of cider in his hands thoughtfully as he started to give his answer,

-For me the case of danger and losing limbs, here or there is all relative. It can happen anywhere: the angel Daniel is a proof of it. He lost his leg in Wilton Town. But I happen to know something which may help to reduce the pain and grief that the good people of Boston are enduring. Raguel, I must say that you did build up your case convincingly enough for me to be willing to join you in your venture. My only hope is that my lack of angelic training will not be a hindrance to you. I also appreciate the fact that my Whil' will definitely be reassured by seeing where her Georgia will reside. She considers her as family not as a maid. But your word and promise were most appreciated because I would hate if anything happened to my Whil' when we are there. But I would not be able to live with myself either knowing that I could have helped to resolve a situation which creates traumatised, destitute orphans like our Ivy and now the young Rick. So I will go to Boston and help out to the best of my abilities for whatever they are worth.

Raguel gave a winning smile to his son at the answer of Odell while Sebastien warned his father a last time,

-Make sure, he comes back. Intact!

#

For Mr Berry and Tyrell to eat and drink at the same table as angels was educational. First they learnt that they were not looked upon for being humans. Second that they were fully in the confidence of the angels. If they couldn't join very well any conversation regarding ghosts and demons, however the others tried to include them as much as they could.

The Great Being took a particular interest in Tyrell whom he knew his son and grandson wanted as an angel, so he engaged conversation with him in a casual manner during the dinner,

-So Tyron, how is your business doing?

The publican answered with his usual simplicity and honesty,

-It is not doing too bad but it is not doing too well either since the departure of Doctor Valdi for his honeymoon. But your grandson has been infinitely helpful. It is all about security you see. My tavern has been targeted by the local gang in the past few days and they have methods to weaken even a strong man.

After taking a sip of his cider, the Great Being commented,

-I can see that. You didn't answer my question earlier on. How are you doing? By the way that cider is delicious.

Opening up Tyron replied,

-I import my cider from Normandy, it is complex in style, with a pleasing sweetness and has a decent effervescence to it. To answer your question, I am doing as well as one can do with my injuries. I am coping well. Sebastien gave me Rob and Callum for a few days and they have been a great help to me, moving the casks, dealing with the heavy weight duties so much so that I can not complain. Let's not forget I also found homeless Rick who has been ever so eager to help since I fed him and gave him a roof.

The Lord looked at the publican with benevolent eyes as he stated,

-It is very kind of you to give that boy a home and your surname. You seem to enjoy your line of work very much. What is your favourite tipple and may I try it?

Tyron putting his fork down answered with some passion,

-Of course, I do enjoy my line of work. Don't you like yours? What is yours, if you do not mind me asking? I know your son is dealing with justice and your grandson is a surgeon but what about you? You have to do what you love to do to make life worth living for in my humble opinion. To answer your question my favourite tipple at the moment is a little creation of mine. It is made partly with whiskey, partly with apple liqueur and the rest is filled with cranberry juice. But you can't have it.

Raguel who had paid attention to their conversation eating silently raised his head with a deep interest. He saw a bemused smile on his father's lips. He enquired with deep interest,

-Why can't my dad have your favourite tipple, Tyron? I thought you were all about generosity.

Tyrell replied firmly,

-It has nothing to do with generosity or being greedy. I served you my best cider, knowing that you will all keep your minds about you when it is time to protect the town. From a humble publican with experience, don't change drinks half way through the night for it is a recipe for disaster, especially if you go for stronger alcohol. I am minding your father, here, not disrespecting him. I want him to stay safe tonight. He can have my favourite tipple tomorrow when everything is over by all means. I will be pleased to serve it to him.

This outburst pleased the Great Being endlessly. He touched the hand of the man and tapped it in agreement before he said,

-I will take your offer for tomorrow then, Tyron. We do admire your good intentions. I am sure I will enjoy your creative tipple, if I do, I will order you to provide that interesting drink on a large scale for the wedding of Father Odell and Miss White which will take place very soon. You will be paid handsomely for it. You see it will be my wedding present to dear Theo, I will take on all the cost of his wedding. I have to find the people who can cater for that event on a short notice and I was thinking of you because you give an excellent service, you care about your customers, you have a very discerning palate concerning food that would be crowd pleaser which is reflected on the menu on the board and for the drinks, you shown to me that you were an expert. I would entirely trust you and your creativity, your flair, to host the wedding banquet and the ensuing party. My line of business is creation and if you want to join me to create Father Odell and Miss White's special moment, I would very much welcome your input my human.

Timidly Theo tried to put a word, struck by the generosity falling upon him,

-Surely, I can't accept. This, this is too much.

Raguel corrected him,

-Yes, you can accept the Lord's generosity when it comes towards you. Beside that, you gave your home in the blink of a eye to my son. Did you think it you be forgotten?

A blushing Odell looked at the Great Being with almost begging eyes who were silently screaming 'Surely No', while the Great Being told in a manner which couldn't be contested,

-Theo, if you haven't noticed how my son and grandson argued about you, well let me tell you that you are one of the most loved angel at this table. Your good heart speaks for itself. Everyone here wants to protect you and nurture you in your first steps in the angelic community. Now, you can't refuse my gift for multiple reasons. First, because you are my servant and I will be truly offended if you do so. Second, you truly deserve it for multiple reasons. Thirdly, you have to think of Miss White, Georgia, Mina and the rest of that household. Raguel, tell him about all the particulars of that third point while I carry on talking to Tyron to arrange everything.

His son took on that charge with pleasure as he explained to Theo with details that if the reception took place in the hotel, all the women would end up working for it, and not truly enjoying it, whilst if it was in town, in the tavern, if everything was taking care of for them, they could truly have a special day without worry on their minds. At the end, Theo could only agree to everything.

Meanwhile Tyrell who had agreed very willingly to host and and cater for the wedding was discussing the details with the Great Being. While the atheist still didn't know who he was truly talking to, the Great Being truly enjoyed his interaction with that human.

However, an alarmed Callum putting a platter down full of baked apples on the table warned Raguel,

-Master, Rob isn't back from his round around the building. He is not responding to my telepathic message. It is unlike him.

Raguel stood up straight away and his move was followed by his son and Valdi. The Great Being ordered to the others,

-You stay put until you are ordered otherwise. Ted, tell my son what is happening outside. Telepathic message only, for you are to stay by my side by the order of the Mighty One. For the rest of you do not panic, stay calm and eat your dessert.

Henry reluctantly obeyed to give the example to the others whilst he was worried. He saw Valdi and Sebastien rush outside at a signal of Raguel who lead the way. He demanded,

-Ted, please talk, tell us. I am on tender hooks right now. Look Callum is guarding the entrance door now. I have got to get involved.

Ted with wild eyes replied with severity,

-No, you don't, not until you are asked for. You are part of the strategical team and the reserve. If it gets out of control you and Theo have to lead the people out of town into the safety of Miss White's hotel.

Henry protested,

-You can at least tell me what is happening!

Ted complied with blood tears in his eyes,

-Darren Bell couldn't set the tavern on fire because it is magically protected. Rob found him trying to do so on his round and Darren poured oil on Rob instead and set fire to him.

Henry stood up, despair in his eyes, as he shouted,

-No, not Rob! I have to go.

This time it was the Great Being who ordered him,

-No, you don't. Be patient. Sit down and wait for your call from the Master.

Ted informed with emotion,

-Valdi is dealing with Rob. He rolled him on the ground to extinguish the flames. He ripped his clothes apart with his bare hands, he is getting burnt himself but he doesn't care, he's got to do what he has got to do, and I think, yes, he has his wings on. I think Valdi is going to take Rob straight to the river to save him. I have his thought process. Yes, he is taking Rob to the river. He is lifting off with him. Rob is badly injured, but he is alive and conscious.

Trying to reassure everyone, Theo commented,

-Vincent knows how to deal with burns and fire. He even saved a cat from a cottage on fire once. He wouldn't let that old lady's pet die. After saving the widow, he went back in to get her pet, he wrapped it in a blanket and gave her back to her alive and well with just a few burnt whiskers.

Tyrell joined in to lighten the mood at the table,

-Yes, she renamed her cat Fireball after that event. I remember. Well, that cat had a long life for a cat: wasn't it eighteen or nineteen?

Henry asked Ted, in an urging tone,

-How is Rob, Sebastien and the Master?

Ted told with some certainty,

-Rob is in good hands. Sebastien is dealing with Darren and the Master with the others. We need to send reinforcement to the Master. They are like a pack of hyenas upon him. He is dealing well but he is alone.

The Great Being stood up and ordered straight away,

-Victor, Charles, Bernard, go straight outside to fight by Raguel.

The three angels left the tavern immediately and rushed outside to follow their orders. Ancient musketeers of centuries past, the three angelic soldiers provided the right reinforcement for the old wolf that was Raguel. A pleased Master asked to one of them fighting beside him,

-Who sent you?

Victor replied,

-Your father following the advice of Ted, the angel in charge of the logistic team. Ted is still a bit shy to give orders. He will get there eventually. He just needs to grow a little confidence on his judgement.

Raguel nodded as he carried on fighting better than ever flanked by experienced angelic soldiers. Alone with his son he had managed to separate Darren Bell from his gang. While his father contained the gang, Sebastien was going all Punisher on Darren Bell.

Without his gang, Darren was running through alleyways and streets, trying to light fires as he went, sometimes succeeding, with Sebastien in his hot pursuit. In the tavern, Ted received a telepathic call from Sebastien, he stood up and urged,

-Darren is putting the town on fire. It's early, we can save the day. Henry, Theo, Matthias gather all the people of the town and lead them to the hotel. For the rest of you, we need to extinguish the fires Darren started. Callum, Mr Berry, Tyron, we have to prepare the tavern to receive the animals left behind. Any people who are seriously wounded are to be taken to the presbytery to Mrs Cotton who will look after them. Go, Go, Go.

When everyone went to their duties, Ted sat back down holding his head in his hands, blood tears pouring from his eyes. The Great Being put his arm across the shoulders of the angel and reassured,

-I know what you've just seen. Sebastien has just been ambushed by Darren and they are three against one. They just poured oil all over my grandson ready to set him on fire. But don't despair. Send him that message for me: Dana's Mirror. He will understand.

In the street, a cornered Sebastien drenched in oil, dreaded to face a similar fate as Rob as he saw matches being struck up in front of him. But he received the telepathic message of Ted at that very moment. Suddenly he felt strong once more. Sebastien put quickly a hand to the wet cobble stones of the street, then rose that hand to the sky saying out loud,

-Dana, scáthán aonbhealaigh!

He stood up and walked without fear towards Darren telling him off sternly,

-So you think you can burn animals, houses and people without punishment, do you Darren? Do you? Well, you have something else coming your way: Your retribution day.

Scared beyond belief that Sebastien didn't show any fear, Darren enjoined his gang members,

-Set him on fire, set him on fire, now!

Both threw their matches onto Sebastien but instead they bounced back upon them. They realised they were covered with oil as they transformed themselves within seconds into human torches. The Mighty One turning to both of them ordered in an acerbic tone of voice,

-Didn't your mothers warn you to not play with fire? Go and get sorted, you will find a barrel of rain water at the bottom of the street. Run for your lives, before I catch you and punish you.

Both men ran away as fast as they could, trying to extinguish the fire spreading on their bodies. Facing Darren, Sebastien smirked as he commented,

-It looks like you are all alone Darren. You have a few options in front of you. The first is run as fast as you can because I am not very pleased with the way you treated a lot of people, animals and just now houses. The second is trying to burn me to death like you attempted with my friend Rob. But you just saw what will ensue to you if you try that one on me. Third, you can try to fight like a man, but if my friend Callum beat you up nicely last time, you do not know what is coming to you this time. Have you seen my fighting scars? You have no clue what you are dealing with Darren, no clues at all.

Sebastien removed his shirt full of oil to reveal his torso but also to take away the danger of being extremely burnt. Darren gasped at the sight of the well muscled angel which he still thought was a man. He threw his match desperately onto the trousers of Sebastien then ran away, cowardly without a word. As the legs of the Mighty One started taking fire, his wings appeared, and he shouted,

-Darren Bell, you shouldn't have done that. I am coming

to get you and you are going to be punished very severely. Let's start now!

Sebastien put his hand on the ground again and then towards the sky incanted the same magic formula as before. The result was immediate: the running man before him started to have his legs equally on fire. As his legs were burning Darren with fear looked back only to see the angel flying in his hot pursuit. He understood at that instant the meaning of Sebastien's words that he didn't have a clue who he was dealing with. It took no time for Sebastien to fall upon him from the night sky like a ton of bricks. After a couple of punches going his way, bruising heavily his face, Darren fell on the ground, fright in his belly. Sebastien pinned him down between his legs on fire, burning further the body of Bell as he told him with great anger,

-Let's watch you burn, shall we! Do you want to know what it feels like to have inflicted such death on people and animals? Tonight was retaliation night, Darren, it was for you, it is for me now. Stay grounded and burn.

The sheer fear, the pain of the fire eating at his flesh made Darren cry, and also pee in the same time,

-Please, please, please, no, no, no, no.

Sebastien commented lighting up a cigar casually above the burning man,

-You, filthy coward, you peed in your pants. How many times did you watch someone die and you didn't listen to their pleas? Tell me before I burn your tongue with that cigar.

It was a straw too much for the human who passed out. Checking the pulse of Darren and finding none, Sebastien removed himself from the burning body and talking to himself said,

-I guess I just killed a human. I only started his punishment.

He heard a vague clapping noise from the shadows of the alley way then a tall silhouette moved forward to confirm,

-I think you just did but his comeuppance was overdue. That one has a bad soul which I am coming to collect my dear Punisher.

Coming into the moonlight, the Being was none but Lucifer. Sebastien stood his ground while he demanded,

-I will be damned! Lucifer! What are you doing in Wilton Town?

The fallen angel corrected Sebastien,

-No you won't be damned, you are too much of a goodie, goodie, two shoes to be damned. Beside that human would have done much worst if you didn't stop him on his track. He had a weak heart condition. Funny, how he could traumatised many but couldn't stand being traumatised himself. Well, his soul is dark enough to burn in hell for eternity, that is why I came forward.

Lucifer stopped to consider the angel who had still burning legs and started to have burning wings, then he went toward him making a blanket appear and gave it to him, while he ordered,

-Put the fire out before you end up a living torch. I am afraid to say but for an angel with human blood inside you, you are extremely brave.

Sebastien accepted the blanket and started to sort himself out while he asked,

-So, you are not killing me tonight?

Lucifer smirked as he replied,

-With all the best intentions, I couldn't kill you myself anytime soon. There is a new angel in the angelic world who happened to have broken my wrist with a single hand. I am an invalid at the moment.

Tapping the last flames out at the tip of his feathers, Sebastien teased,

-It must have bruised your feelings a little if like me he had human blood in him.

Lucifer opened up all of a sudden,

-No, I am not like that any longer. My pride is rather gone. I do admire your army made from human angels and you as well. It took time but I do understand better the scheme of things.

Putting the large blanket on top of the corpse of Darren, the angel commented with a sarcastic tone in his voice,

-Good, I am glad to hear it. Having some understanding is good and does help. I am afraid I can't return the flattery, having fought for my life for the past few days and I will have to end the chit chat here, if you don't mind. I will return to my work and I suggest you return to hell and take that filthy soul away with you.

Sebastien was about to depart when Lucifer confessed,

-Mighty One, I am glad you are alive. I am happy you made it.

This made Sebastien turned around only to reply,

-Look here, you and I are not the best of friends. You can't kill me today, fine, when you are fit for fighting, I will give you a good one. Now, why would you be glad to see me alive?

Lucifer smiled widely as he answered,

-If you are no longer here, I will not be here either. I would be dead and just a pile of ashes. Your grandfather unleashed your father upon me when you were down. It felt like an attack of a thousands rottweiler dogs all at once.

Sebastien commented with a giggle,

-I believe that.

The fallen angel added,

-The Lord destroyed the pact of Archangel Michael giving me his soul for your death. You are safe from any attempts from me. But a word of advice, for all it is worth, do not trust the five archangels that were created before your father.

Looking straight into the eyes of Lucifer, the Mighty One stated,

-But that is including you.

Lucifer nodded positively as he answered,

-I have to play a double game to tell the Lord who are the culprits. I have to be powerful to be believable. I must warn you about something else, something important.

Sebastien demanded in a non amused fashion,

And what would that be?

-And what would that be?

With a deep sigh Lucifer revealed,

-Michael is upset that you are still alive and so is Raphael, they are both going to kill all the healing angels, tonight.

This made the Mighty One fly away into the night to warn the others. On the ground, Lucifer grabbed the soul of Darren Bell in the alley way before he could escape and become a ghost, and he scolded him,

-Where do you think you are going, Darren apart from straight to hell with me? I have the right punishment for you and I can tell you straight now that you will suffer for eternity. So you tried to burnt that angel? Did you? Did you? Well let me tell you that you don't burn a Punisher, oh no, you do as they tell you to do. For you my dear, it is going to be burning in hell forever.

While the soul of Darren was being dragged to hell, Sebastien made it by his father who enquired whilst being pleased to see him,

-How did it go? You smell like burnt coal and, and piss?

Sebastien seeing a dozen individuals knocked out in the street answered,

-Darren Bell is no longer a problem. Gosh, did he rally all the scum bags in the area? I swear they are stronger in numbers than last time. Darren tried to burn me like he did with Rob, I was even ambushed with two more of his gang members. I dealt with them then went for him in a punitive way. Before I was done with him, his heart gave up on me. He is dead, Dad. None, than Lucifer came to pick up his soul to take him to hell. That's how bad he was.

His worried father demanded, taking his son away from the middle of the remaining ongoing fight,

-You saw Lucifer? Did he talk to you?

Sebastien confirmed,

-Yes, he did. He warned me about Archangel Raphael and Archangel Michael wanting to kill all of our healing angels. Touch my hand and you will know exactly what he said.

The Master of all angels shook his head in desperation

as he stated,

-That is a true threat. You must go and protect Doctor Williams, your wife and Jack at the presbytery. I am sending Henry, Matthias and Theo to protect Miss White right now. I am going to check on your uncle who saved your life and is saving the one of Rob. He will be one of their prime targets.

Flying away to his home, Sebastien had fear within his heart, for his new family and for Doctor Williams whom he considered as family just like his father did. When he saw a large feather by the doorway, he knew that an Archangel was within his house. He used the magic of his grandmother Dana to become invisible and transport into his home without opening any doors or windows.

Silent he witnessed the scene. Doctor Williams was attached on the table, ready to be killed in a ritualistic fashion which would prevent him to become an angel again and to reincarnate. As for his wife and adopted son they were roped on to chairs tightly. Jack, however bravely lifted his chair up with him and went to attack the archangel frantically with all his little might he had in his human body. He kicked the chair back and forth onto Michael, shouting,

-You can't! You can't! You can't do that! Michael! Wake up! What are doing!? What are you doing? What are you even thinking of!?

The distraction it caused was enough for the invisible Sebastien to free Doctor Williams and to order him via telepathy,

-Free my wife, I want you to both go the tavern right now and stay safe by my grandfather. I will deal with the situation.

Williams was only too pleased to be saved in extremis. He freed the little Ivy from her chair and told her via telepathy to stay quiet because her husband was here and invisible and to not blow his cover. He ordered her to follow him. She did as she was told but she had tears streaming down her face as soon as they left the house. Her hand and arm were pulled and she was forced to run with the old servant in the streets on fire but she cried,

-What about Jack? What about my boy Jack? We have to save him!

Doctor Williams scolded her,

-Leave it to Sebastien. There is an angry Archangel in

there who wanted to kill you, me, and the boy. It's beyond your capacity and mine to save Jack but it's not beyond the Mighty One. He ordered for us to run for safety and that is what we will do. Come, Ivy, come, be brave and don't look back. Don't let Sebastien lose you. We will cause more trouble than good by getting involved.

Soon they were at the tavern, a devastated Ivy fell on the floor as soon as she passed the threshold. Callum and Williams made her stand up and walked her towards the Great Being. He opened his arms to her,

-Come here my child, come here, there. Stay safe, you have to stay safe for Mighty. He will look after Jack.

Ivy cried upon his chest and recounted,

-It was so scary. Doctor Williams had just arrived, minutes earlier. He told me that the angels will soon bring casualties, that the fire in town had started. We were all ready to receive them. I opened the door to the first angel with a wounded man in his arms. He was extremely tall with curly black hair flowing upon his shoulders. I didn't recognise him from belonging to Sebastien's army but I recognised the man he was carrying. It was an old homeless man that arrived in town from Boston a few days ago. I was feeding him bread and ham everyday. The angel threw me against a wall, with just one arm. He was so powerful. He closed the door of the house, and killed the homeless man before me. I was petrified. Then, then Doctor Williams hearing the noise came into the hallway enquiring if we had our first wounded. He said 'Michael, I wasn't expecting you to be part of that operation'. And the horrible angel said it was because he was not, and he bashed the head of William until he was unconscious. It was terrible. I tried to help, but I was thrown against a wall again. Jack realised something was up but the poor boy got battered when he tried to help. Jack and I were attached onto chairs while Doctor Williams was attached on our make shift operating table, the one I prepared to help the wounded. That, that horrid angel said he will eat all of our heart out. He was ready to proceed on Williams but Jack intervened with all his might, still tied up to his chair... We left Jack behind, my Jack is still behind...

Comforting her as best as he could, the Great Being demanded to Williams,

-There is no mistake that it was Archangel Michael?

Doctor Williams replied with certainty, kneeling by the Great Being and presenting him his hand to read,

-Yes, my Lord. It was him. I can attest of that.

When the Creator touched his hand and saw the entire event, he vented,

-Despicable. Mighty arrived just on time, a minute or two later you would not talk to me. Stand up, Williams, and look after Ivy, she is badly shaken up by the entire matter. Her baby is not hurt and alive inside her. I will still have my great grandchild. Callum, Tyron you are going to be in charge of the protection of this place. Williams, Ivy, you will tend to the gravely wounded here. Mr Berry, you can either go home or be of help to the two Doctors. Ted you stay here to monitor the operations. I am going to demote an Archangel in a brutal way.

The Great Being stood up and left the building with no further a do worried about the stand up between Archangel Michael and his grandson. When he arrived at the presbytery he could hear glass breaking, and noises which amounted to a great fight going on. When he stepped into it, Jack still attached to his chair was fighting with all his human strength to help Sebastien. He had a dagger in his chest but it didn't stop the boy. Bleeding thoroughly, the boy was helping bashing his chair against the Archangel, disturbing his focus. Sebastien, despite his badly burnt legs, ruled the fight, he had cornered Michael with the help of little Jack. Mighty was shouting from the top of his voice,

-You do not touch a single hair of my wife, you do not attack my boy, you do not threatened my friends, you do not kill humans without repercussion, Michael.

Breaking a clay pot on the wall, Sebastien crushed it on the manhood of the Archangel unexpectedly, immobilising his opponent for a moment. He used a chard to free the child from his chair and ordered him,

-Jack, ran to Ma and Doctor Williams! They will look after you my boy!

The teary child, left the room, passed by the Great Being sobbing, but fell on the floor before reaching the door of the presbytery. It was enough for the Lord to come into play. He pushed his grandson out of the way, and before Michael knew what was happening to him, his wings were torn away from him. The Great Being ordered Sebastien,

-Your boy collapsed in the hallway, use those wings to carry him safely to the tavern. I have a demoted Archangel to bring to Lucifer for eternal punishment.

A desperately worried Sebastien obeyed, but turned around at the door. He saw Lucifer by his Grandfather. The Great Being ordered to the fallen angel,

-You know what to do with that one.

-Yes, My Lord.

Michael was dragged to hell without any further notice by Lucifer. Sebastien picked up the bleeding Jack and put him carefully upon the wings. His grandfather followed him with Doctor Fair's medical leather satchel. Together they flew to the tavern. When they arrived they were welcomed by Doctor Williams who announced,

-We have a table ready for Jack. What we are dealing with, Sebastien?

A tearful Sebastien replied,

-Stab wound and collapsed lung. He breathes but his pulse is low.

Doctor Williams reassured,

-We have seen worst together, Sebastien, we can deal with that one, despite Jack being so young. Be strong for him. We need your surgery skills here. Lay him on the table.

When Sebastien did so, he saw his wife and told her,

-Michael stabbed our Jack. Jack kept fighting by my side. He was a tremendous help. He was so brave. I managed to free him but he collapsed. We have to fix his little lung my love. Are you ready to operate on him with me and Doctor Williams?

Ivy retaining her tears, nodded positively as she enjoined,

-Let's sort out our son. I am ready.

Painstakingly, they operated on Jack throughout the night. While they were doing so, a few houses were burning down in town but no other casualties were reported as of yet. Tyrell, Callum and Anthony Berry at the doors of the tavern however started picking up the animals left behind saved from the flames by the angels. Soon Tyron thought that his tavern had become a Noah's ark while the young Rick tended to the animals with diligence, giving them water.

Meanwhile, most of the inhabitants of Wilton Town with scarcely any belongings at all were making the long walk through the forest to reach the Crying White Doe Hotel of Miss White under the guidance of Father Odell. He was walking his flock, his parishioners with great compassion reassuring them along the way. He told about community spirit and if anyone's house was lost to the flames that everyone would assemble together to rebuild it before the winter. While some were devastated, others were strong enough to comfort them. All were scared that the fires in town would reach the woods but it didn't. The rain kept pouring from the sky so heavily that they were all drenched by the time they arrived to the hotel. From the top of the hill they could see that only part of the town was on fire, about a quarter of it and the forest was remaining intact.

At the door of the hotel Miss White was there to welcome everybody. She asked Theo with anxiety,

-Is there anyone hurt that needs immediate assistance? I saw the town burning from my windows. It was worst than now. They are tackling it down. It is not spreading any longer. How is everyone coping?

A partly exhausted Theo who was relieved to see her briefed,

-We have a teenage boy with a broken leg. He went to save his little sister and had to jump out of a window with her. She has a broken wrist. An old lady is suffering from a sprain ankle which happened in the woods. The rest are fine, just tired, wet and fearful.

Whilhelmina nodded to him as she told him,

-Show me the three that need immediate physical care and take the rest to my ballroom. I have prepared make shift beds there and the room is warm. I have enough soup ready to feed all of them, nothing fancy, only potato and leeks but I hope it will comfort them a little. Maximilien did lots and lots of bread rolls to go with the soups. How is it on the angelic side?

With a deep sigh, Theo answered,

-One is injured, Rob who was protecting the tavern. Ted sent us a message saying that Sebastien had damaged legs, and that his little boy had been stabbed in the chest. Jack's life was in danger. Another angel sustained massive burns saving a cat. Vincent took care of Rob but we have still to hear from both of them. Vince still doesn't know how to use telepathy very well. I think he needs practice. And if Rob doesn't use it that means he is not well at all. Raguel went to check on them both. I have much more to tell you my Whil'. Come, let's bring all those people in.

When everyone walked inside the hotel, Mrs Toad was helping Miss White to welcome them all, Pamela Toad couldn't help expressing herself,

-Oh, good Lord, the poor things! Come on in, come on in!

Henry passing by her, carrying the teenager who had a broken leg in his arms, informed her,

-Dear Mrs Toad, you will be happy to know that Mr Berry is safe and well. He is helping to look after the animals those poor people had to leave behind. Given the choice to leave or help, Anthony Berry decided to help. He is a brave man. When he marries you, I will be there. You can start thinking of your wedding bouquet, because I will travel far and wide to fetch all the flowers you want for it. The help you are both giving us tonight will not be forgotten.

It warmed Pamela's heart right up. She thought of her Anthony Berry in the midst of the chaos in Wilton Town on fire. She loved him dearly, and yes, she wanted to become his future Mrs Berry. She soldiered on with renewed vigour.

Once all the refugees from Wilton Town were settled for the night, once the three wounded were seen too, Father Odell did a thorough count of his parishioners and quickly established that five were missing. He knew that two refused to leave their homes but it left three individuals unaccounted for. It was not past midnight yet, when Henry, Matthias and him flew back to Wilton Town for the missing five.

#

When Rob was found burning like a living torch, Vincent Valdi took care of him immediately. He rolled him on the ground to extinguish the flames. He ripped his clothes apart to prevent the textile to burn onto the skin of the angel then he carried him to the river. It was not the largest river by all mean, but the river Wilton nonetheless was a tidal one and could become dangerous very easily. It snaked its way through the lower part of Wilton Town delimiting the northbound boundaries of the town. Only one bridge existed upon it but a bigger and larger one was being built which used innovative technologies further down the river where the Wilton River was wider and deeper.

Valdi flew the injured angel midway between the two bridges. He plunged inside the river with him. Rob had lost consciousness during the flight. He was not doing well at all. With a sense of urgency, Vincent tried desperately to revive the angel. The dip in the Wilton River helped not only to soothe the burnt flesh of Rob but also brought him back to consciousness. Valdi reassured him straight away,

-Hold on to me, Rob, I've got you. You've been burnt in a very bad way. I will look after your recovery. I am a Doctor. I was trained by Doctor Williams.

His head maintained above the water, Rob tried to gather back his inner strength but couldn't at that precise moment yet he managed to speak, and to guess,

-You are not Sebastien. It's not his voice. Are you an angel?

Vincent was ever so happy to hear Rob so he encouraged him to make him talk, he knew the angel was still with him, alive,

-I am a new one. Did you hear of Doctor Valdi?

Rob tried to look at the face of who was holding him but couldn't see. He settled to answer,

-I heard of you. You are the Protector. I can't see you. I can't see.

Valdi told with authority,

-Catch your breath, I am going to put your head under water a few times. The aim is to try to save your eyesight. At my count one, two, three.

Rob did as he was ordered, but at the end of it all, he could only see from one eye. He said with resignation,

-I think I lost one eye Doctor Valdi. I can see from the other now. It will do, it will have to do.

But Vincent wasn't going to give up and told him,

- Let's do it a few more times. Try to open your eyes under the water. Catch your breath. Here we go.

Submitting himself to the treatment Rob could finally see from both eyes, but with one less well than the other. He smiled with thankfulness to Valdi telling him,

-I am indebted to you now.

Looking at the badly burnt angel, Vincent teased,

-Of course, you are not. But if it makes you feel better, I will accept a pair of mating rabbit to feed my family on the long term.

This made Rob smile despite him suffering. He engaged the conversation to forget about his pain,

-I heard, well, it will be no mystery to you, that you and your friend Theo as new angels are on the top of the angelic gossips at the moment, I heard that you only started to have a family because you waited for the woman you loved truly for years to be available. Is it right?

Vincent who was rather private when it concerned himself personally opened up to the injured angel he was holding in the river to cool his burning skin, he admitted,

-This is right. I would have staid a bachelor if my Amelia didn't become a widow.

Rob sighed deeply partly because of his physical pain and partly because he was thinking about his own life as an angel in a reflective way. He vented in almost a whisper,

-She must be extremely beautiful... your Amelia...

Carrying the angel in a part of the river, closer to the banks, less deep, Vincent corrected him, knowing how important it was to keep Rob conscious and talking,

-You would be wrong. External beauty isn't everything, not at all, the internal one is. I have never been interested in physical attributes only a beautiful mind and heart will do for me. Now, I want you to gather some strength, stand on your two feet as firmly as you can, and hold on to me for support. I need to remove the rest of your clothes. Some are burnt into your skin but it is necessary to take everything off to prevent infection. The fact that we are in the water will relieve some of your pain. Be strong for me, Rob. You are going to get through this. If you need to shout in pain, feel free to do so, because it is not going to be easy.

Rob obeyed as he vented,

-What a bloody human bastard! I saw many in my lives but this one, I think this one had mental issues. He just enjoyed seeing others suffer. The cruelty of his intentions! I mean I was killed by mistake on a battlefield by Henry who couldn't load a gun properly. No bad intentions there just clumsiness but here, Darren Bell had those evil eyes, the rage, the anger, the will to see you suffer. And he stood there you know just watching me bursting into flames. Ouch! Ouch! Make me talk of something else, I am getting upset.

Vincent took the hint and prompted as he removed the burnt fabric from the skin with great care,

-So you were one of Sebastien's musketeers then?

Rob admitted proudly,

-Yes, I was. Robert Louis de Montignan, one of the King's Musketeers under Louis the thirteenth, the Regent Queen Anne and then under the brash and glorious Louis the fourteenth.

Taking the last bit of clothing, Valdi commented,

-That must have been quite a time to live in. I guess by the 'de' that you come from a noble family.

Rob nodded positively as he answered,

-My father was made a baronet under Henry the fourth. He was a distinguished soldier and was given land by the king of France in the Rhone area. He built the castle of Montignan, planted vines and had three sons. I am the middle one. In those times, the eldest inherited the land, the others were meant for the military, which I chose, or priesthood which my younger brother embraced, bless his soul, he was the quietest of us all.

Happy that he had removed all the fabric from the skin of the injured angel, Vincent enjoined,

-Let's get out of the river to check you out thoroughly. I need to see how extensive the damages are. Hold on to me.

From behind them a strong voice rose,

-Hold on you two! The end of the road or shall I say river ends here for both of you.

Both turned around only to see a majestic angel above the water. A rather panicked Rob whispered quickly to the ear of Valdi,

-This is Archangel Raphael. This is not good news. He sold his soul to the devil.

Raphael shouted,

-Robert de Montignan, I will drown you.

Robert retorted,

-On which ground? To serve God faithfully unlike you!

Plunging in the river and going to them, Raphael warned,

-Make a prayer to your Lord and see if he will save you. I am going to kill you on the ground that you are a filthy human angel. Angels should be made of fire not humans.

Valdi pushed Robert behind him in a protective manner and argued without fear,

-Oh, yes! Says who? Are you making your own laws down here? Are you a bit angry that the Lord decided to make human angels because the angels made of fire were not up scratch or to the standards he desired? What can I say? Don't they lack a bit of heart? You see, this is the important bit that you are lacking off: A heart! You will not kill Rob. Over my dead body!

Raphael replied in an aggressive fashion,

-Over your dead body will be fine by me! I will kill anyone healing human angels.

An appalled Vincent was getting ready to be attacked, but the physical ghost of Abraham Wilton-Cough came out of him and threw himself upon Raphael. Abraham shouted at him,

-Take Rob out of this river as fast as you can, Vince.

The disturbance Abraham caused was enough for Valdi to put the injured Rob on safe ground. He reassured the angel when they reached the banks,

-You will not drown tonight, Rob. Wilton-Cough said no,

and when he says no, he means no. Look at him fighting that archangel. I have got to get back in there.

A hand landed on Valdi's shoulder at that very moment. He turned to see his eldest brother accompanied by his servant Doctor Williams. Whilst William took Rob away from the scene, flying him back to the tavern, Raguel told his brother,

-You will have a lesson in punishing tonight. I am going to demote an archangel. His punishment is to become what he hates the most: He will become a human before sunrise. If he dies in his human skin, he belongs to hell unless he does something extraordinarily redeeming.

Vincent was only too happy to see Rob being carried to safety. He briefed quickly his brother,

-Rob is going to make it. He will be in pain for a while but he will make it, I made sure of it. How did you know we were in trouble?

Raguel told him sternly,

-I will tell you later. Make your wings disappear to protect them and do as I say. Raphael can be tricky and lethal so watch yourself. He is out to kill healing angels which you happened to be one. I will want you to pin him down with me under water so I can deal with him. Come.

Archangel Raphael was struggling with Abraham Wilton-Cough who would not let him go out of the river. It made the Master smile as he addressed Raphael whilst going inside the river with Valdi,

-My dear Raphael, you can not kill that one. He is already dead.

Trying to remove the pestering Wilton-Cough who kept slapping him with all his might, an angry Raphael vociferated,

-Where did you get that annoying thing from?

It was Abraham who answered as Raphael was getting distracted and worried by the two angels coming toward him, one of which he knew was a Punisher,

-That would be a grave, you, idiot! What part of dead didn't you understand?

This was the last straw for Raphael who threw the ghost

as far away from him as he could. That moment of inattention allowed Raguel to close the distance between him and the dissident archangel. Grabbing Raphael by the collar, the Master of all angels let his wrath entirely out,

-So you think you can get away with murder, Raphael! You are pure angelic trash and watch me as I trash you out! Oh, dear Lord, you are going to be so sorry for yourself. Let me tell you one thing straight, traitor to the Lord: There is no forgiveness for you, just hell, pure hell. This is what you get when you sell your soul to the devil!

At those words Raphael knew every scheme of his had been unfolded. He tried to fight back but the fist that reach his jaw dislocated it, it came with lots of anger,

-That's for my Gael, you bastard! Did you think you could plot the death of my son with impunity? You've got something else coming!

The something else was a kick in Raphael's sensitive parts, which immobilised him for long enough for Raguel to throw him down under water. The Master ordered via telepathy to his brother,

-Now, Vincent! Hold him down for me as I remove his wings. Beware he can still be dangerous. If he fights back, punch all you like.

Abraham who had received the same call moved as fast as he could to be by the side of Valdi. Vincent held with all his strength the struggling archangel. A large scythe appeared into the hand of Raguel who propped up one wing of Raphael and removed it. The archangel tried to get up, but was pushed right back down by Vincent and Abraham. Raguel removed his last wing. When he had finished he ordered,

-You, two, get out of the river. The job is done. Raphael is now just human, a fallen angel that will have to live like the creatures he hated the most.

While Vincent and Abraham obeyed, they kept looking back. They saw the Master shouting, pushing the head of Raphael up and back in the river,

-So you thought it was a good idea to kill all my healing angels, did you? So you thought it was very angelic of you to want to drown a few of my angels? How do you feel getting your threats enacted upon you? How did you feel when you faked healing me back in the days? Were you proud of how clever you were? Especially since I saved you, were you proud? You disgust me. You disgust my father. Live as a human, die as one and go to hell. As for any healing, you will receive none, and I am going to send you to the human charity and we will see if they will have the good heart to care for you until the day you die.

Finishing his sentence he broke both arms of Raphael and left him floating there. Raguel joined Valdi and Wilton-Cough on the banks. The old ghost asked worried,

-Is he going to drown? He can't swim without his arms.

The Master replied,

-This is the least of my concern. He killed my son. He wanted to kill my brother and all of my healing angels. I have no pity for him, I am sorry. Thank you for your brave intervention by the way, Abraham. You may just have saved Vincent and Rob for putting your ghostly neck on the line.

Walking by him and by Valdi, Wilton-Cough asked baffled,

-But you said because I was already dead, he couldn't kill me?

Raguel answered with a slight amused smirk,

-But they can drag you to hell at any time, my dear Abraham. But I will try to make sure they don't. Just keep on the good work and look after my brother. Now go back inside him and rest your energies. Just to let you know, for the future, when you are in your physical shape you can get badly hurt and to fix you up would be quite a challenge. Only my servant and I would be able to do so. Of course, my father as well could do so if he is indulgent to you. But we will train Vincent to be able to do it.

A thoughtful Abraham commented,

-So, what you said to Raphael about me was in fact to protect me.

The Master admitted,

-Yes, I didn't want him to batter you in your physical state. So a little white lie prevented you to get hurt. Those archangels may claim they are superior all they want but they are not the cleverest. If they think they can fool anyone, they have something else coming. I am very good at that game too.

Smiling with emotion Wilton-Cough stated,

-So you cared for me a little then...

Raguel demanded brashly,

-Do you even care if I do or don't?

Abraham answered straight away, tears appearing in his eyes,

-I do care because you are the angel that can redeem me and I will do whatever you say to be redeemed. I never thought you would care for me in the slightest way because... because...

Raguel stopped walking, put his hands on the shoulders of Abraham Wilton-Cough, and made him look at him before he told firmly,

-Abraham, I want you to put, print this in your mind: You are under my wings. I will protect your soul. We may not have seen eye to eye when we first met and started on the wrong footing but I do care for you and will forever. If I have your soul commitment, know that you have mine to you just as well. Now, be at peace and rest inside your Master. What you did tonight was courageous and I thank you for it. Again if I am wiping your tears, it is because I care. Go and take a rest.

The old ghost obeyed and disappeared inside Vincent, fairly soothed. When he disappeared the Master of all angels commented to his brother,

-My dear Vincent, you have a very loyal servant in Abraham. He is a bit brash but he is brave, I like that.

Valdi smiled as he replied,

-In fact he is a bit like you, brash and brave.

Raguel gave his brother a dark look but also a sad smile as he enjoined,

-Let's go back to the tavern. Jack, the adopted son of my Sebastien has been stabbed. They are operating upon him and I truly hope he can make it. He is only eight, you know, and frail.

Both flew away into the night. In the dark water of the

river was fallen archangel Raphael, in pain and unable to move properly. A bitter Raphael reflected on his punishment and cried. He didn't think he would survive the night. He thought of his pact selling his soul to Lucifer. He expected to be dwelling in hell very soon. But what he didn't expect was for a little human girl to spot him. She swam to him and brought him on the river bank under the bridge. She made sure he was breathing and noticed that his jaw was dislodged. She told him with certainty,

-I know how to fix that. I did it for my mum and I did it to myself. It is an easy fix but it will hurt.

Without further a do, she proceeded. Feeling ever so human and the extreme pain all across his body, Raphael didn't mind any longer what happened to him. His jaw was put back into position. He suffered silently. The girl moved away from him and sat on a blanket as she said,

-You don't look too good with your face black and blue. It looks like you've just been beaten up and thrown into the river. Either you got mugged, either someone was really cross about you.

Raphael wanted to smile at her last sentence but couldn't. It took him a good fifteen minutes before he could start to talk again. His first sentence was,

-Who are you?

The young girl who was trying to warm up by holding her folded knees with her arms answered,

-I am not talking to strangers.

Raphael this time managed to smile as he replied,

-But you can save them and talk to them without realising it for the past minute or so. I am Raphael, see we are not strangers any longer.

Crossing her arms on her chest the little brunette argued,

-It doesn't work that way. It is not because you gave me your name that we are not strangers any longer. Anyway you are Raphael, who? You didn't give me your surname Mister! You are a stranger under my bridge. Go under the other one in construction. I helped you not because I wanted to but because I had to. If I didn't know how to swim I would have had a ready excuse to let you drown for my conscience. But as it happened that I know how to swim, I had to get wet on a chilly night to fetch you.

A slightly bemused Raphael told with sarcasm,

-So you have a conscience, that certainly puts things into perspective. Well, let me put that to your conscience then, I have two broken arms therefore I can not swim to the other bridge, so why don't you go there? As you know how to swim and you are already wet, you will hardly feel the difference. Then you can remain a stranger that refuses to do acquaintances all by yourself. By the way, I didn't asked to be rescued.

Standing up, putting her hands on her hips, the girl scolded him,

-That is such an ungrateful way to thank your rescuer. If I didn't have a heart I would push you back in the river. Anyway you couldn't ask for help with your dislocated jaw so your point is not valid. This is my bridge and I will stay here. By the way, I can't take my blanket across to the other bridge without getting it wet. So Raphael Whatever, I will tolerate you under my bridge under my rules, I want you to stay in that corner there and to stay put while I will be in the far corner. Know that my scream can wake up the dead. If you don't want to be chucked out, I demand to know your surname.

Raphael considered the youngster before him. She couldn't have been more than five foot tall. Rather slender and pale, she looked like she had missed a fair few meals in her life. Her dark brown hair were kept very tidy in two neat pigtails. She was wearing a black dress which didn't reach the ground indicating that she was still a young girl by all means, probably a twelve years old one. Her black woollen stockings had holes in them. Her white apron had multiple patches of different coloured fabric to repair it. The beauty of her olive green eyes was such, even if they expressed annoyance and anger, that the fallen archangel tried to compromise. Raphael realising he was now fully human and had to adapt to his new situation, knew he didn't have a surname. He looked around him in desperation. He saw the reflection of the moonlight upon the water then replied,

-I am Raphael River. Whoever you are, you mustn't fear me. I will not harm you, I can assure you of that, due to the fact that both of my arms are broken and that I have no will to do so. I just want to sleep, rest and lick my wounds.

The girl went to the far corner taking her blanket and wrapping herself inside it as she commented,

-Lick your wounds! That is disgusting! New rule: No licking of wounds under my bridge.

This made Raphael laugh and hurt as he did so. He settled in his corner while he corrected her,

-This is an expression, Miss Whoever you are, of course I am not going to physically lick my wounds. Don't you go to school?

She replied unwrapping a handkerchief bag containing a little food,

-I do on occasion. I must confess I am not assiduous. It is not that I am not clever or anything. If I put my heart at it, I reckon I could even become a teacher. Did you have some dinner? I have a little bread, a couple of plums and a pint of milk that I can share with you.

Her simple offer touched the heart of the archangel who didn't expect it. He refused politely,

-It is very kind of you but unfortunately I can't put anything in my mouth until my arms are sorted. Now tell me how a young girl like you got to claim the underside of a bridge? Don't you have a home?

She approached him with her little bag of food as she answered,

-I have a home, I also happen to have a violent father. When he is in a bit of a state, drunk and all, the best place for me is under the bridge. I can feed you, you know, I did feed my younger brother to bring him up. We can share half half. I can see you've been through something and you need something in you to recover. I haven't got the earth to offer you, I have only that, but it is still better than nothing.

Her words shamed the archangel without knowing it. He was faced with human generosity and he thought of his punishment, losing his wings for his hate of humans, human angels, and all his past crimes. Tears appeared at the corner of his eyes, despite himself, he demanded,

-Miss Whoever you are, I will not accept you feeding me if you do not tell me your name. I have my pride and I can't accept being fed by a human stranger.

The girl was quick to pick up on what he said as she

wondered out loud,

-Human stranger!? Who do you think you are, God or something? Have you got a god complex to talk about? You know there is a nice church in town. Father Odell is an excellent vicar, he will listen to you.

This outburst made Raphael smile but he decided to show to the child his damaged back with the stumps of his former wings, then he revealed,

-I am sorry, Miss Whoever you are, I used to be a something, an angel. I am only human now.

The young girl inspected his bleeding back, assessing the truth of the matter before she came up with her answer,

-I have an expression for you: Nobody is perfect.

Raphael laughed at her comment however with deep sadness in his heart and tears running down his cheeks. He was scolded too by the human child,

-And you must stop calling me Miss Whoever you are! It is annoying me. My name is Marguerite Bouchon. My father is French but he changed our family name to Cork so we could fit better in the new continent. So now I am Daisy Cork. But you can call me Margot, this is my nickname. Now that I am no longer a human stranger to you, I can feed you so your pride will stay intact. Let's share the food I am starving. You have to be careful when you eat, because it will be painful. Just do a mouthful at a time, small chunks and not big ones. I am going to dunk the bread in the milk so it will be easier for you to swallow.

The young Margot fed the angel just a fruit, half of her milk and half of her bread but it was enough to warm Raphael's heart up and to make him understand how wrong he had been all along about humanity. He kept crying with sorrow in his corner that night. However he opened up to the human girl and they shared their stories. She shared more than he did or was willing to do. He didn't tell her that he was a big bad archangel, no just a little angel that lost his wings for having done one mistake too many.

But he learnt that Margot's mum was called Ellen Stone and was English, that she passed away recently hence Margot's black attire. The cause of her death was said to have been a bad fall in the staircase whilst in fact her pregnant self was pushed by her husband during a violent fight. The little brother whose name was Peter was also dead and buried. He was only seven when he died of Chicken pox. Through all of that, the young Marguerite tried her best to cope with life but she told the fallen angel that she didn't think she would last very long. She confessed to him that she would not kill herself but that her father probably will one day. He also discovered that she had been abused repetitively by her father, hence Marguerite preferred sleeping under a bridge rather than in her home. Her story filled Raphael with sadness but he also comprehended why Margot was so guarded and had a bit of a character to her.

He watched her as she finally fell asleep in her corner under her weathered blanket. He cried of sorrow for her, not for himself any longer. He slept in his corner, full of hurtful realisation. He wished he could speak to the Master of all angels again but knowing that he was the instigator of the death of his eldest son, and that he influenced Michael to do the same to the youngest son of Raguel, he believed it was a desperate cause. With that he closed his eyes full of remorse, his human body full of pain.

#

As the sun rose, the extent of the fire damage became clearer. No houses were burning any longer. The army of angels did manage to extinguish all the flames overnight. When the Great Being and his two sons Raguel and Vincent walked the streets of Wilton Town inspecting the losses, they all sighed deeply. Abraham Wilton-Cough appeared by the side of Doctor Valdi, although he was tearful, he told them,

-It is not as worst as I expected. A quarter of the old town is gone. To be honest, those houses made of wood were the most vulnerable. We need to rebuild those houses, but in stones this time around. This was the house of the Wells. It was too small for them. Alistair Well is a father of twelve. He is courageous enough to take the knock down. He has never been out of work and has never been sick nor his children. With some help, he will get through it. There is a plot behind his burnt house which belongs to no one any longer.

He pointed to another burnt down house only to comment,

-This small house was owned by the poor old widow Mel Brown. She gets by by making socks and scarves and selling them on market day. This will be a very hard blow to her. She has no one, no one whatsoever to look after her. She is most likely to struggle with her loss. She had a cat. Did you manage to save her cat?

Wilton-Cough's evident concern but also deep knowledge of the town's inhabitants was picked up by the Master who went by him to reply,

-We managed to save her cat. The angel that did it however is very badly burnt. Come with me Abraham and tell me everything about the losses and the people that will be affected by them. Have you got a map of the town by any chance?

A willing Abraham answered,

-Yes, I have. In my bank, if the bank is still standing that is.

Raguel ordered,

-Let's check that, shall we. You and I are going to rebuild that town together. We are going to mastermind the reconstruction with a care for the people. You know them by heart, I don't know them all yet. I want you to teach me about all of them. I will reside here from now on. One thing I noticed is that you have no sheriff in town and I think, seeing what happened last night, is that you can do with one. It will work as a deterrent mainly. But I am going to take on that job. Vincent check if Jack is waking up and do something about my son's legs. He is so worried about his boy, he hasn't been looked after for his burns. Pa, tell me if Jack pulls through, please.

He called a few angels who followed him and Abraham, whilst his father and Vincent went back to the tavern of Tyrell. The Bank was still standing tall in the corner of two streets to the joy of Abraham Wilton-Cough who confided to the Master,

-I am happy to see that my bank survived the night. You know, I am not materialistic any longer but I would have extremely sad to discover that the building I created for this town which was my pride had been destroyed. Let's not stand too long on that spot, this is where I was shot in the guts. It brings back bad memories. Come, let me show you in.

In a very polite fashion, Abraham held the large double doors open and invited the few angels to enter. He came in last and saw that Raguel waited for him in the middle of the great room. The Master told him as he considered the high ceilings,

-It's quite an impressive bank for a small town like Wilton Town. I like the little sculpted figures at every corner of your pristine white ceiling.

Coming to him, Abraham said with eagerness and pride

in his voice,

-I commissioned those from an Italian immigrant who came from New York, a charming fellow who was an excellent sculptor. I helped him as much as I could during his life promoting his work because he was truly talented. He was called Carlo El Bambino. He did a beautiful bust of my Angela which is in my office in the bank so I could look at her even when I was working. Anyhow the poor lad fell from a scaffolding one day when he was working to decorate a rich household and that was it. He broke his back, fractured his skull and he passed away a couple of hours later. Valdi was fairly upset when it did happened. You know, there are not many Italians in Wilton Town. So you see there, in all the corners are depicted fortune deities, you have the Greek Caerus here and Fortuna there. In that corner is the Indian Lakshmi and in this one is a representation of Mammon from the New Testament.

Raguel commented,

-I thought your bank would be a very dry and dreary place to go to. Clearly I was wrong.

A rather piqued Abraham confirmed,

-Clearly you were. Have you heard that to assume makes an ass of you and me? To tell you the truth I gathered a little taste and culture in my life by travelling with my aunt Josephine Cough when I was a child. Now, come with me to my office, I will show you the map and a few documents which may be useful to rebuild the part of Wilton Town which has been burnt. Make sure your angels don't ruin my oak floor. It was pretty muddy out there with that constant rain.

If this made the Master giggle, his angels following him were more cautious and all cleaned their shoes on the mat at the entrance. When he entered the office, Raguel was again slightly astonished because it felt more like a cosy living room than a working office. First he was struck by the mural paintings covering every wall representing cherry blossoms, dragons, koi carps, clouds, waves, trees, mountains and pagodas. He couldn't help asking Wilton-Cough,

-Did you go to China or Japan?

Abraham going to what appeared to look like a bookshelf replied casually,

-I did, with aunt Jo, we visited both and India as well. Those frescoes have been done quite recently, I didn't have time to enjoy them truly. They are really nice, aren't they?

Raguel looking at all the details agreed,

-They are quite exquisite. The colours are so vibrant.

Wilton-Cough replied as he opened the book case like a door,

-I splashed out when I commended that one. You would not believe it, but it was made by Chinese Railway workers. They were working up north from Wilton Town. I really wanted to have a train station for the town so I would have done literally anything. So I was doing a bribery and corruption scheme at all levels to get every one on my side. Having the rail road passing very close to the town or through it could have helped to put Wilton Town on the map but unfortunately I died and no one will pick up that scheme. It has too many inconveniences to work out, which I was keen to look into to make things work but it is not to be.

Not paying attention to the ghost any longer, the angel was mesmerised by the sculpture of a woman on the mantle piece. He demanded,

-Is it your wife's depiction, Abraham?

This made Wilton-Cough turn around immediately to answer,

-Yes, this is my Angela. This is the bust I had made of her.

Raguel commented,

-She is a true beauty! She has a truly angelic name that suits her. How did she end up with a man like you?

Going to the mantle piece, Abraham grabbed the bust and protectively hid it from scrutiny against his chest. He replied with emotion,

-She is mine, my wife. Stop looking at her like that. I often wondered why she married me, all my life in fact.

Correcting him the angel said,

-She was yours. She is now your widow and available to make a more informed choice loving wise. I wonder if she would be interested to fall in love with a rather dashing angel.

He checked himself in the mirror above the mantle piece and smiled at his reflection, fastening his collar a little. Wilton-Cough sighed deeply before confessing with great sadness,

-Raguel, you'd better remove the bust from my hands before I go all poltergeist on you with it. I still respect you too much to batter you with the bust.

Whilst putting back the bust on the marble mantle piece, the Master saw the tears running silently on the cheeks of Abraham Wilton-Cough, he comforted,

-Abraham, I was teasing you. Can't you recognise a tease or a joke?

Still crying, Abraham confided,

-No, I can't. I never been able to.

Feeling bad Raguel told putting his arm across the shoulders of the old ghost,

-Come, come. You have to be more confident about yourself. Do you know that my father heard a prayer made for you by your wife which sounded like a love letter?

Drying his tears, Abraham asked with curiosity,

-I don't know that. What did it say?

Raguel replied,

-I don't know the particulars, you will have to ask my father. He has a soft spot for you so if you beg him politely I am pretty sure he will allow you to hear the entire prayer of your wife. But I know that he said that it was one of the most beautiful prayer he received for someone. Come, let's do some work. Where is the map of the town?

Wilton-Cough who had gathered up together answered,

-It is inside my cabinet. We need the key which is inside that Chinese vase on the mantle piece. It is under the fake porcelain bottom.

The Master retrieved the key with a smile as he commented,

-Ingenious. You and I are going to get along very well I

think, as long as you accept being teased once in a while. I can teach you about recognising jokes.

The angel winked to Abraham before he enjoined,

-Come and show me that cabinet of yours.

Raguel followed the ghost into a small room hidden behind the fake book case. It was full of cabinets of different sizes and chests. While Abraham went to a large elaborate mahogany cabinet, the Master asked with sheer curiosity,

-No one could have guessed that you had such a room by your office. What do you keep in all those?

Wilton-Cough taking three rolls and large manuscript before closing the cabinet revealed,

-Important documents mainly, legal ones, wills and such. The chests contain artifacts, jewels and precious stones.

Raguel stroking the beautiful wood of certain cabinets made with intricate and exquisite marquetry enquired,

-Are they all yours?

But Abraham answered with a sad smile leading the way back to the office,

-I am dead, Raguel, all of the content in this room is my legacy to my family, my wife, my boys and my little Abi. I was also safe keeping a lot of my Aunt Josephine's belongings. They are safe in there. Mainly you will find that everything is the accumulated wealth of the Wilton and the one of the Cough which was consequential. I didn't live too lavishly so I could leave a good fortune to my children. Come, let me show you the maps.

The Master followed the ghost who closed the fake bookshelf door with great care behind him. In the office, Abraham went to his lavish Napoleonic era's desk and opened the map of the town. He held it down at every corner using paperweights which were actual rocks. Lifting the cluster of amethyst Raguel commented,

-Those are very interesting paperweights.

Wilton-Cough confided,

-When I was a boy, I did collect rocks and stones from

my trips with my aunt. It was a hobby of mine. I didn't have many hobbies to tell you the truth, I was a pretty dull child. I was certainly not like my talented Josiah who can play Beethoven faultlessly, no, no, I did just collect pretty stones and interesting rocks. Look at this one, this is a fossil given to me by William Smith on a trip to England. It looks like a snail but it is a very ancient snail apparently. It is my favourite in my collection. My second best is this large piece of amber with a curled fern inside it. If you look closely enough, you will see an ant in there. You can see my entire collection on those shelves between the two windows.

Raguel could feel how enthusiastic Abraham was speaking about his stones. He checked everything he collected over the years Wilton-Cough lived then came back to the desk with glistening eyes. The angel told with some emotion,

-I don't think you were a dull child at all. Look, wherever I go in this town, I have people still talking of you, and very highly of you. Some refer to what you said and even can quote you, like if you had been their teacher. In a way, I believe you have been a teacher to a lot of people in this town, a teacher of life, maybe a harsh one but still a good one. I know you wanted to put this little town on the map and did strive to do so. Well, I just had an idea. Why not creating a museum here, one in your memory? It will have your collection and I am sure my Henry on his flying trips can pick up interesting pieces to add to it. The little school children could go there with their class on a day trip or with their parents and learn about fossils or amber. So, you, my dear Abraham will be remembered, and I, personally want to make sure of it, for generation and generation in this little town that was so central to your heart. What do you say?

The old ghost only cried in front of him. The Master went straight to him and comforted embracing Wilton-Cough in a bear hug,

-My dear Abraham, I can feel your soul, you know. I know how much you care and I know how much you hurt but know that you have a friend in me. With all my heart I will help your spirit. I have a little secret to tell you: I don't want to just redeem you, I want you to have wings and work with us, be part of us. It will be a tough challenge but somehow, deep down, I believe, you, Abraham Wilton-Cough can make it. Now, dry your tears for me and let's work on that map.

Abraham pulling himself together explained with renewed zeal,

-You'd better take notes because it will be lots to take on

board.

Doctor Williams appeared straight away by his Master with a pad and pen in hand. This made Wilton-Cough wonder out loud,

-I swear he was at the tavern looking after that little boy!

Taking a good look at the map of the town, Raguel confirmed,

-He is still looking after Jack. My servant, like me, can be in multiple places at any time. Your master, Valdi, will possess that gift therefore you will do too in order to serve him well. Now, here, on that map, I can see lots of plots of land but the main name is yours on them.

Not shamed, Abraham answered boldly,

-I guess that is what you get when you are the heir and descendant to the person who created the town in the first place. Please, pay attention, this street and that one were the ones affected the most by the fire: houses totally burnt down. There, there and there, the damage is consequential but it can be fixed before winter I reckon. Here, in this street, to be honest with you they are paupers living on shoe strings. They have been hit by the fire, mildly, but they will not be able to repair their roofs. They will not be able to afford the material nor the labour. They are good people, hard working ones but the hole I saw on the roof of Mr Dunnock will be enough to cause pneumonia to at least two of his little children. Now, some land can be redistributed and even used. Let me go into the details.

Wilton-Cough was extremely thorough. He knew every inhabitants of Wilton Town by heart down to all of their children, their pets and their material circumstances. He explained in great detail who could possibly help in the reconstruction of the town and who absolutely couldn't. The Master of all angels and even his servant, Doctor Williams were fascinated by the amount of knowledge the old banker had of people. Abraham knew them by heart, by name, from their psychology down to their last penny. William pointed to the map with his pencil to a plot and stated,

-Do we all agree that the widow Mel Brown is the one requiring the most help at this moment in time? She is now completely destitute with only a cat to cry upon. If we have to prioritise, this old lady should come first. She is all alone in this world, no family whatsoever.

Abraham replied strongly,

-I agree and disagree all the same. If we work on priority, we will lose time. It is the end of the summer, the start of autumn, we need all of those people sorted before winter. Dealing with them in a queue will not do this time around. For all involved who have fallen into hardship, we can enjoined them in a community effort to rebuilt their part of town or help each other. Melanie Brown who will not accept charity easily can for example do blankets for the others and scarves. We can put her in charge of a group of very capable ladies touched by the tragedy whose knitting and sowing skills are demanded and needed right now. Their team will unsure that everyone affected by the fire has at least one blanket for the winter. For Helm street, I call it the paupers street, they have minimal damage but substantial enough to give them hardship in the cold seasons. What we need to do is to employ the men in the reconstruction of the town and for their wives to participate in creating a large canteen to feed all the workers and all who were affected by the fire. We can ask Mr Tyrell if he would consent for his tavern to be used as a canteen twice a day. He is a man of great integrity and has care, right here in his heart.

He made a quick gesture tapping his chest while Raguel approved,

-I think you are right, Abraham. It has to be a community effort. William did you write all of his ideas. It's important. We will use them as a contingency plan for the time being. For all who lost completely their houses, I know Miss White has already given her consent to home them until we rebuild their homes. For Mel Brown and her cat, I am going to ask my Sebastien to home her in his presbytery. Now if we have the help of my angels and the community effort to rebuild the part of the town affected by the fire, we still have to find the materials...

Wilton-Cough opened another scroll revealing a map of the woods and cut the angel's sentence,

-Here, here and here, you will find the materials. Those are quarries belonging to me which I inherited from the Cough family. They all are in my Zach's name now but he will never say no to let them be used under such circumstances. You will get proper stone from that one, there, and here you will get slates which will be adequate to repair the roofs of houses. I had a lucrative side business when I was alive from those quarries. The Wilton Forest belonging to the Wilton-Cough can be used as well but I would hope sparingly because my father loved his woods. I would not like to see his forest destroyed. Building the houses in stone is preferable than wood anyway. Let's keep the wood just for doors and window frames.

Raguel smiled at the intervention then said,

-Williams, it will then be left to you to furnish those household with the essential, beds, tables, chairs, stoves.

The old angelic servant agreed,

-That will not be a problem. I would also suggest having water pomps or, and wells for every house that were completely burnt down. The fact is they were destroyed because their only access to water was here, a single well, quite far from them and our angels couldn't extinguish the fire in time. That only source of water is ridiculous for such a wide area of the town. We need to correct that as we redesign the town.

Abraham sighed deeply, as he told,

-You will find an underground little brook going through town. It's been built over, over time, because it was full of mosquitoes during summer time. I remember seeing it in my childhood. It came from the river Wilton but it was safer than the river. My father took me there to fish for crayfish. If I remember right it goes from here to roughly there where you still have a little swamp area only good for wild geese and ducks. But you have also pikes, catfish and carps in there. I saw a catfish swallow an entire duckling once, I had nightmares about it. You could possibly tap into that brook to provide water to the households of this street, this one and that one. That would be exactly where the fire was the worst.

A pleased Master stated,

-It sounds like we have the birth of a plan of action. I will let you two devise it further. Williams, I expect you to report to me about it in an hour. Abraham, you will disappear within Vincent in about an hour but leave it to me, I will try to have you as a corporeal ghost for much longer than twenty four hours. I do want you to hug your family once more. You deserve it.

Raguel left the room with no further a do. Doctor Williams saw Wilton-Cough welling up. He gave him his handkerchief with a few words of comfort,

-Keep it up, Abraham. The angel of justice is hard to please but you are doing it. He didn't like me at all when we first met. He always live almost like a monk while I live lavishly. I have no shame about it as well. But here, see, I am his servant, accepted. You have already been accepted by him, I can tell. If he wants to do you a favour, that is a big deal. It means you are definitely in his good books. Help him and serve his brother loyally and you will see the best from Raguel. If he gives you his friendship, you will never lose it.

Opening another map after drying his eyes, Abraham mentioned,

-If I can I want to be and stay in Raguel's good books for I have seen him punish archangel Raphael. It was not a correction, you stand up back from easily, if you know what I mean. And in hell, Raguel was quick to protect me against Lucifer. You should have seen the way he did fight. It is the moment to say, it was scary as hell.

A smiling Doctor Williams revealed,

-For Raphael, he had it coming. First, Raguel and him were never friendly to one another. It was cold shoulders all along. Then the way Raphael treated me always displeased Raguel. He was fuming internally, I can tell you that, for a long time. The thing with Raguel, he can bottle up a lot, but he always keeps track of any mistake, bad action someone does and when he decides, enough is enough and it is the moment to lash out, you'd better run for cover if you happen to be the guilty party for Raguel doesn't take any prisoner then. Regarding Raphael, he committed the crime not only of plotting against Raguel's father, he sold his soul to have Raguel's son Gael killed. Well, let me tell you about the Master of all angels, he adores and loves his family. You should have seen him when he single handedly raised up Sebastien in his first human life. There is the expression mother hen, but father hen would have been applicable to him. He never spoilt the boy but he taught him values that would be embedded in his heart for all the rest of his incarnated angelic lives. You know I wanted to rest in peace, going to heaven, until Raguel told me he had another little boy and showed him to me. The pride, love and tenderness Raguel had in his eyes for his baby boy made me stay forever to serve them. By the way, Raguel has a very paternal attitude to all of his angels. We can turn to him when we are not doing too good. I did it many times and he has been ever so supportive. You can do so as well, because he told you to consider yourself under his wings. Just remember one thing, don't put a pretence in front of him for it will not pass, just be yourself. What is that new map?

Wilton-Cough explained,

-This is the sewer system underneath the town. It is not the best but it is not the worst despite how basic it is. The thing is we have a chance to develop it further and improve it.

As Abraham carried on with his plans to rebuild the town, Raguel walked through it in his natural fast pace. He considered the damage but was more hopeful that all could be sorted. His attention was caught by a little noise. He knew straight away it was an animal in pain. He went to the area of a collapsed house, he moved a few beams and rubbles only to found a dead old man with an injured little dog by his side. His heart sank, realising he had found the first casualty that the town suffered. He called his angels to order them to deal with any potential dead and to bring them to the church to be identified. Raguel picked up the wounded Fox Terrier with care and carried on to the tavern of Tyrell.

When he arrived, Raguel was welcomed by Callum at the door who told him,

-Not another animal! Tyron's tavern has become the Noah's ark of Wilton Town.

Tyrell by him commented,

-I don't mind it at all. What has to be done, has to be done.

Raguel answered sternly,

-That one is injured and has lost his owner. I found the poor old man dead under a beam.

It brought tears to Tyron straight away who expressed his emotion,

-That's the dog of Chris Jones. Don't tell me old Christopher is dead!

The angel held his hand briefly sharing the vision to Tyron of the discovery of the body of Jones as his answer. Tyrell shouted out loud,

-The bastards! Jones would not even harm a fly! But Killy was killing the mice in his house.

Raguel asked,

-Is it the name of his dog: Killy?

A crying Tyrell only nodded his positive answer. Whilst the Master stroke the dog gently, he approached the table which concerned him the most. Upon it was Jack who had be operated upon. Sebastien and his wife were caring for the child with all their mights. His servant, Doctor Williams briefed him,

-Jack is not waking up. We are not giving up on him. Valdi is trying something which is quite bold but which may work. We tried it many times in my Boston hospital with some success. Sebastien has refused to be seen to until he knows Jack is safe. Ivy is standing strong and has been helping us in a steadfast manner. Your father went alone in hell to punish personally Michael for what he has done to Jack and what he did to Sebastien. Rob is in a very poor state but we have good hope for him. Luke, who saved the cat of Mel Brown will recover, but he will suffer for a while. Abraham Wilton-Cough is being incredible on his will to rebuild his town. If I have to say just a word about him, Master, is that I value his opinions. He cares. I am pretty sure you will make an angel out of him one day. So I overheard, we have one dead in Wilton Town?

Raguel giving him the dog replied,

-Yes, we may have others. Some didn't want to leave the town when asked to and took the chance to live or die. The owner of that dog perished under a burning beam. Can you see if you can save his dog. I think Killy has just a broken back leg but his flank is open.

While Doctor Williams took the Fox terrier to another table to inspect him, Raguel reached the table where Jack was. As soon as Sebastien saw his father, he went to him, crying,

-I don't think Jack will make it, Dad. We did everything.

Opening his arms to his son, Raguel scolded as he hugged him,

-You've got to stay strong for Jack, Mighty, just as he was strong for you. Go and get some water, a bucket full. Come back, and pull yourself together.

As his son obeyed, Raguel saw the sadness upon Ivy's face. She was clearly retaining her tears while helping Doctor Valdi. He went to hold her hand with compassion as he asked his younger brother,

-How are we doing with Jack, Vincent?

Valdi who was busy trying to save the boy briefed,

-We are doing as best as we can. Jack had a couple of

cardiac arrests but I just managed to get a pulse again from him. It is touch and go. But I can tell you, he is still fighting. I am not going to give up.

Biting his lower lip with emotion, Raguel went to hold Jack's little hand firmly. Vincent told,

-Whatever you are doing, Raguel has a positive effect. His heartbeat is getting stronger.

Raguel answered,

-I am just sending healing energy to him.

Vincent asked wildly,

-Talk to him. We need Jack to wake up.

The Master of all angels did as his younger brother suggested with faith,

-Jack, Jack, if you can hear me, it is the Master, Raguel, your adoptive grandfather. My dear, dear boy, you've got to come back to us. We want you near us and with us. Jack, I never told you how proud I was to have you as an angel but I should have. You were such a good angel and even when you lost your way and your wings, you tried to do good in your own way preserving a little girl's soul. Jack, you are part of us and you know it. Don't leave us. Fight back my angel, fight back.

As he felt the little hand grasping his with more pressure, Raguel stated with a glimmer of hope,

-Vincent, he is responding. Jack is responding. He is pressing my hand. We've got him!

His son was back with a bucket of water while it happened. A tearful Sebastien went to hold Jack's other hand as the boy slowly woke up. Valdi put water on the cheeks and forehead of the boy who came around. The first thing Jack said as he saw Sebastien was,

-Pa.

Jack closed his green eyes once more before reopening them then told,

-I can't see them no more.

Sebastien stroking the child's forehead with tenderness

enquired,

-What can't you see my Jack?

The boy answered as he gave a long tearful look to Raguel,

-The fields full of flowers. I am here Master, I heard you. Am I still your angel?

Despite all his efforts to remain strong for everyone, Raguel shed a tear when he replied,

-You are, Jack, in my heart you never left. You are my angel and always will be.

He tugged the hand of the child before he added,

-Beside I need your caring heart to look after something for me. It is a small mission but I know your big caring heart will take it on board.

Always ever so eager to please and help Jack enquired, his voice still weak,

-What is it Master? I am here for you.

Recognising the strong allegiance that still existed between the fallen angel and the Master rendered Sebastien emotional. He knew at that very moment that Jack was giving himself back to the Master of all angels. He went to hold his wife who cried upon his shoulder finally letting go of all the stamina she displayed whilst operating on Jack.

While Valdi started to bandage the torso of the child, Raguel said in a soft voice,

-Jack, I got you a dog. Like you, he got injured during the night. Doctor Williams is looking after him as we speak, mending his broken paw and pierced flank. The name of the dog is Killy. He lost his owner tonight. The man died under a burning beam. The injured dog was by his master when I found him. Will you care for him for me, become his new owner?

Jack replied with enthusiasm,

-Oh yes, yes, I will that is if Pa and Ma let me have a dog!

Ivy came to the boy and was the first to answer,

-Ma says yes, and Pa will have to say yes, because you and I can do with a little dog warning us about strangers at the doors or even helping us in a biting way against an attacker. How are you feeling my Jack? Now, you must listen to mummy when I say don't exert yourself.

She kissed the forehead of Jack with tenderness before asking her husband,

-We can have a dog, can we?

Sebastien nodded positively as he replied,

-Yes, I can't see why not.

He then went to hug the boy, scolding,

-You have been too brave for your own human body, my Jack. I have been on tender hooks all night about you. Ma as well! I am still shivering about it. I don't want to lose you. Do you understand me? I don't.

Jack sobbed gently on Sebastien's shoulder,

-I am so sorry. I am not a fighting angel, but please teach me how to fight.

Raguel answered firmly,

-Sebastien will see to that, and give you tuitions but first you must get better. Let me bring you home where you can rest and I will look after you. Ivy would you mind carrying the poor Killy, you need a rest as well. Both of you have done enough overnight. Come with me.

Then he ordered,

-Vincent, William look after my son and sort out his legs.

The Master took Jack into his arms and waited at the door for Ivy to follow him which she did diligently with the wounded dog. Somehow, she felt confident by the presence of Raguel by her and Jack. She confessed on the way to the presbytery,

-I am quite worried to step back in the house. I must sound stupid.

Raguel looked at her and noticing how she shivered

uncontrollably, he replied,

-You are not stupid, Ivy. You, Jack and Doctor Williams faced a terrible attack in this house. Look, Jack is not walking, I am carrying him. He nearly lost his life tonight. If Sebastien didn't arrive just in time William would have been dead. To worry is not stupidity. I am going to live at your home, and know that I am a punishing angel. If you want a guard dog, you will not find a better one than me. I will always stay and guard your home. I will watch it from now on.

A large rottweiler appeared by Ivy's grey skirt, who followed her obediently. She looked at her father in law baffled and asked,

-That dog is you?

The angel smiled to her as he answered,

-Yes, give him a good name. I can be at any places, at any time in any shape or form. I can multiply myself as I wish or want to. You wanted a good guard dog and I am afraid the poor half burnt Killy will not do that job until he recovers from his accident that killed his owner.

Ivy considered the rottweiler by her and stroke his head before she proposed,

-What do you think of Ludwig?

The Master giggled as he replied,

-I can read your mind my human, and as it is after Beethoven, I have no problem with that name. So you prefer his seventh symphony. Interesting, mine his the fifth and Sebastien loves the ninth. My father loves all three of them but he includes the fourth in his choices and the moonlight sonata.

Little Jack resting upon his strong chest confided with a very feeble voice,

-I like the moonlight sonata. Are you staying with us for good?

In his rough way yet securing the boy against him, Raguel demanded,

-Yes, I am. Is it a problem?

Jack sobbing on the shoulder of the Master of all angel

confided,

-It will be safer with you with us, much safer. I saw bad things in my past, bad ones but an archangel that anyone trusted turning bad like that... If I didn't need to react and help, I think I would have been sick. What he wanted to do to Doctor Williams was atrocious and to Ma, and to Ma...

Ivy put her gentle hand on the child to reassure,

-It is all over my Jack. Please don't aggravate yourself. Grandpa Rag is with us now.

Raguel gave a look at the young woman at hearing his new name that she had made up on the spot but didn't tell her off for it. He just took it on board with a smirk thinking that she will call him like an old carpet from now on. He wondered what their family life in the presbytery will look like but in all honesty, he was looking forward to it.

When they arrived at the presbytery, Ivy and him put Jack in his bed in his bedroom. While Ivy was putting the boy in his pyjama, Raguel prepared some scrambled eggs for him. He brought the bowl up to the bedroom with a smile and did let Ivy spoon feeding the child, despite wanting to do it, himself. He considered the simple bedroom, walked about it and thought about all of the people of Wilton Town who lost their homes. His angels managed to contain the spread of the fire, the cost of lives and restrict the number of wounded but for everyone affected the Master grieved deeply. He looked at the little injured fox terrier laying on the bed of Jack and sighed.

When Jack was finally asleep, the angel Ted came into the bedroom and told,

-I am ready to take my shift, Master. I will keep an eye on Jack for you. Henry is downstairs ready to brief you about the entire situation. It will be a mournful and quiet day. Everyone has been dealt with. However I had a vision. You must not let Sebastien and Ivy go alone to the clinic today, you must go there too. You will be surprised but nicely surprised. Someone important will come begging. A young human girl needs help but I can't see her survive in any way, shape or form. She needs all of our prayers. She lives in a dangerous situation. She is suffering in silence. I can't offer you any solution for her but she created a miracle overnight.

Ted held the hand of the Master, sharing his vision to him. It was enough for Raguel to swear,

-Good Lord!

A nodding Ted confirmed,

-I know. Only you can deal with him.

The Master ordered,

-Jack is stable and sleeping but monitor him with eagle eyes. I do not want to lose that angel. Anything from temperature to drop in his pulse, I want you to call Doctor Williams for him. Ted, I trust you with Jack until I come back, do not lose him. Ivy, come with me.

While Ted sat on the stool by the bed of Jack, Ivy followed her father in law. He had such a commending tone about him that she never thought to argue or ask why. He offered her his arm to hold as they went down the stairs together which she accepted straight away. Raguel asked her,

-Do you want to rest, Ivy? I can manage the clinic with Sebastien today.

But she replied strongly despite being a little tired,

-Not on a day, after the night we had. I am pretty sure plenty of people will need help and I am ready to give it. I will rest later.

Happy with her answer, the Master knew why his son had decided to marry the young Ivy Fair. He took her to the kitchen where Henry was preparing breakfast. He gallantly pulled a chair at the table for her before he acknowledged the presence of the Messenger,

-Tell me the toll, Henry.

The angel turning to the Master told,

-We have two human deaths. Compared to the initial visions of Ted, we managed to save most of the people of Wilton Town. One young girl is unaccounted for and we have one woman who has been severely wounded. What happened to her is atrocious. We found her Theo and I in a backstreet unconscious, bleeding her guts out. We took her to Doctor Valdi and Doctor Williams. They are on her case right now. The woman is a young lady called Rose according to Theo. He said she was a street worker in Wilton Town. She fell on hard times and guess what, she comes from Boston. The sad thing is she became destitute by the gangs of Boston and raped and nearly killed by the gang of Wilton Town. Valdi said she did bleed for hours and that her chances of survival are slim. On the angelic side Rob is pulling through nicely. I was able to talk to him and he told me to reassure you. It is not the same story for our angel who saved the cat of Mel Brown. He didn't have the straight intervention of a Valdi. He is poorly. Doctor Williams says he will make it but he added eventually at the end of his sentence. So I can only guess that the life of young angel Francis is in question. In the hotel of Miss White, the situation is fine. She dealt with the emergency superbly along with the human Mrs Toad who has such a gentle soul. Whenever I am near Pamela, I am touched by her humble kindness.

Sitting by Ivy, Raguel commented,

-I am not surprised about Pamela. My father talked to her. He doesn't talk to humans if they are not worth anything. My son, who is a fairly good judge of character, liked her almost straight away as well. Can you tell me who was the second casualty?

Henry replied as he put bowls of scrambled eggs in front of the Master and Ivy,

-Apparently, he was a man known as Denis. He rented a room above the empty shop that completely burnt down. He was a bit of a gambler and a bit of a drunkard. He worked here and there. His last reported employment was at the construction of the new bridge in town. Prior to that he worked on the dockyard in Boston. Not surprisingly, like many who came from Boston, he was fearful during his life to give his surname and told people to just call him Denis. Given his gambling addiction I guess he had been hiding in Wilton Town to escape from the gangs of Boston. Theo said he will look into it. He knows the parish where the man came from. Unfortunately, it seems that Denis missed the call to evacuate the town. He was not in his lodging then. But we found him dead in his bed later. Odell said that today was the week day the workers for the bridge received their salary. He suspect that Denis went to drink in a pub out of town, not very far away, came back drunk, as he was a heavy drinker, and died in his sleep during the fire.

Raguel ordered,

-Take a seat and eat with us Henry. Don't forget to feed Ted, he worked all night and he had another vision. We know how badly it affects him. He seems alright but keep an eye on him for me. I am going to leave you in control of this household today. Jack is still a big concern of mine as well. What happened today did not only hurt him physically but it did affect him emotionally. When I carried him here, his pain was so intense, I did hurt. Jack is only eight and human. He may have the intelligence and the memory of an angel but we must not forget that he is a human child now. The trauma he went through is considerable. I gave him a dog to look after. I hope it will keep his mind off things. You and Ted take turns to read that little boy stories. Now, Ivy tell me exactly what happened yesterday night.

Ivy stopped eating and she started to be emotional as she complied with the request,

-It was horrible. You have to bare with me if I cry. We were preparing the house to receive the possible casualties with Doctor Williams. When the bell at the door rang, I went to open it. I didn't recognise the angel but I knew he was one. He was carrying a homeless man I knew. Sebastien and I were feeding the man everyday since we arrived in Wilton Town, giving him bread and ham. I knew something was wrong straight away because the tall angel killed the poor wretch in front of me. He broke his neck with such strength that I was in chock. I was paralysed almost on my feet with horror and fear. I wanted to comprehend what was happening but I couldn't. With just one arm, the angel threw me out of his way against the wall. Doctor Williams went to check what was happening in the hallway. He recognised Archangel Michael and he was attacked by him. Poor Doctor Williams, his head was bashed against the wall so many times that he lost consciousness. I did intervene when I recovered my senses, trying to make Michael stop what he was doing, but I was thrown out of the way like a rag doll, and I did hurt my back. I still don't know how bad my back is. I am a Doctor so I know it isn't broken but it will probably be black and blue. Little Jack went to see what was the commotion all about. When he witnessed what was happening to Doctor Williams and me, he tried to help with all his might but he was battered for it to the point of unconsciousness.

Feeling emotional, catching her breath, Ivy paused before she carried on,

-Michael dragged me on to a chair. I tried to defend myself but it was to no avail. I was attached on to the chair and he bragged, that I didn't see all of my loved ones died but he will make sure of it. He said I was cursed to lose anyone I had affection for. He attached my Jack by a chair next to me. Jack was starting to come around but he had been so battered, the poor thing. Michael told me that after killing Jack, it will be the time for my baby in my belly and then me. I felt so sick. I was so terrified. Michael then brought Doctor Williams who was still totally unconscious. He attached him on the operating table and he said that he will eat all of our hearts out so we don't come back. Jack whispered to me that it was a very dangerous ritual. I don't know about those things, you see. Next thing I know was Jack rebelling and trying to stop Michael by using his chair as a makeshift ram to protect Doctor Williams who slowly was coming around. Then Sebastien came and saved us. Well Williams and myself first. I had to leave my Jack behind. I was so distressed about it. He got stabbed. He was such a brave, brave boy.

Raguel held her hand in a comforting way when he explained to her,

-What you have to understand, Ivy, is that Jack will never be a normal little boy. He has knowledge beyond your imagination, an angelic memory that has centuries behind it. He also has the will to get back his wings. Despite him being human now and just a child of eight, he will act like an angel. Now, eat your breakfast while I tell you more about Jack because we will have to go to the clinic. Sebastien and Doctor Williams will already be there.

For some reason Ivy could not say no to her father in law. She felt his strong personality and was subdued by it. She obeyed and ate then Raguel said,

-Just by touching someone, a hand, a shoulder I know what they did, their past and also their intentions and feelings. I carried Jack here. I can tell you right now that the boy is truly devoted to you and my Sebastien. He is ever so thankful to have been adopted by you two. That fallen angel felt ever so lost. My son and you by giving him your care and a home gave him back hope. Back in the days, Jack was an excellent guardian angel. He made a few mistakes that distraught him very much, he lost his ways and his wings. But unbeknown to us he tried to repair his mistakes all alone, and attached himself to Mina White to protect her soul and to prevent her to kill anyone. I can tell you straight now that Jack has still the heart of the protective and caring angel he was. You should have seen him back in the days. He was one of the most loved angels. Like my William, he is not an angelic warrior or fighter but he has his special way to talk to people to make them cope and feel better. For him to get involved into a fight tonight was a big deal because he is rather a pacific being at heart. But he didn't want to see any of you hurt if he could help it. He nearly gave his life for all of you. I can't tell you how happy I am to have seen him finally pull through from his operation. He has a spirit and a heart that I do not want to lose. My Sebastien knows how much I value Jack. He and Williams were ever so glad to have finally found him after all those years.

Henry commented,

-I remember the day when he came out from the little Mina White. Doctor Williams performed big magic there. And here you had in the corner of the room, Jack in human shape, naked and so frail, it was heartbreaking. Most of us had tears in our eyes when we finally found Jack back. I never personally met him before but the rumour in the angelic world was that he was an angel with a heart of gold. That's quite a reputation to have. Beside that I always heard praises about him. I also knew that Sebastien and Doctor Williams have been questing for Jack for an extremely long time, it was the quest for the missing angel if I recall.

Raguel confirmed with a sigh,

-Yes, I gave my son and my servant that task, that quest because I wanted to give second chances to Jack. The truth is I missed Jack terribly, his good nature and heart. They found him only by chance, but I was over the moon when they did so. So, you see, Ivy, your little boy is a very special boy to the angelic community. He matters to us a great deal so much so that Michael who stabbed him is in hell right now. I can see that you have finished your breakfast. Let's get your shawl, and go to the clinic for we will have a busy day ahead of us. Henry, keep a good watch on this household. The rottweiler is called Ludwig and will help you guard the house. The dog is an incarnation of myself but I promise he will not growl at you nor destroy or bite your legs.

Henry smirked, patted the dog's head and stated,

-Thank god for that.

#

Ivy walking by her father in law through the street of Wilton Town felt safe. She realised the amount of damage that went on overnight and confided to him,

-You know, father Rag', sometimes I fail to understand the world and how violent it can be.

Despite being called Rag again by the young woman, the Master of all angels cared to reply to her,

-Ivy, you mustn't believe that it is always like that. Remember that the trouble makers are always fewer than the gentle folks.

Looking around her, Ivy stated,

-Despite being fewer in number, they can make a hell of damage. Will they be brought to justice? They destroyed so much overnight.

Raguel looked at his human daughter in law with compassion. He knew she was intelligent but that she was mainly ignorant about the angelic world. She only knew bits and pieces of it: The scraps of information given to her by an angel here and there. He decided there and then to make sure the young Ivy was always fully informed as he told her,

-They will. We are detaining all of them but one, the main culprit of the fire. Your husband dealt with him. My son and I are angels called Punishers. I am the angel of justice, you see. We are allowed to punish and give a comeuppance to anyone at anytime. Darren Bell who caused the fire is dead and in hell. He was so bad that Lucifer came to pick up his soul himself. Lucifer doesn't do that very often, only to the worst. He also took tonight Michael who stabbed Jack. I dealt with another angel, Raphael, who planned to kill Doctor Valdi and had organised the murder of all the healing angels and Doctors used by the angelic army of my son. So you can guess his plan included Doctor Williams and yourself and he sent his friend Michael to do the task. However little Jack was there to save the night and my son arrived just in time to help you all. Lucifer gave him the head's up whilst collecting the soul of Darren. Look Ivy, the people are returning back to town led by Father Odell. The ones who lost their homes have been told to stay at Miss White's hotel.

When the people of Wilton Town walked through the streets most started to cry but they realised it could have been much worst than a quarter of the town lost to the flames. Odell took them to the tavern where Tyrell offered them breakfast and explained to them in brief terms that the gang which was persecuting the town, had been tackled with overnight and that its pyromaniac leader was dead. He also announced the names of the casualties. Whilst this was happening Doctor Valdi along with Abraham Wilton-Cough fully briefed Father Odell in the alley way about the reconstruction plans for Wilton Town. Odell was put in charge to rally everyone spirit up but also to organise the teams that will create the community effort to rebuild the part of the town that had been affected by the fire. With the maps given to him, Theo went back to the tavern. He not only explained the how the reconstruction would take place, but he assigned specific task to everyone. Everybody knew their team and what they had to do. When the people of the town left the tavern with their saved animals, they had hope back in their hearts.

Sebastien approached Mel Brown who didn't have a home to go to, but she had her cat in her arms and was only too happy to have been reunited with her pet. She had consented to be the leader of the knitting team that would create blankets for all who where affected by the fire during the meeting. Sebastien, with his natural French charm, stroke gently the cat which started purring under his touch before he addressed the widow,

-What is the name of your cat Mrs Brown?

Still in the tavern, taking the only comfort from just having her cat, Mel replied,

-She is called Poppy, Mr Cotton.

With a beautiful smile Sebastien commented,

-That is a pretty name for a pretty cat, an Angora cat, isn't it?

Mrs Brown falling for the charm incentive answered,

-Yes, she is. Do you know about cats?

Continuing deliberately to make sure the destitute widow would accept to be homed in the presbytery, Sebastien told,

-Well, yes, I have two. My wife has a nice fluffy one and my little boy has a little stray one.

Paling the widow enquired,

-I heard that something happened to Jack during the night, is the rumour true?

Sebastien confided willingly,

-The rumour is unfortunately true. My little Jack was fighting by my side, bravely and was stabbed. My wife, another Doctor from Boston and I had to operate on him to save him. We have good hope that he will make it. He is recuperating at home. He is not the only one that was injured tonight. I was, my legs are in a pretty bad state, burnt all over, almost. Rob who was helping at the tavern had oil poured all over him and was set on fire. Then there is young Francis, he is upstairs lodging at the tavern like Rob, recovering. He is the young man that rescued your Poppy. Do you want to meet him? I am afraid to say that at this stage for Francis, we are not sure if he will pull through. I have seen to him and I can say he has extensive burns. He is stable at the moment. We made him comfortable as much as we could.

Mel Brown accepted the invite with emotion,

-Yes, please, I must thank that young man.

She followed Sebastien to the bedroom given to Francis and at the sight of him she had tears in her eyes. But Francis smiled to her just at the sight of the cat in her arms, he welcomed from his bed,

-I am pleased to see that that poor cat is finally reunited with its owner.

Mrs Brown told straight away,

-Poppy and I thank you from the bottom of our hearts.

Sebastien presented with some formality,

-Francis, this is Mrs Mel Brown and her cat Poppy which you saved last night.

Francis presented his burnt hand to hold,

-Nice to meet you both. Good morning Poppy. Mrs Brown, she has been a good cat. When I took her from under the bed where she was hiding from the fire, she did let me handle her. I wrapped her in the bed cover to protect her because I knew I had to go through a furnace downstairs to get us out. We made it, though, both are alive.

Mel shook the hand of the young angel asking,

-How can I ever repay you?

The amiable Francis told her with gentleness as his upper body went to lay back on the pillows with considerable pain,

-You do not have to pay me back, Mrs Brown but if you really want to you can knit by my bedside, visit me with Poppy until I recover.

The widow accepted willingly. Francis started coughing violently and Sebastien was quick to react and gave him a soothing potion to swallow then an order,

-You must rest now. No more talking for the day. You inhaled far too much smoke last night. Callum will check on you every half hour and I want his report to be that you slept like a good angel, like a baby. It is important that you do so for your recovery.

His throat soothed, being tucked in bed properly by Sebastien, Francis waved politely good bye to the widow and her cat. Sebastien walked out of the bedroom with Mel Brown and after he closed the door, she confided to him,

-What a very kind young man! I didn't catch his surname though. He is not from Wilton Town, is he? I never met him before.

Sebastien walking down the stairs with the widow answered,

-Yes, Francis is very kind. He has an extremely gentle personality that likes nothing more than helping others. But I must tell you, he has no surname whatsoever. He was abandoned as a baby at the doorsteps of a church. The priest who found him brought him up. He named him after the patron saint of the day he found him. The vicar passed away a while ago and Francis is alone in the world, however he has friends like me. To be honest with you, Francis can only have friends because he is so kind and helpful. When I said there was a problem with a gang in Wilton Town, he was one of the first to come over to see that the situation get resolved and to give a hand.

Mel Brown who was already touched by having met the rescuer of her cat, was also moved by his story. This was the intention of Sebastien who had already a scheme to make the lonely and childless lady adopt in her heart Francis as her son. His plans were elaborate and he envisaged that in the near future, when she had her new home, Mrs Brown would lodge Francis which meant that by keeping Francis in Wilton Town, he could keep an eye on his poorly young angel. The widow said with a good and willing heart,

-I will certainly visit Francis with my Poppy everyday. If I had a home I will invite him over for dinner.

Sebastien took his opportunity to propose,

-Then we will invite him for dinner for you, my wife and I. It will be a privilege to have you stay with us in our large presbytery until your house is rebuilt. We have many rooms and we are an household who loves animals.

The widow, sensitive to the invite, knowing she was being given a generous helping hand answered shyly,

-Surely, I can't. I was thinking of paying a room at Miss White's hotel for the time being. But I do not know if she accepts animals...

Falsely scolding Mrs Brown, Sebastien went for the kill,

-Don't be silly, Mel. You are more than welcome in our home. If you really want to pay for your living in our room, my wife is with child, and to have some knitted garments and clothes for our future baby will help us tremendously. You will find us humble people, getting by day in and out. As for Miss White, she does accept animals in her hotel. She did accept to take on all who lost their homes however she is lacking bedrooms to fit everyone in. Lots are going to sleep in her ballroom on the floor, like you witnessed last night. It is better to be in a heated room than being outside in all weather I must admit but with us, you will have a room at the very least and you will sleep on a bed. Not only that you have been put in charge of the knitting team, can you imagine coming to town through those woods everyday whether it rains or shines and going back up hill to the hotel at the end of every long day of work?

Stroking her cat, the widow admitted,

-Mr Cotton, I think you made your case very clear and I will not argue with you whatsoever. I accept to be lodged in your humble home.

A very pleased Sebastien led her away from the tavern and took her to the presbytery. Soon after he left to go to the clinic which he found already opened but not busy. He saw his father in the empty waiting room and addressed him straight away in a slightly angry fashion,

-You, a rottweiler in my house! The cat of Mrs Brown was spooked. I took it out of her arms before it could claw her but it did claw me! You couldn't chose to appear as a less ferocious dog, could you? There is plenty of choice out there! But no, you chose to guard my house as a rottweiler! I am not happy about that one, Dad. I will remind you what you always said to me: discuss before making a decision. Bad decision! Bad one! But I managed to deal with the situation with Henry and the widow Brown is settling herself nicely in our home with her cat.

The Great Being appeared in the room demanding,

-Are you two bickering again?

Defending himself Raguel replied,

-No, I haven't said a word yet, father, I was just letting him vent, while wondering why did I chose a Gallic woman to have him?

His father smiled giving his answer, deeply amused,

-That would be because you loved the woman as soon as you did set your eyes upon her. Now, your son is right, although you had good intentions in creating that guard dog to protect the family of your son, you could have chosen another breed of dog.

Raguel argued,

-Why do you always take his side?

Taking a seat in the waiting room, the Great Being answered with great calm,

-That would be because Mighty is most of the time right when he is upset about something and can justify why.

His grandson took his opportunity to exhibit his fresh new scars to his father as he said,

-Here, look my justification. I have been clawed by Poppy. Not only my legs hurt badly, now my arms do so as well.

Raguel retorted with a smirk,

-You will survive. You always do. Just think that you have nice new scars to show to everyone.

This made the Great Being laugh while Doctor Williams entered the room with a very serious and sad face. William asked,

-Have they been bickering?

To which the Great Being nodded positively before explaining to the loyal servant of his son,

-First Raguel had the generous idea of homing Mel Brown and her cat in the Presbytery until her home is being built. Because he was warned of her proud mind which may refuse charity, he sent his son to go on the charm offencive to convince the old lady to be re-homed. Of course, Mighty delivered the good, he is a better negotiator than his father. Second, my Raguel who is clearly upset to what happened yesterday night to you, Ivy and Jack decided to create another version of himself as a guard dog for the presbytery. The dog is looking so fierce, that it scared the cat of Mrs Brown who was brought by Mighty. Of course Mighty controlled the cat so it will not injured Mel Brown and he has been clawed doing so. But he has more pretty scars on his arms to show off according to his father that he will survive from.

Doctor Williams couldn't help smiling and with a snap of his fingers, he made his medical bag appeared, then demanded,

-Sebastien, show me your arms. I will disinfect them. So you managed to make the widow Brown accept a new home for the time being, well done. According to Abraham Wilton-Cough, she is a poor but proud lady.

Sebastien came to him willingly and presented his arms. The old Doctor started to treat his arms straight away as he commented,

-I can understand why you were upset. But you will survive. It will heal.

Smirking Raguel teased out loud, pointing at his son,

-See, I told you. Who is being a drama queen because he has a big nice guard dog to protect his house?

Sebastien gave his father a dark look however he smiled as he admitted,

-I know I will recover from that one, but trust me, I will make you hold a cat facing a rottweiler to make you feel how it was.

The Great Being and Doctor Williams couldn't help laughing while the Master retorted,

-I fight demons for a living, my dear son, I will not struggle as much as you did holding Poppy being scared. At least you managed to deliver the old widow home safely, she didn't claw you as you showed charity to her.

Sebastien started to laugh as well but he complained,

-I can't deal with a father like that!

But Williams scolded him as he finished treating his arms,

-Of course you can! Listen to your father and stop being a drama queen! Now, tell us how did you convince Mrs Brown?

Looking at his bandages Sebastien told his father off,

-Are you pleased now, dad? My legs are all wrapped up in bandages, now, my arms as well, part of my chest and my wife will believe she is sleeping with a mummy tonight! You could have warned me at the very least that you would be a rottweiler in my home. But no, oh no, archangels are taking such liberties these days!

Raguel only replied sternly,

-Answer the question of Doctor Williams, Sebastien before I start telling you about my grief that despite being given the magical formula to protect yourself, you failed to use it properly yesterday night and ended with seriously burnt legs. I haven't even mentioned you, being near Jack when he got stabbed. You will not escape a very serious conversation with me tonight. Some angels are failing expectations.

Sebastien sighed deeply and this time, his beautiful smile abandoned him. His grandfather came to his rescue in a soothing way,

-Don't be too harsh on your son, Raguel. You should have seen what he faced last night. He did well, especially since he is not fully recovered of his last injury. Without him it could have been much worst. Williams, Ivy and Jack would be dead and Wilton Town would have been almost completely burnt down. Now, for the question he has to answer, I can do it for him because your words did hurt him. What happened to Jack last night upset Mighty greatly. So for Mrs Brown, he just had a simple convincing conversation with her. He presented her the young Francis who saved her cat. Because the widow is all alone, because Francis is all alone, the intentions of your son are to make them a surrogate mother and son. Then they will be two looking after one another. Also he will keep his young angel in town if Mrs Brown feels motherly enough towards the wounded Francis to lodge him in her future rebuilt home.

Williams commented,

-That is what good intentions sound like.

A dubious Raguel stated,

-It sounds like another of his match-making ventures, with an adoptive twist to it.

The Great Being stood up and scolded,

-Raguel, that's enough of you sounding like an old rottweiler!

They were interrupted by Ivy who came downstairs quite alarmed as she announced,

-I think I am losing Rose. She is not making it.

Her husband demanded,

-Let me check upon her. I will try to save her. Where is she?

Ivy replied quickly,

-In the bedroom upstairs where it is quiet. Follow me. She has just become unresponsive.

Sebastien rushed upstairs accompanied by Doctor Williams and his wife. Alone in the waiting room, the Great Being told to the Master of all angels,

-Mighty is an extremely good son, Raguel, who could do with a little paternal love and praises sometimes. Think about it when you live in his home.

The bell at the door rang interrupting them. A young girl entered with some determination and demanded,

-Someone needs the assistance of the replacement of Doctor Valdi. It's a Mr Cotton, I think.

Raguel recognised the girl from the vision of Ted straight away. He demanded,

-Where is that someone and what is your name, pray? Mr Cotton is dealing with a dying patient at this moment in time.

A shivering Margot, wet and cold from spending the night outside, replied,

-The someone is a strange man, I saved from the river yesterday night. He has two broken arms that need to be looked after. He had a dislocated jaw as well but I fixed that. He is not from town, I don't recognise him from being from town. Something happened to him last night, I don't know what but he is in a pretty bad shape. He told me his name was Raphael River.

Despite all the informations he had received, Raguel was dissatisfied and he asked again with some impatience,

-Where is Raphael River? Why is he not coming in person? And what is your own name young lady?

Margot pointed at a tall man across the road from the window, who stayed in the shadow of an alley way and answered,

-There, that is the man. Somehow he turned all shy for some reason. He doesn't sound shy at all normally. I told him he needed to be seen to and that Mr Cotton and his wife had a good reputation in town. But this is as far as he would follow me. You don't need to know my name if he is the patient, do you?

Raguel agreed,

-No, I don't, but as all the inhabitants of Wilton Town were evacuated last night to escape the fire in town, a missing girl was reported, about your age, your height, with your hair colour and the same eye's colour, so little Miss Daisy Cork who previously was Marguerite Bouchon, I am glad to see that you are alive and well, and standing before me. Go and get, Raphael, tell him he will be seen to. Then warm yourself up a little by the fireplace in the waiting room. I am sure you will not refuse a hot cup of tea and some biscuits.

At the commending tone, Margot nodded positively and ran outside to get Raphael. Raguel turned to his father and told,

-Like Ted saw, the fallen archangel and the young girl who saved him are here this morning.

The Great Being recommended before tending to the fire in the small fire place,

-I know it will be hard for you to do so, but you need to show some clemency on this occasion, just a little, Raguel, just a little, but it will go a long way.

He then left the room to prepare a breakfast for the young girl in the kitchen upstairs. Five minutes later a reluctant fallen archangel Raphael stepped into the clinic dragged by the good willing Margot. When the door closed behind him, locked itself, and he saw Raguel standing tall, his arms crossed upon his chest, behind the reception desk of the clinic, Raphael stated,

-I knew it was a bad idea.

He tried to open the door but couldn't with his broken arms. Raphael thought then than his humiliation was complete. He turned back with despair written across his face. Raguel smirked as he asked,

-Mr Raphael River, I suppose you seek a little medical attention, do you?

Raphael walked backward with fear, putting his bleeding back against the door. He answered with tears in his eyes,

-No, I don't. Margot told me about the nice people in this clinic, but I know what you told me too last night. I was stupid, please I beg you to let me out. I will never ask for help, I promise.

Still behind the reception desk, the Master moved some paper casually as he said sternly,

-The nice people in this clinic are my youngest son and his little wife. Michael who you incited to join you to kill all the healing team is in hell right now. You sold your soul to kill my eldest son, do you think I am going to let my youngest who did face death by your scheming to look after you?

A shamed Raphael sank on his knees and begged again,

-Please, let me out. I was an idiot.

The Great Being coming in the room with tea and biscuits commented,

-Yes, Raphael, you were an idiot. It is nice to see you on your knees. Were you by any chance apologising?

Margot came to Raphael and to the astonishment of everyone in the room slapped him harshly before telling him off,

-You tried to kill people and you dared to share my bridge yesterday night. Now I understand why you ended up face down in the river. When I asked you why you were beaten up, if you were mugged or if someone was cross with you, you didn't answer because it was the later. I shouldn't have repaired your dislocated jaw. You tried to kill the good Mr Cotton and his wife, the healing team of Wilton Town.

Raguel smiled at her action, although she was not totally correct she was not far off from the truth. He commented,

-She is good. Where did you find her, Raphael?

Before Raphael replied, the Great Being took Margot by the hand and led her to a tray, he had put on the small table. He told her,

-Come and warm yourself up before you catch a cold, Margot. Breakfast is here. Help yourself to everything. The individual very cross with Raphael is in front of him right now and we must let them talk to each other.

The intelligent young girl enquired giving a good look at Raguel while doing as she was told,

-He is an angel, is he? I know Raphael lost his wings yesterday. His stomps are still bleeding today.

Taking a seat by Margot, the Creator revealed to her,

-The cross angel is actually the angel of justice. He is a very important archangel and as the Master of all angels, he had to punish the criminal Raphael by removing his wings. Raphael is the instigator of the death of the angel of justice's oldest son, he convinced another angel to try to kill his youngest and last child who happens to be Mr Cotton. That other angel stabbed a little adopted boy of Mr Cotton, Jack Malt last night, who is only eight and nearly died, but he was saved by his adoptive Pa and Ma.

A tearful Margot stood back up, went to Raphael, slapped him again with all her might this time before going back to her seat after she warned him,

-You will not sleep under my bridge tonight, you can wander about, you disgust me, stranger.

Raphael was actually aggrieved by that gesture, not because his cheeks did actually hurt but he did like the young human girl that saved him. He finally answered to Raguel, looking straight at him,

-Margot is a very good girl. She has an honourable conscience. She is just about twelve and saved me last night as I was about to drown. I was just minutes away to do so, not that you will care for that. Good riddance comes to mind. I understand how untrustworthy I have become to your eyes. But what happened yesterday, your punishment and meeting Margot made me comprehend a lot of things. It is too late, I know that. But can I recommend to you to keep an eye on that girl. Her father is violent and killed her mother. She sleeps under bridges because she is so scared of him. I believe she was abused by him. Please, look after her. Her only possession is a blanket under the old bridge. I believe she will end up dead if she is reunited with her father. I beg you to keep her away from him.

Coming from behind the reception desk, his arms still crossed upon his chest, the Master demanded,

-So you have decided to finally care about humans now that you are one?

Raphael intimidated by the approaching Raguel stood up and tried to step back but he was already the furthest he could be, and against the door. He trembled with fear helplessly but rallied up his courage to try to tease,

-You know I am not that good, Master, the generalisation doesn't apply here. I am just concerned about her because she saved me and by just about my own skin.

Raguel being now right in front of his enemy could feel Raphael's true fear of him. He asked with sarcasm,

-So is this the great amount that you comprehended over night? I am sure it must have taken a vast amount of effort in your part to consider having concern for one human and not just you. Bravo, I applaud you, you made one little step away from your narcissistic ego centrism and your belly button. By the way, you don't have to call me Master any longer, because your human brain needs to adapt that you don't belong anymore. You are all alone in this vast world. With your stinking attitude, I reckon you will not belong to any group of humans either. You may just call yourself a tramp that is only fit to live under bridges, Raphael River.

Raphael's head lowered with shame. He had a sad side glance towards the Great Being who was not missing anything of the exchange. He then said, his lips trembling,

-I want you both to know that I am sincerely sorry for everything. I am not asking for forgiveness because I know I will not get it but all I am saying is that I apologise for what I have done and the failure as an angel I have been.

An incensed Raguel retorted,

-Failure is an under estimation of what you were as an angel. Archangel shouldn't have been your title, never! You have been the crass of the angelic world, a murderous traitor, a fake, a scheming cheat, lowest of the low that is what you are, the maggot rotting any apple... You are lost, forever lost...

Margot came and intervened,

-Stop! Stop! I know enough to know what is going on. Mr angel of justice, I am ever so sorry to have brought that filthy individual under your nose. I didn't know the, the, depth, is it the word? Of his crimes. Let me remove him from your sight. He is bleeding all over the nice floor. How much is it to buy some bandages? I will work to get them. I will come later to clean that floor too. It was a big mistake to bring him here I am so sorry.

She turned to Raphael then told him,

-You, you are better be on your best behaviour, but you can share my bridge. The Sir over there allowed me to take two biscuits, so I will give you one for your lunch. Come with me, let me open the door for you. And just know that I don't want to hear a word from you because I am truly upset with you.

She turned the lock of the door open and ordered,

-Come on you, follow me, you despicable angel.

Margot courtesied and apologised,

-I am honestly sorry to have brought him here. I didn't know how bad he was. Thank you for the breakfast, Sir, it was most appreciated, and, and the fire, to let me sit by it.

Raphael bowed profoundly to Raguel then to the Great Being before following the young girl through the burnt street of Wilton Town. Raguel closed the door behind them before turning to his father with a smile to ask,

-What do you think of that? That Marguerite Bouchon is a right little character, isn't she? But upon my words, I never would have thought Raphael capable to ever say sorry.

His father stood up to look at the window and see the two on their way back to the old bridge, he answered,

-She is a tough but good hearted young girl. Faced by her simple human generosity will only be good to Raphael. We may in time even recover him. It depends of how long she survives. It depend on her free will. If she goes back to her father, she will most certainly die, be beaten to death. If she stays under the bridge this coming winter, Raphael will wake up one day, finding that she died of cold during her sleep.

Raguel commented with some emotion,

-Surely there must be another outcome for Marguerite.

The Great Being replied,

-Yes, there is. It involves you listening to the first wish, the first free will wish of the human Raphael. He asked for you to help that girl. He knows he can not at the moment in his state. You will have noticed that he didn't feel he was able to ask for anything for himself. Your punishment did hit home in his heart. He was honestly sorry. But I did sense his strong feeling of wanting to talk to you somehow. He thinks, he can't and that he isn't allowed to. But he wants to make up to you. You can go to him, you will have humble pie from him. If you ever give Raphael a hand, or show him a little kindness, he will be responsive to you. It may astonish you to finally see a honest Raphael, but as he is stripped of everything, this is what you will get. His heart still considers you as his Master.

Biting his lips, Raguel confessed,

-This is asking a lot from me. For the young girl, that is not a problem, I will step in to save her. For Raphael, I have only contempt and disgust for him. However I will give him a hand just for you and you only.

Sebastien came downstairs in the waiting room smiling as he announced,

-I think we managed to save Rose. Doctor Williams and Ivy will keep a good eye on her but I managed to stabilise her.

Then seeing the blood on the floor by the door, Sebastien grew worried and went straight to his father, taking both his hands within his, he demanded,

-Dad, what happened? Are you alright? Say something! I can smell archangelic blood. Did you fight a demon? Do you need me to tend to you? Straight away, come, in my consultation room, I will see to it.

Raguel felt the caring love of his son and felt so blessed to still have him. He gave a knowing look at his own father who told him what a good son Mighty was. He reassured,

-Mighty, it is not my blood. It is the one of archangel Raphael. He was here a few minutes ago. He offered his apologies.

Sebastien commented,

-For instigating the death of my older brother, and causing much more damage by his scheming, apologies are just a bit slim to my liking.

His father told sternly,

-To me as well, but do not forget that for someone as proud as him it is a first step. He just did recognise that he was wrong all along and for someone who thought he was always right, this is something to be considered. Do not forget, I punished him very severely last night. He is only human now, from the stumps of his wings that I did cut, he is losing all of his archangelic blood. It is a slow process and a painful one at that. I didn't expect him to survive his punishment at all. I told him that his life was in the hands of the generosity of humans when I threw him without the capacity to swim within the river.

A puzzled Sebastien enquired,

-But we evacuated the population of Wilton Town, yesterday. Who saved Raphael?

Raguel replied,

-We didn't round up everyone. As you know, we have some casualties and there was a missing young girl. She happens to live under the old bridge to escape her violent father. She saved Raphael from drowning. She has a good but tough temperament. Raphael actually showed some genuine concern for her welfare. Somehow he is still sentient. He told me he believes she has been abused by her father and asked me to look after her because otherwise she would be beaten to death like her mother was by her dad. The girl, who is named Marguerite, believe me or not, slapped Raphael twice in front of us in separate occasions. She was telling him off and he accepted it. It was astonishing to see. He followed her back to their bridge almost like a puppy.

Turning around, the Great Being added for the information of both his son and grandson who were Punishers,

-I was next to Margot and I briefly touched her hand

while giving her biscuits. Raphael is right, she has been abused by her father since the death of her mother. She is strong and courageous but she constantly lives in fear. She has no hopes whatsoever for her future. She suffered a dislocated jaw herself and did lodge it back in on her own. She didn't go to anyone about it because she is scared of her father but she still doesn't want him to be dealt with. She knows how to swim because her entire family was in a sinking ship. The father helped all of them to survive. Margot is a complicated case but if a human can show forgiveness, it is her. Raphael was not only saved by her yesterday, she fed him half of whatever she had which was not much. He was touched by that small gesture. She knew he couldn't feed himself, so she fed him like a small child. He could have cried of gratefulness at that moment in time but he retained his tears until she was fully asleep in her little corner under the bridge.

His son sighed deeply before he ordered,

-Mighty, where do you keep your bandages? I need to cut Raphael's wings properly. I wanted him to have a reminder of what he was, that would hurt his feelings so I left stumps upon him. I think we can remove them and make sure that his back heals with time. The process is not sightly and we need to wait for the young Marguerite to come back here. I don't want her to see what we will do to him, even if it will help him in the end. She said she will come back to clean the floor of the clinic by the door.

His father told,

-I can keep her busy here until you two sort Raphael out. Margot badly needs to be fed, I don't think she will refuse a little something after having cleaned the mess by the door. Raguel, stay and deal with the reception until she comes back. Mighty, prepare all the medical equipments you will need to deal with Raphael. I will remind both of you that he is now human and that he hasn't got angelic strength any longer. If he dies under your hands, he will go straight to hell, but we are all agreeing that we are giving him a slim chance to redeem himself if he can. As for me I will fix something to eat for Margot and a basket of food she can take with her when she leaves from here later on.

Already gathering bits and pieces and putting them in his satchel, Sebastien advised,

-Granddad, you will find all you need in the little garden at the back of the clinic which belongs to Doctor Valdi. My Ivy, my Jack and I have been tending it whenever we had time.

Vincent's hens must have given some eggs which will be ready to be collected. With some of our potatoes, our lettuce and some hard boiled eggs, you can prepare a nice salad for Margot. I will help you as soon as I have finished to prepare my satchel.

All of them didn't have to wait too long to see Marguerite Bouchon enter the clinic once more. This time she was unaccompanied. Only a couple of hours had passed. Raguel behind his reception desk was ever so pleased internally to see her stepping in. She addressed him straight away with some politeness,

-I am coming to clean the bloody mess the bad angel left on the floor, Mr the angel of justice. Again I am so sorry for earlier, I was so embarrassed. If I ever knew what he had done, I would have never coaxed him that he needed to be seen to for all his injuries. I managed to get employment to pay for the bandages. Will you accept part payment, or payment little bit by little bit?

The Master liked the spirited girl he had in front of him. She was so poor, grieving, but so strong at the same time. He replied,

-We will strike a deal by a repayment, little bit by little bit. Forgive me to say this but I didn't think you would ever come back.

An offended Marguerite answered strongly,

-When I give my word, I give it truly Mr angel, it maybe Margot's word but it is as good as any since I abide by it and make sure it is done.

Raguel couldn't help smiling despite himself as he enquired,

-I didn't mean to be disobliging. So you said you did find some work to pay for the bandages. May I ask which kind of work?

Margot looking at the large stain of blood on the floor by the door replied almost casually,

-Farm work. The kind Mr Berry is employing me to milk his cows twice a day. I will get two pints of milk everyday on top of my salary. I have a second mouth to feed now since you've broken the arms of your bad angel, he is pretty useless as a human. Where can I get water, Mr angel of justice? I think this stain is going to be a hard one to remove. But I done it before, so I know I can do it.

The Master knew straight away that she had been cleaning the floor after the death of her mother and felt extreme sadness for the young girl. He answered,

-You will find water in the back garden. My father will be there to help you. See at the end of this hallway, this is the door leading to the garden.

He warned by telepathy everyone about the presence of Margot while she followed his instructions to go to the garden. Doctor Williams was soon behind the reception desk, by him, saying,

-I will look after the clinic for you, Master.

His son came next with a full satchel and announced,

-I am ready to go with you, dad.

Raguel ordered,

-Then let's do it. Come with me. Let's check what a fallen angel under a bridge looks like.

#

Arriving at the old bridge, Raguel and his son spotted Raphael crouched upon himself in visible pain. The fallen angel, his head nestled within his knees, crying didn't see them coming until they were about a couple of metres from him and Raguel told,

-Here is the maggot!

The stern voice of the Master recalled Raphael from his tearful daze. When he realised that the two punishing angels were coming towards him, great fear settled in his heart as well as a sense of hopelessness. He made the fast decision to kill himself by throwing himself into the river. It prompted Sebastien to comment,

-I don't want to know what you did to him yesterday, father, but you certainly scared the shit out of him.

Raguel retorted,

-Look who is talking! Oops, the human Darren Bell dies of a cardiac arrest in my hands while I am punishing him!

His son complained,

-That's not fair! I didn't know that human had a weak heart. If we have to play comparisons I spooked a human to death last night, yes, but you, you managed to scare the living daylight of an archangel that used to be an excellent warrior. That is a proper suicidal stunt he is pulling in front of us. We'd better go and get him.

Their wings appeared on their backs. Raguel smirking teased,

-Do we really have to? We can let him struggle in the water a little longer.

Putting his satchel on the ground, Sebastien scolded,

-Dad! You broke both of his arms. He can not swim. What happened with the giving him a little sliver of chance? Was it to sound good in front of grandpa?

It was enough for Raguel to start flying where the struggling Raphael was. He was closely followed by his son. Yet, they continued their conversation, with the Master telling to Mighty,

-Grandpa is fond of the S-word, that's why that rotten angel is being given a chance.

Sebastien asked as they arrived by Raphael,

-What would that be?

Together, father and son, pulled Raphael out of the strong current of the river while Raguel replied,

-That scumbag managed to say sorry.

They flew together back to the banks under the bridge carrying a fearful Raphael. They threw the fallen angel on the river bank rather than depositing him kindly. Sebastien stood back slightly leaving the talk to Raphael to his father. The angel of justice lost no time at all to tell off the fallen angel,

-Have you lost your mind as well as your wings, Raphael? You sold your soul, a suicide is your straight trip to hell right in the hands of Lucifer. If you ever think he will be kind to you, let me tell you that you are stupid and totally misguided. For your information, Lucifer is the whistle-blower who warned my father and us the two Punishers of your traitorous plans and the ones of Michael. He gave us a hand yesterday as well and I can tell you he was extremely joyous to take Michael to hell when my father handed him over to him. If you think Michael will have a pleasure ride in hell, you live under an illusion. Let me warn you that the deepest wish, ambition of Lucifer is to be a Punisher of angels and not only of humans. He wants to be like my son and I. And there is a little technicality which will ensure a rough ride for you in hell, you are now human. But you can stay deluded and imagine that Lucifer will be your best friend down there.

A shivering and wet Raphael looked at the Master and stepped backward from him. Fear in his throat, he asked,

-You punished me already, why are you both here?

Sebastien opened his satchel and showed some bandages to him as his father told firmly,

-Do you remember what I said yesterday that you were left to the generosity of humans? Young Marguerite got an employment at the farm of Mr Berry in order to pay for your medical care, bit by bit. We are here to deliver that care. I am going to do a cleaner job on your stumps, remove them completely so it will allow you to heal instead of them rotting slowly on your back, which will give you an infection that would eventually kill you. Sebastien will look after your arms and put some cast on them so they will mend over time. Come and be looked after, and yes, you have already been punished.

Trembling, looking at the hand tended to him by the Master of all angels, Raphael went towards it in a shy way. Raguel scolded,

-Faster, I haven't got all the time in the world, I am a rather busy archangel, if you don't remember. As for you, you were a good archangelic warrior at one time. I expect you to be a bit more brave than that. As I said we are not here to kill you, we are here to help you a little. Sit down and present me your back.

The fallen angel finally did. He sat by the Master, who straight away took the wet and bloodied shirt with care from the former angel. Raguel warned,

-It will hurt but it is essential that I do it, human. It will allow you to heal as I said. Stay still and be brave for me.

Raphael cried throughout the all process not because

he was in pain which he was in, but because he knew he was now fully human with nothing to remind him of his past as an angel. When the last of his stomp was cleanly removed, he told Raguel sobbing,

-I am ever so sorry for all I did to you. Would you ever task me like if I was still one of your angels?

The Master threw the bleeding stomps in the river as he replied,

-Your apologies are not accepted, Raphael. I lost my eldest son because of you. You will never be treated as an angel by me ever again. However I will give you a chance as a human. Show me if you can make your human life count. If you repent properly throughout it, I may, just may consider to try to reclaim the soul you sold because of your hatred of humans. But you will have to be working very hard for it, well, let me change that to extremely hard for it. I do not know if you are even prepared to do so because, let me tell you, that I simply don't trust you.

Sebastien who was disinfecting the back of Raphael diligently proposed,

-Look human, the town you are now in has been partly burnt overnight. The inhabitants will need help to reconstruct it before winter. You can start to make your human life count here. But it will be probably an excruciating thing for you to do who is allergic to humans.

Despite himself, it made the fallen angel smile. He commented wryly,

-With two broken arms, how can I be of help?

Raguel retorted sternly,

-When there is a will, there is a way. But with the like of you, my crawling maggot, you will find it difficult to figure out that you are now human and not a pretentious archangel anymore. You can stay a tramp under a bridge by all means, it is a clever thing to do instead of helping humanity. You can use something else apart from your arms, your brain. You, that is so used to scheming, I thought you would know how to use it, but there again you were played with beautifully by Lucifer.

Raphael deeply sighed as he made another paltry excuse with emotion,

-But I don't know anyone here.

Sebastien corrected Raphael when he bandaged him,

-Stop being a Prima Donna! You do know some people in Wilton Town. First, you did manage to get acquainted to that young girl, Marguerite Bouchon, so you know how to talk to people, so my only advice is for you to keep practising being sociable to other humans. Then you know my father who is taking on the role of sheriff in this little town. Sure, he doesn't like you a great deal with good reason and I don't think you will be able to chat about the weather with him any time soon but if you are in trouble or if you happen to know of someone in trouble, go to him, he will listen. If it is for someone else than you, he will act, as for you it will all depend of your circumstances. Then there is me who is the surgeon in this town, whom you instigated to kill with your pal who ended up in hell last night, Michael. Yet, you see me today, looking after your wounds. This is the difference between a good angel and a bad one, a good one cares. Now if you don't want to care about your fellow human beings in this town, you are free to do so, just like you are free to get lost and go anywhere you want in this earth.

Considering everything that has been said, the fallen angel asked,

-Will you talk to me if I stay in this town? What can I do to help?

Mighty gave his father a knowing glance as he was finishing off fastening the bandages at the back of Raphael. They knew then that they had made some progress with the fallen angel at his questions. So Sebastien replied to Raphael in a firm tone continuing to work on his physical body but also on his mindset,

-Raphael, what have I been doing for the past few minutes if not talking to you. Look, here, we will not be best friends but I will never ignore you and if you need help, you can come to me. If you need to talk, I will be here for you. I work at the clinic and I have a little back garden behind the presbytery where I live with a bench. It is very private. Whenever you feel the need to talk, confide, confess, say sorry, you can go there, sit on that bench or even sleep on it and I will come to you. You can't knock on the door of my house, because you will not be invited there. You will be refused entry point blank. My father is guarding my house. Now, let me tell you that your friend Michael, nearly killed my adoptive boy last night, Jack, who is a fallen angel turned human just like you. I had to operate on him with my wife to save his life. I will never forget that and I am not ready to forgive yet what happened last night. So your only points of communication with me, if you need me, are my back garden and the waiting room in my clinic. Now tell me why is it important for you to talk to me? May I remind you that you plotted to kill me, my wife, my Jack, Doctor Williams and succeeded to kill my eldest brother Gael.

With a heavy heart, Raphael told, tears in his eyes,

-I am extremely sorry for what I have done to both of you. I didn't know you adopted a fallen angel turned human.

Raguel vented,

-You wouldn't know because you only cared about yourself, Raphael, let's be honest here. Now, answer my son, why is it important for you to talk to him?

Looking at Sebastien who was applying a cast to one of his arms, the fallen angel replied with emotion,

-Because he makes angels out of humans.

The Master of all angels came straight away to confront Raphael lifting his chin in order to make him look at him straight in the eyes,

-Do you Maggot entertain a dream to be an angel again? You can carry on dreaming. It will never happen. First, you have been found disloyal to my father. Second, you have shown a total lack of morals. Third, your vanity stinks. Fourth, last but not least, your hate of humanity goes against the very creation of my father. Just try to be a good human so I can get back your soul but forget to be an angel ever again. Who would want an undermining traitor in their ranks, especially you who considered human angels like a disgrace and crass and undertook to kill them? Your lack of respect is atrocious. Now that you are a human, the idea of angels made from humans sounds appealing, doesn't it? You lost your very wings because you killed my first son for creating human angels. How pathetic are you? It's unbelievable.

Raguel dropped the chin he was holding with disgust. Raphael sighed deeply taking the blame laid at his door in. Sebastien having finished the cast on one arm went to the other one told in a soothing voice,

-Just try to be a good human. You do know the good old saying of taking one step at a time, don't you? Right, your left arm will mend quite nicely in about four to five weeks. You have to bare in mind as you are no longer an angel any healing will take much more time. For your right arm, I have to put the upper bone back into position, into a proper alignment. This will hurt. Are you ready?

The fallen angel nodded positively and Sebastien proceeded. Raphael did not cry, nor shouted, he just took the pain in. As the Mighty One started to cast that arm, Raphael asked,

-What can I do to help the people of this town? Just tell me, order me anything, I am your servant.

The Master turned to correct him, his arms crossed upon his chest,

-You are no one's servant for no one wants you as one. Lack of trust you see. No, Raphael, you are your own man now. You can do what you want. If you want to help go to the church tomorrow and ask to see Father Odell. He is in charge of the reconstruction of the town. He has been creating teams. He will assign you to one of them upon your capacities. Your main skill is scheming but just tell him that you have a sense of organisation instead. You are good at persuading angels to do the worst, maybe you can be good at persuading people to work toward a greater good. Just try to sell yourself for what you are worth. But know that there is no money involved, so if you want a roof above your head, you will have to find another employment on top of that community effort. Right, Sebastien, are you done with the Maggot?

His son told as he helped Raphael to stand up,

-Almost, dad.

He made a shirt appear in his hands and covered the torso of Raphael with it, cutting and rolling the sleeves in order to adapt it to the two casts Raphael had on his arms. Taking the time to button the shirt up, Sebastien said to Raphael,

-Come to me in three weeks time to check your arms. As for your back, if you come weekly or twice weekly at the clinic, it will be better. As for paying work, I know a sheep farmer, Mr Yards, who broke a leg. He needs help to take his flock in the pasture every morning and back every evening. Now, just rest. Tomorrow is another day.

The Master made a blanket appear and gave it to Raphael before his son and him went away. As they walk through town back to the clinic, Sebastien enquired,

-Why did you keep calling him maggot? I never saw you so mean.

His father replied sternly,

-This is how he used to call our Williams for centuries. Raphael didn't complain because he knows it is part of his punishment. He demeaned a lot of human angels, calling them by degrading names.

Nonetheless Sebastien commented,

-I know we both don't like him for good reasons but have you seen his thankful eyes to us before we departed when you gave him a cover. I heard him whispering thank you Master with some emotion.

Raguel scolded his son,

-Mighty, your problem as a Punisher is that you were born with an excellent forgiving heart not unlike the one of your grandfather. I heard Raphael as well but I didn't acknowledge him for the simple reason that it is no use for him to show me some respect now when he has lost all of my respect.

Arriving at the clinic, Sebastien opened the door to his father and reminded him,

-We have to give him a sliver of a chance, Dad. Your heard grandpa.

The Great Being welcomed them from behind the counter of the clinic,

-Speaking of me? How did it go?

Raguel going straight to the reception desk, putting both hands on it in a firm manner briefed,

-Not speaking of you, no, Mighty was just mentioning you. It went rather well. Where is the young Margot?

His father replied with a smile,

-She has already left the building, about five minutes ago, with a basket which I prepared that will give her food for her and Raphael to share tonight. Marguerite went to the farm of Mr Berry to help him with his dairy cows. She wanted to go early so she could go back to her bridge before sunset. Margot had lunch with Ivy and I after she cleaned the floor by the main door, so she was fed.

Ivy coming in the waiting room and picking up on the conversation, readjusting her sleeves, commented,

-Marguerite is such a brave girl. She was so hardworking and polite in her funny little way. She didn't leave until she had cleaned the dishes of the lunch with us, she said it was her manner to say thank you for the meal.

A thoughtful Raguel told,

-We must find her a home. I will pick her up from the farm and walk with her to her bridge to unsure she is safe crossing the forest at dusk. I will have a good conversation with her then to convince her to be re-homed.

Ivy announced in a shy way, twisting her hands together,

-Sebastien, I know we have only small means, and we adopted our Jack and I have a baby on the way, but if you would consider taking on board that young girl, making our home, her new home, I would love it. She would then lodge in the same home of two Punishers and surely it should protect her from the worst from her father.

Coming to his wife, Sebastien held her in a fashion where he could feel the baby inside her, before he announced,

-Pa, my Ivy has spoken. Bring Margot to our home. We will look after her together.

Raguel nodded positively and said with a winning smile,

-Then I will bring her home tonight.

Before he left his father demanded,

-Raguel, why did it went just rather well with Raphael?

The Master of all angels replied reluctantly,

-When he saw us, Raphael tried to kill himself. His fear was great. You can imagine that I didn't go easy on him yesterday night. I expected him to die afterwards and not to be saved by a human. However we rescued him in time from his suicide attempt and like you said we dealt with a very subdued Raphael. Mighty will give you all the particulars. I will see you all tonight.

When Raguel was gone, the Great Being asked his grandson,

-Will you be less elusive than him? Come and let me do you a cup of tea, Mighty. Ivy would you be ever so kind to man the reception desk?

Ivy gave him a smile with a small obliging courtesy and her answer,

-You can count on me.

Leading the way to the kitchen upstairs, the Great Being told his grandson in confidence,

-You have chosen such an excellent wife, Mighty. So, tell me more, how is Raphael?

When they arrived in the kitchen, Doctor Williams joined them and started to prepare the tea for all of them. Sebastien briefed,

-Raphael is very emotional to say the least. Being demoted in such a way did hit his mind and heart very hard. My Lord, I can tell you that what my Pa did to him worked. But I still think it is a work in progress. We need Raphael to adjust as a human first of all. When I touched him to mend him, I could feel and see that he was struggling with it all. My father was so harsh with him but he accepted everything without complaint. I can tell you that Raphael is truly sorry, that he wants to make up to us, but he had no clues how to do so. He even had a wish to be an angel again, but a human angel of course, which was crushed by my father who told him to be a good human first of all.

Williams putting the tea on the table to let it brew commented,

-I know this would have been the reaction of the Master. He surely was offended by it as well. A demoted angel usually don't ask to get back his wings the following day. But we are talking of Raphael, who never had a sense of proportions.

The Great Being smiled widely at his input only to add,

-True, but it shows willingness. Mighty, do you think there is hope for Raphael?

Fiddling with his empty cup of tea, Sebastien replied with honesty,

-I truly do not know. I am mitigated about that one. Raphael is a difficult case to deal with and solve. We did made progress with him this afternoon. It is up to Raphael now to start to be a good human. He hurts, he is pretty much down and under, and at rock bottom really. We had to save him from killing himself, as we said earlier. My dad took a strong stance on him but I think Raphael needs that to be corrected properly. However, I saw in him glimmer of hope that we could retrieve him as an angel at some point in the future. First, Pa will have to get back Raphael's soul and he said he would do so if Raphael makes himself count as a good human. This is the first stepping stone. However my dad told Raphael to not hope nor dream about getting his wings back.

Serving the tea to everyone, Doctor Williams commented again,

-Well, your father doesn't want a traitor in your army in that case. The Master is just being protective of you. He already lost one son, and he also nearly lost his own life at the hands of Raphael who faked healing him. If Raphael passes away, and goes wherever he earns to go but not to your army, it will appease the concern of your father.

Sebastien told while he held his cup of tea and was about to drink it,

-This is what I think. My father has suffered emotionally too much at the hands of Raphael to deal with him fairly. However he is the best one to do so. He is aware of the trickery Raphael is capable of.

The Great Being, putting sugar in his own tea, answered in a commending way,

-Raphael is a case for all of us to deal with. We can all have our input into it. But for my son to be willing to retrieve the soul of that angel shows that he cares about what happens to him despite whatever Raphael did to him. Like you said Mighty, the situation will be a work in progress with Raphael but I will add, with Raguel also. He is intensely protective because he lost so many he loved. I am sure you will understand that because you also suffered heavy losses during your first human life.

Sebastien replied with emotion,

-I do. But let me tell you what I did not expect this afternoon: I saw my father giving a blanket to Raphael. It did move Raphael a fair bit and he keeps calling my father Master although my dad doesn't want him to do so, telling him that he doesn't belong any longer.

Sitting at the table Williams interpreted thoughtfully,

-If the Master gave him a blanket, it is very symbolic. It is like telling to someone that they are still under their wings. A cover means that you will protect them if they fall into hardship. Your father will recover that angel in one way or another but it is up to Raphael to do the hard work.

Serving Doctor Williams, the Great Being stated with a smile,

-That would be my Raguel at work. He will give Raphael a hard time, yes, but he will offer him a life line down the line. Hopefully Raphael would have learnt his lesson by then.

While the discussion was going on at the clinic, the Master passed by the hotel of Miss White to check on the situation there. Whilhelmina welcomed him with an anxious face,

-Is Theo alright? He hasn't come back since dawn.

Raguel briefed her,

-We had some casualties in town, yesterday night. Father Odell is only performing his duties as a priest doing their funerals. He has also been tasked to rally the people together to rebuilt the part of town which has been burnt. He will come back home to you, probably exhausted. Make sure you have a nice supper ready for him.

Whilhelmina sighed deeply as she enquired,

-How many are dead?

Presenting his arm to her, the Master replied,

-Come with me and let's have a little talk in your garden.

Miss White put her shawl on and followed him willingly, her pale hand resting within his strong arm. She listened attentively as he told her, while leading her in her garden,

-There were three dead, last night. One was an inhabitant from the town, one came from Boston and was working to build the new bridge, the last one was the one who caused the fire in town, Darren Bell. The gang has been entirely dealt with. However they caught a woman of low virtue because she didn't have any resources, called Rose who is between life and death. They raped her repeatedly in an atrocious way. My Sebastien managed to stabilise her but, if she survives, she can do with the moral support that you could give her, because you have been through a similar situation back in the days. Come to town to meet her tomorrow at the clinic. She is in a pretty bad state. Doctor Williams thinks that she may survive after the intervention of Sebastien but he is staying by her just in case.

The white witch reassured him straight away,

-I will go and see her. You can count on me.

Raguel smiled before adding,

-She is from Boston and has been made destitute by the gangs there. If you can learn any information from her, come and tell me. I have to deal with the Boston situation which is festering badly. Secondly, I may require your advice for a very young girl of twelve who has been abused by her father. Her father did beat her mother to death and abused her ever since. She escaped and lives under a bridge. My son and his wife are willing to home her. But she has a strong character, one that doesn't accept charity willingly. However if she meets her father again, she will be killed, and if she stays under the bridge, she will die this winter. My angel Ted who has visions do not see a future for her which is alarming. However my father said there was a third option and that would be me helping her out. I am going to pick her up from the farm of Mr Berry to walk her back to town safely and convince her to live at the presbytery.

Whilhelmina enquired,

-You are talking about Daisy Cork who was amongst missing last night? So she made it.

As they walked together under the white rose tunnel, the archangel confirmed,

-She did. Margot is a brave human being.

Miss White confided, as pale as her roses,

-I know she is. Last year, Doctor Valdi and I had to tend to her. She gave birth to a still born child at just eleven with great difficulties. We managed to save her. Valdi battered her father for it, very severely. I guess that with the news of Valdi gone on his honeymoon, her father may have raped her again.

And yes, if she falls pregnant, he will kill her to hide what he did to her. That man, her father is an evil drunkard. No wonder she went to live under a bridge, poor thing.

This made the Master sigh deeply with great sadness. He reacted straight away,

-I must go and get her. Please, Whil', I want to know how the human victims are doing. Use telepathy with me, and keep me informed. How is Amelia doing with the book?

Whilhelmina answered,

-Great progress since Vincent came back by her side. When she saw him alive and in one piece, she soldiered on with renewed vigour. Her anxiety lifted all at once. I am not going to tell you how they greeted one another, but it was very moving.

Raguel scolded her,

-Miss White, you can not tease me like that. I want to know, now. Hold my hand so I can see what you saw.

The white witch obliged the archangel who smiled blissfully as he commented after his vision,

-Those two are definitely a perfect match, just like you and Theo. You must prepare something to eat for Theo. He will be exhausted when he will come back here. His favourite dish is sausages, onion gravy and mash potatoes. When you step into your kitchen, you will find all the ingredients necessary for it on the table courtesy from the Master of all angels. Your future husband is my newest angel but I must say, he has conquered the hearts of all angels, they would all give their lives for him. Tomorrow, I will unite you both. Get prepared. You will find your wedding dress on your bed. It is a magical dress so you can wish all the alteration to it to make it the one you really want. Doctor Williams is already on the coach with Mina, Georgia and Emily bringing them back. They had all a great time in Boston. Emily has her glasses. Mina saw the sea and Georgia, well, she fell deeply in love with my William and we will have to both cope with it, I guess.

He kissed the hand of Miss White gallantly, then clapped his hands to repair the destroyed white roses of the witch before he asked,

-How are my injured angels doing?

Whilhelmina reassured him,

-Maurice is doing really well, so well he has been helping us all night with everyone and he is still up. He is such a soldier. Lawrence is pulling through. What Valdi did with him, worked. Vincent checked all of your angels when he arrived, giving them medicine and changing bandages. Daniel's state did not deteriorate but I would say, he could do with another good talk. The loss of his leg is clearly depressing him. He will need monitoring day in and out, not because of his leg but because of what he could do to himself. He just needs to learn to cope with his injury. It is early days but those early days are crucial.

Coming outside of the tunnel Raguel with a worried face said,

-I will send my father and my Williams to talk to Daniel tonight. Be prepared to receive them. By the way both have wedding surprises for you. So my present is the magical wedding dress but you have to wait for theirs. Now tell me, how have you been coping tonight with all that pressure?

Miss White confided,

-Pretty well, and I didn't have my Georgia or my Mina by my side. I have been extremely busy, yes, but I managed it all with Maurice, Max and the excellent Mrs Toad. I actually spoke to her about becoming a nurse. You know she is definitely set on marrying Mr Berry and therefore living in Wilton Town, just like Sebastien wanted her to do. I told her about the plan to create a hospital for the town and seeing her great care, patience, and nurturing nature all night, I think she would make a perfect nurse for it. I can teach her everything I know. The thing is she is very willing. Her answer was a resounding yes. Apart from that, to be honest with you, I was anxious each time I went outdoors and saw part of the town burning down the hills. But when I received almost all the inhabitants, I felt a bit of relief. Counting the heads with my Theo felt like: one is safe, and one more, and one more... But of course there were the missing ones and Theo, Matthias and Henry went back in the burning town to find them. I haven't heard from Theo since and I have been anxious for him.

Putting his arm across her shoulders in a paternal fashion, the Master stated,

-You did extremely well. I am glad you spotted the skills of Mrs Toad. This is good to know. Remember keep in contact with me for everything and anything. You can think of me as your good genie in a magic lantern and your confidant. As for your Theo, let me reassure you once more that he is well, but just very busy. You should have seen how he rallied those downhearted people at the tavern. His speech to form teams to rebuilt the part of the town that was destroyed went down a storm of applause. The plan for the reconstruction of the town has been devised mainly by Abraham Wilton-Cough. He knows the town and its inhabitants by heart. I need you to make him physical for much longer. You must find a solution for him and me, for it is my will. Abraham is ever so useful, I can not even start to tell you. Render him invisible to the people who do not know he is a ghost. But I want him, I need him in the logistic team of the angelic army of my son.

The white witch smiled to the Master as she commented,

-It sounds like you have been stung by the hardworking bee that was Abraham Wilton-Cough. He gets under your skin yet you can't help admiring him, and his self sacrificing ways. During his life, I liked the man and his tough ethic. Well, I knew where he came from, his family background and how he was brought up, poor little thing. He was unloved by his own parents. Yet, he never gave up and did something of himself and something good for the town. Yes, I will work on that spell for you and for him. If you get to speak to him before I do, send him my regards.

A satisfied Raguel walked toward the ruins of the Ogin cottage with her,

-Most certainly, but you will see him before me because he is back within Vincent. I agree with you Abraham gets under your skin but I still want his spirit to work for the angels forever. Let me tell you, that he protected my younger brother, Vincent and a very injured angel Rob against archangel Raphael who had sold his soul to the devil and was about to drown them yesterday night. Rob who had been very severely burnt, set on fire by Darren Bell, had been looked after by Vincent who plunged with him to the river. You know Doctor Valdi, for longer than I do. He did an emergency rescue on Rob and we have good hope that my injured angel will recover well due to Vincent intervention. Now, Raphael had a plan with Michael to kill all of the healing angels yesterday night, as if we didn't have enough to deal with, with the gang and the fire in town but I think this was used as a distraction. I just need to get to the bottom of the affair at some point, but I think I am not wrong that the fire in town was a diversion. Anyhow to come back to Abraham, he jumped out of Vincent to fight with the archangelic warrior Raphael, giving precious time for Vincent to take himself and Rob out of the water of the river to save their skins. What I have to say for Abraham as I arrived just in time on the scene, is that he was fearless and so protective. In my heart, he saved the lives of Rob and brother last night. Of course he does not know how to fight, but his pestering was sufficient.

Whilhelmina facing the dilapidated walls of the cottage, concerned, told,

-It sounds like you had quite a night in town, all of your angels and you. Is the problem with the archangels resolved?

Sitting on the stone wall and asking her to take a seat by his side, Raguel informed her,

-Yes, it is resolved, as far as I know. But there are more archangels and I do not know how many have been perverted by the schemes of Raphael. You are in danger as well as all of my healing angels. Apart from me, I do not want you to accept any archangel in this hotel at the moment. If I give you the all clear on them, it will be fine but be on your guard until I say so. Stay safe for Theo and me, Miss White. I do not know if you have heard but Michael wanted to reap out the heart of Doctor Williams, do the same to Jack, then take the baby out of Ivy before killing her by removing her heart too. Sebastien arrived just in time to prevent this to happen however Jack was stabbed during the fight while Williams dragged the pregnant Ivy to safety. Our Jack is alright. We saved him but it took a long operation. I do not want you to open your door to any archangel apart from me for the time being. Do you understand? This is for your security.

Miss White agreed, then the Master continued,

-Lucifer came twice in town last night, helping out but we always have to bare in mind that he has double standards. I need you to protect your entire property against him. His manuscript is here. It puts everyone here in great danger. You need to work out a spell to keep him out of your property. My Father and my Williams will come tonight to deal with Daniel's case, but they will help you to secure the hotel. Just find the right spell, and find it fast. When Lucifer is out and about, it is no laughing matter. You have been warned. If you ever see him, give me a telepathic message and I will be right by your side to protect you. He is a smooth talker so do not discuss with him, just think of one thing only, which is that you will be a prey to him. So as soon as you see him, tell me. Have we got an understanding?

Whilhelmina could only agree again, then Raguel stood up, kissed her hand before he said casually,

-I have to pick up the young Marguerite. Keep in touch Miss White, keep in touch. I hope you will like your wedding dress but as it is from me, it may lack the feminine touches here and there. My Williams can show you how to alter the magic dress at your will. He always has a few tricks up his sleeves to make things better.   I will see you tomorrow and have the great honour to unite you to Theo. Take care until then. By the way, plant this entire area between those ruined walls with flowers and ferns. Close properly its dark chapter. Again my Williams is a bit of a botanist and can advise you on the choice of plants for this specific area and type of ground in your garden. But from me here is your first plant: a Boston fern. And with that I must say goodbye until tomorrow.

He offered the potted plant who magically appeared within his hands to Miss White with a bright smile then left. Miss White planted it straight away before going back to her hotel to find a spell against Lucifer. She went to the small private parlour where Amelia was with her husband decoding the manuscript of Lucifer, she begged,

-Amelia, I need to protect you and this entire house against Lucifer. He has been seen in town twice yesterday night. He has been helping but he is like a sword with a double edge. Try to find if he wrote in his manuscript how to defeat fallen angels or even better archangel.

Amelia adjusted her glasses immediately saying, turning pages of the manuscript very quickly,

-There is almost a chapter about that. Let me transcribe that to you, it will take me about half an hour to a good hour.

Valdi putting his hands on the shoulders of his wife adjusting her shawl told,

-I will help you with all my might my little bit. We will translate everything together.

Popping out of Vincent, the zealous Abraham Wilton-Cough proposed his services as well,

-I can help!

But Miss White revealed to him,

-I am glad to see you, Mr Wilton-Cough. I heard that you have been extremely helpful already yesterday. So helpful in fact that the Master of all angels as demanded of me a special spell concerning you. Come with me, I will tell you all about it

Abraham. But just let me tell you that you have impressed that major angel big time. There will be no Rest in Peace for you, Raguel wants you to work for the angels full time. Come, so I can sort you out immediately. It will not take long, then you will be able to offer your help to the Valdi couple.

A slightly emotional Abraham took his top hat off, and turned it within his hands shyly, and asked for confirmation,

-Really?

Whilhelmina smiled kindly to the ghost, put her fair arm under his, and repeated as she led him away from the room,

-Yes, really, he said he wanted you, then corrected himself, he said he needed you in the logistic team of the army of his son. That means you will work under the angel called Ted like our little group of Wiltonians, Theo, Valdi, Amelia and me.

#

While the white witch was dealing with all her orders from the Master of all angels, Raguel was ringing the old brass bell at the gate of the farm of Mr Berry. The good natured dairy farmer came, half running, half walking, and welcomed,

-Raguel, it is a pleasure to see you. How is the situation in town now? I was thinking to bring part of my milk to all the homeless people still at the hotel, kindly homed by Miss White, part of it to the poorer part of town who have damaged roofs, and the third part to the canteen that will be established at the tavern that will feed the workers and all afflicted by the fire. I am bringing to all of them some butter too. I hope it will smooth a little everyone's spirit up. What do you think?

As the farmer showed his carriage which was three quarter full, the Master approved,

-I think it is a good idea. Not only that, it is generous of you to do so. All the fires in town have been extinguished. Most of the inhabitants are back in their homes but in a state of shock, I must say. I must also thank you for your tremendous help you provided to keep all the animals safe in the tavern of Tyrell and for looking after them over night. How are you coping? Are you not tired?

Walking alongside Raguel towards his stables, Anthony Berry replied,

-I am tired but my rest can wait. Beside that, I had help

today to deal with all of my cows. The young Daisy Cork asked me if I could give her some work and I did. She is efficient and hard working. I am taking her on as a farm hand. May I tell you something, something privately, out of ear shot?

The Master stopped walking, and paid more attention to the human farmer who twisted his cap in his hands, he answered,

-You can tell me anything of course, Anthony. Know that I am a sheriff in this town from now on.

Anthony looked anxiously to his stables, then confided in a low voice,

-Well, I think her father is a horrible drunkard. I think he battered her recently. When she rolled her sleeves to milk my cows, the colour of her arms was not what it should be. Listen, the poor thing have just patches of white on her arms, the rest is black, blue and green. I retained my tears when I was working beside her. I think she needs to be seen to by your son, or his wife who is a Doctor. Daisy is a head strong little thing, and I don't think she will tell easily what happened to her but I can tell you that something very bad happened to her recently. It is painful to see.

Raguel replied in a same tone of confession,

-Anthony, we have been made aware of her situation. She has been sleeping under a bridge at least for a good couple of days, escaping the home of her violent father. My son and his wife are going to take her under their roof. I am going to take the little thing there before the sunset. That is why I came to pick her up. We will let her carry on working for you because I think she needs that incentive in her life. We think that she dropped school. Come, lead me to her.

Mr Berry took the angel to his barn and he announced to the young girl who was milking his last cow,

-Daisy, there is someone to pick you up to walk you back to town.

Margot fell from her stool and went to hide behind the cow straight away. But then she looked above the back of the cow and saw the Master of all angels, she sighed deeply, and confessed,

-I thought it was going to be my dad.

She came forward in apologetic manner adding,

-I hope I didn't drop any of your good milk Mr Berry. You can take any spillage out of my wages.

The farmer reassured her,

-You only dropped the stool kiddo, no worries there. It is time for you to go home. I took the liberty to put a couple of pints of milk in your basket and here are your proper wages. Now come back tomorrow around ten in the morning.

Accepting her wages with a smile and thanks, she then went to Raguel,

-I never would have expected you here, Mr angel of justice.

Seeing her tidy pigtails again brought an irresistible giggle on Raguel's face as he said,

-No, you wouldn't have. I had to go and check many human victims at Miss White's hotel. I thought you could use a walking companion to go through the forest when it starts getting dark. As where you were was not far from where I was, I decided to pick you up: pure kindness. Pick up your basket and let's go.

Margot did so without a word of contest. She said farewell to Mr Berry and followed the angel.When they were far away from the farm, Raguel looking at her arms demanded,

-Margot, you can talk to me. I am an angel. I can see your colourful forearms. Tell me what happened? Why do you have to live under a bridge?

The young girl put her basket on the ground and rolled her sleeves down. She pleaded,

-I don't want to speak about it, please.

Raguel took the rough approach, took her basket from the ground and told her,

-That's fine with me because I already know what happened. Come. You will not return to your father. I found a home for you which is better than living under a bridge.

He had the interest of Margot straight away who had tears in her eyes, she asked shyly,

-Where would I be wanted?

The Master replied presenting her his hand,

-My home, the home of my son and his wife. We are offering you a roof.

The young Margot grabbed his hand kissed it and cried. The Master felt emotional and hugged the young girl as he told her,

-We will look after you, Marguerite. No more fear for you my child. We will protect you.

She dried her tears bravely, but she replied firmly,

-I still have to live under the bridge.

Raguel was amazed by her response and demanded,

-Why? We are offering you a roof and protection.

Margot, picking berries, hazelnuts and chestnuts and putting them in her basket which Raguel was holding, explained,

-Raphael can't feed himself. I have to live under the bridge until he can.

Intrigued by her response, the Master enquired,

-Did he put any pressure on you, Marguerite?

She corrected him strongly,

-No, he didn't. Please, call me, Margot. He is despondent at the moment. I am really worried for him.

Starting picking up berries and nuts like the young girl and putting them in the basket, Raguel commented,

-I would not worry for him whatsoever but I worry for you.

Margot put lots of chestnut in the basket as she told,

-This is your problem, Mr angel of justice. You see, some people can be very good one day and very bad the next day. Does all of the bad actions weigh more than the good ones? Myself, I do not know, truly, my father rescued many people from a sinking ship, including myself. He killed my mother, and he abused me. I escaped from our home but still I will not accuse him and see him hanged. I just can't. It's difficult. I am thinking could it be possible to salvage those people? For you it would be your former angel Raphael, for me it would be my father. I am completely torn on the matter. For me, I don't want to see the like of my father ever again yet I want him to understand what he did and how it did impact upon our family. It broke us apart. Strangely, if my father was reduced to the state of Raphael, therefore if he posed non longer any danger to my life, I would go back to him and help him out despite whatever he had done.

A sighing Raguel stated,

-Margot, you have more forgiveness in your heart than I have in mine. Now, I can't let you live under that bridge. Winter is only a season away before you know it you could die of cold out there.

With some emotion, Margot confessed,

-I already considered that and it doesn't really matter. It is a better death than being battered to death. Everyone has to die one day or another. There is no cure for death unfortunately.

Raguel corrected her sternly,

-But the later, the better. Don't you want to enjoy a long and fruitful life?

Their steps had led them out of the forest on the large path leading to town when after a silent while Margot decided to reply to the angel,

-Mr angel of justice, I think I have seen enough. I think I don't really want to see more than I need to.

The Master of all angels felt extremely sad for that young girl of only twelve who had such despair about life. He was more determined than ever to bring her to the family home of his son in order to give Margot a better life and maybe, another love for life. He followed her to the bridge carrying her basket.

Raphael was sleeping rolled in his cover when they arrived. He woke up scared at the sight of Raguel and moved against the wall. Margot reassured him passing by him,
-It is alright. Mr the angel of justice just accompanied me through the forest, which was very kind of him. What

happened to your arms?

Giggling, giving an amused look at Raguel, Raphael queried,

-Mr the angel of justice? Margot, my arms and back have been looked after by his son. They came this afternoon to tend to me. What are you doing here?

Margot putting her hands on her hips replied to him with a scolding tone,

-This is my bridge, Mr the bad angel! How many times do I have to remind you?

She then went to the Master to gave him all the coins she earned for her work at the farm telling him,

-This is for your son, the good Mr Cotton. Please, thank him for me to have done such a thorough work on Mr River. I am indebted. I know this is not the full payment but I will repay him bit by bit like we agreed upon.

Raguel told firmly,

-Please, call me Raguel, Margot, not Mr the angel of justice. We know each other enough to call ourselves by our first names or nickname in your case. Beside that you need to give that payment to my son himself so he can give you a receipt and you can then explain why you refused his offer to give you a roof.

Raphael rose to his feet, shocked, and scolded,

-Margot! Are you out of your mind, my girl? You can't refuse such an offer! Sebastien is a major angel, he will look after you very well. He is full of kindness, he perspires kindness. Margot, you must accept to be homed by him. You must join his family. He has a big heart. He adopts everyone even fallen angels. The winter will come soon, your blanket will not protect you as much as a Sebastien!

The Master gave a deep glance to his fallen angel, feeling his deep concern for the welfare of the young girl. He explained to him,

-Raphael, you are the reason why she will stay under a bridge. She knows you can't feed yourself so she doesn't want to leave you just like that.

Raphael cried silently, then proposed,

-We must solve this. Margot needs to be homed. She can't call a bridge a home. Your son said I could sleep on his bench in his back garden, will I be allowed to do that every night so Margot accepts to live in his home? Margot, you must accept that compromise, if Sebastien says yes to it, you must. If you don't, if I am just your excuse to refuse a good home, I will remove myself from this earth, remove your excuse and go to hell.

An arguing Margot told him off,

-That is not fair, Raphael! Will Mr Cotton accept that deal? I will agree to those terms because I could feed your bad helpless angel, Raguel.

Giving a winning smile and a wink to Raphael, the Master took the basket and ordered,

-Margot, we can only ask my son for his decision on the matter. Pick up your blanket, pick up Raphael's one and let's go to his home. As for my fallen angel Raphael, he has never been really fair, this is why he lost his wings. Come, follow me.

The young girl obeyed, then walking by Raguel, she commented,

-I could swear that you, angels, are playing mind games.

Raguel replied firmly,

-Not that we have to caution a human that is being very unreasonable. We are just looking after your welfare, here.

Margot only bit her lips, while Raphael following them smiled blissfully. He heard Raguel saying 'we', and it just made his heart sing with hope. It was now dusk. The rain was still falling steadily. The cobbled streets were slippery and they saw a man, obviously drunk. Margot shivered at his sight. She warned Raguel quickly,

-This is my father.

Soon enough, her father recognised her and shouted in the street, breaking the bottle he held in his hand on the pavement,

-You! Little bitch! I have been worried sick about you for

two days! Two entire days! Where have you been? There was a fire in town last night! And here you are! You are going to get it!

Raguel pushed the young girl behind him protectively, before his voice stormed upon the man, demanding,

-She is going to get what? More battering? More rapes? She is alive and she is staying with us from now on.

The father came to challenge Raguel. He was a tall and strong man, fearless and drunk out of his wit. Raphael put Margot behind himself and ordered her,

-Stay put, stay safe and let Raguel deal with him. Do not intervene whatever happens.

Margot was crying and shivering behind Raphael but she shouted,

-You did hurt me, dad! You did! I am not coming back! I am not! I don't want to end up in a grave like mum!

Her father attacked Raguel without fear. The tackle was a powerful one as the man proved himself to be very strong. Cork promised his girl as he was thrown aside,

-You do not know yet what hurting means, Marguerite. I will break your every bone if you do not come home.

Raphael answered back with deep anger,

-I will break your every bone if you take her back!

The Master turning to the injured Raphael with a puzzled and amused look, asked,

-How do you intend to do that with two broken arms?

Raphael replied shrugging his shoulders which still did hurt badly,

-I am just saying. You will do that for me. One of my first human prayers and wishes is to save Margot. Watch yourself, Raguel, he is coming back for you with the broken bottle! On your left!

A fierce fight ensued. Raguel was stabbed several times with the broken bottle. Raphael joined the fight to protect him, using his cast arms as weapons, he kept asking,

-Master, are you alright? Break his arms! You must neutralise him like you did with me

The Master was soon back into the fight, giving a severe pounding to the father of Margot, and breaking one of his arms. Raphael helped, and made the man unconscious with a serious head butt which left himself dazed. Raphael saw Margot, still standing, safe and not hurt. He saw Raguel above him, bleeding badly, but still strong and he closed his eyes with exhaustion.

Raguel ordered,

-Margot, I want you to fetch my son, Mr Cotton straight away, he will be at the presbytery by now.

The young girl obeyed. The Master of all angels carried in his arms the unconscious Raphael and started to walk to the presbytery, leaving behind the nasty and dealt with Mr Cork. Soon he was met half way by his son and also Doctor Williams. Sebastien took Raphael in his arms while Williams started to give first aid to his Master. By now, Raguel was bleeding profusely, however he held firmly the hand of Margot and told her,

-You are not going back to him and don't even think to check upon him. I can tell you, he will be fine. He has only one broken arm not two. I have been measured. You, young Lady are staying with us from now on. If you want me to kill your dad to make a fact of it, trust me, bleeding like I do, I can at this moment in time. I know what he is capable of and you will definitely be killed by him if you go back to him. You stay by my side and Raphael's side, this is an order. Look at your Raphael, he will need some good looking after, especially after that fight. You are coming with us, whether you want it or not.

A shivering Margot hugged Raguel, thankfulness in her heart, as she whispered,

-I will stay with you. Please, be well.

Doctor Williams answered,

-I will see that he is, Miss Cork. Sebastien, we need to go back to the presbytery. Your father is losing a lot of blood. He needs multiple stitches almost everywhere on his chest and neck.

Henry, full wings on, appeared and helped Williams to carry the Master faster to his new home to be looked after. A worried Margot asked,

-Mr Cotton, will your father be fine?

Sebastien reassured her,

-Yes, he will be fine. This is not the first time he lost a bit of blood. He kills demons for his leisure, you know.

Following him Margot told him off,

-Now, you are teasing me! This is not the right time, you know. I am very worried.

Giving a glance at the girl, Sebastien explained in a very pondered way,

-My father and I are punishing angels. We punish humans and other angels when they do wrong. But we are also demons killer.

Waking up inside his arms, Raphael blinked at his sight, and mumbled,

-I know that, Sebastien.

Sebastien smiled to him in return, a good welcoming smile, then commented,

-Sounds like you are back with us, Raphael. You passed out on my father. He told me via telepathy what happened to you and him. I was just explaining things to Marguerite. I wasn't talking to you. You were out of it.

Raphael begged,

-Please, put me down, I will try to walk beside you. Please call her Margot, she likes being called Margot. How is your father? Tell me he is alright. He fought like a lion again.

Once he was on solid ground Raphael put one of his arm across the shoulders of Sebastien to help him stand and told,

-I think her bloody dad wrecked again one of my arms and damaged my thigh. He used a broken bottle as a weapon. He was fierce with it. How is your father?

Sebastien noticing the bleeding thigh of Raphael replied,

-He will need some stitches but he is strong. He carried you almost to my home. I will have a look at your thigh. The man may have ruptured one of your main arteries that will explain that you passed out. I think you should forget a bit of pride and let me carry you all the way home. Margot, come and run with me, we need to sort out your bad angel as soon as possible. Let's bring him home.

Holding her basket and blankets, Margot ran behind Sebastien as fast as she could while he was carrying Raphael. When they entered the presbytery, they were welcome by Ivy who informed her husband,

-Your father is going to be fine. It is mainly just lots of scars and lots of blood and it will be lots of stitches. How is Raphael?

Sebastien taking the fallen angel to his drawing room replied,

-We have to take a look at his thigh immediately. He managed to regain consciousness but he is loosing a lot of blood. You must find me a garrot.

Margot entered that strange home lived by angels. She closed the door behind her and took a deep breath. She entered the drawing room where all the action was and proposed her help. Ivy took her to the kitchen and asked her,

-Boil some water for us, dear girl. Bring it as soon as you can.

And then it dawned on her that the household she stepped in was the one of a surgeon and the one of a Doctor, and she took on board the helping pace. She saw how the leg of Raphael was saved. She witnessed the stitches done on the chest of Raguel and when he asked her,

-Are you staying with us, Margot? I will protect you with my life.

She went to him and kissed his cheek with her answer,

-I will stay with you. Thank you so much.

Raguel gave a sigh of relief. Raphael smiled and went outside to the back garden bench silently. What followed was a nice meal which everyone enjoyed but Raphael. However Sebastien, Raguel and Margot at the end of it went to the back garden, all carrying dishes. Raphael cried when the three of them fed him in turn. When Raguel spoon fed him a chicken soup, Raphael was in tears. When Sebastien gave him some bread and butter pudding by the spoonful, Raphael had hope in his heart. When the young Margot gave him her humble chestnuts which she had roasted within the fireplace, the fallen angel smiled. Sebastien told holding the shoulders of Margot,

-You are a welcomed guest, Raphael. I will build you something better than the bench for you, a good shelter to protect you from winter. Young Lady, it is time for you to say good night to Raphael. Let me show you to your bedroom. My Ivy is still in there preparing it for you. Your blanket will be on your bed and she will have prepared a nice little fire to warm your bedroom up.

Margot went to kiss the cheek of the fallen angel, and told him,

-Thank you for protecting me. I will see you tomorrow.

Margot took the presented hand of Sebastien and was led back into the house. Left alone in the garden was the Master and the fallen angel. It was a beautiful night full of stars in the sky. A small breeze moved the branches of the trees surrounding them. Raphael dared to break the heavy silence between them,

-How are you doing, Master?

With mixed feelings, Raguel replied,

-Why would you care? I told you not to call me Master.

Raphael tried with pain to sit on the bench rather leaning upon it. He sighed deeply before he confided,

-I couldn't bear the sight of seeing you bleed tonight. I would have given my life for you for whatever it is worth. And I will keep calling you Master, because this is who you are for me and old habits die hard. Forgive me, if it offends you because I do know I am a reject.

Raguel sat by Raphael on the bench and told him frankly,

-You have always been a problematic angel. How is your leg?

Raphael looked at it before he answered,

-Your son did a good work upon it. I am not bleeding to death any longer and I will not meet Lucifer in hell tonight.

A teasing Raguel commented,

-I am not sure if it is a good thing or a bad thing.

Raphael took a turn in the small back garden considering it from all angles as he replied,

-Good thing or bad thing, you were hurt, Master, yet you didn't leave me behind. My head is spinning.

Raguel went straight to Raphael and made him sit down on the bench ordering,

-Stay put for this evening, you can visit the place tomorrow. You suffered a concussion when you head butted the human we were dealing with. Your head butt was so strong you rendered that man unconscious. What you have to realise is that you are human now and I told you that before. Your strength is not the one of an angel any longer so you have to be careful when you enter into a fight. Use a little bit more strategy.

Sighing the fallen angel confided,

-In the heat of the moment, it was all emotions. I didn't want to see you hurt and I didn't want the man to attack Margot. I am glad you found her a nice home. Your son is kindness personified. She needs kindness.

Raguel confessed,

-You helped because she didn't want to be homed. That girl has a strong conscience and she didn't want to know you were out there not able to feed yourself. I heard that last year she gave birth to a still born baby. She was abused by her father since her mother's death. Doctor Valdi who had to help at the birth of the dead child gave a correction to the father. The abuse then stopped but when Valdi left town for his honeymoon trip, it started again. I saw her arms today when she was milking the cows of Mr Berry. They were black, blue and green. The worst thing she told me in essence that she didn't mind dying because she had seen too much. She is such a sad and hurt little human being. Hopefully, here she will blossom. So you will have to stay as well, so we could keep her here and not let her live back under a bridge. I must say that I am ready to make you adjust to human life. I still hate your guts but not enough to see you dead. I want you to have a good and decent human life that counts.

You know what, I think you can do it. One young girl asked me today: is it possible to salvage bad people? Think about it. I will give you a hand, take it.

His head lowered down, tears in his eyes, Raphael told,

-I must thank you, Master. You punished me and you shamed me. But everything, literally everything you said did hit home. I am trembling saying that to you. But I do disgust myself. When I think of what I did to you and your family, when I think of how undermining I was, I am more than ashamed, I am sorry. I can tell you straight that I will have difficulty to live with myself. But I will hang on in there for you.

Getting up from the bench, Raguel simply answered,

-Try to sleep, now. Tomorrow is another day: a clean slate to be written with good actions.

Whilst the Master left the garden, the large guard dog of the household came by the bench and sat by it. Raphael had no idea that it was in fact Raguel keeping an eye upon him, who was worried about him taking his life. The fallen angel when he saw the dog was impressed by its size, and said for himself and to the rottweiler,

-You are quite a beast, aren't you? Whatever you do, don't bite my fingers off. I am not an intruder, your master Sebastien allowed me to sleep on his bench.

Raphael did lay on the bench with sheer pain, tried to put the cover upon himself with difficulty as he carried on talking to the dog,

-Don't even think that I am growling at you, I am not, I just hurt, that is all.

The rottweiler kept staring at the fallen angel and when Raphael slept, he lay by his side on the ground, still keeping a good watch upon him. Because Raguel knew that Lucifer had been seen in town the previous night and that Raphael as a human would be an easy prey for him to be killed to collect the soul Raphael sold.

Indoors, Raguel was met by his son in the stairs who briefed him,

-Margot is settling in. She is in bed and Ivy is reading her a fairy tale. She has a glass of milk and some biscuits by her on the night table. She is awfully tired. She will sleep soon. My

Jack woke up. He is still so weak. I am fetching a bowl of chicken soup for him. Will you keep him conscious for me until I come back? Ted badly needs a rest. Send him to bed and take over. He has eaten. Henry accompanied Theo back to the hotel because it is getting late. They are flying there and he wanted to make sure that Theo didn't crash land in the middle of the forest in the middle of the night. I will stay up until Henry comes back. Where is your father? I haven't seen him since we've finished our dinner.

The Master smiled to his considerate son and told him,

-Your grandfather is looking after Peter O'Neil. He also knows Henry is going to go to see the human to make sure he is alright. A big conversation is about to take place between him and Henry and then between him and you. I know all about it already. In fact we discussed everything at length my father and I. Go and get the soup for Jack. I will keep him awake and we will talk with your grandfather later.

While Sebastien obeyed, Raguel stepped into Jack's bedroom. Ted had been monitoring the child the entire day, he welcomed the Master with the good news,

-Jack is awake again. It is the third time only since his operation. He managed to finish a full glass of water just now. He will make it for I saw him many times as an adolescent in my visions. He will pull through, Master.

Putting his hand on the shoulder of the angel, Raguel ordered with kindness,

-Thank you so much, Ted. You need to rest. I am taking over for the night. Did Jack said anything I must know?

Ted held the hand of the Master of all angels to share what he saw and heard with him. He warned,

-Jack was delirious then and had a very high temperature which I struggled to bring down. He was speaking about the Ogin boys that needed to be stopped and found. I had a vision of them. They are on an island in the Atlantic. I can't be precise about it at the moment. But you must speak to your brother and his wife Amelia about everything concerning the Ogins brother. They know more than I do. They researched the case. It need to be dealt with, Master. As you can see, those boys are serial killers.

Raguel nodded before he said,

-I will deal with it, rest assure of it, Ted. Thanks for the heads up. I will need you tomorrow to keep track of Lucifer and his whereabouts. My Williams will help you to do so. For now, I just want you to have a well deserved sleep. Recuperate. Thank you again for looking after our Jack all day.

Ted bowed to the Master before he retired from the room. Raguel rekindled the fire in the fireplace, place the pillows so the child could sit in a better manner in order to eat his soup later then sat by the bed with a kind smile. He asked,

-How is Killy?

Jack stroke gently the head of the fox terrier, who was on his bed along with his kitten, as he answered,

-He is missing his owner. Sometimes I can hear him doing the wolf on the bed and my cat goes under the cover next to me. Ted took him out regularly for his needs. Killy is going to be a poorly little thing for a while until he gets used to me. I have been asleep most of the day so I couldn't give him all the love he needs at this moment in time.

Raguel commented,

-Well, both of you will heal together. It always takes time. How are you feeling tonight?

The brave Jack replied,

-My chest hurt but I can cope Master. Like you said it will take time.

Doctor Williams appeared in the bedroom with his medical bag and asked,

-How is our boy?

The Master turned to his servant to tell him,

-Jack is awake. He had a temperature for part of the day and was delirious according to Ted who monitored him. Ted managed to bring Jack's temperature under control. Jack just said his chest did hurt. Hold my hand to see the full brief, William.

His servant obeyed then he snapped his fingers and made a lots of things appear inside the room. First Doctor Williams prepared an orange juice from nice fresh oranges and as he did so, he advised,

-Raguel, your son needs to have his own proper vegetable garden to feed his family. When Doctor Valdi will come back properly in town, he will reclaim his own garden for his own family. I suggest you ask Wilton-Cough for any available good land near the church which could be bought for your son and turn into a garden. Look, Mighty took on board Ivy, Jack, Ted, Henry and the young Margot plus he has a baby on the way, let alone, he invited you to live in his house. Then there is the mouth to feed of a fallen archangel in the back garden. I am not counting his animals...

Raguel agreed,

-I will get Mighty some land in the area. I know how generous he is. He will keep adopting anyone needing a good home. I know him. If he listens to his heart, he will tuck everyone under his wings.

A giggling Jack commented,

-I will help Pa with the new garden.

Doctor Williams gave the child the orange juice and told him,

-First things first, Jack: you need to get better. Show me if you can drink on your own or if I have to help you. It is important to establish if your mobility of the top of your body has been impaired. I hope not.

Jack obliged him. He held the glass and drank, then announced,

-It feels all weak up there Doctor Williams but I can do it. I am a bit wobbly around the edges, just like jelly. I tell you what, Mrs Marlow, Georgia makes awesome jellies. Mrs White over the years bought her nearly all the moulds possible to do jellies. Give her summer berries and a little champagne then she will do her special number with them, first it looks stunning then it tastes divine.

Looking at the boy's mobility and being satisfied with it, Williams smiled as he said,

-Looks like you know already that Georgia and I are going to be courting each other. Drink all of your juice. It will do you good. You must eat your food, finish it off, even if you have no appetite. It will bring your strength back. From tomorrow, you can start walking around the house and the garden but don't push it as of yet until your Pa, your Ma or I tell you. Just do half an hour at a time for the time being every now and then, but I still want you to rest mainly. You could take that little fox out with Ted for example and bond with Killy by doing so.

Stroking the head of the poor little terrier, Jack confided with some glee,

-That is a jolly good idea! I like that, I will walk little Killy. Doctor Williams, I am not an angel anymore but I am still very much sentient. I can see things a little like Ted, maybe less so. I can feel things too and people around me, almost as if I could read their minds. I know that you are on the coach on the way to Wilton Town tonight, one manifestation of you, Mina and Emily are sleeping, shoulder to shoulder, and Georgia is resting upon your own shoulder and you are holding her hand in a protective way. I know Sebastien did facilitate the match.

He stopped before he added putting his empty glass down with difficulties on his night table,

-I know there is a young girl living here now. She has multiple names. She is in trouble. She was raped not so long ago, violently. It was horrible. When she regained consciousness, she only took her bed cover and escaped from her home. I can see all that did happen to her. Miss White lived a similar ordeal. Marguerite is pregnant. It is early days, extremely early days, but she is pregnant from her father. I can see and feel things, Doctor Williams, like yesterday, I knew the intentions of Michael, when you were on attached on the table. I knew he was going to reap your heart out whilst you were still alive and eat it. I also saw what he was going to do with Ivy.

At this point, Jack sobbed. The Master went to him and hugged him. He revealed in a reassuring way,

-Jack, listen to me. It is not unusual for a fallen angel to remain sentient but when they usually remain so, it is because they are still deep down angels and will regain their wings. The visions can be a burden, but they can save lives. Yesterday, what you did, helped to save Williams, your Ma and the baby inside her. As Ted will be living with us all in this house, I want you to speak to him about your visions. He can help you to learn how to deal with them. He has extremely powerful ones. It sounds like you are in the same league as him. That gift is not given to everyone. It is a very special one to possess. From now on, whenever you have a vision, I want you to come to Sebastien or to me to share them. They are important. Come, my Jack, you must be strong for us all. Let's dry your tears because you were a big pat of saving the day last night.

Raguel was wiping the tears of the boy when his son arrived in the room with a large tray. Sebastien had a bright smile on his face as he announced,

-Dinner is served, Jack. For starter, I have a little potato salad for you. For the main, it is a very nice chicken soup to give you plenty of strength back and for dessert I made some pancakes, just for you. They are served with a little compote of bramble berries that were picked this afternoon by my dad and Margot in the woods. How does the menu sound to you my little angel?

Jack perked up straight away by seeing Sebastien. He answered,

-It sounds really, really nice. But what about my dog and my kitten?

Sebastien put the tray on the bed while he replied,

-I thought of them. Your kitten gets a some chicken pieces dipped in a little milk and Killy gets some leftover chicken. Pa, would you take care of the pets while I look after my Jack.

Raguel took the pets off the bed and fed them without any arguments. He actually smiled to see his son embracing family life once more after so many centuries of mourning. Sebastien sat by Jack and insisted on spoon feeding him, telling his boy that he needed to keep all his strength for another day. Jack didn't argue and complied. He was blabbering all along his supper with his adoptive Pa about the weird dreams he had during the day. Sebastien listened attentively to all the chatter. Then when the supper was over, they changed the bandages of little Jack, him and Doctor Williams. Sebastien told a story to Jack from his time as a musketeer and the little boy finally fell asleep. The pets were put back upon his bed. The covers were tucked nicely. Kisses on the forehead were given. Then Sebastien left the room with his father whilst one of many Williams's manifestations remained to look after Jack overnight.

The father and the son found Ivy in the drawing room preparing some tea, she welcome them by asking,

-How is my little angel?

Sebastien gave her a kiss on her cheek before he replied,

-Our boy is pulling through nicely. He is very weak but he is making it. I fed him and he ate with some good appetite everything. He is asleep now under the supervision of Doctor Williams. How is Margot adjusting to her new bedroom?

Giggling Ivy told presenting a chair to her husband then to her father in law,

-Well, she admitted that it was better than being under a bridge and that in her former home she slept on the floor by the fire place. To have her own bedroom is actually a novelty to her. She will adjust, yes, she has a strong character. But the way she talks sometimes makes me smile and sometimes makes me sad. I gave her one of my old nighties and helped her into it.

She stopped talking, and stirring the tea, she tried to compose herself, to retain her tears, then she finished,

-We have got to assess that young girl tomorrow, she is almost thoroughly black and blue to the point where you can start counting the white patches of skin which are not bruised. I talked to her about it and she is very reluctant to be seen to. She doesn't want to speak about what happened to her as well. I have to get her confidence. She likes me but I think her personality, because she has been hurt, is one that will take time to give her trust to anyone.

Her father in law took over with an order,

-Take a seat, Ivy. You worked all night and day, let me serve the tea. Let me tell you as well, that you are right. Margot's trust will always be hard to gain. But she has to seen by you and I would say not by Sebastien but by Miss White. I talked to Whilhelmina about Marguerite's case and she has agreed to get involved. Ivy, you see, Miss White was raped a very long time ago but she knows the effect it has psychologically and physically. Mina White is the result of her rape. Now, let me tell you both what I learnt from our sentient Jack: Margot is pregnant. She probably doesn't know it yet for it is early days. What you two do not know is that she gave birth to a still born child last year, that Doctor Valdi and Miss White managed to save her, and that Doctor Valdi corrected her father for it. Then her father didn't touch the girl, up until Doctor Valdi went away from town. Now I encountered and fought with her father tonight, by all means, he is one of the strongest human I ever met.

Watching his father pouring the tea into the cups, Sebastien giggled as he teased,

-That is quite something for you to say about a human. Do you want to show me all the scratches Mr Cork did upon you?

Raguel argued, putting down the tea pot, and exhibited the scars he sustained that night,

-You can not call them scratches, Mighty, those are scars, proper scars, and done by a bloody human. To add to my shame, Raphael intervened to help me. He was, I dare say quite brave because with two broken arms, he can't fight that well. But he put Margot out of the way behind him during the fight to protect her. Then I must say the head butt he delivered to that man was quite something to witness. You can tell he was angry with that human and what he did to his daughter.

Entering the room with Henry, the Great Being commented with a smirk,

-I know why your son is exhibiting his battle wounds all the time, Raguel. He took it from you. The apple didn't fall far from the tree.

The Master of all angel fastened his shirt back up with red cheeks and defended himself,

-I was literally pushed into it.

Ivy welcomed the new comers, getting up and pulled chairs for them, with a lovely smile on her lips,

-Please, come and join us. We are having some tea to wind the day up.

Following the invite, the Great Being and Henry sat at the round table while Raguel served them and asked,

-How did it went at Peter's?

The Messenger answered,

-It went well. The man is recuperating and he is very eager to start his work for Miss White. He couldn't stop to talk about it. How did it go with homing Raphael on the bench in the backyard?

Raguel sat back at the table after serving himself last and replied,

-It went remarkably well. From archangel Raphael who

was haughty to human Raphael who has eaten humble pie, there is a dramatic change. For one thing, he keeps saying sorry, which would have been a word ignored by him as an archangel. This evening, I saw him care, more than I ever saw him do so before.

The Great Being turning his tea with his tea spoon stated,

-Your punishment worked, Raguel. Raphael meeting the charity of the human Marguerite helped as well. She achieved wonders to his heart that hated humans. He started to care. It can only develop from there. He is human now and we will have to watch what he does with his free will.

Agreeing with his father, Raguel commented,

-So far so good in my books. But he has a suicidal tendency which is worrying me. He needs to adjust to his human status fast. I am keeping a good eye on him of course.

Ivy proposed,

-I would say, and I know that you will not like my proposal, because all of you do not like Raphael and it is understandable, that we involve him into our household. I remember of one dinner we had in Boston with Doctor Valdi and his wife at Doctor Williams's and Valdi explained the way Abraham Wilton-Cough made paupers move on with their lives and getting back in there. There was a story of a young lad which was begging on the street. Wilton-Cough asked him to sweep the front of his bank and his bank then he invited the lad for dinner in his own house to feed him. He managed to get the young man out of begging and found him a proper work eventually. I suggest we do some incentive like that with Raphael. Autumn is coming we have plenty of trees in the cemetery, he could sweep the leaves and we can invite him for dinner to give him a little of moral support and comfort as a reward.

A giggling Sebastien told her,

-Apart that my father broke Raphael's both arms, your idea could work in theory, my Ivy. We can always ask Raphael to try to go on all four and blow the leaves on one side of the cemetery.

Ivy's brows frowned as she responded,

-Mr Cotton, you are impossible.

While Henry couldn't help laughing, Raguel commented with a slight smirk,

-Yes, he is impossible. He did get that from his Gallic mother. We are condemned to live with him, I am afraid to say. Now, Ivy, I do have a plan in mind for Raphael which doesn't involved his arms, which indeed I did break rather badly, but his brain instead. We need an overseer for a quarry in the woods which we will have to use to rebuilt part of this town. To be honest, Raphael will be perfect for that role. If he puts his heart into the job, he will be very efficient. But the first question is will he wake up tomorrow morning, follow the advice that my son and I gave him? He is a human with free will now. He can stay a tramp on the bench outside for all I know. But I think that rewarding Raphael by having a meal with us some time to time, inside this house, should not be discarded. It is a good idea. He responded well to human generosity and to my son and I generosity.

His father stated,

-Making Raphael a human was the perfect punishment for him. Ivy, your idea is a good one. When Raguel and Mighty are out to man the clinic tomorrow, stay behind for a little bit to provide breakfast for the children and Raphael. Doctor Williams will stay with you. Ludwig the rottweiler will be by you. I will stay here as well. I can help with the breakfast and my sight will be enough for Raphael to be tamed. Invite him in kindly. We will see first if he accepts the invitation and how he behaves inside the house. My bet is that he will be on his best behaviour, and it can only be so because of his two broken arms, courtesy of Raguel who doesn't like him at all.

Everyone laughed around the table but Raguel corrected,

-Although it is difficult for me to speak about it, or dare I say admit it, father, I must confess that as a human, Raphael wins my compassion. His first steps as a man have been good ones so far. Suicide is on his mind though, so he will need help to adjust. But I can see a glimmer of hope where he could one day retrieve his wings. Angelic ones, not archangelic ones this time around, but Raphael made enquiries and would be keen to join such an incentive. Of course, I dismissed his hopes, being a punisher and all that, first you have to make them pay dearly, then you have to make them cross the desert. But we gave him directions my son and I and I think I can say with assurance that Raphael is not lost.

Sebastien putting down his cup of tea replied with a giggle,

-No, he is not lost. He is in my courtyard garden. So we are all agreeing on giving him a chance then?

His grandfather nodded positively before he ruled,

-Most definitely. To be human was the best lesson Raphael could have been given.

After sipping a little of his tea Raguel told firmly,

-To all of you, especially you, Ivy, for your protection, do not reveal that Ludwig the rottweiler is in fact one of the many physical apparitions of myself. Ted and Jack can be in our little secret but keep Raphael and Margot out of it for the time being. As for the widow Mel Brown, she is very assertive and we need to discuss upon disclosing to her that we are in fact an angelic family.

Ivy commented shyly,

-I am not an angel. I do not fly like you all.

Sebastien smiled to his wife as he said softly,

-You do not need to fly to be an angel, my little bit, you are one already to my eyes.

Putting his hand in a paternal way over the one of Ivy on the table, Raguel confirmed,

-For once I can only agree with my son: Ivy, you are our angel, you are this family's angel.

Ivy blushed and went shy and silent on them all so her husband knowing exactly how she was feeling took over the conversation,

-To be honest with you, dad, I rather not tip toeing around someone in my own house. I think we should come clean with Melanie and tell her who we are. She has to stay with us for a decent amount of time until her own house is rebuilt. It will be hard to keep the secret that we are all angels with all the events that happens here on a regular basis. Since you wanted me to invite her to reside here, I think you should be the one to deliver the big news that we have wings on occasions, fly, fight demons and so on. But I would keep from her the news that you are in fact the big rottweiler that scared her cat. That would be too much information for her.

This made Henry laughed. The Great Being giggled, sensing that another father and son arguments will be on the way, he stated his position on the matter,

-I think Mighty is entirely right.

Raguel argued,

-You always take his side! He should do the talking to Mrs Brown because he can smooth talk anyone including you.

Henry put down his cup of tea and started to participate,

-I agree with the Master. Sebastien will cut the rough edges of the conversation with that poor widow.

A thoughtful Ivy told,

-She was very silent during dinner. I think that the fact that she has nothing but her cat just sank in. She should know who she is living with but we also have a duty of care on how we will tell her. Sebastien, I know you can tell her in a gentle way so she will understand and fit in our household better for the time being.

Faced by the demand of his wife, Sebastien surrendered,

-For you Mrs Cotton, I will do it.

With a bright grin on his face, the Master said casually,

-I know now how to make you do anything, my dear Mighty.

Sebastien gave a dark glance at his father and pointed at him as he warned,

-Don't you dare using my Ivy in that way under my roof to get all your ways! I will make you share the bench with Raphael, outside, and you can take your rottweiler with you that scares all the cats in this household.

His father retorted gleefully,

-It was one cat! Just one! You drama queen of an angel! Do you want to show us all your scratches just for the pleasure of it?

A giggling Great Being scolded them both,

-Children, would you behave in front of the Lady of this house! Lord almighty, I will start swearing by my own name with you two. If you don't cut your bickering I will put both of you in the corners of the room, facing the wall.

A laughing Henry told as he stood up,

-I'd better head to bed as it felt like rather long forty eight hours.

The Master came to him, patted the back of his angel while he said,

-You do deserve a rest, Henry. Thank you for everything. I will need you to get a few things for the wedding of Theo Odell tomorrow, but try to keep everything secret from Theo and Miss White. So there will be a fair few errands of a nicer kind for you to do. One of them will be to invite Peter O'Neil to the wedding. He will work for Miss White soon and Theo has always been kind to him. It will touch his heart to be invited. Make him part of the preparations. Get the wild flowers he will chose in the fields and we will decorate the tavern of Tyrell with them. Good night, see you tomorrow at the early breakfast with my son and I.

Henry bowed to him and left the drawing room. Raguel sat back at the table and confided,

-I do like that angel. He has such a good nature and temperament.

His father announced,

-I told Henry that he will be put through the training to become an archangel. He was very humbled and pleased about it.

Putting his cup of tea down, Sebastien said,

-You should have told me, I would have congratulated him.

Raguel looked at his son intensely before he revealed,

-Mighty, you will have plenty of time to tell him. You do know that Michael is gone to hell so we have to replace him. Therefore we have something very important to tell you. You are taking his place and you are an archangel from now on. You need to kneel by your grandfather so he will anoint you as one.

Sebastien did so, but kept looking to his father for reassurance. When he was on his knees by the Great Being, he was knighted and his forehead was touched with something which made him look in awe at his surroundings for a few minutes. His grandfather told him,

-You have been an excellent angel for a little more than eighteen centuries now. I have observed you closely over the years and I can't think of a better archangel than you. You are ready to be the first partly human archangel. It will set a new order of archangels where human blood and humanity will not be considered as trash any longer. Now why don't you have a well deserved rest and take your little wife with you, because she worked so hard for more hours that her condition should allow.

For once Sebastien was emotional and speechless for a fair few seconds. When he stood up, he embraced his grandfather silently before he went to his father. He stood before him before hugging him, tears in his eyes, then told,

-I owe everything to you, Dad. Do you know that? Thank you, just thank you to have brought me up the way you did.

Raguel became emotional himself as he ordered,

-My Mighty go and rest. You are one brave son. I am so proud of you, always ever so proud of you. Go before I cry in front of you.

Sebastien went and took his wife by the hand in a very gallant manner. Both left the room after saying goodnight. Raguel started to clear the table with his father. He confided to him,

-Thank you for saving my boy. Mighty is so important to me. I know we do enjoy a good bickering almost constantly but Mighty is my pride and joy.

The Great Being confessed,

-I was fond of your Mighty since the day he was born. The way you raised him single handedly has to be praised as well, you brought a great part of who he is now and what he has achieved as an angel. He deserved the title of archangel since a while to be honest but with your desire to keep him modest, I waited for as long as I could. With our current archangelic situation, it couldn't be delayed any longer.

#

At dawn, Ivy woke up in the arms of her archangelic husband. She looked at him with pride as he was still asleep before kissing him awake whispering into his ears,

-I missed you Mr Cotton, really, really, missed you.

Sebastien opened his eyes, returned the kiss in a very loving way before he whispered,

-And I missed you, my little bit. Do you know that you are in great danger of becoming the mother of at least a dozen children?

Ivy laughed yet kissing him answered,

-Where will we put those children? We already have nearly a full house.

Stroking her belly with love and care, Sebastien replied with a wink,

-I can think of one place, most certainly. How is our little one on the way doing?

Getting up, his wife told,

-He is certainly alive and kicking. He kicked me awake a few minutes ago. I am pretty sure he is going to be as lively as you. If he has a little bit of my father in him, he will also be witty and as you are also witty, I will no longer be able to say a good word in this house.

Sebastien laughed before kissing her again,

-Without a nightdress like you were tonight, I will let you have all the good words in the world.

Falsely offended Ivy slapped his cheek without any strength at all,

-Mr Cotton! You know I had to give my only nightdress to the poor Margot.

At the mention of Margot, Sebastien got dressed up and said,

-She is only twelve and pregnant by her very own father.

Mr Cork disgusts me. If I ever meet him... My father was in a bad state last night because of him. Mr Cork is strong and malicious. You must be careful today, my little bit. The man has a broken arm but he is dangerous. I advise you to keep Ludwig by your side and the one of Margot. Instead of going to the clinic today, I prefer you to stay at home and give a full assessment on Margot's state. I will arrange for Miss White to come this morning to give you a hand. There is also our little Jack to look after. So I will take care of the clinic today with my father and Doctor Williams but please look after our adoptive children for me, both are needy right now.

Ivy nodded positively as she started to clean herself up. She confirmed,

-Trust me I will look after them. What time is the wedding of Theo and Miss White?

Sebastien fastening his waistcoat answered,

-It will be about mid afternoon. My father and my grandfather have decided to organise everything for it. I must say Theo Odell has impressed them both and not only me. Theo will be in his church this morning which has become, like the tavern, a centre to organise the community effort to rebuild the town. We have the wish, my father and I, that Raphael will go to Theo to ask for work today in order to help the town. It will be a big first step for him. But Raphael is human now, which means he has free will, he can very well chose to behave like a moping tramp and not move from our bench at all.

Drying herself, his wife told,

-Well, I can use my free will as well, I can try to convince Raphael to do your wishes. Do you think I have a chance?

Her husband smiling as he brought her dress and petticoats, answered,

-I think you do. If you haven't realised yet, like my dad did, I can't say no to you. I am pretty sure you can convince anyone to do things or at least influence them. I remember when I was a little suicidal and you visited me day in and out. You gave me the strength to hang on in there by doing really simple little acts of kindness, like reading to me, bringing me the newspaper and telling me what happened in the big world, and I remember your little crumbly biscuits that you did with salt instead of sugar. I swear I was one step closer to the grave on bed sheets full of crumbs.

Ivy blushed thoroughly. She said,

-You are not fair! This was a genuine mistake those biscuits. I was crying when I made them because of you, my archangel. You want me to wear the red dress? It is my best dress.

Sebastien kissed her cheek before he replied,

-There is no better day to wear that dress than a wedding day, my little bit. Just don't wear your corset because of our baby. When you talk to Raphael, remember that he is suicidal since his wings have been cut. My father and I had to save him from his attempt to kill himself yesterday. I think I should come with you to invite him in the house for breakfast because I clearly told him to stay outdoors.

Putting her dress on, Ivy confessed,

-I will feel less anxious if we do it together.

Her husband helped her fastening the red dress on, then enjoined,

-Let's go and get him. Remember, he can be quite demeaning towards humans. He hated them for years. He hated angels made out of humans. He schemed to kill all healing angels with Michael. However he has been punished, made human, and left to the charity of humans. The death of my older brother Gael is due to Raphael selling his soul to Lucifer. You will not see my father being very kind to Raphael very often, so be prepared. But we need to keep Raphael here, to keep the little Margot safe.

Ivy understood and followed her husband like a good soldier to the back garden. On the bench fallen angel Raphael was still asleep. By his side was Ludwig who stood up and wagged his tail to Sebastien and his wife. Ivy embraced the large dog with a smile while Sebastien woke up Raphael, putting a hand on his shoulder,

-Raphael, wake up my human.

His gentle words had the desired effect. Raphael opened his eyes and blinked before saying,

-Sebastien!

Smirking Sebastien answered,

-Yes, that would be me. How are you doing? Cold and hurting throughout?

Raphael painstakingly assumed a sitting position however he grinned,

-Cold and hurting resumed my state fairly well.

Sebastien then announced,

-Well, I have good news for you, when my human wife has finished to play with our dog, she will invite you to our home to warm yourself up and have breakfast with us. Human charity obliging, I will let her have her human free will. She wants to give you a breakfast. So I am inviting you in as well, this time around.

A baffled Raphael looked at the earnest eyes of Sebastien and bit his lips with remorse. He confided with some emotion,

-I don't know if I can or should. I feel bad.

Sebastien scolded him firmly,

-Of course you can, I told you so, and of course you should, because I would be upset if you disappoint the good will of my wife. As for feeling bad, of course you should. Let's get you inside and warm you up a little. We will bring your cover in to make sure it is nice and warm for tonight.

Thus encouraged, Raphael stood up, he tried to pick up his cover but dropped it on the floor. Ivy picked it up for him then presented herself,

-Hi, I am Ivy, Sebastien's wife, a Doctor in this town, one of the healing people your friend tried to kill to fulfil your evil scheme. Come and have breakfast with us, I promise I will not attach you on a chair and want to eat your heart out like Michael did to us.

Despite himself, the fallen angel smiled at the gutsy young woman. He found her pretty in a subtle way. He already knew that it was her character that did make her the wife of Sebastien by this first introduction. He presented her his hand with difficulty,

-Raphael, it is a pleasure to meet you.

Ivy looked at his weak hand but didn't hold it. She enjoined him,

-The pleasure is not reciprocated but come in nonetheless. I will not have an evil fallen archangel starve in my back garden. It would make a pretty interesting skeleton sculpture on my bench, but as a talking point in my garden, I am looking for a magnolia tree.

A giggling Raphael followed her as she called the dog to come. When she opened the entrance door of the presbytery and invited him in, Raphael turned his head to Sebastien to have his consent. He was anxious to say the least. But an amused Sebastien told him,

-Come on in! You heard my little lady, she wants a magnolia tree and not a skeleton in our back garden.

Raphael stepped in with great shyness in the home of Sebastien. He looked around as he followed the couple, finding their home an old vast cosy place. He was led to the kitchen. There Raguel was standing by the stove preparing breakfast while the Great Being was seated at the head of the large kitchen table. The Master of all angels welcomed him,

-If it is not our good old traitor.

Raphael stepped back but Sebastien pushed him forward in an friendly way commenting,

-It is only my father, go and take a seat at the table. He can't do any worse to you apart from breaking your legs to prevent you from running away.

The fallen angel bowed to Raguel then the Great Being before taking a seat silently at the kitchen table. If no one talked to him, he was given a strong and warm coffee by Raguel himself. The conversation was very much about the town, the people who needed help the most and the coming wedding. Then Sebastien and the Master left to go to the clinic. If Raphael had remained silent throughout the conversation, he had nonetheless paid attention to it. The Great Being finally addressed him when they were alone with Ivy,

-Did you sleep well last night, Raphael?

The fallen angel couldn't look at the Creator as he replied,

-No.

The Great Being grinned as he answered and went to help Ivy who putting her apron was starting to prepare the breakfast for the other members of her household,

-Well, the hard wood of a bench is not a bed made of feathers.

Raphael corrected,

-Oh no, my Lord. I could sleep on the ground, in the mud, on feathers, what hurts is what Margot calls a conscience. It did catch up with me and I am crying inside for the things I have done.

Getting up from his chair and leaving the kitchen, the Great Being answered,

-Good. Ivy, I leave you with that scumbag while I check on Father Odell. Do not worry, Ludwig is by you.

The large rottweiler went to nudge his head on her dress. Ivy turned to see Raphael whipping. She came to him and dried his tears. She scolded him,

-Listen to me, new life equals new days to do good. They didn't throw you in hell despite their want to do so. Grab your chance. So what are you going to do with your human self today?

Raphael managed to gather himself up. He replied,

-They said to see Father Odell.

Ivy started to prepare scrambled eggs and commented,

-You will find Father Odell in the church this morning. Theo is a very good man, so good that he has become an angel during his lifetime. He gave my husband and I his own house. He will not bite you. Theo is a very welcoming type of person. I can only advise you to go and see Theo Odell. He will arrive early.

As she chopped chives, she added,

-The Master is performing the wedding for Theo this afternoon. Father Odell has his esteem. For one thing, Theo killed five demons in front of Raguel in the space of a few minutes.

A very impressed Raphael was deeply interested but Jack came into the kitchen with Ted, Henry and Doctor Williams. He felt that his time to ask questions had run out. Ivy embraced her little boy with joy,

-How are you this morning my Jack? You are up!

Doctor Williams replied for the child,

-He is better. He had a good night of sleep and he was craving to see you so much so that I couldn't keep him tucked in his bed any longer. So I allowed him to have breakfast with us instead of in bed.

Jack told,

-I am a bit sore, Ma, but I can stand up. Do you want me to help with anything?

A smiling Henry who held the little fox terrier scolded the boy,

-It is my turn to help your Ma! You just need to sit by Doctor Williams and keep an eye on Killy.

Jack contested,

-Since when are we taking turns in this house?

Henry presenting him a chair answered firmly,

-Since I said so and since you need to recuperate. Keep Killy by your feet that's your duty.

A smiling Ted informed Ivy whilst holding Jack's kitten in his arms,

-I knocked on the door of Margot. She is preparing herself for breakfast. She will be joining us soon. As for Mrs Brown, I didn't knock on her door because I could hear her crying. Maybe a quiet breakfast for her would be better. I am going to feed your two cats, Mrs Cotton, in the drawing room.

Ivy scolded him,

-Ted, how many times will I have to tell you to call me Ivy? You live here. Thank you for the cats in advance. We will leave them in the drawing room today. I will have to check on Mrs Brown. Thank you for telling me.

Ted bowed to her before leaving the room with the kitten. Henry started to prepare the food for the dogs by Ivy as he enquired,

-I guess the Master and Sebastien are at the clinic already?

Nodding positively, Ivy answered,

-They got up at the crack of dawn and left soon after for the clinic. My father in law left a letter for you. It is on the shelf.

Henry went straight to it and read it quickly then told,

-I am going to be a busy bee today, it looks like. I hope I will be back in time for the wedding of Theo. I would not want to miss it for the world. But I may have to miss breakfast.

Ivy replied,

-You are going nowhere unless you have something in your belly, Henry. If I tell Sebastien, you skipped your breakfast, he will pull your ears tonight.

A laughing Henry fed the dogs before sitting down by Jack at the table. He said,

-Ivy, I will do anything to escape the punishment of a punisher even eat your breakfast.

Falsely angry Ivy retorted,

-What have you heard about my cooking? I know how to recognise salt from sugar now!

Everyone around the table started to laugh even Raphael who had remained silent. Margot came into the room. Ivy welcomed her with a kiss on her forehead,

-Good morning Margot, take your seat by Raphael. I am almost ready to serve breakfast.

Marguerite smiled to Ivy and proposed,

-May I help you?

A pleased Ivy answered,

-Yes, you can. Bring the bread and butter on the table and let Henry cut it and serve it to everyone. He is punished for teasing my cooking. You will find everything on the shelf.

Margot obliged her while everyone kept giggling at the table. Henry argued,

-It is not my fault if Sebastien don't talk very highly about your cooking... You fed him a fair few odd things. I shouldn't be punished to say some home truth.

Ivy bringing plates on the table, gave Henry a dark glance and demanded,

-What did my Sebastien tell you, so I can pull his ears tonight?

Ted was back in the room and brought the pan full of scrambled eggs to the table and started spooning everything to everyone. Henry slicing the loaf of bread and buttering every slice for everyone including Raphael, was happy to oblige Ivy with a huge smile on his face,

-I heard about your crumbly biscuits full of salt and about a soup which was seasoned with sugar. When he invited me to live here, Sebastien reassured me that he would be in charge of the cooking.

Ivy sat at the head of the table with a pout then vented,

-The rascal! Those things were supposed to stay between us.

Doctor Williams made a couple of books appear in front of her telling her,

-Ivy, don't despair. Here are some culinary books from my library. Learn from them. I know for a fact that they are the favourites of your husband. Everyone knows that you didn't have a mother to teach you anything in the kitchen so you are fully forgiven for your mistakes here and there. Are the scrambled eggs sugary or salty today by the way? Did you make sure eggs have been used?

Although Ivy smiled, she answered,

-If you were not such a good friend of my late father...! Eggs have been used. I did my scrambled eggs the way Sebastien taught me with a little black pepper and some chives and a little milk and of course eggs. There was some salt added to the eggs but I didn't taste the salt like he suggested I did for the foreseeable future and the welfare of our children.

Everyone looked at their plates with some worry. Doctor Williams asked with a grin,

-Who wants to try first?

While Henry was laughing, Ted remained politely silent. Raphael who has been enjoying sitting with them all and their interaction silently proposed,

-I am willing to try. I saw Mrs Cotton make everything and she prepared everything very nicely. Sugar or salt, it will not poison anyone.

Margot sitting by him fed him a spoonful. Raphael gave the all clear,

-Those are nice scrambled eggs. I like the addition of the chives. Margot, eat yours while they are warm.

Margot took his cue, and everyone around the table followed suit. Raphael gave a kind smile and a wink to Ivy while he waited patiently to be fed the rest of his scrambled eggs. They were cold by then but he still liked them thinking that beggars couldn't be chooser. He saw Henry leave first the table bowing to Ivy and asking her,

-What can I bring you to contribute to this household?

Mrs Cotton asked with desperate eyes,

-Can you bring us a hen that lay eggs? Because we can't all live on Doctor Valdi's hens. When he will come back, what will he eat with his young family?

Henry demanded,

-Where will you put the hen? There is no space in here.

Doctor Williams ordered,

-Just bring the hen, Henry. I will get the land to feed this family. We will build a chicken coop there together. We can always put the hen in the stable for the time being.

Henry bowed to him then left. Soon afterwards Ted went with Jack to walk the dogs. Doctor Williams departed to go to the clinic. Before he did so, he made a few things appear and presented them to all intended,

-Ivy, your husband told me that you would end up with a dozen children if you didn't possess any nightdress. This is for you. I went a little lavish upon it because I was such a good friend of your father that I consider you a little like my daughter. The lace on the collar and the pretty red velvet bow will suit you very well. This is for your little boy Jack, a couple of good shirts to replace his one that was damaged. Miss Margot, this is for you. I know you are still grieving but there is a wedding this afternoon and you are invited. Consider this little dress as your best dress and your Sunday dress. It is the same colour of your eyes and you will be very pretty in it. It is a present and you do not have to repay me, however if you keep feeding Raphael, like you are doing, I will consider myself paid back. Finally Raphael, this waistcoat is for you. Let me help you to put it on. It comes from one maggot for another maggot. It will give you a bit more warmth than just a shirt. Winter will be coming soon enough and we don't want you to catch a cold. Especially if you perverted other archangels to kill healing angels, I will not be here to look after you, my heart would have been eaten and you will have to cough a lot then. Have a good human day.

When Raphael saw Doctor Williams leave, he had tears in his eyes. Ivy came to him and scolded,

-Come, come, no crocodile tears in my house, Raphael. You look smart in that waistcoat, good enough to be invited to this afternoon wedding. I will see if they will let you go. It is not a given but they allowed me to invite you in the house for breakfast. You have to understand that it is the household of major angels.

Checking her given dress, Margot commented,

-We must not forget that Raphael has been a bad angel as well. It is not like he is the virgin Marie. But he has been given a chance by the Master of all angels and not sent straight to hell that must be considered too.

Ivy went to her and looking at her dress, she told,

-You, young Miss are going to look so pretty in this. Come, go to your bedroom and put it on. That petticoat is so elegant as well. Doctor Williams has always been a man of taste. He is from Boston, you know, Margot. Look, there is even the shoes to go with the dress and a pair of white stockings. Go and prepare yourself for the wedding of this afternoon. I will prepare your hair. I know a way to make them fall on your shoulders into pretty curls.

Margot smiled and ran rather than walked to her

bedroom with her brand new dress. Left alone with Ivy, Raphael stated,

-I think she is going to be very happy here.

As she started clearing up the table Ivy confided,

-I hope so. What happened to that young girl distresses me. If I ever see her father, I will give him a piece of my mind.

Raphael said,

-Mrs Cotton, I saw the man yesterday with your father in law. Mr Cork is very tall, well built and a very violent man. Raguel is strong yet that bastard of a man repetitively plunged a broken glass bottle in his chest. Such aggression was painful to watch to tell you the truth. I strongly advise you to stay clear from such a man. That comes from me who have been a warrior in my days as an archangel. We had the upper hand but 'just'. I kept Margot behind me, and I can tell you, she was shivering like a leaf at the sight of her fighting father. She was petrified and terrified. I don't want to know what the man did to kill his wife and what he did to his daughter but I can confess to you that I had fright in my chest for Raguel, Margot and myself yesterday.

Cleaning the dishes diligently, Ivy only replied,

-It doesn't deter me for one bit. I tell you what, that man needs to be publicly shamed in broad day light. Yesterday, you three were alone in the street at dusk. He is a coward in my view. He does his attacks, abuses at night or behind close doors. If I ever see him during daytime I will still shout at him. But yes I will avoid him if it is dark out there.

The fallen angel shook his head in desperation before stating,

-With all the due respect to you being stubborn, Mrs Cotton, I will have to inform your husband and your father in law of your intentions for your protection.

She couldn't answer to him as a knock on a door was heard. She ran to the door still wearing her apron and opened it. A surprised Ivy welcomed the visitor warmly,

-Miss White! Come in, please, come in. I am sorry, I am totally disorganised this morning. I have nearly a full house and well, I am learning to deal with an entire household. How is it now at the hotel?

Whilhelmina scolded Ivy,

-Ivy, you must call me Whil'. At the hotel it has been busy as hell, but I have only the families who have lost their houses now. One has twelve children so you can imagine how lively it is up there at the moment. I heard that you have homed Daisy Cork, the little Marguerite Bouchon.

Ivy led Miss White to her kitchen and once there she spoke freely in front of Raphael, as she explained,

-Yes, I am giving her a home. But she wants to be called Margot, so please call her Margot. Did Raguel tell you that we need to check her out, medically? She has been abused again. Look, I helped her to my nightdress yesterday, the poor thing is almost all over black and blue. You could count her patches of skin which are not bruised. I hope I will make her happy here. You know I didn't have a mother to bring me up. So I hope I will still be a good surrogate mother to her or a kind of sister. We have more information, of the angelic kind, Margot doesn't know it yet, we haven't told her, and we, us two, need to assess if it is true or not. There is a very high possibility that she is pregnant.

A thumping was heard, as Raphael kicked the table, venting out,

-Poor thing! She is only twelve! The bastard!

Ivy took the opportunity to present him to the surprised Miss White,

-This is our back garden host, fallen archangel Raphael, he was saved from drowning by Margot. We tolerate him here as he adjusts to be a human.

Whilhelmina just nodded to him before paying her full attention back to Ivy, informing her,

-We just arrived with Theo. We put our phaeton and Rosalie in your stable. As you see I have my medical bag with me, so I am ready to take a look with you at Margot. I dealt with her last year and she will be confident to explain everything to me. Let's go.

Ivy turned to Raphael and told him,

-Let me let you out. Father Odell is here. Go and meet him. Tell me how it all went later. You will find him in the church.

When Raphael was out, he saw Ted and Jack walking the two dogs. He went to them and addressed Ted,

-Ted, I have something important to communicate to the Master and to Sebastien. Can you please send a telepathic message for me? It concerns the little wife of Sebastien. She may run into trouble. Please read me, you will see her intentions. Warn the Master and her husband.

Ted held the hand of Raphael to assess what he heard and seen then agreed,

-I will warn them both. Thank you for telling me. If you ever need to send a message to them, please feel free to tell me or either the Messenger, we are both living here permanently.

Raphael added with some emotion,

-That man killed his own wife. Little pregnant Ivy will not last long within his hands. A confrontation between him and her is to be feared and prevented. But she would not listen to my advices against it. May be she will listen to her husband? But she must stay safe and away from that violent man. I understand her anger, I have the same one concerning to what happened to Margot. But she will put herself in such a dangerous position. You need to tell Raguel, he will know what to do.

Reassuring him Ted told,

-Leave it to me. What are you doing with your human self today?

Biting his lips, Raphael answered,

-I do not really know. I am going to meet Father Odell then he will probably decide if I am good for something despite my two broken arms. I do not know my worth as a human yet.

Ted said leading Raphael to the church,

-Let me open the doors for you. You will find Theo to be a very nice angel. Don't be anxious, just do your best loving wise. The heart is the rule.

Despite that advice Raphael was nervous when he entered the church alone. Ted closing the door behind him confided to Jack,

-Well, since he became human Raphael is learning to

care. This is something.

Ted patted Ludwig's head sharing all of the informations he did get from Raphael, therefore sharing them straight to the Master of all angels then he send Raphael's message to Sebastien. Then he told,

-Jack, it is time for you to have a big rest before this afternoon. I will stay with you.

The little boy gave his hand to Ted and followed him back indoors. In the meantime Raphael walked inside the church. He saw Father Odell working actively by the altar. He went there and somehow his voice failed him at the right moment. Odell, however addressed him,

-Good morning. I don't think I ever saw you in Wilton Town before. May I help you? Are you here to confess?

This made Raphael smile sadly before he replied rather awkwardly,

-Good morning. Are you Father Odell? I have plenty to confess, yes, but I am not here to confess. You are right, I am new in this town.

Theo paid more attention to the tall newcomer. He noticed his two broken arms and commented,

-It looks like you ran into a spot of trouble. I am indeed Father Odell. Take a seat, please. What brings you here?

He went to touch the fingers of Raphael as he added,

-You can call me Theo like everyone. Pray, what is your name if you don't mind me asking?

On the account of the affability of Odell, the fallen angel took a seat on one bench of the church. He could perceive what everyone had said about Father Odell, that he was kind. So he replied with total honesty and sincerity,

-I am the former archangel Raphael. My spot of trouble is that I met the angel of justice and I was punished according to my crimes. I lost my wings and I am now human. My human name is Raphael River. The Master of all angels condemned me to be human, but also to death apart if I met human generosity. He throw me into the river, with two broken arms, so I could not swim. I never thought I would meet human charity but the young girl called Margot, or you may know her as Daisy Cork, saved me. So I am here, as a human, and rather lost. However I live on the bench in the backyard of Sebastien and his father, him and his wife have tolerated me and shown some kindness to me. When I think of what I have done to them or tried to do, I am disgusted with my own self. But the Master demanded of me to be a good human. He said because this town had a fire, they would need help to rebuild it and to ask you to give me some work.

Theo considered the fallen angel, walked passed him many times then told him with slight anger in his voice,

-I don't think I have anything for you. You are the one that wanted to kill my best friend, Doctor Valdi, when he was trying to save the heavily burnt angel Rob. You are the one that schemed to kill all healing angels. You are the one that hate humans so much that you incited others archangels to follow suit. Guess what? I am a human angel, everything you do hate. I suggest you walk out of my church immediately.

With great difficulty Raphael stood up with no will to argue, downhearted, but also with the knowledge that the angel in front of him was a demon killer despite how kind he was supposed to be. But then he heard a voice he recognised, scolding,

-Theo, my good Theo! If the Master sent him to you, there must be a good reason. That piece of trash isn't asking you to like him, he is only asking for work.

The ghost of Abraham Wilton-Cough came from behind the altar holding a rolled map. Theo retorted,

-What can he do without his arms?

Abraham replied straight away,

-He can use his brain.

Then he asked the question to the fallen archangel,

-Can you? What are your skills and credential? You do know that rebuilding the part of the town that was burnt is a community effort, don't you? Therefore you will not be paid for it.

Then the old banker intimated out loud to Theo,

-Father Odell, we do need all the help we can get to make sure the people have houses for winter. The Master knows that. Look they use prisoners to build the railways further north.

Raphael was slightly intimidated by the fact that he was facing the very physical ghost who prevented him to kill Valdi and Rob and had maintained him to be dealt with by Raguel. He also took the cue that the old ghost seemed to know the Master of all angels quite well. In front of Raphael's silence Abraham prompted,

-Come. Respond to my questions. Have you lost your tongue as well as your wings? Don't just stand there like a sore thumb or a useless human! Sit down and tell us what you can do.

Somehow the authority in the voice of Wilton-Cough made Raphael comply. He sat back on the bench to reply,

-The Master told me to say that I was good at scheming.

Theo laughed out loud and ordered,

-Out of my church!

Wilton-Cough's voice stormed over the one of Odell,

-Patience! The Master is not one to make fun or joke of his leftover of enemies. He would not send him to be ridiculed but to be redeemed instead.

He then asked again to Raphael,

-Is it really what he said?

The fallen angel replied with a positive nod but added,

-He told me to say they were organisation skills instead.

Abraham turning to Odell pointing to Raphael, stated,

-Here it is, Theo. The Master wants us to employ him. You've got to get over the fact that this piece of trash wanted to kill Valdi. He didn't at the end of the day because we saved Valdi and Rob. Moreover Raphael has been punished very severely by the Master, who is the angel of justice. I know it all because I was there and trust me when I say I never thought Raphael would be able to stand alive before us today.

Sighing deeply Theo sat by Raphael on the church bench while taking the map from Wilton-Cough's hand. He rolled the map open and said in a more compassionate tone,

-Right, Raphael, our community effort is taking shape nicely. We have plenty of hands to dispatch. We have formed specific teams according to what they could do best. Now we are missing a couple of overseers, one for the reconstruction work in town, and one to organise bringing the material in town. I think you could help with the later. Let me explain to you what it involves with the map. Here, we have a stone quarry. We have a good team formed to work there but they need leadership. We also have a very large forest and we will need to fell some of the trees to make doors, window frames and furniture for those who lost everything. That team is rather small, split in two, one that will fell the trees, and the one that will transform them into what we need. That small team will need some organisation. We also have a problem, between the quarry and the main road to the town there is no path to bring the stone upon carts. Right here.

Raphael commented,

-The team needed to fell some trees will have to start right there and make that path to lead to the road for the carts. It will facilitate everything. I am up for it, if you want to give me the work. I can oversee that operation, control the quarry and your forest team. We can get things done before winter. I controlled armies before.

Then he stopped talking abruptly. He bit his lips. His head lowered and tears appeared in his eyes. With a gulp in his throat he begged,

-Please, let me help you.

Theo stood up and replied,

-I will. I will help you as well. The bench in Sebastien's garden is uncovered and you will face all the elements from wind, rain and snow. Sleep on the church's benches at night. It is still quite a drafty place but it will be warmer than outside and you will have a roof above your head.

Taking the map back, Wilton-Cough added,

-Stop mopping, Raphael, come with me. I will show you where the quarry is. It is a bit further afield but I will give you all the markers to know where you are in the forest. I used to go there with my father often. He was a keen hunter. Your work will start from tomorrow. I will tell you about everything you need to know about everyone on your teams on the way. They are a very good bunch in general but there are also about three or four to look out.

Raphael stood up and offered his hand to Theo with a few words,

-I am truly sorry, Theo. Please don't give up on me. Help me to become a good human.

Odell held his hand briefly before he replied,

-I will help you but you must work hard to prove yourself to me. No one touches a hair of Doctor Valdi without facing my wrath. You and I will never be friends. I am just agreeing to give you some work and a roof above your head. Now, go.

The fallen angel bowed to Theo and obeyed. He followed the physical ghost of Abraham willingly. Outside on their way to the woods, Wilton-Cough told Raphael,

-I never saw Father Odell being so cross. But you must understand, that Doctor Valdi is not only his best friend, Theo considers him as an elder brother. They have been through thick and thin together looking after the people of this town. When someone is born they are usually there, when someone dies they are usually there together. At my death, I had them both at my bedside.

The fallen angel asked,

-I heard the name of Valdi very often since I am here, who is he? He seems to be highly regarded. I thought he was just an healing human angel. And of course I regret deeply my atrocious intentions towards him and Rob who he was saving.

Wilton-Cough sighed deeply as he stated,

-You are a totally lost fallen angel in Wilton Town if you do not know who Doctor Valdi is. Vincent Valdi since he came into this little town twenty odd years ago, made changes, good ones. He was our first Doctor and we needed one very badly in town. Then his morals, ethics are right up there. This is why he became an angel during his lifetime just like his friend Theo. But Valdi was first to earn his wings. Doctor Valdi not only helps people, he protects them. When he went on his honeymoon, away from the town, all the scoundrels in town thought they will have a good time. Hence the fire we suffered recently. However what they didn't expect was that we had angels coming into town and settling there. And you, you, chose that night of fire to plot to kill all the healing angels! Despicable!

Without any notice, Abraham kicked the fallen angel.

Raphael lifted his broken arms up in the air before saying,

-I am truly sorry.

The old banker stopped and demanded,

-Prove me how sorry you are. I will keep checking upon you. We are giving you a chance and you'd better be good at it because otherwise, it is hell for you.

Raphael answered,

-Please, show me where we are on the map now. I will deliver. I don't want to fail the Master ever again. Can I ask you what is your connection to Raguel?

Wilton-Cough replied proudly, before showing the map,

-I serve him. I serve his brother. I serve his son. I serve his father. We are here, by the four ancient oak trees. It is like a cross road in a sense. Now, you see this oak tree marked with an A and another A entwined in a heart, this is where you need to turn right to go to the quarry. Come with me, the path hasn't been used for years, so it has almost disappeared.

Looking at the tree and getting a good sense of his surrounding, Raphael asked,

-Who marked that tree? What is in the other direction?

The ghost answered willingly,

-I did mark the tree when I was young and alive. One A stands for Abraham, my first name, and the other for the first name of my widow, Angela. We made love by that tree very often, so often that she became pregnant with my first son and I add to marry her despite the disapproval of my family. Angela was my ray of sunshine during my life. The other way leads to a lake, a small one. The path is overgrown as well but, it would be a good idea to clear it. The lake is full of fresh water fish which could provide the inhabitants of the town with some much needed food in their time of struggle. If you reestablish that cross road to its former glory, you will have achieved something. Just leave the four oaks standing.

The fallen archangel followed Abraham, thinking that he could see why the Master of all angels and his family took a servant like Wilton-Cough. He listened carefully to all of the advices of the ghost even the simple ones, like when Abraham told him that when cutting the undergrowth, to keep all the nettles and to not discard them because they could be used as soup to feed the people who did fell on hard time. When they reached the disused quarry. Wilton-Cough showed him the dangerous parts and the ones which were fine. They sat on an old rock together and Abraham explained to him the entire situation in very complexed details. But when they went back together into town, Raphael was fully clued up about everything and was very certain that he could do a good work as an overseer.

It was past noon when they arrived in Wilton Town, passing in front of the clinic, they were called in by Raguel. Abraham encouraged the anxious Raphael to step in the clinic. When both entered, Raguel locked the door behind them which unnerved the fallen angel greatly. But the Master ordered,

-Raphael, sit down and stop trembling. Abraham, please tell me how did it go this morning? I have three small missions for you following this one.

Wilton-Cough bowed to Raguel, while Raphael sat silently and watched the interaction between the ghost and the Master of all angels. Abraham told Raguel,

-It was not a given. Theo did have a good conversation with Vincent yesterday night. Of course, Vincent confided what happened to him to his friend. I never saw Theo so cross in my entire living life. He literally was upset for Vincent. But as you sent me to help Theo this morning, I was able to control the situation and his temper. So Raphael is appointed as the overseer for the quarry and the woods. I showed Raphael where everything was and briefed him fully about his role.

An appreciative Master demanded,

-Thank you so much, Abraham. I will take it from there with Raphael. I need you to go to the presbytery and to check on the situation with Margot. I want to know the result of her examination by Mrs Cotton and Miss White. Then check on Jack. Is he strong enough to attend the wedding this afternoon? Come back to tell me everything. Afterwards I just need you to go and get Valdi and his wife. They need to be ready for Theo's big day.

Abraham bowed again saying,

-I will get it done, Master.

After letting the physical ghost out of the clinic, Raguel locked the door again. He then turned to Raphael to ask,

-So Father Odell gave you a hard time it seems?

The fallen archangel nodded positively. He complained,

-You should have warned me...

The angel of justice cut him short,

-Did you warn anyone when you did plot to kill all healing angels? Right, let's get back to our matters. I am pleased to know that you have managed to be appointed as overseer of the quarry and the woods. How do you feel about it?

Sebastien and Doctor Williams came into the waiting room, nodded to Raphael to acknowledge his presence then Sebastien told,

-That's it Dad, your turn to have lunch we are done. Did anyone come apart the Maggot?

His father smiled to him only to reply,

-Just our good old banker Wilton-Cough, so you haven't got any patient to look after at the moment. However be prepared, Ted had another vision, just about a minute ago. He thinks it was happening when he was seeing it. You must expect at lest two casualties if not three, a father and two of his eldest sons, from the poor street in town. Their roof which was badly damaged by the fire collapsed upon them. I sent five of your angels to the location to check upon the situation. They will bring them if they retrieve them from the debris. So get ready. Doctor Williams, did you prepare the soothing cream for the bruises of the young Margot? The Messenger is on his way to pick it up to bring it to Doctor Cotton and our nurse Miss White.

Williams answered diligently,

-Everything is ready, Master. I did large quantities of the cream for that poor child. However, Henry may have to do a couple of trips to bring all the pots to the presbytery.

A satisfied Raguel ordered,

-Warn him, Mr Berry is in town this morning and can help him with his carriage. Anthony will never refuse, he is such a good human.

Then he turned to fallen angel Raphael, helped him up, and told,

-Come with me, my Maggot.

Raphael followed Raguel willingly and silently in the corridor that led to a vegetable garden. Once outside the Master turned to him to say with a deep sigh,

-I'd better give you a good lunch because we will all be at the wedding of Theo later this afternoon and the chances of you being invited are very slim, it seems. Odell is a good angel, but if you wanted to harm his friends, especially his best friend, that will certainly not sit well with him. Come with me and respond to my initial question, how do you feel about being an overseer at the quarry and the woods?

The fallen angel saw his former Master pick a basket and a gardening tool, then pick up pea pods and dig up some carrots. He replied to him with honesty,

-I think I can help and help well, Master. Wilton-Cough did give me not only the full brief of my duties but also lots of ideas. I went with him to see everything from the woods to the quarry. He briefed me even about every single member of the teams I will be dealing with. It was very informative and, yes, I think the ball is in my camp. This is something I can do.

After collecting some parsley and putting a bunch in his basket Raguel answered,

-Good, after lunch, I will make you meet your teams. Come with me upstairs. Don't be afraid I will not bite you, I am not a vampire. I am just going to feed you. But don't speak too loudly because there is a bedroom near the upstairs kitchen where a young lady called Rose is resting. She is in a very bad condition, not because of the fire in town, but because of the gang who did horrendous things to her. Sebastien who is a surgeon for this town managed to save her but we don't think she will be able to get up for a while. She has an appalling story, destitute, all alone in the world. She escaped to Wilton Town to be safe from the gangs from Boston but here, she suffered the most vicious attack by the gang of this town. We tackled that gang the very night I punished you and my father sent archangel Michael to hell forever with the help of Lucifer. Come, but don't be loud.

Once in the small upstairs kitchen, looking at the humble surrounding Raphael asked in a quiet voice,

-Who lives here?

Presenting him a chair at the table, Raguel replied,

-This is the home of Doctor Vincent Valdi, the angel you wanted to kill in the river along with my human angel Robert. If it wasn't for the intervention of Abraham Wilton-Cough and me arriving in time to punish you, if you had killed Valdi, you would have faced my father's wrath. He would have come to pick you up himself with Lucifer and you would have faced the hell punishment like Michael forever. Take a seat.

Raphael obeyed while he enquired,

-Doctor Valdi seems to be so important in this town?

Presenting three bowls, putting the pea pods in one, the Master ordered,

-Time for you to regain some dexterity in those fingers, Raphael. This is just a small exercise so your fingers don't go totally numb on you. Take all the peas out of the pods. Peas are going into that wooden bowl, pods are going to the other, simple logistic. To answer your question, Doctor Valdi is not only important in this town, he is very important in the angelic world. If you were an angel, I would tell you precisely who he is, but as you are my maggot, rotting things up, I will not tell you. If you are clever, you will work things out, eventually, for the time being, take the peas out of those shells if you want to eat. We haven't got all day.

Doing as he was told, Raphael complained,

-You are always such a tease. But thank you for accepting me in your vicinity. I must confess that I need your help more than ever. Being human, well, being human, I would say hurts more physically and mentally. If I did know that before I would have probably been more compassionate to human kind.

Raguel cleaning the carrots then chopping them laughed,

-It took you an eternity to realise that.

The fallen angel retorted,

-No, it took you! So, your son is adopting fallen angels and you have ghosts working for you, what is going on there? If I may ask. Apart if you want to carry on being a tease, you may give me another non answer.

Raguel replied by asking,

-How are you doing with your manual task?

With a deep sigh, Raphael confided,

-It is more tedious rather than hard to do. But the pain in my left arm is more acute than the one on my right. I can manage it though. Will you ever answer my questions, Master, or keep leaving me in the dark now that I am a human?

The Master of all angels told sternly,

-I am not keeping you in the dark because you are a human, but because you are a traitor to my father. Your current status is not affecting your past actions. They speak for themselves as... well I will lack adjectives to describe them really but let's settle for despicable for now. As for the Mighty One, he always had a good heart and he gives more chances to angels to redeem themselves than I do. Jack, his adopted son, if he is a fallen angel has worked for centuries to protect the soul of a little girl which he did successfully on his own. Jack deserved his chance. For you, it is extremely early stages. We don't even know if we can trust you. You have to earn your credentials. Pass one human lifetime or many and earn your flying colours. Although you did hurt me beyond belief by taking one of my sons away from me I am not going to ignore you if you ever try to regain your wings. As I said first you need to live a decent human life, a helpful one. I will be there to judge you at your death. Then I will decide if you need more human lives or if I can't get the soul you sold, to just let you go to hell.

Raphael gasped but then replied,

-Master, I will try my best to regain your trust. I said sorry to you but I am ready to spend one human lifetime or many to say sorry to you. I will start to do what you did ask me to do. I will try my best to live a good human life. I will serve you during it. You can ask me anything, even shelling peas for your family or growing them. You can call me your Maggot because I will spoilt you rotten, because I cry tears of sorrow for what I have done to you. I am your slave, your servant. I am here to stay by your side forever.

The fallen angel tried to dry the tears flowing on his cheeks but couldn't. Raguel came to him and did it for him, scolding,

-Concentrate on your peas so we could eat one day our lunch and stop working yourself up. I got your message loud and clear when despite your state you intervene against Margot's father. I am taking it into consideration, it is all that I am saying at this stage. Now, tell me what do you plan to do as an overseer?

Pulling himself together Raphael explained, with some enthusiasm,

-There is a crossroad in the woods. It is disused but it leads to the quarry on one side and to a lake on the other. The road it crosses is the one that goes to Wilton Town. I will put some men to work in the quarry straight away because it will take them some time to chisel the stones for the houses. Whilst that will be done, the other team will clear the path to the quarry and make it large enough for carts. Your ghost did give a lot of savvy tips, like using nettles to do soups for the people who fell on hard time, also not to just use the trunk of a tree to do doors but to remember that the branches and twigs can be used as firewood for them for the winter. Once the way to the quarry is cleared, I will make them open the other way leading to a lake. The lake is fed by a little stream coming from the main river. You have fresh water fish in there to feed the locals according to Wilton-Cough. Creating those two ways should provide enough wood needed to rebuild the houses burnt down. I can oversee that easily. The harder task is to make sure the humans in the quarry stay safe because some parts of it are dangerous. I will have to keep a close eye on them. Can you tell me more about your ghost? He was so helpful and knowledgeable.

The Master went to the stove, put his carrots in a pan of boiling water before he replied,

-It sounds like you have a good plan, Raphael. When I presents you to your teams this afternoon, I want you to explain the plan clearly to them. Now, as for the ghost his name is Abraham Wilton-Cough. He was the descendant of the man who created this town. He, himself, created the first bank here. Abraham was a banker through and through, he knew all of his customers by heart as well as what they did possess or what they did lack of. He was the main landowner of this town, selling or lending lots of plots of land to newcomers. People appreciated him, but also feared him and respected him. Abraham died because he protected his customers in his bank from a robber. He saved everyone but his own self. He was shut in the guts and died in agony hours later. He doesn't rest in peace because he wants to look after his family from beyond the grave.

Handing all of his shelled peas with difficulties, lifting the bowl and bringing it to Raguel, Raphael commented,

-Here, Master. To be honest with you, I like his non sense approach. Although my first encounter with him was when he stopped me from doing the worse, I appreciate his courage to do so greatly. In the way he speaks to you, he is a servant of the angels, isn't he?

The Master of all angels admitted, while he prepared the meal,

-He is and he is a good one at that. He has the will. He is brave. But more importantly he has a good heart. My father rates him very highly. Prepare me some parsley, just tear the leaves up. It doesn't matter if it is roughly done. Only the flavour is important here.

Taking back his seat Raphael obeyed and confided,

-Master, if I fail to meet your standards, if I fail to get some wings, if I simply fail, would you let me be a servant ghost if I can't be a human any longer?

Raguel gave a long deep look at the fallen angel before he replied, half teasing,

-Of course, I will send you to hell at the first opportunity, a hell of slavery by my side where I can call you maggot everyday and make suffer for eternity.

Raphael smiled despite himself. Soon the meal was served by the Master who presented it on the table with some gusto,

-Here, my Maggot, I hope you will enjoy that because you probably will not have any food until tomorrow. We have fish from the river which was cooked in the oven with cream, breadcrumbs and some herbs by Sebastien, crushed potatoes with a knob of butter and your roughly teared parsley and our boiled carrots and peas. We mustn't forget a little soda bread done by my son to share between us. Now open your gob, like a good human, and let me feed you.

The fallen angel submitted himself to be fed willingly. His eyes moistening at the thought that the Master of all angels kept looking after him despite it all.

#

Coming back from the tavern meeting, side by side, the Master of all angels told Raphael,

-That didn't go too bad. In fact, it went better than I did expect. For your first interaction with a lot of humans, I would rate it as a six and a half and to be generous with you a good seven.

The fallen angel argued,

-That was a ten out of ten. I did have them all involved. All do know their tasks for tomorrow. They are mentally prepared and ready for the mission ahead. I answered all of their questions. I gave them the schedules and time frame. I even went to the very minute details à la Wilton-Cough of the waste nothing...

An amused Raguel retorted,

-I agree with you on those points, my Maggot, but you muddled their names which is worth minus one point.

Raphael looked at him bemused and kept arguing,

-They were so many! They all look like working ants to me. I can't recognise them all from day one, can I?

The Master responded by a sharp slap on the back of the head of the fallen angel,

-You are one of them now, Raphael River, do not forget about it. Treat and speak of humans like insects, and I will carry on to treat you like one. Respect them, you will then earn my respect. Learn the names of everyone in your teams, recognise them, most importantly respect them as individuals and spot their specific skills. You will then know how to deploy everyone more efficiently.

Taking the advice on board the willing Raphael queried,

-Where did I lost my other two points then Master?

Raguel told sternly,

-Your big fat lie, that was a minus two points, about your two broken arms. You didn't help during the fire in town, you were a hindrance.

Raphael protested,

-I was trying to protect you. I didn't want to say you broke my arms.

Laughing the Master replied,

-Trust me, if you would have told the truth, that you suffered your broken arms because you wanted to kill Valdi and Rob, the town folks would have accepted it. They probably would have tried to drown you in the river afterwards but I may have enjoyed it. Anyway, I am their sheriff now. If you would have told the truth, it would have sent the message that I will not mess about. But I accept that you shied away from the truth, that is what cowards do. It is to be expected with you, my Maggot.

A sighing fallen angel felt relieved when he saw Wilton-Cough coming towards them. The ghost bowed to Raguel before briefing him,

-Master, the young Margot is definitely pregnant. Mrs Cotton and Miss White are extremely upset about it. What hasn't been noticed because she is such a tough girl is that Margot had a couple of broken fingers. Those have been seen to by Mrs Cotton. Jack is having a good rest, he is asleep since his walk with Ted, this morning after breakfast. However, Ted wants Sebastien or Doctor Williams to check him before Jack is allowed to get up again. He said it would be preferable to let him rest than go to the wedding. He also said that he will keep looking after him because the boy has visions or had visions which are draining him. Jack will be fine but he needs to rest. I am now on my way to fetch Valdi and Amelia.

The Master thanked Abraham who disappeared from the view of everyone. A concerned Raphael confided with emotion,

-Poor little thing pregnant at that age, it is disgusting. Mrs Cotton was very upset about the possibility of it this morning. Now, she will be really upset. You must watch her, Master, because she will probably put herself in great danger if she ever see that man.

Raguel told him,

-It is not the first time it happened to Margot. She nearly lost her life last year giving birth to a still born baby. Ted failed to see a future for her. She has been placed in a home with a surgeon and a Doctor so I hope for a better outcome. Look, we have devised a plan to reconstruct the town with Wilton-Cough. As you know I am the sheriff here now, I will have premises, office and jails built. Individuals like Cork will be sentenced, judged and put in prison in the near future, I can tell you that.

After your spell as overseer, if you really want to stay in this town, if you don't find some work by yourself, I can employ you as a jailer. It is not a bed of roses work but someone has to do it nonetheless. I know that when your arms are healed, you will retrieve part of your past strength you had as an archangel. It will not be the same, but it will be enough to deal with nasty humans of the like of Mr Cork or the gang I had to deal with and threw out of town. The thing is you are also canny enough to not let them fool you to escape. You always had your wit about you so you can outfox the criminals. I sincerely think you would be perfect as a jailer and this town will need one with me taking charge of doing the law.

The fallen angel giggled despite himself as he commented,

-I bet they would need one... But jailer is not a very glamorous work to do. Everyone will hate me.

Smirking, the Master retorted,

-Look it is no longer the centuries of knights in shinning armours. As I said it is up to you. The offer will remain on the table. And by the way for your information, everyone hates you already because you hate everybody. You will not lose your status of being not liked whatsoever.

Raphael argued with some passion,

-This is not true any longer, this is not true! I like poor Margot, I like Ivy, I like your Sebastien, I like you, I even like your Williams and I like your ghost. I do not hate everybody any longer. It's finish! I have feelings, I do have feelings, Master. As a human, I feel, I started feeling and I can feel it...

With his emotions rising, Raphael started crying. Raguel put his arms across his shoulders and comforted,

-Come, come, don't cry on me now. Good Lord, aren't you an emotional thing since you are human? It is good to have feelings. Now, you understand where everyone is coming from but also the wrongdoings you have done for centuries and how hurt everyone was when you did them. Now, you must dry your tears for me. Be strong and be a good human. It is a new start, a fresh start with nearly no mistakes in it, except for your little lie this afternoon to your teams about your broken arms but I will generously pass on that.

Walking to the presbytery together, Raguel continued,

-Why do you think you like Margot? Think about it? She saved you from a river out of her good conscience and heart. The girl has nothing and had to be given a roof above her head. She had fled bad circumstances, violence and yet that little human took the care to save you and share her bridge and food with you, and she didn't have much, did she? You finally saw the good side of humanity in her. She has nothing and yet you like her because she helps her fellow humans. Now, you have nothing, just like her but a blanket and the clothes upon yourself but you can be liked at some point, because you can follow her example and help your fellow human beings. Feelings are a good first step now you need to transform them into positive actions.

When they arrived in the church yard, they saw Margot holding the little fox terrier Killy, she came to them and announced,

-Jack can't go to the wedding, Doctor Williams said. He is running a bad fever and Doctor Williams and Ted are dealing with it. So I have been walking Killy for Jack. I hope Jack will get better soon. Are you both coming to the wedding? They did big preparations in the church. It looks beautiful.

Smiling to her, Raguel replied,

-I am sure it will be a very nice wedding. Seeing your very nice dress I know you are invited. It suits you very well. It matches the colour of your eyes and I like what you did with your hair. How are you doing, my young friend?

Margot gave him a welcoming hug as she answered emotionally,

-I could be better but Ivy looked after me so well. I, I may have a baby in nine months time but the first time I failed to deliver so I know it is not a given. Ivy said that I will go nowhere but staying under her roof. She said she will take care of me and my baby and that she will protect me. And Miss White was ever so nice to me, she always has been. She asked me to be her bridesmaid. I have never been a bridesmaid before. Mrs Marlow, Mina and Emily will also be her bridesmaids and so is Ivy and Amelia Valdi. It will be quite something. Oh, and I have two broken fingers but Ivy said they will mend well. Mr the angel of justice, how are you doing today? I have been worried for you all day since what my Pa did to you last night. Are you coming to the wedding?

The Master led her back to the house whilst he said,

-I am the one marrying Father Odell and Miss White, so yes I will be there at the forefront.

A disappointed Margot confided to him,

-I wanted to sit by you on a church bench during the ceremony.

Sensing her fear, Raguel reassured her,

-No, no, you are participating so you will be standing up most of the time. When it is time to take a seat, take it by my son Sebastien, he will protect you. I gave the orders to three of my angels to guard the doors of the church during the ceremony so if your father ever comes, he will stay outside. You will be alright, just like last night, I promise you that.

She nudged the hand of the angel, she had been holding, as she replied,

-Thank you Mr the angel of justice, it is most appreciated. If I ever grow up, I will demand you in marriage on one knee to show you how thankful I am.

Her answer surprised the Master who lost his usually stern face all of a sudden. It softened his heart to the point that Raguel smiled when he ordered her,

-A lot of water would have pass under the bridge before that can happen. Now, my dear Margot, let's concentrate on the wedding at hand. Please, tell all the ladies and the bride to be all ready for the ceremony which is due in one hour while I will be preparing the altar. And please, if you really want to marry me, just call me Raguel in the future.

The young girl kissed his hand before running inside the house, with some joy carrying the little fox terrier as she said,

-I will get it done for you, Raguel.

Once the door was closed behind her, a baffled Raphael asked,

-Did she just said what she did? You literally had an almost complete marriage proposal, here, Master! Or shall I say Mr the angel of justice? The gusto of that young Margot keeps amazing me.

Walking with him towards the church the Master stated,

-You heard it as well as I did. The fact is she had her hand in mine at that moment and I can reveal to you that she was in earnest and that she meant it. I read her mind.

Now, very curious, Raphael demanded,

-What did she think of?

Raguel was happy to reveal,

-She feels safe by me. She wants protection and she wants to be a good wife to me in exchange. The degree of her thoughts were quite mature, she wanted to clean my house, clean my clothes, prepare me nice meals, be devoted to me and give me a family. I can tell you she was all very serious about it.

A little miffed Raphael commented,

-Well, she should have chosen me, really. Not that she did a bad choice on the contrary, she did a very daring one. But I met her first and I protected her too.

The Master teased him,

-Do I sense another of your bouts of jealousy coming towards me? Look, here, I am called Mr the angel of justice and you are called the bad fallen angel. Maybe she is just using reason as well as heart on that one?

Despite it, Raphael couldn't help giggling but intrigued he demanded,

-Come rub it in! But will you ever consider that human for matrimony?

Raguel told with assurance,

-If she ever propose to me again when she is of age then yes, I will not only consider her, I will give her my hand, I will give her my protection. Look, she will be a young woman then with a young child to raise. No man in town will want that burden especially if it is not their child. She will have very little chance to find a husband willing to accept her as a wife knowing that she is not a virgin any longer, that she has been damaged and raped. But I am actually very willing to look after her, care for her and if she doesn't give a still born baby, care for her child as well. If she marries me in the future, me, being the sheriff in town, it will give her an instant status in town, for her and her child. To be honest, I consider it as taking her under my wings.

Opening the large doors of the church, the Master let Raphael in with him. Raguel was amazed by the decorations from the ivy garlands decorated with white roses running all around the pillars of the church, to the huge elaborate tapestry behind the altar representing a white rose and a white dove with a golden ring between them, passing by the red carpet going to the altar covered with white and red rose petals. Henry came to him with a smile and briefed him,

-We are only doing final touches to the arrangement, Master. I managed to get everything on your list. Literally everything, so much so that my wings hurt. Your father has organised everything for the celebration at the tavern. He is still there at this moment in time but he will come, for he doesn't want to miss Theo's wedding. The beautiful tapestry behind the altar is a gift from him to Theo's church. He said it has to be used for every wedding in Wilton Town from now on, because it carries a blessing for every couple in its threads. The people in town have been informed of the wedding of Father Odell to Miss White, and so many are coming. They are putting their best attires for it. The three M will be guarding the doors of the church for you but I will give them a hand if needed and report to you if any trouble happens there.

The Master tapped the shoulders of the Messenger with gratefulness as he said,

-I bet you are looking forward to the feast tonight at the tavern? I thank you, my son.

With delight, Henry replied,

-Yes, I am looking to rest my wings definitely but I heard Sebastien did profiteroles towers, filled with cream, covered with chocolate and caramel. Now, that is something to look forward to. He did some for me for one of my birthdays in a past life, a little stack of them and they were delicious. So, yes, I am full of anticipation for those. Can't you suggest him to do those every Sunday as a treat for all of us in his house?

Raguel laughed however he answered,

-If he does that dessert every Sunday, you will not be able to fly any longer my angel. So no, you are too useful to me to become a plump turkey flying in the sky. I will not suggest any such thing. Beside that my Sebastien is poor, he will not be able to sustain his growing family if we don't intervene. I know he wants to feed us all but he hasn't got the human means. Williams is going to get him a piece of land which we can transform into a garden. But I aim to get him another plot for grazing animals, like cows, sheep and goats. Then maybe he will have cream everyday to be able to indulge us with profiteroles every Sunday. But if this happens, I will make you fly a lot to lose your weight. I will make you cross the Atlantic ocean twice a day, flying during any kind of weather.

Henry pouted and vented,

-Alright then profiteroles are just a treat for every now and then. But can I say you are mean without punishment?

Corking his brows, the Master replied with a smile,

-You can try and see what comes to you.

The Messenger had slopping shoulders at that moment. He commented,

-I'd better get back to work. You can task me again Master because I did all you wanted.

Raguel told with a sigh,

-I do have a small mission for you. But it is very precise and I want you back for the wedding. Williams send me a message just now that he needs something from his house in Boston to look after Jack. Jack is running a fever right now and Williams has the potion which could help our boy in his laboratory cabinet. Go and fetch it as quick as possible. Hold my hand and you will see where everything is. He wants you to fetch a few more things as well. Jack is struggling to recover as you know. If I ever lose that fallen angel I will cry rivers. Please, be quick, fast and thorough.

Henry held his hand then went after doing a silent bow to the Master. Raguel went where Father Odell was. Raphael was following in his tow without a word. The Master of all angels asked a busy Theo,

-How are we all doing?

Theo Odell looked at him and replied,

-It is pretty much ready. I didn't do the altar though. I am not dressed up yet and I am suffering from a bad case of anxiety. I am going to marry my Whil' though, it is just belly butterflies before the moment, that is all. What is he doing here? I told Mrs Cotton that I didn't want him at my wedding whatsoever, not after what he tried to do and all his plots. He can enter my church to sleep in it tonight and every night when no one is here, not beforehand, and do not plea to me to accept him like Ivy and Daisy did. My answer is simply no, not after what he tried to do to Vincent.

Raphael bowed to the Master and simply said before he went away with a great deal of sadness in his heart,

-I will be on the bench outside, Master.

Once the fallen angel was out of the church, Raguel told Theo,

-This is the second time I find you vindictive, Odell.

Theo retorted,

-Justifiably so! Don't tell me you didn't go all vindictive upon him as well with the state he is in. I will give him a hand but I don't want to see him during my wedding day. He tried to kill my Vincent! Vincent is an older brother to me. I can't bear the thought of ever losing Vincent, I just can't, not with the amount of times I cried upon his shoulders. He has always been the strong one. You don't understand. I rely on him. He is my guiding hand, my compass, my north pole, my moon and my sun. I learnt by following Vincent for fifteen years and yes, the joke about me is true, I would have lived on tea and biscuits offered by old ladies if Vincent didn't took the time to teach me how to cook a little for myself.

The Master scolded him gently patting his back,

-Right, I understand you are still very upset about it all. But I want you to understand one thing as well, a very important thing: Raphael has been punished and very severely too. My eldest son is dead because of Raphael selling his soul yet I know I punished him thoroughly. Raphael is now just a lost human upon earth. I can assure you that Raphael's sorrow is so real that he is suicidal. He is on the edge. He paid by his punishment. As for my brother Vincent, he is still alive. You haven't lost him. Abraham and I saved him. So I am afraid you will have to get over that anger of yours, in time. If I can get over mine, who has really lost someone, I am sure you will be reasonable enough to get over yours who didn't lose anyone. Now, go and get dressed for your wedding while I prepare the altar. You will find some very dashing clothes in the cloakroom of your church, which Henry brought during the day. They have been tailored just for you and they are a gift from the human angels army of my son. You will also find a lovely white rose, to put inside the top pocket of your tail coat. I chose it myself from the garden of Miss White. Let me tell you something, your future wife is as anxious as you. She also has the belly butterflies.

Sighing Theo told before obeying,

-Bless her.

Little by little, everyone from the town arrived and took their places on the church benches. After what had happened in town with the fire, the inhabitants needed a happy event and most certainly the wedding of Theo Odell was providing it. The joyous chatter amongst everyone stopped when they saw their elegantly attired priest, not in his usual frock, take his place by the altar to wait for his bride. Perceiving the anxiety of his new angel, the Master went to him and adjusted here and there his attire, before tapping his shoulder as he reassured,

-Here, my Theo, you look dashingly the part. You must count your blessings not only because you get to marry the most elegantly beautiful lady in this town, but also because you are an angel who get to marry for eternity. It doesn't happen very often in the angelic world to find an eternal being as a companion. I can tell you that for only having married humans and having to grieve at their eventual death. You, my lucky angel, is escaping grief with your other half. You just face eternal happiness.

Doctor Valdi arrived by the side of his friend Theo along with Sebastien, both were bickering yet smiling. Vincent demanded,

-Theo, tell that angel that I am your best man, he insists that he is your best man.

It was the Master who resolved the issue by ruling,

-Sebastien, you will sit with your wife and Margot on the front row. The young Marguerite is scared and you must sit by her side to protect her. I do not want want to hear any 'but' from you either. I know you like your Theo so much that you could have become his wife if you didn't have one already that also need some looking after. So stop being childish, my son, how many centuries do you need in order for you to become an adult? Vincent, you are the best man of your best friend.

Valdi couldn't help giving a winning look and smile to Sebastien who in turned couldn't resist pulling his tongue to him. But at the angry glance of his father Sebastien retreated to the bench without any argument. The Master vented,

-Children! I knew that both of you would be trouble together. You've both similar personalities. Good Lord, I wait to see the day when you will both start working together properly at the clinic. I can already guess that there will be a lot of slamming doors and objects thrown at each others.

Valdi arranging his own tail coat and his cravat denied,

-No, I am always well behaved with perfectly good manners. It is my nephew who is the trouble maker...

The angel of justice warned him,

-Are you really sure you want to persist in that line when you are talking about my son?

Looking at the stern face of his older brother, Vincent desisted with a giggle,

-No, I think I will stop at 'you have a perfect son who can hold so many good or bad arguments that he could have been a lawyer instead of a surgeon'.

Raguel couldn't help smiling at his repartee and ordered,

-Prepare the rings, Vincent. You will find the small red velvet cushion on the stool by the altar.

Then the Master turned his attention back to Theo who was smiling. He asked him,

-Are you ready, my angel? Are you sure in your heart?

Theo nodded positively to him and replied a firm yes. Raguel stated,

-Good, because your future wife just stepped into the threshold of your church. My father is giving her a way and she looks splendid. Turn around, and look how magnificent she is. Take a deep breath because she will take it away.

His heart pounding in his chest, Theo obeyed. An organist and a small orchestra started playing the 'Sarabande' of Haendel. At every step of Whilhelmina walking up the aisle, at every note of the music, Theo's emotions rose to the fore. He, who had always been teased, had found the way to the heart of a most magnificent woman, a life saving nurse, a caring midwife, a beautiful soul. When she was finally by him, she saw a little tear at the corner of his pale blue eyes. She smiled shyly to him as she wiped it with her finger delicately, softly saying,

-My Theo, I love you so much.

Her touching tenderness rendered Theo even more resolute that she was in hers and his heart already his wife. He gave a nod of the head to the Master who started the ceremony fully.

In the meantime when the church's doors were closed, trouble arrived in the shape of a Mr Cork looking for his daughter. However, the doors were heavily guarded by Matthias, Maximilien and Maurice, the former musketeers, now angels in the army of Sebastien. Cork tried to force his entry but was soon rejected, however he had managed to give a concerning bleeding black eye to Matthias. The father of Margot decided to see if there was an unguarded back entry to the church and as he walked around, he came across the little backyard garden of the presbytery. On the bench, a down hearted Raphael was having a nap. He didn't see the man coming but he heard him when Cork shouted,

-You! Where is my daughter? I want my daughter back! You are the bloody bastard who helped the one that was taking her away.

He started battering Raphael who was just coming back to his sense. Whilst one of the three M took his injured brother to see Doctor Williams inside of the house, the other stood in guard by the church doors. Williams at the news that Cork was nearby ordered Maurice,

-Release the rottweiler. He will find your man and get rid of him. I will look after Matthias. Go with the dog but be careful with that man, he is nasty. It looks like your brother may have lost an eye. I am sending a telepathic call to Henry to come immediately.

Maurice didn't lose a minute to do as he was told. Ludwig the rottweiler ran as soon as the door was open where the trouble was. Maurice had difficulty to keep up with the dog. Ludwig went ferociously for the calf of Cork as soon as he found him. The human stopped battering Raphael straight away and tried to deal with the dog harassing him. He took a tomahawk from his belt and was ready to plunge it into the rottweiler who was still having a good go at his leg. But Henry arrived upon the scene, and in a fast move removed the tomahawk from the hand of the man from behind. Henry, now the holder of the axe, warned,

-Get yourself out of here before I start playing with your tomahawk and scalp your head raw.

Facing a fierce Henry, Cork released a large dagger from his belt as he said,

-Let's just see who will get more skin out off each others heads, shall we?

Maurice arriving in the backyard garden tried to tackle Cork to make him release his knife, but was in great danger doing so. A badly bruise Raphael managed to get up from his bench and punched the man with his cast in his balls, then stated,

-I really wanted to do that.

Cork dropped his dagger straight away in pain. Henry gave the tomahawk and the dagger to Raphael with the order,

-Look after those while we get rid of this bastard from the property.

Maurice and Henry threw Cork back into the street and close the gate of the church yard. Henry stroking the head of the rottweiler commented,

-I wish I thought of that kick in the balls, Master. I am sorry I came a little late for the wedding, there was an exhausted cow in trouble in a muddy ditch. Of course, I had to help. You know me and animals. I was many of them before.

Dusting his shoulders, a baffled Maurice queried,

-Henry, what are you talking about? I am worried about you sometimes. This is a dog, not the Master. Have you really been animals before? And what was that about scalping that human? Truly this was scary. You nearly ended up in a massive fight there. But that human, that human is nasty, truly, truly nasty. My entire body hurts just by wrestling with him. Thank god for the quick thinking Raphael.

Henry revealed,

-The guard dog of Sebastien is a manifestation of the Master, but you must keep it secret from Raphael. I had the warning from Williams but I knew exactly where to land because the Master was there already attacking Cork and he told me the exact location to be fast. And yes I was an animal spirit before being human and an angel. If you want to sit by me at the wedding banquet, I will tell you all about it. Now, go and check on Raphael. I think he is pretty beaten up but he will never admit it. Go with Ludwig. I have to deliver some remedies for little Jack to Doctor Williams.

While Henry entered the presbytery, Maurice went to the backyard garden where he found Raphael in sheer pain. But, as soon as Raphael saw him, the fallen angel put on a brave face and asked,

-Is that man out of here?

Ludwig went to put his large head on Raphael's lap looking at him. By doing so the Master of all angels was assessing Raphael's body fully, just by the skin to skin contact. He was already sending messages to Doctor Williams and Doctor Valdi about the state of Raphael. Maurice replied,

-Yes, he is out of here. Thanks to your intervention. How are you doing? Because I can tell you that this man is so strong that my muscles are in pain right now.

Making a great effort to present the weapons of Cork, the fallen angel answered,

-Same here. The bastard caught me asleep and unaware. That human is so violent. I can't imagine what his poor daughter went through. Here, give those to the Master. I can feel terrible things from the tomahawk. It is very blurry because I am not an angel anymore but I can say that the man used it, his father used it and his grandfather used it. I can feel the blood of many humans upon it. The Master will know what to do with them. Thank Henry for me for intervening and thank you for coming to help. I am indebted. I haven't got very much to offer but if you need any errands to be done, anything that I can possibly do, please, both of you, feel free to ask me.

Maurice took the weapons and told,

-Thank you, Raphael. Keep Ludwig with you. The guard dog of Sebastien will keep an eye on you.

Stroking the head of the rottweiler Raphael said,

-He already did. Cork stopped battering me when he intervened. So his name is Ludwig. You are a very good dog, Ludwig, I like you.

Maurice smiled before he left the courtyard. He came back to the presbytery to check on his brother. He saw two Doctor Williams at once in the room of little Jack. One physical manifestation of Williams was looking after a feverish Jack, whilst the other was looking after Matthias attentively trying to save his eye desperately. One of the Williams asked fervently as he saw Maurice,

-How is Raphael doing?

Maurice replied as he deposited the weapons upon the chest of draws,

-He is putting on a brave face like I do. I can tell he is sore and he is in pain. That man, Williams, that Cork, he is atrocious. Something is wrong with him. No one can be so violent like that. Raphael said he could feel that Cork's tomahawk was used by Cork, his father and grandfather, and that the blood of many humans is upon it. He couldn't see that much further though. He said it was blurry.

Doctor Williams commented,

-Well, if Raphael is a little sentient, even just a little, there is hope for him to gather back his wings. Watch this space. The Master told me, Raphael sustained more broken ribs, a couple. But Raphael is brave as you said. We are going to tend to him after I have finished with your brother. I think I may have saved his eye but only time will tell. I want him to be seen by a specialist in Boston. I am afraid I will keep Matthias with me tonight and he will miss the big wedding reception at the tavern. But I am sure you will be kind enough to bring us some food from the party for your brother, Ted, Jack and I, if only just some profiteroles that Sebastien made this morning. Now, go and stay with Max to make sure he is alright and that Cork didn't come back.

Maurice bowed to Williams and obeyed. However when he arrived at the doors of the church, they were flung opened. The bells were ringing madly. The newly married couple was about to come out. Henry had brought the little phaeton of Father Odell out from the stable. He was holding the old Rosalie which had been nicely decorated for the occasion with red and white ribbons and flowers on her mane and tail. There was no sign of Mr Cork in the vicinity, Max came to him and told him,

-The coast is clear. Henry, you and I are going to accompany the couple to the tavern, leading the way.

It was just time as everyone was leaving the church full of cheers. The newly wed couple followed suit. Whilhelmina was beaming while Theo was amazed by the attendance at his wedding. The bride threw her white and red rose bouquet to the crowd before climbing into the little phaeton of her husband.

Georgia Marlow caught the bouquet before it reached the ground to the applause of Mina White who said joyfully,

-You caught it, Georgia, you caught it! That means you are the next one to be married!

The good old Georgia commented with a blush and a smile,

-I do not know about that.

But Mina retorted with a giggle,

-I think you know that a certain Doctor Williams is sweet upon you. He kept smiling at you in Boston and in the coach. You've got to marry him so Emily and I can ring the wedding bells again. Wasn't it fun Emily?

The shy Emily answered her jubilant friend,

-Yes, it was. That very tall gentleman was very kind to let us do so.

The Great Being behind her said,

-The very tall gentleman is here to escort the three of you to the wedding reception. Let us follow the phaeton. Will you do me the honour of holding my hand, Emily? So you all enjoyed a good time in Boston, I heard?

The enthusiastic Mina responded straight away,

-Don't be afraid Emily, take his hand. You are with Georgia and me. We had a lovely time in Boston, Sir. Emily got a pair of glasses she needed. Miss Marlow has a new very fashionable hat and we saw the sea. I have a collection of sea shells now, because I collected so many of them and Doctor Williams was ever so kind to teach me all their names.

Smiling at the former young vampire, the Great Being carried on the conversation all the way to the tavern with the three of them. Meanwhile in the church, an anxious Margot was holding the hands of Ivy and Sebastien tightly. They were waiting for Raguel who was tidying as much as he could. They were the last within the church. But Sebastien urged his father,

-Pa, Raphael is hurt, outside, on a bench. We've got to go and see him.

The Master told sternly,

-And we will, in time. Do you know that back in the days, this excellent warrior faked to be injured and in trouble on the battlefield? Protecting him, I was the one who got injured. He, the only healing angel at the time, pretended to heal me but I was getting worse. When I stopped to be under his hands, I slowly got better. Raphael can wait a little. At least, we will not fake our care for him when we are giving it.

Paying attention to the conversation Margot demanded to know,

-What happened to Raphael outside?

A little annoyed by the question, Raguel nonetheless replied,

-Your father happened. He recognised Raphael from yesterday and decided to batter him. My angels did successfully not let your father enter the church. Although   it was almost at the cost of one eye for one of them. Your disgruntled father subsequently took it upon Raphael when he found him on his bench.

An upset Margot with tears in her eyes exclaimed,

-But Raphael couldn't defend himself with his two broken arms!

Getting angry as well Ivy told,

-That man need to be stopped. He is despicable.

Sebastien intervened strongly,

-Ivy, you must go to the tavern. Doctor Valdi and his wife Amelia are waiting for you in the courtyard. You will be escorted by Maurice and Max. My father and I will look after Margot. We will not be long to join you all at the wedding reception at the tavern. I just need to attend to Raphael first. The man wanted his daughter back, so we will keep her safe my father and I. She has two punishing angels as bodyguard. Remember, stay safe for our little ones.

A disgruntled Ivy did as she was told but kissed the forehead of Margot before she left the church. When the church doors closed behind her, Sebastien confided his worries to his father,

-Dad, my Little Bit is definitely upset. We must pray that

she doesn't encounter Cork. I know Ivy by heart, when she is angry, anything can happen. In the Boston hospital, we did operate on a man with a bullet in his chest. We saved him. He had been attacked by that gambling gang. One of the member of the gang dared to ask for his money back whilst the man was recovering. Ivy was there and she threw scalpels at him to get him out of the hospital. She was fierce and calling him a scoundrel was not enough for her. Doctor Williams had to prevent her from chasing the man in the street who was running away from her with a scalpel stuck in his leg.

Smiling Raguel told,

-It is better to go to the tavern as soon as possible then. Let us check on Raphael.

Sebastien's medical satchel appeared in his hand straight away while his other hand took the one of Margot with great care as Sebastien enquired,

-How is your little mitt now?

Margot replied with certainty,

-It will be alright. I have seen worst. Ivy mended it. She said it will take about three to four weeks for my fingers to be back to normal.

On the way to the back garden of the presbytery Margot pleaded to Raguel,

-Mr Raguel, is there any way we could take Raphael to the wedding party so we could feed him a little tonight?

The Master sighed deeply as he replied,

-It is not my choice that he was refused point blank to be invited at the wedding. Raphael wanted to drown the best man of Father Odell only a few nights ago, who was not only his best man but also his best friend. So you must comprehend that Theo Odell doesn't want to see Raphael on his wedding day whatsoever.

A pouting Margot retorted,

-What I also understand is that if Raphael had been inside the church, he would not have been battered.

Sebastien commented,

-She has a point, there, father.

Giving a dark glance at his son Raguel replied,

-So am I to understand that you are both prepared to ruin someone's wedding day for a bad arse fallen angel?

His son replied firmly,

-For a severely punished angel who is now a rather lost human with two broken arms and has just been battered, yes.

The young Marguerite added passionately,

-And I know what my father can do! He can break spirits, souls and lives. We must take Raphael with us otherwise my father, knowing where he sleeps, will go and finish him off. He is, he is vindictive, that is the word. My father will kill him tonight.

They arrived at the garden and saw a suffering Raphael on his bench. Sebastien asked him with compassion,

-I heard about what happened. How are you doing? I am here to treat you.

The fallen angel didn't expect to see the three of them and asked,

-Shouldn't you all be at the wedding?

The Master answered,

-We are all concerned about you. We will go later after Mighty makes you a little bit more comfortable. Will you come with us? You still haven't got an invitation, but I will ask again. You can stay in the alley way by the tavern until I tell you the answer. You will be protected by the angels Callum and Maurice. Ludwig, our guard dog, will stay by you as well.

While Raphael couldn't help tapping the head of the rottweiler in a gentle manner, he commented,

-He is a good dog. He helped me greatly. He was fearless and I was fearful for his life. The man had a tomahawk and he was going to go for the dog. I was struggling to stand up but the Messenger came right on time and saved the situation. He challenged Cork in a manner in which I was then scared for him. I can not start to tell you, Master.

Raguel told,

-I do know everything. Just answer my question, my Maggot. Do you want to come with us? I can not promise to you that I will succeed to get you inside the tavern with an invitation. But I can guarantee your protection while you are out there in the alley way. I can also promise you to feed you my leftovers.

Margot added as she went to hold the hand of the Master of all angels,

-And I will keep you some good bits to eat as well. I am used to not eat a lot anyway. You must come with us, Raphael.

A smiling Raguel commented winking at the fallen angel,

-Maggot, you can't refuse the charity of a human.

Sebastien who had started to remove carefully the waistcoat and the shirt of Raphael told him,

-You are coming, Raphael, it is not a question any longer, it is an order. Now let's see what Cork has done to you. That doesn't look really good. It's manageable however.

Snapping his fingers, he made a pot of cream appear by his side and asked,

-Father, Williams must make more of his cream for bruises. I have just taken an entire pot of his supply because this fallen angel will need it. Raphael will be alright. However, he will be in pain for a while. We can only soothe him, I am afraid at this point.

Making a few more things appear he continued,

-Raphael, I am not going to lie to you, it will hurt you when I will apply the unguent to your skin but you badly need it. I will massage it in. Now, as you have broken ribs you will be in pain when I do so, but you will feel the effect and the relief within half an hour. Then I am going to bandage your chest in a slightly stronger bandage than the initial one. It will allow your ribs to heal by maintaining them in place. It will still allow you to move but in a restricted fashion to prevent more damages. Do I have your consent to proceed?

The fallen angel agreed and thanked Sebastien when it was all over. He then followed the group on the way to the tavern asking the young girl,

-Did you enjoy the ceremony, Margot?

Margot told him with her natural honesty,

-Yes, very much. I made two new friends today, Mina White and Emily, both are roughly my age. I knew Emily from before, at school but she was always very reserved and timid, a shy thing really. But I don't know if it is the influence of the bubbly Mina, she was opening up a little more today.

Sebastien explained to Raphael,

-The little Emily had a poor eyesight. She couldn't see things properly and it gave her trouble at school. The teacher, she had in the past, punished Emily so severely repeatedly that Emily has appalling scars on both hands. According to Valdi, one day, her father who unfortunately passed away since, brought her to the clinic to have her hands seen to because you could see the bone on one of her fingers. The teacher's cruelty stopped there because Doctor Valdi intervened and got the man sent away from the town. Emily who didn't want to return to school is now a little companion to Mina White and lives at the hotel of Miss White.

His father corrected,

-The hotel of Mrs Odell now, my son.

Although he had not desired that much informations, Raphael understood the level of care that existed for humans between the father and the son. He reflected that when he was an angel, he despised humans so much, that he didn't care at all about their individual stories but now that he knew Margot things were dramatically changing. Somehow he had began to feel for the human plight and he wondered if he followed the example of the Master and the Mighty One, he would one day regain his wings.

When they arrived in the alley way by the tavern, Callum and Maurice were already there waiting for them. Both angels bowed to their superior before Maurice briefed,

-Everyone is indoors safely, Master. We have kept the places where Ivy is sitting free for the three of you. For Raphael we have a barrel of ale outside to sit upon. But we also have a glass for him courtesy of Tyrell. We told him that we may have an extra guest but that he may not be invited in by Father Odell. We explained him why. We also told him the mitigating circumstances about Raphael having been battered. However he said that if Theo persisted in his choice of not inviting Raphael, he will respect Theo's will, because he is, himself, a good friend of Doctor Valdi. But he said, as the plea was made from angels, he was willing to make the fallen angel feel a little better and warmer with some good ale, hence the cask and the glass. He told us if Theo refused entry to Raphael which he approved of, he will prepare nonetheless a plate of good food for our fallen angel to be fed in his alley way.

A worried Master enquired,

-So you did tell Tyrell the entire truth about Raphael?

Callum replied,

-Yes, we did. When Sebastien sent his telepathic message to us, he said to us to consider Tyrell as his next angel and part of us, so we informed Tyrell fully.

Sighing Raguel ordered,

-Raphael take a seat on that cask for now, but I have a deep feeling that you will stay out there up until we take you back with us at the end of the reception. But at least you will be fed and protected. Ludwig is by you and you have my two angels. Maurice, please help Raphael drink. He can't do that on his own yet. But don't let him become a drunken mess for he is starting work at the quarry tomorrow and he will need his wit about him. Callum guard the entrance of the alley way.

Callum bowed respectfully to the Master and gave him a large key. He pointed to a small back door to the tavern and said,

-Tyrell is giving you the key of the back door for the night so you can look after your fallen angel easily, Master.

The Master of all angels nodded to before he enjoined,

-Margot, Sebastien, let's go in then.

#

Inside the tavern a cheerful ambiance reigned. Beers, Champagne, Wines were flowing aplenty and the people were joyful. While Sebastien and Margot went to sit by Ivy, Raguel went to find Father Odell. He found him on a quiet table in the corner surrounded by red velvety benches. It had been especially decorated for the wedding with a garland of white and red roses and ivy. The husband and wife were sharing a happy moment together, drinking Champagne and touching hands looking at each others with love. Both were blushing when Raguel stood by their table when he commented,

-My new angel, I think you can kiss the bride once more for you are both devouring each other with your eyes.

While Whilhelmina remained silent but couldn't hide your thoroughly red cheeks, her husband delivered a kiss on her hand gallantly before he told firmly,

-Master, my answer is still no. Tyron had the courtesy of warning me about the matter. My wife and I are long time friends of Vincent. I will not tolerate the fallen angel that tried to kill him to be enjoying himself at my wedding reception.

Raguel demanded,

-May I sit by you and talk to you both for a very little while?

Odell nodded positively and made room for the Master of all angels by him. He then poured some Champagne into a glass for him. Raguel commented,

-I will agree with your decision, Theo, do not fret about it. Something happened outside the church while I was marrying you two and Raphael was battered by Mr Cork. We sorted Raphael out, giving him medical attention. Well, my Sebastien did. I have a big conundrum for you, Theo. May I share it? Or is it not the right place and time to do so?

A curious Whilhelmina told,

-I would love to hear it, if I am allowed that is, Master?

Raguel replied firmly,

-You are allowed because you are part of my son's army.

With a deep sigh Theo answered,

-You may share it. I would have preferred another time but we are your soldiers at the end of the day.

A pleased Raguel clinked his glass with the ones of the couple before he shared,

-As you know I am a punisher and the angel of justice. I fell on so hard on Raphael, that I have true sorrow from him in front of me. He hated humans and I rendered him human to punish him. It works. Now the conundrum is this: he sold his soul when he was an angel. He had his punishment. He is now human and weaker and if he dies, he will go to hell despite having paid for his sins.

Theo took a deep sip of his Champagne before he answered,

-We have to keep Raphael alive before we find a solution. I offered to him to sleep in my church at night so he will have a roof above his head against the elements. Now, what else could be a danger to his life?

His wife responded,

-Theo, the man has just been battered by Cork this afternoon. Cork is a danger to his life. I've see the true state of Margot this morning and I was retaining myself from crying. What are the damage on Raphael right now, Master?

Sighing the Master replied,

-A couple of broken ribs, but he already had a couple of broken ones before from my punishment.

Theo smiled despite himself as he commented with sarcasm,

-Ouch, that is going to hurt!

Raguel scolded him,

-Compassion, my angel, compassion. I do not like him either but I recognise true sorrow when I see it. He has it aplenty. I made him human and now he will be lost in this world if not for us and the charity of humans. Not only that he will be lost forever if he dies. I have to find a way to retrieve his soul while we are keeping him alive.

Intervening the white witch told,

-I know who can help! Jack preserved the soul of my daughter for centuries. He can tell us how he did it. I can also dive in my witchcraft books and try to find a solution.

Odell proposed,

-If well accompanied to be able to get out of hell, Wilton-Cough could possibly steal the deal, the selling of soul deal, he has seen it, like you, your father and Vincent. You can trust Abraham to remember where Lucifer kept his souls deals. It is not something that would have escaped his attention. Once retrieved, we can burn it and void it. It will put Abraham in great danger though, but he is canny. I am sure he can pull that one out of his bag. He will need proper diversion which you can provide with Vincent. May be just another rough and tumble fight with Lucifer could do the trick?

The Master commented,

-I prefer investing in the Jack solution but I am not dismissing your one, my Theo, not at all, I think it is a very good one. My last fight with Lucifer ended with me having a dislocated shoulder so if the less brutal way works, I am all for it. Thank you both for your advice. I will leave you two to enjoy your reception.

Taking his Champagne glass with him, Raguel went to inform Tyron about the decision of Father Odell regarding Raphael. The good tavern owner nodded positively before he confessed,

-I am not surprised. Valdi and Odell are like two fingers beside one another on a hand. If you ever hurt one or think of hurting one, you will have the wrath of the other on your hands to deal with. Raguel, you are new in town, but there is one thing you must understand straight away, Vincent and Theo are such friends that they would lose their life for one another. I have seen them in my tavern many nights from the early days of their friendship till now. An exhausted Doctor Valdi, coming from a long day of work, was teaching painstakingly and hilariously at time Father Odell to play cards and chess. They were having conversation about everything from politics to god passing by the latest fashion on how to fasten a cravat. But mainly Valdi was making sure his friend had a proper meal at least once a day. With them, it is friendship on the highest level. You can't mess with one without getting a repercussion from the other. So I will prepare something for your fallen angel. I already kept a few bits aside for him because I guessed what would be the outcome of trying once more to get him invited. Now, I know he will help at the quarry as an overseer and I know he lives on a bench at night. You can tell him one thing, if he comes to my tavern from tomorrow, I will feed him in the evenings. It will not be free, I will expect him to repay me later. I understand he is newly human and a little lost at the minute but that he has to learn to earn a living.

The Master commented,

-That's right. You have been very well informed.

A smiling Tyrell answered,

-I just pay attention to everything. Like today when the supposedly Mr River who is in fact fallen archangel Raphael was asked about his two broken arms, I knew he was pulling a tall tale out of his bag by the expression on your face. But I also noticed that you, having severely punished Raphael, you stood by him to get him started with his human life. I can help you do that. I can do with some help in my tavern in the evening. My tavern is rapidly becoming a place where people eat rather than solely drink. I can do with another waiter therefore I can employ Raphael. I will pay your fallen angel for his work. What do you say?

Raguel finished his glass of Champagne before he replied with some glee,

-I only hope that Raphael will accept your proposal. I will put it to him. He has an offer of work from me to become a jailer when my sheriff offices are done and the prison for this town is built but this will take some time. If he is a waiter until then it will keep him nicely occupied. Let me tell you a little angelic secret, Raphael did hate humans with a passion. Now that he has been punished to be one, his mind is turning around on the matter. To have him serving humans for a while, is not only pleasing me, it is also amusing me greatly. But on the serious side of things, I think it could be just the exercise he does need and requires to help him to recover his wings at some point.

Tyron refilling the glass of Champagne of the angel told,

-I am always happy to help. Raguel, during your stay here in Wilton Town, I want you to know that you can count on me. I owe to you and your son to have kept my tavern, my livelihood. It will never be forgotten.

The Master of all angels served the man a glass of Champagne as he said,

-This is good to know. You have my appreciation and the one of my son. By the way my son wants to make an angel out of you so be prepared to have a conversation with him in the next few days. As the Master of all angels, I am ready to welcome you in our midst.

Both smiled as they clinked their glasses together and Raguel was about to go outdoors when a window of the tavern was smashed, and Mr Cork stepped inside through it, shouting,

-I want my daughter back!

It was so close to the table where the family of his son was that he rushed to intervene. But Ivy had already stood up to the man and shouted back,

-You will never get her back! Over my dead body! You, rapist! Have you seen what you did to her? Ladies and Gentleman, I present you a despicable man who after killing his wife raped his daughter. Mr Cork is not a man to respect, he is an animal of a man.

She lifted the sleeves of the young Margot to prove her point. The exhibition of the arms of Marguerite was sufficient for others to know that Doctor Ivy Cotton was right. Ivy went further, she challenged directly the intruder. She slapped him in front of everyone before anyone could react, as she added with great anger,

-Ladies all with me! We will keep his daughter protected together. This man has no place in this town. He blinded a man from one eye. He battered a tramp sleeping on a bench. He stabbed my father in law with a broken bottle. He is a nasty piece of shit!

Cork punched her in return causing an up row. Sebastien pushed his wife in the arms of Henry ordering him to look after her, while he went in a full fight with Cork. Raguel took the young Margot out of the way and through the back door. As he opened the door, he announced to his angels,

-Her father wants to claim her back and is causing a brawl in the tavern. Keep Margot safe for me, all of you. Maurice, Callum and Raphael, I am counting on you three. I have to go back in there and fight. The bastard did hurt Ivy. He punched her in the face. Margot, stay with them and stay safe. We will protect you.

Whilst Raguel went back inside the tavern, Margot cried thoroughly. Raphael went by her and made her sit on his barrel. He reassured,

-It is going to be sorted, Margot. Please, dry your tears. We are not letting you going back to that monster of a father. Stay with us and all will be alright.

Marguerite tried her best to be brave whilst she was wondering what was happening inside the tavern. In there Sebastien was helped by Valdi to prevent Cork to touch Ivy ever again with his fists. However the young Doctor was not done with Cork. She was truly upset that he did punch her. She went back to fight the man, anger in her eyes. She shouted, as she broke a bottle in half,

-You bloody bastard of a man, you will never touch a woman or a man or a child the way you did. This is for the harm you did to my father in law!

Raguel stopped her in time before she lashed out fully upon the man. However if he took the broken bottle from her and held it high up in the air, he warned,

-Mr Cork, if I was you, I would run away now. You raped your child, you killed your wife, you did hurt lots of people and I am about to teach you everything about comeuppance. Punching the Doctor that is looking after your girl was a wrong thing to do. Punching Ivy will cost you dearly. Sebastien, Vincent with me.

Raguel came like a bull into the ongoing fight. He threw Cork back into the street by the window the man had came in to disrupt the reception. The angel of justice jumped into the street followed by his son and his brother as he continued,

-Do you want to know what it feels like to be stabbed by a bottle, like you did to me, do you?

Everyone in the tavern went to the broken window to watch what was going to happen. The newly wed Whilhelmina shouted,

-Break his fingers, like he broke the ones of his poor girl!

An incensed Ivy agreed loudly,

-Yes, and punch him for me, punch him hard! I never saw a child so bruised in my life!

Theo and a few men jumped in the street by the window. They watched the fight ready to intervene but Raguel had the upper hand. At every punch he told Cork this was for this and this was for that. The Last punch was delivered by Sebastien saying,

-This is for punching my wife. We will look after your daughter from now on and that is all there is to it. If you ever try to claim her, rape her or kill her, you will face your death penalty. Now, I suggest you leave town before the mob stones you to death the next time you appear in the streets.

Like a dog running with its tail between his legs, a properly battered Cork left as fast as he could the scene. If he still wanted a revenge, he knew he would not get it that night. When the man was out of sight, Sebastien turned to his father to proudly say,

-I think we have secured the safety of our Margot for a few days if not more. Good Lord was he a tenacious bastard!?

Raguel smiled to his son as he answered, bleeding from one eyebrow,

-Yes, he was but that mustn't allow you to swear by your grandfather's name. Let's get back in. I will fetch Margot. By the way, you have a beautifully blue tumefied cheek.

Checking Valdi, the Master commented,

-He went for your eyes too. Cork nearly blinded one of my angels this afternoon. Let me see. This is just a pretty black eye. It will hurt for a bit but you will be fine.

The three came back to the tavern by the main doors to a round of applause. Amelia threw herself into the arms of Vincent, kissing his cheeks. Ivy did the same to her Sebastien, yet giggled,

-You've got a similar cheek as mine, Mr Cotton. Thank you for protecting me.

Sebastien couldn't help smiling as he said,

-Next time you want to have a big fight my little Bit, tell me first, please.

She kissed his nose laughing. Raguel gave a side glance at Ivy adding his own advice,

-I am begging you likewise, Ivy. I need you to understand that we will always be on your side. Put your love and trust in angels, Ivy, we will fight for you.

Ivy held the hand of the Master with tears in her eyes as she said simply,

-Thank you, thank you so much.

Raguel went to the alley way, opened the back door to

it. He told sternly,

-Trouble is over. Margot come with me back inside. Callum, stay on the watch. Maurice, you can have a meal. Raphael, thank you for your help. I will feed you later.

But Margot corrected him,

-We will feed you later, Raphael.

So with a smile, Raguel confirmed,

-We will feed you later. You must stay here, I have something important to tell you. Beside that you have a plate set aside for you, my Maggot, and it is not of leftovers.

Raphael came to the Master and with great effort wiped his forehead and face from the blood with an handkerchief. He asked,

-You've been hurt?

Raguel shrugged his shoulders as he replied,

-It is not the first time and it will not be the last time. Don't you start to worry for me.

Looking at his split eyebrow, Maurice told casually with a smirk,

-Your servant is on his way to sort you out, Master. I took the liberty to warn him that you required a good couple of stitches if not three to not bleed all over your plate at the wedding reception.

A smiling Raphael added,

-Callum had a prime view of what went on outside the tavern. He told us everything, from the punches you delivered to the left to the ones you delivered to the right. I can tell you that one young girl on my barrel said a lot of yes, yes, yes at the description of each punch you gave.

A fully winged Doctor Williams landed in the alley way, his medical bag in hand and asked immediately,

-Who are the casualties, Master? Let's look at that nice scar of yours first. Go and sit on that barrel so I can have a closer look.

Raguel complied reluctantly while Margot demanded with anxiety,

-Doctor Williams, will he be alright? There was a lot of blood coming from his eyebrow.

If the concern of Margot amused Raguel, Doctor Williams took care to answer her,

-Yes, Mr the angel of justice is eventually always alright. That's merely a scratch for him.

She swore,

-That was a bloody hell of a scratch! The blood ran all across his face. Raphael cleaned it up. Look his handkerchief is a bloody mess now!

Raguel ordered,

-You must go and have your meal, Margot. I will not be long. Please, reassure Ivy that you are safe and well. Maurice, please show her the way in and enjoy your own dinner.

When both left the Master and all the other angels in the alley way couldn't retain their laugh. Raphael commented with a broad smile,

-Master, I can tell you that Margot likes you very much. You, kicking her father up, was like giving her own back. Callum can tell you how difficult it was to keep her in the alley way, hidden from sight. She wanted to join you to fight her father. I managed to coax her to go back on the barrel but it nearly took all my wit.

The Master smiled to him as he told,

-I can bet it was the case. You were very right about Ivy as well. She was all out with her anger and temper. She was a woman on a mission. It was hard to stop her getting hurt. She only had a good punch on her cheek but she could have been hit so much more, however she did what she aimed to do. She publicly shamed the man. I don't think he will stay in town for long with the reputation she gave him. Sebastien added his stance to protect Margot which was listened to by many. All in all, I think we have a good chance to keep that young girl safe with us.

Raphael made a winning punch in the air which did put him in pain, however he was pleased with the outcome of the fight. He asked with some anxiety,

-Your Sebastien and Ivy are definitely going to keep Margot?

Whilst Raguel's eyebrow was being stitched up, he replied with certainty,

-Yes. I've always known my Sebastien to take on board people. He never has been humanly rich but he has always done so throughout the centuries. He is a carer, he homes people, future angels or not. His new wife, Ivy, do not have any mother from birth and recently lost her father. She has no one in the world but us. Sebastien took her on board.

Joining the conversation Doctor Williams commented,

-I am glad your son married Ivy. I have known her from a very young age, well since she was an infant. She has always been such an intelligent woman and as a Doctor, she always manned up. When some of my medical students were skirmish about doing this or that, she was not. Autopsy, amputation or operation, she can always stand bravely there.

The Master smiled as he told,

-You should have seen her going for the man, my William! She even broke a bottle to do to him what Cork did to me the previous evening. I stopped her just in time. If that broken bottle had changed from her hand to his, I can't tell you, how our Ivy would have been hurt! I gave her to Henry to be maintained and well protected. He wasn't able to. The only solution was for Mighty, Valdi and me to really go full on on the man, throw him out of the tavern and bring the fight on the street, to make sure there was a fair distance between him and the pregnant Ivy. It was the only way to keep her safe because she would have staid involved in the fight otherwise. Raphael, again, thank you for warning us about Ivy's state of mind this morning. It gave us the heads up.

Finishing neatly his stitches Williams stated,

-That will be a beautiful scar for you. Soon you will be able to compete with your son on the amount of battle scars you two have. I am sure Sebastien will enjoy that game.

Raguel scolded him straight away as he stood up,

-William! Do not ever suggest such a competition to my last son! He will get himself hurt and I will be ever so upset. Last time when my father had to take him away to be seen to was upsetting enough. I lost my first child, I don't want to ever lose my Mighty. Come with me, you need to look after the eye of Valdi and the cheeks of Ivy and Sebastien. But do not chat silly non sense to my son.

Both left the alley way by the back door of the tavern. Alone with Callum and the rottweiler, Raphael confided out loud,

-I am ever so sorry for what I did to the Master. I want to repay him but I can't bring his eldest son back. If I could, I would. I have been such a stupid, evil angel. I hate myself, I really hate myself.

Callum came to him and filled his glass with ale and said,

-Raphael, you are working yourself up. The Master, since he found you were still alive and have found human charity is tolerating you. You have a chance to make it up to him. I don't want to give you a bad advice but I think that something could be tried regarding the eldest son of the Master. Here drink a little and sit back on your barrel. Try to contain your tears, please. Now, I am not a mastermind but I know you are quite one, so you may work everything out from my idea.

An interested fallen angel retained his tears to ask,

-What is your idea? Spell it out.

Callum lit a cigar before he told,

-The soul of Gael, the Master's eldest son, is not lost. He is in heaven. Us, excluding you because you are solely human now, the human angels can reincarnate as many time as we want to serve the Mighty One and the Master. There must be a possibility for Gael to reincarnate. I have heard, but for the specific you must ask the Messenger or the Great Being, that something is preventing that scheme. However Doctor Williams is a wizard and the new Mrs Odell is a powerful eternal being and a white witch. With their efforts combined together may be they could come to a solution.

He helped a thoughtful Raphael to drink. The fallen angel then answered,

-I will work upon it. I want to repair my mistakes. I owe it to the Master. But please don't tell him. I would love it to be an anonymous surprise so he could accept it better. I can only dream to see the smile on his face at the sight of his eldest son coming back to him.

Unbeknown to Raphael, the Master knew all his intentions already, having one of his physical manifestations as Ludwig the guard dog by the beer barrel. Inside the tavern the banquet was in full swing. The conversation were now less about the wedding than the fight that ensued. Ivy was having her cheek looked after by Doctor Williams who told her,

-Your father would have been proud of you. You stood up to a monster of a man. I am proud of you.

Sebastien holding her hand on the table added,

-I am proud of her too yet I was so scared for her.

Doctor Williams replied with confidence,

-I do know. I just looked after your father's eyebrow. With an angelic touch you see what happened. You went all fists and fight again.

Still full of fire, Sebastien answered,

-Yes, the man dared to touch my little Bit! I wasn't going to let that pass! My father made sure Margot was safe before coming back while I dealt with that bastard. Doctor Valdi was a massive help meanwhile, he dived into the fight. I would have been hurt more if it wasn't for him. Then father came back and went all angel of justice on the human. So you can guess the man had a pretty good punishment.

Only smiling a little, Williams said,

-Ivy, you will be fine. It is bruised but there is no broken bones. He didn't go easy on you that Mr Cork. You may lose a tooth in the next few days. I tried to heal it but I would say a little prayer to the Lord might work better on that one. It is only one of your wisdom tooth so you will still keep your pretty smile if you ever lose it.

Margot who had a seat between Sebastien and Raguel asked quite shyly,

-Does this mean, the fight, does it mean I am definitely staying with your family?

An adamant Ivy replied,

-Yes, we claimed you. You are staying with us and we

will protect you. You are part of the family now. Maybe it is too early to say it but I will say it nonetheless, I will consider you as my eldest daughter. My Sebastien and I already adopted our Jack. We can adopt you fully so your father will never, ever hurt you again. That goes for the little one inside you. We will look after that child as well. You can always count on us to never let you down, Margot. We will be there with the love that will shelter you, with the support that will see you through. We will care and comfort you my darling girl. We are here for you.

Margot went to the hurt Ivy straight away. She put her arms around her neck and cried upon her shoulder. She sobbed,

-Thank you, thank you so much. I was so afraid with my father. I thought I would die like my mother. I saw partly what happened to her and, and, I still shiver at night when I think about it. I lived in a world of fear, Ivy. Thank you to take me in. I will be a good girl to you, helpful and everything. I am not afraid of hard work.

Comforting the young girl, Ivy said,

-Instead of hard work, how do you fancy reading with Jack fairy tales to me by the fire place while I learn to knit some little socks and little hats for our babies with Mrs Brown? We can also learn to cook together, make biscuits and cakes.

Sebastien giggled as he commented,

-Little bit, please don't teach her to make salty biscuits.

Ivy slapped his hand in a playful manner then replied with some pride,

-I will not, Mr Cotton! You are impossible. Your father agrees with me as well. No, Doctor Williams has been kind enough to give me some culinary books to learn how to cook.

When Sebastien's cheek was tended by Doctor Williams, her husband swore,

-Good Lord! Williams! That's a recipe for disaster! You didn't give Ivy cookery books?! We are all going to be poisoned in my house! Dad say something.

The Master couldn't resist laughing as he answered,

-Stop swearing by the name of your grandfather! How many times will I have to tell you that?

Henry who was at the table started laughing joyfully as well, feeling that there was going to be another father and son bickering looming.

Giving a dark glance to his father Sebastien retorted,

-Taste her biscuits then you will learn how to swear like I do! No, giving Ivy recipe books is a bad idea, a very bad idea. She doesn't recognise her salt from her sugar for a start then when she uses Cayenne pepper as paprika, I am sure you will enjoy washing your mouth in a bucket of water repetitively. I speak from experience.

However Raguel replied with great composure but also a giggle,

-Everyone has to learn and start somewhere.

Sebastien pleaded,

-I don't want to taste the somewhere! I tasted plenty of somewhere that went nowhere! Who's idea was that to give her a cookery book? It is evil! Pure evil! I can do the cooking in my home, it is fine, I love cooking. At least I know which ingredients I am using to not poison everybody.

Doctor Williams scolded him, as he looked after Sebastien's bruised cheek,

-Come, come, this was not evil, this was angelic. It was my idea. You can't let this poor young woman without cooking knowledge when she has to feed an expending family. She expressed the wish and I delivered.

Sebastien pouted with his argument,

-As long as she doesn't reduce the family members with the salty biscuits, I may cope with the idea.

Still laughing Henry told,

-Ivy did a decent scrambled eggs breakfast this morning. It was seasoned properly. Raphael tasted it for us and as he didn't die, we knew it was alright to eat.

Then Williams proposed,

-Why don't we label everything in your kitchen and pantry? It will help Ivy and with experience, she will learn taste and different flavours.

The Great Being at the head of their table stated,

-Well, I have to command Doctor Williams to you two, my dear children, for instead of bickering like you both do, he thinks of solutions instead.

With that praise which felt like an accolade to him, Williams bowed to the Lord then announced,

-Your grandson jaw will be sore and bruised for a little while but he will cope, I have seen much worst upon him.

With a smirk, Raguel commented,

-I am sure you did, Mighty shows his battle scars to everyone, even to the world if he could.

Sebastien gave another evil look to his father while the good Williams happy to defuse the upcoming bickering said,

-No, he wasn't flashing his wounds to me with pride, it was because I had to tend to him and mend him regularly. I know what his angelic body went through and it went through a lot.

Instead Sebastien took the opportunity to challenge his father,

-There, you see, I am right, you are wrong! I don't flash my scars at every opportunity!

A laughing Ivy by his side commented,

-Oh! Yes, you do!

Sebastien giggled to her with sympathy yet scolded her,

-Don't you start, Little Bit! I know everything about you too! Can you explain why, after a few years, you didn't develop a proper sense of taste? Now, I want the truth Mrs Cotton, nothing but the truth, because I know the truth full well. Why don't you taste as you go your own dishes like I told you to do since you were fourteen trying to feed your father who couldn't afford a cook any longer due to his gambling debts?

Put on the spot, Ivy blushed thoroughly, however she replied with great shame,

-I stopped tasting my dishes because they didn't taste good.

Her husband then told everyone at the table,

-I raised my case, I am right and you are all wrong. I had to come regularly to Doctor Fair's house for dinner preparing the dinner to unsure that father and daughter were eating something decent and were fed. When I wasn't doing that Doctor Williams was inviting his friend and daughter for dinner at his house, so we both worked out a way for them both to have proper meals every day. William, tell me if I am wrong?

Doctor Williams sighed deeply before he admitted,

-You know I can't say you are wrong because we devised that plan together.

However Raguel intervened,

-I would say, on the contrary, you are very wrong, Mighty. Basically, you are sending a message to your wife that she is hopeless in the kitchen rather than giving her hope that she can learn to cook. Doctor Williams's approach is far better because it doesn't remove any chances from her. So for one salty biscuit someone is a bad cook forever? I don't think so. Ivy, I will help you to gain confidence cooking wise because this is what you need, and practice makes perfect. Together Little Bit and with Margot, we will cook everyday and prove that French angel wrong. We will make him eat his words and apologise to you for not giving you a chance in the first place. Williams, thank you for giving Ivy books. Tomorrow I want you to label everything in their kitchen and pantry and teach our two young ladies all about ingredients doing so.

If this brought a smile on the face of Doctor Williams who was happy to receive that new task, a sad Sebastien turned to his young wife and simply said to her,

-I am sorry in advance Little Bit and do apologise to you. I will give you another chance to kill me with another salty biscuit.

His big grin at the end made his wife kick his hand on the table gently as she scolded him,

-You are impossible, Sebastien, but I love you so I will learn all my ingredients by heart, just for you.

Raguel ruled,

-We have a compromise then. My William, go and check on Valdi. Although he is not complaining, I know his black eye is giving him pain.

Ever so pleased his servant bowed to him and asked in a pleading tone,

-After I have done so, may I eat at their table?

Giving a quick glance across the room at the table of his younger brother where Amelia, Georgia Marlow, Mina and Emily were seated, the Master smiled. He answered,

-Yes, you may. The seat by Georgia is still free. I think you should claim it. Thank you for everything, William.

His old servant went to look after Vincent Valdi, and put his medical bag on the free chair by Georgia Marlow without further a do.

Raguel sighed happily, before confided to his son,

-I never thought I would ever see my William falling in love after what happened to him. Mighty, I will admit one thing to you. It pains me to say it. But your match making is working for him and I am happy about it.

Sebastien gave a winning smile to his father as he desired another confirmation,

-So at least, at the very least, I did one thing right according to your eyes.

A large platter of cooked crayfish arrived at their table along with a couple of sauces when Raguel responded to him,

-No, you did, over the years, a lot of things right, my son, a lot of things. You can't begin to imagine how proud I am of you because I tend to keep praises away from you in case your head become as large as the inflated balloon of the Montgolfier brothers. Anyway the proper dinner has finally started. Eat.

The Master of all angels not only served Margot beside him, he shelled her crayfish for her telling her,

-You must try those, they are delicious. You can have them on their own or dip them in the sauces. Let me put some sauce on your plate. So this one is a parsley and chive creamy sauce, while that one is called a mayonnaise. It has got a little lemon juice in it which goes well with seafood in general. Tell us, how good are you at cooking? My son is so much of an expert that he is overbearing about it. Ivy didn't have a mum to show her, teach her anything cooking wise, and I will let you in a secretive gossip, Father Odell used to only eat biscuits until Doctor Valdi taught him to cook a little.

The young Marguerite smiled to him gratefully. She knew she couldn't have done the shelling with her two broken fingers, but Raguel saved her pride and didn't make her ask for help, he just gave it in a manner which she could only accept. She replied willingly to him,

-I think I know how to cook a little. I can make bread, sourdough bread. I am good at making pancakes and I can roast a chicken. Also I can do soups, when my mother was alive she taught me how to do a leek and potato soup, a chicken soup and a squash soup. I also know how to do apple pies and pumpkin pies.

Sebastien nodded his appreciation before voicing it,

-That is far better than my Ivy who didn't know what to do with eggs at fourteen.

While his wife was kicking his leg underneath the table mildly, he enquired,

-So, Margot, tell us, what does your father do for a living?

The young girl sighed deeply before she answered,

-He is a man of all trade, really. My mother used to complain about it. She said he couldn't keep any work for long because of his temper. He has been a baker, a miner, a smith, a thatcher, a butcher, a sailor and finally a brick layer for the new bridge, here, in Wilton Town. He also does boxing where people bet. He has always done so.

Touching his bruised cheek, Sebastien commented with a point of sarcasm in his voice,

-What a surprise! I thought he had a very strong left for a human.

Raguel added,

-Cork is stronger and taller than your average man.

The Great Being told casually,

-Because he is not one. He is a cambion. He is simply a wild cambion at large in the world. He doesn't know it himself and it is better if he stays ignorant about it.

A puzzled Margot asked,

-What's a cambion?

All the angels at the table wished she didn't asked that question. Yet, the Master of all angels replied to her,

-It is the offspring of a demon and a human. Cambions are unusually strong. They resemble humans but can live much longer than them. They can bestow some magical powers as well. Did you ever see your father do anything strange, something out of the ordinary?

It took time for Marguerite to answer, but she did,

-One night, the day my little brother died, he was upset with everything and everyone, and underneath our feet it was like the earth tremble. We thought it was an earthquake.

Shaking his head in disbelief, Raguel announced,

-That is a strong cambion on our hands then. Margot, you will have to stay with me and my son at all cost. Cambions can be very dangerous beings. Your father is an instinctive one which can be the worst kind to deal with. Now, eat a little while I will go with my father and Sebastien to feed Raphael.

The Master didn't tell her that it was why her father rendered her pregnant but he knew that Margot would be a breeding mare for her father if she ever fell back under his hands. This was why Cork wanted her back with desperation. A cambion natural demonic instincts were to reinforce their demonic side in their children, hence their tendencies were to interbreed and be incestuous.

Putting some crayfish and some sauce on his own plate, Raguel went outside followed by the Great Being and his son. Once they were in the alley way, the Great Being revealed,

-Lucifer managed to create a powerful demon to do most of his dirty work. However he has lost the entire control of his creature. Mr Cork is the offspring of that incubus demon.

The Master shook his head in desperation as he started shelling crayfish for Raphael who was remaining utterly silent upon his barrel. Then an exasperated Raguel vented out,

-An incubus! They breed like rabbits! How many Cork will we have out there to deal with? Creating an incubus and then he can't control it! Stupid fallen angel! Most of those fallen angels are like that: full of pride, vanity and stupidity. They want some power but then they fall flat on their faces because they can't deliver anything but the worst. They are creating mess after mess after mess to correct. Lucifer wanted to be me and to be your son, father, so he is plaguing my life by envy and jealousy.

Turning to Raphael aggressively, Raguel demanded,

-What is your excuse? What mess do I have to tidy up after you? We have definitely lost an archangel that is not retrievable because of your duplicity, just because you couldn't cope being the only healing angel any longer, just because you couldn't understand we were creating a team of them. What type of fallen angel are you going to be? A totally lost one? A messy one?

With a knot in his throat Raphael answered with sincerity,

-I have no excuse, Master. But I want to tidy up my own mess. I don't know how to quite do so yet but I will try to figure it out. As for lost, I am out in the woods, lost. I can't deny that. I will try my best to be a good human for you, this is all I can say for now.

Raguel told sternly,

-I will accept that for now. Here, have some of those. By the way, you are not lost, if you haven't noticed, you are still very much with us. I will not be here feeding you if it was not the case.

Sebastien who had been holding the plate for his father throughout his rant confirmed,

-Raphael, you mustn't feel lost. Even if my father and I are both Punishers, you can approach us to talk or to confide anything you want. Moreover we will help you. You can ask us for help or we will just give it but don't feel shy to come to us when you feel you need to. You met the charity of a human, so you are still alive, therefore you are still with us, and when I say with us, it is the big 'us'.

While Raphael nodded his appreciation, the Master of all angels corrected his son,

-Technically, Raphael hasn't been saved by a full human which was the condition of my punishment. However I will not hold it against him.

With a deep sigh the fallen angel dared to enquire,

-So I understood that Cork was a cambion? Am I right? That would explain his strength but also how full of stamina his daughter is. At twelve to save me from a river with strong currents, did require, well, some muscles. We also must bear in mind, Margot was solely and recently beaten up when she helped me.

The Master feeding him replied,

-You understood right. Cork is a cambion. So his daughter has some demonic blood in her. Cork doesn't know he is a cambion but his daughter will work out in time that she has some demonic blood in her because I was open about it with her.

It made Raphael think for a while before he said,

-She will have no place in your son's household then and is going to be back under the bridge.

An outraged Raguel kicked the back of the head of Raphael gently as he scolded,

-We have more heart than that, you, Maggot! No, she is staying with us for good, like you can if you want to.

The fallen angel teased,

-Yes, the back garden bench can be quite comfortable when you are not battered randomly upon it.

Giving him a dark glance the Master ordered,

-Eat and don't knock the hand that is helping you. Remember that beggars can not be choosers.

With his good heart, Sebastien proposed,

-In light of what happened to you, Raphael, will you sleep on the sofa in my drawing room from now on? That is until we build you your own little cabin. I know Odell proposed to you the benches of his church, but it is a drafty place that little church. It is still a roof above your head though and it will be quiet. On the other hand my home is a family home and partly an angels dormitory, with my father, Henry and Ted residing there permanently. However it will not be quiet, I have children, cats and dogs running about the house. I am uncomfortable with you staying outside when we have a strong cambion in town. It took three of us to deal with him tonight and you can see the damage on our faces.

Raphael was surprised by the proposal. He bit his lips with emotion before he answered,

-If you would have me, yes, please. I will make myself small.

Smiling kindly to him, Sebastien told,

-We have a deal then. It will be more comfortable inside for you and warmer. Father, he has finish his plate, let's go and eat ours. I hope Henry didn't eat the entire platter of crayfish and left us some. With his albatross past I don't trust him.

His father laughed before turning to Raphael,

-I will be back with the next course. I hope you enjoyed that one. Apparently, crayfish are abundant in the river. Fishing can be a way to feed yourself when you become independent in your own cabin.

The fallen angel thanked the Master of all angels but couldn't catch his hand in time. The father and the son left the alley way chatting together. Raphael sighed deeply and cried, not realising that the Great Being was still there who recalled him,

-Raphael, gather yourself up. Stop crying. What are those crocodile tears for?

Almost choking the fallen angel replied,

-Sorrow, pure sorrow for what I did to your son. If he would have me as his slave to serve him for eternity, I would agree straight away. I am so sorry, it hurts. I will devote myself to him and his son. Even if they don't want it, I will serve them and help them silently. Both are so good, I am so ashamed of myself. I want to repay, I want to repay so much.

Coming to him and touching his hand gently, the Great

Being told,

-Do as you said. The Master of all angels never forgets any of his angels, even a fallen one. You did hurt him very severely, more than anyone but I know that Raguel has deep down a forgiving heart. It will take time, a lot of time, but don't give up.

He went back into the tavern leaving Raphael alone with Ludwig the rottweiler who put his large head on his lap. Callum at the end of the alley way offered his opinion, smoking casually his cigar,

-You should perk up a little, Raphael. Don't give up because it is clear that the Master hasn't given up on you. Just don't let him down this time around.

The fallen angel went by the human angel and engaged a good conversation with him about how Callum did become a human angel and what did he do in his human life to get his wings. Raphael noticed that the dog had followed him and sat by him as he was chatting.

Inside the tavern, Raguel, the Great Being and The Mighty One were relaxing a little at their table enjoying their meal. Raguel confided to his father,

-I never thought I would say this to you, father, but I think it is possible to retrieve that archangel of yours. It annoys me greatly to admit it but he is truly repentant.

The Great Being smiled as he stated,

-Making Raphael human is the best thing you could have done for him. He will learn everything back from scratch but essentially humbleness and compassion, the two qualities he lacked the most as an archangel.

The young Margot who had finished her plate joined the conversation with her comment,

-When we were under the bridge, when Raphael was hurting all over, when he thought I was sleeping, I heard him saying: 'what have I done dear Lord?' And that he should have died for it. I could hear him sob too.

Raguel told the girl when the main course arrived on their table,

-Do not worry about him, Margot. I will do the worrying.

My son and I will look after him now that he is human. He will
have a little cabin for himself. He will also be employed. He will
be fine at the end of the day. Here, let me serve you. What piece
of chicken do you want?

Margot went shy on him and replied,

-Can I chose my piece after everyone has theirs?

The Master of all angels accepted her answer and
carved the roasted chicken then served it to everyone around
their table. Then he shared the last leg with Margot. Soon
everyone where eating and chatting together. Whilst most were
enjoying a conversation betting who would be the next couple to
be married, Raguel and the Great Being were probing Margot.
What transpired was that the young girl was bright, caring and
loving but that she also did believe that she wouldn't live very
long. She explained how bad it was when she gave birth to a still
born baby and that she doubted to survive giving birth another
time. Almost at the end of their conversation and the main
course, Tyron brought a plate to Raguel saying,

-This is for your fallen angel. I managed to save some
pieces of chicken breasts, some mash potatoes and some onion
gravy. I couldn't put aside some vegetables because I didn't
have enough for everyone. However I kept three profiteroles for
him for dessert for later.

Standing up Raguel welcomed,

-That is more than enough for him, Tyron. He didn't
expect to have food tonight. Thank you for your help. I will give
your proposal to him and see what he says about it. I hope he
will not be stupid to refuse it. I will tell you about it shortly.

Taking the plate, he enjoined,

-Come Margot, let's feed our scoundrel of an angel.

The young girl went with him carrying some cutlery. She
asked him with great shyness as they went to the back door,

-Mr the angel of justice, will you still tolerate me knowing
that my father is part demon?

The Master holding the plate on one hand and opening
the door with the other scolded her,

-Of course, I will tolerate you as long as you remain a
good being. Now, Miss Marguerite Bouchon, I told you to call

me Raguel especially if you want me to carry on calling you Margot.

He invited her to pass before him while he held the door. Margot smiled as she asked for a confirmation,

-So we are still on good terms then?

Raguel replied as he closed the door behind them,

-Yes, we are. You can count on me to protect you. I am used to deal with beings, humans, angels, archangels, demons and else.

Margot put her hand in his, and held it tight before she simply said,

-Thank you, Raguel. There are a couple of tares in your shirt since the fight, I can repair them for you tonight. Will you let me do so to show you my appreciation?

A smiling angel agreed with a condition,

-You can do it, yes, but tomorrow only. You had a long day and I want you to rest when we are going back home.

If Margot agreed, she became worried when she saw no one sitting on the beer barrel, she asked wildly,

-Where is Raphael? Has he been killed by my father?

#

Raguel reassured her straight away,

-No, he is with Callum at the entry of the alley way.

He called out,

-Maggot! Come here! We have your dinner courtesy of the owner of the tavern. Come and sit back on your barrel. You are worrying my Margot if you are not staying put on the barrel.

Raphael came immediately with a smile upon his face and the rottweiler following him. He bowed to the Master before putting himself back upon the barrel as he said,

-I am here, Master. You mustn't worry about me, Margot, I am not worth it.

Raguel corrected him,

-Maggot, you are not worth it, yet. So I see that you have started befriending human angels. It was about time that you did so, and a punishment to make you human to remove your preposterous vanity.

The fallen angel having heard the emphasis on the word 'yet' became full of hope. His eyes search desperately in the eyes of the Master of all angels if there was hope for him. But Raguel turned his head to Callum and ordered,

-Go and get your dinner Callum. Tyrell reserved you some and my Sebastien kept you a place on our table. I will look after the Maggot. Trust me when I say it is highly unlikely that we will see Cork causing anymore trouble tonight.

Callum extinguished his cigar against the wall of the tavern, with a smirk, as he replied,

-I trust you, Master. I saw how you dealt with him. My bet is on him taking about a week to recover fully from his sore body. The Maggot's bet is on a good couple of weeks if not three weeks. Maurice's bet was lower, he went for three to four days because he said the man was unusually strong. But now that we know he is a cambion, it explained how powerful he is. However I still maintain my bet.

Smiling Raguel repeated,

-Go and eat, Callum, otherwise I will bet safely that your food will be cold when you arrive at the table. Thank you for your service tonight.

Callum bowed to the Master and obeyed. When he left, Margot enquired full of curiosity to Raguel,

-Why are you all calling Raphael the Maggot? Surely that is not very nice, is it?

The Master replied sternly as much for the intention of the young girl as for the one of his fallen angel,

-It is not intended to be nice. For your information, when an angel loses his wings, it is not because he has been particularly nice, on the contrary. Raphael demeaned lots of human angels and humans by calling them maggots during his time as an archangel. This is why he has earned this nickname in punishment. Shall we feed him before his meal is cold? Give me the cutlery then hold the plate steady for me. I will do the spoon feeding. You must rest your broken fingers.

Margot did as she was told but scolded Raphael,

-It hurts me to hear you being called Maggot, Mr River! Why did you have to be so mean by calling people like that? I wish you were not so bruised and battered, because I would truly slap you for it. Make sure that in your human life you call people correctly.

An exchange of knowing looks and smiles happened between the fallen angel and the Master of all angels. Raguel told in a more gentle tone, as he started feeding Raphael,

-I hope you will like that. The tavern in this little town serves decent meals. This is simply some whites of roast chicken on a bed of mash potatoes with lashes of an onion gravy which is delicious. Try it, it is very decent food. The onion gravy is a favourite of Father Odell so it had to be on the menu for his wedding reception.

A grateful Raphael ate, trying desperately to retain his tears. He was just the picture of a contrite fallen angel. Raguel kept wiping Raphael's tears as they appeared, and he knew at that moment that he could retrieve archangel Raphael for his father. He also realised that if they were no witnesses Raphael was ready to fall on his knees in front of him. When the plate was empty, Raguel ordered,

-My Margot, bring the empty plate to Tyrell and ask him for the profiteroles that were kept for Raphael. Bring them to us, please.

The young girl obeyed. When she left the alley way, as he expected the Master of all angels saw the fallen angel drop on his knees before him. Raphael was full of apologies and he begged again and again,

-I am so sorry, Master. I am ever so sorry. Please, let me be your slave. Let me make it up to you. I will be good. I promise I will be good. I learnt my lesson. Please, keep me by your side, please, I beg you to keep me by your side. I will work hard, very hard.

The fallen angel's head went to sob upon Raguel's legs who put a hand on his head and told sternly,

-I have lost a son because of you, Raphael. I will allow you by my side but you will need to deserve to be my slave or servant for truly and honestly you have been a plague in my entire life and worst a traitor to my father's creations. Come, get up, pull yourself together before the little Margot return.

Raphael tried his best to obey. He composed himself as best as he could then Raguel said to him,

-I know your sorrow is real, my Maggot, if you don't let me down, I will not let you down as well.

Returning to the alley with a bowl of profiteroles, a smiling Margot told with glee as she handed the bowl to Raguel,

-There are three towers of them in the tavern, three!

The Master smiled to her as her stated,

-And they are delicious. My son prepared them this morning. Go back by Ivy to eat your share. I would not want you to miss that delicious dessert. I will look after Raphael.

Margot was only too happy to oblige him and ran back inside. It made Raphael giggle, then he commented,

-At least with your son and his little wife, she will have a chance to be well treated and have a childhood. Now, I wonder if she ever propose to you again, when she is older, if you will still consider her, knowing that she has demonic blood in her veins.

Taking no time to answer Raguel replied,

-Yes, I will. The fact is Marguerite has a conscience and a soul and a rather good one at that. If she ever ask me again, I will say yes, demonic blood or not.

Raphael looking at the closed back door of the tavern asked pensively with some curiosity,

-What will your father say? After all you are a demon killer, just like your son.

Sighing deeply, the Master confided to his ancient enemy,

-I will see. I still have to have the conversation with him. Whatever he says my consideration for Margot will remain. The last time I married the daughter of a Goddess without knowing her origins I ended up his slave. However the outcome of the union was the Mighty One which my father can't help dotting upon. I was only supposed to marry a human to replace my Gael who was in charge of creating human angels for my father.

I can't fall further down than being a slave so it is alright. Just eat.

Being almost force fed a profiterole, Raphael took his time to chew it before he said with some sadness,

-Yes, you can fall further down. You can lose your wings and be refused to even be a slave.

Raguel scolded him feeding him another little choux bun,

-Did you really need to say that my Maggot? Eat. Anyhow my issues are not yours. Lets talk about you. I have a proposal from the owner of this tavern for you. Tyrell is a good man which we helped as he and his tavern was targeted by a gang of Wilton Town. We dealt with that situation. Tyrell, whose first name is Tyron, is a potential human angel and knows about us. We have been introducing him to the angelic world as per say. He knows exactly who you are and that you are a fallen angel.

Taking a slight pause, the Master gave the last profiterole to Raphael, then he continued,

-Right, as I said, you were falling under human charity, well, this is one for your consideration. Tyrell is willing to feed you dinner at his tavern. If you come to him, he will not turn you away, he will give you a meal. However, he will want you to pay him back when you can. He knows that you will work at the quarry during the day so he will feed you in the evening but in return, when you can use your arms that is, he wants you to pay back for your meals working as a waiter. He said, he could do with some help at the tavern and if you carry on working in the evenings for him, he will pay you once you paid for all the dinners you had when you had no money for them. This is a good offer for you in my opinion. But it is your human life, and you have to do what you want with it. What do you say?

The fallen angel reflected before he replied,

-I will accept. I don't want to be a burden on the family of your son. I know he has many mouths to feed and I already feel ever so guilty for having been fed by you all. But when you have built the prison for Wilton Town, I want to work for you as a jailer.

Raguel nodded his approval and told,

-That could be arranged. Now, the prison will be the last

thing to be built in town. The houses for the people who lost their homes take priority on the reconstruction plan. It will mean a spell of six months to a year for you as a waiter but the way I see it is rather positive. It will give you the opportunity to know the inhabitants of the town and vice versa: the inhabitants will get to know you as a new resident of Wilton Town. So if you are intelligent enough to be amiable and friendly with the humans, when you take on the work later on as a jailer, you will not suffer from their hate but instead perhaps you will earn their appreciation.

A thoughtful Raphael could finally envisage his future in Wilton Town in a more positive light. Henry stepped in the alley way then bowed to the Master. He informed,

-The bride and groom are ready to leave the tavern. I can tell they are longing to be in one another's arms. I will lead their Rosalie and their little phaeton back to the hotel. Mr Berry will accompany us with his carriage. He proposed to take the two tired little girls, Mina and Emily back to the hotel along with the pregnant Amelia and Mrs Toad. Valdi will sit by him. Doctor Williams and Georgia Marlow however are walking to the hotel. Williams is escorting Georgia. He is properly courting her. They didn't stop talking all night. As for your family, your father has already left with Peter O'Neil. I will come back with him on my return back from the hotel. Sebastien and Ivy are ready to go home as well. Margot, who must be tired, has started to lean and doze on the shoulder of Ivy. Beside that some people are leaving and some are still enjoying themselves.

Acknowledging everything Raguel ordered,

-Go now with the Odells and send me a message when you have left the building. Theo didn't want to see the Maggot at all during his wedding day which I can appreciate. Then I will be able to bring Raphael inside and take my family back home.

The Messenger bowed to him as he left to obey his order. A few minutes later the Master told,

-Here we go my Maggot, time for us to go home. I just received Henry's message. Now, I want you to respect Theo Odell in the future. He is a new angel, yes, but he is one that we all esteem greatly hence my very own father attended his wedding. I need you, want you, order you to be on good terms with Theo. I do not know how you will achieve this, you will have to work it out for yourself. But Theo is essential to this town, not only that he is one of my potential demon killers. He thinks fast and acts likewise. You, who has sold your soul, will be plagued by demons or, and possessed humans ready to kill you and carry you to hell to Lucifer who will have a great time torturing you. I strongly suggest you to befriend Theo, Vincent and Henry who are very good demon killers. Maurice, one of the three M, musketeers of my son who became angels in his army can cut the mustard as well with demons. Of course now that you are a vulnerable human, you have your free will to chose who you want to be friend to or with but I am just giving you angelic suggestions for your welfare.

Raguel opened the back door to the tavern to let Raphael in who followed him quietly. The fallen angel was taking all the informations in and was ever so appreciative of what the Master of all angels was doing for him. Inside the tavern Raguel went first to Tyron, Raphael in tow. He announced,

-Tyrell, my fallen angel has accepted your offer.

The owner of the tavern smiled, shook gently the hand of Raphael conscious that both of them were seriously hurt. Tyron welcomed,

-I am happy to hear it. Now, Raphael, you can come in my tavern whenever you want in the evening and I will see that you are fed. You will have to pay for your meals only when you can and are able to do so. As you can see, I suffer from injuries as well and I know what it is like. I will be patient with you. Once you are my waiter, and you have repaid your meals, I will give you a salary weekly. Customers give tips and any that you earn for good service will be yours to keep. There is one condition, I want you and I to be clear upon: I don't want any fib, lie, trickery from you at any point or it will be you out off the door straight away. Just tell me the plain truth all the time even if it is bad. I know you are a fallen angel, I know you lied through your teeth this afternoon when you presented yourself to the good people of this town, but I am willing to give you a chance. However at your first lie to anyone else or myself, your welcome in this tavern will end. Do we understand each other?

Whilst Raphael agreed and then discussed further with Tyron about the conditions of his future employment, Raguel went to the table his family was. He saw the sleeping Margot and announced,

-It is grand time for us all to go home. I will carry Marguerite.

However the Master warned Margot before doing anything,

-Margot, it is me Mr the angel of justice. We are going

home. You are very tired and I am going to carry you there. So you can sleep in my arms on the way.

Full of trust, Margot presented her arms and did let herself to be carried. She soon went back to sleep on the angelic shoulder. While Sebastien fastened Ivy's shawl on her shoulders, the Master called out,

-Raphael, we are going home, come with us.

The fallen angel finished immediately his conversation with Tyrell politely to follow the Master of all angels and his family. In the street, the rottweiler joined them and walked by the side of Raphael, who made a great effort to stroke his head, despite being in pain. Raphael confided to Raguel,

-Everything has been arranged Master. After my work at the quarry and the woods, from tomorrow, I will go to the tavern for my dinners. Mr Tyrell has given me some explanations about the work I will do as waiter. Tomorrow, he will show me the way around the tavern and tell me fully what he will expect of me.

A satisfied Master replied,

-Good, now tell me what are your first impressions of him? Can you feel that you can work with him, bearing in mind he is human?

The fallen angel who kept stroking the dog's head told,

-Definitely Master, I can work for him, I am human too. If you remember, since a couple of days I am no longer a pedantic archangel. I can learn a lesson, you know. It did sink in. As for my first impressions, after seeing the man twice, they are good. I find Tyrell amiable and of a pleasant character yet I would not be one to step on his toes. I am pretty sure he is a man that knows what he wants and also to hold his ground if he has to do so. He is straightforward, which I like a lot. You can also tell he is a very observant human. He has an attention to details which reminds me of your ghost Abraham Wilton-Cough. He is a people person although, tell me if I am wrong, he is alone because he lost someone not so long ago. His heart was attached to a young lady but she died. I had a flash of an accident passing before my eyes when I was talking to him. I think he saw what happened to her and he is still sad and distraught about it. But he carries on because so many relies upon him. As if I was still an angel, from his handshake, I could feel he is generous, caring and courageous. Speaking of Wilton-Cough, Mr Tyrell did arrange a deal with him. I couldn't ascertain the nature of it like I use to but it gave me good vibrations. The fact that Wilton-Cough is dead, Mr Tyrell has not been able to help people as much as he used to.

Sebastien and his father gave each other a knowing look. They knew from what Raphael said that he would become an angel again at some point. The Master commented,

-I am glad you appreciated Tyron. Just to let you know, my father likes him a lot, hence he will probably be the next human angel. If you are curious of the process of how we are creating human angels, I can only advise you to watch and learn how Tyron will get his wings.

The fallen angel answered still petting the dog by his side with pain and difficulties,

-I certainly will pay attention, Master. I... I... I really want to learn to be one of your angels again. I will learn to be a good human too, first of all.

When Sebastien opened the double gates of the churchyard, he told,

-Raphael, you seem to like our Ludwig a lot. I want you to take our dog with you when you go to the quarry tomorrow morning for your protection. Until you get back the use of your arms, it will be better for you to have our dog by your side.

As soon as he closed the gate he saw a pale little Jack standing at the doorway of the presbytery, Ted, behind the boy, explained,

-Jack felt that you were all coming back. He was so happy, that he couldn't stay in bed.

Sebastien and Jack ran to one another. Lifting the boy into his arms, Sebastien asked tenderly,

-Did you miss me? Because I can tell you that I missed you greatly. Did you eat your supper? How are you feeling now?

A smiling Jack replied,

-I feel better, Pa. Doctor Williams gave me something that Henry brought and it was like magic, my fever went away. But I didn't feel like eating.

Ted confirmed as Sebastien and everyone went inside the presbytery before closing the door behind them,

-Jack didn't want to eat anything. He was scared for you all. He only wanted to see you all back and safe. He had visions of the fight with the father of Margot.

Sebastien scolded the little boy gently,

-My Jack, my father and I can fight. We can fight hell demons and dust them. You mustn't worry like that. We may get scars and bruises but we will always stand up at the end of the day, together, strong, forever. Let's make sure you have something to eat before going back to bed. Little Bit, I will be looking after Jack and putting him to bed after he has eaten. Ted, I am sure you must be starving, come with me and Jack in the kitchen. Dad, please help my Little Bit to put Margot to bed. Raphael, I would love to say just stand in the hallway with the dog, but I will invite you in my kitchen. You can warm yourself up by the stove. I will prepare hot chocolate for my Jack and you can have some as well.

His words were followed. Soon Margot was in her bed sleeping profoundly. Soon Jack was fed and back in his bed resting. Ted took his leave once having eaten and retired to his bedroom. In the drawing room, Ivy prepared the large velvet sofa for the night for Raphael, saying,

-Here, your blanket is nice and warm, Raphael. You can use this cushion for your head.

Raphael thanking her couldn't help feeling sorry to see her cheek so intensely bruised,

-Thank you Mrs Cotton. I am sorry for what happened to you tonight.

Kindling the fire in the fire place to warm the room up, Sebastien commented,

-Don't be sorry. For once you were not the trouble.

His father who was serving tea, proposed,

-My Maggot, will you have some tea with us? We tend to have a very late night tea together in this house, just to close the day. We are also staying up until my father is back with Henry.

Raphael accepted and sat at the round table with them on the chair presented to him by the Master. Seeing his shyness, Ivy engaged the conversation with vivacity,

-You shouldn't feel sorry, because I got to do what I aimed to do: I shamed this evil bastard publicly. Everyone now in this town is aware of him and of his crimes.

Sebastien smiled as he commented,

-Raphael, don't be sorry for her. She knows how to pick up a fight. Why do you think we took her far from the Boston gangs to hide her in Wilton Town? She did a public shaming on a couple of their members, once in the hospital where we were working, once in the street when she was alone with her handbag. It was during the day. I wish Williams was here to describe to you her state when she came to us at the hospital that day. She was bruised, badly bruised but she said to us that the man was as bruised as her. With the ruined state of her little medical bag, I believed her. Of course I went to punish the man later on but I can tell you, he did have his share of bruises like Ivy said.

Joining in the conversation, the Master told firmly,

-But nonetheless, Ivy must be careful when she picks up a fight. First she needs to tell us so we can be here to protect her. It could have been worst than a bruised cheek if we didn't have the heads up from Raphael this time around. Like us she didn't know she was facing a cambion, part demon, part human. So I will advise you, my Ivy, unless you want to have fighting lesson with me to know how to defend yourself properly to stop slapping people in public however bad they are. Beside that you are pregnant, which means you could have endangered another life, the one of my grandchild.

Appearing in the room, a fully winged Doctor Williams added,

-Not only that, I don't want Ivy to receive death threats like she had in Boston.

An astonished Raguel demanded,

-What are you doing here, my William? I thought you were going to return back to Boston tonight.

Williams, his wings disappearing from sight replied,

-No, I will keep the multiple physical apparitions for a while. I am already looking after Jack upstairs, looking after the human victims in the hotel and I am still in Boston doing my night shift at the hospital, and I am here by your side to announce that Georgia Marlow said yes to me. I wanted you to be the first to know, Master. It happened when I was walking with her in the woods. I dropped the question but I didn't expect to have a yes straight away. But she didn't think about it, she just said yes holding my hand and kissing it.

The Master gave a manly hug to his old servant with some emotion,

-You have all my congratulations. I am so happy for you.

Ivy clapped her hands happily exclaiming,

-Yes, another wedding! Doctor Williams, I am so pleased to hear your news. Sit with us, have tea, tell all about it!

Somewhat her enthusiasm made William blush a little yet he accepted the offer and took a seat between her and the Master. Sebastien had a winning smile on his face when he said,

-I knew it! I knew it would and could only happen. Congratulations, William! I have to be your best man, I just have to.

Raguel argued straight away,

-No, you just don't have to Sebastien! On what ground, pray? I want to be his best man!

The Great Being appeared in the room with the Messenger, he told with an amused smile,

-Just in time for another bickering, Henry. I told you we would make it. Take a seat by Mighty.

While he sat by Raphael at the round table, the Great Being asked the fallen angel,

-Please explain the subject of the new bickering between my son and my grandson for the pleasure of Henry.

A shy Raphael obliged him,

-Both want to be the best man of the Wizard, Henry, because Doctor Williams is going to marry a lady called Georgia Marlow.

Henry nodded to Raphael in an encouraging fashion before he informed the fallen angel,

-Georgia Marlow is an excellent woman which we saved by making her an eternal being. Sebastien did match make her with our Doctor Williams. So, it did work!

He turned to Williams with a pleased smile,

-Congratulation, my friend! So you did pop the big question in the woods, when you were walking Georgia back to the hotel, didn't you?

Blushing again, Doctor Williams answered,

-Yes, I did. I was anxious to be honest with you all. But I took my courage from two things: first, Georgia had just spent a few days in my Boston home with the two little girls and I know she enjoyed them. Second, the good feelings to see Miss White finally being married to Theo Odell did help me, I think. Georgia was in he right mood to accept me. I decided to go for it when the iron was hot. Now, that she is an eternal being, Georgia will need a lot of learning to know how to deal with eternity, I can teach her that. I can also as an angel look after her for eternity. She will not be alone to face anything, she will be loved in her own right throughout centuries.

Taking the moment to point out to his father and argue, Sebastien told,

-This is why I should be the best man, Dad, and not you! I made the match! And you must perform the wedding like you did today, anyway.

Raguel retorted with a smirk on his face,

-What is it with you wanting to be a best man, Mighty? You nearly caused trouble today in church contesting Vincent Valdi, the best friend of Father Odell, to the post right by the altar. Beside that, you forget that my father can perform the ceremony of William as well, therefore it will allow me to be a best man to my Williams. I can argue than I know him for longer than you did, much, much longer.

Henry started to laugh but tried to hide it by lifting his cup of tea. The Great Being ruled,

-Children, you all had a very tiring day, why don't you settle this with the most concerned? The choice belongs to you my dear Williams.

Trying to be diplomatic, the old servant answered,

-Master, I would love you to do the ceremony for me, like you did for Theo. It will mean so much to me. Mighty, please be my best man.

If the father and the son both agreed to the proposals, Sebastien dared to give a winning smile at his father. Raguel putting his cup of tea down, commented with irritation,

-You can smile all you want, Mighty, all I can see is a beautiful bruised cheek on your face.

Henry who couldn't help giggling finished his cup of tea and excused himself. He bowed and left the room. The Great Being told,

-Raguel, your Messenger is truly exhausted. I will suggest you do not task him tomorrow until after noon. You mustn't forget that he is still recovering from a severe injury. He is putting on his generous and helpful brave face on at the moment. He will never say no to you or your son but I am telling you this time, he needs a rest. With Henry it is always hard to tell because he is so hardworking and pushing himself almost to his limits with a smile on his face.

Putting his cup of tea down, the Master agreed immediately,

-I will see that he does. By the way Ivy, after the long day you had today and made us have by picking a fight with a strong cambion, I suggest you do go to bed after this cup of tea.

A pouting Ivy could only replied,

-I am not a little girl!

Sebastien giggling advised her,

-Do not pick up a verbal fight with the angel of justice, my Little Bit. Trust me on that one. I have the experience and I very rarely win.

His father commented,

-Let's be honest here, Mighty you never do win, only when your grandfather happens to side with you and by respect for him I give up the argument. As for you, my Ivy, two years ago, you were still a teenager. So when Grandpa Rag ruled it is well past your bedtime, it is probably because it is. But let's not part on bad terms, come and give me a kiss goodnight on my cheek, I deserve one for getting a split eyebrow for your sake.

Ivy gave him a smile and conceded,

-Alright then, Grandpa Rag.

She obliged him before leaving the room after her husband said,

-I will not be long Little Bit.

After she closed the door behind her of the drawing room, Sebastien started laughing as he repeated,

-Grandpa Rag! Where does that come from? You sound like an old carpet, dad!

Everyone around the table started to laugh even Raguel despite giving a dark glance at his son, he pleaded, before he gave an explanation,

-Don't you start calling me like that, Mighty! Your wife came up with it. It was when I was carrying little Jack back from his operation to your home. She was trying to find comforting words for your boy and as I am now a adoptive grandfather to Jack, she started calling me Grandpa Rag. Although, I thought it sounded like if I was an old carpet, I didn't have the heart to suggest her something else at that trying time. So I guess I am stuck with that one now.

Williams, who was still giggling, commented,

-Bless her, she is only so young and learning to be a mother. We have to bear in mind all the time that she never had one, no example to follow.

Looking directly at Doctor Williams, Raphael, very shyly said,

-I agree with you, Doctor Williams. Having seen her preparing the breakfast for so many this morning, I can tell that she is strong young woman that has a heart which can take on board many. She has a caring soul. She may not have had example but she has the maternal instinct. She will be, is already a good mother. In fact she will be mothering almost all of you before you know it. She is the heart of this family. I can feel it. It radiates from her. She is upright and generous.

Sebastien welcomed his comments,

-My Little Bit is definitely as you describe and so much

more. I hope you enjoyed your breakfast this morning.
Apparently she managed to season properly the scrambled
eggs for once. You could have eaten sugar flavoured ones... But
my father, Grandpa Rag, and Williams will make sure she learns
how not to poison anyone by sheer mistakes. But most of the
time, I will do the cooking in this house to unsure everyone stays
alive. However, as a Doctor she is brilliant like her father was.
And if you want to see a poker face, a proper one, you must play
with us poker with Ivy. Her father was a gambler, but to her
credit, she is better than him at the game. She could win me a
fortune if I let her play on a proper gaming table and not just with
coloured buttons. But I would never let her do that due to what
happened to her father.

Doctor Williams added, engaging with friendly talk back
with the fallen angel whose plans had nearly murdered him a
few days ago,

-Raphael, you definitely must play poker or any card
games with us with Ivy and you will understand how clever she
is. I taught her chess as well when she was fourteen. Now, that
she is twenty-one, I have a hard time to win against her. Mighty,
would you agree with me that she thinks outside the box?

Serving more tea to everyone, Sebastien agreed,

-Yes, my Ivy does. Tomorrow night let's settle to have a
game of cards, even with our children, Margot and Jack. It will
take their minds off our last trying few days. So once you had
dinner at the tavern, Raphael, come back home between eight
and nine. Williams, I will expect you here and I would love you to
invite your Georgia. It will give you another occasion to walk her
back to the Crying White Doe Hotel and if my grandfather
answers my prayer to make it a beautifully starry night, without
clouds and rain, it would probably be for you another romantic
night.

The Great Being told casually,

-You've got it, Mighty. It will be fair tomorrow night. My
dear Doctor Williams, where will you have your wedding, in
Boston or in Wilton Town and when?

Blushing, Williams answered in a timid fashion,

-We didn't discuss a lot yet. It is early days, well a very
early night of having my hand being accepted.

With benevolence the Creator said,

-Then a romantic walk is a must for you to probe the wishes of the good Georgia. With the Master of all angels, I will look after the details of your wedding, William. You are an angelic servant which I am most proud of. I would have been extremely sorry to have lost you. But Mighty saved the day like he usually does.

His grandson was quick to replied,

-You intervened too to deal with archangel Michael, you and Lucifer.

The Great Being sipped his tea before he stated,

-Michael sold his soul for your life, Mighty. His soul now gone to hell, you are relatively safe. I also do deals with Lucifer when I am displeased with the actions of my creations. You may be surprised to know that Lucifer is still my servant despite it all but it is the case. As for you Raphael, try to redeem yourself as fast as you can. Lucifer will be extremely fierce on you if you die and if he can have your soul to play torture with it. But I guess my son was angelic enough to warn you about that?

Put on the spot the fallen angel answered with a knot in his throat,

-Yes, the Master was kind enough to warn me. I will try my best to be redeemed, my Lord. I want to serve your son with all my heart.

With wrath in his voice the Creator stormed,

-How long did it take you to do so? Centuries, thousands of years? What did it take you to realise it, the loss of your wings, being human? I do not regret the loss of Michael, and at this moment in time I will not regret your loss as much as I regret the one of my grandson Gael. If you lose your soul for having plotted against my very own family, I will not lift a finger to retrieve you. Listen to me very carefully, pay, re-pay, and pay again.

A pale fallen angel bit his own lips to the blood whilst shivering. Raguel putting his hand on top of the one of Raphael tapped it gently as he said,

-I will see that he does, father, I will see that he does. It will take time, of course. He is only human now. He needs time to adjust to his new situation and to move forward in the right direction. Stop shaking Maggot, my father is not going to call Lucifer upon you. You have a chance, a slim chance, but nonetheless, a chance. Let me help you finish your tea. You have a big day tomorrow. It will be the first day at the quarry, leading two teams of men. It will be a long day especially since what happened to you today. It is time for you to rest.

Raphael obeyed like a child. He welcomed the help of the Master of all angels. He remembered how he had been fed by him all day and as he drank the tea given to him, he couldn't help his tears rolling upon his cheeks. Sebastien extinguished the lamp closest to the sofa then rekindled the fire in the fire place and said,

-You will be safer here than outside, Raphael. Ludwig will stay with you as well. It will be warmer. My father or I will tell you when to get up tomorrow morning for breakfast.

The exhausted fallen angel soon went to lay on the sofa. He could feel pain not only all across his body but also in his mind in the form of deep sorrow. But as soon as his blanket was put over him by Doctor Williams, he fell partly asleep. Raphael could only vaguely hear voices over him.

-He is clearly unwell. His battering by Cork didn't help this afternoon. I think I will have to stay here tonight to monitor him overnight, Master. I don't think he will have a fever because he has been made a strong human but he has more than one broken bone in his body so it can not be dismissed.

-Can he do his work at the quarry tomorrow?

-With a good night of rest, surely. We are talking about Raphael, Master. I can prepare something to alleviate his physical pain for tomorrow.

-I can feel his sorrow from here, father. He almost fainted upon us. He is emotionally exhausted that's what it is.

-Most certainly, your grandfather didn't go easy on him with all due right. But he is certainly weak from my punishment, the encounter we had together with Cork and when Cork found him on the bench and attacked him. It is a combination of physical pain and spiritual one. We must let him have a good rest. My William, stay by him, monitor him for me. Don't let him deteriorate. I don't want to lose my Maggot...

Raphael's consciousness sank at that moment to sleep properly and deeply. Sebastien closed the curtains in the room, then blow out the remaining lamps only leaving one at the table for Doctor Williams. He proposed while closing the door of the drawing room,

-Let's carry on talking in the small garden. Go ahead, I will join you, in a minute giving a last little walk to Killy. The Great Being followed his son who led the way in the garden. Raguel confided,

-Father, like always you were right with Raphael. He is responding well to help and charity. I saw him kneel to me in a very dramatic way this evening in the alley way. I could feel his repentance. He even wanted to be my slave.

The Great Being sat on the bench by his son,

-Of course you refused him.

With unrest Raguel stood up and confessed,

-Yes, you know me and what he has done to me in the past. There is still a high level of revulsion in me towards him. However with him being human, with him responding so well to the punishment he had received from me, I must say that I was torn when I refused him as a slave or a servant. I have already my William who is an excellent servant at that. I can forget or even forgive the treatment of Raphael toward William. Raphael even wanted to put William to the sword, to kill him and managed push Michael to try to do his deed in the most cruel way possible. Both would have obliterated my William. Their plans disgust me. I know I am a hot head and that we did save the day but just, just. Our poor Ivy was dragged away in tears from that house by my William and they had to leave Jack behind. My son and his boy fighting in their own home. Michael debasing himself to stab a boy of eight. I am still very angry about it all. How could Raphael become my slave? He will have to work with William who he hated with a passion for centuries enough to plan his murder and sell his own soul.

His father smiled to him before coming to him, telling,

-Raguel, my Raguel, think, you had the two of them at the same table this morning and tonight. On both occasions they were not at the throat of one another. You will find in Raphael a willingness to be forgiven by William. He doesn't know yet how to go about it but when there is a will, there is a way. My solution would be, if Raphael is daring enough to ask you again to be at your service, to accept him on the equal footing as William, as a servant, but with the condition that he becomes the slave of William. I dare say that you will be surprised by his answer. You will have no need to be torn then. It will resolve everything.

The Master of all angels embraced his father. Sebastien

stepped in the garden holding the little injured fox terrier in his arms and demanded,

-Did I miss something?

Once Sebastien had put the dog on the ground, Raguel held the hand of his son to share the conversation he just had with his father. Sebastien nodded positively afterwards before commenting,

-I think this will work in my humble opinion. You know, father, there is great hope for Raphael. Callum told me during the dinner that Raphael asked him how to become a human angel. Due to the tenacity of Raphael, I do believe we will count him back in our angelic ranks at some point in future. What was amazing was although unable to fight properly, he did intervene to protect you when Cork was stabbing you with the broken bottle. I do believe, if you accept him as a servant, like grandfather said, under a condition, you will actually find him to be a good and willing servant. I know how angry you are with Raphael but you have a way with him. He desperately wants to make up to you. Let him do so. He is different. I can feel he is different. Of course he has still got his wit about him but for the good not for the bad. The fact that he warned us about Ivy's intentions this morning as soon as he was aware of them shows that he cares or is willing to care.

Raguel sat back on the bench and sighed. He revealed,

-Raphael did hurt me the most but I must admit that I am willing to give him a hand. A manifestation of me in the form of Ludwig the rottweiler has been by him for a while and is laying by him now. All I heard from him, in that shape, did let me know that he is changed. I even feel sorry for him. He wants to stay by me, and I can't push him away. I just can't.

The Great Being sat back on the bench, started petting the little injured fox terrier, then told,

-I smell forgiveness is on the way. My son, it will heal you, him and William. Raphael wants to bring back your eldest son. Now the problem with that, to be truly honest with you, may not be with Raphael trying this huge task being only human, but with Gael who had a good taste of heaven and find it rather peaceful there. To make Gael exchange his holiday of his after life time for the hard life of being a demon killer and a punisher again is a tall task. Gael is completely different from our lively Mighty. I know you would love your eldest son back but does he want to be back, this is the question.

Walking and turning in the small garden the Master acknowledged,

-The last time I visited Gael, he was more interested by ants than what I had to say. I don't want to assume that he has become lazy, no, disconnected with the angelic world, most probably, yes. In many aspects, I find him similar to my William who is an angel that is of a peaceful kind. Strangely enough, the two human angels that Gael created were peaceful ones, William and Abigael. On the other hand, Mighty created a proper angelic army but it suits his character. If my Gael comes back, he mustn't be a punisher or demon killer. We should have a different proposal on the table for him. I will have to think about it.

Making another turn around the bird bath Raguel proposed,

-Father, what if we just let him make human angels? He was good at that. William turned out to be a most excellent angel and Abigael is archangelic.

Sebastien sitting by his grandfather commented with a smirk,

-Wouldn't it be ironic if once Raphael gets Gael back, but I don't know how he could manage to do that, Gael turns Raphael into a human angel?

His father gave him a dark glance for the suggestion whilst his grandfather simply answered,

-It is a possibility that can not be dismissed.

A smiling Sebastien added,

-That would be interesting, don't you think so, Dad?

Raguel vented,

-It will surely annoy me deeply. However, if Raphael pass everything with flying colours, and become an angel again I will welcome him back.

Smiling his father stated,

-You have no option but to do so, my son. Anyhow, by the time it happens, you may be surprised that you have befriended Raphael, especially if he has become your servant.

The Master of all angels could only confide,

-I think it is already happening, father, since Raphael is human, he hangs on to me like a lost toddler to a father.

The Great Being commented as he petted the injured little Killy,

-I know what kind of father you are. You will take him on and bring him back to me.

Nodding positively to his father Raguel said,

-I will bring him back to you. Sent, sealed and delivered, you will have his soul back on a platter. I know a way to bring back Michael as well but I want him to pay first. There is nothing better for him than a spell in hell.

His father gave the dog back to Sebastien before he stated,

-I agree. As much as one archangel did encourage the other to do bad, when Michael will come back from his spell from hell, he will discourage Raphael to turn bad again. It is fool's proof. Now, I know you have to tell me something that you deemed rather important, something personal. Why don't you take back a seat by me and just uncover your heart to me? Do you want your son to know and stay here?

Giving a look at Sebastien, Raguel told,

-Yes, I want him here. He can take everything in with his big heart. So I received a marriage proposal from Margot. So if she is so inclined to renew it when she is of age, I am willing to accept it.

His son dropped the dog, surprised by the news but Raguel caught it before Killy touched the ground just in time. The Master scolded his son,

-Pray, Mighty, don't break another leg of that poor dog! Killy suffered enough.

Sebastien retorted his excuse,

-You can't tell a news like that without consequences! Blimey! Father! She is the daughter of a cambion, a grand daughter of a demon created by Lucifer himself. Are you in your right mind?

His father explained while cuddling the fox terrier,

-I am. The way I see it, is like you adopting Ivy and Jack. Margot will have a child with demonic blood. Someone strong will have to keep an eye on that child and bring him or her up. I can do that and make sure that her child doesn't stray in the wrong paths. For Margot, she has a conscience and a good one at that. The fact that she does trust me is a very good thing. We mustn't let her fall into the claws of her father who will use her like a breeding mare. You know me, I will protect her. You have a family to look after, Mighty, and I have to stay in this town like you, so if she wants me to take her under my wings when she is a young woman with her child, I am just saying that I will do so. She will become the wife of a sheriff and have a better status that her present future reserves to her. With what happened to her, no one will want her. If you can give her a proper childhood, I can make sure that the rest of life is happy.

Turning around the bird bath in the small garden Sebastien conceded,

-I can see where you come from. But still! But I kind of agree with you. I did notice that Margot likes you a lot.

Raguel told simply,

-Well, Mighty, when we walked back, Margot and I, from Mr Berry's farm through the woods, I got to know her a little. Then I defended her twice, protecting her from her father. This is not love as per say, her proposal came from her need for protection because she thinks I can give it to her. To be honest with you, I am willing to do so.

The Great Being commented,

-Like your son, you have been grieving for so long that it will make a change to see you marry again, Raguel. Do you intend to have children with her?

His son nodded negatively as he answered,

-If she ever ask me to marry her, when she is of age, my intentions are just to care and protect her and raise her child. She has been raped in a brutal fashion more than once, I will never touch her unless she wants to make love to me. I can tell from the touch of the fingers the true intentions of someone, if they feel obligation or something else. I don't intend to have any children with her at all.

His father told firmly,

-I approve of your decision to marry Margot if she ask you again. If an offspring or more come out of your union, I will embrace and accept them all. I have seen how you brought up Gael and Mighty. I have good faith in you, Raguel, that you will know how to deal with children with demonic blood. Therefore, although very early, you have my blessing.

The Great Being hugged his son before saying,

-Call me if you need me. Do not hesitate. I will always be here for you. The same goes for you, Mighty.

Standing up he embraced his grandson briefly before vanishing into the night.

#

Meanwhile in the Crying White Doe Hotel, Theo and his wife were deeply asleep in the arms of one another. Doctor Valdi had taken charge of the human victims for the night to allow one of Doctor Williams's physical manifestations to rest. Mina and Emily in the same bedroom for the night could not sleep and were chatting happily about the wedding in their large bed. Most were sleeping nonetheless in the hotel, but Amelia Valdi was awake.

With a candle by her side, she had returned to her task of transcribing Lucifer's manuscript. Georgia who could not sleep was by her, helping as much as she could, but mainly she was telling her all about the declaration of Doctor Williams. As all the ink had dried for the part of the book of how to deal with demons Amelia had already copied, she asked Georgia to hide all the pages inside an armchair cushion. The good old Georgia was only too happy to oblige and was sewing without knowing what type of pages she was hiding within a cushion. She only vaguely knew they were important pages and that the now Mrs Odell had the knowledge about what they were. But Georgia was only interested in recounting to Amelia all about her journey to Boston, all about Doctor Williams, and how he asked to marry her in the woods.

Amelia, who enjoyed every gossip in town, was pleased to have a companion to keep her awake whilst her husband was upstairs tending to the many wounded. She was very tired but she was as inquisitive as usual. Dealing with the transcription of the angelic side of the manuscript, she was still able to join the conversation,

-Doctor Williams is so clever, properly educated and intelligent. When we stopped by Boston, Vincent, Zachary and I had dinner at his house. That is when I met him initially and Mr Cotton and Ivy. The evening was so entertaining and there is so much to see in his house. Good Lord! It is not a house, it is a museum!

Georgia smiled as she replied,

-I know! I loved every minute I spent there. I learnt so much in the space of a few days.

-I bet, I did too just visiting his house. His greenhouse is magnificent. I can't remember the name of all the plants there but there was a little fountain in his greenhouse with a statue of a mermaid which was so delightful. Purple lotuses were in the fountain. I can only dream to have something like that in our garden. But I will talk to Vincent about it. I will see what he says. It must be so expensive to have something like that.

The good Georgia acknowledged,

-For sure Doctor Williams is very wealthy and lives in luxury. I was a little uncomfortable within that beautiful house at first but Doctor Williams made so much efforts for us to feel at home during our stay there. I can ask him the cost of his fountain for you and where you can get a similar one.

A few hours passed with the two ladies chatting together. Amelia completed the work, she gave her transcription for Georgia to hide in another cushion. She went back to the desk and try to verify if she had been thorough with the manuscript. She saw a shadow on the white pages of the book. She turned around immediately and saw a beautiful angel with black bat looking like wings. A knot formed in her throat. However Amelia reacted immediately, she took the inkwell from the desk and threw the ink upon the eyes of the fallen angel while she ordered,

-Georgia, run away from here. Tell my husband that Lucifer is here. Hide and protect yourself.

Georgia hid behind the back of Lucifer all the pages she didn't have time to sew in a cushion inside her bodice and did as she was told, she ran away from the room. To protect Georgia's escape Amelia slammed the manuscript upon the momentary blinded Lucifer, she shouted to him,

-You come for that! Here it is!

She did hurt him again with the book hard enough for him to step backward. Not letting go of the book that she was using as a weapon to protect herself, Amelia moved away from the desk and managed to placed herself as fast as she could in front of the fireplace. She threw the manuscript within the flames. Lucifer full of wrath told her,

-You will regret that, woman, you will regret that very dearly!

Amelia seized a poker, pushed the manuscript further inside the fireplace then turned around to the menacing Lucifer who was coming towards her. Her hot poker lifted right up, she warned him,

-Don't you dare touching me.

Lucifer smirked at her gutsy courage. He demanded,

-What is your name, human? Do you know the price of touching my manuscript? Do you have any idea of the punishment for burning it in front of my nose?

The brave Amelia fearing for her safety as the fallen angel undeterred came closer to her replied bravely,

-I am 'Human', just 'Human'. Why do you need my name? Is it just to have an entry in one of your log books on how to kill an Amelia?

Lucifer laughed when he attacked her fully,

-Let's learn together how to kill you, Amelia. I think you deserve a little trip to hell and a great amount of torture, don't you?

At that very moment Valdi came into the room, having heard everything. But he was to far to reach his wife who was transported to hell and disappeared from the room with Lucifer. Abraham Wilton-Cough manifested from him and ordered him,

-Fast, wings on, get your brother, he will know what to do to retrieve Amelia! I am going to hell to protect her as much as I can. Go, on my son, go.

Vincent Valdi wanted to follow his ghost but he knew that strategy was key so he did as he was told. The commotion in the house was noticeable enough for a few to get up. Theo as soon as he knew the matter insisted to come along with Vincent, dressed only in pyjamas and his jacket full of bottles of holy water. They flew together to the presbytery whilst the three M accompanied Georgia Marlow away from the hotel safely with the copy of the manuscript of Lucifer.

With crying eyes, Vincent rang the brass bell of the presbytery strongly in the middle of the night. Sebastien was the first to answer and open the door, dressed with only a pyjama bottom. When he saw a distraught Valdi, he knew something was wrong and invited,

-Come on in. What's up?

An overcome Vincent couldn't answer. But Theo told everything for him,

-We need to act fast, Sebastien. Lucifer abducted Amelia. He took her to hell. He said he will torture her. Abraham went in there to try to protect her. We need a big operation to retrieve her safe and well. Whilhelmina checking the room where it happened said that Amelia burnt the Manuscript of Lucifer right in front of him. The copy is safe and with Georgia Marlow. The three M are taking her here on my phaeton. But Lucifer saw Georgia. We need to get her out of town so she doesn't get the same fate as Amelia.

Sebastien ordered,

-Go to the drawing room. Theo warn William about Georgia. Vincent, your wife needs your help right now, not your tears. Pull yourself together and get ready to go to hell with us. I will wake up my father.

When Sebastien arrived in the bedroom, his father was already awake and getting dressed up. Raguel asked,

-Who rang the bell so late at night and so frantically? Is it that cambion wanting his daughter again?

But his son corrected him,

-No, it's your brother and Theo. Amelia Valdi has been abducted by Lucifer. They need our help to retrieve her from hell. She burnt Lucifer's manuscript in front of him. He said he would torture her for it.

An alarmed Raguel ordered his son,

-Wake up Henry, we will need him, if just for diversion rather than fight. Where is Vincent?

Sebastien replied with a deep sigh,

-In the drawing room with Theo. He couldn't talk. He is fairly distressed. I briefly touched his hand and saw what he witnessed. It is bad, father. Amelia is in deep trouble. One more thing, I saw is that Abraham Wilton-Cough went to hell to protect Amelia and he told Vincent to get you because you would know what to do.

Fastening his shirt, Raguel said,

-Good old Abraham is buying us time. I know how much of a good hindrance he can be, but he is as much in danger as Amelia on this occasion. You must put a shirt on my boy to go to hell with me. You are covered in bandages and that screams out the weak one at this moment in time. They will go for you down there. You will find me in the drawing room. Get Henry ready. Tell Ted of what is going on so he can brief Ivy. Be sharp and short, we need to retrieve Amelia and Abraham as soon as possible. Be fast.

He made a shirt appear for his son before he went downstairs. When he entered the drawing room, Raguel saw his younger brother being restless and doing the hundred paces around the room. The usually slightly sun kissed Vincent was livid. Coming to him the Master told him,

-Vincent, we will get her back. Now, you must get a good grip on yourself otherwise I will have to leave behind because you will jeopardise the rescuing operation. Sebastien informed me of what happened. Now, let me tell you one thing. It may not be that reassuring but Lucifer will not let Amelia being touched by his demons. She will not be tortured or harassed by them. The simple reason is that she knows far too much, things he doesn't want his demons to know. He will deal with her himself and privately in the same place we went before. Secondly, remember that you broke his wrist. For one thing Lucifer will not be able to tie her down. Crucially with Abraham by her side, she does possess a fair chance to not get hurt. Think of how fierce he was when Raphael wanted to drown you. You mustn't forget that Amelia is the mother of his daughter. Trust me when I say, he will protect her.

His talk had the desired effect on his brother who pulled himself together and nodded positively as he said,

-I want to come, I need to come. My Amelia will want to be with me after her ordeal as soon as possible. I will be able to reassure her. When are we going, it kills me to be here.

Raguel was quick to respond with authority,

-When we have have the right numbers to deliver a swift rescue mission. Henry is coming with us and the three former musketeers of my son and of course Mighty. Let me call my father, he has a way to deal with Lucifer which is effective. We will get out of hell without leaving anyone behind, that is my plan.

Father Odell told firmly,

-I am coming too. I am well prepared.

Turning to Theo, the Master couldn't help giggling as he retorted,

-With your pyjama and your slippers, my dear Theo, you are screaming I am a real target for demons. No, you are staying here to defend this household. I can see you have your ammunitions on so you will be most useful. If you give me a minute I will give you your mission which is a very important one.

Awake Raphael who had paid attention to everything, sitting on the sofa, proposed,

-May I help in any way, Master?

A surprised Raguel nagged,

-Yes, you can butt head any demons coming here. But you are not coming with us in hell because Lucifer will definitely keep you there for he has done his part of the bargain. Your soul is his until I claim it back. So, Maggot, you've got to sit that one out. Keep an eye on this household with the dog for it may come under attack. But please, don't let demons drag you to hell. Try to outwit your enemies if you can.

Sebastien followed by Henry and Ted arrived in the drawing room. Sebastien announced,

-We have an update on the situation, father. Ted had a vision when I told him what happened. Go on Ted, tell him.

The angel told the Master,

-Amelia is behind Abraham Wilton-Cough right now. Both are fighting Lucifer together. She has a hot poker in her hand, they are close to a fire place in a very monastic chamber. Abraham is throwing hot burning logs at Lucifer. He told Amelia to burn one hand of Lucifer with the poker which she managed to do. It was the only good hand of Lucifer. They are still in deep trouble but they are managing it well so far.

The Great Being appeared in the room when Raguel said to his brother,

-I told you Abraham would manage to protect her. Father, your Lucifer has abducted Amelia. We need to retrieve her.

His father ordered,

-Mighty informed me of the situation. Let's go. I ordered the three M to come when they can as our back up to return from hell.

The Master turned to Williams to give his last orders,

-William, I leave you in charge of this household. Hide what you will receive for it is important. Theo, you know how to kill demons, if they come forward, I trust you to deal with them. Ted, communicate with me anything that is happening here or any visions you do get. Raphael, go with the dog at the main door of the house and guard it. Raise the alarm if demons are coming by ringing the bell thrice. But be careful and try to stay out of harms way because you are unwell.

Making a cape appear out of thin air and fastening it on the fallen angel, Raguel told him,

-This should keep you warm when you stand outside as a warning guard for this house.

Soon the Great Being, the Master, Henry and Valdi disappeared from the drawing room to be on their way to hell. All left behind looked at each other in dismay. However Doctor Williams took the lead with ease as he said,

-Raphael, I will bring you a stool. You are still weak and I don't want you to stand outside like that for part of the night when you should really rest. I know of a hot beverage that can keep you warm and awake to be sharp on your duty. Theo, Ted, take a seat at the table we can all do with that beverage. I hope the three M will arrive soon.

Willingly taking a seat Father Odell asked,

-Don't they know the trick of Sebastien, the one that make a horse fly by putting their angelic wings upon it? They are coming on the phaeton pulled by my old Rosalie and I tell you that she is not the fastest horse in the world. She would never win a grand prix or any race for that matter. But she knows how to fly because Sebastien made her have wings on occasions.

Williams exclaimed, clapping his hands,

-Excellent idea! I wish I would have thought of that before you did. I taught that trick to Sebastien when he first became an angel. I will send them the message.

Taking a stool covered with blue velvet, he ordered in a kind voice,

-Come with me Raphael, lets make you comfortable at the entrance.

Raphael came, followed by the rottweiler who he had noticed was never leaving his side. Somehow he felt more secure to have Ludwig by him. He confided to Doctor Williams in the hallway,

-I never knew about such a trick to make a horse fly when I was an archangel.

Opening the door for the fallen angel, Williams explained,

-Raphael, you were so demeaning of human angels, that we kept all the arrogant archangels in the dark of all the angelic magical tricks we learnt over the years. We developed many. We have an entire repertoire of them but we teach them to angels who have done at least one or two incarnated angelic lives on earth.

Williams put the stool by the wall and bellow the brass bell with some care while Raphael enquired,

-So some archangels, the ones who were not arrogant did know about all that? How many are they?

Doctor Williams sighed deeply as he answered,

-Since you developed a pernicious culture amongst the archangels telling them that they were better than any one else, only one, the son of the Lord himself, the Master of all angels is aware of all the things we can do as human angels and what we have developed or created. Of course, now they are two, since the Mighty One passed his grades as an archangel. Now show me if you can reach that bell and ring it in any danger, remember the code: Once for visitors, twice for angels, thrice for demons or deep trouble like Cork.

Raphael lifted his arm with difficulty but eventually did ring the brass bell with pain. An observant Williams made a long string appear and attached it to the bell, then ordered,

-Try again by pulling the string. It should hurt you less.

An obliging Raphael did so with much less difficulty and pain. The fallen angel smiled as he said simply,

-Thank you, Doctor Williams. You know I never said sorry to you personally, and I will understand if you refuse my apologies. But I want you to know that I am sorry for having been such an arse toward you. You didn't deserve any of my hatred whatsoever. I was so jealous and so envious of you. When I think of how I behaved, I am disgusted by it. So I am sorry, really sorry. I am getting emotional again, I guess that is the plight of being human but at least I feel something better than when I was an archangel. I lost my sense of superiority at the hands of the Master but I feel better for it. It is like my head was in a fog and he removed the fog. Now, I understand how wrong I was and always has been. I think of what I said and did in the past constantly in utter shame. I want you to know that William.

Doctor Williams nodding positively stated,

-Trust me we all know that you are repentant. Why do you think the Master tasked you this evening? Come, take a seat. You can rest your back on the wall. It will give you a correct posture which can only help your bones to heal. Remember, you are our eyes tonight. But do not go into any fighting, let the dog bite and retreat inside the house. If a dangerous situation happens and, it may well be the case, go inside the drawing room where Theo and I will be and stand behind us. We will protect you. Theo is canny dealing with demons and me, I know a trick or two magically wise. To tell you the truth, we did acquire, steal is probably a more appropriate word, something very important to Lucifer, which Amelia Valdi did burn in front of him. This is why she is facing torture down in hell. Now we are going to retrieve her, but if you know the game of tit for tat, Lucifer will try to get his own back by either seizing our ghost Abraham Wilton-Cough or you, who are so vulnerable at the moment, that he can order your death and then take your soul. Lucifer will only feel glee to possess the bigger stake of a fallen archangel. So as the Master said you must outwit your enemy. If you want to regain your wings, you must stay alive at all cost. Now, I will not close the door fully therefore you can just push it with your shoulder and run back in.

For a split second Raphael held the hand of Williams

with gratefulness but he remained speechless still full of emotions. The old angel felt the true sorrow of the fallen angel. Their eyes met and Williams said before he left the threshold,

-I will come to check on you regularly tonight. Remember, if you are in danger come to me straight away. If you focus on the horizon, you might see an old mare flying in the sky. A horse with wings is quite a sight. Although you are not an angel any longer, I am pretty sure if you ask Sebastien, kindly of course, he will take you on a night trip on one, one of those days. But you need to get better first.

Doctor Williams left the door as he said slightly opened and Raphael sighed deeply. Once alone the fallen angel talked to the dog as if he was an old friend of his,

-Do you know what my dear Ludwig? I was a fool, a utter fool, a complete fool. Doctor Williams is such a nice angel. To just think that I planned his death, I disgust myself. Given two arms back, I might end my days, hang myself and get the punishment I deserve for having been such an horrid archangel. I feel terrible.

The rottweiler put his large head on the lap of the fallen angel and licked his hands which made Raphael caress the dog. A few minutes later, he saw the black mare flying towards the church yard pulling a phaeton whilst two angels were flying by her side, one guiding her. Soon everyone made a safe landing. Maurice helped a lady out of the phaeton with care. One of his brothers took charge of taking the old mare into the stable whilst Matthias came to the presbytery door. He gave a small bow to Raphael as if he was still an angel before saying,

-You can announced that we are here, finally arrived, to Doctor Williams.

Standing up Raphael pulled the string of the bell twice. The diligent servant of the Master came straight away at the door and invited,

-Matthias come straight in so I can brief you all up with the orders of the Master.

Matthias did as he was told, while Maurice with a bright smile walked Georgia Marlow to the door. Maurice told,

-This was an interesting trip which your future wife enjoyed very much, Williams. As soon as Rosalie took off her worried face was left behind to be replaced by a smile from one ear to the other.

Georgia retorted falsely offended,

-No, I am still extremely worried! You can't give me flying horses to make all things better when Mrs Valdi is in deep trouble.

Doctor Williams taking the hand of Georgia explained with a giggle,

-It was not for your enjoyment my dear, unfortunately. It was just to speed things up. The three M need to go to hell as reinforcement to help for the safe rescue of Amelia and Wilton-Cough. Come on in.

Georgia saw the tall Raphael who bowed to her at the door like a servant but she realised he was in pain as he did so. She asked Doctor Williams,

-Who is that? I never saw him in town before. Is he alright? He seems to be suffering.

Doctor Williams made the presentation willingly,

-Georgia meet Raphael River. He is in fact the fallen archangel Raphael. He was battered today by the nasty Mr Cork. He suffered a few fractured ribs as a result. He is strong, he will recover soon enough despite being now just a human. He is still being looked after by angels. Sebastien is giving him a home for the time being until he adjust as a human. So yes, Raphael is new in town but he will help to rebuild the burnt part of the town. Raphael, meet Georgia Marlow, my future wife. She works at the Crying White Doe Hotel on the edges of Wilton Town. She has recently been made to be an eternal being.

Smiling to Georgia, Raphael said,

-Nice to finally meet you. I heard about you since I arrived here. Everyone says that you are a very fine cook.

The good Marlow replied,

-I do know how to feed a crowd nicely. If my future husband invite you in my future home, you will be able to sample my food. It is mainly comfort food, heart warming stews, pies and roasts. I am sorry I never heard of you before.

With a sad smile the fallen angel commented,

-It is probably better that you never heard of me. The

less said about me, the better it is really. I lost my wings. This speaks for itself. I do not sustain the hope of ever be invited in your future home. But nonetheless it has been a pleasure to meet you.

Georgia gave him a clumsy courtesy with the word,

-Likewise.

Then she followed Doctor Williams indoors who asked her,

-Have you got everything?

When she entered the drawing room and then closed the door, Georgia answered,

-I have. Amelia did make me conceal part of it in a cushion which is all sewn up. Then there is another part which I managed to hide from the sight of Lucifer in my bodice. When she handed me the last part, she said that she had finished her work. But she kept checking a large book to make sure she didn't forget anything then Lucifer arrived behind her.

Georgia lifted her skirt up and removed the cushion from her crinoline skirt where it was tucked in. She gave it to Williams blushing as she said,

-It was not my idea to hide the cushion there to hold it. It was the idea of Whilhelmina to hide it. I don't wear crinoline skirt so she lent me her crinoline and fitted me with it.

Williams dared to tease her,

-Well, it was an excellent idea which allowed me to have a good glimpse at your lovely legs. You will have to thank Mrs Odell for it for me.

Now red as a lobster Georgia put her skirt down doubly fast, and she scolded,

-You are suppose to be an angel, Doctor Williams.

He smirked to her as he retorted,

-Angel doesn't mean being a monk. You look very nice in a crinoline skirt. Knowing a little of the future, it will be extremely fashionable in the years to come.

Georgia confided,

-That is why Whilhelmina always sets trends and elegance in this town. She played with her crystal ball. She knows the future as well and is always ahead of everyone fashion wise.

Williams told her,

-As much as I would like to talk fashion with you my dear Georgia, the longer you carry those papers upon you, the more at risk you will become. I surely don't want to see you being dragged to hell like Amelia was. I need the ones in your bodice.

Blushing again Georgia replied somewhat shyly,

-They are too well tucked in. I can't.

Nodding his understanding, Doctor Williams ordered,

-Theo, Ted, would you please both face the wall. Now, Georgia, you are going to be called Mrs Williams and you can trust me. Let me help you. You mustn't stay in danger with those paper. You can remain a prude after you are prudent.

Georgia gave her consent and let William undo the laces of her bodice. He freed the pages which contained all the informations about killing angels. He held them in his hand with some relief. He gave his next order with a smile,

-You can fasten your bodice back up. But let me tell you that by protecting those pages where you did put them you have been a mother hen to all angels.

The good Georgia was wondering what he meant and turned around to be presentable once more. Doctor Williams went to Ted and Theo, he told them,

-We need to hide those as fast as we can.

Theo replied immediately,

-For the cushion, you can let it in plain view. To Amelia's credit, she was clever when she thought about that stratagem. The cushion could do with more padding inside it. Put it on the spare chair in the corner that is rarely used. For the other pages, I have a good hiding place for the time being. But I suggest that we do the same at a later date, hide it inside a matching cushion.

While Odell lifted the carpet a little by the fireplace, Doctor Williams did put the cushion in place as he was told. It did look innocuous enough there, then he went by Theo and asked,

-So what is this hiding place?

Lifting a slab from the floor, Theo revealed,

-Only Valdi, Whilhelmina and I know of it, and my priestly predecessor of course. This house was the one of the founder of Wilton Town: Noah Wilton, before it became a presbytery. He did hide his diaries under this slab. Those diaries contained what happened at the start of Wilton Town. It was not all very rosy, I can tell you that. The first settlers faced a famine of a few years which had dramatic consequences, some people did eat their dead, some did kill others to eat. Noah Wilton tried to control the situation with great difficulty. My Whil' was already an eternal Being at that time and know exactly what happened then. One of her darkest sorcery book, the one which allowed her to become eternal is also hidden in this cache. Noah did put it there for safety reasons after it was used by the neighbour of Whilhelmina.

Doctor Williams deposited the pages in his possession inside the hole in the ground while he enquired,

-The neighbour who is now the crying white doe and doesn't rest in peace for having curse the town?

Father Odell corrected as he placed back the slab,

-Not exactly. We solved that problem. But her sons are troublesome vampires somewhere in the world. For her to rest we need to resolve their cases. Valdi and Amelia were working together on the matter. They have some clues.

When Theo covered the slab back with the carpet, Williams did a small incantation over it. Odell asked,

-May I ask what was that for?

Smiling to him, William answered,

-Yes, you may, I have just restricted who would be able to open that little cache. No demons, no humans and no fallen angels will be able see its content. It will be sealed closed for them. Now only angels have access to its content but I will say that we will only share the existence of the secret niche to the Master, Sebastien and Henry. Ted, you have to keep your mouth close about it and Georgia, the same goes for you. It is our secret.

Odell and Williams stood up satisfied that they had hidden the most important part of the copy of the manuscript. Doctor Williams went to prepare his beverage for everyone by the fire place when Ivy stepped into the room and sighed with despair,

-I can't sleep, Doctor Williams. I am so worried for Sebastien. Where is he gone again? He is covered in bandages already.

Looking at the young woman in her nightdress, covered with her shawl, Williams told her the blunt truth,

-We have an emergency situation on our hands, Ivy. The wife of Doctor Valdi has been abducted by Lucifer and is in hell. Your father in law, Valdi, your husband and Henry went to rescue her. The three ancient musketeers of Sebastien just went there as well to give them a hand. You must be strong for your husband, Ivy. You know he is a fighting angel. He has to do what he's got to do. Sebastien always comes back, maybe with more scars an bruises, but at the end of the day he will be proud to show them to us.

This succeeded to make Ivy smile again. She conceded,

-I've got to get used to it I guess. But the worry, oh, the worry!

Doctor Williams admitted,

-I know. But they have to save Amelia Valdi at all cost. Here take this warm beverage to Raphael who is guarding the entrance.

Ivy obeyed straight away, so used she was to follow the orders of Doctor Williams to whom she was a medical student. She went outside and offered the hot drink to Raphael. She helped him drink but she asked,

-What are you doing out there? You were supposed to sleep on the sofa.

The fallen angel could only focus on her sore cheek as he replied,

-There is an emergency situation going on, Mrs Cotton.

I have the same question for you, what are you doing out here? Please, go back inside. I can feel something coming. It's only minutes away. We will be lucky if we have half an hour. Please, go back inside, run to the attic and take the children with you. Lock yourself in there with Miss Marlow and the old Lady who has a cat. Something is coming. Don't go near any windows. Please Go and stay safe.

Ivy went back in. She stepped into the drawing room and reported what Raphael said to Williams who turned to her and advised with confidence,

-Listen to Raphael. He is still sentient my Ivy. If he says something is coming, it will be here soon. Run upstairs, take this with you and throw it all over the floor in the attic. It will prevent demons from smelling where you are in the house. Now, you will all need to be silent and to stay still, until I, the Master or Sebastien come to get you. Go, Ted, go with them, make sure they follow the orders and stay in the attic with them to protect them if needs be. Do you feel something coming?

His hands holding his forehead, Ted told sternly with some fear,

-Yes, definitely, it is the father of Cork, the unruly demon that Lucifer created. I must take them upstairs now, call Raphael back in. He has no chance to survive if he is staying out there.

Ted stood up straight after what he said and enjoined,

-Ivy, Georgia, go and get the children and Mel Brown. I will bring some knives and save the animals. You must make sure to all be quiet.

The two ladies rushed upstairs without further a do while Ted went to fetch knives in the kitchen as fast as he could. Williams went to the entrance door of the house and ordered,

-Raphael, come back in straight away. You happened to be right. We have a demon from hell coming in our way, a very dangerous one. Go and sit down on the chair in far corner of the drawing room. Let us deal with the demon. He is going all out for your soul. You will not last long under his hands according to Ted, our visionary angel. Go now, take the dog with you.

The fallen angel obeyed. Williams took the stool then closed the door behind him. He secured the door with a short spell before going back to the drawing room. He warned,

-Theo, be prepared to fight and fight hard. If this is the

father of Cork, we will all end up in a bloody mess. By securing the door, I only bought us a few minutes to secure the children.

Thinking forward, Theo gave a couple of bottles of holy water to both as he advised,

-Aim for the eyes, it blinds demons momentarily. Then you can either make a fighting move or run away from a bad situation. Raphael, use the stool to protect yourself. Here. Do you know a bit of fencing? Can you be as good as an Amelia Valdi with a hot poker?

The fallen angel smirked at the suggestion as he replied,

-I am a consummate warrior. Of course I will know how to use a hot poker in a normal situation but I have two broken arms. I can hardly feed myself as it is.

Odell asked wildly,

-Is there any chance that you can come up with a spell to sort out his arms, Doctor Williams? My Whil' managed to render Wilton-Cough physical for long period of time, surely you can do such a feat.

The wizard thought for a minute before he replied,

-I can, but he has been punished. My spell will go against the will of a Punisher, my Master.

Looking at Raphael, Theo argued,

-Raphael has been punished, and given a chance to do good by the Great Being and the Master himself. Please, let him defend himself. Sort out his arms now. I am pretty sure that the Master will approve of that move and decision. Even if you do a momentary spell for his arms and physical body, please I beg you to do so, right now, for the Great Being doesn't want to lose Raphael's soul for whatever it may be worth. We are his front line right now to protect that fallen angel. You know he likes to retrieve them. Please, I can't beg you enough! We have seen how tough the son of that demon is. We are going to deal with the father of Cork... Please, save Raphael from a straight death.

His compelling plea was listened to by Williams who performed the spell by holding the hands of Raphael. The wizard told sternly,

-Raphael, you owe me one. Fight for your life. The spell

will last for a dozen of hours. You can you use your body fully for that time but remember one thing, you are still very human. So I have to warn you to be careful. Stay behind us. If the demon is coming for tit for tat and for you... Just try to stay safe behind us.

The fallen angel nodded his agreement to Doctor Williams as he started feeling strength back to his muscles and back. He had glistening eyes as he gave a look at Theo and William to only say,

-Thank you.

Odell gave Raphael a hot poker with his advice,

-Use it wisely. Aim for the parts which will disable your enemy even momentarily. There is no shame to aim for the sexual parts of your opponent when he is a dangerous incubus demon who creates the likes of Cork. Then when he is hurt, blind him and move away from his wrath. We are all in it together. We will protect each other.

Having an idea he then turned to Williams to ask,

-Do you still possess the control of the animal spirits of Sebastien, Doctor Williams?

The old angel smiled as he replied,

-I do! You are a blessed angel Theo! We can do with a sabre tooth cat and a cockerel bothering a demon. I will conjure them.

In the meantime, Ivy went to get her two adopted children, Jack and Margot. Margot took Killy in her arms as she followed Ivy while Jack carried by Ivy didn't part with his kitten. Georgia woke up Mel Brown and warned her of the emergency situation. Mrs Brown didn't argue. She followed Georgia with her cat in her arms. Soon all were snuggling to one another in the attic with some fear but no one dared to speak. Ted came, a kitten in his arms, knives in his pocket. He handed the long haired kitten to Ivy with a,

-Look after your little fur ball. I see that we are all here. Let's secure that trap door then.

He lifted the ladder to go to the attic, closed the trap door, put the ladder upon it and then secured it to close the trap door with a couple of large chest. Ivy exclaimed,

-We haven't got Ludwig!

Ted went by Jack as he answered,

-Ludwig is going to protect those downstairs. Do not worry too much for him, Mrs Cotton.

Then he ordered,

-Now, we must all stay quiet and put. For all who have pets in their arms, make sure they stay silent.

He gave knives to everyone by their side and said,

-If an angry demon managed to come here, do not hesitate to use those. I doubt that it will happen but there is strength in numbers. If we all go for him at the same time, we will do him some damage rather than him doing damage to one of us. He will not be able to focus if we are all attacking him together.

Ivy could see a couple of large butchering knives at the belt of the angel. She then knew that the situation could be very serious indeed. She went to open a large chest who was behind them. Putting her large shall inside it, she ordered,

-Jack, give me your kitten. We will keep our two kittens here for the time being. So we will have our hands free to fight properly you and me. They will sleep in there.

The little boy obeyed straight away. The two kittens snuggled to one another upon the shawl within the chest. Ivy closed the chest and said,

-Ted, you have us on board.

Margot told,

-I want to be on board too!

Ted replied strongly, pointing to an almost dilapidated wardrobe in the attic,

-This is your demonic grandfather coming to us. Hide in that wardrobe right now, keep the dog quiet, and keep the knife by you. If he takes you away, you will end up breeding demons after demons. They will abuse you endlessly, him and his son. Hide, Margot, hide.

Despite having a strong character, Margot did as she was told because she knew all so well what it was to be abused.

She was shivering when she closed the doors of the wardrobe. She held Killy tightly upon her young breasts to give herself some courage. Then she heard a commotion coming from downstairs. Her grandfather had arrived with some fracas.

The demon, who could not pass the front door who had a spell on it, broke a window of the drawing room to step inside the house. Raphael threw the little stool by him at the colossal demon, wondering out loud,

-Why does Lucifer has to make them big? Williams, throw everything at that one!

Theo helping out, blinding the demon with some of his holy water, enjoined,

-Williams, that is a sabre tooth cat moment! I saw some large demons but never that large.

Doctor Williams who couldn't believe the size of the demon they had to tackle conjured the spirits of the cockerel and of the sabre tooth cat. The cockerel appeared first. The bird went straight to attack the face of the demon, but if it clawed it, it was also thrown like a rag doll on one side in a great array of feathers by the entering demon.

Raphael commented when he saw the bird almost lifeless on the floor,

-Short and sweet, that's one line of defence gone and one enraged demon still left.

Giving him a dark glance, Williams ordered him,

-Shut up Maggot! This is not helping. This is!

The sabre tooth cat appeared into the room and stood in front of all of them taking a protective pose between them and the demon. Raphael couldn't help saying with an irresistible smirk,

-That is more like it, yes. I agree.

The demon shouted,

-Give me the things I want and I will let you live. We do not have to fight, I do not need to disembowelled you, and dismembered you piece by piece when you are still barely alive if I get what I want.

Stepping forward without fear, his magic wand in hand, Williams demanded,

-What do you want?

Flanked by Odell and the sabre tooth cat, the Wizard tried his best to contain his nerves. From his first assessment, he assumed that the demon may be a very strong one but not the cleverest of them all. He sent a telepathic message of encouragement to Theo and Raphael,

-Stay strong and together. We can outwit that one.

The demon replied strongly,

-You two, you and you can escape with your lives if I kill this one, Raphael. Lucifer wants him badly. I heard that my granddaughter was living here now. I want her very badly for my son and I to breed. She is ours.

Raphael threw with great impulsion of disgust a vase onto the demon, shouting,

-Breeding bastard! Son of the devil! You will never get me and you will never get her back! Never! I will kill you before dawn! Mark my words!

The demon said simply,

-So, I am right, you are Raphael. Thank you for clearing things out for me. My Master wants your soul. And I want you dead for delivering my granddaughter to angels.

He made a move forward to attack Raphael but Theo blinded the demon with holy water. Odell ordered,

-Poker in the fire, Raphael, you will need it burning hot.

The sabre tooth cat went to protect but it was too late. Theo had received a punch in the jaw which rendered him unconscious. Williams positioned himself in front of Raphael who had followed the advice of Theo to the letter and was making his poker very hot. The sabre tooth cat and Ludwig the rottweiler both were attacking the demon. The dog was having a good go at the legs in a ferocious manner while the prehistoric cat dug his teeth into the shoulder of the demon. In desperation the demon ran away from the room and upstairs trying to escape the animals.

Raphael enjoined Williams,

-Check that Theo is alright. He doesn't look too good. He is properly out of it. I am going to go in the chase of that bastard.

While the animals followed Raphael every step of the way, Doctor Williams had to attend to Theo. With water, Odell eventually came about. His first words were,

-Bloody hell, I will only have teas and soups for a week.

Williams ordered to him,

-Hide under the sofa. Your head did hit the wall rather badly. You have a severe concussion. And yes, your jaw did receive a nice blow. This will hurt for a while. I need to go upstairs. Stay safe, Theo.

An unwilling Theo obeyed feeling extremely dizzy. He dragged himself under the sofa then lost his consciousness again. But Williams was already out of the room chasing what was happening upstairs. He could hear a lot of noises. Doctor Williams arrived to a scene where Raphael was bleeding heavily but still standing. Ludwig was laying on his flank and the sabre tooth cat was still fiercely alive but with clawing marks throughout his body. Raphael told him tears in his eyes,

-We tried to stop him. He is in the attic. I can not fly there to help them all. Take me there we need to save them. He is a monster. He is going to kill them all.

Williams held his hand and teletransported Raphael to the attic with him. There they saw Ted, Ivy, Georgia and a poorly Jack harassing the demon together. The cat of Mel Brown was clawing the face of the demon. However the strong demon threw Jack away from him but Raphael caught the boy before he could hurt himself on a chest. He ordered him,

-Put the ladder in place and go and hide yourself. Run and save your life, Jack. Williams save Ivy and Georgia.

Williams knowing the great danger the women were in pulled them away from the ferocious fight. Both of them were bleeding but if Georgia followed him willingly, Ivy kept punching the demon until the demon threw her aside unconscious. Williams carried Ivy and teletransported her downstairs in the drawing room. He deposited her on the sofa. Georgia who had run downstairs with Jack went into the room asked with great concern,

-How is she?

A worried Williams replied with urgency,

-Try to revive her my Georgia. Use water on her forehead. There is some tonic on the table. Give her some. She has a pulse. I have to go back upstairs to save Mrs Brown and Margot. Where is Margot? I couldn't see her upstairs.

Georgia answered,

-She is hiding in the broken wardrobe up there by the order of Ted. She was keeping the little dog quiet for us.

Williams nodded before he ordered,

-Lock and block the door until you hear my voice back. Jack hide yourself behind a curtain for the time being.

He rushed out and teletransported back to the attic. Ted and Raphael were fighting the powerful demon. Ted was visibly injured yet he wasn't giving up the fight. Williams made the large sabre tooth cat appear in the attic which took no time to attack the demon then Williams rushed to the terrified Mrs Brown. He guided her away from the attic took her back to her bedroom and told her to lock herself in her room and to hide herself there. She cried for her cat to him, that it was still up there. Williams told her that he will try his best to recover her pet. He rushed back to the attic and saw Ted on the floor bleeding badly. However Raphael was still fighting the demon. The sabre tooth cat was laying on his flank, stabbed. The cat of Mrs Brown was lifeless behind a chest.

Raphael was using his poker with great dexterity. Williams with his magic wand rendered the poker very hot with a simple spell. This pleased Raphael who thanked him. This little gesture renewed his fighting spirit. Thinking of the advices of Theo, Raphael attacked the private parts of the demon with no further a do and burnt them totally. The demon screamed in pain, momentarily immobilised,

-You are going to die for that!

Williams threw some holy water blinding the demon and ordered,

-Raphael, now, his heart!

Reacting fast Raphael planted his hot poker in the chest of the demon repetitively. The demon knelt knowing he was now dying in pain. Raphael went behind him to finish him off, taking a butchering knife from the floor, he cut the throat of the demon deeply. When the demon fell forward dead, Raphael said with emotion to Williams,

-We did it! Where is Margot? We need to look after Ted as soon as possible.

Doctor Williams went to Ted and started to give him first aid on the floor, he told,

-Ted is breathing. He still has a pulse. Margot is in that broken wardrobe with the little fox terrier. Ted had ordered her to hide in there. Go and get her, the poor thing must be terrified.

Raphael opened the doors of the wardrobe and found Margot trembling, crouched upon herself holding Killy tightly. He reassured her,

-It is all over, Margot. You can come out now, give me the little dog and hold my hand. We can go and reassure the others.

Willingly Margot gave him the dog as she confided,

-I saw everything from a crack in the door. I was so, so scared. I think I did wet myself when the demon killed the cat of Mrs Brown.

Smiling kindly to her the fallen angel told,

-It does happen, one more reason to get you out of that wardrobe. Come and take my hand. It is finished, you are going to be alright.

As Margot came to him, Raphael saw some blood where she had been sitting. He called out,

-Doctor Williams, please, there is something I want you to see, in the wardrobe. Margot did bleed. She thought she was weeing but she bled.

Leaving the side of Ted for a few seconds who was now in a sitting position, Doctor Williams came immediately. When he noticed the dark pool of blood, he put his leather gloves on. He went to touch the blood and found a very small embryo of a demon, dead. He gave his conclusion straight away,

-She miscarried in the wardrobe that is what happened. Ivy and I will have to look after Margot to unsure she is not having a subsequent hemorrhage. Margot, you are definitely a bit pale. We will have to tend to you. You lost your baby I am afraid.

The strong Margot commented with some emotion,

-It is probably better like that.

Raphael nudged her little hand and agreed with her,

-Probably. You may go back to school like all the other children and with little Jack once he is better.

The young girl managed to smile this time around at the idea as she asked him, following him,

-Do you think I could ever have a normal childhood from now?

Williams sighed deeply hearing her question at the same time as Raphael did. They exchanged a knowing look at each other. Williams enjoined,

-Truly, we do not know about that whilst your father is still out and about. But with the punishment Raguel delivered to him, he will be calm for a good while. But what I can promise you is a few angelic tricks for tonight. Ted let me help you to stand up. Carry Mrs Browns cat. Everybody hold each other by the arms or the hands. Margot, in just a few seconds you will be in the drawing room without even walking.

She said with a smile finally appearing on her face,

-It is not possible.

But Raphael corrected her kindly,

-Oh, yes it is possible. Just hold my hand tight and see what Doctor Williams is capable of.

Before she could even replied, Margot stood amongst everyone in the drawing room. There was even the sabre tooth cat there which was still on his flank. Georgia announced to Doctor Williams as soon as she saw him,

-Ivy and Theo came around. It took a great deal of tonic. What is the situation upstairs?

A pleased William replied,

-A large demon is down and has been dealt with courtesy of Raphael. The incubus of Lucifer is dead. Now let's look at all the damage that demon did to us. Jack you can come back from your hiding place, the danger is over.

The little boy came and ran into the arms of Ivy who praised him,

-You have been a brave boy my Jack like usual. Have you been hurt in anyway? Let me check you out.

Jack said with a smile,

-Well, I haven't got any battle scars like Pa has but I have just a couple of bruises. I wanted to show off a little to him you know.

Ivy demanded with a kind giggle,

-But you can show off to your Ma. Show me your impressive bruises so I can look after them.

Doctor Williams made their medical bags appear by their sides whilst the child exposed his bruises. He came by Ivy to inspect Jack with her, and after a few minutes delivered his diagnosis,

-Nothing is broken. You had a lucky escape, Jack. Ivy, rub this unguent on his bruises. He will be fine if a little sore then put him back to bed and come straight away back downstairs because we need to do a fair few stitches on Ted. Now, I want you to carry on being brave, Jack and sleep with all your little pets for the rest of the night. You are going to be their little guardian angel for me, your Pa and your Ma.

Jack replied with some anguish,

-We left our kitties up there, in a chest, they are in Ma's shawl. We put them out of the way to protect them. We need to get them back.

Raphael who had made Margot sit by Ted on the couch proposed,

-I will go and fetch them.

Williams asked,

-Can you go and check that his bedroom and all others are safe, and bring Mrs Brown downstairs with us?

Bowing to him, Raphael answered,

-I will.

Raphael did everything with diligence. In the attic, he opened many chests before finding the right one with the sleeping kittens. He enveloped them within the shawl with care, and noticed that the demon was disappearing into a pile of dust decomposing itself. He gave a sigh of relief as he locked back the attic. He went to fetch Mrs Brown who was crying. He reassured her that all was over, that the demon was killed. But he didn't have the courage to tell her that her cat was dead. He thought that probably Doctor Williams would have more tact than him to break the news to the woman. However, when they arrived in the drawing room, her cat was alive and well on the lap of Theo. Mel Brown rushed to her pet and hugged it,

-Come to Mummy, my poor little thing! You clawed that nasty demon very well. Now you need a good rest, just like Mummy.

She excused herself and went back to her room with her cat. When she was gone, Raphael stated,

-She could have stayed a little longer with us. Her cat was killed, I saw it happened. How can it be alive now?

Doctor Williams explained to him,

-Theo has been given a gift by the Great Being not so long ago. He can revive animals. The cat wasn't dead long enough for its spirit to not be recalled to inside its body. As for Melanie Brown, she lost her home and everything, apart from her cat. You must excuse her for being a little uncommunicative at the moment. But the Master made his son lodge her here to make sure she comes over her trials. We gave her the responsibility of the group of ladies who will creates the blankets needed for the winter of all who lost their homes to the fire. So she has an incentive to not give up, and to take her mind of things. Her human case will be tended to, do not worry.

Theo added,

-Mel is a very good woman living one of her roughest time in her life. She went through many like the loss of her husband. We have to give her a little time to recover from the loss of her house. I can assure you that Melanie is more communicative than that normally. She usually run a stall on market day where she sells all   the knitwear her crafty hands made. She made a small but decent living out of it. People of the town always come to her when they need socks, gloves, scarves, shawls, blankets, woollen hats, clothes for their babies. She is talkative normally, Raphael, a popular individual in town. She has just fallen on hard time and has to come to term with it. I will go and talk to her now. With what we endured tonight with that demon, she must be still distressed.

The fallen angel bowed to Theo as he left the drawing room. Ivy asked Raphael as she took the hand of Jack,

-Come with us with the kittens, Raphael. I am going to put Jack to bed. Then will you bring Killy to my boy and stay until my Jack is fully asleep?

Willingly following her, Raphael agreed, saying,

-Yes, of course I will. You will be happy to hear that your two little kittens are fine. They both just slept throughout the commotion. But how are you doing, Mrs Cotton?

Ivy looked at him as she replied,

-Please, as you are going to live with us for a while, just call me Ivy. I will be fine, I just took a bad knock and fainted. In my condition, it is to be expected at some point. But I will survive, maybe with one more bruise for the day on my elbow, nothing to worry about. No, really the question should be how are you, you, Raphael, who managed to kill that demon, because I can see blood upon you?

An embarrassed Raphael who was hurt lied,

-Like you I will be fine. It may be just the demon's blood and a few scratches.

He watched as Ivy put Jack to bed, and smiled tenderly as she tucked him in. He deposited the kittens on the bed and gave her back her shawl before he went downstairs to fetch the fox terrier. He noticed that the rottweiler was guarding the entrance of the house and somehow was pleased to see the dog alive. He briefly went to stroke his head, and talked to the dog,

-Good dog, keep watching the main door. We need to protect this good home and its family.

#

It was dawn, Georgia was brought back to the hotel by Father Odell. She was so exhausted that she was sleeping on

his shoulder all the way. An anxious Wilhelmina was so happy to
see the little phaeton, the good old Rosalie and its two
occupants. She came running towards them and demanded,

-Is everything alright? Where is Amelia? Where is
Valdi? Where are the three M?

Theo lifting the sleeping Georgia in his arms responded,

-Georgia is exhausted. If you show me her bedroom I
will carry her there. We had to deal with a demon at the
presbytery, an incubus, the grand father of Margot, a demon
created by Lucifer. It was quite something. I am tired beyond
belief. It was such a struggle but Raphael managed to kill the
demon. As far as I know, the rescue expedition to save Amelia is
still in hell. We are still waiting to hear from them.

In the drawing room of the presbytery, only Doctor
Williams and Raphael were still up. Williams was attending to
the wounds of the fallen angel scolding him,

-Only scratches! That is a gaping wound here, and
there. You are as bad as Sebastien to describe your wounds.

Raphael managed to giggle as he replied,

-I will take that as a compliment if you don't mind.

Smiling back Williams ordered,

-Stop moving Raphael or my stitches will look like some
kind of lace work.

A recognisable voice in the room said,

-They always are pretty lace work! I am next, along with
my father, Valdi, Henry, Maurice, Matthias and Maximilien.

Doctor Williams stood up straight away with joy and
tears in his eyes. Raphael couldn't help doing the same.
Williams invited,

-Please, all of you take some chairs. Where are Amelia
and Wilton-Cough, Sebastien?

Valdi replied as he entered the room carrying his wife
who was asleep,

-Abraham is back inside me. Amelia is fine but the strain
of everything took its toll. She has some bruises but nothing to

worry about. She is just tired. Abraham protected her like a lion down there. She also did her bit. We saw her fighting, there was no way Lucifer could get close to her. She was throwing books at Lucifer, everything on his shelves and Abraham was throwing burning logs and coals towards Lucifer.

Coming inside the room with his father, the Master told,

-Oh my William, she fought for her dear life! All along she did, ready to survive at all cost. When she threw the books at Lucifer, she never missed a hit as she said, 'you want your books, here they are'. Whilst Abraham shouted to him, 'burn with them' as he was throwing incandescent coal on the books. We stepped in such a scene.

Henry commented with a giggle,

-Well yes, those two, a ghost and a woman managed to set the feet of Lucifer on fire. That's going to be quite a gossip for a while in the angelic world.

With disapproving eyes, Raguel ordered,

-Henry, take a seat and wait for your turn to be seen to. I am sure that you will spread that gossip like the fire on the feet of Lucifer very fast over the next few days with great delight.

His father commented as he sat by Henry,

-You can't blame your angel for being your Messenger, Raguel. I will personally not disagree with such a story being spread. For all the archangels who are looking to lose their souls in the hands of Lucifer, it may discourage them to do so.

The Master smiled as he said firmly,

-I am quite inclined to arrange a trip to hell for them all to see what torture Michael is enduring. That will teach the archangels what kind of treatments Lucifer reserve to them.

While the three M took their seat on a little curved velvety bench by the fire place, Sebastien took a good look at the state of his drawing room and of Raphael. He stated,

-It looks like you had some enjoyable fun as well. Let me help you with those stitches on Raphael. I will do his other wound. Did you clean it or have I got to do it, Williams?

Doctor Williams replied welcoming the help of the angelic surgeon,

-Both of his wounds are now clean. I did put an anti poison unguent on them as a precautionary measure. They just need stitching. What I am worried about is that he didn't have much sleep. He is supposed to work at the quarry today. The spell I did to fix his body to make him able to fend for himself will wear out in about eight hours. He will be in great pain after that.

The Master of all angels who was still standing, approached the chair where Raphael was looked after. He considered the fallen angel before telling sternly,

-I am sure the Maggot will withstand the pain. If his friend ended up in hell because of him and is going through the atrocious torture of having his heart being removed for eternity by demons, let alone the constant stabbing they are inflicting upon him, he can do with some suffering as well.

Sighing deeply Raphael answered,

-Yes Master, I will and can.

Sebastien enquired in a much kinder voice than his father,

-So do you want to brief me about what happened here?

The fallen angel recounted everything while his wounds were looked after. He finished by saying,

-Everyone is in bed now, sleeping. Everyone has been tended to and is safe.

When Raphael was all stitched up, Sebastien sat on the chair to take his turn with a small wound on his upper arm. The Master demanded,

-Maggot, come with me.

A worried Raphael followed Raguel to the back garden of the house. At the invite, he sat by the Master on the bench yet remaining silent. Raguel started,

-In the light of what happened tonight and how you dealt with it, I am willing to take you on as my servant but I have a condition. Before I elaborate, do you still want to serve me?

The fallen angel fell onto his knees in front of the Master of all angels with great eagerness with his response,

-I do, Master, I do. Let me serve you. Let me make up for it all.

Raguel pursued,

-Right, I will let you be my servant. I will expect you to regain your wings and to become a human angel at some point, the sooner, the better. Now, there is a condition, which could be a heavy price for you, I want you to become the slave of Doctor Williams, just like I am the slave of my father. I will consider you both on an equal footing as servants, but I want you to serve him as well.

The question that came from Raphael surprised the Master of all angels,

-Will he ever accept me as his slave? I have been so horrible to him. I apologised, I did. I said sorry to him, Master. But yes, if ever wants to give me the chance, I will serve him and I will serve him well.

Raguel ordered,

-Take a seat, Raphael. Let me tell you that Williams and I are almost constantly talking via telepathy. I know everything about what happened tonight, every single detail. He praised your courage but also the care of everybody in this household you showed throughout. I know that you held the hand of Jack until he fell asleep. I know that you prevented him to get very badly hurt by the demon. I know that you were concerned about the young Margot bleeding in the wardrobe, I could carry on ... Trust me for I am a watcher. So I believe that if you ask him, he will accept you. Williams is a gentle angel. He has kindness in abundance. He will not treat you like you mistreated him. He will definitely task you because he is always busy in multiple places and he could do with someone helping him who is intelligent and efficient which I think you are. Once he has finished dealing with all our wounds, we will ask him if he is willing to take you on board. But I can tell you already that he will. I know my William. Now, I have to ask you what is the state of your jealousy and hatred towards him?

Sitting by the Master, the fallen angel confided,

-I am making a complete U-turn. I am ashamed of what I felt before towards him. I also feel utterly stupid. Working with him tonight to make sure we protect everyone as best as we could made me realise how wrong I was about Williams. I can tell you that I appreciate him now.

Raguel nodded positively before he told firmly,

-Good. Now if he accepts you as a slave, you will become my servant. I will be fair to you but I want you to acknowledge, that I am giving you a chance, but it is the one and only. There will be no other in the future. It goes without saying: don't mess it up and don't deceive me. I am not going to be lenient towards you. But I have something to show you.

Taking a scroll from inside his jacket and unrolling it, the Master, holding it, presented it to the fallen angel,

-I possess your soul. To be honest with you, it has been a tremendous fight for it with demons and Lucifer. You will have to thank first Abraham Wilton-Cough who remembered where Lucifer was keeping your deal with him then all of us angels who got injured, making, forcing Lucifer to change his deal. He reluctantly did it. But I think during our struggle this is when Lucifer launched his henchman demon to collect your soul before we could retrieve it. However we were successful in our fight. We killed the personal guards of Lucifer, all of them. He has to train new ones now that he will have a little confidence with. That will take time especially with demons. If you look here, we forced, my father and I, Lucifer to sign that whatever happens to you, hence death, but also from that point on, presently during your human life, that your soul is mine. See there is the seal of my father, here is my seal, and here is the blood signature of Lucifer. So my dear Maggot, your soul belongs to me now and not to Lucifer. I told you I would fetch it back. But justice being justice, for you to become once more custodian of your own soul, you will have to work hard to prove yourself to me and earn your wings back.

Raguel enjoined while he put the scroll back in his jacket with a winning smile,

-Let's go back in my Maggot. You do not know how close you were about to end up in hell tonight but you fought very well on your side for a human. We all witnessed the demon that came out of a cage in Lucifer's bedroom. The cage was hidden by a door looking like a wall. Lucifer also called out his guards to impeach anyone of us to leave hell so we couldn't come to your rescue in time. So the plan was to subdue Lucifer to change the deal on your soul as fast as we could.

The Master of all angels stood up, left the garden with Raphael who followed him to the kitchen of the presbytery silently. The fallen angel was thinking of all the implications of his soul belonging to Raguel. Within the kitchen, he stood by the door, looking at the strong angel, who was preparing breakfast, before he asked rather shyly,

-Does it means that I am out of trouble, Master? May I help in any way?

Raguel turned to him and said,

-I was wondering when you would open your mouth again. I was getting worried that you had properly lost your tongue along with your soul. You may help, I have a few injured angels to feed. Now that you have the usage of your arms for a little while, yes, you can render yourself useful. Bring the basket of eggs from the pantry.

Raphael obeyed without a word, putting the basket on the kitchen table. Raguel ordered,

-Get the large bowl on that shelf and start breaking eggs in it. We will be making omelettes. Now, to reply to your question, you are not out of trouble whatsoever. First, with me, the angel of justice, live a human life which is less than good and I will have no problem at your death to drag you to hell. Second, Lucifer always try to get his own back in a manner or another. He may be badly injured at the moment but he can recover just like the way you did overnight by a spell. He doesn't trust his entourage so he doesn't have a wizard as a servant like I do. But nothing will stop him to try to abduct one or a witch for that matter. He will not hesitate then to try to kill you, so you must be constantly on your guard. Another of his way to get to you could be to pervert you, turn you back to your old horrendous self again, then you will be in his hands and I will have to give your soul back to him as a completely lost cause. But as I said, do not believe any seductive words he can throw at you because the aim of the game for him will be to have you in hell and torture you. Thirdly, you killed one of his pet creation. When you take something away from Lucifer, he tries to take something away from you. Tit for tat. A life for a life. So if he kills you now, you haven't lived enough as a human to prove yourself to me, hence, it only means hell for you. All in all, it is not the end of your trouble. You have to stay alive to keep all your chances alive. That will mean hard work.

Stepping into the kitchen his son told with a smile,

-You read my mind, Dad. After all that fighting, we are all ravenous. I am stitched up. Look another long one, but smaller than the last by at least an inch. Let me take over. You need a fair few stitches as well. Doctor Williams is fixing up the arm of Maurice at the moment. His wound is not as bad as we thought. One of his arteries was damaged hence it caused so much blood loss but I attended to that. William is doing the closing up work. But you are next. What are we making?

His father came to him and fastened back the shirt of his son with great care as he said,

-I fancy your omelettes with mushrooms and lardons for all of us this morning. I am a little peckish.

Sebastien agreed,

-Get mended, I will see to it.

Once his dad left the room, hearing the crack of an egg, Sebastien noticed Raphael,

-I thought you were gone to bed?

The fallen angel replied with a white lie,

-No, I couldn't possibly sleep with a night like we all had. Beside that, Mrs Valdi deserves a good rest after her ordeal in hell. I heard that she defended herself very well.

Sebastien remembered that the sofa who was supposed to be the bed of Raphael was occupied by a sleeping and exhausted Amelia. He confirmed,

-She did. Her former husband was a soldier. He taught her how to protect herself when he was not here. Well, the man is dead and buried now since a little while, about a year and a half to a couple of years ago. You know, Raphael, I have still a spare bedroom, but it is not the best one in the house. I am still repairing it when I can. It used to be the one of Father Odell who kept all his best bedrooms for everyone but himself. First it lacks a fire place. Second it is rather humid, but as we repaired the guttering outside, it will be much better. I intend to redecorate the room at some point. But there is a rather good bed in it. You are welcome to use that bedroom in my house for protecting my family when I was not here to do so. I will try to get you an iron cast fire stove for you to stay warm this winter. You can't stay in the drawing room on its sofa with that large window broken. It will be drafty. What do you say?

Cracking another egg in the bowl, Raphael said,

-I say thank you. I accept the bedroom, I will help you decorate it. How many eggs do you want in that bowl, Sebastien?

Sebastien made appear on the table a smoked ham and some wild mushrooms before he replied,

-We are feeding my angelic soldiers, put twelve eggs in there. Then we will repeat with another twelve eggs. We will do batches. I heard that my father was considering you to be his servant. That must have cost you a fair amount of begging and kneeling. I remember the day you tried to kill yourself in front of us. He was not inclined to fetch you as fast as I was. Do you realise that it will be servitude to the angel of justice that you have been asking for? I am his son, I can tell you that I don't get away with anything. Nothing passes his scrutiny, will you be able to cope with that? How sure are you to pass his grades as an angel at some point?

The fallen angel sighed deeply as he answered in all honesty,

-I trust your father more than I trust myself. I want to serve him because I have a lot on my mind about what I did to him which I am not forgiving myself with. I want to try to repair what I can repair. In my heart I know that I will be a good servant and that when there is a will, there is a way. At the end of the day, Sebastien, I was a sick angel which went astray. Your father punished me severely for it but it is his duty as the Master of all angels. I don't resent anything at all, I appreciate what he did to me. He put me back in my place and showed me the right direction, one which I want to follow. I need to stay by your father and it doesn't matter if he is harsh on me. I want to be a better angel than I was an archangel and for the time being a good human. I know I need to find how to adjust properly as a human but somehow now, I think I can do it. I understand now where you were all coming from and your aim. Being the servant of your father and the slave of Doctor Williams is all I want at this moment in time. I will be reeducated by them to serve your grandfather properly.

Sebastien smiled kindly to Raphael while he commented and ordered,

-There is no need to season the eggs with your tears. Dry those up. My grandfather is stepping into the kitchen. Go and fetch some salt, some pepper and a bunch of parsley in the pantry. Compose yourself in there and come back so I can feed my angels that fought in hell.

Obeying Raphael went to the pantry, but bowed to the Great Being before he did. Sebastien welcomed his grandfather and asked,

-How is it going on in the drawing room? Is Dad badly damage? He didn't want to tell and was putting a brave face on. I know he was worried to get us all out of hell and to check if Raphael was alright.

The Great Being took a knife and started cutting the ham into lardons on a wooden board as he replied,

-He will survive. However he had sustained a nasty bite on his left shoulder which can get infected as well as the bad cut on his thigh. The leg is getting the stitching treatment. You and Williams will have to make sure that you keep an eye on that bite in the following days to keep it clean. How is Raphael?

Sebastien whispered with some compassion,

-He is a little emotional, grandpa. I tried him a little about his will to become the servant of my father, but he is determined to do so. I reckon he really needs my father right now. I will home him for a while until he feels ready to live on his own but very nearby us.

He stopped talking when Raphael came back from the pantry with all the items requested then stated,

-You found everything, I see. It is important that you get to know your way around this house. Although your are a guest here, I want you to feel at home. Here, put everything on the table. You know we were all worried about you not making it last night. Lucifer really tried to snatch your soul, he threw so many demons at us to prevent us to come to save you. But here you are, standing tall, having killed that large pet incubus of Lucifer.

Doing as he was told, Raphael went back to deal with the eggs and commented,

-I was greatly helped to survive, Sebastien. I could not have done it on my own. Father Odell gave me precious advice before the demon arrived upon us and he pleaded for me to at least be able to defend myself to Doctor Williams who was good enough to accept to do the spell to give me back my healthy body for a while. I will lose it soon. Then Ted was efficient in hiding and protecting everyone upstairs. The only thing, Ivy was given a magical packet of salt and herbs to throw on the floor of the attic, but in the heat of the moment she forgot to do so. It would have prevented the demon to smell their human scent and the one of his grand daughter. We were trying to tackle the demon downstairs, Williams, Odell and I but, he was so strong he knocked Odell unconscious. So we lost someone important to help with the fight, momentarily but minutes, seconds count in a battle. The conjured smilodon may have been too much for the demon so he ran away from the drawing room. That's when I think he detected the scent where everyone else were hidden and we saw him go for them, I ran after him with the smilodon while Williams gave some first aid to poor Odell and hid him.

Raphael stopped and gave his bowl to Sebastien, who asked him,

-Please chopped the parsley for us, Raphael, while I beat those eggs up. Let me tell you that Ted is at the head of a new team within my human angelic army: the logistic team. Due to his visions, he has always been able to help us throughout the centuries. He is able to give us the heads up. However he is not a fighting angel. His visions hurt him physically. But he often chose to be in the midst of things to tell us when a next move his coming. So he stays in the front line despite knowing he will be at risk.

The obeying fallen angel doing his new task commented,

-He fought rather well. There were a few movements he did which left him exposed but against the demon we had to tackle it was difficult to fully concentrate. The idea to harass the demon from multiple angles and together was from him. I must say there is always more security in numbers. He did give some knives to everyone to be able to defend themselves or be able to attack. Most of the humans chose to attack, your brave Ivy, your courageous Jack, and Georgia. Mrs Brown was terrified in a corner of the attic. Whilst Ted had the good sense to tell to Margot to hide in a broken wardrobe you have in the attic, prior to the demon coming. She was holding the little fox terrier in there. When I will get better physically, if you want me to, I can teach a few defencive move to your angel Ted. He is not that bad as I said. I saw the few mistakes he made which did result in his injuries but the remedy to that in the future is simple coaching and training.

Sebastien welcomed the proposal,

-I would be happy if you did so, but I can only warn you that I tried. Ted in his very first human life was a boy given away to a monastery. He became a monk subsequently then my angel. He is not of a solid constitution and he tried to cope with his visions using alcohol and tobacco. He lives under my roof because he needs help and I do not want to lose him. We gave him a better clean bill of health not so long ago. He has a tendency to keep himself for himself which dates for the centuries where he has been a monk time after time. However he has started to open up a little, life after life. Henry is going to train him how to fly properly because compared to my other angels Ted never mastered that skill.

Laughing his grandfather told,

-It didn't help that you threw him of a cliff by desperation, Mighty.

Pouting Sebastien replied,

-Dad, told you about it! He shouldn't have. No, it was to make Ted's survival instinct kick in, deploy his wings and fly. All other methods did fail.

While Raphael started to giggle, the Great Being explained to the fallen angel,

-My grandson, although he has a lot of quality, like generosity, being courageous, is also rather impatient and fiery at time. Shall I say as impulsive as his father?

Coming back into the kitchen, mended, the Master retorted,

-I am not impulsive!

Sebastien laughed,

-Oh, yes, you are! You've just proved it.

Raguel demanded,

-How are things going? Everyone is getting sorted and will go to the dinning room soon, however Amelia is still sleeping thoroughly. Vincent is staying by her side. He said he will eat later with her, and your family when they are up and his Amelia wakes up.

His son replied,

-I can do with your help for the breakfast, Dad. I must say when those two were reunited, Valdi lifted her in his arms, cried and held her tight. I really was so moved by it all, I nearly lost my concentration to fight.

His smirking father checking the stove commented,

-Well, I know I was there to recall you to the demon coming to attack you.

Raphael giving the chopped parsley to Sebastien told shyly,

-It sounds like we had all quite a night.

Doctor Williams arrived in the kitchen to brief,

-Everyone has been seen to, Master. The three M and Henry are in the dinning room. Valdi will be staying by his wife. She needs a good rest the poor thing. I agree with you, Raphael, we all had quite a night. But today is another day.

Taking the opportunity Raguel stated,

-Yes, it is. My Williams, I have something important to ask you. I received a plea from our fallen angel Raphael to become my servant, but I will only accept him if he becomes your slave. The final decision is for you to make: Do you want to take him on or not? I acknowledge that you have centuries of not getting along together and that it is a big ask for both of you. What do you say? Come and take a seat by my father.

The old angel looked at the fallen archangel and asked,

-Will he have to live in my household?

Sebastien replied as he seasoned and put some parsley in the eggs mixture,

-No. You will not have to worry about his lodgings. He will live in my home for the time being, when he can become an independent human being, he will live close to where my father ever chose to live. Raphael needs a proper angelic reeducation which my father can provide to him with your help.

Sighing Doctor Williams said with honesty,

-I don't know. This is an angel that wanted my death so much, threatened me constantly, with a pure hatred towards me that I nearly lost my heart to Michael, that Gael was murdered and Jack was stabbed. I need to reflect upon this. I feel like I will have another wife to poison me at the idea of it all.

His hope dashed in an instant, Raphael walked to the Master and knelt by him, presenting him a knife, tears in his eyes, he begged,

-Please, Master, end my human life. I deserve hell. Do you remember the technicality you talked about? I shouldn't be here and entertain hopes of being redeemed, I am ready to be tortured. I am begging you, just let me go. I am a broken angel, I don't deserve any chance.

A moved Williams went straight to remove the knife from Raphael's hands and scolded him,

-Don't tempt the angel of justice like that! Have you lost your sanity as well as your wings? What part of I need to reflect upon the matter you didn't understand? Put your trust in angels a little, would you, human? You need to keep going on. You need to regain your wings. You mustn't give up at the first hurdle. Go and take a seat. I need to reflect.

The fallen angel took his seat by Sebastien, who put his hand upon his shoulder and tapped it gently, with his advice,

-Just wait, Raphael. You will always be more emotional as a human, but also as a human angel. Don't feel low, you are still with us. We have some dealing to do. We know about your guilt, and the weight upon your soul. We will help you deal with it all, so you have to stay with us. Don't have a hard time on your mind because of the technicality, because it is not on ours. We are ignoring it. We have dismissed it. Why do you think we ended up all with scars to retrieve your soul deal as well as Amelia and Wilton-Cough from hell?

The Great Being going by his son who was manning the stove, giving him the prepared lardons added out loud,

-We want you to be, Raphael, it is as simple as that.

Deeply sighing, turning around the table thrice, Doctor Williams finally stopped by the Master and told,

-I will accept him as a slave but I have my own condition.

Smiling Raguel asked,

-That you don't bite more than you can chew?

Everyone in the kitchen giggled even the downhearted Raphael. Doctor Williams replied firmly despite a smile on his lips,

-Master! No, I am willing to give him one trial, one only, this current human life he has. Then I will make my mind up if he can remain my slave or not, and endorse him as my angel, like I am yours, like you are the one of your father. Does he even know what it involves?

Raguel, cooking now with his son and father, answered,

-You can always ask him. He always comes up with clever answers. If he doesn't know, you can teach him. I didn't let you train my son for no reasons. You can educate better than any other. I am accepting your condition, so do you accept him for a good life long trial, my William?

The old Doctor accepted and Raphael went to hold his hand gratefully without a word to say. The Master stated,

-Raphael, you are now officially my servant. Don't mess up your trial period of a lifetime, otherwise you will lose your post. Go with William in the dinning room, tell the others that breakfast is nearly ready.

Once his now two servants left the room Raguel turned to his father to confide,

-I feel like swearing by your name, father, and to say Good Lord, I do not know if I can cope with an emotional Raphael. When I think of the arrogant warrior he was and his state now, it is like comparing the sun with the moon. I didn't expect him to give me a knife to finish him of. I felt so sorry for him at that moment. But my good William as always reacted properly and swiftly.

The Great Being asked,

-Would you have done what he begged you to do?

Raguel confessed,

-No, I could never have done so. I was ready to tell him off instead. Within Ludwig the dog, I observed all the actions of Raphael so far and, I think, father, that we are going to retrieve your creation, your archangel.

Satisfied his father said,

-Exactly what I trust you to do with Williams. The two of you are like an iron hand in a velvet glove.

Dishing out the first omelette on a plate, Sebastien giggled,

-I know who is the iron hand of the two. Pa, I had a very short conversation with Raphael. I was trying him a little and you should know the result, well his answer. I think you would be as pleased as I was with it. Touch my hand to know all.

Sharing his conversation he had with Raphael in the kitchen with his father by just the contact of their hands, Sebastien continued,

-I don't think you will see him default on you as your servant apart if Lucifer interfere in our scheme to redeem Raphael.

Raguel dishing out a second omelette agreed,

-I share your opinion. Somehow like my father said Raphael responds well to kindness. Who would have believed that a strong archangel needed maybe a little attention all along to not go wrong?

The early morning breakfast amongst the angels went well. All were chatting together of the events of the past few nights. Raphael noticed that he was no longer just an observer and listener of the conversation at the table. All the angels were involving him in the conversation, just as if he was still an angel himself. When it was time for Raphael to go to the quarry, Raguel and Doctor Williams went at the door of the house with him.

Strangely enough Raguel felt like he was letting go to a child on to his first day of school. He impulsively readjusted the shirt of the fallen angel. Snapped his fingers and made a white scarf appear and put it on Raphael with care with his orders,

-Now, my Maggot, you are a human so there is no need for you to have an appalling attitude with humans any longer. Be nice to them. Although you are managing two teams, make sure you are fair with them all. Do not abuse them physically, by that I mean, overwork them and do not abuse them verbally for trust me I will know if this happened and you will be back on my bad books. Wilton-Cough warned you of some bad elements in your teams, who could be troublesome, but remember some have dozens of children to feed, lost their houses, and they are giving their labour for the reconstruction of the town for free. But I trust that you will be able to manage them well. Don't forget that they are only humans, so you must sent some for their lunch at the impromptu canteen but not all of them at the same time to keep the work going. Last but not least, be on your best behaviour. Oh, and you must go and eat at the tavern tonight. Get properly acquainted with Tyrell. I will come and fetch you at around eight or nine tonight there. With that cambion still alive and you having killed his father, it is better if you are walking home with someone at night. Keep the dog with you, Ludwig will protect you. Tyrell will accept him in his tavern. Go and have a good day.

Turning to Doctor Williams, the Master told,

-Accompany him to the quarry, William, for his first day of human work, then you can come back and teach our young Ivy to recognise ingredients in her pantry.

The old angel giggled as he commented,

-I will have a busy and fun morning by the sound of it.

Sebastien rushed to the door,

-Wait, we forgot to give him his lunch!

He presented a satchel to Raphael, made of black leather, with the silver letters R entwined with another R embroidered onto it,

-Your lunch is in here. It's just some buttered bread, ham, and cheese. There is a flask of water and an apple as well. It should see you through up until tonight. Don't forget we have a card game on with the children and Ivy.

The fallen angel thanked Sebastien, shook his hand, then impulsively hugged Raguel, retaining his sob, before he went on his way with Doctor Williams. After they left the church yard, seeing that Raphael was emotional, Williams broke the silence between them,

-You will be alright. Do not worry. If you managed to kill the pet incubus demon of Lucifer, you can manage two teams of humans. By the way, your satchel comes from the Great Being. He bestows one to all his human angels. So I guess it means that he expects you to be one, one day. The content however will be from Sebastien who love feeding his eternal beings, humans and angels within his army.

The fallen angel confided,

-For today, I think I will be alright. I have no fear of me being despicable again. I am just so grateful to be accepted by you, the Master and his son. It makes my heart swell. I don't know what it takes to be a human angel but I will certainly aim for it. I will have to wait until my death to know if I made it.

Looking at the long muddy street before them Doctor

Williams commented,

-Or you could achieve it faster than the normal like Doctor Valdi and Father Odell did. They both became angels during their own human lifetime. There is a chance that Tyron Tyrell will do so too. I can't see why you couldn't give it yourself a good go. Beside that you have the knowledge from previously being being an archangel.

Raphael sighed deeply as he said,

-Yes, I have the knowledge of how to be a bad angel but the one of being a good angel I need to learn.

Williams couldn't help smiling with his reply,

-We can teach you that. In one word, I would resume it to helping. But the Master of all angels may differ on that matter and chose the word caring instead as for the Mighty One, his son, he will chose most certainly loving. For the Great Being, my humble guess would be that he will do a magical concoction, creation of the three words together. But I guess that will be a successful recipe for getting wings. What do you think?

Approving, the fallen angel answered,

-I can only agree with you. May I ask you, do you mind me being your slave?

As they entered the long path leading to the forest that went along the cemetery, the old angel confessed,

-Yes, I do mind but I have a duty of care and I will do my utmost to help you in your rehabilitation as an angel. One thing is I am glad you will not be living in my home, that the Master and his son decided to look after you in their home. However, for your reeducation, I will want you to spend a weekend at mine, in Boston, once a month to start of with. You will work with me in the hospital. It will give you a full grasp of human plights. It can be hard and sad, but when you save a life, it makes your day. I trained Sebastien and Doctor Valdi there. It will also help you to understand your new body as a human.

Raphael accepted, and reassured,

-You don't have to worry about me any more, Doctor Williams. I will do as I am told and I will also be good. We did work well together last night, didn't we? I must say when Ted did fall almost unconscious in a pool of blood I was so worried for him, I thought the fight would be over and the slaughter would happen for everyone but you saved the night by making my poker hot again. I remembered the advice of Theo Odell and we smashed it together. I appreciate what you are doing by taking me on board. Will you call me names, like a maggot during my slavery?

Laughing Doctor Williams replied,

-No, I will not be like that with you whatsoever. I know the Master enjoys calling you that because you called me like that when you were an archangel. But have you noticed that what started as a payback punishment, you became 'his' maggot? And when you almost collapsed on us yesterday, the Master of all angels said that he didn't want to lose 'My' maggot. Although you are a fallen angel, he will care for you. Did you know that the Master and his son always try to track any fallen angels and to retrieve them somehow, to give them another chance? So with me, there will be no name calling, although it is tempting to get my own back, I am not like that. You will be called just Raphael, maybe by your human surname if I am upset with you, and if we ever manage to be on good terms, maybe one day I will say what do you think of that Raph'.

A thoughtful fallen angel confessed,

-I heard when the Master said that he didn't want to lose me, calling me his Maggot. I must say to you, if you don't mind, that it warmed my heart and made me fell asleep that I was still his in his mind. I will work hard for you both. I can only hope I will pass all my grades during my human life.

The old angel told him,

-If you succeed you will need to decide what you want to be in the Mighty One's angelic army. There are three teams, the fighting one, the healing one and the newly formed logistic one. As you know I am part of the healing one. Doctor Valdi whom you wanted to kill is part of the three teams. He is a versatile angel. I think you can aim to be one as well. But I will leave the choice to you. When you make your decision, speak to me about it. Take your time, there is no rush. The Master and I will then focus your training to help you accomplish your duties. What you need to understand is that human angels are more hands on with humanity. We help humans in a more direct way but we usually don't tell that we are angels apart to selected humans, the ones who are part of our families, the ones that will become angels, or the ones that will become eternal Beings. We keep our secrecy that we are incarnated angels most of the time otherwise. It does happen, but not often, that a human will guess that you are somewhat different and then you will have to bring him or her, if needs be, into the secrecy.

Turning to Williams with anguish, Raphael said,

-I didn't say sorry to Valdi yet nor to Rob... I must do so, I must do so.

Doctor Williams replied sternly,

-Yes, you must do so. For Valdi, he will probably be gone by the time you come back tonight. But you will have plenty of time to make amends to him when he will be back, if you managed to not get killed beforehand. As for Rob, he is lodging at the tavern, and he is back there, recovering. He is a strong human angel so he will be back up on his feet in a couple of days. He just got badly burnt, well, really badly burnt. But Valdi saved him in extremis. Rob works at the tavern as a doorman with Callum. They are also behind the bar on occasion monitoring the place. So when you work there as a waiter, you will be able to say sorry to him. I am sure he will accept your apologies for your threats to drown him when he was in a desperate need for help.

Looking ahead, watching the leaves which where already starting to take their autumnal shades, Raphael confessed,

-I am not proud of myself, Williams, definitely not proud.

The fallen angel stroked the head of the dog by him. The old angel did smile with some kindness to him as he announced,

-Here we are at the quarry. Make sure the humans do not work on the side of the quarry that is dangerous. I do not want to see any casualties on your watch. The same goes for the felling of the trees to create a carriage path. Be vigilant. Look after yourself as well. To make your work as an overseer easier, I did spell your satchel this morning with the authorisation of the Master: Whenever you touch it, it will extend your ability to move well for three hours. But it doesn't fix your body totally so you must keep your arms' cast for your bones to heal properly. I will see you tonight at the house. Take care of yourself. Last but not least, we know you don't bestow telepathy any longer. So if you are in danger or see that nasty cambion Cork, you can call Sebastien and myself by touching the two Rs on the magical satchel, so keep it upon you at all time. The two letters stand as much for Raphael River as for your rescuers. The one on the left is to call me particularly, the one on the right is to call the Mighty One. But you can call us both and we will both come forward. Now, it will be hard work for you today as your first human working day, but try to see the positive, you are not in hell, you are still with us, so chin up and get on with it.

Williams was about to leave him alone when Raphael asked with some anxiety,

-Am I allowed to call the Master as well?

The servant of the Master turned back to the fallen angel with compassion to reassure, certainty in his voice,

-Raphael, don't forget that the Master of all angels is a watcher. He will be the first by you and to know what is happening to you. There is no need to call him. New angel Doctor Valdi is struggling to use telepathy, yet when he was in danger to be drowned by you, the Master came to the rescue. He knew what you wanted to do to Valdi and to Rob. Be at ease, you are a servant of the Master, now, he will be there for you in your times of need. See you later and remember to have a good day.

Raphael told quickly,

-See you later, Williams, and thank you for everything.

He saw the old angel fly away above the woods then took a good look at the ancient disused quarry. He assessed for himself the dangerous parts and when he realised how easily the rocks and stones could fall down, he came up with an idea. It was still the early hours in the morning when men, young and old, came to work. Some were in a deep visible state of poverty, whilst others if they were not in their fineries, had manners indicating of their higher status in society, but all had come together to rebuild the town.

The fallen angel shook the hands of everyone warmly thanking them for coming. For them he was only Mr River, the overseer. Being taller than average, Raphael inspired authority. His lie about getting injured the night of the fire trying to extinguishing it, that he told at the tavern when meeting his two teams, had spread in Wilton Town without his knowledge. He was regarded as a benevolent new comer. As soon as Raphael spoke, everyone was silent and listening,

-Right, we have a lot of houses to build and lots to repair. We must get it done before winter comes. This is not a small task, this is a big one. We need to provide homes for your wives and children before the worst of the weather comes upon us all. We need to get on with the job in an orderly fashion and I will not tolerate laziness, arguments or fighting which could slow us down. If any petty fight occurs come to me and I will resolve it. We are here to rebuild a town and not to pick neat at each others. Now, that this is clear, loggers team go on this side.

When the two teams were separate. Raphael looked at the men with military precision. He started with the loggers. He saw a lot of young teenagers, even one little boy within that group. He separated them from the adults, keeping the youngest by his side. He ordered to the youngsters,

-You are my loggers sub team. I need great efficiency from you lot. We need to clear a path to allow carriages to bring the stones to the town. So you will take care of clearing the undergrowth. Do not throw anything away, I want you to make neat piles of whatever you find in this area of the quarry: A pile of nettles, a pile of pine needles, whatever mushrooms, nuts, berries, twigs. This will become food for the makeshift canteen to feed us all, some will become firewood for the winter for everyone. You, my boy you stay with me, I have another duty for you.

He turned to the adults then told them,

-Start by marking all the trees that we need to fell to create that carriage path with a cross. I want you to do the same thing to create a path to the lake so the cross roads will be there again. Access to the lake will provide fish to all of us. Now, loggers start working. I will check on your progress regularly during the day. Remember no felling of trees yet, just marking them to create a clear path.

The two teams of loggers went to their duties. Raphael then tasked the others working for the stone quarries. When everyone was working but the child by him, he demanded,

-Shouldn't you be at school?

The kid answered,

-I've never been at school. We couldn't afford it. The books and the slate and the chalk, they are too expensive.

A curious fallen angel who could feel that there was something wrong with the little one enquired,

-What is your name? Where do you live? Who are you parents?

The more he observed the child, the more he noticed he

was extremely pale and thin. The pale blue eyes boy answered,

-I have a name but I don't remember it. He called me 'you'. I haven't got a home anymore. But I turned up the night of the fire at the hotel where everyone in town went to escape it. I sleep in the big ball room there like all who lost their homes.

Raphael kneeling by the child held his shoulders to ask further, worried,

-How hold are you my boy? Who called you just 'you'?

The child replied in a secretive voice,

-I don't know how old I am, may be I am six or seven, I don't know my birthday. Can I tell you something but you can't tell it to anyone because I will be scared?

Through his fingers the fallen angel could feel vaguely the traumatic childhood of an abandoned child. He noticed burnt marks on his neck, wrists and hands. Raphael encouraged,

-Please tell me. But I will have to speak about you to the surgeon of this town and his wife. You are burnt and need to be looked after. They are very kind.

The boy confided,

-I was kept in the basement of Darren Bell. He is the one who burnt the town. On the night, he burnt his cottage but he released me from the basement. He said to me to try to escape the fire if I could. I saw the priest rounding up people to save them, so I joined them.

Raphael enquired further,

-Are you related to Darren Bell?

Sighing the child replied,

-I do not know. But he tortured me and did things to me.

Without further a do, Raphael touched the letter R on his satchel to call Sebastien, before saying to the boy,

-Stay by me. I will keep you safe until the good surgeon of this town arrive. Do you know where you are?

The boy answered,

-I heard it was called Wilton Town.

#

It was not long before Sebastien came to the quarry on his appaloosa. He descended and smiled when he saw Raphael holding the hand of the little boy. Approaching the fallen angel, he teased,

-Are you in great danger to have a heart, Raphael, so much so that you need to be rescued from a little boy?

Raphael smiled despite himself but corrected,

-It is not me that need attention this time around, it is this child. He doesn't know his name or his age. I think he suffers from amnesia. He was kept in the basement of Darren Bell, whoever that is, who burnt the town, and who tortured that little boy and done probably worse with him. I don't want him to work in the quarry, he is far too young and emaciated. I wanted to beg you to look after him. I can't check everything here, but he shows signs of burnt marks old and fresh on his skin. He needs to be checked out. He currently lives at the hotel since the night of the fire because Darren Bell did let him go when he burnt his own cottage down. Do you want to hold my hand to know what the boy said to me when I questioned him?

Briefly doing so, Sebastien told,

-I will take him on. To be honest with you, I think you are right, he is suffering from amnesia. Thank you for warning me about him, Raphael.

Offering his hand to the little boy, Sebastien proposed kindly,

-Do you want to have a lovely ride onto my horse?

The child looked at the stallion with awe, then asked,

-Really, can I? But I don't know how to ride.

Sebastien smiled to the curly brown hair boy as he answered,

-Of course you can. I will be with you and teach you how to ride.

The child left the hand of Raphael to reach the one of Sebastien at that moment. But he looked back at Raphael to ask him,

-Is he the good surgeon you were talking about?

The fallen angel reassured the little boy,

-He is. His name is Mr Cotton and his wife is a Doctor in this town. They will look after you. You will be alright under their care.

Sebastien putting the child on his horse said to Raphael,

-Thank you for calling me. I will see you tonight.

Climbing on Fair Wilton, behind the boy, Sebastien made the animal start his journey back to Wilton Town in a slow pace. It gave him the time to get acquainted with the poor little fellow. He engaged the conversation,

-My wife and I have adopted two children so far, you will be a welcome third one. We live in the large presbytery by the church. Hold on to the reins, it will prevent you from falling. You see what I am holding, that's those.

The boy obeyed then confided,

-I don't know where the church is. I haven't been in town. I remember just that I woke up wrapped in a cover, completely tied up, that I had something in my mouth to prevent me to shout and was at the back of a carriage. Then I was in a basement of a house for very long. So, you have children?

Sebastien tried not to feel emotional at the account of the unknown boy for he needed him to feel confident that he could talk to him, so he carried on,

-Yes, I have. First, we adopted our Jack, who is eight, and very clever. I can bet that he can teach you how to read and write if you don't know how to. Then, very recently, we gave a home to our Margot. Her real name is Marguerite, but she prefers being called Margot. She is twelve. Her real father has been extremely bad to her, very violent, so she needed a good home to go to. She is a very courageous young girl who did suffer a lot, like you did. But she is recovering with us now like you will do so.

The child sneezed, before he said,

-Darren Bell wasn't my father, I know that. I don't know if

I have parents but I don't think I have. But I can't be sure of anything, since, since the attack.

Sebastien enquired,

-Do you want to talk about it? What can you remember?

Feeling somewhat not intimidated by Sebastien, the boy opened up in a half hazard way,

-I remember bits. It was in an alley way. It was almost dark. I was doing a wee wee in the gutter. He attacked me from behind. I couldn't see him, I couldn't see his face. I struggled to get free from his grasp but I wasn't strong enough. I was hit with something on the head and then all turned dark and then I remember I was in a carriage tied up. But I don't remember before the attack.

The angel reassured the boy,

-It may come back to you one day. When you suffer a knock on the head like you did, it can happen to people to suffer memory loss, sometimes it is permanent, sometimes it is not. Whatever your case is, we will help you and look after you.

Soon they arrived in the church yard. By the door of the presbytery was the Master discussing with Henry. When he saw his son back, Raguel came to him, followed by Henry. Sebastien gave him the child which the Master put on the ground safely. Raguel asked the boy,

-Did you enjoy your ride, little one?

The child was slightly intimidated by the tall Raguel and shyly answered,

-Yes, I did, Sir.

Presenting his hand for the boy to hold, the Master of all angels told,

-You can call me Grandpa Rag, not sir, just like my other adopted grandchildren. Henry, see to Wilton Fair.

Sebastien descended from his stallion and took the other hand of the child then he confided to his father,

-It is as bad as it can be, Dad. He is a lost little thing.

His father corrected,

-No, now, he is a found little boy, Sebastien. Come on in, little one, you will meet our other children and the pets, because my son rescues cats and dogs as well.

The child followed, feeling in safe hands. He entered the house with great awe and confided to Sebastien,

-I don't think I ever been in a big house like that before.

Tugging the child's hand, Sebastien commented,

-There's a start for everything. Now, that will be better than a basement. Did he ever let you out?

Sighing the boy revealed,

-I was attached onto a wall. He never did let me out. He never detached me.

Raguel comforted,

-This will not happen here. We are all in the kitchen at the moment. I will prepare you a little something to eat. Are you starving?

Smiling to him, the child answered,

-I've been fed by Mrs Odell this morning. She is very kind. I had a piece of bread with butter and even jam, and, and some hot milk with honey. It was so nice. I am used to, I am used to...

The boy fell silent. Sebastien told firmly,

-Little one, it will be completely different here.

When they entered the kitchen, Ivy looked at the emaciated little boy with tears in her eyes. She came to him wiping her hands upon her apron and welcomed him,

-Hello! Welcome to your new home. Take a seat at the table by Jack. I am Ivy, and this is Margot. This gentleman here is called Doctor Williams. He is a very good friend of the family. The little dog on Jack's lap is called Killy, he doesn't bite so don't be afraid of him. Come. Make yourself at home.

The child took her hand willingly and sat by Jack. Despite being shy, he said a timid,

-Hello, everybody. I am You.

Margot turning a long wooden spoon inside a large pan stated with her natural determined little mind,

-No, you is not a first name.

An intervening Sebastien explained,

-The little one doesn't remember his first name. He suffers from memory loss, Margot. Someone did hurt his head badly.

Doctor Williams went to inspect the head of the child immediately. Putting his hands above the head of the boy afterwards, he revealed,

-I know his name, he is called Tobias. I can hear a woman, his mother calling him Toby. She is not alive anymore since a few years, three or four. The boy will not retrieve the memory of his past. His brain has been damaged. He suffered a fractured skull. It healed itself but badly.

Ivy ruled,

-Then you are going to be our little Toby. I am making a nice compost, I will give you a bowl of it when it is ready.

Rolling his eyes, her husband corrected her with a smirk,

-Not compost, my Little Bit, you and Margot are making a 'Compote'. Did you use sugar for it and not salt?

Raguel replied for her,

-I am teaching her the basics and I made sure that she did use sugar. Now, go and open the clinic. You are late already. I will look after the children with your Little Bit. I will send you Doctor Williams after he has examined Tobias with Ivy.

Sebastien kissed his wife on the cheek, whilst Jack went to give him a hug. Then he asked Margot kissing her forehead,

-Are you going to Mr Berry's farm to milk his cows today? If so be careful on the way.

His father again answered this time for the young girl,

-She has decided to go and help him, yes. But I will walk her there and back. Don't worry, I will make sure she stay safe.

Sebastien gave a last order before he went,

-My Jack, make sure Toby feels home. He will share your bedroom.

When he left, Williams proposed to the Master,

-I can rearrange the bedroom to accommodate the two boys.

Raguel nodded his ascent to his servant who went immediately to do so. Doctor Williams liked nothing more as a wizard but to use his magical talents and taste to redecorate rooms. Having read the little Tobias fully, almost like a book, the old angel knew that the child Raphael found had an appalling childhood so far. Tobias was the child of a whore, who passed away when he was only about four. He became then a mendicant in the streets before being abducted a year later by Darren Bell. The little boy had intelligence and survival instinct. Williams was rather happy that the poor boy ended in the home of Sebastien whom he knew to have a big heart.

In Jack's bedroom, Doctor Williams went for the full magical transformation, which he knew he would have to explain as charity to the Master of all angels. First he covered the oak floor with a lavish dark blue carpet full of gold and silver foliage pattern which was surrounded by white, gold and silver fringes. Then he attacked the walls, covering them with a panoramic theme wallpaper in the style of Charvet representing a landscape of a tropical island in the Pacific Ocean. Satisfied with the result, he went on to refurnish the room entirely, replacing the single bed by a double bunk bed made of oak, with goose feathers mattresses and pillows, white sheets adorned with a dark and light blue wave pattern at their upper ends and large blue and white quilted covers.

Not stopping there, the generous angel, who was feeling sorry for Toby and Jack, placed an oak wardrobe and a chest of drawers in the bedroom. He carried on with two desks place side by side in a corner of the room, and a book shelve. He added a beautiful white rocking horse with grey spots and a black mane in the middle of the bedroom. Then his magic wand turned to the finishing touches, he added an oak chest at the bottom of the bed for the boys to hoard some toys and navy blue velvet curtains to replace the old ones of the only window of the room. His last gifts were a set of tin soldiers and a book:

Robinson Crusoe of Daniel Defoe. He added two wicker baskets, with blue velvet cushions for Jack's dog and kitten, then went back to the kitchen with a smile on his face.

Eagerly Williams told Jack,

-I think you should show Tobias the bedroom he will share with you. If you want something else ask me because I am still here and very happy to provide.

Jack took the hand of the younger boy and enjoined him,

-Let me show you our bedroom!

The two boys ran together outside of the kitchen. The Master asked his servant,

-What have you done up there?

Holding the hand of Raguel, Williams showed what he did, and shared what he saw from the past life of Tobias, then simply said,

-I tried to make the life of a little boy better than it has been so far. He has been living in the streets with his mother since he was born, then a basement where he was abused and tortured.

The Master of all angels was saddened by what was shared to him, he swore out loud,

-Poor thing! Stay down here and make sure Ivy do not burn the compote. I will check on the boys.

Raguel opened the door to the bedroom only to find the two boys standing still in the middle of the room mesmerised by it. He asked,

-Do you like it then?

Jack was the first to respond with gusto,

-Oh, yes we do! Look Grandpa Rag, we have even a rocking horse, and our individual desk to study together, and a book shelve. And, that wallpaper is awesome, it looks like we are in a paradise island... What do you think Toby?

Shyly the young boy said,

-I don't remember sleeping in a bed before.

The encouraging Jack took him to inspect the bunk bed as he told,

-Toby, you must chose your one. If you take the top one, I will be here on the bottom one to protect you but if you are scared of being too high up then take the bottom bed. Look at the embroidery on the sheets, that represents waves. Those aren't straw mattresses either, we have feather ones. We are going to sleep like babies on those.

Toby smiled timidly when he asked,

-Can I have the top one?

Jack giving him a gentle hug answered,

-Of course you can. I will look after you. Do you know how to read and write?

When the little boy nodded negatively, an enthusiastic Jack told him,

-I will teach you. Pa and Ma are going to send us to school with Margot. I will help you. Look we have desks and a book. We can learn together. When I am older, I want to become a Doctor and a surgeon like Pa and Ma, someone who save lives. What do you want to become?

Tobias replied a little confused,

-I don't know.

Raguel going to the boy held his hand and told,

-It is alright, Toby, it will come to you later. You are very, very young my dear child to make up your mind. So do you like your bedroom?

Toby nodded positively to him. The archangel then enjoined,

-There is a rocking horse that is waiting for you two to be named and a chest of toys which is longing to be opened. When you have finished come back to the kitchen.

Satisfied with the work of his servant, the Master stepped back in the kitchen stating,

-The boys are pleased with their bedroom. You went all out, didn't you, my William?

The old angel smiled as he replied,

-I haven't got any children, Master. The ones that your son are taking on, are a little like mines in my heart. Consider me like their godfather.

Raguel went to the stove and confided to Ivy,

-Little Toby had such a poor childhood so far that that bedroom upstairs is his first one. He only knows streets and a basement. He hasn't got his mother, she passed away and he doesn't know who is his father is, but I can tell you that he is dead as well. We have a true little orphan, here. How are you feeling about taking him on? How is the compote doing?

The young woman smiled as she answered,

-Grandpa Rag, at this rate you will have lots of grandchildren. My Sebastien and myself have heart enough to welcome everyone. I was an only child and somehow one of my dreams was to live in a large family, vibrant with life, joy and laugher. Well, I think this will happen. We will bring up Toby and if tomorrow Sebastien take to me another child in need of help and love, my heart's door will still be open and I don't think it will ever close. As for the compote, I managed to not burn it so far. Do you want to taste it and tell me what do you think of it?

With a giggle Raguel replied,

-Do I really have to?

Ivy laughed as she scolded,

-You are supposed to help me, not to behave like your son. My little family is growing by the day and I need to learn how to feed it. Oops! Your other grandchild gave me a little kick. I think, I will assume that he is agreeing with me.

As she touched her belly with tenderness, Raguel took a spoon and tried the compote. After a few seconds, he stated,

-It is not bad. It needs a little more sugar and it could do with some cinnamon infused into it. Then we will have a delicious compote of apples and plums to jar.

Margot brought the sugar and suddenly asked Ivy,

-Here, I labelled the sugar pot. Can I call you Ma just like Jack?

The young woman hugged Margot with some emotion, giving her answer,

-Of course you can! In my heart you are already my little girl. I will fight for you to make sure you are safe.

Touching with gentleness the tumefied cheek of Ivy, Margot replied,

-I know. You did so already. Ma, I admire you.

Ivy smiled stating,

-And I admire the way you are doing your pigtails, my Darling. When I was at boarding school, it took me ages to learn how to do them properly.

The two boys came back to the kitchen hand in hand. It was clear that the fallen guardian angel Jack had resumed his role as guardian by his way he was looking after Toby. Barely two years older than Tobias in human years, he could relate to the timid child and was encouraging him already to talk, read, write and play. Raguel asked jack as he was showing Toby how to juggle with the apples,

-Did you find a name for the rocking horse, Jack? Stop playing with the apples, you are going to drop them and bruise them and your Pa will not be very happy with that if I tell him. Teach Toby how to write and read the word apple instead.

A giggling Jack answered,

-We named the rocking horse like the appaloosa of Pa, it is called Fair Wilton. I need slates and chalk batons to teach Toby to write properly. Surely Pa will not be upset with a couple of bruised apples.

Raguel couldn't help smiling when he replied with great half faked seriousness,

-You don't know your Pa like I do. He is a born Punisher. He also love his food a great deal to be perfect. If he notices blemished apples on the apple pies tonight, he will turn to your Ma to say again that she is a dreadful cook. We are aiming to win him over about her cooking so you need to help us and not undermine us. Williams, give the three children slates.

Magic wand in hand, his servant obeyed. Three slates and chalk batons appeared on the table to the amazement of Tobias who jerked backwards and asked,

-What did just happen?

Holding the hand of the frightened boy, Jack tried to explain,

-Doctor Williams is a magician, a great wizard.

A baffled Toby demanded,

-You are kidding me?

It was time for explanations and the Master of all angels went by the little boy, holding reassuringly his shoulders. He told in the gentlest manner,

-The household you are in is a peculiar one, a very nice one, but a peculiar one. My son who brought you here is an archangel like myself. The friend of the family, Doctor Williams is an angel, so is Henry which you met in the churchyard. Jack is a fallen guardian angel aiming to retrieve his wings. Ted also living here is an angel and Raphael River which you met this morning is a fallen angel living with us for the time being. He noticed that you were poorly and all alone so he sent you to us to be well looked after. You will see us with wings at times, and yes, we do make things appear out of thin air. Doctor Williams is the most proficient in that matter, and yes, he is an angelic wizard. But there is nothing to be afraid of. We will offer you care and protection here.

Ivy added,

-And lots of love, tenderness and affection. If you have no mum, no dad, you have us Toby, we will look after you.

Looking at the young woman, her kind air and her simple attire, Tobias knew that she was not like his own mother had been who had always been outrageously dressed. However seeing her tumefied cheek, he asked,

-Did a man beat you, Mrs Cotton? My mum used to be beaten up, one day it was so bad that she didn't wake up at all.

Then he looked at the authoritative and paternal figure that was Raguel, with glistening eyes, he confided to him feeling all of a sudden emotional,

-I've just remembered something from my past! Usually I can't! I remember now what my mother looked like. It is the bruise on the cheek of Mrs Cotton, it made me recall my mum. She is dead.

Ivy ran to give a hug to the little boy, who willingly went into her arms. She lifted him up and cradled him, gently as the little boy cried upon her shoulder. She comforted tenderly,

-There, there, Toby, I am here. If you want to share anything you can remember, we are here for you.

Returning to the stove, carrying the crying child, who was holding on to her, Ivy took the spoon to turn the simmering compote. Doctor Williams gave a knowing smile to Raguel, sending him a telepathic message,

-The wife of your son may not have been brought up by a mother, but she has the maternal instinct. I reckon she will be such a good mother for all those children. Master, I still remember her, sitting on the lap of her father, learning how to read in medical books with him at about four. She was so bright already, so precocious. That at six Doctor Fair decided to further her education in a very good boarding school in England. While the other little girls started to learn to write and read, she already knew Latin and Arithmetic. So they did decide to put Ivy in a higher class. I wish her late father could have seen what she had become, a Doctor, a kind hearted mother. He would have been so proud of her. I know I am.

The Master of all angels reprimanded his old servant out loud,

-You are in great danger of being emotional, yourself, my William. Help Margot with the labelling of the jars. We need twelve.

Then he stepped by Ivy, demanding,

-Let me carry little Toby. How is everything going on?

Giving the child to Raguel, the young woman replied,

-I didn't burnt the compote yet, it has the added sugar and the cinnamon and dare I say it is smelling rather nice. Toby managed to stop sobbing. It was a big realisation dawning upon him, I guess.

Reminiscing of the time, when Sebastien was a child, Raguel confided,

-My Sebastien asked me what happened to his mummy when he was about six, the age of Toby. Although he was too young when his mum did pass away and couldn't remember her at all, being only a baby, he cried a lot the day I told him.

Toby enquired timidly,

-Did Mr Cotton lost his mummy too?

Raguel told the boy,

-Oh, yes, he did. He was only a little baby of six months, when his mother passed away of a very bad injury. Mrs Cotton, Ivy, also lost her mummy, but that happened when she was born so she never knew her Ma at all.

Joining in, Margot said,

-Toby, I lost my mum as well. My new Ma, my adoptive Ma is now Ivy. You can call her Ma, like Jack and I do.

Jack added,

-You can also call Sebastien, Pa, because you are being adopted. I am your big brother now, and Margot is your big sister. Come and let me teach you how to read and write your first word.

Putting the child down, Raguel watched Toby running rather than walking towards Jack. He smiled then turning to Ivy, he asked her,

-So let's resume, what we were doing my dear Ivy. We did decide on an apple pie for tonight, what did you decide for the rest of the menu to impress my son? I will fetch the ingredients for you as I take Margot to the dairy farm.

The young woman showed her anxiety there and then as she confessed,

-Sebastien is such a good cook, I don't think I stand a chance to impress him with my culinary skills. I decided to go for something I think I could manage. In the book there is a soup recipe I like the potato and leek one with a little bit of cheese within it. That would be the starter. I can try to do soda breads to go with it. Doctor Valdi's garden has the ingredients for the soup. For the main, I do not know if we could afford any meat because we used almost all we had on the ham. If Sebastien gets paid today at the clinic then we could afford something otherwise, we will rely on the hens of Valdi and their eggs. I could do something with ham and eggs, I guess, but I do not know what.

Raguel after tasting the compote told,

-This is ready. Let's give some to the children now and jar the rest. You have a good dozen conserves ready for the winter months here. Now, I like your idea for the soup. I will get you everything you need for it and I will find some meat for tonight. We will do the dinner together, so you mustn't feel anxious about it.

Soon once the children had eaten their compote, the Master of all angels enjoined,

-Who is coming with Grandpa Rag walking Margot to the dairy farm?

Jack posited himself straight away to do so and invited Toby to follow suit. Soon all three children were with wicker baskets and followed the angel into the forest. Ivy and Doctor Williams went to the clinic to help Sebastien. On the way, Ivy couldn't help sharing her thoughts to Williams,

-Raguel is very much a family man, isn't it?

The old servant answered with a sigh,

-Oh, yes, he is. I can tell you how happy he was that his son invited him to live with you two as you were building your family. First, Sebastien, who was single handedly brought up by his father, knows full well how good Raguel is at educating children, with life skills, common sense, and also recognising right from wrong. Secondly, sometimes, Raguel may seems to be on the harsh side but to tell you the truth, when we are speaking family, children, his angels, he is almost a father to us all and never ceased to be one. He deeply cares, he always did. Look he took your case on for you to learn how to cook. He will supervise you until you gather your confidence. He has kindness in abundance. He even spoon fed Raphael who he doesn't particularly like.

The young woman confided,

-I must say, I feel secure by him like I do with my Sebastien. And I love the way he gave a nice rough and tumble to that Cork bastard of a cambion.

Doctor Williams couldn't help smiling as he replied,

-Well, you are married to a Punisher and his father is the strongest of them all Punishing angels. Raguel has put himself as sheriff of this town so you might see a lot of action from him. But you and I will probably have to mend him many times. With your husband and him, you will be very skillful at stitching.

A laughing Ivy entered the clinic who was fairly busy. All the chairs of the waiting room were taken. Sebastien welcomed his wife and Doctor Williams with a bright smile and took them in the consultation room to brief them. Once he closed the door, he informed them,

-It looks worst than it is, really. Most complaints are from individuals who wants to escape the voluntary work to rebuild the town and who don't want to help. They just need a valid excuse from us. Most of them are fine, honestly just fine. If they want their house or roof back, they need to pull their weights as well as the others. So do not give in to lies, both of you. However we have three who really need our help. The young Miss Freeman, I leave her case to you, my Little Bit. She is an orphan and a servant girl in a good household of this town. She woke up bleeding, and hurting. Obviously, she is having her first periods. Please teach her all about it and how to deal with it. Williams, I want you to see to a man sent by Raphael from the quarry. It is one of the volunteers to rebuild the town who didn't know how to use a hammer, a Mr Sutton, well to do. He managed to crush one of his fingers under his hammer. Assess him for me. It may be a case of removing his finger at the end of the day but if you can use a little magical trick while talking to him to render his bones fixable, it would be welcomed. He has a good heart. I have a logger who axed his thigh open to deal with. The rest can truly wait for a while until those three are seen to. Let's go.

While the day at the clinic was going on. Raguel was holding the hands of Jack and Margot walking through the forest. Toby was holding the hand of Jack. Showing the trees, the angel was teaching all of the children the different names of them and how to differentiate them from their leaves to their trunks. Soon they left Margot at her work at the dairy farm of Mr Berry. But seeing the children, Anthony Berry couldn't help to give them some hot chestnuts and a couple of pint of milk.

With the midday sun soon approaching, Raguel couldn't resist to go to the quarry to check on Raphael. With the two little boys in tow, he found the fallen angel quite alone, sitting on a rock eating his lunch. Raphael stood up and bowed as soon as he saw him with a sheepish look on his face. He welcomed,

-Master, I didn't expect you here.

Sitting by Raphael casually, Raguel told,

-I had to pass by, so I decided to check on how you were doing?

Raphael replied giving a full brief,

-Not too bad but not too well either. I did have two humans with injuries this morning. One absolutely can not work in the quarry. He has good intentions, yes, but he is out of his depth here. We need to relocate him. He crushed his finger under a hammer. I was hurting for him when I saw the state of his finger. I sent him to Sebastien to be dealt with. To be honest, that human is intelligent rather than manual. I need someone to organise the carriages that will go from the quarry to the town in a diligent pace. I think, he could be the one to supervise that operation. Then one logger, a rather experienced one, suffered from an axe blow from an inexperienced logger. I was in the quarry when it happened. He was sent to your son straight away. Apart from those dreadful accidents, we are making some progress. We have fire wood for the winter piling up. We have nettles kept aside for soups, but we need some barrels for them. We are working on a project to break down the dangerous part of the quarry. If it falls we have immediate access to stones to carve. It will not be even, yes, but it will be plentiful. So, on overall there is some give and take. I can see the little boy is with you.

Stroking gently the brown curly hair of Tobias, Raguel answered,

-Yes, Sebastien is adopting him. We have a little something for you. Not much, but it is just for you to keep on the good work. Jack, do you want to give it to Raphael?

Jack obliged with a bright smile,

-Here is a pint of milk for your rest of the day, then some nicely roasted chestnuts and we brought you a little pot of Ivy's first apple and plum compote. It is well nice! Here is the spoon. Toby learnt to read and write his first word today.

Raphael looked at Tobias with great kindness and said,

-Well done. So you have been called Toby?

Tobias answered with some confusion,

-No, it is my name.

Raguel explained,

-Doctor Williams checked the child. He managed to know well see what happened to him in his past. His name is Tobias. Let me show you, give me your hand. Toby is an orphan which now has a home, thanks to you.

The Master of all angels held the hand of the fallen angel who then saw the miserable past of Tobias. Raphael commented with a deep sad sigh,

-Maybe it is best and a blessing in disguise that Tobias do not remember his past.

He then asked the little boy,

-Do you remember the word you learn to read, Toby?

The question did cause some difficulties for the little boy who fidgeted as he tried to remember the word but then he saw the apple by the side of Raphael so he replied,

-It is apple! Yes, it is apple! I know how to write apple.

The fallen angel nodded his satisfaction, before proposing,

-Toby, I will give you my apple if you spell that word for me.

Tobias concentrated for a good minute before he advanced full of uncertainty,

-A-P-L-L-E.

Playing with his apple Raphael teased,

-Close enough, but not quite there. You doubled up the wrong letter, Toby. I give you another chance and a clue, you need to double up the other consonant in the word.

A baffled Tobias asked,

-What is a consonant?

Jack went to hold the hand of the confuse little boy and told,

-Vowels and consonants are part of the alphabet. I need to teach you the alphabet. The alphabet are all the letters that we use to read and write. The letter you need to double here is P. Try again.

Jack shaped the outline of a P with his fingers to help Tobias, who nodded then said,

-A-P-P-L-E.

A satisfied Raphael gave him his apple with his praise,

-Well done, Toby, you earned that apple, here, take it and enjoy it. You must continue the good work and learn to read and write. It is important.

While the little boy ate his apple, Raphael observed to Raguel,

-Toby's memory is visual at this moment in time. He remembered the word by seeing the apple and the letter P, by seeing the shape of a P. He will have difficulties learning but he will catch up with everyone eventually. The way to make him learn faster will be to put images in front of him or physical objects.

The Master stood up, appreciating the comment of the fallen angel,

-We will make sure to educate him with the consideration to what happened to him. You are welcomed to participate in his education and to join in. We will certainly value your opinion. Now, try not to have any casualties in the quarry or the woods this afternoon. If you see someone too clumsy to hold a tool, keep them with you and task them to another duty. Get to know your men and their abilities, fast! This is the order of the day, so no one gets hurt. Is that understood? I am looking forward to see you tonight at home.

Turning to the children, Raguel enjoined,

-Come on, boys, let's go fishing! We need to catch some fish for your Ma to do a decent fish pie.

Raphael saw the two boys, hand in hand, following the Master of all angels and he couldn't help smiling. He also sighed deeply. Within his mind was the predominant idea to give back the son he took away from Raguel. He recognised what a father figure Raguel was to all, and also to him. He finished his lunch thoughtfully, giving good bits of his sandwich to the rottweiler by him. He stroke the dog and said,

-Ludwig, I wish I was a guard dog to the family who owns you, just like you. Sebastien and his wife are so kind and the Master, well, the Master, I would lay by his feet, all the time. I would protect him with my life. I've got to get his son back, I've got to. Shall we try what Ivy made? It sounds nice, but does it taste nice? The proof is in the pudding.

Raphael tried his pot of compote and surprised, smiling, he told to the dog,

-Sorry my friend, this is too good to be shared.

His workers came back by little groups into the quarry, having finished their own lunches in the canteen. During the afternoon, the fallen angel received another visit, this time by the Messenger driving a carriage. Henry stepped down and attached the cart horse to a tree. Raphael came to the visitor and bowed to him. The good natured Henry commented,

-Please, Raphael don't bow to me, you will only make me feel uncomfortable. I haven't got an ego that requires bowing every time you see me. Now, I have got what you requested.

A puzzled Raphael answered,

-I didn't request anything.

Henry who started unloading the cart corrected,

-This is not what the Master messaged me. He said you needed some barrels. I got you some, six. The cart and the horse is yours to use at the quarry. It is a very docile, strong and sturdy animal called Buttercup, due to its almost yellow colour. If you find the right driver amongst your men, you can start bringing things from the quarry to town like the fire wood which must stay dry. Anyhow, I have a large waxed cover to protect that wood for the time being. I will try to find you another cart and another good horse to add to this one. The presbytery stables are large enough to keep them safe overnight. With those two carts, bringing the reconstruction materials and else to town will be easier and faster. I must say, your workers did do a good job with that overgrown path for the first day. I have been able to use it.

The fallen angel looking at the path told and winked,

-This is due to my sub-team of teenagers and

youngsters. They move fast. Youths for what could be back breaking for older adults is the key you see. They can bend to clear the undergrowth without pain. Do you happen to know how are my two injured humans? I am quite worried for them both.

Winking back to Raphael, the Messenger replied,

-I do. Mr Sutton who crushed his finger with a hammer didn't lost it in the end. Doctor Williams applied a little magic trick to save his finger. He made the man talk so much, that Sutton didn't realise he was under a spell to repair his bones. He will come to the quarry tomorrow morning to report back to you. For the logger, Mr Dunn, Sebastien dealt with him. He had to have many stitches. His thigh muscle is going to be weak for some time. If you want a driver, use him. But pair him with someone who can do the up and down from the cart. Dunn is determined to keep helping, Sebastien said. He is one who lost his home to the fire. He has a small family which is lodged at the hotel for nothing at the moment. He looks after his two children, his grandmother, and the old father of his wife. His wife did pass away a few years ago. Dunn is an excellent man according to Sebastien. I need to dash. I have just received a new order. I will see you tonight at home. Make sure you bring Buttercup back to us so I can feed her. Take care.

The angel went to the forest and disappeared from sight. Raphael sighed deeply. He longed to be an angel again but this time to help, just help, he touched briefly the head of the dog by him and vented,

-If only I didn't mess things up as an angel.

The dog licked his fingers which made Raphael smiled sadly,

-So you agree with me, my friend. Come. Let's put all those nettles inside the barrels.

Soon enough it was dusk and Raphael called the end of the working day thanking everyone for their hard work. He was surprised to find at the cross road, Raguel carrying Toby who was asleep on his shoulder, with Margot and Jack carrying baskets which looked very full. He stopped his cart by the Master and told,

-Step in. I will drive you all back home. Children, you can pet Ludwig who has been an excellent dog. He protected one of my worker from a snake. Jump in the back.

Jack helping Margot up in the cart asked eagerly,

-Was it a big snake?

Raphael replied,

-Not big, but it was a venomous one, a rattlesnake. The tail of that snake rattles and if you ever see one you must stay well out of its way because its bite is dangerous. How did the fishing went?

Putting the little Toby between Jack and Margot in the back, Raguel answered,

-We eventually caught something.

Then he stepped by Raphael on the driving seat and added,

-At least the two boys learnt how to fish.

A giggling Raphael enquired,

-If I remember right, this is tonight the dinner that Ivy is preparing? Am I lucky or not to eat at the tavern tonight?

Raguel laughed with his reply,

-We've got to give her a chance. It is all about education. I am more patient than my son on that one.

Making Buttercup advance, Raphael commented,

-I agree with you, Master. The little pot of compote she made this morning was delicious. What is on the menu tonight for all of you?

The Master revealed,

-Well it will be a potato and leek soup with some cheese in it which we got from Mr Berry's farm, to start of with. It will be followed by a fish and crayfish pie with pan fried cabbage and cream then an apple pie for dessert. I will help Ivy throughout. She is not hopeless by all means. She just need to be shown what to do in the kitchen. I reckon she will pick up whatever we are teaching her fast. Ivy is a clever human, a little stubborn and strong headed, but ever so kind and righteous.

Seeing the end of the forest, Raphael told,

-Yes, Ivy is all that. You know what? She suits the

temperament of your son so well, if you don't mind me saying. I do like her a lot. Seeing her damaged cheek hurts me. So Toby did learn how to fish. How easy was it? He will face learning difficulties all his life but repeat and proceed could do the trick with him. Otherwise maybe Doctor Williams could apply a little of his healing magic on his little skull like he did to the crushed finger of Mr Sutton.

His eyebrows lifting, Raguel demanded,

-Did he use magic on a human? It is supposed to be used for angels and eternal beings only.

Raphael bit his lips, realising he said something that other angels knew but didn't tell the Master of all angels. Knowing that they could face the wrath of the angel of justice, Raphael said in a pacifying manner,

-Look, the man didn't even realise what Doctor Williams did to him. For Sutton, it was just a talkative trip to the Doctor. His attention was kept on your skillful wizard's conversation. So don't go all harsh on your Williams for a silly rule. At the end of the day, your servant helped a good man to the best of his abilities.

But Raguel argued,

-They are not silly rules! He needs to be careful that's all.

The fallen angel retorted, as he engaged the cart on the wide path between the cemetery and the forest,

-Well, what I heard is that he was careful. So don't go all worked up over it, please. Beside, it is still to my eyes a very silly rule. A human is suffering less for it to be broken, this speaks for itself.

Raguel looked at the tired Raphael and stated,

-You are fatigued, Raphael, and not capable to sustain an argument with me, so I will let you off the hook on that one.

However with a giggle the fallen angel insisted,

-No, please don't. Hear my points: First there is the old adagio that when rules are no good they are meant to be broken. Take your father, yourself and your sons, you did stop making angels out of fire and made them out of humans instead. You would not have punished me the way you did if this was not an ancient rule who deserved to be broken: No more angels of fire but instead angels made of blood, flesh and a human heart. Second, heart is the key to unlock those rules which are almost blind to love and humanity. I believe Doctor Williams listened to his heart and just showed great compassion to that human. Thirdly, and this is my weakest point which will not have any value to your eyes, I am now human and therefore I would be very sorry if an angel could not use all of his skills to make me feel better if I am injured, just because I am human. When you taught me harshly to have consideration for humans, you want to deny them the help of your healing angels? It doesn't make sense to me. I understand about the secrecy that all incarnated angels needs to maintain but they are ways your angels can learn to help humans with their full potential yet to stay undiscovered as angel. I think your servant just demonstrated it today and should not be blamed whatsoever for it.

Arriving at the gates of the churchyard, they saw Henry standing there smiling. Raguel turned to Raphael briefly to order,

-Go to the tavern and have your meal. Henry will accompany you and have dinner with you. I will come and fetch you both in about three hours time. By the way Raphael, I appreciated your conversation and I honestly think that you scored a point.

Raguel helped Margot and Jack to stepped down from the cart, and took a sleeping Toby within his arms. While all of them made their way to the presbytery, Henry stepped in the cart by Raphael, took the reins from him, and said,

-Time for you to rest a little. Your first day as a working human is over.

#

When they arrived at the tavern, Callum was waiting outside. He greeted,

-At long last, here you are. Henry, I will deal with the barrels, just deal with Buttercup and the cart. Raphael, you can go inside, Tyron is waiting for you.

Entering the tavern, Raphael saw a lot of his men at the bar or sitting around tables. They saluted him and he saluted them back. Somehow he was slightly anxious. He went to Tyron who was behind the bar and asked, with shyness in his voice,

-Hello, Mr Tyrell. Could I see Rob, please? I don't want to eat before talking to him.

Tyron, knowing what it was all about nodded positively and just said,

-Follow me. How was your day at the quarry?

Raphael answered,

-It could have been better. We had two casualties: Mr Sutton and Mr Dunn.

Leading Raphael up a rather narrow staircase, Tyron commented,

-To be honest with you, I am not surprised about Mr Sutton. I heard already what happened to him. He is more of a gentleman than a worker. He is an educated fellow not skillful with his hands whatsoever. Give him a hammer and he smashed his finger. However we do like him a lot in town. For one thing he is extremely kind so much so that no one believes that he could kill a fly. As for Mr Dunn, it is a crying shame. He is a very good logger to lose on the first day.

Raphael agreed but told,

-He is not lost. He will be the driver of the cart that brings the stones and goods in town. If he can't do that I will make him be a supervisor of the team of loggers. But in that case I will need to find him a seat so he doesn't stand all day.

As they went through a small corridor, Tyrell said firmly,

-For him, your second option is the best. You can take one of my stools for Dunn. He can make sure that no accident happens when the men are felling the trees. For good cart drivers, you have Mr Hardy which is in your quarry team. He raises horses for a living and sell them. He trains them like no other. Then you have Mr Davis in town. He didn't want to participate to the rebuilding of the town. We consider him like a grumpy old man to be honest with you. His house wasn't affected by the fire whatsoever so he doesn't care for the rest. But he is a very skilled driver. He makes a living out of delivering goods from one town to another.

A smiling Raphael replied,

-I think I will pay your grumpy old man a visit. Where does he live? I need two drivers because we will have two carts to move things fast and forward.

Stopping by the bedroom door of Rob, Tyron asked,

-How will you convince Davis? He saw the fire in town, he didn't care.

The fallen angel confided,

-An angel is always an angel deep down, wings or no wings. I have ways to convince him, trust me. I may send him to a guilt trip of a lifetime before you know it. Now, open that door, and let me apologise to Robert. You don't have to wait. I will recognise my way to go back downstairs.

Tyron let Raphael in, but remained standing by the door he closed. The fallen angel as he saw Rob went to the window to close the curtains as he demanded in a gentle voice,

-Hi, Rob, how are you doing?

Robert vented,

-How do you think I am doing? It could have been worst.

Inappropriately Raphael couldn't help having a smirk on his lips as he confirmed,

-I know.

But he then sat by the bed with a serious face and told with true sorrow in his voice,

-Robert, I want you to know that I am sorry for what I intended to do that night. I don't expect you to forgive me, and I accept that, but I need you to acknowledge it. I am sorry. I brought you a little something, I had one and kept the rest for you.

From his leather satchel, he presented to the burnt angel, some roasted chestnuts in an handkerchief. Robert dismissed,

-I can't shell them. Keep your sorry tail between your legs and go away.

With a heavy heart, Raphael peeled all the chestnuts and put them upon the night table, then he repeated,

-Robert, I am sorry. I was awfully wrong. I know it now because the Master corrected me. If you want to give me a hard time whilst I am in my human shell to get your own back, you can. I will not protect myself. If you want to use or abuse me like a servant, you can. I will not utter a word of protest. I would love your forgiveness but I know I don't deserve it.

Seeing a tear on Raphael's cheek, Rob asked,

-So it is true then you are a fallen archangel?

Raphael presented him with a chestnut, nodding positively,

-Please, have one.

Robert accepted as he scolded,

-Don't cry on me, I will not know what to do. Human, hey, I love the irony of the Master. That will teach you right!

Drying his tear with the palm of his hand, Raphael agreed with a sad smile,

-The Master knew what I needed. I could have been sent to hell instead. It could have been harsher much harsher. But the angel of justice's hands when they are punishing you, they are giving you back clarity. I can tell you that, still shivering. I do understand my mistakes, all of them. I would not be by you saying sorry if I didn't. Did the angels told you that Darren was dead and in hell?

Eating the chestnut, then smirking, Robert answered,

-Of course they did. The Messenger gave me the entire feedback of what happened to him. Sebastien went the all punishing way on that nasty human, but he couldn't finish, Darren's heart gave up before the end. Apparently, this is a secret, Sebastien felt short changed on that case as a Punisher.

Raphael commented,

-Surely, this is rumours. Sebastien has an extremely good heart.

Robert corrected him as he took another chestnut,

-He has, but at the end of the day, he is still a Punishing angel. You can't mess about around him. Ask the three M who were his musketeers or even Henry and Ted. They will tell you that he has an iron fist in a velvet glove. However we all find him slightly kinder than his father. But they both work together with similar ethics. I heard that you have been staying close by the

Punishers, the two of them, even the Master?

Nodding positively, Raphael confided,

-Yes, I am staying by them. I want to redeem myself and I am sure they can show me the way to do so. The Master took me on as his second servant and I am the slave of Doctor Williams while Sebastien is giving me a temporary home under his own roof.

Smirking Robert teased,

-You are going to have fun under the roof of two punishing angels.

The fallen angel gave another chestnut to the burnt angel as he confessed with a giggle,

-I actually find it rather pleasant. Both are really kind deep down. If I don't make it back as an angel, somehow I wish to reincarnate as a dog to follow the Master. Seeing him and his son bicker constantly is also rather amusing. It is a constant battle of good points and wit. Myself, I would struggle to say one is right and the other is wrong, because usually both are right to some extent. The wife of Sebastien is such a nice human. She is so welcoming and generous, young but learning how to run a household. She also has a character that suits him perfectly: strong, clever, and kind. She is a little bit like him in a sense. Then there are the children, they adopted. Their house is very lively and I am rather lonely, so seeing them all, somehow comforts me.

Rob looked at Raphael straight into his eyes and ordered him,

-You must go and have your dinner, Raphael. You are not my friend and you never will be after threatening to drown me. I accept your apologies so now do me the favour of going from my room and to stop making conversation with me. Thank you for the chestnuts.

Biting his lips, Raphael stood up, accompanied by Ludwig, he went to the door silently. His heart was heavy as he opened the door. He turned around, wiped a tear, and said,

-Thank you for accepting my apologies. It means a great deal to me. I am going to come everyday to the tavern in the evening, is there something which I can bring tomorrow for your comfort?

The softness of his tone, the sadness on the fallen angel face who was visibly retaining his tears, and the kind offer touched Robert somehow so he replied,

-I am not a very patient angel and staying in bed annoys me deeply, but I have to for a fair few days. Bring me a book, not just any book, one which is full of adventures and fights. Can you find me some gloves so I don't see my burnt hands and to protect them as I use them? I would also love something else than water. Not alcohol, it will burn my throat, but apple juice or pear juice will do. Can you do that? If you really want me to tolerate you longer than five minutes bring a deck of cards with you tomorrow.

Raphael regained his smile as he answered very willingly,

-Yes, yes, I can do that. I will see you tomorrow, Robert, with everything you want.

Once the door closed, the Great Being reappeared into the room onto the chair by the bed of Rob. Robert confided to him,

-Well, that was an unexpected visit. I did hear that he was now an humble pie Raphael but I didn't know to what extent. Although I loath him, I felt sorry for him. I don't know. Is he truly reaching out like the Master said?

The Great Being replied with a kind smile,

-Yes, he is. His punishment worked. Now we can resume our conversation, apart if you need to speak about what just happened, and I feel you need to.

Robert nodded positively as he asked genuinely,

-Can a foe become a friend?

Giggling, the Creator replied,

-You should ask the same question to my son. You two can find out together. All I will say to you is that if that fallen archangel dies without having a chance to have regained his wings, by accident, in his human shape, my son will shed tears of sorrow for him. If next to no one would attend the funeral of Raphael, I know my son would be there, directing it, and Williams, his trusted servant would have provided a coffin fit not for a fallen angel but for an archangel. I will let you in a little secret, if I would not have attended the funeral of archangel

Raphael, I would attend the one of the human Raphael River.

The burnt angel commented,

-That's telling. I must confessed, I was compelled when I saw him. I know that to help Raphael win his wings again is the aim of the Master of all angels. I am ready to give him a hand in that project.

Giving a chestnut to Rob, the Great Being told,

-Raguel will be happy to hear that. But for the time being, I must enlist you to be the bodyguard of Doctor Valdi who saved your life. You are going to depart in a couple of days, with him, his wife and I. Vincent is doing a grand tour of Europe for his honeymoon. His wife still needs protection because she knows too much and can end up in hell again. Let me tell you a little secret, Vincent is my youngest son. So, as you need some holidays after what happened to you, I want you to tag along with him. As a Doctor, he will be able to ease your condition and help you to get better faster. As for you, I know you are desperate to be useful again and feel bad to have been injured on duty. You mustn't. Now, Vincent knows he is my son and an angel only since a few days ago. He needs to learn the basics of being a human angel and I am giving you that task. When Vincent will return from his honeymoon, my eldest son and grand son will finish off his angelic education. Now, depending on your result on the task, my plan is to elevate you as a teacher of human angels, a little like Doctor Williams is one, but the difference is that, you can focus on the physical training. You are an excellent fighter. You can teach so much to new recruits in Sebastien's angelic army. Here are my orders. Rest, and be prepared to travel with us in two days time.

He held the hand of the angel who smiled to him full of gratefulness then left the room. Rob finished the chestnuts thinking of the opportunity he has just been given. Of course, he didn't know Vincent Valdi very well, nor his wife for that matter. But he remembered vividly how Doctor Valdi acted fast to save him when he was engulfed by flames. When he himself had a sense of panic, Valdi remained calmed and in control of the situation and helped him in a way that he would never forget. If Rob would recover from his burns, it was entirely due to the quick thinking and actions of Doctor Valdi. To be able to be a bodyguard and teacher to Valdi was a superb occasion to show his appreciation to the new angel that saved his life.

Meanwhile Tyron was giving a tour of his tavern to Raphael from the kitchen to the cellar passing by the attic and the stables. Back behind the bar Tyrell explained in great details what he expected of Raphael as a waiter. The fallen angel found that his work description was slightly more than what his assumptions of it was, but he was undeterred, and determined to do it when his arms were mended. On the third encounter, he also still liked the personality of Tyron and was willing to work for him. When he was finally asked to find a table to eat by the tavern owner, Raphael looked at the buzzing room, full of chatter and tried to spot an empty table, a little corner where to put himself, but instead he saw Henry making a gesture for him to come over and presenting him an empty chair at his table. As he approached he noticed that at the head of the table was the Great Being and opposite Henry, was Callum. The fallen angel bowed respectfully to all of them before taking the seat presented by Henry silently.

The amiable Messenger presenting him a piece of paper where the menu was written told with a smile,

-Mr River, this dinner is on me. I arranged it with Tyrell so you can not argue. It is to inaugurate your first working day as a human. Chose what you want. We are all ready to order but we were waiting for you. If you care for a little insider's tip, which I have from Tyron, the best dish tonight is the grouse served with a Port jus. We are all having it. It's served with sautéed wild mushrooms and potatoes.

Callum added,

-I took the adopted boy of Tyron hunting this morning and foraging. We were very successful. Rick is a good shot. He rarely miss his target. Hence Tyron was happy with what we brought to him for tonight. So there are enough grouses for them to be on his menu.

A shy Raphael, feeling included immediately, said simply,

-I will have what you are all having.

Standing up, Henry announced,

-Right, I will go and place the order at the bar and bring the drinks over.

When he departed, the Great Being gave a long stern gaze at Raphael and asked,

-How was your first day at the quarry?

Stroking the head of the rottweiler by him to give himself

a little confidence, the fallen angel answered with deep honesty,

-Not as good as I would hope, my Lord . There were two injuries this morning, quite serious ones for two workers. Sebastien's dog also averted what could have been a fatal incident by killing a rattlesnake this afternoon. We did make some progress clearing the cart way to the crossroad and we managed to have three decent blocks from the quarry to work on tomorrow to plenty of brick size stones. I have an idea, a project, but I need to discuss it with the Master before going ahead with it. It can be potentially dangerous, but well executed, it can give us lots of stones fast to carve to rebuild the town before winter. I think it could eliminate the dangerously unstable part of the quarry and make it safer for the workers. But as I said, what I have in mind can't be rushed and needs to be well thought out to keep safety paramount.

The Great Being nodded his approval before he posed his next question,

-How did you feel interacting with humans?

Henry came back to the table with pitchers of red wine and glasses on a platter and started to serve everybody, commenting with a smile,

-That is an interesting question. Being an ancient animal spirit, my reply would be bad when I was hunted and good when I was petted.

Callum started laughing while the Creator giggled before saying,

-The question was for Raphael, my Messenger. Take a seat.

With sincerity Raphael answered,

-I felt bad inside because of what I thought of humans before. But I saw them in action, helping one another, giving guidance when it was required, the old teaching the young, and a spirit of solidarity in their time of hardship which was pleasing to see. When Mr Dunn was injured by the axe of a youngster, badly injured, he didn't blame the lad, he just said to him to work doubly hard to compensate for him as a logger. The young Albert was inconsolable, and I had to make him sit down by me until he composed himself. He had a good cry, I comforted him. I am not the mothering type, but I just felt compelled to do so. Being human is making me have a heart, and I can't help it. I could be full of sarcasm about it, but I can't I am just full of emotion. I must confess that it is a novel thing for me to feel. I will need time to adjust because it is overwhelming me at the moment. The 'How could I have been so wrong all along' is still hammering my soul and crushing me deep down. But I am starting to understand humanity's plight, and my own question has been how can I help and help better and further all day. I had lots of examples in front of my eyes and I think it starts with little gestures and acts of kindness to one another. My plan is to do just that with my fellow human beings.

Callum commented,

-I will drink to that! Raphael has finally a right angelic human heart.

He lifted his glass which was met by the others, while the Great Being encouraged Raphael to do the same. The fallen angel managed to smile shyly feeling once more accepted amongst angels. Their dinner arrived at the table and Henry vented,

-I am glad you told me you caught some grouses today, Callum, because Ivy is cooking tonight. I wonder how the meal at home turned out.

Callum scolded giggling,

-You will never know you coward your way out of it. Ted and the children are braver than you.

The Messenger retorted,

-I have god by my side. The Lord is eating at the tavern and not at home. Do you want to know why, my dear Callum?

An amused Great Being replied,

-No, it was not by the fear of Ivy's first dinner, it was to make sure her children ate their fill. Jack is still recovering and the young Marguerite along with Tobias are far too slim for my liking. Both suffered malnutrition and need to put food in their stomachs, whatever food they can get. The less at the family table, the more they can eat.

Henry commented,

-They will probably be able to eat the portion for Sebastien. Knowing his fine taste, he will probably leave it all on the plate under the disapproving eyes of his father. This is what I will miss the most the bickering between father and son. I am sure there will be a good one tonight at their table. Sebastien is too quick to advance his opinion and the Master is so fast to correct him verbally.

Tucking into his grouse with poise, the Great Being confided with a broad smile on his face,

-This is what I am escaping from. Bon appétit, let's eat. But to be honest, as my Raguel helped Ivy to do the meal tonight, I think they will all have a substantial, digestible and reasonable dinner. But of course, we will know how it went when we come back home, you, Raphael and I. I am pretty sure my grandson will be keen to tell us. I only hope he will remain sensitive to the feelings of the learning Ivy. He mustn't crush her will to learn how to feed her ever growing family. Three adopted children with another one on the way, this orphaned young woman must keep her strong heart. Henry, how did your endeavour went this afternoon?

The Messenger putting his wine glass down replied,

-Rather well. I managed to find a good cart and horse for the quarry, tomorrow I will get another cart. I heard that Mr Hardy who lives on the edges of the town breeds excellent horses. I am pretty sure he will have what I am looking for. I will meet him before he goes to the quarry, check his horses and buy one if he has a decent one to be a good cart horse. I also spent some time late afternoon with Abraham Wilton-Cough. He showed me the two plots of land that we need to secure for your grandson. They belong to his eldest son at the moment but he assured me that Zachary will be willing to sell and grant us the plots or rent them up until we reach the amount they are worth and then they will be ours. The soil is fertile but the land is partly covered by trees. It is close to the river but on upper ground, so safe from flooding. The advantage is that the access to water will be there. There is a closer plot available to us, a third one, but this one is by the river and can suffer from floods on occasion. My advice would be to secure the three plots of land. They have all decent sizes and as I said fertile. You can see it by the vegetation growing there. Your grandson would not be short changed by any means.

Watching attentively the fallen angel, the Great Being scolded him,

-Raphael stop looking at your grouse, it will not fly away from your plate any longer. Eat. If you need strength in your arms, just touch your magical satchel that we gave you otherwise I will have to cut the roasted bird for you and spoon feed you in front of everyone. As they are a lot of your men working at the quarry and the woods in the room, you will not want that. Henry, please, help him to grab his satchel, then just pour some of that nice port jus on his plate. I am afraid, my son never punishes lightly and that fallen archangel is in pain right now, suffering silently in front of us.

Henry obliged straight away while Raphael apologised,

-I am sorry to be a pain. I forgot to hold the satchel before the end of my a bit well spell.

Callum commented,

-Don't start to be a forgetful human on us, Raphael. When you are given an angelic satchel, you need to keep it upon yourself at all time. Look at the Messenger and myself, we never put ours on the ground or by our feet. It is one of our rules.

Filling his own glass with more wine, the Great Being told sternly,

-He doesn't knows the rules for human angels, not yet. We will have to babysit him through his human life and teach him the ABC of becoming a human angel. In the first place, he wasn't meant to stay alive after his ordeal. But with human free will, by chance he met someone, who saved him. I can tell you the face my son did when he met Raphael again. The chances of that fallen archangel to stay alive were so slim. Anyhow, Raphael has been punished and is meeting our charity and compassion now. His soul belongs to my son and he became his servant but also the slave of Williams.

Henry smiled as he said,

-There will be no real slavery with Williams, he is kindness incarnated. I can already bet safely that Raphael will be treated very well by him. When William sees someone suffering, he can't stand it. That is why he became a physician and a Doctor in the first place. He is one of the most pacific angels I ever met.

Turning to Raphael, Henry added with confidence while putting sautéed mushrooms on the plate of the fallen angel,

-Doctor Williams will treat you right and not as an inferior. It is simply not in his nature to do so. However he is a good teacher and I can predict that he will teach you how to become a human angel. After all the Master and him have been the tutors of the Mighty One. I think the aim of the game here is how to bring back an archangel from the brink. I have been fighting along with the Master and his son down in hell to retrieve the deal about your soul, and I know for a fact how fierce they were to not let that soul of yours to be lost.

Callum stated, then asked,

-That's compassion for you, Raphael. Henry, how many demons did you have to tackle with down there?

The Messenger, who was only to happy to give the details of any news, told with some excitement in his voice,

-Between two dozen to three dozen. In the midst of a fight it is always hard to tell. We all did suffered some blows, but we killed them all. Fair play to Lucifer, he ordered for the demons not to attack Amelia Valdi. She stayed safe behind her husband and Matthias. Wilton-Cough knew where the soul deal was kept. He is so observant. He made a bee line for it. We protected him. Lucifer was willing to take our ghost away. But the Lord intervened. So Lucifer had to back off from attacking Abraham. Then with the deal in hand, with Amelia, and our good old ghost, we had all to fight our way out of hell as fast as we could. For Mrs Valdi, she fought with a hot poker almost like a musketeer. It was quite something to watch. Maurice said she dusted one demon with it. I haven't witnessed all of that, because I was engrossed in tackling my own demon which was trying to pull me back down. But the Master came to my rescue and killed him for me. We all came out at the end of the day, with everything we wanted. It was a tough challenge to look after each others back and to ensure that no one was left behind, but we did it. Raphael's life is in the Master's hands now. If Raphael dies too soon, he will still end up in hell but give him the time of a long human life and he has a chance either to go to paradise or pass the grade to be a human angel. The decision belongs to the angel of justice.

Holding a drumstick of his grouse, Callum pointed to Raphael,

-You'd better do as you are told from now on until the end of your human life. The Master of all angels took you back on so don't let him down ever again. I saw how he was feeding you in the alley way. He is giving you a chance of a lifetime. So don't you dare missing it.

The fallen angel nodded positively with his answer,

-I will do my best. At least if I die too early, I will have died trying to do so.

Henry scolded him straight away,

-Look here, stop thinking of death and start thinking of living decently and properly. We understand how miserable and guilty you feel at the moment but you have been punished and you need to shake that weight off and move on. I killed a man in my first human life, by mistake, but still. The guilt stays for a very long time but you have to pull yourself together, be accountable and make all the acts you do from now own count in a positive way. What is done, is done, past is past, punished is punished, so you must start to get a mindset as soon as possible to ensure that all your human days have a positive impact upon humanity. If I have done it, you can do it as well. Trust in yourself a little. For me I was just a clumsy, incompetent human to start of, coming from the animal kingdom. Your advantage to start your human life is that you will be far from clumsy, you have an intellect which can challenge almost anyone, and the memory of your past as an archangel has not been removed. You have plenty of experience which you can tap upon, not even get like I had to do. So I can not stress enough, move on.

The Messenger paused to drink. The Great Being agreed and added,

-Henry is right. Raphael, you need to start thinking of your human life and what you can do with it rather than the end of it. My son will expect that of you.

Then Henry carried on,

-Listen, if you need moral support, I am here for you, Raphael. We will live in the same household for a while so you can come and talk to me when you need to. As I said I killed a man and faced terrible remorse. Sebastien got me through it and helped me every step of the way. I ended up being an angel at the end of my human life. Living under the roof of two punishing angels will not be a bad thing for you, because I will let you on on one of their little secret, they always make a point of retrieving the fallen angels.

Callum commented,

-I remember how happy they were to find Jack back. His disappearing act did worry them greatly. They were searching for him endlessly. Sebastien adopted him straight away. Ted was in a bad patch and about to lose his wings in this current incarnated life and now he is living under the roof of the ever so caring Sebastien. Now that port jus was delicious. Henry are you coming back here for dinner tomorrow night to eat with me and Raphael?

Putting his knife and fork on his empty plate, the Messenger replied,

-I definitely like the food coming out of this kitchen. I will have a busy day tomorrow so I can't promise anything but I will try my best to make it. But you can't count on me for the day after tomorrow. However I will come back after all my duties the following day. Right, it is eight, we'd better go home before the Master gets impatient, Raphael. My Lord, are you coming with us?

Folding his napkin with extreme precision, the Great Being stood up and said,

-Of course I am.

After Henry paid Tyrell for the meal all but Callum were on their way to the presbytery in the cart pulled by Buttercup. Henry confided,

-I sensed that Callum was missing Robert although Rob is just at the tavern upstairs recovering.

The Great Being agreed,

-Yes, he does. Callum is so used to work in pair with Robert. But I am afraid to say that I will be taking Rob on a long trip with me the day after tomorrow.

Henry, driving the cart, concluded,

-He is coming with us then.

The Creator confirmed,

-Yes, but he will stay with me for the long journey the Valdi couple are undertaking in the old continent. While you will return to Wilton Town to give all your help possible to Raguel and Sebastien.

At the back of the cart, Raphael was sitting, listening to the conversation thoughtfully, stroking the rottweiler by his side. He had found the talk at the tavern inspiring. He also knew now that he would not eat on his own, that some angels in town or just passing in town would not shun him and share their table with him.

When they arrived at the churchyard, they saw the

Master and Ted sharing a cigar at the entrance of the presbytery. Raguel smiled at the entrance of the cart and was quick to pass the cigar to Ted as he announced,

-Here, they are finally. Crush that fast.

He came to help his father to step down from the driving seat, but his father refused point blank,

-Help Raphael instead! You smoke? You know what your son think about that. You gave an angel which was destroying himself by that habit the very thing that rendered him extremely weak? The very angel, Mighty has struggled to save.

At the mounting wrath of the Great Being, the Master went to help Raphael down,

-Come here my Maggot. Go inside, everyone are in the drawing room. Ted, go with him. Henry, look after the horse.

Once everyone was dispatched the father and the son were alone in the courtyard. The Great Being started,

-I am waiting for your explanation. What have you got to say for yourself?

Raguel confessed,

-I was a bit upset and I needed to calm down. Ted proposed to me to have a cigar. It was his last hidden one. I accepted. I actually searched his room with Williams and it is his last one. So we shared it him and I waiting for you all.

His father probed,

-What caused the upset?

Kicking a pebble from the cobbled courtyard Raguel told,

-He managed to make Ivy cry. She worked so hard for that dinner but it was not good enough for Sebastien. His Little Bit is in tatters in their bedroom where she locked herself in admitting no one. I tried, Mighty tried, the children tried, Williams tried to make her open the door, but we just hear her sobbing, and she doesn't answer. The thing is the food was not that bad at all. The soup was good and a success and the apple pie was very nice, but the main, the fish pie... Well, it was not entirely Ivy's fault, it was mine as well and a bit of Margot's one as well. Margot was in charge of labelling all the jars and spices for Ivy.

She didn't know how to spell Cayenne pepper. So she wrote simply pepper. I didn't supervise her at that moment in time, and feeling shame to not know how to spell that word because she did stop to go to school, she told no one about it. Now, Ivy didn't know the sizes of her spoons. I told her to put one to two tea spoons of pepper, she did put two table spoons of Cayenne pepper. I was checking the progress of Tobias writing the word Plum at that moment in time. And here you have it in a nutshell a recipe for disaster. The main was extremely spicy. All the children reached for water putting on a brave face while my fiery Mighty didn't go easy on demeaning his wife in front of everyone. I told him off strongly. But Ivy retreated to her bedroom very upset. She lost her father not so long ago in dreadful circumstances, she just took on three children, she has just become a wife with a family, everything almost overnight and I am afraid what I heard from my son lacked comprehension and even kindness towards her. I am cross with Mighty.

The Great Being told calmly,

-It is just a storm in a tea cup, my Raguel. Let's go and resolve it. Come with me.

Stepping in the drawing room, the first sight, they saw was three forlorn children clutching pets for comfort. At the round table were Doctor Valdi, his wife, Doctor Williams and Ted. In the far corner of the room was Raphael sitting on a chair making himself small and unnoticed. Raguel demanded,

-Where is my son?

Williams replied,

-He is cleaning up the dishes in the kitchen, Master. He is upset with himself since what you told him. He wants to be alone too, now. I proposed my help to him but he refused it.

While Raguel gave a desperate look at the ceiling, his father ordered,

-Go to your son, I will deal with little Ivy.

The Master went to the kitchen and found his son crying, he demanded,

-Are you shedding crocodile tears now?

Seeing his stern father, Sebastien replied with emotion yet humour,

-No, it is the Cayenne pepper. I keep wiping my eyes. I have been such an arse, dad. I tried again and she will not talk to me. She is in that bedroom all upset and I caused it, like a complete stupid arse. And you, you are right as always. I am kicking myself right now. I love my Little Bit so much. I am annoyed with myself. I am supposed to give her a very nice home here in Wilton Town and I gave her grief tonight, my poor thing. She didn't even argue with me, she took it all in, and to see her face so, so sad. Father, I am upset with myself. I am trying to think of what to do, but she will not see me. I want to say sorry, I said it at the door but there is no reply.

Raguel dried the tears of his son as he stated,

-Finally you realised you were too harsh upon Ivy. Words are powerful, Mighty, they do have the power to hurt. You must be careful with whatever you say even if sometimes your aim is just teasing. This time you went too far. Your Little Bit is not overly confident and you have been her staunchest critic so far. She needs nurturing, help and love not constant put downs and embarrassments in front of people. If I see that attitude ever again from you towards her, I will come upon you like a ton of bricks. I will never let it pass. Now, what you can do is apologise to her. Your grandfather is with her at the moment, dealing with the situation. Another thing you can do is to simply teach her how to cook rather than going on a stampede about her cooking skills. Her soup was nice and her apple pie was delicious. It was all done under tuition but it will help her building her confidence if you were appreciative of those facts. Why picking the mistakes only and put them on the forefront when she had two dishes out of three right? Is it to make her feel bad? Just think, my boy, think before you talk. If you take my advice: just take the time to teach her. I noticed that she didn't know her spoon sizes. That is just a simple thing that you can remedy easily. Teach her, don't harass her and tell her that she is useless in the kitchen. Do the dinner with her tomorrow night. Look, you have centuries of practice, and she has virtually next to none. Give her the practice she needs.

He stopped for a minute then ordered,

-I have the message from my father. Come with me. Now, be on your best behaviour. Make up with Ivy, she is ready to see you. Do you want me to stay with you or can you do it on your own properly? Whatever you say to her I will know anyway and pull your ears afterwards if it wasn't right. Remember, no teasing, she is sensitive and went through a lot.

Sebastien asked,

-Don't tell me the rottweiler is in the bedroom?

Smirking his father replied,

-No, Ludwig is by the feet of Raphael who remained very silent since he stepped in and is in a little corner of the drawing room worried to be a hindrance to anyone. No, I have eight eyes in your bedroom which you will not find.

Sebastien swore,

-Good Lord! No! Not a spider! I will clean that bedroom tomorrow and you will be out of that room. Have you been watching me when I made love to the Little Bit?

His father laughed, slapping the back of the head of his son, then scolded,

-Stop swearing by your grandfather! Of course I didn't.

Sebastien commented,

-You are so sneaky.

By the bedroom door Raguel corrected him,

-No, I am a Watcher and your father. Now, get in there and do the right thing. I expect you to bring Ivy in the drawing room within half an hour to join all of us and enjoy herself a little once more.

He knocked at the bedroom door and the Great Being opened it. Ivy was standing in the middle of the bedroom, looking forlorn but she was drying her tears. Sebastien stepped in while his grandfather stepped out, giving him a dark glance. With a sheepish heart Sebastien faced his wife. He went straight to her, and held her tight with emotion in a big hug, saying with a sob in his voice,

-My Little Bit, I am ever so sorry.

The Great Being closed the door behind him and enjoined Raguel,

-It will be alright, come. Let those two make peace with each other. As I said it was a storm in a teacup.

His son enquired walking by his side in the corridor,

-How did you manage to resolve the deadlock?

Sighing the Creator revealed,

-I conjured her father. He told her that sometimes her mother had arguments with him, telling him that he wasn't good enough but that love always prevailed and that he was in paradise with her and that they were watching upon Ivy together and being ever so proud of her. His simple talk did the trick.

Raguel demanded with astonishment,

-Just that?

His father nodded his confirmation,

-Yes, just that. But as you said, Ivy is such a young woman, an orphan, and yes, Mighty is now her family and he needs to be supportive of her in every way. She puts him on a pedestal in her mind, so whatever he says goes straight to her heart. Any criticism he has coming her way, she is taking it very seriously. She has no parents so yes, Sebastien is her world at the moment. Doctor Williams is her only friend and she is getting acquainted with you from only a few days. However she trusts and likes you already. You are a father figure to her. I suggest for you to become her confident and give her moral support.

They stepped in the drawing room and seeing the concerned faces the Master reassured,

-It will all be alright. Williams, I need a little of your magic done tonight. I want this table to be large and oval and be surrounded by as many chairs we need. Then I want you to deal with that broken window. Being all boarded up doesn't do it for me. I could see a beautiful stain glass window with two white doves sharing a laurel branch on a blue back ground. We also need some baskets with cushions for the pets in this room. I want a vase on the mantle piece and one on the table to replace the ones that got broken during the fight with the demon and don't go magic out on me my Williams.

Behind him his father stated,

-You are a bit tense tonight, Raguel.

His son retorted,

-You don't understand I was sincerely at two fingers away from going the punishing way with Mighty, two fingers. I know it is not like he has been violent with Ivy but there are limits in what you can say.

Coming with one of the kittens, Margot told him,

-Here, Mr angel of justice hold the kitty, it will appease you a little. It did it for me.

Her simple gesture almost disarmed the anger of Raguel who took the cat in his arms. Then he saw Margot turned to his father and explained,

-What Sebastien said to Ma, was not really nice at all. Considering she had been trying her best all day and working at the clinic as well, she did deserve more credits than critics. Also it wasn't entirely her fault whatsoever. I didn't know how to write Cayenne, so I think I should have taken the blame for the bad fish pie.

The Great Being took her hand and tapped it gently as he commented,

-Look, my grandson made a big fuss out of little nothings, I would say a small incident. Trust me when I say he is sorry for it. None of you should take the blame for what happened when you all tried your best. Now, let us see a very important wizard in action, children come by me and watch.

Jack revealed with some excitement, holding the hand of Tobias,

-We did get to see some magic already today when Doctor Williams decorated the room for Mr River. It was awesome, wasn't it, Toby?

The young child with glee in his pale blue eyes confirmed,

-Oh, yes, it was swell! The floor boards were clean in an instant and covered by a very thick carpet which came from, from, I can't remember...

Jack helped him with a kind smile,

-It came from Persia.

Raphael looked at Doctor Williams and remembered what Henry said about him, that he will not be treated as a slave by him. He was very curious to see his room in the house. But first he witnessed with awe the magic wand appear on the left hand of the old angel who proceeded to please everyone especially the Master and the children. Williams created the large stain glass window with the two doves in the middle of the room then put it in place. The window floating in the air went to its final position. He then changed the table with a slight move of his wand, it became a very lavish white marble top table with gold painted legs finished by lion paws which seemed to claw the ground. Tobias had his mouth wide open and when Doctor Williams had completed to transform the room, he went to the little boy and made a toy appear in his hands which was the representation of a little steam locomotive made out of wood. For Margot, he presented her with Noah Webster's dictionary, and he told her in a kind way,

-I don't expect you to learn this by heart, Margot, but this book will help you to write all the words you do not know how to spell.

When he turned to Jack, he gave him the Encylopédie of Diderot and D'Alembert with this advice,

-I don't expect you to know French, Jack, but your adoptive Pa do know it by heart. And your grandpa Rag knows the language very well as well. It is grand time for you to be reeducated by very major angels, sit with them and learn what you can. I do know you are well educated already but if you have just a hidden desire of becoming my apprentice and an angelic wizard, you need to learn even more. In time I can take you there.

The green eyes of Jack lit up with joy, he turned to the Master of all angels to enquire,

-Can I?

Giving him the kitten Raguel told,

-If you want to become one you can, but you will have to either stay under my guidance or the one of my son or the one of Doctor Williams forever. No disappearing act like you did for centuries. You will be accountable every day just like Doctor Williams is. I can start your tuition with Williams and you can make your mind up, if it is really what you want to do at a later stage.

The boy impulsively hugged the Master of all angels taking care of not hurting the kitten. Raguel ordered,

-Children, put all your pets away in their baskets and all your presents away in your bedroom then come back downstairs to play cards with us.

The three children obeyed straight away which made the Great Being smile. While he and his son went to take their seats at the new table. Doctor Williams told Raphael,

-Let me show you your room.

The quiet fallen angel followed him. Doctor Williams said as they walked upstairs,

-You must know, it was not the best room in this old house but I fixed the problems. You should feel comfortable here. Did you enjoy your first working day as a human?

Raphael opened up with a sigh,

-Two of my workers got injured this morning and I do feel ashamed about it.

Williams told reassuringly,

-It will take you time to adjust to your human life but accidents do happen constantly, I know it all too well because I am running a hospital.

Raphael said,

-I am going to use Mr Dunn as an overseer for the team in the woods because I can't be here and there. He will be my eyes in the woods from now on. Mr Tyrell did give me a stool for the man so it will prevent him to hurt if Dunn stand up for the work.

When they reached the bedroom door, Williams gave the key to it to Raphael,

-Here, open it. I changed the lock for you to have privacy. Only me and the Master can enter that room without you.

Raphael noticed upon the white painted door, a ceramic little rectangular plaque with the name 'Mr River'. He smiled to Williams and confided,

-I couldn't think of a human surname for myself when I was saved. All I could see was the river where I was pulled from. How was your own day?

Doctor Williams looking at the fallen angel opening his bedroom door for the first time was astonished by his question, he stepped aside and demanded,

-Would you even care if I told you how my day went?

Holding the door, Raphael answered with sincerity,

-I would, yes. William, I am not an archangel any longer. I am not who I was any longer. I will serve you and I will serve you right, with care and diligence. I am determined to make my amends to you. Please do enter before me.

Doctor Williams stepped into the room telling the fallen angel a vague reply,

-I was here and there and almost everywhere at the same time. I am still here and there. It was a rather busy day but it is always rather busy when you work for the Master of all angels. Here, check your bedroom. Tell me if you want any change done to it.

A speechless Raphael followed the old angel, and looked around the room. It was more than just a bedroom. He came straight back by the side of Williams, held his hand briefly with emotion and simply said,

-Thank you.

Doctor Williams smiled to him and commented,

-You are most welcomed. That room suffered from humidity before but Sebastien solved that by repairing the guttering outside a few days ago. Because there was no fire place, I got you a little iron cast burner to keep your bedroom warm. On the top, you have a little copper kettle, which you can use to boil some water for either tea or coffee. In that corner, you have a desk and a standing bookshelf. In there you will find some books from Rousseau, Diderot, Voltaire and Goethe, in case you want to know what humans have been up to this last hundred years. If you want to read more, feel free to ask me, I will provide for whatever you fancy reading. In the other corner of the room you have a little gueridon and a cosy armchair to either rest, read or drink whatever you want.

Raphael went to the leather armchair and tried it looking at a decorated cushion upon it. Embroidered were two blue fish their heads going either way and amongst their blue scales, each had a silver R. Williams explained,

-Like your satchel, the two letters stands for Raphael River but if you touch the letters we will come forward. The R from the top fish will call either the Master of all angels or his son. The R from the bottom fish will call me. It is a magical cushion.

Going to sit on one of the two decorated stool by the little table and facing the fallen angel, Williams told,

-Raphael, you must feel free to conjure us at anytime. If you feel the need to either talk or just even chat when you feel out of place or lonely, we will come to you. If you had a bad dream or had a really bad day, we will be here to comfort you. You are not alone, the angels know your human plight and we will help you through it all. Now, if you have two stools along with your armchair around that table, it is because I want you to invite people. You can start by inviting the two little boys of Sebastien for example, Mr Dunn which you want to task to look after your men in the woods, Callum, Henry or Ted, or why not Mrs Brown who lives for the moment on the same floor of this old house like you? She didn't come to have dinner with the family tonight. She lost everything but her cat. However she went to pay a visit today to the young angel Francis who did save her cat on the night of the fire. You could invite them both. Consider it as your first task from me: reach out to people and invite them in your personal space. I give you two weeks to get it done. But it will not be a done and dusted task, it will be a done and carry on if you achieve that small mission by the due date.

For Raphael who was not highly sociable indeed it was a mission but he could see himself achieve it with flying colours. He asked,

-But what can I offer them?

With a small sigh the old angel replied,

-First and foremost: your time which is a very valuable commodity in human terms. Second: your conversation. For example Mrs Brown could do with opening up a little. So does the little Tobias. Third: your friendship, if you chose to do so to any you invite. I know Callum will feel acutely the departure of his best friend Robert for a few months. Henry already warned me about it. Callum is a very good angel which society you may appreciate and learn from. In a reciprocal manner he may learn from you, not that I am calling you an old dog of a former archangel.

While Raphael giggled, Williams continued,

-Here, behind you, this is my fourth: Tea or coffee with biscuits. In this Japanese tea cabinet, you will find everything you need. Open that door, you will have your porcelain tea set for three. I kept it simple: blue and white with the fish theme who are jumping above the waves. This door opens to your coffee set for three, all is silver plated. The little door in the middle, this is your sugar pot for the two sets. Porcelain white and blue, the fish above the waves and a silver lid with your initials R and R. It is filled with brown sugar already. Here, on the bottom you will find a bag of coffee beans of good quality, and next to it a grinder. On the other side, you have tea leaves of different kind on different trays, and a little silver strainer in that drawer. The bottom middle door opens to a jar of biscuits matching the sugar pot. It is filled with Brandy Snaps biscuits. You can be lavish and fill those biscuits with cream to indulge your guests. So here you are all kitted out.

An amazed and fairly impressed Raphael simply said,

-I love it. I love all of it. The bed, the picture on the wall, everything. I love it all. Thank you. Thank you so much. How can I thank you enough?

The old angel told with compassion,

-Be an angel again.

#

The fallen angel gave a look around his bedroom, finding other details, like the wicker basket and cushion for a large dog, and a fish bowl with two colourful goldfish in it on a shelf. Williams told him before disappearing,

-Why don't you get acquainted with your room a little and come downstairs once changed? You have a cleaning bowl and jug on that chest of draw and some soap. In that wardrobe, you will find some outfits and, at the bottom, some shoes which are not muddy by the quarry and some slippers. Now, do not be afraid to ask me for anything, anything whatsoever, from the trivial to the important. However there is one thing the Master will not let you do for the time being, which is shaving yourself. He will do that for you. It is a question of trust which you need to gather from him. He is worried that you might do something stupid to yourself. So I will repeat, I am a providing angel for the army of Sebastien. He is homing you therefore it is more than likely that you will become one of his angelic soldiers so just ask me anything like them. See you downstairs in a few minutes.

Once alone with Ludwig the dog in his bedroom Raphael said,

-Looks like you are going to tag along with me, Ludwig.

Your basket is right here. I will not be too long.

Fifteen minutes later, Raphael made his way downstairs followed by the rottweiler. He entered the drawing room and was happy to see Ivy standing there in her pretty red dress welcoming Georgia Marlow. Doctor Williams in an affable manner invited him,

-Come and join us. We are going to teach the children how to play cards.

Margot presented the chair next to her to him,

-Sit here Raphael, you can help me. I don't know a thing.

Tobias between her and Jack said shyly,

-Me, too.

The fallen angel taking the deck of card in the middle of the table presented the cards to the children and disposed them into suites. Patiently, he showed them every card but he focused on Tobias, teaching him how to recognise numbers and on how to count up to ten. Soon the chatting Ivy and Georgia sat at the table still talking about the wedding to come of Georgia. Doctor Williams sat by his future wife and informed Raphael,

-The Lord and Henry went to pay a visit to a certain Peter O'Neil. They will join us later. Ted is gone to bed. He is still rather poorly to be honest from the incubus attack we had. The Master and Sebastien are in the kitchen preparing some mulled wine for all of us and some cranberry juice for the children. Mrs Brown declined to play with us.

The fallen angel proposed,

-Maybe I can bring her glass of mulled wine to her bedroom?

Sebastien entering the room holding a tray with a large jug and glasses, followed by his father carrying another tray with another jug, glasses, biscuits and a slice of apple pie disapproved,

-With the rottweiler following you everywhere, Raphael, I can only discourage you to do so.

Raguel smirked with irony as he commented,

-Oh yes, because the cat of Mrs Brown is lethal when it sees Ludwig apparently. Maybe, it is a good idea to send Raphael up there after all.

Putting his tray down, Sebastien scolded,

-Father! If I am not allowed to tease in my own house, I don't think you should do so, grandpa Rag.

Williams, his eyes to the sky, in false desperation, ordered,

-Raphael, it is a nice gesture. Go to her room with a glass and a couple of biscuits. I am sure she will appreciate it. I will keep the dog by me.

Pouring a glass of mulled and putting it on a small silver tray, he found on a small table, the fallen angel stated,

-I don't mind being clawed, Doctor Williams. It is quite alright. I like having Ludwig by me. I am talking to him like if he had always been my friend.

The Master told firmly,

-Raphael, the dog will stay downstairs with us. Mrs Brown will not bite you. She is an elderly woman not a demon. Mighty, go with him.

His son and Raphael obeyed and as they left the drawing room, Raguel served everyone, Ivy, Georgia, Amelia, and Margot first. He started the conversation in a jovial manner,

-One thing is for sure I am going to be very happy to direct your wedding, Miss Marlow, or can I call you Georgia? My William is almost my grandson. He has been created by my eldest son Gael, who is no longer with us unfortunately. So you, inevitably, will become part of my family, just like Ivy and Amelia are. Ivy for being the wife of my son and Amelia for being the one of my younger brother.

The good Georgia turned her warm glass in her hands and said with her deep honesty,

-Of course you can call me Georgia. Will you let me call you grandpa Rag in return?

The Master of all angels gave a desperate glance at Ivy who had created this name for him for her children in the first place. He smiled irresistibly, knowing that he would be called that way for years to come. He also knew that his son will find great pleasure to tease him and call him the old Rag every now and then, which sounded like an old carpet. Despite it all, Raguel agreed with good spirit,

-Yes, you can. You can also use my name, Raguel. I know it is too early to ask but I will anyhow, do you want to get married in Boston or here in Wilton Town? It goes without saying that both have their pros and cons.

Georgia replied with her characteristic clarity of views,

-It is preferable if the wedding happens in Wilton Town. It will be intimate, amongst friends and family and not grand amongst strangers in Boston. I am also thinking for the safety of my future husband who has been the witness of a dual not so long ago. I rather prefer us to have a very understated wedding rather than one that could bring the attention of the gangs of Boston to him.

Holding her hand with tenderness, the old William added to the attention of his Master,

-In Boston, she will behave like she is my maid and not my wife to protect her from being abducted and have her fingers cut one by one. So yes, it will be a small and private wedding here in Wilton Town. Whenever the gang situation is over and resolved in Boston, then and only then, we will declare that we are husband and wife. It is just for protecting one another. I haven't got Sebastien any longer under my roof and I can't leave my hospital unattended.

Sitting by his brother, Raguel told,

-I will deploy two angels for your protection in Boston. I know that you love the home you made in Boston dearly, but would you consider having one in Wilton Town as well, just for the sake of your wife, so she could be protected until we resolved the situation in Boston?

Doctor Williams answered with uncertainty,

-Of course I would but how?

Springing from the body of Doctor Valdi came the ghost of Abraham Wilton-Cough. He bowed and took his tall hat off then replied,

-I know how.

Raguel smiled at the physical appearance of Wilton-Cough, for him, now, it was like seeing a good genie coming out of an oil lamp. He invited,

-Abraham, go and take a seat by my servant and explain yourself.

Doing so an eager Wilton-Cough announced his solution to the dilemma,

-Master, I showed you the map of the outskirts of Wilton Town belonging back to my family, where we will build a hospital in the near future. There is a very large field, the one, where Henry was shot in his wing from which can be bought by Doctor Williams. It is only at a walking distance from the hotel which would be extremely convenient for Georgia to stay in contact with Mrs Odell and the little Mina, which she does consider as her family. Now, this plot would be very near to the hospital. I heard Doctor Williams has been an apothecary in his past life as well as a physician and a Doctor. He could open the first pharmacy of Wilton Town there. Not only will it help to protect his wife to have a home here, it will help the inhabitants of the town to get medicine. The plot is also large enough to grow medicinal herbs. If we build a multi storey house, we can save some land for cultivation. A basement that will be cool enough to store the goods, above a shop, a small office and maybe a little consultation room like in the clinic in town, then upstairs, the lodgings. On the first floor, of course, a kitchen, a drawing room and a dining room and maybe a large balcony or terrace. Somewhere where you could put a panel with the name of your shop or simply 'Chemist', but also somewhere where the couple can have breakfast together on warm days and grow more of those useful plants. On the second floor could be their bedroom, a bathroom and a little snug and we could build a third floor with a laboratory, another store room and a guest room.

The Master commented,

-This sounds like a plan. Submit the drawing to my William or better work with him to draw it with his future wife tomorrow before you leave with Vincent the day after.

The idea pleased Georgia greatly as she said,

--I would love a pied à Terre in Wilton Town. Not that I do not like Boston, for one one thing, I love the sea but to be close to Whilhelmina and Mina will mean a great deal to me. I am good at concocting things so you can show me how to prepare medicine and unguents for our shop. Give me a recipe and I will do wonders.

If her enthusiasm pleased Doctor Williams, it made Ivy sigh deeply. Raguel proposed to the young woman,

-Shall we walk Killy together, Ivy, in the back garden?

She accepted willingly and apologised saying that she did forget about the needs of the poorly dog. She went to fetch him and followed her father in law. In the hallway, Raguel told her in a soft way,

-I can feel you are still upset. Let's walk together and you can tell me all about it.

Descending from the stairs, Sebastien who was followed by Raphael, asked,

-Are you going somewhere?

His father replied,

-Ivy and I are going to walk the dog in the backyard. How is Mrs Brown?

Sebastien taking the large shawl of his wife from the coat hooks and fastening it upon her answered,

-She accepted the mulled wine and the biscuits. We talked to her a little. Raphael invited her to have tea in his room tomorrow evening. He said he will try to invite Francis as well, but it all depended on that young angel being better. But she accepted the invite nonetheless. I think Raphael is right, that we do need to find out what she likes as well as giving her time to process that she lost everything. But she appreciated us visiting her. Little Bit, I know you do worry about her, but she will come to term with her loss and we will be building her a beautiful home to replace her old one.

Raguel commented,

-Good. Please, make sure the guests are entertained in our absence. By the way, Wilton-Cough, our favourite ghost, decided to make a physical appearance. He is with us tonight. He means to help as always so just make him feel welcomed. I can feel he is still extremely tired from his hell spell when he protected Amelia but he wanted to help Doctor Williams and Georgia Marlow for their future home. I will tell you all later.

The Master of all angels was about to step outside with Ivy when Raphael presented a plant with a nice potential root.

The fallen angel said in a shy way,

-Mrs Cotton, please accept this, it is to thank you for your delicious apple and plum compote. It was the highlight of my day. It is a variegated ivy. It will grow well on your stone walls in the back garden and decorate them.

The young woman thanked him before going outside holding the plant with care. Alone walking side by side Raguel asked kindly,

-How are you holding up, Ivy? Do you know that I was very concerned about you?

Gliding one of her arms within the one of her father in law, Ivy offered him a sheepish smile with her answer,

-Grandpa Rag, you shouldn't worry for me like that. But I am really sorry to you all. When I cry, I usually cry in my little corner away from everyone to not upset anyone. But it had the opposite effect which I am ashamed off.

Tapping her hand on his arm with kindness, Raguel told,

-Don't be ashamed, but as I am your 'Grandpa Rag', next time, come to me, and cry on my shoulder, you will not upset me, I will only endeavour to appease and comfort you. Know that I am here for you. In my heart you are my daughter. Did my son apologise properly to you?

They arrived in the back garden, sat on the bench. Killy waging his tail ran as much as he could around. Turning the ivy within her hands, Ivy replied,

-He did. He was really sorry. I don't think he is used to me locking myself up to my bedroom, well our bedroom now, when I cry. I used to do that at dad's home because I didn't want my father to see when I was sad. I always get over things eventually and come out when I am composed once more.

Raguel confided firmly,

-My dear young Lady, I didn't like seeing you upset for one bit, it pained me. If there is any next time, come and talk to me straight away. I will take you to another room where we can have a heart to heart conversation privately about it. Consider me as your confident from now on. Are we agreeing on this point?

Ivy smiled and touched his hand while she confirmed,

-We are and I thank you for it.

A satisfied angel commented,

-Good, now, my son is not always right. It would be a fallacy to believe so. But he can impose upon people if you give him the leeway to do so. I am not agreeing with him constantly. You must have noticed that we do bicker quite a fair bit. We have done so for centuries, believe me. But he will always be my son and I will always love him, and I know I will always have his filial love. For you, I noticed that you didn't dare to answer back to him, you just folded, retreated, broken hearted by his comments. But you had ground enough to reply to him on this occasion, I would have protected you and also Margot would have, if she did dare to admit in front of him her own little mistake. He would have backed off, trust me. Anyhow you saw me telling him off before you left, did you?

The young woman nodded positively so Raguel continued,

-He heard from me how well you did all afternoon. Look, you did a very nice compote which will give the children delight over the winter months. Your soup was a success and your apple pie was delicious. So you had three out of four nailed, so you mustn't give up learning to cook for a genuine mistake and the fuss of a Gallic angel about it.

This made Ivy giggle, her father in law tugged her hand when he enjoined her,

-Let's plant this ivy, my dear Ivy. Where do you want to put it? You see Raphael enjoyed your compote so much, he brought you a token of his appreciation in his satchel. I am thinking of you as well and I really do not want you to feel bad whatsoever. You are building a family with my son and there will be bad times and good times, but we always must build strength on the good times. Did I tell you about Sebastien's mother?

They planted the ivy together as Raguel told her ancient stories of his own family. They went back arm in arm back to the house minutes later and Ivy was smiling again and this time surely. Her father in law was so caring that before she stepped back in she thanked him. Raguel was satisfied enough that the young wife of his son had regained her spirits.

Entering the drawing room, they found Amelia in a vivid conversation about weddings with Georgia, Williams already drawing plans for his Wilton Town new home with Abraham

Wilton-Cough, Sebastien and Doctor Valdi were talking about the case of Mr Dunn in a very medical manner worried about the implication the injury of the man would have upon his life while Raphael was teaching the children how to play with cards.

The fallen angel was the first to notice the presence of the Master back in the drawing room. He welcomed him by announcing,

-Master, Tobias knows how to count up until ten! Show him, Toby.

The shy boy put his little fingers up one after the other reciting what he had just learnt,

-One, two, three, fo-four, five, six, seven, then I don't remember, then nine and ten.

Ivy smiled and went to kiss Toby on his forehead, approving,

-Well done, that's my boy! The missing number is eight. You deserve one more of those nice biscuits that your Pa did.

She gave a glance at Sebastien across the table who smiled back at her, he presented a chair by his side asking,

-Will you take a seat by me my Little Bit? I kept you a chair.

Willingly she went and took a seat by her husband whilst Raguel ordered,

-Let's play. Raphael, sit next to me, so I can ensure you are not cheating.

The fallen angel obeyed but complained,

-I do not cheat!

However Raguel retorted,

-Old habits die hard, same as lies it seems.

Raphael giggled knowing he would not win a verbal fight with the angel of justice. It was lost in advance as he couldn't even remember the number of times he cheated people as well as angels in his eternal life as an archangel. It was so numerous, that he could only admit defeat and just sighed deeply.

Within half an hour it was clear who was winning. It was Ivy who had retrieved her smile. She was also helping all her adopted children to play and to play well. Amelia folded and lost, soon afterwards. Raphael followed suit but he was given the slice of apple pie which Raguel said he had kept for him to celebrate his first human working day. For the fallen angel it was something he didn't expect and somehow it mellowed him and rendered him totally quiet. He knew he was amongst major angels, and to be just sitting by them still moved him. He listened with some fascination at the conversation which was lead mainly by Raguel who clearly wanted to know better the future wife of his old servant. Georgia who usually kept herself for herself was still in the happy mood of 'I am getting married' therefore she submitted herself to the inquisition of the Master of all angels willingly. If the story of Georgia was not as extraordinaire as the one of Doctor Williams, it moved somewhat people around the table that she had been abandoned twice in her life, once as a baby and once as a eight year old girl.

Doctor Williams recounted stories of his life in Egypt as a physician, architect and minister back in the ancient days where he helped creating the pyramids. It was mainly aimed at the children around the table who were fascinated by them. He spoke of crocodiles in the Nile having tears watching their preys. He told how he did meet Alexander the Great and had to attend to him when Alexander suffered from a fever. He described in details the great library of Alexandria. If Tobias was fascinated by crocodiles and how they could drag an entire animal under water to eat it, Margot took a morbid interest in the process of mummification which Williams confessed he had performed many times in his past lives. As for Jack, he took his opportunity to ask lots of pertinent questions to the brilliantly knowledgeable angel he had before him.

Abraham Wilton-Cough joined in the conversation about Egypt and told all about his infamous fall from a running camel to the great hilarity of the children. When Tobias showed his first signs of tiredness, Sebastien stood up, and ruled pointing at the clock on the mantle piece,

-It is well gone passed your bedtime, children. It is after ten. Toby, Jack, Margot say goodnight to everybody. I will put you to bed.

If Tobias and Jack obeyed, Margot contested,

-But I haven't lost the game yet! Can I stay?

Coming by her chair Sebastien looked at her cards then stated,

-You have a losing hand, Margot. It is not worth staying and getting more tired for it. Take a biscuit and a glass of juice and you can rest reading in bed for one more hour. Don't forget that you need a good night sleep because you are working at Mr Berry's farm tomorrow, keeping Margot's word who is as good as anyone else's. Ma will check on you in an hour.

Feeling defeated Margot stood up and said her goodnight too and followed Sebastien who was holding the hands of Jack and Tobias. He took the children upstairs. In the drawing room the game and conversation carried on and Raguel probed Georgia again,

-Will you plan on having children?

This made the good Georgia almost choked on her mulled wine as she replied,

-I am too old to have children.

The Master corrected her,

-Not any longer since you became an eternal Being.

Nodding her acknowledgement, Georgia confided,

-Your son and daughter in law are adopting children and I am considering doing the same thing with Doctor Williams if he wants to do so. When I came back from my little trip to Boston, I saw all the victims that you found in Amos's farm at the hotel. My heart feels so sorry for one little boy missing half his arm, half his leg and his tongue. He is just about five.

Raguel smiled with compassion as he said,

-You are talking about the little Meat.

An offended Wilton-Cough argued,

-Don't call him that. No, the boy with no name is now Mitchell.

Smirking Raguel retorted,

-Agreed only if you call this time your bedtime for the ghost that you are.

Abraham, still on his high horse of a temper, told in a firm reply,

-By respect for that poor boy I will, but it will be only for tonight, and you have to meet me half way through there, by giving me the promise that you will call him Mitchell from now on forever.

The Master went to shake the hand of the ghost commenting,

-It is a hard bargain but I will accept it, Abraham, with pleasure because you need to rest. Also I need you to show, on the ground, the plot to acquire by Doctor Williams, to him and Georgia tomorrow. It has to be done before your departure the day after tomorrow. There are the deeds for the lands for my son and my Williams that you have to do as well, because you are the most qualified to do them for your son to sign. So it will be a busy day for you my dear ghost tomorrow.

Abraham, lifting his top hat, bowed to the Master before asking,

-Did you see the plots of land reserved for your son? Are they to your liking?

A smiling Raguel answered,

-According to Henry they are more than fine. I will confess to you something, which I thought I would never say, I trust you, Abraham. If on that one only, I do trust you. I will go and see the land tomorrow with Ivy, Henry and the children.

Wilton-Cough bowed again before disappearing within Doctor Valdi who stated,

-That is a ghost who badly needed some energy back. I can feel him and I can feel it.

His older brother winked at him as he commented,

-I knew he needed a rest by his aura depleting fast. But he did entertain us with his Egyptian adventure with his aunt Jo. The children couldn't stop laughing.

Ivy putting her cards down with a bright smile claimed,

-I win!

Everyone who was still not out of the game already

checked their own hands. One after the other they admitted their losses. Ivy was cheered. Doctor Williams soon announced that he needed to walk Georgia back to the hotel and departed with her. Sebastien came back to the drawing room only to state,

-I missed something!

His father told,

-Yes, the end of the game: your Little Bit did win hands down like you predicted. Do you want to prepare us some tea, my Mighty?

Sebastien bowed to his father and left the room then Raguel turned to his younger brother,

-Are you going to the hotel as well or staying with us tonight, because you can? There are no bedrooms left to spare but we have the sofa, and it is a warm room.

Before Doctor Valdi could answer, Raphael proposed,

-There is my bedroom, Master. Mrs Valdi can sleep in the bed and there is a comfortable armchair for Doctor Valdi and my blanket. Doctor Williams put an iron cast stove there so it is warm too. I can sleep on the sofa.

The Master felt the eagerness of the fallen angel so he ventured,

-Or there is his bedroom.

Valdi looked at the pregnant Amelia and knowing how busy was the hotel with all the victims of Amos's farm and the families who had lost their houses to the fire, he accepted but somewhat reluctantly. Raphael invited immediately,

-I must walk Ludwig. Would you do me the favour to walk him with me, Doctor Valdi? I have something important to tell you.

Vincent agreed despite cringing at the entire idea. He had sat at a table where Raphael was the entire evening but had noticed his humble demeanour throughout. So he went to walk the dog with the fallen angel. The night was clear. The moon was bright and the path by the cemetery was rather dark. They walked there very silently for a few minutes, then an impatient Valdi demanded,

-What have you got to say to me? Let us be clear, I will

never enjoy your company.

This made Raphael sigh deeply as he replied,

-I do understand. I am not asking you for your forgiveness, but I need you and want you to know that I am truly sorry for what I did or ever wanted to do or said to you in the past.

A hot headed Vincent kicked a stone in the path before he announced,

-Like wanting to kill me. I am sorry but your poor apologies are not accepted. Thank you for doing them and giving your bed to my wife tonight but that is all you will get from me. If the dog has done what he needed to do and you are done with saying sorry, let us not waste time at trying to make friend with each other which will not happen and go back in.

All of a sudden the dog stood still, his ears perked up and Raphael warned in a low voice,

-There is someone in the cemetery. Let's go back in quickly. I can sense who it is. Someone in the house is in danger. If I was an angel I will know straight away. Come quick, and stay low.

Valdi confided as he moved along the fallen angel,

-I wish I could warn my brother, but telepathy is still something I am struggling with.

Raphael reassured,

-It will come to you with experience. Don't beat yourself up for it. Here, I can see him. Can you see him? I think this is the father of Margot. Can you recognise him? He may have come to get her.

Vincent took a good glance through the iron railing and scarce bushes and said,

-It is that bastard. I thought he would be out of the way for a while.

Giving him a dark look, Raphael corrected him in a secretive voice,

-You would be wrong. Cambion are strong and mend themselves fast. This is the offspring of a demon created by

Lucifer. Look, I need you to run as fast as you can back to the house without being seen, warn the Master and Sebastien. I will challenge our intruder with the dog to give you some time. Margot will need to be protected. Tell them that. They will need to hide all the children because a demon or a half demon can kill everyone in his path to get to his own child. They are in danger, right here, right now. Go!

Valdi went without further a do using his wings to go faster. While Raphael went with the dog back inside the cemetery by the crooked little rusty gate as silently as they could. They made their approach as the cambion had reached the back garden. Ludwig rushed to tackle Cork as he tried to climb the wall of the presbytery. The part of the wall of the presbytery was right bellow the window of the bedroom of the young Margot. Raphael then knew he was right all along about his suspicions. He went all in and threw the cambion off the wall to the ground. The dog attacked Cork biting his arm to the blood. While Raphael took his chance to try to render the cambion unconscious but Cork single handedly attempted to strangle him. In a bad spot, Raphael remembered Theo's kick to save a situation. He delivered a hard kick in the balls of the cambion who released his neck.

Trying to grasp his breath, Raphael saw the dog being handled in such manner that he was fearing for his life so he went back in and punched the cambion so strongly that Cork ended up back on the ground. He vociferated angrily,

-What are you here for, Cork?

The cambion replied that he did want his daughter back. To which Raphael replied ponding Cork,

-To do what with her? Do you want to tell me? To do what with her? The poor thing miscarried again, you bastard! As long as I am alive you are not touching her ever again. Never, do you understand me, never!

The half demon answered with a smirk, his hand suddenly becoming full of claws,

-Then I just have to kill you.

It was a very rough fight on the ground but then Henry appeared along with the Master, he gave a knife to Raphael while Raguel intervened to save his servant. The fallen angel managed to stab the cambion through his heart in the heat of the moment. Cork finally gave his last breath. Raguel pulled Raphael from underneath the dying cambion. Raphael confided in the arms of Raguel,

-I did my best. He didn't enter the house and harmed any of your family.

Henry told,

-We have to bring him in. He is bleeding badly. He needs immediate attention.

Raguel lifted the fallen angel who slowly lost consciousness in his arms and he could see how damaged Raphael was. He deposited him with care upon the kitchen table soon afterwards. Doctor Valdi was immediately called to the rescue and Ivy came forward to help out. The Master ordered,

-Henry, get my son and Williams. Please, as fast as you can.

The young angel obeyed and left the room while Vincent and the Master uncovered the chest of Raphael. Valdi gave a deep sigh as he stated,

-He needs a lot of attention. The puncture points are deep, it is clear to see.

Raguel commented,

-The cambion used claws at the last struggle.

Valdi sternly told,

-Then it could mean that we have a potentially poisoned fallen angel. Mrs Cotton, I need hot water. Call my wife, she will help as a nurse. Raguel, retrieve one of the claws of the cambion and check that he is not missing one or more. I need to open Raphael up and fast because he is turning rapidly grey.

Ivy brought her medical bag to Valdi then followed the rest of his orders. When the Master came back into the kitchen, he announced,

-Cork is definitely dead but he is missing two claws. Here is one from his hand.

Doctor Williams appeared in the room asking,

-What happened?

But Vincent ordered,

-Williams, I need a counter poison as fast as you can do one. We are losing Raphael fast. He has two poisoned claws inside him. He is only human. Raguel, give him the claw.

Doctor sensed the urgency and worked on a counter poison immediately. Amelia was soon by the stove keeping surgery tools sterilised and clean which she handed to her husband who started operating on Raphael with Ivy. A few minutes later, Sebastien arrived saying,

-The children are all back in bed. Margot is in quite a state. Father, you have a way to deal with her. Please go to her. She knows something did happen. We have got to tell her that her father died tonight. Valdi, how is Raphael doing?

Vincent replied as Raguel rushed upstairs to the bedroom of Margot,

-Think of the worse and you will be close to it: Multiple puncture points with probably poisoned claws. Two claws are embedded in him. We need to find them fast. My educated guess would be his vital organs. He has a deep puncture by his right lung and another one by his left one. I am sure we will find the claws of the cambion there.

Washing his hands quickly, Sebastien went to help in the operation under way. Meanwhile a frightened Margot was found by Raguel under her bed. He pulled her gently out of her hiding place and cradled her in his arms. He comforted her,

-Margot, you are safe now. You mustn't fear your father any longer. He wanted to take you. He was climbing the wall to reach your bedroom. But Raphael managed to stop him. A fight ensued, a big fight. I must tell you that your father is no longer with us but that Raphael may also not make it tonight.

Marguerite cried thoroughly upon his shoulder. As she sobbed, she said,

-My father was bad, very, very bad. I was so scared of him. I will not miss him. But I will always miss my mum he killed.

It took a while for her to stop crying and a lot of reassurance from Raguel to tell her that it was all over and that she was now completely safe before Margot finally felled asleep in his arms. He put her in her bed with care, then went downstairs. A good couple of hours had passed since he went upstairs. Worried, he went to the kitchen. A pale Raphael was still on the kitchen table. The Master demanded,

-How is he doing? Will he make it? Who is coming with me if he is going to hell to retrieve him?

Doctor Williams who was cleaning his own hands with hot water over a metal bowl replied,

-Raphael is still breathing, Master. We managed to retrieve the two claws inside him. It is too early to say if he will survive or not.

Finishing stitching the chest of Raphael with Sebastien, Valdi gave his opinion to his brother,

-I think he will make it. Although he is human, we acted in time. We injected the counter poison straight into his veins. Since his skin colour has improved for the better but also his body temperature. If he take a turn for the worst, I will come with you, but I don't think it will be necessary.

Sebastien agreed,

-I am of the same opinion as Vincent. Raphael has improved under our hands not declined. But if needs be, you know you can always count on me, father. How is Margot doing?

Coming closer to the injured Raphael, Raguel replied,

-She was very distraught. It took time for her to finally cease to cry, cease to be scared and just to fall asleep. She can't possibly work at Mr Berry's farm tomorrow. I will keep her by my side.

Valdi commented,

-That will be for the best. Margot looks strong, seems strong but she went through a lot. It will take its toll upon her. We are talking about a girl who has been raped, miscarried twice, whose mother has been killed, whose little brother died untimely to illness. Now, she has lost her brutal father which is for the best but it will dawn upon her that she is now an orphan with no ties to her past. You will need to get her grounded into this new adoptive family fast.

Ivy who was cleaning the chest of Raphael with great care could only agree,

-Sure, we will do so. She has started calling me 'Ma' this morning. I didn't expect her to do so but she asked me if she could and I said yes. It was a small step but it is a good step in

my view. I have a good bond with her so far and she listens to
grandpa Rag but she calls him occasionally Mr the angel of
justice, then as we have seen she does what she is told to do by
Sebastien. Is Henry back with the bandages?

Smiling to her from the doorway of the kitchen, the
Messenger answered,

-Yes, Ma'am. I have everything you ordered me to get
from the clinic.

Ivy couldn't help saying,

-Henry, you are an angel! Raphael's chest is ready to be
bandaged. Oh! Oh! He is pressing my fingers! Sebastien, he is
coming back to us! Raphael is regaining consciousness.

Raguel immediately took the other hand of the fallen
angel and when he felt some pressure on his own fingers, he
smiled with relief and stated,

-He is definitely still with us. Let us hope for the better.

With great struggle, he got an answer from Raphael
himself. It was feeble and almost inaudible but it was there,

-For the better, Master.

Raguel ordered,

-Let's wrap him up. Put him in my bedroom for the night,
I will monitor him with Williams.

Doctor Valdi put the bandages with Ivy being careful
and he instructed Sebastien,

-As Raphael lives in your home keep a very good eye
on him especially for any signs of infection, internal or external.
Change his bandages daily, check his scars and stitches on his
torso. Keep him clean. But if he goes outside, like I have seen
him walking the dog, make sure he has enough layers to stay
warm. You don't want him to catch an illness of the lungs right at
this moment in time because he will struggle to fight it. Be
worried at any signs of fever. Keep giving him the anti-poison at
least twice daily for a good couple of weeks.

Soon Sebastien put Raphael upstairs with the help of
his father. Ivy and Amelia tidied the kitchen with the help of
Doctor Valdi. Ivy asked still incredulous,

-So that nasty Cork is dead then?

Henry replied to her showing her from the kitchen window,

-And he is buried as we speak. Raguel decided that his grave will not be unmarked for the sake of his daughter and because the cambion did save people from a sinking ship back in the days. However, Cork will not be brought back to the living. The ceremony the angels are doing around him are turning him to ashes of a certain type. Lucifer can't claim the spirit of that cambion. The Master and his father claimed it.

Putting her hands on her hips, Ivy scolded,

-Henry, you are talking to me all angelic gibberish. You can just tell me the man is properly dead-dead and will never annoy our Margot any longer.

Henry giggled at her reaction and conceded,

-Alright the cambion is properly dead-dead. But I will have to remind you that being married to an archangel, having the Master of all angels for father in law, you will not escape the angelic gibberish, you will live in the midst of it. But when you get lost with some of our terms, come to me and I will break it down for your understanding. I was an animal spirit for a very long time and I had to pick up first to become human then to become an angel.

Ivy held his hand for a brief moment before she said,

-It will be most appreciated.

Soon all activities stopped in the house and everyone was sound asleep but one Raguel.

#

It was past midday when Valdi knocked on the bedroom door of Raguel. The Master welcomed him,

-Come in, Vincent.

Doctor Valdi saw Williams asleep on an armchair. In the bed was Raphael. Vincent asked,

-I am coming to check upon Raphael, and Amelia is carrying a tray with some lunch for all of you. How has our patient been doing during the night?

While Vincent put his medical bag by the bed, Raguel replied,

-Pretty well. He had a nightmare but no temperature to go along with it, however we had to maintain him so he would not hurt himself and fall off the bed Williams and I. He was reliving his fight with Cork which was quite something to witness in real life. I think if we didn't give him a weapon, Raphael would not be alive today. But he is pulling through nicely.

As they spoke, Raphael woke up and went in a panic as he saw the time on the clock upon the fire place. He claimed out loud,

-I need to go to work, I am late, I am extremely late.

The Master came to him and reassured,

-Calm down. There is no need to worry for today. Callum is replacing you at the quarry until you do get better. Now, Doctor Valdi and Williams, Ivy and Sebastien had to operate on you yesterday. It was touch and go but you made it. Do you remember anything?

An upset Raphael answered,

-Yes, the fight. How is the dog? Did he survive as well?

Raguel showed him Ludwig sitting by his bed and Raphael smiled. He made a great effort and went to stroke the head of the rottweiler. Vincent commented,

-At least we know Raphael can move. It is nice to see he appreciates dogs more than healing angels. Maybe it is a start in his humanisation.

This made his brother laugh then order,

-Raphael, Doctor Valdi is here to check you, stay still please.

The fallen angel stood up and came before Vincent Valdi with an apologetic smile as he corrected,

-Maybe it is a start. But before I did appreciate healing angels but probably too greatly to the point that I became jealous of them. Imagine if you were the first one being created then others were created and they prove to be better than you are. I must confess I hated Doctor Williams with a passion because it was clear he was brilliant. I wasn't made a teacher and mentor of healing angels, he was, and with good reason. It really got to my head and I acted like an imbecile, a stupid, jealous, angry, imbecile. I could have retrain myself, learn from him to get better instead. And here I am with no wings, no friends, a past villain and a foe with for only friend the good kind eyes of a dog. If I fail to be a good human, if I fail to earn my wings again, if I escape hell, my only wish would be to be reincarnated as a guard dog of the Master's household.

Doctor Valdi smirked and told with sarcasm,

-Tell me when I need to play the violin to accompany your litany. Come, you have been accepted in a decent household. The very angel you hated has been up all night looking after you. Look how exhausted he is. In my honest opinion, I think you have very forgiving friends all around you. I saw how the Master fought in hell along with his son in order to save the soul you sold in a stupid manner. I also saw him carry you unconscious indoors with great care for you to be seen to yesterday night. Now, just lift your arms as much as you can. I need to check your scars.

He turned to his wife briefly to order,

-You can deposit your tray on that console, my Darling. Would you fetch me the hot water I prepared for me to clean Raphael? It must be ready now.

Amelia obeyed and went away. When they were alone, Vincent started to remove the bandage surrounding the torso of Raphael with great care. He inspected the scars and was quite satisfied with them. He commented,

-Raguel, although he moved a fair bit in his sleep, he didn't damage his stitches. The redness is to be expected but I can't see any sign of infection. Your son will know when and how to remove those stitches. However if any complication arises on this case, do not hesitate to let me know and I will come despite the distance. Now, I can't stress enough that his bandages will need to be changed everyday and that his chest need to be cleaned daily with hot water. When Amelia comes back I will show you the process. Will you be his carer with Williams and Sebastien?

The Master replied firmly,

-I am his main carer. Doctor Williams has plenty to deal with at the moment with his hospital in Boston and all the victims from Amos's farm. Sebastien and also Ivy will help when they are not at the clinic working. When can Raphael work again at the quarry?

Valdi told looking at the eyes of Raphael,

-His mobility is good. He is just an overseer isn't it? To be honest with you, he didn't suffer from collapsed lungs. He can move about and you don't have to keep him in bed. However I would keep him around you for another day, tomorrow, just to observe how he is doing. You must remember that the claws found within him were poisonous. He is only human now, hence his constitution will be weaker. However with the anti poison, he has been responding very well so far. But make sure he drinks the counter poison twice a day for a couple of weeks to keep him with the living.

A worried fallen angel demanded,

-What poisoned claws? Did the cambion had poisoned claws?

When Amelia knocked, Raguel took the bowl of water from her and thanked her. Once alone again Raguel bringing the bowl by his younger brother explained to Raphael,

-It is a rather long story, my Maggot, but if you care to listen to it, I will let you in the know. Once upon a time the Creator created Archangels and the sixth one who happened to be his son, me, was put at the head of all of the previous ones and was able to create angels. Envy and jealousy flowed in the ranks of the other archangels. Lucifer who thought it was not fair caused great discontentment amongst the ranks of Archangels, with you being a prime prey to listen to his persuasive talks. Hence you later didn't cure me when I was wounded saving you from a battlefield. You kept me sick and ill despite your knowledge of how to make me recover. I had to go away to look after myself to prevent myself from dying. I returned to havoc to resolve and Lucifer became the first fallen angel. His jealousy of me didn't stop there. Still a servant of my father, he was put in charge of hell. And you will get the rest of the story later.

A disappointed Raphael retorted,

-That is not fair! What is the rest of the story? What is the link with the poisoned claws?

Ignoring him Raguel asked his brother,

-Show me.

Vincent demonstrated,

-You start by tapping gently the wounds. Your water is clean and hot at that point. Once this is done, you need to change the cloth you are using and do the rest of the torso finishing by the armpits. For the rest you do not need to tap, you can scrub him clean.

Waking up Doctor Williams looked around the room and saw Raphael, up and being attended to, he vented,

-I napped on duty!

The Master smiled as he commented,

-I did let you do so because I know you were exhausted. You have stretched all your physical apparitions of late. Here, Amelia Valdi brought us some lunch, eat then you must go with Wilton-Cough and your Georgia to check the plot of land for your new house. That will be a brand new chapter in your life my William.

Clapping his hands together the old angel said with glee,

-Indeed it will. How is our Raphael doing? I can see him standing up straight which is a good thing. He is fully awake which is another good thing. What do we have for lunch?

It was Valdi who responded to his queries,

-He is doing much better than I thought he would. He has been responding well to the counter poison. He is alert, talking, also can move. No infection are setting on his scars but this has to be monitored daily. So far so good, our patient is still alive. What we did to save him yesterday worked. For your lunch, I am afraid Williams we did what we could do with what we had. But the children enjoyed it. You have buttermilk pancakes, creamy spinach, poached eggs and some bacon. I hope you will appreciate it. I know it is not lobster like you can find in Boston but still you have to give us credit for the effort that went into it. By the way, I taught Ivy to do all of it. I made sure she used a pinch of nutmeg and not one of Cayenne pepper in the spinach. It is highly edible.

His answer made Raphael laugh but he held his chest in pain doing so. As fast as an arrow, the attention of Valdi was on his patient as he told him,

-Laughing and coughing will be painful for you for a little while, Raphael. Your lungs are damaged. They will recover with time. But you must avoid at all cost to catch a cold. If you ever see blood when you cough, you must tell Sebastien, Doctor Williams or the Master. If they tell me about it I will come straight away to make sure you get better. Now, here you are clean, with new bandages. I fastened them tighter this time around because your ribs are still on the mend. Your arms are getting better much faster. Keep exercising them, maybe not by killing a demon or a cambion everyday, but maybe by just using a knife and a fork to eat lunch. Let me put your new shirt back on.

The fallen angel was thankful. He smiled to Vincent,

-I thank you with all my heart for saving me. How can I show you my gratefulness?

Valdi replied,

-Keep being like that dog, who yesterday night alerted us of upcoming trouble, keep protecting the house of my nephew, like you did. Keep protecting my brother. And go and eat your lunch.

Vincent left the room before he had an answer, his medical bag in hand. Raguel called the fallen angel to his side,

-Come and eat with us. This is nice. You should try it while it is still warm.

Once Raphael took his seat by the small round table, he stated,

-So Valdi is the son of the Lord?

Raguel answered with a smirk,

-Yes, it was a big mistake for you to try to attack my younger brother. Now, eat. I am taking you this afternoon along with Ivy and the children to see some plots of land by the river.

Although he started to eat the fallen angel kept enquiring,

-Let me tell you that your brother reminds me of you and your father. Don't get me wrong when I say that because I imply it as a compliment, but one can feel you can't mess around with him. I had no idea that the Lord would have another child. He is a very strong minded one at that, like you. I remember him standing up to me that infamous night to protect Robert. I am so ashamed of what I said to him that day, even more now, having been saved by him on the kitchen table. He was so brave you know?

The Master replied,

-I know. When my son arrived in this town, he kept hearing how much Valdi was policing Wilton Town almost single handedly. Doctor Williams did guess when he had met Vincent for the first time that he was rather special as well. I remember him telling me that I would get a human angel during his first human life. I didn't believe him at first. But Valdi's name kept ringing into my ears on and off during the past twenty years. Then my father told me who Vincent was, only recently. I think it was one of his best kept secret of all time. The first time, I met Vincent, not knowing who he was exactly, he prevented me to touch something poisonous, strongly holding my hand. Not only did I feel his strength there and then, listen to the valid point he was making to protect me from doing a mistake, I just knew he was different from all of my angels then.

Doctor Williams who had finished his plate, and wished he had some more upon it, commented,

-Now this was nice, if Ivy can reproduce that recipe without supervision, you two are in for a treat in this household. I could see it working with salmon instead of bacon, or even lobster or crayfish. I must say Vincent did remind me a lot of Sebastien when I first met him. Yes, they both have the common points of cooking well, and to know how to look after themselves and others really well. What did strike me was that both had great aptitude to fight but also could save someone with their medical skills. It is like they were born fighters and healers and this made me question if Vincent Valdi was in fact an angel in formation. His uprightness was so impressive even as a young man of twenty. I kept writing to him throughout the years because I felt there was something in him, something different. In the end I was proved very right. It fills me with joy that he has been one of my medical students. But do not tell him that he surpasses me now in every way medically. He loves teasing just like Sebastien does. To keep up I have to visit the future now.

With a giggle but also a dark glance Raguel scolded his old servant,

-You do know what I am thinking of travelling to the future, my William. It is forever changing by our actions right now so you can not take it for granted. I will let your little time travelling adventures pass this time around because I need you to go on one for me. One of the vision angels of my son, Ted couldn't see a future for the young Margot. She seems to believe that she will pass away soon as well. I want you to tell me how relevant this is now that her father and grandfather are no longer with us because Raphael managed to kill them both. Is she safe for good? She miscarried this time around very early on and she is doing fine so the fear of losing her to child birth is over. But is there something else we need to worry about? I need you to answer those questions for me.

Williams stood up and bowed to the Master with his answer before he disappeared from the room,

-I will see to it, Master. I will try to provide you with some answer by dusk. The waistcoat on the bed is for Raphael. It is for him to have shown bravery once more yesterday night.

Finishing his own plate, Raguel went to the bed, lifting the waistcoat to consider it, he commented,

-It is a bit red but like Williams always does, he went all out for it. It has silver buttons with your initials and a lining made of rabbit fur which should keep your chest warm. He picked up on the advice of Doctor Valdi obviously.

Raphael stood up and started tidying the empty plates for everyone to put them on the tray. He quoted with a smile,

-Beggars can not be choosers. I will take whatever I am given, Master. Beside that I do happen to like red. Back in the days when I was a flamboyant archangel I did wear red very often. But when I think about it now it was probably style over substance because whenever I did look at you, you had that understated style, but you could deliver a blow like no one else.

Looking at the fallen angel who was making himself useful without being asked to, Raguel asked,

-How are your arms? Let's put your waistcoat on, your cape and go out with the family.

Coming to him the Raphael answered,

-Like Valdi said my arms are getting better. I can feel it. But I do not know if it is due by the magical satchel or by true physical healing.

The Master put the waistcoat on Raphael and fastened it as he said,

-Or it could be due to an angel who did hold your hand most of the night to thank you to have put your human life on the line to protect his family, one who has been creating healing angel by order of his father. Put your cape on and let's go.

Soon Henry was leading most of the family to the plots of land that Abraham Wilton-Cough showed to him the previous day. He was his usual chatty self, walking by Raguel who had offered his arm to Ivy and had given his hand to the very silent Margot. Behind them, Raphael followed with Jack and Tobias. The cheerful Henry told trying to bring a smile to everyone's faces, knowing of the trying night they all had,

-You will like what you will see. I promise you that. The good thing is that the land is at a short walking distance from the presbytery. It is highly convenient. One plot can be used as a garden and the other as a grazing field to keep animals. Wilton-Cough was very precise about it all.

Jack who held the hand of Tobias on one side and the hand of Raphael on the other asked with joy,

-So we will have more animals?

Turning to him Raguel replied,

-Yes, my child, this is the aim of the game. Doctor Valdi managed to sustain himself by having a garden and keeping hens. We will do the same to make sure our little family has some food on their plates every day and a little bit more.

Jack ran in front of the Master and demanded full of excitement,

-What animals are we going to get? I will look after them, you know I will.

Raguel took the boy in his arms and carried him for a distance as he explained,

-First, we need to have a lovely chicken coop, a sustainable one, just like Valdi has. Henry will get us some good hens for it. Depending on the size of the field which will be used by Wilton Fair to graze, we want to have a couple of dairy cows if it is possible and maybe, just maybe a couple of little goats and sheep. If we could have a pig pen and some ducks added to that, it will be very good. But one thing is sure we will have some rabbits but as they will be for the pot you mustn't get attached to them or named them. However, you, Tobias and Margot can give names for all the other animals we will have in the future.

Once Jack was back on the ground he asked,

-Can we have a goose too?

Henry answered,

-It is possible. There is a Canadian goose which can't fly at Amos's farm. He shot it but he didn't manage to find where it landed. I have been feeding that bird for the past few days. It will never fly again but she will give good eggs and her feathers could be used to fluff up our pillows.

Turning to Henry, Raguel ordered,

-Bring that bird to us tonight. We will keep it in our stable for the time being.

Happy Jack was bouncing all around Henry clapping his hands. The Messenger commented,

-It will have to be Jack's bird.

Raguel replied with a smile,

-Obviously. Jack, I entitle you to find her a name.

Tugging the hand of the very quiet Margot, Raguel asked her,

-Now, my Miss Margot, is there a particular animal that you would like?

The young girl almost woke up from her day daze. She looked at Raguel with her sad eyes. He repeated the question, knowing that she was lost in her thoughts for the past few minutes since they had left the presbytery,

-My dear Margot, every one of you are getting an animal to name and look after. Which one will be yours?

Marguerite with her usual seriousness said simply,

-I think I have already some animals. With my father being dead, with myself being the last of my family, they belong to me now. We had a dairy cow, not as good as the ones of Mr Berry. She is called 'Blanche'. It means the white one. She has just a speck of brown on her head otherwise she is completely white. I used to look after her. Can we retrieve her? Then we had some chicken, they don't have names. It is just a cockerel and three laying hens. We did have a dog, but my father killed him one day when the dog was barking too much and when he was too drunk. There is a cat, we used him to kill mice, but it is almost a stray cat, always outside or in the barn, never inside.

A sighing Raguel proposed,

-Will you come with me, Sebastien and Henry tonight? We will go and retrieve your animals.

Margot accepted just with a positive nod then Raguel added with a smile,

-You still can get a new animal and can name it. What will be your choice?

He managed to get a glimmer of a faint smile from Margot who pondered out loud,

-I would love to have a pony or a horse but I do not know how to ride whatsoever so it would be useless because I will just look at it. However it would be preferable for me to have another dairy cow. I am very good with them. Not only do I know how to deal with them, I can make some good cheese for all of us to enjoy. You know if I took employment at Mr Berry's farm it is also because if I can reach adulthood I would love to make dairy produce like butter and cheese and sell them. I am learning a lot with him. I already knew a fair bit. I can make a butter with garlic and chive which is awesome with roasted chicken and I know how to make a soft cheese which is very nice on toasted bread. Mr Berry has a recipe for hard cheese which I am learning step by step. I want to be 'une laitiére'.

Raguel could feel the will and the passion of the young Margot but he also remembered with great pain that his last wife, the mother of Sebastien died because she suffered by being crushed by cows. He sighed again not willing to turn away the aim of Margot for her own future by his own internal fears. He proposed,

-I think you can have both. One will not rule out the other. Sebastien is an expert with horses and he can teach you how to ride. We are looking to get some nice dairy cows so one could be yours. But you will have to promise me to be careful with those large animals.

Margot tugged his hand in agreement. Raguel then turned to Tobias who was now holding the hand of Raphael only to ask,

-Which animal do you want, Toby?

The little boy replied straight away,

-I want a crocodile.

Raphael and Ivy started to laugh while a still composed Raguel commented,

-It will be extremely hard to get especially since it can eat little boys. Let me rephrase the question, which farm animal do you want to look after a little and name?

Tobias thought long and hard before asking genuinely,

-What is a farm animal?

Feeling ever so sorry for the child who had problems with his memory, Raphael took him in his arms, carried him and told,

-Well they are animals who live on a farm. There are horses who are pulling carts or ploughs. There are cows who give milk and say 'Moo-Moo'. There are sheep who give wool and say 'Baa-baa'. There are goats who can give milk and cheese. There are chickens which can have eggs, like the poached eggs you had for breakfast. I think you, my little friend, should have a pony to learn how to ride along with your adopted sister.

Toby smiled as he was put back on the ground. He answered,

-I will have what he said.

Raguel asked in a gentle manner to exercise the memory of the little boy,

-And what did uncle Raph' said? Which animal should you have, Toby?

While Tobias thought hard to remember the name of the animal, Raphael felt slightly emotional by being called uncle Raph' by the Master. A tear ran freely upon his cheek as his eyes met the ones of Raguel. He dried it as fast as he could then tried to give himself a countenance by helping the child,

-It starts with 'po'. I will give you a clue, it looks like a horse but it is smaller. You have seen a horse because you went on Wilton Fair the stallion of Sebastien.

Toby finally asked with a bright smile,

-Was it pony? Can ask you what is a stallion?

Raphael tugged the hand of the boy as he replied,

-It is a pony, well done, Toby. Of course, you can ask me anything. A male horse is a stallion, a female horse is called a mare and a baby one is called a foal.

The ever so helping Messenger proposed,

-We can take the children to see and chose the ponies at Mr Hardy's. Being there, early this morning, I can tell you that he has very nice animals, Master. He treats them so well. Hardy mainly has horses, and I did get a very fine cart mare from him this morning for the quarry at a reasonable price with some respect. She is a beautiful grey Percheron called 'Snow White'. I saw her first thing in a field, and because she has such a good temperament, she was with seven ponies in that field, the only ones Mr Hardy has. There is a pretty white pony with a grey mane and tail and a white and brown one slightly smaller which is absolutely adorable. I am sure those two would be perfect for the children. Sebastien who is a superb handler of horses would need to come with us to chose them.

Raguel agreed with a nod as he said,

-Let's do that tomorrow morning, first thing after breakfast. Ivy, you will have to man the clinic up until Sebastien comes back. But Doctor Williams will be with you. As for you Raphael, you can chose either to come with me to Hardy's or to stay with Ivy and Williams and give them a hand at the clinic.

Henry pointed with some glee,

-Here is the first plot. It goes from that rough line of hazelnut trees to that hedge of blackberry bushes and from that path to the start of the forest in the distance. As you can see, it is huge. Wilton-Cough said this one would be perfect for grazing animals. Let me show you around.

Flicking his fingers the Master of all angels made wicker baskets appear on the arms of everyone to the great amazement of little Tobias. Then Raguel ordered,

-Raphael, go on that side and pick up as many hazelnuts as you can with the two boys. Ivy, Margot, you are in charge of picking the blackberries. We want enough to make some jam, at least a dozen pots for the winter months. Henry, show me around but most importantly tell me what did old

Abraham explain to you.

Everyone obeyed to him without any complaint. The fallen angel with his own basket in hand led the boys to the trees followed by Ludwig the rottweiler and Killy the little Fox terrier. Jack asked him,

-Are we picking up the chestnut too, uncle Raphael? Because there are a fair few on the ground.

Knowing how important it was to feed and establish the growing family of Sebastien in town, Raphael told,

-Yes, let's not leave anything we can eat behind. Look Toby, this is an hazelnut, and this is a chestnut. We want both in our baskets. If you look up this is an hazelnut tree and this one is a chestnut tree, which is larger. Do you remember how to count up to ten? I want you to put ten hazelnuts in your basket.

The emaciated little boy obliged him with great effort remembering the numbers with the help of Jack. The counting game started in full swing on their side. On the other side, Ivy was having a good conversation, a heart to heart one, with Margot. The young girl was grieving her father despite her fearing him when he was alive. She cried as she explained everything to Ivy in her own honest way. Ivy hugged her and told her about her own father who had died not so long ago, who was not perfect, but who was not all bad either. But the difference were that Margot's father wasn't a human. He was a dangerous cambion who had to be stopped before he did more harm. Margot understood but felt closer to Ivy than she ever did after that good talk.

Walking across the field, the Master was listening attentively to the Messenger who described the plot of land to him,

-Not only the trees and bushes on the edges will belong to Sebastien, right here, here, here and here, roughly in the middle, you have fruit trees. Abraham said they will provide shade for the grazing animals in the summer and should stay there, so they mustn't be cut down. You have a couple of apple trees, a plum tree and a cherry tree right there. He suggested for your son to plant more fruit trees in the field. A pear tree would not go amiss for example. Near the forest, there is the outline made out of bricks of an old cottage. Those foundations can be used to build an animal shed or a pig pen. Then here you have ample space to create a chicken coop, a large one at that. Abraham did advise to build a tall fence or even a wall between the forest and the field first to protect your animals from the ones from the forest but also to prevent yours to run into the wild. Now, Mr Berry, he said, would be the perfect man to employ to create such a fence but he also did say that animals will be animals and that maintaining the fence regularly would be needed. Let me show you the other plot.

Leading the way Henry told,

-There you could create a little gate to access the second plot from the field or you can access it from the road. Here, you have less trees. The plot hasn't been managed for years but it is rich and fertile. Abraham remembered that in his childhood it used to be a field full of golden wheat. You can see some wild wheat here and there now to attest of his memory. This is your perfect plot for a garden: Large and wide. Now, you see the hedge that the blackberry bushes is creating on that side, well, Abraham suggested to plant hedges of fruit bushes all around the plot. Here, it could be raspberries, there redcurrant, blueberry and gooseberry bushes and there a row of hazelnut trees which could be used for fire wood, sticks to grow beans and peas and also fencing. Can you picture it? It would be a large garden enough to sustain your family. The fact is it is elevated but close to the river, so to water that plot of land will be easy, a true advantage. But Wilton-Cough suggested to have a well in that corner. In the past, there has been some very dry weather in Wilton Town which caused a terrible famine, so he said it is better to be safe than sorry. If you come with me I will show you the third plot of land which Abraham suggested you acquire.

Jack and Tobias walked inside the would be garden with some excitation and called out,

-Grandpa Rag, grandpa Rag! Come and see, what we have got, come and see. We found a crocodile! Uncle Raph' is holding it for us.

Raphael following the children reassured Raguel who gave a worried glance towards him,

-Master, it is not a crocodile.

When everyone were around Raguel, the two boys harassed him with questions,

-Can we keep it? Can we keep it? Will it grow big? Will it eat us at night?

A smiling Raphael displayed the creature in question, which was on top of the nuts in his basket. Raguel took the poor animal in his hands with care and ruled,

-No, we can't keep it, boys, but you saved it. This is a salamander, it usually lives by rivers. So this little fellow did stray further inland than it should and probably did lost its way. So what we will do is to return it by the river's banks and give it back a chance to survive there, because it will perish in your bedroom even if you spend all day trying to catch flies to feed it.

Tobias sighed deeply while Jack took a more grown up position on the matter as he said,

-Grandpa Rag is right you know, Toby. We've got to let that little salamander live where it should live.

Offering his hand to the disappointed Tobias, Raguel proposed,

-Come, let's do it together. I will let you hold the salamander and release it.

The child smiled again and asked reaching out for the presented hand,

-Does it bite?

Raguel reassured him,

-No, it will not bite you. But you will have to be gentle when you hold it. If you draw a picture of the salamander for Doctor Williams when we are back home, he will be able to tell you about them. Do you know how to draw, Toby?

Replying negatively Tobias was led by Raguel who ordered to Henry,

-Stay with Ivy and Margot, Henry. Make sure you tell them where we are. Keep an eye on them and protect them if needs be. Raphael, you stay with me to look after the boys.

An eager Jack went to help holding the basket of Tobias and proposed,

-I can teach Toby how to draw.

The Master welcomed,

-I will love you to do so. Jack, you don't how much we missed you.

The little fallen angel nodded positively as he replied with a very serious air,

-I think I do. When I saw the faces of Pa and Doctor Williams when I first appeared as a human, I think I realised then they had been looking for me all along. They recognised me straight away.

The Master of all angels smiled to the angelic child commenting,

-No one can forget the angel you have been and the memories of your deeds you left us with. We all entertain great hope for you because we all know you can do it.

With frowning brows Jack enquired,

-Hope of the wings kind?

Raguel confirmed,

-Yes, of the wings kind. My brother and his wife may have found the hideout of the result of your mistake. It is early days but it could mean that you can potentially correct your failures. We will all help to correct them and clear your slate, all of the human angels are behind you, but also my father and myself.

Jack went to nestle his hand in the spare one of the Master. Walking behind them, silently, Raphael was moved. Running towards them down the path were Ivy and Margot, with Henry flying above them, giggling, holding their two baskets. They were shouting,

-Wait for us!

Raguel turned around. Ivy was the first to reach him. With very flushed cheeks she told him,

-We want to see the salamander and it being released.

Then Margot arrived and trying to catch her breath confirmed,

-Yes, yes, we do. I never saw one before.

He couldn't help smiling as he fastened back the bow of the dishevelled plait of the young Margot. He enjoined,

-Toby, show the salamander to your sister and your

adoptive Ma.

The little boy showed his basket with great care and said,

-It is in there. It doesn't bite. But Grandpa Rag told me to take care when handling it but I don't remember why.

Stroking gently the brown curly hair of Tobias, Raguel said,

-It would be because it is a fragile creature, Toby. Now let's all put it where it should live by the the river banks.

It was a small adventure that pleased not only the children, but also Ivy who couldn't help clapping when she saw the salamander walking away from them and the basket. Her three adopted children followed her in her enjoyment and it reminded Raguel that Ivy was still such a very young woman at heart.

However while the children and Ivy were witnessing the departure of their salamander with deep interest, soon the attention of Raguel turned to Henry who was describing to him the last plot of land to acquire,

-Master, it goes from the river banks to the would be garden, from here where we are standing to over there. It is a very decent plot of land. The downside is that it can be prone to flooding on occasion every decades or so. However to have access to the river banks is not to be neglected according to Wilton-Cough. First, it is primordial to have access to water. Secondly, fishing can bring food back home. Abraham knows of your intentions to build a cabin for Raphael. He suggested that at the bottom of a cemetery will be dreary but here, with good pillars of stones or bricks and mortar, you could elevate a house, cabin of substantial size. It could have a terrace and even a balcony over the river. He thought of a two storey cabin, up from the ground which would not be damaged by floods. Below the cabin, he suggested that we kept a barge or two for fishing. He also mentioned that we could create a little pier and make people pay a little fee if they wanted to use it to take their goods to Wilton Town. Well, he had lots of interesting ideas as always.

The Master of all angels sighed with a smile as he agreed,

-Yes, I am starting to know Abraham Wilton-Cough very well. I must admit he is very astute. We will purchase that plot as well as the other two. Go and tell him so he can draw the deeds for his son to sign. Go now, Henry.

When the Messenger left, Raguel turned to Raphael to ask him,

-Do you rather see yourself living at the bottom of a cemetery or here? We will make you a nice cabin wherever you chose it to be, my Maggot.

Raphael stroked the head of Ludwig the dog impulsively while he replied,

-I prefer it here, Master, by the river. It is close to your family home still. Faced to graves everyday, I may just want to end up in one if I live in the cemetery. I, I, I...

His voice failed him. The Master demanded,

-I 'what'?

The fallen angel confessed,

-Raguel, I am suicidal and my soul is in your hands. I am trying to cope, I am just trying to cope. It is the guilt. It is choking me everyday. I find it hard to live with myself and what I have done.

Raguel scolded sternly,

-Well, you have to live with it and repair. Just like little Jack, we will help you fix your mistakes. Instead of suicide, start to think positively of what you can do to improve or just to mend what you have done. Start by taking one basket left by Henry.

As Raphael picked up the basket full of blackberries, Raguel added in a more soothing tone, taking the second basket,

-I think it is fitting that Raphael River should live by the river. I can actually see your house. We will build strong pillars for it to keep you safe. A little spell from Williams will not go amiss to make sure they stay put. Then a large decking area where you can eat outside when the weather is nice, or even have a hammock to rest. The house will be simple, with two rooms downstairs and two rooms upstairs.

Looking at the Master, Raphael enquired with some surprise,

-Four rooms? I thought I will have just a one room cabin

to live in.

Raguel replied with a smile,

-If we are acquiring a decent plot, we might as well use its full potential. With the flooding risk, using the land as a garden will not be reliable, but many houses have been built on pilotis. You could have a living room downstairs along with a small kitchen and upstairs a bedroom and a small bathroom but also a little balcony to look upon the river. When you will work with me as my jailer, I swear you will need some time to breathe, go to your home, sit on a chair on your balcony and just watch the sun go down. If you ask my Sebastien, I am sure he will allow you to keep Ludwig as well. I can always find him another guard dog when the time comes. Of course your house will not be a grand house but you are welcome to design it with us all to make it yours. My main concern is that it needs to be a warm place for you to live in. But I know Williams will make sure of it.

Ivy and the children ran to reach where they were and Ivy told joyfully,

-We made a little grotto with mossy stones for the salamander and it went straight in there!

Her father in law couldn't help the innuendo as he said looking at Raphael,

-That slippery little thing did lost its way, I am sure it was eager to find it back and a little shelter to call home. Come on all of you let's gather some more blackberries. We want enough for making jam but also a blackberry and apple crumble tonight.

All of the children clapped their hands with joy.

#

When the sun almost disappeared in the horizon, whilst the Master, Ivy and the boys were preparing dinner in the presbytery, Sebastien, Henry and the young Margot went to collect the animals from her old home.

Margot pointed from the hill down to the almost derelict cottage and said,

-Here it is: my old home. It doesn't look like much. When my little brother passed away, my father went all wrong, and he couldn't deal with anything anymore. He became violent, so much so he killed my mum. The state of the house is due to a storm, a couple of years ago, but he didn't bother to repair it and he refused any help from anyone.

A sighing Sebastien commented,

-Grief makes people do a lot of things they will regret later. Come Margot, let's rescue your animals. If you feel up to it, take your belongings from this house. I will come with you if you want to.

Holding his hand tightly, Margot replied with anxiety,

-Yes, I want to go back in, but I don't want to go alone. There was a portrait of my mother which I want to retrieve. It means to me.

Sebastien reassured before turning to Henry,

-Then we will get it together. Henry, you are going to be in charge of the animals: Poultry first, then secure the cow to the cart, then fetch the stray cat.

Driving the cart and the yellow mare Buttercup, Henry smiled at the prospect of his mission while Sebastien headed with Margot inside the old cottage which was partly made of stone and partly made of wood. When she passed the threshold, Margot shivered, and stepped backward with a knot in her throat. She confided, fear in her voice,

-I can't. I know he is no longer here but I am still frightened. Shall we come back another day together with Mr the angel of justice?

Sebastien feeling how terrified she was through her hand asked her gently,

-Will it reassure you if my father was here?

The young girl nodded positively giving her answer,

-Yes, it will.

The kind Sebastien revealed to her,

-We do not have to wait. Let me tell you a little secret. My father is one of the angels that can be summoned. So whenever you need him, or need his protection, you can call him. All you have to do is think intensely of his angelic name and repeat it in your head or out loud seven times. You can repeat either: 'Please Raguel come' or 'Please Raguel I need you'. Do you want to try it? I often summoned my father to appear like that and he never fails to come by my side.

A pleased Margot replied, but also enquired,

-Yes, I want to try. But he is at home right now. He can not be here fast. Are you an angel that can be summoned as well?

Sebastien explained,

-I can be summoned, yes, but it is different for me. In fact, for all angels that can be called it differs. It works a bit like a code. For Henry who is the angelic messenger you only have to say, 'I need the Messenger' twice. Now, as for my father, he is a special angel who can be physically in multiple places at the same time in different shape or form. In essence, he will be with us, but he will also be present at home looking after the boys and my Little Bit, and he is and has always been everywhere. He won't tell you whatever he have seen or lived, but I can tell you that it is a lot at any one time. But he did let me know a little tiny bit of his importance whenever I was a child, because the bedtime stories he recounts are in fact the moments and adventures he lived. He will tell you it is the story of this or that but somehow you can guess deep down that he did witness it first hand. You and your brothers should ask him for a bedtime story tonight, I am sure you will enjoy it. Now let's summon him together.

The talk of her adoptive father made Margot almost forget her fears of entering her former house. When, after the summon, she saw a fully winged Raguel appear before them, her shivering ceased all at once. She felt instant relief. She ran into his arms at once apologising,

-I am sorry to have called you. I was just so scared. This place is full of bad memory for me. Will you stay with me to visit it one last time?

Raguel reassured her, giving a knowing glance to his son,

-I will stay by you. We will visit it together. Give me your hand. We will be courageous and stay brave. This has to be done. Show me around and you can confide anything to me, good or bad.

Margot gave his hand to him willingly and presented,

-This is the main room of the house. On the left, you have my parents' bedroom. Upstairs, it was my room and the one of my brother. We were sharing it. It was better than the house we had in France. It was more spacious. But we lived more happily there than here.

Despite already knowing the answer, the Master asked,

-What changed?

With tears in her eyes, Margot told,

-The death of my brother. We all survived a sinking ship. My father made sure of it. But my brother wasn't well at all after that event. He struggled to just live. He was coughing and very poorly. My mum and I tended to him as best as we could. My father couldn't afford the Doctor for him and by pride he didn't want to be in debt with anyone or even having to give one chicken away. When my brother died, my mum blamed my father for his decisions. He didn't appreciate her views and killed her. He said she fell from the stairs but she didn't. I saw what happened. I even tried to intervene that night but I was thrown aside. I had a dislocated jaw and a bad back there and then, I couldn't get up from my spot and I couldn't shout 'Stop'. Mum was dead by the time I could say something. Then my father started to abuse me, every day and nights. I managed to go to see Doctor Valdi at his clinic one day. He and the now Mrs Odell saved me when I gave birth to a dead child. Doctor Valdi gave a very severe punishment to my father and everything went alright for a while. But, when Valdi left town my father was upon me like a rash and it was worse than ever. So I left this house to live under a bridge. I never wanted to return.

Sebastien said soothingly,

-Well, my home is your home, now Margot. Pick any belongings you want to keep.

While his father put his arm across Margot's shoulders to reassure her, Sebastien warned,

-Dad, I can hear a slight noise. Someone is here. Keep her safe, take her outside. Look at the fireplace. The ashes are still glowing. That someone saw us coming and is hiding.

Taking Marguerite with him, Raguel ordered,

-Don't be brash, Mighty. Stay safe. I called Callum and Henry will be right behind you.

A worried Margot enquired,

-What is it?

Once outside with her Raguel told her,

-We do not know quite yet. But there is an intruder in your house. It is certainly not a raccoon that can light a fire and try to extinguish it. Did your father invite anybody? Was it his own house or was it rented?

Margot very anxious held his arm tight as she replied,

-My father built this house from his own hands. He bought that plot of land. It took us almost all of our belongings to do so. We started back from scratch here. But my father didn't make any friends in Wilton Town, not with his violent temper. The only guest we had was a young man who worked to build the new bridge in town with him from France, which my dad saved along with us on the sinking ship. He saved others too but if everyone went their own way, Louis helped my father build his house.

Acknowledging what she said, Raguel commented,

-So he is a young man who owes his life to your father. Where does Louis live?

The young girl pondered for a minute,

-I actually do not know. I know he slept in our barn a fair few times and in others' barns as well.

Putting her upon the cart, he ordered,

-Hide between the cages for the hens and stay put. I will stay by you.

Callum landed within the small courtyard. He bowed to the Master shortly before going inside the house without a word. There he found Sebastien and Henry questing for the person hiding in the abandoned house. He enquired,

-Who are we looking for?

Henry replied with a low voice,

-Or what? The blood I smell is part demonic. Here, you see that drop of dry blood. The scent is not totally human but it is not the one of Margot's father. It is very similar, however.

Callum gave a glance at the Messenger with a smile as he said in a similar low tone,

-Sorry, I wasn't a hunting dog in my past human lives. I could not tell the difference.

Sebastien turned to them to order,

-Silence! Henry, we are facing a cambion, you are right. It is a wounded one but do not let your guard down, both of you. The fact that he is hiding doesn't mean that he will not fight if it comes to it. I think he is upstairs. Can you hear it? He is still moving and trying to find a place to hide. All with me!

The charge took place and they arrived into a large under the roof bedroom. There they saw a man with shackles on his hands and ankles, totally naked, who had fairly fresh and horrendous wounds. Henry told,

-That is our cambion.

The cambion went into a corner of the room and crouched pleading,

-I don't mean no harm. I don't mean no harm. I needed a bit of warmth that is all. Please don't tell Mr Cork I used his wood for the fire place. He will kill me.

The compassionate Sebastien came closer to reassure,

-He will not kill you, Cork is no longer alive. He is dead and buried.

Tears poured out of the cambion immediately. Sebastien asked gently as he made a blanket appear in his hand to cover the nudity of the cambion,

-What is your name?

Once covered the very tamed cambion answered,

-My name is Louis.

Sebastien in a commanding tone then said,

-Louis, you can not stay here, all alone, shackled, naked and bleeding. I am a surgeon and my wife is a Doctor, we can see to your wounds. Come with us.

Louis followed willingly the three angels surrounding him. When they reached the cart, the Master demanded to his son,

-Who is that?

Sebastien replied not hiding any truth he gathered from putting the cover on the shoulders of the cambion, the touch of the angel that knows all,

-This is Louis, father. He has been abused by Cork, very recently. His blood is spread almost all around this house. He apologised to have used Cork's wood to lit a fire to warm his naked self up. I have to see to him. He has been flogged, but in such a way that he will have scars for life.

Raguel took a good head to toe look of the cambion in front of him whose demeanour was extremely shy to say the least. Tall and emaciated, Louis had the same vivaciously intelligent olive green eyes as Margot. His messy dark brown hair flowed in locks upon his shoulders. One could call Louis very handsome in an androgynous way despite all his bruises and cuts.

Raguel demanded,

-Pray, what is your age Louis and your surname?

Louis looked at him with a disarming honesty only to reply,

-I do not know. I was found as a toddler lost in the woods.

Climbing on the driving seat of the cart, Raguel, ordered,

-Margot, come and sit by me. Sebastien, put Louis in the back of the cart. Callum, we will drive you back to town, step in. Henry, what's the situation with the animals?

As everyone did as they were told without questions, Henry answered,

-As you can see I did secure the cow and she is attached at the back of our cart. If we drive slowly to her walking pace, it will be best. If Sebastien helps me, we will secure the hens and the cockerel in no time at all. As for the stray cat, he is in the barn sleeping. We will catch him last.

Sebastien was soon by the side of Henry with the cages for the poultry. Whilst they went, Raguel took a glance at the back of the cart where Callum was sitting by the crouched cambion. He asked,

-How is Louis doing?

Callum replied,

-He is shivering, Master.

Snapping his fingers Raguel told making another thick cover appear by the side of Callum,

-Put the blanket over his legs, Callum.

Then he demanded,

-Louis, I heard that you were working at the building site for the bridge, so you didn't go there naked, did you? Where are your clothes?

Looking before him at the planks of the cart, Louis revealed,

-He burnt them. He said without them I will not be running away like his daughter did.

Raguel sighed deeply when he asked,

-Why did you go there?

This time Louis had tears in his eyes as he replied,

-I have no fixed abode, Sir. He was one who did let me sleep in his barn and gave me a meal one evening every week. I sleep in the woods most of the time. I have a bed of moss there. But it rained and rained and rained lately. I started to sneeze and cough so I thought to myself, Mr Cork will have me in. He did, but he was hurt and enraged that night. He kept shouting, crying, throwing things around that 'They didn't let him have his daughter back'. He gave me a look which chilled my spine and said that I will do for the time being until he gets her back. Then I was battered, humiliated and kept prisoner in his house. I was terrified to even move, terrified like I have never been before.

Raguel reassured,

-We will sort you out. First, you need to be seen to medically. Second, a good meal will not go amiss then we have to find a way to remove those shackles and lastly we will have to find you some clothes to wear. Now, dry your tears, your ordeal is over.

Louis took a deep breath and simply said,

-Thank you.

The always paternal Master enquired,

-What did you eat to be skin and bone like that? If you worked at the construction of the bridge for the town, surely you received wages, what did you do with them? I am sorry for asking you that but I am deeply concern for your wellbeing.

His answer was lost within the cacophony of poultry in cages being loaded onto the cart by Sebastien and Henry and when they left, he tried to express himself again,

-I, I, gave them to a destitute young woman from Boston so she could have a room to live in. We, we are not together. I like her a lot but I am very poor myself. And I don't think she likes me, I mean loves me really. I have no muscles to show off and I am not the brightest man around. I have no idea where she is right now, she disappeared since the fire in town. She is called Rose.

Sighing deeply, Raguel told Louis,

-The young lady in question nearly lost her life the night of the fire. She was attacked. She has been in a very bad way for a few days but she is recovering slowly. You will find her at the clinic of Doctor Valdi which is run by my son and his wife in his absence. She may appreciate you paying her a visit because no one came to see her or to make sure she was alright. She is virtually alone in this world, a little bit like you.

The green eyes of the cambion lifted with hope for a few seconds, glanced at Raguel, then lowered back down as he commented,

-Rose was attacked. I told her what she was doing will put her in danger. But who will listen to me? No one.

Sebastien who had returned with a sleeping cat with Henry scolded,

-We are listening to you right now. Here, hold the cat Louis. He will stay asleep on the way.

Then he addressed Margot,

-We have the portrait of your mother, Margot. It is a little damaged, but Doctor Williams will repair it for us. Henry is putting it in the cart. I will lock and secure the house. Henry will drive you all back home and I will join you in a short while.

Henry jumped on the driving seat by Margot and the Master and soon Buttercup was peacefully making her way back to town. While Callum was dropped at the tavern, Raphael stepped in the back, having had his dinner. Raguel welcomed him with a bright smile,

-How was the food tonight my Maggot?

The fallen angel noticing the naked cambion in the back of the cart told,

-Delightful as always. We had, well, I had because Callum didn't finish his meal, jacket potatoes filled with butter, cheese and bacon and it was delicious. Now, who is the man in the back? He has shackles on. Is he lethal?

Henry reassured him,

-Cambion, with a little of animal spirit in him, harmless. His name is Louis.

Looking at the rather forlorn Louis, Raphael enquired,

-Is he a prisoner?

This time it was the Master of all angels who replied,

-No, but he was one. Cork used him instead of his daughter when she ran away. The cambion has been abused badly. We need to free him.

A surprised Raphael couldn't get his head to think as he demanded,

-You are going to let this cambion lose? Just like that? Cambion, half demon, hence danger...

Raguel told with conviction,

-Not all demons are bad, neither all of their offspring, it is on a case to case basis, Raphael. If you were an angel of justice you would be able to tell the difference. This one is different. This one is safe. This one doesn't know how to protect his own self. He is a young cambion with not much clue at all. We will give him the clues and his freedom. Louis, meet Raphael, my most annoying servant.

Louis gave a very shy glance to Raphael and he whispered,

-Hello.

Speaking his mind, Raphael expressed himself out loud,

-Master, that one is damaged, badly damaged! You can't let him lose like that. We met Cork, we know what he was like. I can tell that Louis is going to need more than freedom.

Fast and forward the reply of Raguel came,

-Well, as he is a loner like yourself, I think you could befriend him and set him on the right path if you still have a little angelic kindness in you that is.

Margot turning around added her own opinion strongly,

-Yes, you must, Raphael, you must. You killed enough cambions and demons as it is. This time you have to play nice with this one. No more killing.

Her little rant rather frightened Louis who was ready to jump out of the cart becoming scared of Raphael all of a sudden. However Raphael caught him before he could do anything stupid and ordered him,

-Sit down, Louis. I will do you no harm. You can't run with your shackles and you are rather naked, if anyone apart from us see you like that in town they will not understand and give you a hard time, like a stoning. So stay put and stay down for your protection.

The young cambion obeyed, still scared and shivering. Raphael repositioned the covers upon Louis and said in a softer tone of voice,

-I have been battered by Cork and I pretty much know how you feel. Trust me. The third time, I met him, it was a fight for life. It was either me and the entire family who are now raising his daughter in a safe place or him. I was lucky enough to have the upper hand at one moment but only with help and only because I did a bit of fighting in my time. However like you, I ended a fairly bit wounded. I actually think I broke some stitches just by trying to catch you up.

Raguel picking up on what his new servant said quickly enquired with concern,

-My Maggot, how bad are you? Physically of course.

It made Raphael smile despite himself, he looked at his shirt which started to have blood upon it and replied,

-It can wait, Master. I will survive if you care that I do.

Raguel demanded,

-Henry, can we go a little faster despite the cow?

-We don't have to. We are almost arrived. If you would like to open the iron gates for me? I can already see Doctor Williams at the door of the presbytery.

The Master jumped down and explained,

-Yes, I warned William about Louis but also just now about Raphael. Look after the animals, Henry.

Soon he helped Margot down who went to pick up the portrait of her mother, then he helped the young cambion whilst Doctor Williams offered his hand to Raphael. The fallen angel accepted the help of the old angel telling him as he stepped down,

-You mustn't worry for me, Williams, I have seen worst.

Doctor Williams replied, giving some support to Raphael,

-The more you say that, the more I will. Come inside, Ivy is preparing the drawing room for the two of you to be seen to. Did you have a nice dinner? We kept you some apple and blackberry crumble.

The fallen angel smiled but said,

-You should have given it to the little Toby. He needs badly to be fed.

Correcting him, Williams answered,

-Tobias has been fed. For him it has to be little but often. It will also be the case for our new friend. Just looking at his legs hurts me. What is your opinion upon him?

When he saw the cambion going inside the house with Raguel and Margot, Raphael confided,

-I only know him for a few minutes. It is hard to cast an opinion. But at first glance, I know he has been hurt and badly, physically and emotionally. We have a very frightened being to deal with. Like Cork, I don't think he knows he is a cambion. He may have instincts which we do not know about. Due to the colour of his eyes, he is obviously related to Margot and her father. Having killed the Incubus from Lucifer, I recognised the smell of him in his blood and skin. I will put my bet that he is the younger brother of Cork. That said, like the Master stated, we have to cast our judgement on a case to case basis. He is a cambion yes but a bad one, maybe not. But he is certainly a very weak one. When I stopped him to jump from the cart who was in motion, I was worried I would break one of his bones.

Doctor Williams asked with worried brows,

-Why did he want to jump from the cart when you were all helping him?

Stopping, Raphael thought for a second then answered,

-It was when Margot told me off for killing demons and cambions.

His hand upon his mouth, Raphael realised out loud,

-This one knows he is a cambion! Let's go inside and make sure the family stays safe. Ludwig, come my boy. Williams, the Master may need us. Be observant, like I will be. Where are the boys?

A concerned Williams led the way inside as he replied in a low tone,

-The boys are in their bedroom, Ted is reading a story to them.

Raphael advised,

-Tell Ted to lock the bedroom door and to stay with them. Just a precaution, tell him to put a poker in the fireplace. If that cambion was ready to jump out of a moving cart, when he will realise he is in a household full of angels, he may act to try to save his life at all cost. He will not know the good intentions of everyone towards him. He is a pretty lost thing, I can tell you that. He faced abuse recently. He is on the edge of breaking down.

As soon as Doctor Williams sent telepathic warnings to

all angels in the household and the Master. When they arrived in the drawing room, they saw the naked cambion being cleaned by the Master and Ivy who warned,

-His wounds are very deep, Doctor Williams. One shows signs of infection. It is deep but we can't sow it yet. Not that one at least, but the others are manageable. Cork didn't go easy on him. He has been flogged more than once.

Raphael who was uncomfortable to see Ivy so close to the cambion who he was unsure about suggested,

-Mrs Cotton, why don't you let Doctor Williams take over and check on Margot?

Raguel, seeing the point, insisted,

-Yes, Ivy, Margot had a pretty emotional moment seeing her old house. I think you should go and talk to her. We will take care of Louis, Williams and I. Sebastien will soon return. Raphael go with Ivy to be seen to and stay with her and Margot.

The young woman took her medical bag without further a do and scolded Raphael who was standing at the door of the drawing room with the dog by his side,

-How many times do I have to tell you to call me Ivy, Mr River? Come with me before you bleed on the carpet.

Raphael followed her with a smile as he replied, satisfied that she was out of the room,

-It was out of pure politeness, Mrs Ivy.

Glancing at him she retorted,

-Ivy, just plain Ivy, Mr Raphael, with that smirk of yours, I am starting to believe that you are mocking me.

Opening the door to the kitchen with some visible pain letting Ivy enter first, Raphael, smiling bravely answered with honesty,

-I would not dare to mock you, Ivy and in my opinion you are not plain at all. But why do you insist on me calling you Ivy?

The young woman put a medical bag on the table with some care and ordered,

-Come and take a seat, uncle Raph', I want you to call

me simply Ivy because if you haven't noticed you are part of the family now. Beside that you are living here.

Closing and locking the door behind him with care, Raphael mentioned,

-Yes, at the moment I am living here but what will happen when I am living by the river?

He sat obligingly in front of Ivy and started to open his waistcoat as she answered,

-You will still be uncle Raph' and I will expect you to invite us for dinner at your home and to fish with my boys on occasion, but also to spend every Christmas with us. What do you think Margot, am I not right?

Without really focusing, the young girl told,

-Yes, you are.

She shook her head before paying attention to what was happening in the kitchen, then Margot apologised,

-I am sorry, Ma. Yes, yes, I agree.

Smirking at Margot, knowing she was lost in her thoughts looking at a painting on the table prior to them entering the room, Raphael asked,

-So Margot you are prepared to call me uncle Raph' from now on? Even though you slapped me a fair few times and you argue with me a lot.

Somehow Margot managed to giggle as she retorted,

-It was only two slaps. Is he going to be alright, Ma? He is bleeding a fair bit. Do you want me to help you?

Ivy turning to the young girl replied,

-Yes, please. I just need some hot water. We have to keep changing his bandages daily, now is a good moment to do so. He will be alright. It is just a little tare in the wrong place.

Then looking at Raphael, she demanded in a scolding way,

-What did you do again Mr River?

The fallen angel put his arms up in the air, holding his waistcoat and shirt giving himself up to the expert medical hands of Ivy, only to reply with a smile,

-Of course as usual I am supposed to be the guilty party but not this time. I tried to protect Louis from jumping from a cart in motion. You have seen how bony his legs and hips are, not mentioning his shackles, he would have sustain serious injuries if he had done so. If a certain Miss Margot would have kept her numbers correct, just like she did with her number of slaps given, for my number of cambion and demon killed, I would not have sounded like an ogre to Louis and he would have probably stay put by my side and not go into a panic. She added 's' to both words. Now, I only did kill one demon and one cambion and both times to protect this family from the start of my human life.

Preparing the hot water, Margot reacted straight away,

-I am so sorry! I caused the panic with my silly words... That's why you are hurt now! I am sorry.

A compromising Raphael told in a soothing way,

-You didn't know how he would react. I certainly didn't. But your small mistake highlighted to us the fact that he knew he was a cambion. Now, your father didn't have that knowledge. He only acted on his instincts, the demonic ones, well as far as I understood only from late. But when those starts in a powerful cambion like your father they are pretty much impossible to harness and stop. For this young one we may be able to do something, well the Master mainly. But it will be a hard call. Louis is erratic, has been abused and is hurt emotionally and physically. I can tell you that from the get go. If I closed the door of this room, there is a reason for it: to protect you both. We do not know what the reactions of Louis will be when he learns that he is in a household of angels. Margot, are you related to Louis because you have the same eyes colour, the same as your father and demonic grandfather?

The young girl fidgeted as she answered with honesty,

-I don't know. I did notice. My own mother had the same eyes colour though. Louis has always been accepted as a guest since I can remember but only for one evening during the week and he sleeps in stables and outdoors. He has always been helpful to my family. He followed us on our move from France. My father saved him along with us when the ship we travelled upon was sinking. He saved others of course on the little barge he managed to lower down to the sea. We were in the ocean all of us and dad was struggling to free that barge but he did and he picked us all up, one by one, my brother, me, my mother, Louis and he picked up all who had a chance of surviving but mainly children.

When Margot brought the hot water to the table in a large bowl, she saw the extent of the damage her father did to Raphael on his chest. She gasped,

-How can you stand tall all day when, when, you are so hurt?

The fallen angel reassured,

-It is not that bad. I made it in the end. So your mother, she did have your eyes?

Margot went to pick up the portrait of her mother and showed it to the fallen angel with some pride,

-This was my mother. I do have her eyes rather than me hers. But I can say the same thing with my father's eyes. Especially the eyebrows, mines look like my father's one more than my mum's.

Looking at the portrait, Ivy commented as she started cleaning the torso of Raphael,

-She was certainly a beautiful woman. What was her name? I thought you had humble means in France, but to have a portrait done of that quality shows higher status. Her dress is not one I could have, I think, ever afford.

Margot put the portrait back on the table when she revealed,

-Her name was Mathilde Du Plessis. I was a bit of her confident whenever we had a chance to talk together. What I know is that she was deposited as a baby at the doorsteps of a castle. She was draped in finery and lace, and had a fine cameo upon her, which I have. My mother made me hide it in the heal of my shoe one day. The following day she was dead. I have still got the cameo, on the back three letters are engraved M, D and P. There is a bit of a story associated to my mother but would you care to listen to it?

It was Raphael who answered first and foremost,

-Yes, we would! You owe me that anyway because I have to get more stitches because of the slip of your tongue which revealed that I could kill cambions and demons. It will distract me from the pain of the needle going through and through my skin again and again.

Ivy, caring for her patient but intrigued as well by the story of Mathilde Du Plessis, insisted,

-Yes, we do care and you must tell us. Please, fetch the little silver flask of rum in the pantry first for uncle Raph'.

When Margot left, Ivy explained to the fallen angel,

-I am going to need you to drink a little, Raphael. What I am going to do will be rather unpleasant and I wish my Sebastien was here instead of me doing this operation for he has eagle eyes. Basically, you have bits of bandages and fabric inside your wound, I need to remove them all carefully otherwise you face the risk of a festering infection. It is more the task for a surgeon rather than a Doctor, but I can do it. Doctor Williams, my late father and Sebastien trained me well about surgery. Now, when you stopped Louis to jump from the cart, do you remember him having claws?

Raphael thought for a second before answering,

-I don't remember it. It happened so fast.

Sighing Ivy scolded,

-If you knew he was a cambion, if you are warned about it, you need to pay attention to those details especially since you seem to be a demon magnet.

Raphael contested,

-I am not a demon magnet!

However Ivy preparing her tools and sanitising them with hot water commented,

-This is not what grandpa Rag said.

Interested the fallen angel enquired,

-What did he say? He never lets out much. He talks to you then.

A smiling young woman told as she started to prepare the wound,

-Oh, yes, he does talk to me. We have good conversations together. He accepted me as his daughter in law. I was scared he wouldn't like me at all but he does treat me like his daughter.

Looking at Ivy with kindness Raphael vented,

-Who wouldn't like you to be honest? If you were my daughter in law, I would be ever so proud of you.

Margot who arrived back in the room was ready to give her opinion,

-Well, you didn't like Ma for wanting to kill her and her husband. Your plot was evil, purely evil.

The fallen angel sighed deeply then replied,

-I didn't know Ivy then and I was an ignorant fool, a totally ignorant fool. Grandpa Rag taught me a lesson I will always remember. I am starting to learn how it is to be a human. What humanity is and dare I say to have a heart. I needed it. I really needed it.

Taking the silver flask from the hands of Margot, Ivy told strongly,

-What you need right now is drinking a fair bit before I proceed, Raphael. Margot, you can sit at the table. What I will do is not sightly but tell us about your mum, please.

Margot took a chair but did put it by the one of Raphael. She sat on it and held the hand of the fallen angel as she said,

-I am tough enough to watch, Ma, but I also want to learn how to mend people. Uncle Raph' can do with a little bit of support too. I will tug his hand when the going gets tough.

Raphael couldn't help teasing the young girl yet with a kind smile,

-You are my saviour as always, Margot. Come, so your mum was found at the doorsteps of a castle, do you know which one?

He started drinking but listened attentively to whatever Margot was saying. She started her story with an unpromising,

-My mum and father knew the castle but they never told me its name. It is very complicated. I just know it is located in the Auvergne mountains of France. All I heard is it was nearby an area where a beast killed women and children. My mother said she was frightened to go outside at night because, although the beast which was like a huge wolf had been shot dead years before, the idea of it still terrified everyone. She told me lots of stories about it.

Three knocks at the door were heard, then they all heard a voice,

-Raphael, it is me. Open the door.

Recognising the voice of her husband, Ivy ran to open the door at once. She commented,

-Sebastien, you are back. I am so happy to see you. I didn't know how long you will take at Cork's cottage.

Sebastien went to deposit a few objects on the table before he ordered,

-Please, Little Bit, lock the room. I am here. Raphael summoned me so I came as fast as I could. He said you wished that I was here.

Ivy closed the door and locked it before she enquired,

-How did he do that? He was with me all the time.

Washing his hands with no further a do in the bowl of hot water, Sebastien explained,

-He may be a fallen angel but he knows how to call us and has the ability to call us angels. I will teach you how to do so, Ivy. It is not that complicated. So let's have a good look at you, Raphael.

The fallen angel complied with willingness as he told,

-Fabric went into the wound.

Sebastien commented before he ordered,

-I can see that. Margot, can you bring that candle closer and hold it steady beside me. Little Bit, you are going to be my assistant. Raphael, just take one more sip of rum for me. It is going to be tedious and painful on this occasion. But it has to be done.

With no further a do Sebastien started to take a long

piece of textile from the wound with great care. His wife informed him,

-Raphael doesn't remember if Louis had claws or not. It was a heat of the moment thing and he stopped the cambion to jump from the cart in motion because he thought Louis would hurt himself.

Nodding positively, Sebastien simply said,

-My father told me of the little incident. Check Raphael's shirt for me and his waistcoat, Ivy.

His wife obliged him and inspected the garments,

-His waistcoat has blood stains and one of the culprits, one claw.

Sebastien ordered,

-Don't touch the claw with your bare hand, Ivy. Just leave it to me to deal with, put the waistcoat on the ground for the time being, make sure the blood doesn't touch the stone slabs. We don't want any of our pets licking the blood and being poisoned. So be careful with it. Then can you fetch the anti poison we have for Raphael. He will need a good glass of it.

While Ivy obeyed, Sebastien turned to Raphael to explain,

-We will have to ascertain if the poison is similar to the one of Cork. The fact that you didn't feel being clawed straight away or at all is normal. Some demons and obviously cambions did develop claws which numb the area they rip apart. It happened to me, you think you are alright for a while and before you know it you collapse. I just made the call for Doctor Valdi to assess you. He saved me, and you back from your fight from Cork. I am going to put you on the table. If claws are involved, we can't take any risk, especially since you are now human. Come.

Sighing Raphael got up from the chair and felt much weaker on his legs. The arms of Sebastien supported him. Before he knew it he was upon the table. He asked,

-What was in the rum you gave me?

Ivy, going by the table, revealed,

-It is a special formulation my father created to make his

patients sleepy before a tough operation.

Sebastien advised,

-Just relax yourself Raphael. You need to be still for what we are about to do. The rum will help you to do that. I will need to remove all the fibres one by one from your wound. Just have another sip.

If Raphael obliged him, he nonetheless complained,

-I wanted to hear the story of the mother of Margot.

The young girl told sternly,

-You will hear it another time. What is most important is for you to be looked after right now. Drink.

Soon in a daze, Raphael couldn't open his eyes, couldn't move any limb yet could hear the conversation around him,

-He is nearly out of it, but not quite yet.

-Three knocks at the door, hopefully it is Doctor Valdi. Go and open my Little Bit.

-Is the code, three knocks?

-Yes, only for the time being, until potential danger is out of the house. Louis looks innocuous enough, but as you can see with our friend Raphael, he can inflict a decent wound without being provoked.

-It was my fault, you know. I shouldn't have mention that uncle Raph' killed my father.

-It is not the precise account that was given to me. You just said demons and cambions. Stop beating yourself for it. You didn't know Louis would react like that, did you? None of us did.

The last words Raphael heard were,

-He is out of it now, prime to be operated on.

His wife did let the newcomer in,

-It is only Henry.

The Messenger smiled to her as he commented,

-I am sorry to disappoint, and to not be the man of your dreams Mrs Cotton. Who were you looking for?

A blushing Ivy failed to respond while Sebastien scolded,

-Henry, it is not the moment to tease my young wife. I need her fully focus on the operation. Ivy, I need the tweezers. Now, that the large part is removed we need to do all those fibres. We are going to have fun, I can tell you that. So, Henry, where is Doctor Valdi?

Coming to where the waistcoat and the shirt were on the floor, Henry replied,

-Nice slashes on that shirt, three, I can tell you that Louis uses his three middle claws to attack. But there is a puncture point there, almost like a hawk or an eagle attacking its prey. How is Raphael doing? Doctor Valdi is on his way, winging it. He hasn't grasp the art yet of coming when summoned. He will, given time. Apparently, the Great Being and Amelia are coming as well.

Slightly concerned, Sebastien asked,

-Do you know why is Amelia coming? After what she went through in hell. I'd rather have her resting in the hotel tonight. She has a long journey to do tomorrow and beside that she is with child.

Henry took the clothes from the ground with care, removed the claw from them and put it in a little dish as he answered,

-Amelia Valdi knows something we should know. Well, not all of us of course: The Master and yourself mainly. Then you may disclose it to whom you want or trust. Your grandfather is driving Amelia here on Theo's phaeton pulled by a flying Rosalie so they will arrive after Doctor Valdi. I will dispose of Raphael's clothes, burn them in the yard. Does Raphael have a chance of making it?

Sighing deeply, Sebastien told,

-It is too early to tell. He drank the counter poison, yesterday and about a couple of minutes ago, and this morning as well. The only thing is how many attacks Raphael can sustain as a human? This one was short and swift but can prove lethal.

Biting his lips Henry enquired,

-May I warn anyone about it, like your father?

Sebastien shook his head negatively as he ordered,

-Don't tell Dad. He will be extremely upset about it. Let him concentrate on who he is dealing with. Don't burn the clothes of Raphael yet, I need you to show them to Valdi first when he arrives. Then bring him to the kitchen immediately. Afterwards burn the clothes and wait for the arrival of Amelia and my grandfather then you will have to tend to the old girl that Rosalie is.

Henry bowed before leaving the room. Ivy questioned,

-Why Henry is bowing to you now?

Sebastien replied with slight annoyance,

-I don't want Henry to do so but he feels very obliged to do the angelic bowing because I am now an archangel. Please, lock the door my Little Bit. Margot, please don't sob. If you want to help Raphael, you have to keep that lamp steady so wax doesn't burn his skin. He is already badly damaged as it is. We can fight and save him together. So I need you both to stay strong with me so he can live another day. He fought to protect us more than once now, let alone trying to help someone from getting injured and getting badly injured as a result.

When his wife was by him, she held the hand of Margot and tugged it twice as she enjoined,

-We will save him together. Dry your tears my Margot. Uncle Raph' has seen worst and he always made it.

#
Henry didn't have to wait too long to see Vincent Valdi flying toward him in the courtyard of the church. Making a perfect landing and his wings disappeared, Doctor Valdi demanded,

-How bad it is?

The Messenger told with a deep sigh,

-It could be a matter of life and death according to Sebastien. So it is serious. I was there when it happened, driving the cart. Raphael wanted to prevent the cambion to hurt himself from jumping out of the cart. I can tell you that he didn't feel the pain when the blow happened but he saw the blood afterwards. Raphael did put on a brave face and didn't want to pull a fuss either. But he warned all of us that the cambion may not be as pacific as we thought he would be. All the children in the house are in locked rooms with an angel by their side to protect them if needs be. Let me show you the shirt of Raphael. It has been clawed. There is three lashes and an entry point like the claw of a prey bird. I did feel some animal spirit in Louis, the cambion we are facing with. He is part demon but he is something more, not only human I can tell you that. He is acting far too fast to be mainly human. Bearing in mind that Louis is weak and has been abused, he knows he is a cambion and did let himself abused by one. Obviously we thought he couldn't fend himself against Cork but seeing the amount of blood in the house of Cork, Louis probably did pull up a fight but lost it. Louis was shackled when we found him: wrists and ankles. After what happened to Raphael we are not ready to take the shackles of him yet. If the strong Cork had to restrain Louis, it is probably because he had to for his own purpose. So the unassuming Louis is a young but strong cambion to not be underestimated. Poor Raphael got the bitter hand of the stick on that one. Let me show you in.

Considering both garments closely, Vincent followed Henry who carried his medical satchel. By the kitchen door, Henry knocked thrice, exchanged again the clothes for the satchel and just begged,

-Please, save him, Vincent. He is trying so hard to redeem himself. If he dies now, Raphael is the piecemeal of Lucifer. If you need anything, anything in order to save him, I will fetch it for you. You can message me via telepathy or ask Sebastien to do so for you. I am at your disposal.

Valdi looked at the messaging angel, at his moist golden eyes which were struggling to retain tears only to ask,

-I thought he demeaned all human angels. Why do you give him your consideration and your tears?

Henry replied with his honest simplicity,

-Because this is what we do as angels. He did treat me badly when he was an archangel but not when he was a human. But when he was an archangel, I remember him saving a cat stuck in a tree. He gave the young cat to me and ordered me to deliver his message and to find a nice home for the cat as well. That were his orders. When I accomplished them, he smiled at the one that the cat had a good home. As a human, he brought to our attention the plight of the young Margot and then the one of Tobias. Raphael has eyes to see and perceive people in trouble. He is an asset and we mustn't lose him working for the angelic community. Deep down, he has a good heart.

Shrugging his shoulders Vincent smiled to Henry as he replied firmly,

-Then I will make sure he stays alive, not only just for you, but for me as well for what he did to protect the Cotton family yesterday was selfless.

Ivy opened the door and sighed with relief at the sight of Doctor Valdi. She invited him in immediately,

-Doctor Valdi, here you are! The patient is unconscious but we did that to him. When you see his wound you will understand that we had to do so. Come in, quick. Thank you, Henry. When you have finished with your tasks please come back to us with a large bucket of water.

The diligent Messenger bowed his head slightly to Ivy and told firmly before he left,

-Yes, Mrs Cotton. I will see to it.

Locking the door once Doctor Valdi entered the room, Ivy informed,

-We found one claw stuck in Raphael's waistcoat. It is in the dish over there. Henry retrieved it for us because he always wear or almost always wear his leather gloves. My Sebastien believes there is another claw that made its way inside Raphael, just like it did for him. Come and have a look.

Valdi went to the table and took a good look at Raphael then commented,

-I am allowed to say that I am starting to feel sorry for him? Right, he is really pale. Did he eat something, prior to drink Doctor Fair's special rum?

Sebastien replied with certainty,

-Yes, he had a full meal at the tavern tonight.

Vincent started inspecting the wound then the surrounding areas with great care as he stated,

-Raphael has definitely a poisoned claw inside him. The

main wound is not what we should be attending to right now. Here, look at this side. So easy to miss, here is the entry point of a claw matching the one on his waistcoat. It is nearly sealed up as well. I am afraid we have to open him up and fast.

When the laborious operation started, Henry was burning the clothes of Raphael under the moonlight, outside upon the wet coble stones of the church yard. Its fire served as a beacon to guide the flying phaeton carrying the Great Being and Amelia towards the presbytery. Soon it landed in the yard. Henry bowed profoundly to the Creator who stepped down the phaeton.

The Great Being took one glance at the golden eyes of the Messenger before he stated,

-You have been crying, Henry. Come, stand up, Raphael has always been as solid as a rock. He will bounce back. He always bounces back. How is my Raguel about it?

Henry stood up and informed dutifully,

-He is worried, my Lord, very worried. But I kept away the worst informations I have from the Master to not let him be upset. It was the decision of your grandson that I should do so. You will find Raphael operated on in the kitchen by Mighty, his little wife and Doctor Valdi. The young Margot has been kept with them for protection. The door is locked and three knocks on the door will grant you entrance. The Master is in the drawing room along with Doctor Williams dealing with the young cambion Louis. The boys are in their bedroom. They have no ideas of what is happening downstairs, Ted is with them to protect them but he is also reading them a bedtime story. Mrs Brown is not here, she is being dutifully entertained by Callum and Francis at the tavern to a dinner. We will keep her away as long as we can until we don't have a situation at home. When Callum gets the all clear, he will walk her back home.

Being helped to descend from the phaeton by the Great Being, Amelia commented,

-It sounds like a military operation.

Giving her his arm and leading her inside the house, the Creator told her, before thanking with a nod of the head the Messenger,

-It almost is. My eldest son is dealing with a lose canon of a cambion. Whilst my youngest is dealing with the first known casualty from that cambion. The evening might be long and interesting. I hope you are ready for it. Henry, thank you. When you have finished all your tasks please will you stay by the Master. I am worried for him and Doctor Williams.

Bowing another time profoundly, the Messenger replied,

-Yes, my Lord.

Once the door of the presbytery was closed, Henry turned to the mare and said,

-Come on my good old Rosalie, let's settle you for the night fast in the stable. I am pretty sure Wilton Fair will be happy to see you and you haven't met Buttercup and Snow White yet.

The Friesian horse followed him willingly to the stable. Henry didn't even have to lead her by the reins.

By the kitchen door, the Great Being did the three knocks. The door was opened by Ivy who fell into his arms and cried,

-I think we are losing him.

The Creator ordered,

-Amelia, lock the door behind you. Ivy, please, stay strong. Vincent, tell me what is going on?

But his youngest son didn't reply, busy dealing with the cardiac arrest of Raphael with the help of Sebastien. It was the young Margot who replied through her tears,

-Uncle Raph's heart stopped. It is the second time. He is not doing well, he is not doing well at all. He sustained too many injuries in the past few days, far too many, far too many...

Going to the table and seeing his pasty fallen archangel, the Great Being told in a strong manner,

-He is dying. To any of you, do not ever tell him what I will do now. If you ever do so he will act with contempt. If you stay quiet about it, he will behave the way he did since his first human days. We want him to recover and not to end up in hell. It is our secret. Vincent, move your hands from his heart.

His son did and saw his father just apposed his hand on the heart of Raphael. A flash of light was seen in the entire room which went from the hand to the heart underneath it. Raphael breathed again but didn't woke up. The Great Being stated,

-You can resume the operation. Raphael's heart will sustain the pain of it this time around.

Turning to Amelia, he then said,

-You can go and fetch the book, Amelia. Come back immediately. It is in the drawing room.

Valdi raised his concern,

-Do be careful.

Margot proposed and reassured,

-I can come with you, Mrs Valdi. I have never known Louis to attack people prior to today. I think he acted with unreasonable fear.

A worried Sebastien ordered,

-Take Ludwig with you. Don't linger in that room.

The confident young girl put her hand inside the one of Amelia, and gave her lamp for Ivy to hold. The rottweiler followed them out of the room. A concerned Ivy asked,

-Why do we need a book to operate when practice makes perfect?

Valdi mentioned,

-It is not that type of book Mrs Cotton.

Her grandfather in law added,

-Ivy, we have a suspicion that Lucifer has been creating a specific race of demons and cambions to kill angels. In Wilton town, you have encountered those, in the form of the demon that Raphael killed in the attic, in the cambion Cork and we suspect in Louis as well. The plot goes deeper than that. But Amelia did transcribe an important manuscript for us and she recalls a mention about the race you are facing here and in danger against. Your own husband was attacked by two of those demons and nearly died because of it.

Sebastien agreed as he vented,

-Yes, tell me about it! I swear I never have been stuck in bed for so long in my entire lives. The innocuous Louis must have wriggled his claws inside Raphael with the damage to repair and the amount of fibres in his entrails. He has shackles on though but he did deliver a bad blow to the poor Raphael. This will take time.

Vincent smiled as he removed a large claw from the wounded fallen angel. He boasted,

-Here is our culprit! Now, our man has a chance to survive. Come on, my dear nephew do not despair! We will get there together.

This made the Great Being enquire,

-Is it true that Raguel told the children to call Raphael, uncle Raph'?

It was Ivy who replied to his question,

-Yes, it is true. There are two part to that story though. One is a kind hearted, redeeming one. In this family, we do adopt people. Because Raphael saved us twice, Raguel granted him to be adopted in essence by us. So he came up with the title of uncle Raph'. You should have seen how moist the eyes of Raphael were when he heard being called uncle Raph' for the first time. We were walking altogether and Raguel told us not to look at Raphael because he knew Raphael would be completely tearful then. It allowed our uncle Raph' to gather his composure back. The second part is a little bit of irony on the part of your son. Because I call Raguel, grandpa Rag for the children. It did make Raphael and Sebastien smile many times because it makes him sound like an old carpet. So uncle Raph' was somehow for your son to get his own back. He pronounces Raph' as wrath on occasion.

To that Sebastien commented as he put a lot of textile fibres into a dish with his tweezers,

-It doesn't astonish me at all coming from dad.

A minute later, knocks on the door came fast and furious, three ones with a desperate begging voice,

-Please, let me in, let me in!

Valdi's concentration was lost on his operation. His head jerked up as he said,

-It's Amelia.

Ivy rushed to open the door and did let a devastated Amelia back in the kitchen. She closed the door behind her, seeing the blood pouring from her chest. Out of breath Amelia told as fast as she could,

-There is a fight in the drawing room. It is the Master against Lucifer and the cambion. The little girl is dead, Doctor Williams is trying to resuscitate her. Henry has joined the fight, he helped me to escape. It is a blood bath...

Terrified, she cried. The Great Being ordered,

-Amelia, Ivy go to the pantry and hide. Ivy look after Amelia, she is injured. Mighty, lock them in there and look after the rest of the operation of Raphael. Vincent, you are coming with me. We are going to take Lucifer back to hell. Mighty, lock the door behind us. Be cautious and protect that room with your life. Amelia has the book with her.

His grandson understood straight away. A distraught Ivy took her medical bag and almost dragged Amelia inside the pantry with her without a word. Sebastien locked the pantry and put a large cabinet to hide its door. He then put the large key to it inside the standing clock in the kitchen. He used his newly discovered magical powers to make the key invisible but to him, his father, grandfather and uncle only. Then after having made the kitchen safe again by locking it, he returned to the operation of Raphael, and said aggressively,

-Oh, Raphael, do not die on me! Make it! We need a bloody bastard like you in my ranks. I am begging you to stay with us.

He couldn't help being tearful at the news of the death of Margot. He didn't know what happened which did upset him greatly. Inside the pantry, his brave wife was trying to look after the injured Amelia who was shivering. Ivy took the cushion from her first and did hide it inside a large bag of flour. As she did so, she demanded,

-Amelia, please, Amelia, I need to know what happened to my adopted girl. Please, I am pleading with you, I need to know. I know I will feel low, low forever, but I need to know. I lost my father in dreadful circumstances, so hit me with the truth. Go straight on. What happened to my Margot?

But a trembling Amelia was a bundle of emotion struggled to talk,

-The cambion, he had claws. He killed her... It was so

brutal, so fast.

Ivy came by her and lit the candle lamp advised,

-You and I must calm down despite our distress. We mustn't be heard. So speak as low as you can. I am going to take the top of your dress down and see to you. I need to find your wound. You said Lucifer was in the house? How did he enter?

A sobbing Amelia whispered,

-I don't know. He was in the corridor. He knocked at the door thrice. Margot and I were already in the drawing room. The Master and Doctor Williams were looking after the cambion and everything was fine, everything was calm...

Trying to understand as she undressed Amelia, Ivy asked,

-Are you telling me that Louis was peaceful before the arrival of Lucifer?

Mrs Valdi nodded positively with her answer,

-He was. He was also good mannered and shackled. Lucifer knocked our code: the three knocks. Doctor Williams said that it must be Henry and to let him in. Margot answered the door but it was Lucifer, he pushed her away, making her fall doing so. He said 'here you are' to me, 'let's take you back to hell'...

Amelia stopped talking, wallowing in her emotions. Ivy who had found her wound told reassuringly,

-I will be able to deal with that. It is not that bad. Now, I have no water, but we have vinegar here. This will hurt a fair bit. It will clean your wound. Who did that to you?

When the vinegar was applied, Amelia fiddled with her glasses to give herself a countenance. She replied, trying desperately to be strong,

-It was the cambion. Lucifer said something and Louis was freed from his shackles. He knocked the Master with a set of them and rushed to attack me, but Margot came between me and Louis and told him off. Lucifer ordered Louis to kill Margot, he said she was useless. I tried to move her out of the way and I got clawed. Raguel rushed to the rescue as soon as he was conscious. But it was too late the cambion had put his hand in the chest of Margot and took her heart out. It was still beating and he threw it in the fire. He vociferated it was for all the tortures he received because of her. Doctor Williams tried to retrieve her heart from the fire place. Raguel attacked the cambion. Lucifer made an attempt to abduct me again but Henry arrived in the room behind Lucifer and he tackled him, he ordered me to run for my life. He was strong enough to make sure I could leave. I glanced back once to only see the poor Margot lying on the floor, dead, among all the fighting going on.

Ivy did let her emotion run free when she said,

-Margot was the bravest young girl I ever saw in my life. I will miss her. I will miss her so much. She was so serious that Sebastien told me we should nickname her our serious little bit.

Her tears flowed on her cheeks. Amelia hugged her tight crying likewise,

-Yes, she was brave till the end, so brave.

Meanwhile, when the Great Being left the kitchen to intervene in the drawing room along with his youngest son, Vincent, he didn't expect the ghost of Abraham Wilton-Cough to make a physical appearance. In the corridor, he demanded,

-Abraham, what are you doing here?

The old banker replied sternly,

-I aim to help, my Lord. Even if it is just to cause a diversion of the enemy's attention on the fight.

Valdi tapped the shoulder of Wilton-Cough with appreciation while the Great Being approved,

-Do as you said Abraham. If you get dragged to hell we will claim you back.

The Lord stepped into the room to see Raguel in a dire fight with an exhausted cambion, while Henry was about to lose his with Lucifer. He ordered,

-Abraham, help the Master, now. Vincent, we need to help Henry immediately.

Valdi went straight in. Lucifer never expected him. He cried out loud,

-You!

Vincent punched his face as he answered,

-Yes, me! So you went for my wife again. You do not learn your lessons, do you?

He dragged Lucifer with sheer strength and anger away from Henry and carried on fighting, saying at every knocks he delivered,

-Do you want a piece of my mind? Learn to listen! Leave my wife alone!

The Great Being managed to rescue Henry and led him to the kitchen. He knocked thrice on the door. Sebastien opened it and he received in his arms a badly injured but still walking Messenger. His grand father ordered,

-Call your three M, we need reinforcement. Your father is wounded as well. Williams is on on the floor showing no signs of life but he is still alive. I will go and get him. See to Henry immediately.

Sebastien did as he was told, walked Henry to a chair where the angel lost consciousness for a while. But with vigorous slapping, Henry came back to his senses. He saw the intense eyes of Sebastien upon him and when he ordered,

-Drink this.

He just obliged him. Then Henry told tears in his eyes,

-I heard Lucifer ordering Louis to kill Margot. I was in the corridor. When I arrived in the room she was dead, the poor little thing was dead. I saw her heart being thrown inside the fire place. Amelia was so distressed, she was wounded, she couldn't move. You know, from the shock of what happened before her eyes. I ordered her to escape. And then I wanted to kill Lucifer, just get rid of him once and for all. But he reopened my recent wounds during the fight, one after the other like if he knew all my weakest points, all of them. I thought I was going to die. But Valdi came and tackled Lucifer, and the Lord saved me.

Sebastien took the shirt of his young angel off and said,

-Let's look after you. So the order to kill Margot came from Lucifer?

Henry nodded positively with his answer,

-It did come from Lucifer, yes. He said she was useless. Then I heard Louis blaming Margot for the tortures he received from Cork. I arrived too late in the room, soon enough to save Amelia but not our Margot, not our poor Margot. She suffered a terrible death, Sebastien, a terrible one. I remember Ted saying that he couldn't see the future of Margot. He was worried about it.

Unable to retain his tears, Sebastien replied while looking after the wounds of his angel,

-I know, he told me about it, but he couldn't have a vision. He desperately tried. But Ted has been injured lately and is very weak. His visions take most of his strength away and the one for the fire in town drained him. As for little Jack who has started to have visions, he is not in the best of health either. We couldn't foresee or prevent that one.

In the drawing room, the fight was still going on. Valdi was getting the better out of Lucifer who was under him almost choking. Vincent bragged,

-Did you lost a tooth or two? Is it too hard to swallow? Let me help you.

He turned Lucifer around almost like a rag doll with sheer force and made him cough out his teeth in a violent way. As soon as it was done, Lucifer spat a couple of tooth along with blood then swore,

-You are a bastard!

However an angry Valdi retorted,

-Look, who is talking? A bastard of a failed angel with no heart. Let's see if we can find one in you! I have no claws like your creatures so it will hurt a tad more when I will do the digging.

His father who was carrying an unconscious Williams warned him,

-Keep him alive, Vincent, for I will make him pay dearly for that one.

On his side, Raguel had knocked down the erratic cambion and was putting the shackles back onto his ankles and wrists with the help of Abraham. He ordered to his brother,

-Do as father said, Vincent! I need him alive because he

has questions to answer.

Lucifer gave a fearful look to Valdi and pleaded

-I deserve death, kill me, kill me now.

Giving him an evil smirk, Vincent told,

-It sounds like you are going to get tortured, Lucifer.

At that mention, Lucifer tried desperately to regain the upper hand, putting all his efforts into the fight. However he felt doomed when he heard the Master of all angels saying,

-I am coming, brother. I am done with Louis, he will not wake up for a while. Abraham, guard him.

Lucifer shouted an order in tongue, but it had no effect, he shouted again and again. Raguel arrived by Valdi, pushed him out of the way and delivered a punch to Lucifer which sent him flying across the room. Then he smiled as he boasted,

-Yes, it doesn't work any longer. You can get us once with your magical formulae but not twice. I am afraid your cambion has been freed from your thrall. He will never reply to your orders anymore.

Lucifer retorted frightened,

-How would you know? How?

Smiling wickedly, Raguel approached calmly the visibly shaken fallen angel,

-I happened to know a lot, far more than you can imagine. Vince, grab that bastard and teach me the trick on how to break his wrist in one go. You see, Lucifer, we learn all the time simply by watching others.

A very daunted Lucifer retreated until his back touched the wall. He demanded,

-You are still playing the watcher. Well, you have never been very good at it. You could have spotted that Raphael was a double standard archangel. Hit me with it, what do you know?

Dragging Lucifer towards him and in a fast move that even Lucifer didn't expect, Raguel had the fallen angel in a solid lock. Vincent was already by his brother and broke one wrist of Lucifer. In pain the fallen angel could only hear the comment of

Raguel,

-Neat!

In a fast move he was passed to Valdi who held him in an extremely strong fashion. Lucifer tried to wriggle his way out of the hold but couldn't with one hand disabled and another weak from having been broken not very long ago. The Master stated,

-Oh, you see, Lucifer, you are not the only one with tricks up your sleeve. My commands to my angels are plain and uncomplicated because I have no fear of some rebelling against me any longer. I know all the culprits, and as the angel of justice I will go after them one by one. So let's start by the one with the most double standards under the sky, which happens to be you.

A fearful Lucifer pleaded,

-You are wrong, it is not me at this moment in time, it is Gabriel. I am merely involve with my creations which are awfully not working for me as they should, as you have seen.

Taking the lame hand of Lucifer, Raguel twisted and broke the little finger of it as he commented,

-So removing the hearts of those who are not working the way you want seems a good idea? I wonder what would happen if I did that to my angels: a mutiny? Probably. Remove the wings of a bad one and you have a flock of bad ones following suit. You don't learn, do you, Lucifer? You think you know it all, but in fact, you learnt nothing throughout the ages.

The fallen angel yelped,

-If you read my manuscript you should know I did learn many things throughout the ages! Many, you don't know what it is to try to survive down there in hell.

As another of Lucifer's fingers got broken by a calm Raguel, Valdi mentioned,

-Do you mean the manuscript on how to kill everything? That's very instructive indeed. My only wonder is did you learn the word compassion? You'd better learn it fast. Go for his thumb, next.

His will almost failing him at that moment in time, Lucifer cried out,

-What do you want from me? Just ask. Just ask. I didn't just learn how to kill things, let me correct you on that I did learn how to create them.

The angel of justice broke the thumb of Lucifer with his stern statement,

-Failures like you.

Stepping back into the room was the Great Being who asked with a falsely genuine smile,

-Who created failures?

His eldest son dared to say, knowing he possessed the full support of his father,

-You, obviously. I have a beautiful one, a failure, in front of me. Why on earth did you decide to create things from fire that are so ablazed with hate?

Peacefully his father locked the door of the room before he replied,

-I thought it was a good idea at the time. But giving it full consideration and a great amount of time, I did revise my position on the worth of them all. A little like our good friend Lucifer, I am considering losing some right now.

Coming straight to Lucifer, slapping him and making him kneel right down, the Great Being ordered,

-Tell me all, now. Last chance, Lucifer, last chance.

On his knees, the fallen angel with his two shoulders maintained down by Raguel and Valdi confessed,

-I have been creating. It took me a very long time to know how to do it. I wanted a demonic army of my own, like your son has an angelic army. I wanted true protection down in hell.

The Great Being turned around and pointed to the dead Margot then demanded,

-Can you explain me that?

A blank Lucifer replied,

-She wasn't any good for my purposes. She had too much human in her. She failed to reproduce demons like her mother.

He received a massive punch from Raguel which broke his lower jaw.

Valdi commented,

-I can only guess the conversation is finished, dad. Shall we take him back to hell?

At that moment in time the three M arrived in the room. They bowed in their ancient manner reminiscent of the time they were musketeers. One pointed with his black cowboy hat towards the body of Margot and demanded,

-Who had the indecency of killing that poor child?

This incensed Raguel, who pointed at Lucifer, punched the fallen angel in the stomach and replied,

-Him.

Lucifer argued with great difficulty and tried to point with his broken finger to the cambion on the floor,

-No, it was him, it was him. It's not true!

He bled profusely from his mouth as he did so. His terrified eyes met the ones of the angel of justice who replied sternly,

-You gave the order to kill, Lucifer. You are also her murderer.

Lucifer looked at the dead girl with consternation before he protested with difficulties,

-Why would you care? She was basically made by my creature once removed. She was mine to be disposed off.

The Great Being went to the child and put her upon the sofa with care as he responded closing her beautiful green eyes,

-To be a Creator, Lucifer, you need to learn to care for your creatures. The problem is that you only care for yourself. The rest doesn't matter to you apart to be used or be abused. Did you give your creatures free will?

Trembling the fallen angel answered with honesty for

once,

-No, my Lord, I didn't but they got it anyway as soon as they mixed with the human race. When their blood has human blood I lose total control of the creatures. They have a mind of their own. Her father was a decent cambion, whom I had no power over up until he endured the pain of the loss of his son. It was only then that he responded to the instinct of his demonic blood to do my biding.

The Creator demanded,

-Did you kill the son of Cork?

Lucifer shook his head negatively,

-No, the boy was weak since the sinking of the ship. He was part human like her and he just caught a severe pulmonary disease.

Returning by him, the Great Being asked further,

-So you kept an eye on Cork's family?

With a deep sigh Lucifer gave his answer,

-Yes, but loosely like you do with your humans that kill each other endlessly.

He received a harsh slap from Raguel who carried on the interrogation,

-How many creatures are out there?

Refusing to answer the fallen angel tried in vain to escape by opening a window. But the strength of Valdi caught him by his wings and threw him on the floor. Matthias closed the window and positioned himself by it while his brothers did the same by the other windows. The Great Being ordered,

-Raguel, cut his demonic wings. Lucifer will stay in hell from now on with no access to earth.

The sentence was a blow for the fallen angel who saw the scythe appearing in the hand of the angel of justice. Raguel was fast to execute his order, helped by his bother who maintained Lucifer down on his knees for him. The large demonic bat wings were thrown aside nonchalantly. Tears in his eyes from pain, Lucifer looked at his cherished appendices cut from him laying lifeless in a pool of blood. He then met the severe eyes of the Creator and dared to ask with sheer difficulty,

-Can I make it up to you, my Lord, in any way, shape or form?

The Great Being ordered, ignoring the plea,

-Take him to hell.

Then he turned to Abraham Wilton-Cough to ask,

-I need you to come with me, Wilton-Cough, we need to retrieve the spirit of that little girl and convince her to become a ghost.

Abraham bowed, taking his top hat off only to agree,

-Yes, my Lord.

Only Matthias was left behind to keep an eye on the unconscious cambion Louis. A somewhat subdued Lucifer who had stopped struggling and fighting was brought back to hell to his somewhat monastic apartment there. His pass which allowed him to go to earth removed, he asked,

-Who will be the servant to take the souls who needs to go to hell?

An undaunted Great Being looking at the messy bookshelf in the chamber replied,

-My son, of course. Raguel is experienced and most of all, he can be trusted. You didn't tidy up your place since we left you last time.

Lucifer nodded positively before he said simply,

-Burnt hands, a broken wrist... and know broken fingers and a broken wrist again... I will tidy up when I can.

Out of any will to fight or even argue, the fallen angel sat on his bed. He looked thankfully at Raguel who had let him do so. He paused before he cried out,

-I am lost totally lost, a total mess of a former angel.

He spat some blood at his own feet and sighed deeply. The Master brought to him a glass of water then ordered,

-Here, drink, then tell us about your creatures. You don't

have to hold the glass I will do so. Tell me, have you got a proper servant to look after you? By the state of your room, it looks like you have none. Hours passed since we came last time.

Lucifer gave another thankful and tearful glance at Raguel. He burst out,

-If anyone could be like you down here, I would know where to stand and say my stance. It would be straightforward. But we are in hell, and backstabbing is common place. I have no servant, no true servant, no one I admit in this room but you proper angels, the Lord and his servants. Otherwise my trust level is next to none.

The Master of all angels told sternly despite giving more water to Lucifer,

-You do know I am not going to be sorry for you? You have been around long enough to know about karma and bad karma. Or you must be aware of the old saying that 'What goes around, comes around'. As the angel of justice, I can even mention to you: As you sow so you shall reap. So you can't trust anyone. I will state just this: No wonders!

Despite himself the fallen angel smiled, his jaw in horrendous pain. Then he confessed,

-I created just one demon, Raguel. But I had a hard time to control him. I wanted him to react to instinct but also to orders. But it was a utter failure. He was not fully controllable. Raphael killed that creature. It was called Lucas. That incubus did create Cork, the mother of Margot and Louis with three different human women. Then he fell in love with a succubus and I couldn't get him to work for me for a while until I arranged to kill his sweet heart. I told him to replace her with his granddaughter. That scheme didn't work out. I can't have the army I wish to have.

Valdi turning around the messy room demanded,

-Hold on! If your Lucas mated with a succubus, why are you not using their offspring?

Taken out of pace, Lucifer replied,

-They are not what I wanted. They lack the human loyalty.

Caught red handed, the fallen angel was slapped

roughly by Raguel who asked,

-How many? Are they in hell or upon earth?

A daunted Lucifer answered,

-They are all in hell but one. I lost the track of one, a male demon, an incubus called Dee. He is in Wales.

Another slap hit him with the question,

-How many?

The fallen angel replied with a sigh,

-Thirteen, twelve in hell and one on earth.

#

Hurting all over Raphael woke up on the kitchen table. He saw Doctor Williams, snoring gently by him, holding his hand tightly. As soon as he released his hand the old angel was awake. Raphael enquired,

-William, you have blood on your hands and you are badly burnt? Where is Sebastien? He needs to take a good look at you.

Doctor Williams waking up replied almost a little stunned,

-He did, he did. How are you feeling?

Raphael managed to sit on the edge of the table with difficulty before he answered,

-I am alive.

Williams started to cry at that answer. A concerned Raphael went to him and embraced the old angel, pleading,

-Please do not cry for me, William, I am not worth your tears.

Doctor Williams looked at the fallen angel and his sincere attitude then announced to him the truth,

-Raphael, we lost someone during the night.

The fallen angel instinctively hugged the old angel then demanded to know,

-Who did we lose, who? Don't tell me it is the Master, please, don't tell me it is him, for we need him.

Williams reassured but revealed the news in an almost blunt way,

-It is not the Master. It is the young Margot.

A shocked Raphael collapsed on the shoulder of William and cried thoroughly. Doctor Williams tapped his back gently as he gave more details,

-Lucifer came to take Amelia Valdi again. But Margot protected her. Louis, the cambion killed the poor child. He took her heart out with his claws. I tried my up most to retrieve her heart which was thrown into the flames. It was still beating. But the cambion started to batter me unconscious with his chains. Lucifer did free Louis with a magical sentence. Louis was nice and obedient up until Lucifer came. Then with a few words all hell were unleashed as per say. But Margot is no more. The entire family is in tatters. Raguel punished Louis and Lucifer but I can tell you it was a blow for him. He was an angel of scarce few words. Lucifer is condemned to hell and will remain in hell. He will not walk upon earth until further notice.

Raphael tried to gain his countenance back but he hardly could do so. He demanded,

-Why Margot? Why? She was such a good girl. Upright and such, such...

The old angel answered,

-Margot was so good that she did put herself in the line of fire as per say. She was part human, she had a loving heart. If you did something wrong in front of her she would react. She did just that and lost her life.

Holding the hand of Williams, Raphael enquired,

-Where is the Master? Where is the family?

Doctor Williams informed the fallen angel,

-You will find the family praying by the coffin of the little girl in the church. The funeral will be done this afternoon by the Master himself. As for him, he is injured and to be left alone for a while. He is upset and brooding in the back garden.

Standing up with difficulty, Raphael told firmly,

-I will go to him.

Williams stood up from his chair then stated,

-Then let me go with you. When Raguel is distraught, he may not take any consideration of a word you say. For him only actions speak louder than words.

Watching the slowness of Doctor Williams's moves, Raphael gave him his support. Shoulder to shoulder, almost as if they had never been enemies, they walked together to the little back garden, giving each other mutual help. When Raphael saw Raguel, who was just standing there, broken hearted, he came to him, hugged him silently then knelt to him. With a sobbing voice, he announced,

-I heard, Master, I heard about Margot.

Tears started to stream upon Raphael's face again. Raguel looked at Williams for an explanation only to demand,

-I told you to take him to his room if the Maggot ever woke up? He needs a rest.

A tired Doctor Williams sensing the annoyance in the voice of the Master sat on the bench however replied strongly,

-I know what the order was but he is a human with free will now. He wanted to see you.

Raphael's tearful gaze met the uncompromising one of Raguel. He stood up, painfully, without help. Then the fallen angel said with a sobbing voice,

-I just wanted to say that I am sorry to hear of what happened last night, Master, truly sorry. May I be allowed at her funeral? She meant to me. She just meant so much. She just meant.

Softening up, Raguel held the hand of Raphael for a brief moment as he conceded,

-Yes, of course you can come. Would you do the honour to Margot to write her eulogy? Would you read it for her during the ceremony?

Raphael nodded his ascent before saying strongly,

-I will, Master, I will.

Then a minute of silence stood between them, where a broken hearted Raphael just cried again. Raguel hugged him, and ordered,

-Go and see her before we are closing the coffin. Then write her eulogy. Keep it short, keep it as straight as she was.

Turning to Williams, he added,

-See that Raphael is suitably dressed for the funeral. Keep looking after him for me.

The fallen angel bowed to the angel of justice then followed the lead of Doctor Williams. Out of earshot, Raphael vented,

-I can tell he is upset.

The good William helping Raphael to walk straight up commented,

-I told you he was. You must learn to know when to leave him alone. Apparently, from what I gathered, he went to hell last night to lock Lucifer in his chamber almost forever by the order of his father. Raguel doesn't like to have to do that even to his fallen angels. But this became a necessary measure for Lucifer. You don't want to know all the particulars of Lucifer's punishment but I can tell you it is a matter of life and death for him, a little like it was for you. It was dealing with a traitor's matter.

To be compared to Lucifer did hurt the feelings of Raphael who sighed deeply but nonetheless he turned to William with an honest question,

-What do I have to do to redeem myself in the Master's eyes and then to the Lord's ones?

The old servant looked at the hurt fallen angel before he replied,

-I do not have an answer for you, but you will have it at some point in your heart. Trust your human heart. Let's cover you up before we see the coffin. No one is expecting you to pay respect to Margot and you can't come just with a torso covered with bandages. Here let's give you a nice shirt, a little black tie and a black short jacket. The funeral will be very private this afternoon. Margot did lose all the members of her former family and in town, she was only talking to a few, not many at all. She was a rather reclusive person probably because of what happened to her. Mr Berry knew her and our Mrs Odell. Valdi did know her too but he had to go, leave, mainly for the safety of his wife early this morning. So it will be Sebastien's family, the Master, you and me, Mr Berry and his partner, Theo and his wife and Henry and Ted.

Williams made clothes appear in his hands and dressed Raphael with care then once satisfied, he stated,

-Here, you are presentable my friend. Remember one thing, Ivy is staying strong but she is devastated upon the entire matter. I can tell you that she is just pulling a brave face on.

With a tear running lose upon his cheek, Raphael confided,

-I am just as well. I can't start to tell you how upset I am. Not because Margot saved my life but because of who she was, because of who she was.

Fastening the bow tie of the fallen angel, Doctor Williams scolded,

-Come, come, Margot would have wanted you to stay strong. Within her last minutes, hour, she was holding the candle lamp to help with your operation.

A sighing Raphael put his jacket on before following Williams to the church. When they entered silently, sobs could be heard. They saw the family by the coffin crying together in a cluster. When Raphael saw the pale face of Margot, he did burst into tears again. He knelt on the cold stone slabs of the church. The old Williams instinctively gave him his hand to hold. Raphael reached for it, grieving.

Sebastien and Ivy went towards the newcomers and hugged them silently. If Williams could dry his tears, Raphael couldn't. He kept watching at the young Margot positioned in her little coffin. He kept thinking at the way she saved him against the strong currents of the river, the way she tried to make him do the right things, and the way she scolded him. Raphael then told,

-She needs to be surrounded by holly because she is our holy Margot. Let's get some for her, let's find some. Who is with me?

Jack put his hand within Raphael's hand and Tobias

followed suit. Soon the entire family was in the woods gathering beautiful branches of holly to decorate the coffin of the young Marguerite. When her coffin was closed everyone went back to the house, Theo Odell had arrived and prepared his church for the afternoon ceremony.

In his bedroom with Doctor Williams, Raphael proposed to the old angel,

-Please, William, rest upon my bed for a few minutes while I write the eulogy of Margot.

An exhausted Williams did so willingly. Soon his eyes were closed. Raphael closed his curtains to promote his rest then went to his desk, lit a candle and started to write. He couldn't help shedding tears on the paper as he wrote. A couple of hours later, came a knock on his door. He invited,

-Please, do enter. The door is not locked.

The Master entered and demanded,

-Are you ready for the funeral?

Standing up Raphael dried his tears and bowed with his reply,

-Yes, Master.

Raguel went to adjust Raphael's jacket then commented,

-Here, you are presentable. Have you done the eulogy?

The fallen angel presented it with shivering hands before telling,

-It is done. I hope I am doing our Margot justice in it.

Briefly reading it and noticing the tears upon the paper, the dry ones and the recent ones, the Master said,

-I am sure you did. In the future, I want you to lock your door and assess who wants to come in. The reason is that you are human now and Lucifer will be after you in one way or another. He will not give you time to redeem yourself, I can tell you that. He is ruthless. So you must keep your wits about you. We uncovered a race of demons and cambions created by Lucifer which can be triggered by a simple order of his. Louis is one of them. It is like his personal undercover army upon earth.

So you must be careful. I will brief you more upon it later on. How is my Williams?

Pointing at the bed, Raphael answered in a whisper,

-He is exhausted. He went in the woods with us. He was attacked last night and he still has a full physical presence in Boston. I made him sleep for a little bit to recuperate.

Raguel's eyes met the ones of his fallen angel who were looking at the sleeping servant with compassion for a split second. He ordered,

-Come with me, my Maggot. We will let William sleep a little longer. The funeral is starting in an hour. Father Odell and I will show you how it will go. Take the eulogy with you.

Once out of the bedroom, the Master told,

-Raphael, please dry your tears. You are going to start me on and we need to pull through that ceremony somehow.

Following the strong angel, Raphael obeyed and apologised,

-I am so sorry, Master. I will try to not cry. I can't promise it though. I sincerely can't.

Tapping gently his shoulder, Raguel revealed,

-All may not be lost. My father is working on something. I don't know the outcome yet but I will let you and William know as soon as I am informed about the result. The spirit of Margot belongs to the angels, although she had demonic blood within her, she belongs to us.

Raphael's eyes were full of hope and corrected,

-You mean to you...

The Master held the fallen angel's shoulder firmly before repeating,

-No, to us. I expect you to regain your wings one day.

Both went to the church, where Father Odell was finishing the preparations with his wife. If Raguel went inside straightforwardly, Raphael stood at the entrance at the sight of Theo Odell suddenly unsure if his presence would be welcomed. Ludwig, the rottweiler was nosing him to step in.

Raguel warned Theo,

-Raphael has done the eulogy, he has it with him.

Odell felt sorry to see the uncertainty of Raphael to enter his church when he was present. He left what he was doing and went to welcome the fallen angel,

-Come on in. I heard that you was attacked last night.

Suddenly shy, Raphael replied holding his folded piece of paper close to his chest,

-Yes, I was.

Theo sensed the timidity of Raphael so probed him further to allow him to open up a little,

-How are you feeling today?

He led the fallen angel within his church slowly, walking by his side. Raphael replied in an emotional way,

-I am devastated about Margot. I swear it should be me in that coffin, not her, never her.

Raguel came straight away by his new servant and put his arm around his shoulders in a comforting way as he said,

-Neither of you two should have been hurt last night. Theo meant how are you physically?

Odell nodded his confirmation, realising that the death of Margot was affecting deeply the fallen angel. Raphael tried to withhold his coming tears with his answer,

-I am sorry, I misunderstood. Well, I can just stay I am still standing. I am in pain but standing. Sebastien is a great surgeon. Doctor Valdi also came to my help, I heard. This is probably why I am still alive.

Theo told showing the decorations,

-We thought that your idea of holly was a good one, Raphael, so we put branches on every pillar. Mr Berry went to gather some for us. We also brought the last white roses from the hotel. My wife and Miss Marlow made a beautiful crown of them to go above the coffin. See. Mrs Cotton will recite a poem of Byron. Do you need to rehearse the eulogy? Because you have time to do so.

Witnessing all the preparations coming together to celebrate the life of Margot, Raphael replied,

-No, I don't need to rehearse. I know it by heart. It comes from the heart. The worst that can happen is that I will burst into tears mid way through.

A very serious Theo demanded,

-Raguel, do you want to read the piece in that case?

The Master of all angels declined,

-I will do the exact same thing. No, let Raphael do it. If we cry, we cry and at the end of the day, sorrow being in our hearts, we are allowed to. We are both shaken by the death of young Margot. Theo, I like what you did with the decoration.

Raphael gave a thankful silent look to Raguel before he agreed,

-She would have loved that, I am sure. She did like the white roses at your wedding, Father Odell.

Whilhelmina came by them and embraced Raguel, tapping his back, saying,

-You have all my condolences. I was so sorry to hear what happened. My Mina is coming with Emily. Georgia is bringing them. They were so upset at the news. Emily did go and tell them throughout the town to the households where the classmates of Margot are. We are expecting some parents and many of the school children at her funeral.

A worried Raguel queried,

-What did she say?

Theo reassured,

-What we told her to say. We know what happened but we can't reveal it, so we created a rumour on this occasion, that she did pass away having a miscarriage.

It made Raphael start, shout, and cry out loud,

-It is wrong! Margot died bravely trying to protect Mrs Valdi.

Raguel intervened, putting his arm across the shoulders of his servant,

-Raphael! Don't get incensed, please. Theo, we have to say the truth on that one, we have to reestablish it even if it will hurt and shock everyone to hear it.

Breaking down into sobs, the fallen angel turned to the Master, who put him against him and enjoined,

-My Maggot, please, get a grip on yourself. Theo, you can come with us. I just need to calm him down.

Theo exchanged sorrowful looks with his wife and both followed Raguel into the little room where the priest usually changed attire. The Master made Raphael sit on the dark coffer bench and made an handkerchief appear. Giving it to the fallen angel, he told Theo,

-You have to forgive him. He is unwell and a bundle of emotions right now. Dealing with feelings is a very different affair between being an angel and then being a human.

His arms crossed upon his chest Father Odell commented sternly,

-Do you mean that he has started to grow a human heart?

Whilst Raphael was bowing his head down, the Master accepted but gave a staunch glance to Theo,

-Yes, if we put that in an insulting way for him.

Odell reacted by kneeling down by the fallen angel, putting his hands upon Raphael's knees, he said in a much gentler tone of voice,

-Raphael, I know this will not comfort you at this moment in time with everything we are dealing with but I have a message for you from Doctor Valdi. You know he had to leave early to protect his wife. He told me to tell you one thing: He has forgiven you. I also want you to know something else, all the angels in Wilton Town will unsure that you are alright. At one call from them, Valdi will be at your side to ascertain that we are never losing you. So you have to be strong for us and with us. We will stand by you. I acknowledge that I shun you before, but with Valdi making the step to forgive you, I have no longer the same grievance against you. You have my own forgiveness as well for all that it is worth.

Father Odell stopped, clearing his voice. He met the sorrowful gaze of Raphael then carried on,

-I heard that you have decided to live in Wilton Town. I will make sure you are fully accepted in our small community. Mr Tyrell will do so just as well and Doctor Valdi when he comes back. You have a place here and I am sure you will find a place in our hearts like you already have started to do. Now, dry your tears. I don't think I ever presented you my wife, Whilhelmina. She is the nurse and midwife in Wilton Town. She is also an eternal being. Someone you can talk to if you need to talk to the angels in time of emergency.

Whilhelmina presented her pale hand to the fallen angel who held it briefly by politeness. She proposed,

-Mr River, I am worried about you. Did you eat today? Your complexion is dusky. Do you want something to eat? You mustn't fall or faint during the eulogy.

Raphael answered,

-I can't eat today. I have no appetite.

The replies came fast and forward. The Master was the first to say,

-Tough, you must.

Theo joined in,

-Georgia is bringing gingerbreads, you must have a slice or two before the funeral. I don't want you to collapse during it. Vincent is not here with us and Sebastien and Ivy are so distraught to have lost their adopted girl, so any medical attention given to you will be minimal.

Smirking Raguel said meaning every word,

-It is very simple, if he doesn't eat something and he faints afterword, I will wake him up with an entire bucket of cold water poured over him if that fails to work I will use Margot's method with him: meaningful slapping.

Those words had the power to make Raphael smile and cry at the same time as he consented,

-I will have to eat something then.

Whilhelmina ordered,

-Stay here, Mr River. I know Sebastien is preparing nice cups of hot chocolate for his boys and his wife, and us. I wonder if he will have a spare one for you. If not you can have mine.

Before Raphael could say anything, Whilhelmina had left the room in a ruffle of black satin dress and petticoats. Raguel noted in a complimentary fashion to Theo,

-The black suits her as much as the white.

A sighing Odell replied, officially in love,

-Give her any colour of the rainbow to wear and she will brighten any sky, any day. She prefers white most of all though but I didn't gather why apart that her maiden name was White.

Raphael dared to join the conversation with his comment,

-I can tell there is more into it. Her skin is so pale. It looks like porcelain. She noticed my complexion the first time she saw me. My only guess is that she pays a lot of attention to hers as well. How did she become an eternal being may I ask? Because depending on the method, you can get that very pale skin and wearing white will make her look more human to human eyes.

As Theo was a bit baffled yet thinking that Raphael was right, Raguel explained,

-Theo, Raphael is still partly sentient as a human. He also has all his experience of being an archangel and years behind him worth of memory. However it doesn't impeach him to be stupid from times to times but he does also say something intelligent on occasion.

The fallen angel exchanged a knowing look with the Master of all angels. He couldn't help smiling. Raphael stated,

-Well, the amount of my stupidity is that I do not have wings to show off any longer.

Theo considering Raphael with different eyes, brought a little wooden stool closer to the bench and invited,

-Please Master take a seat we have time to discuss a little. I arranged for some musicians to come for the funeral but they always take time to come.

Likewise he sat in a stool almost in front of Raphael, then Theo queried,

-Raphael, I heard that you wanted to become an angel again, am I right?

Faced by the two angels Raphael felt a little intimidated but replied nonetheless,

-You are right. I am going to work my up most towards that goal. I don't know if I can achieve it but I will die trying.

Raguel added to that confirmation of intent,

-I will make sure he will. He is me servant now, and dare I say, he will have me pushing him all the time until he gets his wings.

Raphael smiled with grateful kindness as he said,

-I know you will.

Acknowledging that moment, Theo told,

-So if you are aiming to be an angel, Raphael, you will be a human angel. We are split into teams in the army of Sebastien and with your definite intelligence and experience, I would recommend that you join the Logistic team. We are not a lot, Ted is at the head of it. Then it is composed of my wife and I, Valdi and Amelia. Apart from Vincent we are not fighters as per say, but we need to plan and think forward. I think you could be a very welcomed member in that team. I will leave that to your consideration.

Raphael stood up and offered his hand to shake to Theo as he said,

-It is all considered. During my human life I will work for the angels.

Odell took the hand presented to him. He felt the firm grip of the fallen angel who simply added,

-My aim is not to deceive anymore.

Stroking his own hands straight afterwards, Theo commented,

-I can feel that you mean your every word. I thought you

had your arms broken?

Raguel smirked at that comment only to reply,

-He had. But he did also exercise his fingers since. Raphael will be slightly more powerful than your average human. However we nearly lost him last night to heart failure. When he recovers and he is fit and healthy, I strongly suggest you to take some fighting lessons with him.

Odell commented stroking his chin thoughtfully,

-I wonder if it is a good idea. I can already guess that I will be on the ground in a matter of minutes.

A reassuring Raphael told,

-The importance is on always standing up again. It is a learning process. It may be tough at first but it is learning to survive. I can make it easy for you initially and then gradually increase the level of pressure until you will be able to survive a one to one with a demon. But you are clever and resourceful, so with close combat techniques added to that, you will be one of the best angels... I would advise never to dismiss something until you try it first. Of course it may not be pure wisdom coming from a fallen angel but if the Master wants you to have fighting lessons it means that he wants you to be fully protected when you are in the thick of it. Because you will be in the thick of and you already have, I heard. Five demons in one day, the other angels would have boasted loud and proud about that feat for ages. That is an achievement.

Coming running into the room was Mina. She threw herself onto Father Odell, crying,

-I saw her coffin, Pa, I saw it. I put my bouquet of lavender onto it. It was attached with my best purple velvet ribbon. I am so, so sad. The school children did start to arrive with their parents, they are all lighting candles for Marguerite.

Theo dried the tears of Mina and enjoined her,

-Well, we have a duty to welcome them, then. Let's do it together.

He then turned to the Master to say,

-I will do the lessons. I am going to send Georgia to you. Make sure Raphael eat a little. I know we have a banquet later on prepared by Tyrell, but he definitely needs something before then. His hands are cold and shivering. Valdi ordered to not let him grab a cold.

Taking the hand of Mina, Father Odell led her to the main part of the church. Left alone with his fallen angel, the Master confided,

-Raphael, we are all caring about you. We may call you names or be annoyed about all your past. But past is past and present is present to build a better future. So far, I want you to know that you have been a very brave and decent human. To be honest with you, my Father and I, and my son as well, will appreciate having you back as an angel when you earn your wings. To have you with us, simply as a human, well, we learnt another side of you, the Raphael who has a heart.

Raphael didn't have time to comment. A diligent Miss Marlow came into the room without knocking. She bowed briefly and addressed the Master rather than the fallen angel,

-How is he doing? He should really be in bed resting.

Raguel reassured,

-He will be fine. The worst is over. We just need to keep an eye on him. He gave his bed to your future husband who is rather exhausted. But we need Williams at the funeral so if you would care to wake him up gently I will appreciate it. He is a little injured as well. He will probably not tell you that so you do not worry but be aware of it and tell me if his condition deteriorates. I don't think it will though.

The good Georgia nodded her ascent then told while cutting some slices of ginger bread,

-I will see to it. I've heard that the boys were not fed this morning? I can prepare something for them.

Correcting her Raguel replied,

-No, they did eat. Sebastien made scrambled eggs for the entire family this morning. But I am sure the boys will enjoy a slice of gingerbread nonetheless. Tobias is so worryingly emaciated. He can do with eating a little, and very often.

Georgia gave the slices to Raphael with her usual simplicity,

-Please eat. This will do you some good. You need to gather some strength back, Mr River. Are you coming to the tavern with all of us tonight? Mr Tyrell is preparing the funeral banquet there.

Raphael gave a wondering look at the Master of all angels who replied for him with certainty,

-Yes, he is coming with us. He is part of our angelic family. Will you make sure all the little children that came to the funeral of Margot have some of your gingerbread?

A smiling Georgia replied firmly,

-Oh, yes I will. I did make plenty with the girls this morning, enough to feed a crowd. Your angel Henry is already giving some to the kids that knew the little Marguerite at the entrance of the church. I gathered, he was hurt last night, but he is smiling and standing and welcoming everybody...

This pleased Raguel who did indulge the curiosity of Georgia,

-Henry suffered injuries last night, yes. But relatively speaking, between you and I, for a young angel of a couple of centuries, he is still standing and living after a big fight with Lucifer. He did hold his own for a fair few minutes and gave Lucifer a rough and tumble both will never forget. One will now be worried of the other, while the other did learn what it was to tackle a major fallen angel. Henry did well to survive the encounter and the one to one. It is all I can say. But you must go now, the funeral will be starting shortly.

Georgia recognised the authoritative tone of voice, she bowed to the Master of all angels then left the room. With querying eyes, Raphael demanded to know,

-Did the Messenger fought Lucifer last night? He is still standing?

A proud Raguel replied,

-You should have seen it. Henry arrived in the room seconds too late, but he did hear the order of Lucifer to kill Margot. While I was tackling the cambion, he took on upon himself to tackle Lucifer and he went for it properly. Henry saw the heart of Margot being thrown into the flames. Disgusted he gave a battering to Lucifer. Not only that he made sure Amelia Valdi could escape from the drawing room. However, you know as I do how experienced is Lucifer in terms of fighting. Henry did well, but if my father didn't arrive in time to split that fight, we would not have a Messenger today. But as I said, that young angel just had the tuition of a lifetime, he knows what it takes to fight Lucifer. I know what it takes, do you?

Putting his half eaten slice of gingerbread down, Raphael confessed,

-I actually don't. Back in the days, I remember Lucifer training a few angels to fight but I was never one of them. Strangely enough all of those became fallen angels. That I noticed. Do you think he has a specific fighting method?

The Master answered,

-Of course, he has. We went to hell last night. We have imprisoned Lucifer there. But he will free himself, he is like a snake that will find his way out of a situation. Valdi and I did injure him greatly but if that puts him out of the way for a few days, it is only days. Lucifer tried to create an army of creatures that he can control like Louis. He simply has to give an order and from a peaceful creature you have an unstoppable killer to deal with. Williams did get the specific magical order for Louis. But it was at a cost, he got injured as well, pretty much like all who were in the drawing room last night. So Lucifer has many creatures out there at his command. He can partially control some. They do reproduce and like Cork by instinct, they are violent but also physically strong. However, they have to breed with humans which weakens their lines so they do interbreed in order to keep strength in their bloodline. They do find each others on earth but we do not know how yet. We took Abraham with us in hell so when we were dealing with Lucifer, he searched through his manuscripts in his chamber. He found two interesting ones this time around. I can tell you one thing, right away: All of the archangels, all of them, former or not are in a target list devised by Lucifer. You and I are therefore in big trouble. It also includes my youngest son. Apparently Gabriel did the same mistake as you did and signed his soul away to Lucifer.

A sighing Raphael confided,

-Gabriel is a prima dona of an archangel. I would not say even worse than I was, but I can understand how the stance of Lucifer worked with him. Master, hold my hand and read me fully. You will see how Lucifer gets us to sign the deals to sell our souls. I hope it may help you and the angels.

Raguel read his servant, then a knock on the door was heard. The Master satisfied that he had seen enough gave the order to enter the room. His son stood with his two adopted boys at the opened door. Jack ran towards Raphael and hugged him silently. The shy Tobias followed suit. Then Sebastien entered and gave a hot chocolate to Raphael asking him,

-How are you? Don't try to be brave with me, I am your surgeon who will be looking after you. So I want the blunt truth, like it hurts here or there.

The fallen angel smiled to Sebastien before he answered,

-Thank you for saving my life. I am in pain but I can stand it.

Sebastien replied as his two boys grabbed back his hands,

-You are welcome. But you must know it was a joint effort between Doctor Valdi, my wife and I. Now, drink. The benches are filling. Father Odell will be starting within minutes.

Turning to his father, he then said,

-Ivy is still in taters about it all, dad. She tried to put on a brave face all night long. But with the heat of the moment gone, the blow did reach home, if you know what I mean. She did put her black dress on but she then sat on the sofa, the one, granddad did lay Margot upon. She said she will come to church but I can tell you, I think she needs you to walk her here and talk to her. I will supervise uncle Raph' for you. Make sure he eat.

Raguel tapped briefly the shoulder of Raphael to order,

-Eat and drink and don't crumble on me when I am doing the service, my Maggot. I will make you sit behind the altar. Theo will be there as well. So, in effect you will stay by me, behind me.

Raphael nodded silently. The Master left the room and the church and went straight to the presbytery. He found Ivy where Sebastien said she was. Alone she was sobbing on the sofa. Her distress was evident. With a soft voice, he announced himself,

-It is only grandpa Rag. Come here, my child, come here and have a good cry on my shoulder.

The young woman accepted and sobbed out loud,

-There are plenty of things I don't understand. Why her? Why, my poor Margot? I keep thinking that I should have accompanied Amelia instead of her in the drawing room. Why did I let her go here? Why?

Tapping gently his daughter in law's back in his embrace, Raguel told firmly,

-Don't you start blaming yourself for Margot's death my Ivy. I am a very ancient angel which lived for many, many years, and I can tell you that why, is very rarely ever answered. I am still mourning my eldest son, I have still unanswered questions about his death, but he lives forever in my heart like Margot will in all of our hearts. But like my Gael, like your father she will carry on living in spirit form. Her soul once created, conceived is eternal. Trust me when I say that my father is dealing with her case right at this moment in time. Margot will never be lost to us, never. Beside that she would have wanted you to be strong for her, like you have always been. She has chosen you, she demanded if she could call you Ma. You had a bond with Margot that will never be dissolved. So you must be strong for her, Ivy. You must be strong for my Sebastien, you must be strong for your two little boys Jack and Tobias and also for me. Are you ready to be our family's soldier?

With a deep sigh, taking everything in, Ivy dried her tears with difficulty but she did. She confirmed,

-I am ready, grandpa Rag.

The Master offered her his arm as he enjoined her,

-Then lets do it together. I will see to the entire funeral and you will see to my boy and the little ones.

Ivy nestled her pale hand within the muscular arm of her father in law and followed him to the church willingly. When they arrived Ivy was surprised to see so many already on the benches, she confided to Raguel,

-I thought it would be a private funeral...

He replied tapping her hand gently,

-Someone decided it would be otherwise, the little Emily who knew Margot from school. She warned the school children and their parents of her death. Therefore a lot of them came to pay their respect to their former little comrade in their class. I guess our Margot was a popular little girl amongst them. She had such a good and strong temperament that it is no wonder.

People bowed to the passing Ivy remembering how she

had defended Marguerite a few nights previously against her violent father at the tavern and knowing she had given the young girl a home, hers. Raguel presented her the first bench where Ted and Mrs Brown were,

-This is the family bench. Take a seat. I am going to fetch Sebastien and the boys then I am going to start the ceremony with Father Odell.

Henry closed the doors of the church and went to take his seat by Ted silently. Soon Jack and Tobias came between them and Sebastien who sat by his wife and held her hand tightly. Going behind the altar were Raguel and Theo. Raphael sat behind them on a dark chest. Raguel started,

-As you all know, we suffered a terrible loss last night. Someone who has been abused by Mr Cork in a despicable manner killed our Marguerite Bouchon, who some of you may know as Daisy Cork, and the more privileged ones who bestowed her friendship as Margot. With him was an intruder, and it was a fight, a terrible one, where our postman Henry got injured and I. But Margot, the brave Margot, who saw the trouble coming stood in front of the pregnant Mrs Valdi to protect her. Henry arrived just in time to save Mrs Valdi but it was too late for Margot. I can't express enough how upset we all are. Father Odell if you want to proceed.

A sighing Raguel sat by Raphael. Odell with his clear voice made his address to the community,

-We do have a problem in this town, a very serious one. We are not the only town to have that problem. We received people from Boston who thought it will be alright here, thinking they were escaping gangs but faced another gang here, one such person is Rose who is poorly on the bed at the clinic who was attacked during the night of the fire. We need a police force of the like of the one which was created in London in 1829, not so long ago. We need to address our issues and we also need a jail, a prison. We will build together a post for the sheriff and a prison. It is not fair that the Doctors of the town faced harassment when they try to protect a young girl from abuse. It is not fair and what happened last night was far from fair it was horrendous. It left an entire family in tatters. Mrs Cotton, please step forward, it is time for your address.

In her warn black dress which she never thought she would wear again so soon, Ivy went behind the pulpit and started with tears in her eyes,

-My husband and I adopt children in trouble. I am

myself an orphan. I am building a family, my family, by helping the young ones that need a roof, a home, food on the table, and someone to talk to, a heart to heart. The poor Margot was living under a bridge, under a bridge! She did leave her real home because of the horrors that happened there. Her killer was taken prisoner in that home and was abused there as well. He took it upon her for what happened to him. Our house got broke into and our hearts broke. My husband and I were operating on the injuries of Mr River and the next thing we knew is that our little girl was gone, dead, by a distressed Mrs Valdi. It was terrible. You want to rush to your child but you can't. You have to hide in your own house. Mrs Valdi was wounded and be seen to and you think that your world is crumbling around you. I have got to speak about Margot, she was brave and strong. More than a daughter, she was the little sister I always wanted to have.

She read the poem of Byron before going back to her seat by Sebastien who hugged her. Father Odell turned to Raphael and invited him,

-Please, come and read your eulogy for Marguerite, Mr River.

The fallen angel stood up and unfolded his piece of paper, before saying its content without looking at it,

-When you met Margot, you met all that was good in this world. I fell in the river and she saved me. I owe my life to her, simply and purely. Our first encounter will stay within my heart forever. As Mrs Cotton said she was a strong young girl. You may not all know that she was the survivor of a sinking ship. You may not all know that she looked after her sickly and dying younger brother. All in all, you may not all know what she went through during her short life, but she went through a lot, a lot... I shared the security of being under 'her' bridge for a night. The following day she took me to the clinic to be seen to for my injuries. I talked about her in the clinic because I knew she was in trouble. When she saved me, she was hurting as much as I did. Yes, Margot was a very courageous being, but she was also generous and upright. When she had next to nothing to eat, when I was destitute, she shared her food with me, a fair share, half and half. She had a most beautiful heart. I must confessed that having met her changed me totally. I wasn't always good in my life but since she saved me, I swear to her that I will always stay upright, loving, generous and courageous like her. Margot will carry on to live in my heart with her pigtails and her beautiful green eyes. She will still say you can do this but you can't do that with her little bossy ways which were mostly right...

Raphael broke down at that moment, taking him aside

Raguel gave him a warm manly embrace and sat the fallen angel down beside him. Father Odell continued the funeral mass. Then he asked for silence for Marguerite Bouchon while Mina played Partita Number 2 of Jean Sebastien Bach with her violin. Many parents and children cried. Jack was hugging Ivy while Toby was crying upon the shoulder of Sebastien. When the sad music stopped, Raguel, his son, Henry, Ted, Mr Berry and Raphael carried the coffin of Margot to the cemetery. Straight behind them Ivy followed in tears holding the hands of Jack and Tobias.

The coffin was lowered down in the ground in ceremony then almost everyone left little by little until Sebastien pushed his wife to go to the tavern because their two boys needed to eat, then the only people left standing by the grave of Margot were Raguel, Raphael and Mr Berry. Anthony Berry had brought an entire holly bush and was planting it with the help of Raguel and Raphael, he said,

-Margot will like that. She did love flowers, plants and animals. I saw her foraging in the forest so often, so often. Will she have a headstone?

Raguel replied with assurance,

-Yes, she will. It will be made of white marble. I am organising it for the family. It will have her three names engraved on it.

The dairy farmer proposed,

-May I contribute to the cost?

The Master of all angels smiled gratefully to Mr Berry before he answered,

-I can't say no to you because my son and his wife are not wealthy but can I ask just for some milk and butter for their two little boys instead?

Anthony shook the hand of Raguel and said,

-I can do better than that. I can give them a decent dairy cow. But I have heard that Mrs Cotton was not so much of a cook so I can show her how to make butter and even cheese for her family.

Raguel accepted then commented,

-The generous Margot would have smiled at you, right

now. She would have also been thankful for that holly bush by her grave. But she would say she appreciated all the small gestures you did to her when she was alive. If there was a man she needed to turn to when she was in trouble, or starving, it was you.

Sighing Mr Berry told,

-I don't have children, but Margot was a little girl I wished to have been able to call my daughter. That is all.

Raguel tapped the back of the dairy farmer who was about to cry. He enjoined,

-Anthony, you must go to the funeral banquet. Mrs Toad might miss your presence there and feel a little lost in Tyrell's tavern.

Mr Berry did as he was told, leaving but holding his hat down to Raguel. Left alone with Raphael, the Master of all angels was arranging the grave as best as he could putting the flowers and the decorations with care with his new servant. Both stood up and considered Margot's grave. Both had tears in their eyes. They remained silent in their grief for a while. Then they felt their hands held. Both looked down at what was happening to them.

They saw Margot standing between them, almost transparent, who said,

-I decided to be a ghost.

When the Angels go marching in:
Part 1 Sebastien's Arrival
Book Three of the Wilton town Series.
The Wilton Town Saga continues. The Angels go marching in Wilton
Town was written when due to unforeseen circumstances, I partly lost
my ability to walk properly. I must confess that I had trouble dealing
with my loss of complete mobility then but also now. 'Marching' in
the title is almost telling the entire tale of what did happen to my
physical life or lets just say giving a clue to the loss of something
important to me. This story took a completely different spin than the
one I had in mind and planned due to what happened to me.
Spread your wings...

Raising IT-666:
The Teenage Beast
Book Two of the young Beast years.
Adopted by the human Walter Workmaster, the Beast is being given a
fair chance to live and learn almost like a normal teenager. 'Almost',
for normality does not apply when It-666 is concerned. Trained to be
a Soldier by the Angel of Death, monitored by Archangel Raphael and
looked after by Archangel Gabriel, It is raised as a Being with the
open opportunity of her own heart, which they will protect. Trips to
Hell and fighting demons make her earn her true colours within the
Angelic Army raising her up in their midst.

By the same author:
Hair Rising, Heir Raising, Erasing.
By Cordelia Malthere.
A vibrant beyond the grave tale which will chill your bones while
warming your heart. When the deadly serious is delightfully hilarious,

you will know you have just been acquainted with
Abraham Wilton-
Cough. His skeletal hand will drag you from grave to
grave, under the
moonlight of the night where many dead are rising...
Could it be the
apocalypse?

About the Author

Cordelia Malthere is riding the wave of her dreams and nightmares
which are translated into tales and stories. Sometimes dark yet
always full of humour, her writing words/worlds are an invitation to
open one's heart and mind fully to simply love one another.
Escaping prejudice age 5 from a school that saw her as a devil child
for being left handed and breaking free from the chair she was
attached to, Cordelia ran away back home and from any restraining
bonds that made no sense at all to her.
Ever since she fought the tough fight to be her own self and not
the person others wanted to impose upon her. She believes in free
will bestowed to all humans, and took full advantage of hers. She
went on to choose everything that suited her best, from country,
religion, sexuality and name.
After studying Literature, Philosophy and Art for her Baccalaureate,
she carried on studying Art in the Fine Art school from her home
town for a couple of years. Her love for drawing especially
caricatures never left her. She uses that skill to draw the characters
of her stories, and be fully involved in the creation of her book
covers.
She came to London in 1996, age 20, in order to perfect her
English, yet fell in love with the cosmopolitan British capital and
never left it. After a Bsc in Archaeological and Anthropological
sciences, the author started to write her imaginary world down bit
by bit, story after story.
The 'Clementine's epic adventures in the After-World'

blog and
        story brought her many fans worldwide. Sadly the loss
of her father
        in 2013, prompted the author to make every day count
from then
        on: 'Carpe Diem'.
        'Malthere Publications' was then created in 2014 to
carry all the
        Born to be Free Loving Voices that want to be publish.
        Raising IT-666 The Teenage Beast 414

Cordelia Halthere

<<<<>>>>